Feather of Maat:
Hatshepsut's Childhood

By Kathy Timpane Medbery

Mystic Mustangs Publishing

Published by Mystic Mustangs Publishing

Acknowledgments

I wish to express my gratitude to the people that have been a part of my journey in writing this story. First of all, to my husband, who has tolerated my obsession with Ancient Egypt and learned more about Hatshepsut than he ever wanted to know. He trooped through Egyptian museum exhibits in NYC, Paris, Luxor and Cairo and lay out under the stars with me 'to see Goddess Nut, swallowing and giving birth to the sun'. I thank him for the time in Egypt together when I insisted on pushing my limits to get a 'sense of place'. He bicycled with me on the West Bank in Luxor, from the workman's village to Deir el Bahari and climbed the cliff walk back to the Valley of the Queens. I'd like to thank Ruth Shilling and her "All 1 World Tours" for our wonderful adventure in Egypt in 2001 and her ongoing enthusiasm and encouragement for my writing. Susanne Davis was very important in showing me ways to sculpt each chapter to create dramatic tension. The women of Susanne's writing group helped by reading my story and making helpful comments. My deep appreciation for Candy Smith, Shaughn Hayes Roman and Mystic Mustangs Publishing for all the detail work to get this story ready for publication.

And finally, I thank Diane McNamara for continuously bugging me to get it published, so that I would write the sequel.

Table of Contents

Acknowledgments   3

Table of Contents   4

Map of Hatasu's World   1

Map of Thutmose Campaign   2

Character List   3

Hatasu's Family Hierarchy   6

Prologue   7

Hail Thoth   9

Part 1   10

Chapter 1- Khamsin   11

Chapter2 - Wadjmose   32

Chapter 3 - The Hawk-in-the-Nest   57

Chapter 4 - The Foreigners   73

Chapter 5 - Osiris's Day   93

Chapter 6 - Horus Day   110

Chapter 7 - Set's Day   128

Chapter 8 - Isis's Day   139

Chapter 9 - Nephthys's Epagomenal Day   151

Chapter 10 - The Oracle of Amun   160

Chapter 11 - The New Year's Day Announcement   170

Chapter 12 - The Valley of the Ancestors   185

Chapter 13 - The Tales of the Heroes   195

Chapter 14 - Preparations for War   215

Chapter 15 - Gold of Honor   237

Part 2   252

Chapter 16 - Neferubity's Birth   253

Chapter 17 - Journey to the Place of Truth   276

Chapter 18 - Beginning of the Nile Journey   298

Chapter 19 - Abedju   312

Chapter 20 - Between Abedju and Zawty   335

Chapter 21 - Trouble from the Oasis   360

Chapter 22 - Setmose   383

Chapter 23 - River Dangers   398

Chapter 24 - Khemenu, City of Thoth   417

Chapter 25 - Usersobek   438

Part 3   458

Chapter 26 - Ankh-Tawy, The White-Walled City   459

Chapter 27 - City of Craftspeople   487

Chapter 28 - The Oracle   510

Chapter 29 - Mutsi and Ferit   525

Chapter 30 - The Pharaoh's Return   547

Chapter 31 - Miriam's Story   574

Chapter 32 - The Elephant Hunt   590

Chapter 33 - The Duck Hunt   598

Chapter 34 - The Judgement of Maat   612

Chapter 35 - The Pharaoh's Announcement   632

Chapter 36 - The Sphinx   652

Bibliography   663

The Author   667

Map of Hatasu's World

MAP OF HATASU'S WORLD

Map of Thutmose Campaign

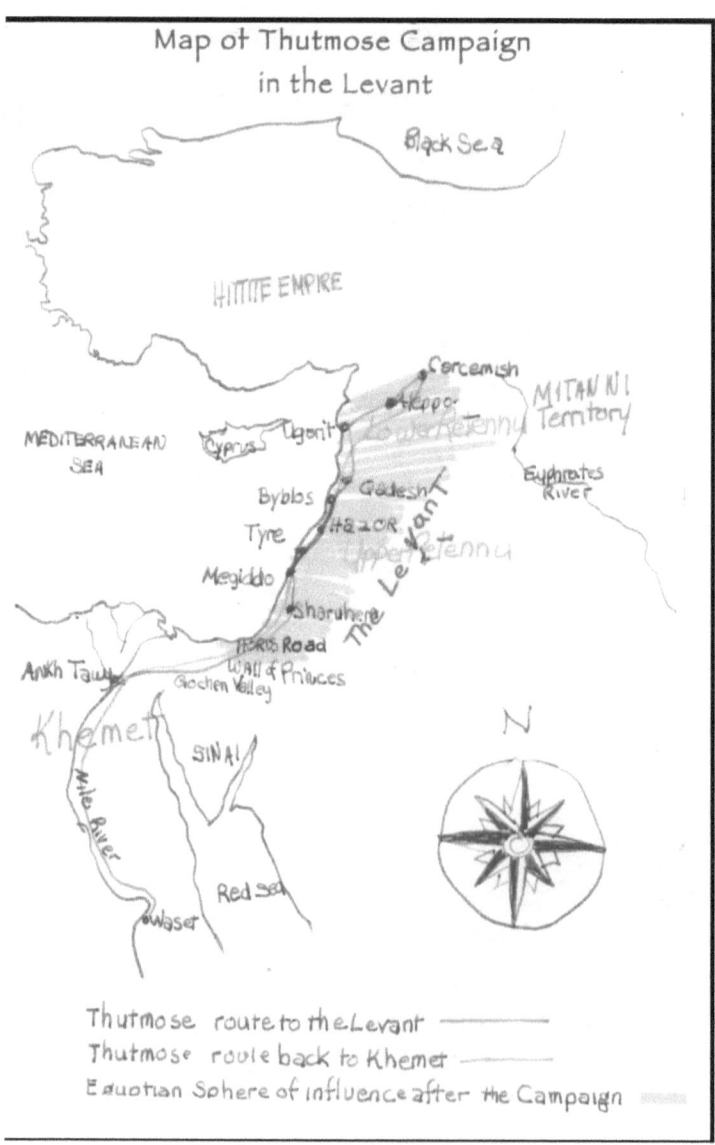

Map of Thutmose Campaign in the Levant

Thutmose route to the Levant ————
Thutmose route back to Khemet ————
Egyptian Sphere of influence after the Campaign ▨▨▨

Character List

Royal Household in Waset

Hatasu	the childhood name of Hatshepsut
Thutmose I	Hatshepsut's father and Pharaoh, name means ;Born of the god of wisdom, Thoth'
Okheperkare	Thutmose I's throne name meaning 'Powerful is the transforming soul of the sun'
Ahmose	Hatshepsut's mother, her name means 'Born of the moon'
Sitre	Hatshepsut's nurse-tutor
Thethi	Hatshepsut's halfbrother later known as Thutmose II
Paheri	Thethi's nurse-tutor
Senisenb	Hatshepsut's paternal grandmother
Satamun	Hatshepsut's maternal aunt and God's Wife of Amun, high priestess
Tao	Hatshepsut's cousin, Satamun's son
Ineni	Pharaoh Thutmose I's brother and visier of the Two Lands
Nefermose	Hatshepsut's aunt, wife of Ineni and mother of Isis, Meryt and Sennefer, cousins
Hapu	High priest of Amun and cousin to Queen Ahmose and Priestess Satamun
Ahhotep	Wife of Hapu and mother of Hapuseneb, Amenmope and Ahm
Wadjmose	Hatshepsut's oldest half brother by father's 1st wife, Mutnofret
Amenmose	Hatshepsut's second half brother by Mutnofret
Neferubrity	Hatshepsut's baby sister
Muthotep	Neferubrity's nurse
Hetep	friend of Wadjmose and Amenmose
Ibana	Army general, granfather to Thethi's tutor, Paheri
Pennekheb	Army general
Nakht	Commander of the guards
Nefermut	Ahmose's childhood nurse-tutor
Hapuseneb	Hatshepsut's friend, Child of the Palace, son of high priest Hapu

Meryt	Hatshepsut's cousin, Child of the Palace, daughter of Vizier Ineni
Isis	Hatshepsut's cousin, Child of the Palace, youngest daughter of Vizier Ineni
Sennefer	Hatshepsut's cousin, Child of the Palace, son of Vizier Ineni
Huy	Pharaoh Thutmose's scribe
Yuf	Queen Ahmose's scribe
Chi-chi	Hatshepsut's pet monkey, a gift from her father
Behka	Thethi's pet dog, a gift from his father

Governors along the Nile

Itruri	Governor of El Kab, father of son, Paheri and daughter, Amensat
Amensat	Daughter of Itruri and love interest of Hatshepsut's brother, Amenmose
Sahte	Greeter at the Place of Truth
Merit	Elder chantress at the Place of Truth
Puya	Governor of Abedju
Puyemre	Son of Puya and friend of Hatshepsut
Rekh	Temple teacher in the Abedju House of Life
Senenmut	Student from the House of Life and storyteller
Djehapy	Governor of Zawty
Kharit	Wife of Djehapy and master weaver
Tutkharit	Daughter of Djehapy and Kharit
Setmose	Rebel from the Oasis, grandson of Teti-an of Itjtawy
Amenhat	Governor of Itjtawy
Usersobek	Treasonous priest of Itjtawy
Tjay	Governor of Khemenu
Maatmose	High Priest of Khemenu
Djehuti	Student at House of Life at Khemenu, Hatshepsut's cousin
Khnumhotep	Governor of Beni Hassan
Rahotep	Mayor of Ankh-Tawy
Nebra	Rahotep's son and hero in military campaign
Sihathor	Priestess of Sekhmet
Hereptah	Master craftsperson
Ptahhotep	Older priest of the oracle
Siptah	Priest at Temple of Ptah
Serit	Peasant's daughter

Simut	Merchant's daugher

Foreigners

Bazor	Amorite delegate
Ynene	Libyan delegate
Mahar ba'al	Delegate from Byblos
Barratarna	Leader of the Mitanni
Mursilis	Hittite Ruler
Mariyannu	Mitanni Warriors
Mashmashu	Wizards of evil magic from the Levant
Samana	Demons of Mashmashu
Ferit	Peasant's daughter
Mutsi	Merchant's daughter

Hatasu's Family Hierarchy

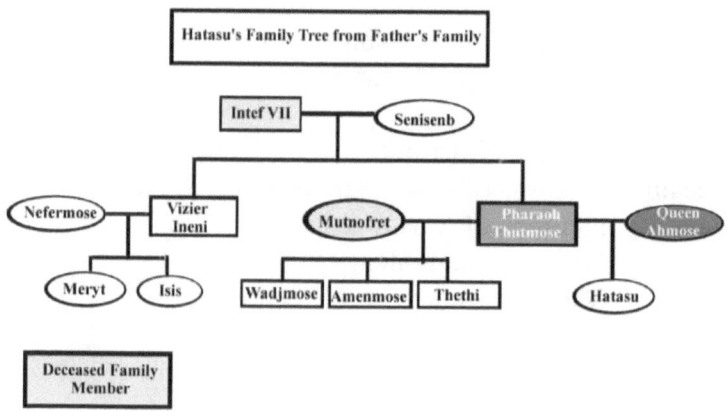

Hatasu's Family Tree from Father's Family

Intef VII — Senisenb

Nefermose — Vizier Ineni — Mutnofret — Pharaoh Thutmose — Queen Ahmose

Meryt — Isis

Wadjmose — Amenmose — Thethi

Hatasu

Deceased Family Member

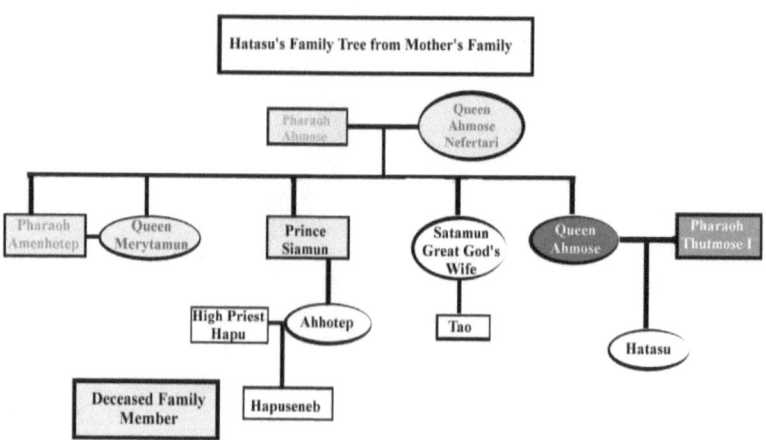

Hatasu's Family Tree from Mother's Family

Pharaoh Ahmose — Queen Ahmose Nefertari

Pharaoh Amenhotep — Queen Merytamun

Prince Siamun

Satamun Great God's Wife

Queen Ahmose — Pharaoh Thutmose I

High Priest Hapu — Ahhotep

Tao

Hatasu

Deceased Family Member

Hapuseneb

Prologue

Divine kingship was essential to Khemet's (Ancient Egypt's) sense of wellbeing and the goddess, Maat (representing the principle of order, justice and truth) was essential to Khemet's kingship. Each pharaoh had the duty to maintain cosmic order and to protect the land from chaos, within or without. The rich array of rituals functioned to communicate and unite the three worlds; heaven, earth and duat (the dwelling place of the gods and goddesses). This kept things in ordered balance and in a way the goddess Maat was honored. This was as important to the kingdom's welfare as doing battle and ensuring fertility.

Our story takes place in Khemet in the early fifteenth century BCE, fifty years after the end of rule of a foreign people, called the Hyksos. The land was still recovering from the chaos caused by the years of occupation by these people with alien ways. The people of Khemet called this chaos and disorder 'Isfet', the opposite of Maat. The armed struggle led by the Tao family had freed them from intruders; however, the land was still in a precarious position, threatened by the return of foreign enemies and vulnerable to internal conflicts.

Thutmose I was the ruling Divine Pharaoh. He was a strong, charismatic military leader, committed to strengthening and protecting the land of Khemet. He, however, was not himself a Taosids...the dynasty of pharaohs that reigned before him. His predecessor left no living children; therefore, he chose Thutmose, a young man who had distinguished himself as a warrior, and in whom the princess, Ahmose, saw future greatness.

Under Thutmose's rule, Maat was honored, but he knew the continued stability of the land was dependent on his ability to produce an heir…preferably with the great royal wife, Ahmose. They had one daughter, Hatshepsut, who assured the line of succession…for it was presumed that she would confer the insignia of royalty through her choice of consort, as her mother had.

The Pharaoh and Great Wife continued to pray for a son of their union for her to marry, for a male heir was the most certain way to quiet ambitious descendents of other branches of the royal family. It was such fractured loyalties that had given the Hyksos a toehold in the first place. Several miscarriages and the certainty that her present pregnancy was a girl, led Thutmose to institute a backup plan. He was grooming Wadjmose (the oldest of Thutmose's three sons by a non-royal wife) for the role of consort and future pharaoh. Hatshepsut's royal blood would make Wadmose the legitimate successor.

Our story begins as Hatshepsut, nicknamed Hatasu, is eight years old.

Hail Thoth

Hail Thoth, architect of truth,

Give me words of power

That the heart of my story

May beat strong enough

For a person to rise up and walk in it.

-The Egyptian Book of the Dead-

Part 1

Chapter 1~ Khamsin

The sandy wind was the first thing that warned the princess of the storm. She looked up from playing with her cat's new brood of kittens to see the invasion of dancing desert sand whirling all around, disturbing the usually peaceful palace garden. Squinting her eyes to protect them from the gritty air blowing in her face, she noticed how the palace servants were scurrying about, fastening covers on the grain bins and closing the wooden shutters over the windows. Eight-year-old Hatasu (ha-TA-su) sensed the urgency in their hurry. She left her cat, Miu (Me-U), under the sycamore tree and went inside the palace to find her nurse-guardian, Sitre (Sit-RA). Sitre was in Hatasu's bedroom covering the bed and chests with linen sheets.

"What's happening, Sitre? What are you doing?" Hatasu asked.

"We have to get everything covered before the khamsin gets here," Sitre said.

"Who's the khamsin?"

Sitre chuckled. "It's a terrible storm with strong winds that gets sand into everything, even after I cover it." Making an exaggerated funny-face scowl, she added, "We'll be cleaning up sand for half a moon." She shook the white linen sheet, having it make a popping noise as it billowed down over Hatasu's bed. It would protect it from the worst of the fine sand floating down from the cracks in the window shutters.

To the casual observer, Sitre looked like Egyptian women everywhere with shoulder-length black hair and kohl-lined dark eyes, wearing the common white linen sheath and the blue faience neck beads. But for her young charge, she was unique in all the world and her face was a marvel of ever changing expressions. The most common of these expressions was the broad mouthed smile that lit up her midnight black eyes and meant there would soon be a new, delightful game. Almost as common, however, was the wrinkled brow accompanied by wringing hands—hands that seemed to be trying to pleat themselves into a tidy braid. On rare occasions her face darkened and the mole on her chin would turn the color of carnelian. At those times, the child knew to stay out of her way, for her beloved nurse's usual soothing words could contain a sharp scolding. Granted, that usually happened at times Hatasu misbehaved. This day, her eyes were smiling.

"Would this khamsin cover up Miu and her new kittens?"

"Certainly, it could."

"Well then, I must bring them into the palace!"

"No, no. Dear Heart, these winds get strong enough to blow away such a small girl." She then added as a cajoling afterthought, "…even if she is the daughter of the Good God Thutmose (TOOT-mo-se)." She was about to shake out a second sheet when she saw Hatasu moving in the direction of the garden in spite of her warning. To deter her, she playfully shook the linen over the child, catching her up in the ballooning sheet and tightened her arms around her in a hug.

Hatasu giggled and squirmed until she'd wiggled her way out of Sitre's arms. Off she went, a big puff of white. Equally engaged in this new game, Sitre took off after her, but the child was small and agile, eluding her nurse by ducking into a doorway and tucking the abundant folds of sheet in around her to secure the secret of her hiding place.

Once the corridor was clear, she headed for the courtyard again. Pushing the heavy palace door open, she was met with a blast of desert air. It was hotter and stronger than when she'd left the garden just a few minutes before. She was glad she still had the sheet on, for the flying sand bit into her exposed skin. Without another moment of hesitation, she pushed forward, her small feet patting across the mud bricks of the garden path. She rounded the corner of the palace and crossed to the sycamore tree where she'd left her cat.

As she ran along the path, she wondered for the first time if this *was* dangerous. The winds were stronger and the sky was darker than she ever saw by day. Her next thought, however, was of her father, the great warrior Pharaoh. She knew he valued courage and she heard him say many times, "The duty of the Pharaoh is to protect those given to his care."

Her cat and kittens were under her care. Surely, he would be proud of her for this act. She pushed through the winds to the sycamore and sure enough, Miu and her kittens were there. The mama cat's body, a deep yellow color with darker striped markings, was curved around three tiny, nursing kittens. The princess gathered the three little ones up in a pocket she made in her sheet. As Hatasu headed back toward the palace, the mama cat trailed along beside her.

The child bent into the wind as she re-crossed the courtyard, amazed at how the storm kept increasing in intensity. The air was so thick, she could hardly see the palace. The wind pulled at hercovering like jealous fingersand tried to spill her precious cargo. Hatasu gathered the folds tighter and held the kittens closer. She felt for the protective amulet her mother had given her. Yes, the small turquoise figure of Bes, the protective god of children, was on its string around her neck, With that assurance, she pushed on.

Noticing that Miu seemed to move with greater ease, she dropped 'cat-like' to her hands and knees. It lessened the resistance from the wind but it meant hobbling along like a three-legged dog, for she still held tight to the protective sheet-pocket containing the kittens. Finally, she reached the palace wall and it shielded her some from the howling, pushing, storm. She edged along the sidewall but the savagery of the wind still bit into her face. She met this challenge by turning, crawling backward, presenting the sheet to the wind. It was even hard to breathe now because there was so much sand in air. The distinct sensation of fear caught in her throat.

Just then, she backed into an obstacle. It felt like two firm columns. She turned quickly. Barely visible through the sand, she saw a pair of men's feet in golden sandals. Her eyes followed the legs. There was the surprised face of her father, the Pharaoh, squatting to examine this wind tossed ball of white sheet at his palace door. Even in this storm, he was regal and imposing with his prominent nose, sharp kohl-lined black eyes and bronzed broad shoulders covered with gold and jewels. His head was bare of his usual royal headdress…and he, and his jewels, were covered with layers of khamsin dust.

She was so glad to see him, for it took all of his warrior strength to get the palace door opened in the wind. The two seemed to be blown inside with a burst of whirling sand. He pulled the door closed, saving them both from the roaring storm. Hatasu wanted very much to please this magnificent father. This was even more important than rescuing her cat. She felt sure her father would approve of her heroic deed and this would earn her his attention. While she could assume her mother's love and protection, she had to earn her father's attentions.

"What were you doing out there?" The Pharaoh's voice held more soldierly sternness than he had ever used with her before.

Still hopeful he would praise her when he realized her bravery, she opened the folds of her sheet and showed him the treasure of the three rescued kittens and the mama cat that emerged from the cloth around her legs. Taking in the situation at a glance, an amused smile spread over his face. He shook his head slowly. Hatasu sat herself down in a pile of sand, her white linen floating to the ground. She looked up into his face…longing for his smile of praise, fearing his displeasure. He stood over her, his arms crossed but she could see a twinkle of amused pride in his eyes. His words and tone, however, showed his disapproval. "That was dangerous, Hatasu."

"But," she said quickly, "if I didn't rescue these pets…these little ones left to my care…well…the sand would have buried them."

"So, you did show courage."

Hatasu smiled as he said these words and her chest expanded again with the warm glow of the acknowledgement she craved. He stroked his chin watching her closely. "But…" Her body tensed as he continued, "it displeases me that you were reckless about your own safety."

"But Father, I *am* safe…and so are the kittens!" Almost desperate to regain his approval, she went on. "You tell Wadjmose to be brave and protect those under his care." There were several moments of frowning silence. A feeling of dread rose in Hatasu's throat. No one spoke back to the Pharaoh!

He squatted down to her level and looked into her face. "It is important that you *not* carelessly do things that endanger your khet, for it houses your royal ka and your divine Akh!" He stood again and moved toward his council room door. "Now, you go with Sitre and stay *out* of the storm."

As he walked away, Hatasu's heart ached. She thought to herself that he was the handsomest of all men. He was the god around whom her sun rose and set. She *almost* had the warmth of that sun shine on her. *Almost*!

She considered the reprimand and thought of what he'd taught her from her earliest childhood. There were different parts of her. The khet, her physical body, was the only part that could be seen by earthly eyes. The ka, pictured in the 'words of the gods' on temple walls as two arms stretching upward, was her spiritual double and her instinctual yearning for her spirit self. A royal ka was unique and special to the rulers of the land. The ba, pictured as a bird with a human head, was her soul, free from the khet and able to travel between the worlds. The final, and most important part, was the akh, her luminous Self, pictured as a crested bird with shining plumage. He had taught her that it was her primary life-task to develop and inhabit this as her highest spiritual potential.

She turned from watching her father leave to see Sitre and her younger brother, Thethi staring at her: Sitre, with her brow furrowed, wringing her worried hands, Thethi (TEE-thi), his eyes wide, was looking at the kittens playing among the folds of sheet around her.

Thethi burst out, "What happened? How did you get out in the storm?" He was only a few months younger but much smaller. His nose, the same shape as his father's, dominated his face. He would no doubt grow into it in time but now it gave him a beak-ish, bird-like look.

She'd barely started to explain to him when Sitre exclaimed, "Oh my, how the wind chapped your skin!" The princess was the lotus blossom in the garden pool of her life and she was ever vigilant for her welfare, a fact often annoying to Hatasu, but as she looked down at her arm, she saw it was, indeed, red with windburn. "Why can't you listen when I say something isn't safe?" Sitre was shaking her head. "*No*, you have to hear it from you father! Well…" She let out a heavy sigh. "We can put some aloe on it. It will heal quickly enough."

Sitre led the children to the family rooms of the palace. Hatasu carried two of the kittens, Thethi carried one. Miu trailed along. As they walked though the corridor, Thethi said to his sister, "You could have come and gotten me if you were going on an adventure. Then the Pharaoh would have seen both of us as brave."

"And he could then be displeased with you, as well," Hatasu

returned.

Thethi started to voice a response but interrupted himself by a series of convulsing coughs.

"I think the sand is making you sick again, Thethi," Sitre said. The coughing reddened his face and slowed his ability to walk. Sitre, whose large heart had long ago encompassed the motherless half-brother of her princess, ceased moving. She squatted to Thethi's level and said, "There, there. We'll get you something to soothe your breathing, as well."

Gradually, he caught his breath and they proceeded to the family quarters. Singing the children a little ditty to distract them…and possibly herself…from the loudening sound of the winds outside, Sitre helped Hatasu get her kittens settled in a woven basket, then rubbed aloe on her skin. For Thethi, she mixed honey and moringa oil syrup. Hatasu's skin quickly felt better but Thethi's cough changed into wheezing as more and more fine sand drifted into the room through the cracks in the shutters.

This family room was the center of palace life. It was large enough to accommodate the extended family and cozy enough to feel like home when just the two youngest children played there. It had four pillars placed a distance from each other. The top of each pillar was in the shape of a papyrus bud. The walls were brightly painted with scenes of the river marshes. High among the green stems and papyrus tufts were images of pintail ducks, red-breasted geese, long-beaked ibises and plied kingfishers, each flying about their nests full of eggs. Closer to the floor, one could see under the water of the marsh, a gracefully swimming collection of Nile fish:

Upside down catfish, Nile perch, and most significant of all, the tilapias, swimming with lotus buds in their mouths.

The tile floor had a light blue design containing the buds and flowers of the lotus. Hatasu and Thethi sat on finely woven reed mats on the floor as they played with the pets. The windows, high up on the cool, thick walls, usually open to let in the light but not the heat, were now closed. The room glowed from within by the light of a multitude of graceful alabaster vessels.

Thethi's wheezing breath kept getting worse. Sitre showed the children how to tie a small patch of linen with a long string and drag it across the floor to entice their cat to play. Miu began to chase it with all her feline passion. Hatasu moved the bait slowly until she saw Miu crouch low, get ready, then pounce! Hatasu moved it just in time. As she began to run after it, the princess, too, ran until Miu leaped upon the pretend mouse. She then held her string high and Miu jumped and twisted to catch it between her paws.

Sitre smiled. The storm was almost forgotten. Thethi jumped up and begged for a turn, too. Quickly, his wheezing forced him to slow down. Sitre said, "Sit still, Thethi. Let your sister pull the string. You watch."

Thethi glanced at his sister's nurse and then set his jaw firm. Hatasu had seen this reaction many times. She knew how Thethi hated the confines of this illness. He regularly behaved as though he could overcome it with the force of will alone. Sitre, on the other hand, was less patient than usual. She took his continued running and wheezing as misbehavior. Her voice got louder, "Come here

19

and sit down, Prince Thutmose the Second. Right this moment!"

Hatasu, seeing her brother's plight, offered, "Hey, Thethi, let's both sit and play with Miu on the floor. This can be our adventure."

Thethi didn't have much choice but to stop. "It's not fair!" he said between wheezes. "You never get sick." He folded his arms.

Hatasu dangled the toy in one place. The cat still leaped and twisted. Thethi's breath got a bit easier as he sat still and she attempted to draw him into the more sedate version of the game. "Look! We can still play." Hatasu lowered herself to her knees and shortened the string. Miu continued her antics.

"Sure... 'we can still play'," he mimicked. "After all, you're the red-haired daughter of the gods." He'd chosen words that he knew would upset her. Whenever he was jealous or annoyed, he picked on the quality she was most self-conscious about—her red hair. She hated being teased about it. It made her different from everyone else. Her mother, at times, had tried to cajole her by saying she must have inherited it from the gods. That didn't help Hatasu a bit and it made Thethi all the more jealous. She put down the string and got up to walk away.

Thethi called after her, "Don't go, Hatasu. I'll stop." Then, with a loud sigh, "I'll play with the string sitting down."

Hatasu looked at his flushed face and cough-reddened eyes and returned to their game.

Sitre made a second cat toy and handed it to Thethi. He moved it slowly to attract the attention of the cat and soon Miu was going back and forth between the two toys and the two children were laughing together again from their seated position. The wheezing slowed down but didn't stop.

Thethi was one of three half-brothers by the Pharaoh's first wife, Mutnofret (MUT-no-ret). Thethi was three years old when she died and it was about that time he started having trouble with his breathing. Clearly, the loss of his mother still haunted him. His nurse-guardian was the warrior, Paheri (Pa-HAR-ree), but he, too, was frustrated with the sickly eight year old and his care often fell to Sitre.

Even with Sitre's medicine and the sedate play, Thethi continued to wheeze. This worried Hatasu. It was unsetting to watch when he couldn't catch his breath. She wished her mother were there, for she always knew what to do when Thethi's sickness got bad…which it did from time to time.

As though responding to the silent call, Ahmose (Ah-moses) entered the room carrying a box containing her magic. She sat on the floor with the children, while Miu went off to nurse her kittens.

Hatasu thought her mother was the most beautiful woman ever. Her face was round and light complexioned like the moon when it was full. Her eyes were dark and round like the moon when it was new. Lovely, long lashes framed her eyes and the customary kohl makeup highlighted them. This was fitting, for she was named after the ancient moon god, Ah. Ah-mose, therefore, meant 'daughter of the moon'. She had traces of the bright-toothed smile of the Taosid family as well as their rich black hair. Her body was slender and soft, graceful and beautiful. There was a noticeable bulge in her stomach that carried Hatasu's baby sister. "Oh my, Thethi. I heard you were having trouble with your breathing again," she said, putting a gentle hand on her stepson's back.

"A little."

"These storm winds are fierce enough to steal anyone's breath away." Rubbing her soothing hand in a circle on the middle of his back, she said, "I'm going to give you a treatment that will help."

She placed her box on a table and took out three things: A bowl of water, a sistrum, and a container of spicy smelling paste. The water was to cleanse Thethi's khet, the sistrum was to purify the environment of hurtful spirits and the herbal concoction was to strengthen his sekhem (inner strength). Once they were arranged neatly in a row, she took the water and washed his chest and back. Then, she began a magical chant. *"As Isis healed her son Horus, so I pray she heals this child."*

Ahmose's voice was beautiful and she accompanied it with her sistrum, a seed rattle with the face of the goddess on the handle. Next, she spread the paste of the herbs on his chest and back, filling the entire room with the powerful scents of frankincense, cumin and juniper berries. These three elements…water, music and herbs…made up a spell far more powerful than any of Sitre's remedies. Usually, when stronger remedies were needed, they turned to the queen's sister, Satamun, the high priestess of healing, but the storm kept her away this day.

Once Ahmose performed her treatment, she told Thethi he must stay still and rest to let the strength of the goddess work her magic. To help him do this, she offered to tell him and Hatasu a story. She gathered the children on her lap, one on each knee, and said, "I will tell you the story of Sekhmet, the goddess of storms." She began,

"Once there were rebellious ones who wouldn't live in harmony with the laws of Maat's (ma-AT), the laws that protect all of us. Ra, the sun god, sent his daughter in her lioness form, Sekhmet (sec-MET), to subdue these troublemakers and protect the righteous people. Sekhmet did his bidding with great enthusiasm. Once she got started, however, she destroyed all in her reach.

"Ra called for her to come home but she didn't want to stop. Ra, turned to the god of wisdom, Thoth. It was he who set the plan to surrounded her with beer. Sure enough, Sekhmet drank it until she got so drunk she fell asleep. Her rampage stopped. When she awoke, she was willing to return home, transformed back to her form as the gentle cow goddess, Hathor, (HATH-or). She had destroyed the lawbreakers."

Thethi asked, "Do you think Sekhmet sent the storm to take my breath, because sometimes I feel so rebellious?"

"No, no, Thethi. It is the wind and the demon of your fear that takes your breath away. Sekhmet destroys those demons. She heals your fears. Can you feel her healing working yet?"

"I do feel better." The wheezing was quieter.

Hatasu, listening to the high pitched roar outside, asked, "Is it really Sekhmet raging in this storm?"

"The wind may sound like an angry lion, but it is only the wind."

Hatasu knew this was the season for winds. It was Shomu, the hottest, driest time of the year, when the river shrank to a trickle and everyone prayed for the returning waters of the inundation. She'd seen windstorms before but never a khamsin as loud or as long as this one. "But Omm (mom), why didn't the rebellious ones honor Maat's laws?"

"The rebellious ones are people who are ignorant of how to live in harmony with the cosmic order or who let themselves be ruled by their own unbridled emotions."

"Do you think there are rebellious ones in our land and that is why the storm is raging?"

"People sometimes do get out of harmony with the divine world. It is the job of your father, the Pharaoh, to maintain the harmony between his earthly people and the gods in the Duat. He is the go-between for the Great Above and the Great Below."

"Is this storm raging because there are such people in our land now…besides Thethi?" She sent a playful grin toward her brother.

Ahmose said, "Usually the rebellious ones are foreigners like the Hyksos, full of ignorance and passions. In your grandparents' time they ruled the North Land without the wisdom of Thoth or the illumination of Ra. There are stories of awful storms during their reign."

"So can the storm be an omen?"

"Unusual storms can be omens." Her mother's brow formed worried wrinkles.

"It could be a curse!" Thethi burst in, looking scared.

"I don't think so, Thethi. It is most likely just a regular storm and will be over as quickly as it came."

"What if it isn't?"

"I think you are scaring yourself, Thethi. It's just a seasonal khamsin."

Ahmose got up to leave but Hatasu pulled on her linen sheath.

"Omm, what about Wadj and Amen? Are my brothers safe from this storm?"

"We have gotten word from Amen that he is overseeing the safety of the horses at the stables."

"What about Wadj?"

"The storm came up suddenly while he was overseeing work on the canals and dykes on the west bank. I'm sure he'll be back as soon as the river is safe to cross."

She had a strange feeling about Wadj in the storm but then she always missed Wadj when he was away. This nineteen-year-old brother was expected to be her consort. She knew of the prophecy that she would 'rule in peace' as Great Royal Wife, married to a pharaoh who would preferably be her full brother from her royal parents. Since Ahmose had trouble bringing her pregnancies to term, and since after ten years of marriage they did not have a male child, Thutmose was training her half-brother, Wadjmose, to succeed him…with the understanding that a marriage to the fully royal Hatasu would legitimatize his rule.

This had become the natural order of things to Hatasu. For as long as she could remember, she understood her future would be as queen to Wadj. Wadjmose was his full formal name. This was okay with her, because things were so much more fun when he was around. He took her for horse rides on his back and taught her how to hunt for frogs. Once, he carved her a toy boat that she sailed on the lotus pond. He made her feel as though things in the world were in their proper place.

Wadj and Amen's absence wasn't the only thing that made

things feel odd. The children were accustomed to spending the evening out in the garden, so the palace room felt confined. It seemed even smaller when her father entered the room and started pacing back and forth.

"I'm beginning to get an uneasy feeling about this storm," he said. "The wind's voice seems ferocious; more disturbed than the usual seasonal khamsins."

Hatasu's father and mother exchanged meaningful glances. "Yes," she agreed. "I expected it to have stopped on its own, by now." Ahmose closed her eyes and tilted her head as if listening to the storm. Nodding, she said, "Perhaps we need some Hathor magic to speak to Sekhmet's rage—magic that can soothe her angry dance. Ah now, where is my frame drum?"

Hatasu watched her mother…her eyes closed, still listening to the voice of the storm itself. Everyone else in the room was silent. All that could be heard was the wail and howl from outside the walls. Then, with one hand holding the full-moon-shaped instrument high above her head, she began to move her body to the rhythm of the wind. At first she stepped slowly around in a circle, her head held high, eyes partly closed, hips swaying and the linen of her dress swirling around her.

As the wind seemed to howl louder in response to her dance, she picked up her speed, turning one-way and then another. The wind roared and her steps turned into whirls as she spun and twisted faster and faster, until she was going around herself, around the room—seeming really like the wind…like the storm itself. She moved around the Pharaoh, twirling, swaying her hips, and extending her arms with the drum over her head. Her dancing arms called to him to join her. His eyes met her eyes and he stepped onto the floor with her. As they moved together across the floor, a smile lighted his face.

Hatasu and Thethi watched as their father began to emerge from his worried mood and to move across the floor with his Queen— this woman who danced to storms. He heard something different in the storm than she did. He responded with a flat-footed stomp that punctuated the rhythm of her drum. He lifted his foot high, turned it at an angle from his body, and brought his whole weight down with a slapping sound against the floor mat. His smile broadened as he did this step again, this time clapping his hands out in front of him as his other foot slapped the floor.

Her steps continued as light as air itself. It almost looked as if she were floating along with the iridescent sand glittering in the alabaster lamp-lit air. The rhythm picked up still more speed. She whirled—he stomped. She was the wind—he was the sand.

Sitre brought out more drums, handing one to Hatasu, and both of them joined in the whirling light-footed dance, twirling and swaying like the Queen. Thethi tried to do the stomp dance like his father but quickly lost his breath and resigned himself to sit and watch. The dance was a rapid tempo of swirling, twirling, stomping and drumming. As the Queen aligned the dance with the goddess of storms, it felt like the storm was inside as well as out. The movement and drumming reached a peak of intensity - linen dress swirling, hair flying, jewelry clinking. Hatasu wondered if indeed Sekhmet had taken possession of her mother…if she had, indeed, brought the storm inside.

Pharaoh Thutmose started a chant. *"I am the voice of Ra calling Sekhmet home."*

"I am Sekhmet dancing for my father, Ra," sang Ahmose.

"Sekhmet, drink the beer of this music. Let it sooth your anger and lead you back to your gentler self as Hathor," sang out Thutmose.

They sang together, *"We praise Hathor with beauty and call to her with dance."*

The dance rhythm began to slow down. The drumbeat quieted, the twirling slowed, the stomping softened.

Ahmose chanted, *"Sekhmet, come home to rest."*

Hatasu was sure she heard a softening of the monotonous roar of winds outside. As Ahmose slowed the dance, Hatasu strove even harder to imitate her movements…the swirl and twirl of it. The drumbeat softened, the dance circles slowed, the movements quieted.

Ahmose slowly lowered herself to the floor, eyes now closed, listening to the storm answer to her chant. Thutmose softened his step, slowed it down, and seated himself on his throne-chair. A last pop of the drum…then quiet. There was still the sound of wind outside, but it was more like a normal wind.

After a few minutes of listening, her father sent a servant to check. He returned saying, "There's some wind but no sands, Your Majesty."

"Ahmose, My Dear, your magic is strong. Thank the goddess."

Hatasu's mother, still catching her breath from the dance

invocation, nodded. Once Ahmose returned to herself, she sat on her throne next to Thutmose. She called Hatasu over to her. "You liked this dance, Hatasu?"

"Yes, you were like the wind itself!"

"You liked doing the twirling, too?"

"Oh, yes!"

"Well, I will teach you some things about dancing for Hathor." She drew her daughter to her with both hands and said, "Hold yourself tall and straight. That's it…for in the goddess's eyes you are standing between heaven and earth."

As she put a firm hand on the top of her head, she said, "Your head is the heavens above." She slid her hands down to her small hips and said, "Your pelvis is the earth below. Can you imagine a stream of water flowing from your pelvis to your head?"

She closed her eyes and saw the image. "Yes," she answered, as she pulled herself to her full height, standing as tall and as straight as a Hathor-headed column.

"Now, let your head rest on your shoulders. Good. That's it."

Holding herself just so, Hatasu very slowly and mindfully began to take a step forward.

"Ah, yes," her mother said. "Beautiful! What gives a dancer strength is the knowledge that the above and below are one…and you, my daughter, are the child of both."

Hatasu glowed at her mother's encouragement. She looked over toward her father and he was smiling at her. Ahmose picked up the drum again and began a gentle beat. "Now, let the music flow into your ears and guide it along your spine, all the way down to your belly. That's it. Fill your pelvis with the music and let the drum beat sing to your feet. Yes, your feet will know how to answer its song."

Hatasu rose up on her toes and began the stepping movement she'd seen her mother do, only slower. All of Hatasu's energy was in the dance and the drumbeat. She felt her spirit soothed by its gentle trance. The drum beat and she danced.

Her father's voice broke into her awareness. "Listen! I can't hear the storm anymore. I think Sekhmet is sleeping."

Indeed, the roar outside was still. The Pharaoh, himself, went to check. He opened the door and they listened to the miraculous hush of the night garden. Thutmose turned to his Great Royal Wife. "Your dance has quieted the winds. You are indeed Mut, the mother goddess who protects her people."

She put her arm around her husband. "Tomorrow it will be your turn to be the god Amun to the people and guide them in setting things straight after this khamsin."

"Indeed."

Sitre accompanied Hatasu to her sleeping room, carrying an alabaster lamp. The light threw shadows on her walls and seemed to animate her mural of the god, Bes. He was the laughing dwarf god with hairy eyebrows and fat cheeks who protected children and guarded their sleep…the same god as the amulet around her neck. The shadows made it look like Bes was doing his own dance to scare away any lingering spirit of the storm.

Her mother came to her room and sat with her. She smelled of lotus blossom unguent and her hands were soft as they smoothed the stray red hairs off Hatasu's forehead. Hatasu pointed out the dancing Bes to her mother. "Will Bes protect Wadj tonight? I wish he were safe here with us."

"I wish he were here, too." There was a kind of sadness in her voice as she tucked the sheet around her daughter. She said no more about it, but in her sweet voice, she began the nightly lullaby that carried her daughter off to sleep.

"May the Wings of Isis enfold you,

Safe may they always hold you.

Near or far,

The Great Mother will hear you call.

Isis watches over us all."

She drifted off into a fitful sleep. The storm continued to howl on in her dreams…and filled her heart with disturbing images of her beloved Wadj.

Chapter 2 - Wadjmose

Hatasu woke up with the dawn, only remotely remembering her strange dream. Shaking off its sad images, her small feet carried her down the hall to Thethi's room. "Wake up! The air is clear—a good day for an 'adventure'."

Thethi's spirit was more willing than his body. His small frame was exhausted from the battle for air. His complexion was pale and there were circles under his eyes. Hatasu reached for his hand and slowed her pace to accommodate his still-shallow breaths.

Unlike the night darkness, the dawn light exposed the remains of the storm's violent romp through the land. It was a dismal sight. The children expected to find the area ready to play in. Instead, piles of sand littered the pathways. The ground was strewn with bruised and sandy dates, figs, persea and pomegranates. The usually clear pool was cloudy and dirty looking. The lotus flowers were broken off their stems, wilted and graying in the murky water. The bright-colored paintings on the mud brick wall around the area were faded with a light coating of sand.

"Sitre, Sitre!" she called, running back into the palace for her nurse. "It is terrible!" Hatasu stood with her small hands on her hips as though she could defy what the storm did.

Sitre was just coming out of the bedroom corridor, rubbing the sleep from her eyes. "What's terrible?"

"The storm ruined the garden!"

"Oh my!" Sitre said, as the three of them walked out the door. "What a mess! Thank the goddess you were unharmed." Her hands went automatically to their worried wringing. Seeing the distress on the young faces, however, she put aside her own upset and pointed toward the sun. "But look there. Ra is back in his barque, moving across the sky. His light has returned. Plants will grow back. See, the gardeners are already at work cleaning things up."

Hatasu looked around her. "The sun's light just lets us see all the trouble the storm made!" Hatasu sounded like a young replica of Sitre, un-fooled by her guardian's reassurance.

Gardeners were, indeed, busy loading the broken branches onto carts and sweeping sand piles into baskets. This area, usually an oasis of beauty, defined the space between the residential palace and the ceremonial palace. The pathway joining the two was lined with trees, alternating sycamore figs and date palms. To both sides of the path were ornamental pools encircled by a recurring pattern of blue cornflowers, purple mandrakes and pink poppies. White lotuses floated in the pools, sending out a fragrance that blessed the entire garden and provided shelter for the goldfish that played hide-and-seek among their stems. This had always been a spot of peace and beauty, the scenery of Hatasu and Thethi's everyday play.

The work areas behind the palace were also awakening with a heightened buzz of activity. Animal herders led their noisy, gangly geese to the canals and large-eyed cows to the pastures. One could hear the distant voices of the kitchen workers as they checked the grain storage bins, preparing the bread and beer for the day. There was the hum of the looms and the work songs of women and children who prepared the palace linens. This day, there were also scribes recording the damage to the palace and garden and noting the repairs that would be required. Amidst the usual morning activities, there were also the frantic comings and goings of messengers. Relatives and friends were sending servants back and forth to ascertain each other's well-being.

The two children saw their grandmother, Senisenb, arrive in her litter. She came, herself, to be assured of everyone's safety. She was the soft-spoken, but strong-willed, mother of Hatasu's father. Her face had the wrinkled lines of age, in spite of years of care with oils. Peeking out from under her wig were wisps of gray. Her body had softer, rounder curves than her mother's and she was cozy to cuddle up to. It was known that she had a special warm spot for each of her son's children: Great pride in Wadjmose's accomplishments, interest in Amenmose's hunting exploits, delight in Hatasu's curious and kind nature and great tenderness for Thethi—especially so, since his mother's death.

Hatasu ran to greet her. Thethi came along at his own pace. She embraced them both, bending down and enfolding them in her ample arms. "Is everyone all right?" she asked.

"We're all right," Hatasu answered. "We are waiting to hear from Wadjmose."

"Everyone's fine at my house, too." She resumed walking and expected the children to follow along after her, and they did. "I lost some plants and trees, but all my servants are fine." She walked with a limp, her hips too stiff to move easily. "The messenger from your Uncle Ineni and his family said they, too, are doing well enough." She stopped and looked down at her youngest grandchild. "Thethi, I hoped you didn't have one of your breathing attacks."

"It's okay now." Thethi didn't want to talk about it.

Taking each of their hands and continuing the uneven stride of her walk, she said, "Well then, let's go take a look at the river. If you haven't had your morning purifications yet, we can do that together." Her voice had a slight quiver but it was still firm and confident.

The three of them headed for the steps of the palace harbor. It was necessary at this time of the year to walk down many steps before they came to the water level. As the children descended and submerged their sand-coated bodies into the refreshing water, they breathed a sigh of refreshment. They splashed and giggled, Senisenb right along with them. Then the three of them sat, drying, on the sun-warmed stone steps.

At this time of year, the river itself was narrow and still. Hatasu's father had taught her to listen to the song of the river and to notice its different rhythms according to the season. This day it was slow; a doleful chant sounding in the sluggish currents. The land around them was silent, sun burnt earth that longed for the wet kiss of Hapi, the Nile river god, and the promise of his gushing song and juicy silt-filled flood. The earth on which the town sat was a sacred place because, like the primeval mound at the beginning of time, it was land that remained above water during the floods.

From the steps of the palace harbor lake, the three of them could look across the river to the expanse of the dark squares—the fallow fields, checkered by the canals and dykes of the ancient irrigation system. In the far distance, they could see the Western Mountains.

Thethi spotted it first. There was a small boat crossing the river toward them. A larger boat followed, accompanied by a minor flotilla. The small boat docked. The boatman headed, somber-faced, toward the palace. Senisenb stopped him. He recognized her and said, "I'm so sorry, Mother of my Pharaoh. I bring the message of Wadjmose's death."

Hatasu stood frozen as the words hung in the air. As if in slow motion, she looked to her grandmother. All color drained from Senisenb's face and she reached for her granddaughter's shoulder to steady herself. The messenger hurried on, leaving them stunned.

Several women, having gathered to do palace laundry on these river steps, overheard the messenger. They put down their laundry, held their arms above their heads in grief, and began making the keening sound of mourning. The sound seemed to reach Hatasu as though through water, distant and distorted.

The barge drew closer and docked next to their father's war ship. Wadj's body lay as though he was sleeping. Accompanied by the messenger from the small boat, the Pharaoh and Queen came out of the ceremonial palace with quick, urgent steps. Ineni (IN-en-ee) was with them. This brother of the Pharaoh was also the Vizier, wearing the long white kilt of his office and carrying the staff of the Vizier's authority. He was tall, like his brother but with uneven features that deprived him of the designation of handsome. What he lacked in evenness and beauty, he made up for in the look of strength and character.

When the royal parents reached the pylon, they looked right through Senisenb and the children as they hurried on to the quay. Hatasu reached out for Thethi's hand, drawing as much comfort from him as she might be giving. Amenmose came running, his thick black hair blown back from his face and his pronounced nose jutting forward. His muscled seventeen-year-old body moved him to the quay quickly where he stood in stiff, silent disbelief as the barge pulled up.

Hatasu's first glimpse of Wadj assured her he was, indeed, just sleeping. It was all a terrible mistake. As the barge docked, however, she could see the red and black matted area on his head and the strange gray-blue color of his skin.

Amenmose reacted first. He let out an animal-like moan and lunged toward his brother's body. He grabbed it by the shoulders and shook it hard. "No! Wake up, Wadjmose! You can't go! We have hunts to go on. We must both be soldiers."

The Pharaoh, the brow of his noble face pinched together indicating his pain, reached down and put a calming hand on his shoulder. Amenmose shrugged his hand off, still shaking his head 'no'. There was a defiant look in his eyes as he stared at the barge platform.

Thethi stood still, his face frozen. He just stared at the body lying on the stretcher. Hatasu felt his hand tighten its grasp on hers. He leaned his small body into hers and she put her arm around him. Queen Ahmose moved as though to touch Wadjmose gently on the arm...as if to wake him from a nap. But she withdrew her hand and squatted down next to the younger children, putting her arms around them.

Hatasu realized her mother's hands were shaking. Hatasu tried to stay very still, barely breathing. Was this feeling for herself, for

Wadjmose, or for the rest of her family's pain? She remembered how the family had been distressed for so long after Mutnofret died. There was a numbness in her chest, an armor that protected her from the full impact this event would have on her.

Other people began to gather around: Scribes, palace workers, servants, and administrators. They stayed at a respectful distance, but their wailing grief moved over the family like a blanket.

As Hatasu stood with her family, a strange sensation settled in her stomach and the thought popped into her head. *Well, if Wadj isn't in his body, then where is he?* There was a particular way he 'felt' inside her heart, and it was by this feeling that she recognized him. She felt his presence now, hovering just overhead, as though he was in the air. This must have been his ba.

It was then that the mayor of the West Bank village, who accompanied the body home, stepped from the boat. He came forth with a sad and nervous explanation. "Oh, Great Pharaoh, Ruler of Upper and Lower Egypt, Beloved of the people, it is my sad duty…" He paused, showing his reluctance to go on with his message, "It is my sad duty to bring to you the khat of your son, Wadjmose." His voice hurried a little at this point, as if he could lessen the burden this news would inflict upon the family. "He died as a great man, in an act of leadership and bravery."

"What happened?"

"He went out in a chariot when the storm first began to rescue my son, Hetep, who had been overseeing work on the far dyke. On the way back, Wadjmose's horses got frightened by the wind and bolted. The chariot overturned on the cracked mud. Wadj was thrown and his head hit a rock. His ba passed quickly. It was a good death."

The Pharaoh looked at the mayor closely—perhaps in disbelief, perhaps waiting to hear more. There was nervousness in the mayor's demeanor and when his eyes made a quick dart to his left, the Pharaoh's eyes followed them to the mayor's son, Hetep.

The young man raised himself to stand at his full height and he looked with great pain at Pharaoh's feet. "Wadjmose and I were together. After he found me in the far field, we were racing against the wind. I was thrown from the chariot, too, but my fall did not injure me." His chin quivered a bit, and a tear ran down a line on his face.

The Pharaoh nodded an acknowledgement. He turned now and addressed the wailing crowd that had gathered. "We all know that we are but visitors on this earth. As birth is a door the ba passes through to life here, so death is the passing through that doorway again back to one's home in the stars. The great sky goddess, Nut, receives Wadjmose back into her starry body. It is up to us now to prepare him for his journey and transformation back to the spirit world." His words were calm and clear, but he clenched and unclenched his fists as though in contradiction to his words. He wished he could grab hold of this son...steal him back from starry Nut.

Hatasu's dark eyes were large and dry as she heard her father speak. She tried hard to make her heart awaken from its numbness and to understand what had happened. She could feel Wadj's spirit there with them, but it wasn't moving his body. *What would happen to her if he were not to be future Pharaoh, and of course, her husband?* This was a thought too discomforting to entertain.

After his initial outburst, Amenmose settled into sullenness. He and Wadj had been constant companions, not just his brother, but also best friends. She knew he still missed his mother terribly. Hatasu overheard Senisenb say once, that he had redirected his devotion to Mutnofret toward this older brother. Now, he raised his arms above his head as the other mourners did but his moans and wails rose above those of the others.

Hatasu felt so sad for him. The memory of his mother's death was close upon Thethi, too. Hatasu knew, because she heard him struggle to maintain his breath. As he leaned against her body and squeezed her hand, they kind of swayed back and forth together and she felt she could feel his pain as well as her own. It threatened to carry the two of them away like the first rush of the inundation.

"What will happen to him now?" Thethi managed to say.

Ahmose bent her head close to his ear and said, "His ba is like a bird and it will be free to fly even as far as the stars. There, the great mother of the gods, Nut, will receive him—embrace him with her starry arms and protect him on his spirit journey. His khet must be brought to the mortuary temple." She continued, "For the next seventy days, the priests of Anubis will prepare his body for its resting place in its house of eternity as his spirit prepares for the great transformation."

Feelings of loneliness were like cold fingers squeezing Hatasu's heart. She wanted to move closer to her father, too, but his attentions were elsewhere.

It was her mother who continued to respond to her grief. "This is a time for us to mourn, to say our goodbyes to Wadjmose. When a person lives and breathes, his physical form is called his khet. When the life force leaves his form in death, we call what is left behind his khat. It is right for us to express to Wadjmose and to the gods how much we miss our loved one who had gone from our embrace to that of the goddess."

Amenmose and many of Wadjmose's friends were crying and moaning.

Hatasu spoke up hesitantly, the confused images in her dream pressed close and she could see the images clearer. "I dreamed of Wadj last night. He stood by my bed and told me that he needed to take a long trip. He said he was going home to the stars. Then, he kissed me on my forehead and just floated away. I asked him to teach me to float like that, but he just vanished."

The Pharaoh's eyes widened. He exchanged a glance with her mother, then looked down at her. "This dream is important, Hatasu. It seems you have the gift of dream magic. You received a visit from your brother's ba and you carried the memory of it into the day."

As quickly as she had his attention, it was gone again. Wadjmose's khat needed to be brought to the mortuary temple for embalming. A small procession of mourners would accompany the family in this sad trip through the town to this temple by the river. There, the body would be cleansed and prepared for its journey to the tomb. News spread quickly, and the extended family left the tasks of their own recovery from the storm and gathered at the palace.

Hatasu, still dazed, gravitated toward the garden. As a youth, she needed little preparation for this procession to the temple of embalming. She wore only the glistening, sandalwood-scented oil on her light nut-brown skin and gray-black kohl highlighted her deep eyes. Sitre sat with her by the murky garden pool and neatly re-braided the red of her youth lock…the braid on the right side of the head that marked royal children up until their maturity.

The child looked at her reflection in the water. She had the rounded face and eyes of her mother and was blessed with her mother's long, dark lashes, her sensuous, soft mouth, and her slightly prominent teeth. But she also had the distinctive Thutmose nose—pronounced, straight, and noble—like her father and brothers. Hers was a bit more delicate, fitting into her feminine face, but it was definitely a Thutmosid nose. Each of these features made her lovely to look at…even her troublesome hair.

Yes, she thought to herself, her hair—her carnelian-colored, flyaway hair—did give her trouble. People reacted as though it were something odd. Her mother said her hair marked her as being destined for great things. Her father said it reminded him of fiery Sekhmet. Amenmose teased her, particularly when she was angry, telling her it was because she was a warrior like Sekhmet. When Thethi was really little, he'd cry, saying he wanted to have 'god's hair', too. Wadjmose would rumple it as an expression of affection. Sitre just complained of its unruliness as she tried to keep it groomed.

This day, Sitre was attempting to form it into a neat braid, while

Hatasu sat, quiet and thoughtful. The memory of her dream came back to her and she wondered how to braid together her dream world and her waking world. Her mother and father busied themselves with receiving condolences from the family and making the necessary arrangements. They donned no formal garb and wore only the simple white linen of ordinary palace activities. Her mother's linen dress reached from her breasts down to her feet and a plain black wig framed her face. Her large, dark eyes, saddened in their grief, were accentuated with black kohl outline. Her collar was simple, with alternating gold and turquoise.

Her father wore a kilt that went from his waist to just above his knees. He wore no crown, but the nemes cloth, straightened now—and around his sad eyes, the kohl was slightly smudged since its morning application. He wore a collar and armbands of lapis and gold that accentuated his broad shoulders and deep sun-bronzed chest. He was the living god, Horus, Son of Ra. Hatasu felt reassured by his grand appearance. No matter the misfortune, he would know what to do—for the family and for the Two Lands (Egypt).

Hapu (ha-PU) was the next to arrive. He was the lector priest, the magician who knew the chants and spell that attuned the living to the dead, the people to the gods. A man of average height, he was several inches shorter than his Pharaoh. His shaved head emphasized its graceful, rounded shape, and he wore the leopard skin pelt of the high priest over his chest—for he came directly from his morning ritual duties at the temple. Most striking in his appearance, were his eyes. They were light...rather gray, almost blue…a contrast to the usual dark eyes of most people of Khemet. These eyes seemed more focused on the other world, rather than on this one.

As he hurried into the palace garden, he had kohl-stained tear lines running down his cheeks. He bowed low before his Pharaoh, and rising, he extended his hand to the Queen. She accepted his condolences and acknowledged their shared grief with an embrace. His son, Saamun, and Wadjmose were the same age, and the fathers and sons had often hunted together. Hapu was particularly fond of Wadjmose. Hapu was the Queen's cousin, of the Tao dynasty. He was married to Ahhotep, Ahmose's niece and the daughter of her deceased older brother, Siamun. The three of them had grown up together in the palace school.

Ahhotep arrived after her husband, walking with purposeful steps. She had the dark eyes and overbite of the Taos, and her sad smile showed the hint of her protruding teeth. She wore the ribbon of the priestess on her head, and the finest of linen flowed over her body. She had two of her three children with her.

Ahm, several years older than Hatasu, stood close to her mother, looking the mirror image of her. She was training to be a chantress at the temple. The youngest, Hapuseneb, stood slightly apart…and this day he looked at Hatasu, his playmate, as though he, too, knew where Wadj's ka was. He had an uncanny way of knowing things, even for a child. He had the same light 'see-through' eyes like his father. In spite of that, or maybe because of it, he was Hatasu's favorite playmate.

Saamun, who wasn't with them, was the oldest son. He had

completed his studies as a scribe and was moving up the ranks of the military administrative staff.

Ahhotep greeted her aunt in a tight embrace, then bowed before the Pharaoh.

Satamun (sat-a-MUN) was not far behind Hapu and his family. The gold ribbon around her black wig identified the Great God's Wife of Amun as the high priestess. She was Ahmose's older sister and her teeth protruded the most of any of the Tao family. She looked like a less beautiful version of the Queen. Two young priestesses bearing sistrums accompanied her. She walked briskly to her sister, Ahmose, embraced her warmly, expressing her shocked grief. She bowed to the Pharaoh, formerly offering condolences.

Once she'd completed the formalities, Satamun's eyes scanned the family group and sought out her niece. They rested momentarily on Hatasu's face and she smiled at her. Unlike Senisenb, who loved each of the Pharaoh's children, Satamun openly favored Hatasu, the only one of the royal children related to her by blood.

The gathering of family formed into a procession and moved out through the town's gateway, toward the funeral temple. The two young priestesses were the 'Kites', who represented the grieving goddesses, Isis and Nephthys, in their bird forms. Each of them carried a sistrum preparing and cleansing the pathway with its sound. Its rhythm was a slow lub-dub, matching the sad beat of their hearts. The priestesses sang chants that aided the ba of Wadjmose.

High Priest Hapu followed. He held a long, thin instrument

shaped like an outstretched human arm, with a cup at the end in which he burned incense. Puffs of sweet-smelling smoke rose toward the sky, spreading out to reach Hatasu's nostrils with the familiar scent of frankincense. The incense protected with scent; the sistrum protected with sound.

Satamun came next as chief chantress. She walked behind Hapu, singing magic incantations, reminding Anubis (an-NU-bis), jackal-headed god of the dead, that the frankincense was an invitation to draw him to their company and to ward off negative energies.

Next came the wab priests, carrying the khat on a pallet. These young priests were all bathed, shaved and dressed in short linen kilts during their three-month rotation in the temple. The royal family followed after the khat. Hatasu, Thethi, and Amenmose walked with the Pharaoh and Queen. The Pharaoh's mother, Ineni, and Ahhotep and her children walked next. After them followed the servants, scribes and workers of the palace and temple. All of the people…young and old, men and women…made a most sad and mournful sound, loud enough for the gods to hear.

When they proceeded beyond the wall of the palace, Hatasu was jarred by what she saw of the changes the storm had made in the countryside and the town. The palace walls had protected her family from the worst of the storm. As they walked toward the village, she saw the damage to the mud-brick houses and the fields. She looked into the sad or scared faces of the peasants and town folk. The frankincense and the sistrums heightened her senses and intensified all of her feelings. Those intensified feelings opened her to the feelings of the people, and blended their sadness with her sadness about Wadjmose's death.

The temple of embalming was at a distance, beyond the palace on the riverfront. Between the palace and this temple, stretched the part of town that contained the small homes of the palace workers: Servants, scribes, and craft persons. The savage winds left behind wreckage to homes and gardens, animal shelters and fishing boats. Groups of men worked to repair each other's homes, while women brushed away the sand from their doorw and tidied up their yards. Children tended to chores and cared for their animals, with shocked frightened faces.

In a distant field a rhythmic work song rang out as a gang of youths labored to reclaim the irrigation canals and the dykes. The procession wound its way through the khamsin-swept town, along the street that led to the mortuary temple. Townsfolk left their work and joined the troupe, mourning for their beloved Pharaoh's son.

A young girl, a little older than Hatasu, broke from her family group and ran up to the princess. She handed Hatasu a single red poppy flower. "I'm sorry about your brother. My brother died during the storm, too." Before Hatasu could even say thank you, the girl dashed away back to her family at the end of the line.

They approached the pavilion of transformation. Hatasu saw the tent-like structure in front of a mud-brick building. The chief ka priest...looking like the jackal god, Anubis...stood waiting at the entrance of the tent to greet the khat and the royal mourners. His black dog-headed mask was large, with a long thin snoot, tall pointed ears, and neat slits for eyes. This was the priest that knew the rituals to help Wadj make his journey through the door of death.

Just inside this tent was a stone table with a lion's head carved at one end and lion's feet at the bottom of each of the four legs.

Satamun saw her staring and whispered, "That's the table of rebirth. It is as though the lion will carry him on his back into his new life."

The wab priests received Wadjmose's khat and placed it on this table. The mourners gathered around, continuing their wail. Three bare-headed Ka priests stood in readiness by the jackal headed priest who, bowing to the grieving pharaoh, said, "We will purify and mummify Wadjmose's khat. He shall be prepared for his transformation."

The Anubis priest continued with a prayer over the empty khat. His voice rang clear so all gathered could hear.

"Hail to this Wadjmose
May you be purified
May your ka be purified
May your ba be purified
May your akh be purified
May you come to your mother, Nut
Behold, you are spiritual
And dwell with the gods."

After more chants, prayers and incense, they left the body to the wisdom of the ka priests. The group accompanied the mourning family back to the palace, where the close relatives would stay to share the grief and to comfort the family. They would have a funeral meal in the evening, and they would call the ka of Wadjmose to join them.

On the less formal procession back to the palace, Hatasu's Aunt Satamun extended her hand as an invitation and the child walked with her. Her long graceful fingers, gently enclosed the soft small ones. While Satamun's hands were lovely to look at, they did not feel good to hold…they were too bony, too hard. Hatasu looked up into her aunt's plain face. When Satamun smiled, her long upper teeth showed. It was her power and intelligence which drew people to her, not her looks. Young priestesses walked a slight distance behind. Their attention and affection for the High Priestess were obvious.

"I know you loved Wadjmose," she said. "This is a very hard time. Many of my loved ones wait for me in the stars…my parents, my husband, and three of my sons. As you grow, you will become more accustomed to having dear ones on both sides of the doorway of death." She said this with softness and the understanding of her niece's pain.

Hatasu knew she was widowed and had chosen not to remarry. She said it was enough that she was the God's Wife. She put all of her energy into her role at the temple. She worked hand in hand with Hapu, performing rituals for the well being of the people. In addition, she was responsible for overseeing the women temple workers and directing the temple school for artists, musicians and chantresses. She had suffered much at the loss of her children and took comfort in her only surviving son, Tao. Her fierce family pride shone, through her love for him.

"I wish your cousin, Tao, could be here today. He loved Wadjmose, too. His studies have taken him to Thoth's House of

Life in Khemenu. He would understand your grief. He was your age when his oldest brother passed to the stars."

Hatasu only vaguely remembered this cousin but he was spoken of often. He was older than Wadjmose. What she could remember of him was that he was stiff, quiet and serious, with looks as uncomely as his mother's.

"What will happen to Wadj at the mortuary temple?" Hatasu wanted to know.

Satamun nodded and said softly, "His body must be purified and prepared for the tomb. It will take seventy days, the same number as it takes the star Sothis to travel the underworld beneath the horizon, before it rises again with the sun on New Year's Day. Once these preparations are done, we will have a funeral service and he will be placed in his House of Eternity on the West Bank."

"So, when his khat is purified, he then goes to Nut?"

"Well, first his ba goes before the assessors who ask the questions about whether he has honored the spirit of life while he walked the earth. Then Thoth, the god of wisdom, weighs his heart against a feather of Maat's justice. Wadj lived a good life and his heart will surely be light as that feather. He will proceed on his way to Nut."

"But why do they do things to his khat? I thought it was his akh that was important."

"You are right," said Satamun. "It is the akh that is important, but when the khat is preserved, then a part of his soul stays close to earth. Whether a loved one is on this side of the door of life or on the other, he is still part of his family. I know you will miss Wadj

50

very much and by having the ka close by, it helps you stay in touch with him. Once his khat is in his house of eternity, the family will make offerings to his ka and have a place to visit with him on our festival of the ancestors. There you will seek dreams and communication with him. This helps us on this terrestrial plain and it helps him on the celestial plain."

She listened carefully to all her aunt said to her. Nodding, she thought of her dream of him and wished for more such dreams.

When they returned to the palace, it was quite late in the day. Thethi went off to his room to rest. Hatasu found herself a quiet hidden place in the garden, along the enclosure wall behind the blue cornflowers. There, she just wished to be alone. She thought about how Wadjmose would miss the things in this world. He loved to hunt wild animals. He told great tales of his exploits hunting the scimitar-horned Oryx in the desert and the hippopotamus in the river. He wanted to be a warrior and do great deeds in battle, and he was content with his role as future Pharaoh. He had always loved the time of inundation…when the waters returned dancing and swirling red…and he enjoyed the festival celebrations welcomin the time of the flood.

Hatasu fell asleep in the garden. The sound of her grandmother's voice awakened her. It was dark all around. Night had fallen as Hatasu slept.

"Hatasu!" her grandmother called. "Where could that Sekhmet warrior be?"

Hatasu realized, in her sleepy haze, that Senisenb was calling her. Hatasu sat up and stretched, rustling the cornflower plant as she stood. The bright stars twinkling in the clear, night sky gave sufficient light for her to see her grandmother walking along the garden path.

"Ah, there you are!" said Senisenb. "I missed you in the hall and didn't find you in your room. I thought you might be out here."

Senisenb moved to the bench by the lotus pool. She smiled, and patting her hand on the bench next to her, invited Hatasu to come sit.

The Sekhmet Warrior did an artful imitation of a stalking cat as she moved to the bench to be with her beloved grandmother. She snuggled up next to her soft, receptive body and made playful, purring sounds.

Putting her arm around her princess, Senisenb asked, "How are you doing, my little one?"

"I wish I could have saved Wadjmose from the storm, the way I saved Miu."

"Oh, Hatasu, there are some things none of us can help. All the magic of the goddesses and gods themselves cannot change one's destiny. We must do what we can to the best of the abilities given us. It was Wadjmose's time to move on to the stars. It seems the gods have destined someone else to be your future husband." It was reassuring to know that her grandmother understood her worry.

The two of them turned their eyes skyward. "Do you see Nut up there, smiling down on us?" Senisenb pointed with her free arm, the other one still holding the young princess close to her. "You see the form of her body stretched milky white across the sky?"

Hatasu nodded.

Pointing to the western horizon, she continued, "See, there's her head." Now, pointing to the eastern horizon, she added, "And there are her legs…and in between all that milky whiteness are stars, the ba of the ancestors."

The child sat still, feeling very small.

Now, turning around behind them to the north, she pointed to a particular group of stars. "Those stars are called the Imperishable Ones. They are always in the sky. Other stars spend some part of the year living out of our sight, beneath the horizon, rising again to visit us only for certain months of the year. The Imperishable Ones, far to the north, never fade and never die. That is where we wish to go, to be eternal like those imperishable ones."

They were silent for a few moments. Hatasu said, "Which one do you think is Wadj?"

"Hmm, there are so many he could be! I see that one there," she said, pointing to the sky. "I think it is twinkling at you. Maybe that is Wadjmose."

Hatasu snuggled closer and smiled. She imagined herself twinkling back at her brother in the stars. "How is it that he is there, yet I feel him here with us?" Hatasu asked.

"Ah, yes. You are blessed to be able to feel such things. Can you feel him missing you as much as you miss him? His ba is like a bird that can fly. It can be here with us, and it can fly to his mother in the sky. The period of time just after death is a hard time for a ba that passes. He's in transition between this world and the next, so he needs help from both sides. The chants, spells and prayers we said today help him, as well as what the priests do at the mortuary temple. All these things are meant to help him make a successful transition. It also helps us to make the transition to relating to him as a spirit. But the ka will stay close, and we will have ways to express our continued love and care for him through the years, as we can make offerings to his ka."

"Grandma, Mama says I am going to have a sister soon. Where will she come from? Does she have a ba in the stars? Father said Wadjmose passed out the door to the other world, just as we pass through it when we are born. What does that mean?"

"Ah, you ask wise questions, Little One. Yes, the ba comes from the stars. Your mother's body gives it a khet, and Khnum, the potter god, gives it a ka…a double."

As her grandmother finished speaking, there came from inside the palace, amidst the jumbled noise of many people, a strange and wonderful sound. Tilting her head, Hatasu's grandmother said, "Ah, I hear the music of the harp. There is no better way to soothe the sadness of our grief for Wadj. There is also food set out, if you are hungry. Shall we go inside?"

A gentle and soft melody floated through the night air of the palace. Following the sound, Hatasu and her grandmother entered the family's living room. The small group that remained was the close family. They sat around low tables spread with the remains of food. They were talking in low voices.

Ahmose, having dismissed the court musician, sat at the harp herself…plucking from it a soothing magic. Thutmose sat on his throne, the base of which showed the weaving together of the lotus and papyrus of the Two Lands. He looked with unseeing eyes off into the distance. Thethi sat on Paheri's lap; his nurse-tutor comforting him with a gentle song…an unusual softness between them.

Uncle Ineni was next to them with his young daughter, Isis, on his lap, listening to the music, too. Cousin Hapu sat with Amenmose and his son Hapusenab, leaning forward in intense, soft conversation…as though he was trying to impart an urgent, if soothing, message to the young men who lost their companion. His wife, Ahhotep, and Hapu's mother were in conversation by themselves a short distance from him. Ineni's wife, Nefermose, and his daughter, Meryt, sat close to the Queen, along with Aunt Satamun who was singing softly to the song of the harp music.

"The Great Mother Watches over us all.

The sparkling stars are spinning.

Listen and you hear them singing."

Groups of servants clustered in corners and serving women, moved through the group, offering to refill cups or plates. The music gently floated around each small grouping and washed them clean, like an outpouring of ankhs.

Hatasu's attention was drawn toward the harp, itself. Her mother kneeled behind the wooden frame and leaned into it, touching the strings with her gentle fingers. She plucked a delightful melody that she played over and over in a hypnotic way. It seemed to encompass everything in the room. Within a short time, the enchantment touched Hatasu, too. Each person present seemed to be softening, as though they could feel their spirits growing cleaner and being released from disturbance.

Thutmose looked up from his reverie and scanned the room until his eyes fell on Amenmose. He called his son to him and putting his arm around his shoulder, held a private conversation with him. Though shaken by Wadj's death, Thutmose had lost none of his authority. Amenmose looked stiff and tense. When the conversation was over, his arm still around his son, Thutmose called for the attention of the family group.

"Our family has a great grief at the loss of our beloved Wadjmose. He cannot be replaced, but my duty to the kingdom goes on. From henceforth, Amenmose will be the 'Hawk-in-the-Nest' and the heir to the great throne." Her father looked tired and her brother looked like he was in an unreal daze. The family applauded this official announcement. It was what was expected.

Folks milled about, patting Amen on the back with congratulations and honoring him in his new role. It was clear they were comforted to have this matter settled quickly. Hatasu did not care who was named as the next Pharaoh; what she did care about was that she did *not* want to marry Amen, this teasing brother. All the more, she missed Wadj.

Chapter 3 ~ The Hawk-in-the-Nest

In the morning, the relatives were gone and the harp stood stately and imposing in the corner…right where it stood the night before, when it had soothed the family's grief. It was a thing of beauty. Made of glowing sycamore wood, the lower part deepening into the form of a ladle covered with a drum membrane. Its underside was painted with a design of alternating lotus and papyrus blossoms. Above this ladle, a wooden arm thinned to a neck that reached toward the heavens and at its tip was a lovely, delicate carving of the feather-topped-head of the goddess, Maat. Strung vertically between the pegs in the upper arm and the rod on the membrane-covered ladle part were eight strings. Her mother was again strumming those strings, issuing forth sounds that were soft and sad, slow, and moving.

When she stopped and smiled sadly at her daughter, Hatasu reached her hand high to stroke the smooth neck of the instrument, all the way to the top. She had to get on her tiptoes to touch the feather of Maat on the very top.

"Do you know why Maat is on my harp?" her mother asked.

With effort, Hatasu took her gaze away from the beautiful head on the harp to look to her mother for an answer. "Maat is the goddess of harmony?" offered Hatasu.

"Yes," said her mother. "When these strings vibrate together in music, there is harmony. Such music can bring peace to the sad and troubled heart, just as harmony and order between the gods and the people bring peace to a troubled land."

Hatasu's fingers slid down the wood to the membrane over the ladle. Her mother smiled as she tapped it with her finger, making a sound not unlike her frame-drum. Hatasu reached to touch a string and her mother watched as she carefully plucked one than another, delighting in each different sound.

Ahmose extended her own hand up to the knobs just below Maat's head. "This is the Great Above of this instrument." Then, moving her hand to the rod over the membrane of the wooden ladle, she said, "This is the Great Below. The strings are the magic that makes them able to speak to each other. This feather of Maat is the celestial Nut, and the lotus and papyrus is the earthly realm of the Two Lands. The Pharaoh is like these strings that communicate between the spirit-world of Nut and the earthly-world of Khemet. There must be a strong, wise pharaoh that can bring harmony between the two. The lotus and the papyrus are Upper and Lower Khemet and like the Pharaoh and his consort. Your father and I are that earthly harmony and the land flourishes under his care. Wadjmose was the most like your father of his three sons. He had the gift and he was learning to be like the strings of the harp, bridging the gap between gods and men. His passing from this realm is a great loss."

"If Amen is to be Pharaoh, I must be his consort, right?"

"That's right. In the royal family our lives are directed by a duty to keep the land and people in harmony with the goddess."

"Mother, I don't want to be Queen to Amenmose," Hatasu blurted out.

"It is the duty of the daughter of the royal line to marry her brother, who is Pharaoh."

"When I think of being consort to Amenmose, I feel like a bird imprisoned in a cage. My heart weights heavy in my chest. He likes his horses more than he likes me." She let out a loud sigh. "Oh…how I miss Wadj!"

"I know. You and Wadj were as twin kas, but now your divine father, in his enlightened wisdom, has chosen Amenmose to be his heir. It is still you, the daughter, who will empower Amen's rule, for as my daughter, and daughter of the dynasty of the Taosids, your position of queen and first royal wife is central. Maat balances the Pharaoh's leadership with the Queen's protection. She is like the protective goddesses Wadjet and Nekhbet to the Pharaoh, and she is the mother goddess Mut to the people. You must find ways for your kas to make harmonious music between the Two Lands and the goddess."

"But, you wanted to be consort to Father!"

"Yes. Your father holds my heart and I his. It might have been more difficult if there'd been a living son of my royal father's family. My oldest brother, Pharaoh Amenhotep, ruled well with our sister, Merytamun, but they left no heirs. Your father shone bright among all the young men in the House of Life. From the first, our kas saw beauty in each other and we were drawn together…like you and Wadj. Pharaoh Amenhotep also saw Thutmose's strength, because he was a great general in the army."

Hatasu sighed, trying to resign herself to what her mother said. Having always had the importance of her royal duties impressed upon her, she could see no other option but to accept this change in her fate.

"Don't fret too much about it now, Dear," her mother said, seeing her distress. "The goddess unfolds the future in unexpected ways. My ka sees you as a Daughter of Amun and as one who will 'rule in peace'. I don't know where Amen fits into this, but I know this about you."

Hatasu was thoughtful of her mother's words. Her sense of duty conflicted with her steadfast longing for Wadj.

The next few days passed slowly. Un-realness permeated everything. It was like trying to paddle a boat through a thick river fog. Hatasu missed not only Wadj, but her larger family. Since his death, she wanted everyone she loved close around her. They seemed scattered: Her father withdrawn into meetings about the storm, Amen withdrawn into the horse stables, Thethi withdrew to his sick bed, and her mother alternated between her sad-songed-harp and overseeing the household. Sitre was the only one available, and even she, her gentle guardian, was quiet…her energies subdued.

There finally came a morning the Pharaoh took breakfast with the family. All were there but Thethi, who was still sick. It was the first time Hatasu had seen her father in days. Her heart tightened in alarm at the change in his appearance. He looked thinner, wrinkles were deeper at the outside corners of his eyes and shadows hung under ther kohl lining.

The Queen's eyes followed him as he entered. "Dear, you must slow down and give yourself the chance to mourn Wadj. No god would fault you for your sadness. Looking at his wife, the Pharaoh answered, "The storm has done so much damage, My Dear. I am receiving reports and requests for help from as far away as the town of Zawty, half-way down the Nile. Clearing the canals and dykes of khamsin sand must be attended to immediately, before the inundation, or there will not be adequate water for the irrigation of the fields. That would threaten the harvest. As Horus, I see afar and must keep the land in alignment with the seasons of the gods.

"The work tax I'd planned to finish my great wall around the temple to honor the gods, must now be used to dig out the main canals and as much of the dykes as can be accomplished before the waters rises. On top of that, the regional governors are restless again, particularly in the Itjtawy area near Memphis. This must not be allowed to develop into dissention fueled by an inadequate harvest."

Sitting in the chair the servant pulled out for him at the head of the table, he continued, "My biggest worry, however, is that the people are frightened by the death of Wadjmose. It has renewed the rumors and doubts that Pharaoh Amenhotep and I struggled to keep at bay. Some are looking for an excuse to question the god's favor on this, my Thutmosid line. The surety of the succession passing to Amen's must be established quickly, even before his first temple initiation."

He turned to Amen and said, "Tomorrow I inspect the work on the canals. It is important for the people to see you with me and feel reassured."

Amen nodded, his eyes still reddened and swollen from his grief. Turning back to his Queen, he continued, "No one can be allowed to doubt our strength. There are jackals who would use any doubt to reach for the Double Crown for themselves. Any division of loyalties would leave the land vulnerable to the expansionist powers warring in the Levant. Even as there is suffering at home from the storm, there are also reports of a troubling nature from our suzerains in the north."

"Yes, all these things are important. Still, you must rest."

"There will be time to rest after the Epagomenal Festival and the inundation. Maat calls to me to make things right, now." He turned back to his son. "When Ra shows his face over the eastern mountains tomorrow, Ineni and I will meet in front of the ceremonial palace. Be there."

"I will," he said.

Hatasu felt a bit anxious as her father talked of all these concerns. She remembered the discussion about the khamsin and bad omens and evil magicians, but when she looked at her father, her eyes could only see his divine majesty, and she assumed his perfect wisdom in handling all problems—tired and sad, or not. After all, he was the god Horus on earth.

The Pharaoh continued talking to her brother, "Amen, you are the Hawk-in-the-Nest now. There is much for you to learn. I know it is more to your liking to race chariots and hunt Ibex. These were skills that suited your training for military leadership when Wadj was to be the Pharaoh, but now you must learn to lead in times of peace, too."

Amen looked up this time and with effort, fixed his sad eyes on his father. "Yes, Father, I know. I'll do my best. It's just that being

Pharaoh suited Wadj so much better. He wanted to be Pharaoh. I just don't understand why he had to die. He would be Pharaoh, I'd be the military General, Thethi would be the Vizier, and Hatasu was to be Wadj's queen consort.

"Yes Amen, that was the plan but now, we must go on. We are the royal Thutmosid family. It is our duty to assure the well being of the land."

"I know," Amen said, holding himself a bit straighter with some pride.

Hatasu had a question she'd been waiting to ask her father. This lull in the conversation was her first opportunity. "Did many die in the storm…like Wadjmose?"

He turned to her and swallowing his breakfast fig said, watching her quizzically, "A few people. One young man drowned in the river. Some of our noble families report injuries and illness due to the storm."

"During the procession, a girl gave me a flower and told me her brother died, too. Her family will get help, right?"

He raised his eyebrows, then turned to her mother and said, "Our daughter has a heart for our common people." He reached his hand across the table and mussed her red hair in an affectionate way. "Amen, your sister-consort will make a fine queen."

Amen nodded politely toward his father, then turned to his sister with eyes that only thinly veiled his irritation. She realized how, even now, as he was the Hawk-in-the-Nest…he so vied for the blessing of their father's approval that he might find his praise of her annoying.

Her father looked at her and said, "I will see to it the girl's brother is buried well and that the family does not need for food or shelter as they grieve him."

Amen finished his breakfast abruptly and said, "Excuse me, Father. I have things to do at the stable."

Once excused, however, Thutmose watched him go with a sigh. When Amen was out of ear shot, he turned to Ahmose again, shaking his head. "Hatasu is more like Wadj than Amen is."

Ahmose put her hand on the Pharaoh's arm and said, "Give him time, Dear. He is so shaken by his brother's death. It is no wonder he can neither focus on anything, nor pull himself out of his sadness."

"I'm sure you are right. But with Wadj's death, and that oracle dream that I wouldn't sire another male child…" He shook his head as he spoke. "Well, the succession must be managed with the children I have, and Thethi's illnesses make him a poor candidate. It is so important that Amen rise to the occasion."

Ahmose continued, "Amen needs to be trained, just as you trained Wadj. While he doesn't have the love of governing as Wadj did, he is a disciplined master of the horse and chariot. He is good natured in a way that makes the soldiers love him as well as respecting his skill. He will just make a different kind of Pharaoh than Wadj."

"Yes, yes…you are right. He is a good son. He will learn what he needs to, to be a good pharaoh. I believe his role in the upcoming Festival will generate more enthusiasm in him. The military display on the Day of Horus, and the hunt on the Day of

Set, will allow him to exhibit his finest qualities."

Hatasu listened silently. This was so important to her father. She knew her duty. She, too, would do her best…for him.

After the meal, her father rose to return to the ceremonial palace. As he was leaving, he paused and turned back. "Daughter," he said, "tomorrow, when I inspect the work on the canals," he nodded his head briskly and commanded, "you will come with us."

Her young heart swelled with happiness. She had never been included in such a trip with her father before.

The next morning came slowly for her. She was ready before either the sun or Sitre were up. She still had to wait for Ineni to arrive and for her father to finish his sacred duties at the temple. She sat on the low wall around the lotus pond and waited.

She thought of Ineni and her father as brothers, like Wadj and Amen. They were both Intefs, whose ancestors had ruled Waset generations ago…and were, therefore, called 'hereditary princes', but as far as the ruling dynasty, her mother's family, was concerned…they were commoners. Amenhotep Tao was Pharaoh as Thutmose and Ineni grew up in the palace school known as the House of Life. Hatasu knew the story well, of how Ahmose loved him, and Amenhotep named him as his heir, making him co-regent with him to secure a smooth transition.

On the other hand, her father's brother, Ineni, was traveling a different path. His love of architecture led him to become Amenhotep's architect and design the great pylon gates of the Amun temple for him. He married a non-royal noble woman, started a family and had leisure time for his hobby of horticulture.

His manor outside the city was a gardener's delight, and as a green haven in the desert, it was a favorite place for her to play with her cousins, Meryt and Isis. Whatever childhood rivalries they might have had, Thutmose and Ineni were now well suited to their differing roles; Thutmose was Pharaoh, Ineni was the chief architect and the Vizier of the whole land. They worked well together. Hatasu understood this was why Thutmose expected his own children to be satisfied in fulfilling complimentary roles.

As she was thinking of Ineni, the litter bearers arrived and placed themselves near the gateway to wait. There were two litters, which meant the Pharaoh and the Hawk-in-the-Nest would both be very visible for the town's folks to see. Hatasu was just as glad to not be expected to be limited by the confines of such a chair. She loved the rare opportunities to be in the village of Waset.

Finally, Hatasu spotted Ineni coming through the gateway wearing his usual long white skirt and holding his staff. Hatasu ran to greet him with a bright smile of expectation. "Hello, Uncle. Father said I could go to town with you today."

Ineni had the odd feature of one eyebrow being perpetually higher than the other. This gave him the appearance of always being both quizzical and amused. Though he was preoccupied with the business at hand, her cheery face brought him out of his reverie. He smiled down at her as she walked along beside him, matching his long strides with two of her half-running steps. Slowing down so she could keep up with him, he extended his hand to rest on her shoulder as they walked together. His chief scribe, pallet in hand, walked a respectful pace behind him.

"You are like a chirping bird this morning, daughter of my brother. So, you shall make inspections with us. It shall be a pleasant thing to have your smiling face to brighten our day."

They paused by the garden pool to wait for the others. Wadjmose had often gone on such trips with the Pharaoh and the Vizier. Her heart fell a little as she thought of her missing brother. The empty ache that seemed to have set up a dwelling place in her chest, grew heavier.

Just then, the Pharaoh emerged from the palace with his faithful scribe Huy by his side. She was again so glad to be going with him that her heart lightened. He stood erect and glorious as he strolled toward them, yesterday's tiredness less obvious. He was wearing his nemes crown and a brightly jeweled collar with matching arm bands. As he approached, his eyes scanned the garden, clearly looking for Amen.

She heard the sound of running footsteps and around the corner came Amen, his eyes still sleepy. He had obviously dressed hurriedly. His white linen kilt was on crooked and the eye kohl was smudged at the corners. He slowed to a more dignified walk as he approached and bowed his greeting to his father.

The Pharaoh eyed him carefully with an almost unperceivable shake of his head and said, "Amen, you will ride in the litter next to me. I want all to see you as we go through the town. When we get to the canal road, Ineni will ride." Hatasu guessed that was because they would confer on the progress of the repairs.

The small group headed off for their inspection tour. There were several ways through the town. One was the ceremonial road that stretched between the two great temples, that of Amun, near the palace, and the other the southern temple of the goddess Mut. The alternate route was the market street that ran parallel to the river. They took the latter, along which was clustered the homes and stalls of merchants, crafts persons, fishermen and servants of the temple and palace.

As they began their day's journey, Hatasu danced along beside her uncle as her father and brother rode royally in the litters. As she walked, she was free to go as she pleased. Sometimes she held Ineni's hand and sometimes she ran ahead to see a bauble that caught her eye or lingered behind to pet a dog. As she went, she recognized the mid-morning smells characteristic of each of the vendors. Her nose rose into the air to take in the smells of fresh-cooked bread. There was the earthy smell of vegetables and animal smells coming from the cages of pigeons and ducks. Sounds rose up to meet her, as well. People were loudly making their transactions. The donkeys brayed, complaining of their loads. Children laughed as they ran after each other or animals.

Though the smells and sounds were similar, the sights were different. Things were still in disarray from the storm. The merchants' wares were scanty, broken pieces lying about. Many people wore bandages. The usual brightly-striped canopies were set up to give shade to the merchants and their produce, but today, some of the poles that held them up were broken and even the sheltering cloth was torn and dusty. Through the stall, Hatasu saw the boats tied up at the shore. Fishermen were working to repair damages to them.

It was a rare occasion for their beloved Pharaoh to come through their streets. He was their good god and it was his job to care for them. The relief measures he set up were received with gratitude, and now they came forward with their love, as well as with their condolences at the loss of his son. Hatasu watched him as he sat tall, accepting their adoration and sympathy. The Pharaoh looked out over the people, their damaged shops and their houses, as he nodded and smiled to reassure them.

Amenmose rode beside their father now, waving and letting everyone see him as their new heir to the Double Crown. The people were receptive—smiling, waving and bowing to Amen, as well as Thutmose.

The small herd of scribes was interspersed among the royal entourage. Foremost among them was Huy, the Pharaoh's personal scribe. He was a man of bright, dark eyes, big ears and fine, long-fingered hands. Hatasu knew he and the Pharaoh had been childhood friends growing up in that same House of Life. Now, he walked near Thutmose's chair and used his reed pen to make note of the Pharaoh's planned improvements and other orders. Amen looked like he was really trying to pay attention. The rest of the scribes were under Ineni's directions and they recorded damages to the canals and wrote down reports given by the villagers.

Once they came to Temple of Mut, they turned toward the east and traveled along a road of hardened dirt that took them alongside the main canal. At this point, the litter bearers were given a rest and the Pharaoh and Amen disembarked. The main canal was as deep and wide as the Nile itself at this, its yearly low.

Here, close to the river, it was clear of sand and ready for the water, but Hatasu could see the straight line it traveled into the desert. About three-quarters of the way out, there was a gang of bronzed-backed men deep in the canal bed, working with shovels. Piles of sand were visible on each of the canal banks.

Thutmose and Ineni stood together looking out over the length of the canal and surveying the system of interconnecting dykes…pointing and nodding and directing the scribes in their records. There was still much work to be done, as this smaller patchwork of the water irrigation system was still mostly filled in with sand.

Amenmose was content to not be part of this conversation between his father and uncle. He absent-mindedly kicked a pebble around on the packed dirt roadway. Hatasu watched him for a minute, and then, reminded of a game she'd often played with Amen and Wadj, she moved over next to him. When he kicked the stone out a bit, she was able to intervene and kick it back to him. He kind of smiled, nodded at her, and passed the stone back in her direction. She didn't miss a beat, but kicked it ahead down the road at an angle in his direction. He kicked it back.

The Pharaoh and Vizier re-embarked on the litters and preceded north again on a canal road outside of the city, while Hatasu and Amen followed along, passing the stone back and forth between them…an occasional giggle from her or a laugh from Amen. This had drawn an approving smile from the Pharaoh.

Hatasu had learned to be good at this with Wadj and she was delighting in a possible camaraderie with Amen. Just at that moment, however, perhaps because he was distracted by knowing his father was watching, he misjudged and kicked it too hard. The pebble went off the road and into a ditch. Amen's mood shifted suddenly to annoyance and he said, "Enough, red-haired Sekhmet!" as though it were she who had miss-kicked, not him. Then, off he stomped by himself.

"Come on, Amen. It's just a game. Here's another pebble."

"Yeah, it is just a game. And I don't feel like playing anymore."

Hatasu was stunned for the moment, almost wondering what happened. Then the heavy-chested loneliness settled into her heart again. Wadj would never have gotten angry with her for his miss-kick. But then, she couldn't remember a time he'd missed a kick.

Seeing her walk by herself now, Thutmose invited Hatasu to ride with him for a while in his litter. She forgot her upset at Amen and delighted in riding with her father. He talked to her about the canals and dykes, and how they worked to bring the Nile water into what would otherwise be the desert. "When the Nile floods, everything is covered with water, as you can see from the palace roof-garden. When it recedes to its banks, the dikes are closed, keeping the water in the canals so a farmer can use his shaduf (levered irrigation device) to lift the water from the canal and dykes, into the irrigation ditches in his field. Now the dykes are open again, waiting for the flood to refill them."

From this vantage point high on the litter, she could see that in many places the irrigation ditches were still so full of sand, that they were level with the fields.

"All this must be dug out to make space for the water of the flood. Do you understand?" he asked her.

"Yes, it is the Pharaoh's job to look after the people, and the people must be able to work their fields for the Pharaoh," Hatasu answered. She'd heard it many times before. He nodded, satisfied.

They continued toward the palace on the northern road. Ra-Atum was about to slide beneath the western mountains as they returned to the palace garden. It had been a long day.

Amenmose, still sad and tired, bowed a respectful goodnight to his father and went in the direction of his rooms.

The last stretch of this journey had been long for a child as young as Hatasu. She had fallen asleep leaning against her father. He lifted her up in his strong arms and, rather than calling a servant, he carried her into her room and placed her on her bed. He kissed the top of her red head, lingering a moment to study her in her sleep.

He could not have predicted the threat she would see the next day.

Chapter 4 – The Foreigners

This was the hottest, driest time of the year, during which the most likely place to get the relief of a faint northern breeze was on the roof of the palace. For the next several days, Hatasu spent much of her time there. It was a pleasant space, shaded by a roof-covering held up with brightly colored lotus-topped pillars, decorated with potted palms, and made comfortable with woven mats and soft pillows. Part of the roof was left open to the sky…for during these hot moons, the family often slept here under the starry heavens. During the day, she could look out over the canals and dykes and watch the progress the work gangs were making in clearing them for the flood waters.

As the days went by and the work went along, it looked like all the dykes would be cleared in time for the inundation. Hatasu noted her father's stressed-look eased as the clearing neared completion. Looking out from her perch, she could also see where…just a few moons ago…the area to the east of the palace had been fields of green waving grains, contrasting sharply against the dull sand of the desert. Now, these same fields were the brown color of cracked earth, almost blending with the wild land beyond. She could see past the canals and would-be fields, into the desert, where the military barracks and the practice fields of the Pharaoh's army spread out in the distance.

On the other side of the roof, she could get a clear view of the river. As expected at this time of the year, it dwindled to a thin ribbon of its former self. She knew that at this low-river time, drinking water was scarce. It was a dangerous time… reminding everyone of the precariousness of life in the face of an encroaching desert. Hatasu's missing Wadj seemed to make the heat and dryness all the more intense for her. The anticipated inundation was the annual blessing that would again relieve the land, the people and, young Hatasu hoped, her own sad heart.

At this pivotal point in the cycle of the year, when the desert seemed poised to invade the cultivated land and civilization itself seemed to be held hostage to the returning river, the people gathered for the grandest of all the festivals of the Two Lands—the Epagomenal Days. This week-long festival included five days that existed outside of the calendar year, between the end of one year and the beginning of the next. During that period, the people remembered the gods and goddesses, told their stories and celebrated the cycle of life, death and rebirth. This festival culminated on New Year's Day, when the great star, Sothis, returned to the sky—rising reborn with the morning sun after its seventy day journey out of sight in the underworld. The star's return predicted the river's return. This sixth day of the festival began the new agricultural year, the New Year's Day, and the whole land celebrated by remembering and honoring the ancestors—thus weaving the beloved past and the hoped for future into the tapestry of the present.

In spite of the heat and the dryness, a lively sense of anticipation filled the palace and the town as everyone joined in the preparations for the festival. Palace women sat in small groups weaving garlands of flowers with which to decorate themselves and the festival hall.

The aromas of sweet breads and ripe fruits being prepared wafted through the air from the kitchen ovens.

There, also, was a great influx of people into the town as the noble families from areas up and down the river arrived to join in the celebration. Exotic looking foreigners arrived as well, bringing their tribute gifts required by Khemet's military treaties in neighboring lands. There was an air of expectation around her everywhere.

Thethi's strength returned and he was again Hatasu's companion in the excitement of the preparations for the festival. Sitre heightened that excitement by her yearly telling of the creation story. She viewed this narrative as essential in her duties of preparing them both for the upcoming festival. Hatasu loved stories, and sitting cross-legged at her guardian's feet, she leaned forward, eager to listen and focusing her attention on the ancient tale that helped to put order in the history of her people and her gods.

This year, the dying of the land was a reminder of her own loss, and she looked to the story of creation and the birth of the gods and goddesses as an invitation into the sacred mysteries; the conquest of order over chaos and the yearly rebirth of the dying river. Before she started, Sitre looked at her two young charges with her eyes shining with her delight in telling this, one of her favorite stories. She began.

"Before the birth of the world, there was nothing. All that existed was the abyss. This was the soundless, boundless, black, watery chaos called Nun. Within this chaos was everything that could exist but did not. It lay still and dormant, resting as unmanifest potential. From the dark abyss rose the primeval mound, the Benben. On this mound came forth the first god, Atum, the 'Completed One', rising alone and unaided. It was Atum's breath that was life and gave life to all else that is."

Even at this young age, Hatasu knew this was the initial victory of order over chaos. There was comfort in hearing this, a reassurance of the renewal of order...again and again.

Sitre went on, "Then, there came forth, the primeval papyrus swamp through which all other things came into being. Standing on this Benben, Atum...male and female within himself...produced all the others. First, he created Shu, the male, who is air...and Tefnut, the female, who is moisture. Mating together, Shu and Tefnut gave birth to Geb, the earth father, and to Nut, the sky mother. Earth and sky lay together until Shu (air) came between them, separating them so there would be room for more creatures.

"Once there was room, Nut gave birth to her first two children: 'Ra', the god of the sun, and 'Thoth', the god of wisdom. Ra did not want his mother to give birth to any more offspring, but...she was already pregnant with five children waiting to be born. Ra wouldn't allow her to birth her children.

"Thoth, the ibis-headed god of time and wisdom, came to Nut's defense. He helped Mother-Nut by challenging Ra to a game of dice. The stakes were a piece of time, won out of Ra's yearly circle, in which Nut could birth her children. Thoth won the game and Nut gave birth to her five incredible children: "'Osiris', first ruler of our land, now ruling the afterlife...'"

(He reminded Hatasu of Wadj, now in that afterlife...)

"…'Horus', the hawk-headed god of kingship…"

(…making her think of her grand father…)

"…'Set', god of the wild and barren desert…"

(…a troublesome god for Hatasu…)

"…'Isis', the goddess of healing and motherhood…"

(…similar to her own dear mother…)

"…and lastly, 'Nephthys', the goddess of divination."

(…seer of the unseen, like her aunt Satamun.)

"It is these gods and goddesses," continued Sitre, "who teach, guide, and help the people of Khemet, and the people of Khemet honor them by remembering and celebrating their great festival of the Epagomenal Days…a day for each of these gods and goddesses!"

Hatasu loved the story so she clamored for Sitre to tell it again, but her nurse laughed and said, "Once is enough today. I have things I must do to get ready for Osiris' Day. Why don't you go to the garden and make your own flower garlands for the festival?"

So she and Thethi amused themselves in the palace garden. Hatasu strung flower blossoms on a strong linen thread to make garlands as Sitre had suggested, but Thethi busied himself by arranging small stones as toy soldiers for the military parade he looked forward to on the Day of Horus, just two days away.

The children were side by side, absorbed in their individual activities. They expected this to be like preparation days they remembered from the festivals of other years. They had not expected what happened next.

The sound of people shouting came from the harbor-lake. This commotion brought foreboding to the children, for they remembered all too well the day Wadj's khat arrived on that very spot. They went to discover what was going on.

Palace servants, herdsman watering their animals, and laundresses washing linens, were shouting and waving their arms at a strange looking boat…telling them not to enter this private area of their Pharaoh. A large high-sided, many-oared ship had lowered its sails and a full crew of sailors rowed into the enclosed space in spite of the warnings. It pulled up alongside 'The Hawk', the Pharaoh's sleek warship.

Hatasu and Thethi exchanged alarmed looks and then turned toward the harbor. A foreigner intruding on this territory was a disturbance to Maat's order. *Was this the omen the storm had warned about?* Though the civilized rules of hospitality meant the people of the Two Lands must give a welcome in his home to one of 'equal rank'. Since none were equal to the Divine Pharaoh, these travelers, assuming to come to the Pharaoh's palace, was a breech of civilized conduct and considered barbarously offensive.

The children watched dumbfounded as an oddly dressed man disembarked. He wore a long, brightly colored purple skirt wrapped several times around him in descending layers. A gray-white cloak covered the bright color underneath. He had black, curly hair…even on his face…and a tight-fitting cap on his head.

She was relieved as her uncle, Vizier Ineni, marched with urgent steps down to the harbor, attended by a small unit of black-skinned Medjay guards carrying spears. Ineni made strong hand gestures indicating the boat leave immediately and dock at the town harbor.

The foreigner responded with a voice that reminded the children of the growl of an animal. Ineni replied in a language the children did not understand, and only when two of the Medjays guards stepped forward with pointed spears, did the foreigner re-board the ship.

Hatasu noticed the gleam of knives tucked into the belts of the men on the boat, again not customary for tribute-bearing delegates. The sailors began rowing out of the harbor lake and into the canal, an eerie stillness on board. Hatasu realized she'd been holding her breath only as the air escaped her as a sigh of relief.

Noble Ineni was standing on the harbor steps, shaven head and face, white-skirted, gold-collared, holding himself erect with the staff of his authority before him. He was a striking contrast to the man whose disrespectful behavior she saw as representing an undefined threat. Ineni stood there with deep frown lines on his face.

Once the foreign ship was safely out of the harbor, the children cautiously approached their uncle and looked up at him questioningly. Ineni's asymmetric eyebrows were exaggerated. The right one was pulled down so far that his eye was a narrow slit. The left one was raised high on his forehead. Both eyes followed the boat as it traveled out into the river.

"Who are they, Uncle?" Hatasu asked.

"Amurru, Canaanites, Hyksos...they are all the same; arrogant, rude, and ignorant." Seeing the alarm on both children's faces, he softened his tone. "They are delegates from the Amurru suzerain in the Levant and they bring their treaty tribute." Then, as though forgetting the children again, he said under his breath, "This is a bad omen. We'd best be wary."

The foreigner's strange behavior and Ineni's mention of Hyksos, heightened Hatasu's worry. She remembered her mother saying these people caused trouble in the past. She knew the suzerains were from the territory in the Levant area of Asia. These lands were originally conquered by her grandfather, Pharaoh Ahmose, the Liberator. Now her father held hegemony over these many warring kingdoms and their subjugated princes. She heard her father say how difficult it was to maintain control there, because no one from their Nile Valley wished to live in the faraway land.

This was unlike their rulership of the land of Kush, to their south. The Pharaohs of the Two Lands had a long history of dominating the Nubians and peoples of Kush. The Pharaoh's people could feel at home there because it was a land sharing the same beloved river. There was no comfort for the men of the Two Lands in the alien lands of the Levant, so, unlike Kush, there were no colonies or military units stationed there. None the less, she had seen delegates from each of these territories arrive for the Epagomenal Days in the past to offer the tributes demanded by the military treaty.

Never before had anyone challenged this arrangement. Once the boat was out of the harbor, the children turned to go back toward the palace. They saw the Pharaoh standing at the top of the steps in a wide legged stance with his arms folded, his eyebrows pulled together and his eyes narrowed. The Vizier approached and stood next to him. They watched together as the foreigners rowed out toward the river.

Seeing the two brothers side by side in the sun, highlighted their family resemblance. Hatasu and Thethi stayed close to them as the two men discussed the incident, hoping for more information.

Ineni started reporting to his Pharaoh, "It is, indeed, Bazor…Hazor's son. It seems the old Amurru king considers his son to have come of age to act as his delegate."

"But Hazor would have trained him. The rules of hospitality forbid it…unless this is deliberate challenge."

"Bazor insisted he was *entitled* to a king's greeting. So, either he does not have his father's wisdom, or Hazor is not well enough to advise his son…or perhaps, Bazor does not heed his father's wisdom."

Thutmose's frown deepened. His eyes flashed with anger. "He expects to be honored as a visiting *monarch*!" He raised his voice in disbelief. After a moment's pause he lowered it again, and said with emphasis, "But he is a subjugated prince!"

Hatasu seldom saw her father so blatantly angry.

"Yes," answered Ineni. "And the message was delivered as a challenge."

"If we suppose old Hazor knows of Bazor's plan, he is letting us know his son and heir has ambitions to a grander kingship than this father's." Thutmose pulled his eyebrows even more tightly together in a thoughtful scowl. "He tests us, to see how we respond to this intrusion. Perhaps he assesses our resolve in order to determine further acts of rebellion."

Then with a decisive nod of the head, he said, "Ineni, once he is settled in his lodging, deliver a message from My Divine Majesty, saying I will see him at the Tribute Procession on the Day of Horus, like all the other delegates and subjugated princes. Let him know he is offered no special privilege."

Ineni nodded briskly. "Yes, it will be done as you say." Then with a thoughtful hand rubbing his chin, the Vizier added, "Thutmose, we must also consider that perhaps he comes to spy. To see if he can find any weakness to encourage rebellion in Amurru or even armed invasion into the Two Lands."

Hatasu spoke up, "Would they do that, Father?"

Looking at his daughter's upturned face, he answered, "I don't believe they would, but you must know that we do have enemies. The peoples of the Levant are always hungry for more land. They wish to overthrow the Two Land's authority over them…and, like all the tribes in the Levant, look with greedy hearts on our grain and our gold."

The Pharaoh's eyes returned to the slow movement of the foreign ship in the canal as he said, "Those people who dwell in the Levant live in fear and are ruled by fear, knowing nothing of Maat or Ra. Their strength over their domain is that of brute force rather than wisdom of the gods or the love of their people…such as they, must never again gain a foothold in our land as the Hyksos did."

They all watched as the boat pulled out of the canal and into the river. As it did so, the sailors unfurled the sail to catch the northern breeze that would carry them upriver to the quay. Thutmose and Ineni saw it at the same time. On the sail, in bright colors and bold design, was a picture of two lions locked in mortal combat.

"That is not the sail of a subject prince come humbly to offer tribute," said Thutmose.

Ineni responded, "No, but it is consistent with the reports the messengers bring of trouble in the territories around the Amurru. We must watch him closely and gather information from him about what is happening where he lives on the banks of his river, the Orontes."

Anger retreated from Thutmose's face and hard resolution took its place. He said to his Vizier and his brother, "My army is strong, Ineni. It is well equipped with the finest of men and horses. The god, Amun, has given me victories in battle before and he will do so again if necessary."

Thethi interrupted at this point and in a strong voice asked, "Will you go to war, Father?"

"Only if I must, son," his father said. "Let Bazor see the military display on the Day of Horus. It will be strategic to remind him to respect Your Divine Majesty. Perhaps then war will be unnecessary."

"Yes, he will bring word back to his father, Hazor…I am too strong to resist or invade. In the meantime, Ineni, double the Medjays in the town around the area where they are staying and assign a man to report on all of their doings. We must know more. Do they come to challenge, to test, to spy, or all of these things. We must also be prepared to mobilize the army to go north if rebellion or invasion is part of their plan."

The children looked at each other, Hatasu's body was tight from the growing tension.

The Vizier responded, "I will see to it immediately. The guards will watch the whole Amurru crew." Then he turned to young Thethi. "But, little prince, I do not think Bazor will persist, once he sees the Horus Day military display. It shall be truly awe inspiring this year. No one could see it and think of disrespecting the Double Crown!"

"So probably no war, right?" Thethi, looking back up to his father, sounded almost disappointed.

"No, Thethi, probably no war, but we will never again be blind to the possibilities of oppression by these peoples. Never again will they get even a toehold in this land. I must be prepared to act decisively."

Once they could see that the foreign boat was docked at the town quay, the two most powerful men in the land turned and walked in the direction of the ceremonial palace, an area the children were not allowed to enter.

Their voices grew fainter but Hatasu distinctly heard her father say, "Yes, and I am also pleased with the way Amenmose has been taking on more responsibility in the army. This is a good way for him to grow in the skills of rulership, for I, myself, learned much in the army of Pharaoh Amenhotep. On the Day of Horus he will stand out as the Hawk-in-the-Nest. This will let Hazor know that we, too, have a strong heir to the Double Crown."

The Pharaoh and Vizier walked on, out of earshot of the children. They were left to decipher these events as best they could. Thethi was particularly agitated. "Hatasu, what do you think will happen? I don't think I've ever seen Father so angry or Ineni so upset!"

"Father knows what to do, Thethi."

"Maybe Father will go to war."

"I don't think so. I think Bazor is just testing. When he sees the army, he will not dare cause more trouble. It will be alright."

"But what if Father really does go to war? Oh, I wish I was old enough to go with him like Amen!"

"The foreigners would be very foolish to go to war with Father. He is, after all, the Good God and divine."

"If Father takes the army to war, Amen would get to go."

"I guess."

"I asked Amen to take me with him to the barracks yesterday morning. He said I was too young…and sick." Thethi scowled. He shook his head and stomped his foot as he said, "I'm *not* going to be sick any more! I'm *not* going to be left behind."

"Okay, Thethi. Stop upsetting yourself."

"I am going to live to be a soldier you know, Hatasu."

She looked at him oddly.

"I know what people say about me. I know they don't think I'll live to be an adult…but they are wrong. I'll live to be an adult *and* I'll be a soldier. You wait and see."

"I do not doubt you. I'm on your side, remember?"

"Okay, just so you don't write me off like Amenmose does. He used to do things with me, like play senet or take me to the stables. He's always too busy now. He says that's what happens when you become the Hawk-in-the-Nest, but Wadj wasn't too busy when he was the heir to the Double Crown."

She nodded, knowing it was true. "Well, Thethi, at least we have each other."

His small frame relaxed a bit. Hatasu and Thethi knew Amen was spending most of his time at the army training field at the edge of the Eastern Desert. She also noticed how the wrinkle lines around Thutmose's eyes lessened day by day as Amen engaged in this aspect of his training for rulership. She felt relief her father had again returned things to order and stability after the chaos caused by the storm. This added to her feelings of adoration for her father. As always, in her mind, he made everything right. For this reason, she also trusted he would take care of the foreigners.

News of the behavior of the Amurru's intrusion into the royal harbor spread rapidly around Waset, and the excited preparation was tempered with anxiety and gossip. There was an increased sense of agitation in the grownups around Hatasu. Sitre, in particular, was not her usual self. As she combed and re-braided the princess's red fly-away hair in preparation for the pre-festival family banquet, she talked a little faster and her hands were less gentle than usual.

"Why are you upset, Sitre?"

"I'm not upset. Why do you ask?"

"Because you are pulling my hair!"

"Oh…I didn't mean to do that."

"I know. So, why are you upset?"

"I'm not afraid of those Asiatics. Really, I'm not."

"So, why do your hands shake?"

"They are *not* shaking!" She put them flat on the child's head to stop the tremors.

Hatasu knew now she just needed to wait. The truth would come.

"Maybe I'm a little nervous. But who wouldn't be with the stories of the Hyksos when I was growing up. My mother would hide on the Day of Horus when the Asiatics brought their tribute. She said they looked and sounded like the dreaded Hyksos who had raped her sister. My mother said my aunt was never the same after that, and I knew her only as a child-like woman who needed to be taken care of. I, myself, never saw a Hyksos but my mother said the Amurru are close enough. They come every year but they never before acted so threatening. Who wouldn't be nervous?"

Hatasu left Sitre wringing her hands and pacing in small anxious steps. The princess rejoined Thethi and thought together they would amuse themselves until their cousins arrived. Just then, Paheri (pa-HAR-i) entered the garden, smiling as he walked toward the two royal children. This was Thethi's nurse-guardian, as Sitre was hers. He had the strong bronzed body of a chariot driver, the fine long-fingered hands of a scribe, and the heart of a nobleman farmer.

But, Hatasu thought as he approached, *he has the ears of a monkey*. Sure enough, both ears stuck straight out from the sides of his head. Actually, she liked Paheri because he often thought of interesting things for Thethi and her to do…other than the dancing and singing and making flower garlands Sitre liked so much. Paheri would take them out on the river sometimes or bring them to the royal horse stables. He also had the patience of a farmer that could wait as things grew in their right time. He applied this to Thethi and watched over his growth.

This day he walked into the garden with two throw-sticks in his hand. "How would the two of you like to learn how to use these today?"

Thethi jumped up from the stone soldiers he was playing with again and greeted Paheri with a huge grin. They both ran to meet him. "Come with me." Paheri said, "There's no one at the stables because they are all off at the desert training camp preparing for the Day of Horus. We can use the practice field there."

The throw-stick was primarily the weapon of the royal sport of duck hunting, but it was also standard issue for soldiers in the Pharaoh's army. These sticks rather resembled serpents. There was a snake-like curve in the body, broadening out at the tip into a snakehead-like point and ending in a tail…leather bound to form a throw-handle.

Paheri drew Thethi close to him first and said, "Here, look how it is done." He took the end of the stick and with a flick of the wrist, he threw it. It went a short distance and then turned and came back to Paheri, who caught it nimbly in one hand.

Thethi jumped up and down. "Let me try, let me try."

"Here you go," he said, handing him the stick.

Thethi threw it hard, but low. It went into the ground and he needed to run and retrieve it.

"Try again," said Paheri. "Throw higher this time."

He did and the stick did indeed return, but traveled only half of the way back to him before it hit the dirt again.

"Let me try!" Hatasu said, jumping up and down in impatience. "I want a turn, too."

"Here's one for you," said Paheri, as he handed the other throw-stick to Hatasu.

She threw it hard and high, but it went to her left and straight into the mud brick stable making a loud thud.

She looked quickly at Paheri, who smiled and said, "The idea is to throw straight ahead."

Thethi was ready to throw again. "If I were in the army, I'd throw so hard I'd get rid of all those Amurrus."

"Well, not this week. They are our guests and we must act civilly even if they don't."

"Did your parents tell you stories of the Hyksos?" asked Hatasu, thinking of Sitre.

"My grandfather has lots of stories because he fought in the war that drove them out of the Two Lands. The Amurru are like the Hyksos but they are not as detestable—only because they have no chance of gaining power here. No, the Hyksos were an abomination…a scar on the face of the land. Anyone who would take as his ruling name Apophis, the enemy of Ra, the one who seeks to destroy light and wisdom, is an anathema to the people of the Nile. That is the name their ruler took and he behaved as though, like Apophis, he wished to destroy our wisdom." Paheri's stuck-out ears had grown red with anger and his head shook back and forth.

"Tell us the story about Apophis again," Hatasu asked.

"Every night as the sun god, Ra, sinks behind the western mountains, he rides in his divine barque through the underworld. Every night the serpent, Apophis, tries to overcome and defeat Ra so he cannot rise anew and light our world each morning, rising over the eastern mountains. Our true Pharaohs take names of blessing gods. Your father, Thutmose, is named for Thoth, the god of wisdom. His name means 'born of Thoth'. Before him was Amenhotep. Amun-Ra is a form of the sun god and hotep means 'satisfied'."

"Wow, those foreigners are strange," said Hatasu.

"Yes, they are indeed strange."

They went back to their practice as Paheri set up targets for them to aim at. They started out standing pretty close to the targets and still it took considerable practice for them to hit it. Paheri promised when they could hit the target from a reasonable distance, he would take them to the marsh for a duck hunt.

Ducks were *not* what Thethi and Hatasu were thinking of hitting as they practiced that afternoon.

Eventually, their cousins arrived. The families of Cousin Hapu and Uncle Ineni gathered at the palace for the family meal celebrated at the eve of the festival days. Hapu, the high priest, and his wife, Ahhotep, came first with their son, Hapuseneb (Ha-PU-sen-eb).

Hatasu and Thethi gave their throw-sticks back to Paheri and ran to meet their friend. He was Hatasu's favorite of the playmates. He looked like a younger, taller version of his father with the same light eyes. Instead of the shaved head of the priest, however, he had a full head of shiny black hair pulled to the side in the youth lock. He was a year older than Hatasu and of a quiet, thoughtful nature with a curious mind. From their earliest childhood, he had liked

Hatasu, too. He liked her ideas, her schemes, and most of all, like her, he loved stories…particularly stories of the gods and goddesses.

Uncle Ineni and his wife, Nefermose (nefer–MOSES), arrived soon after with their children. Meryt (MER-et) was her favorite of these cousins. She was lively, beautiful, cheerful and fun. Two years older than Hatasu, she always knew a little more or could do a little more than the princess could. At the same time, sweet-natured Meryt could be depended upon to listen to Hatasu's schemes and help make them work. There was a natural maternal quality to Meryt. She sought out and helped anyone or anything younger or smaller than herself. Perhaps that was because she was put in charge of her baby sister, Isis. There were five of them who were the core group of the palace children and this evening they greeted each other…happy about the festival and buzzing about the stories of the rude foreigners.

Thethi's play with his stone soldiers now seemed immensely interesting to all the cousins. If there had been sticks around, they no doubt would have developed a game of throwing them at Amurru but in lieu of that, they played at being soldiers. Initially, Thethi led marching maneuvers and he was delighted that Hatasu and the others followed him - holding an imaginary shield and lance - stepping, sharp and precise. Hapuseneb assumed the role of military musician and made imitation horn sounds as he marched. Meryt treated it like a kind of dance but she also clapped her hands to the marching beat,, and that actually helped.

For Hatasu, the military game touched off something unexpected inside her. The marching beat and the imitation horn sounds seemed to shift her anxieties into a mode of challenging these foreigners who had offended her father, upset Ineni, frightened Sitre and angered Paheri. What had been Amen's teasing nickname, 'Sekhmet warrior', now made her feel stronger. Though her movements were still more dance-like than military, within a few minutes of the game she was leading even Thethi…driving an imaginary chariot, imaginary bow in hand and arrow case over her shoulder.

Thethi barely seemed to notice she had taken over but, out of the corner of her eye, she saw Ineni watching their play. He shook his head with a kind of twinkle in his eye. The children were called from their play as the extended family gathered in the banquet hall for the pre-festival feast, knowing these next five days were the epitome of the ancient wisdom passed down through generations to preserve stability, maintain the connection between gods and men, and ward off the ever-present threat of chaos. This year, the threat of chaos was present among them in the form of these unpredictable foreigners.

Chapter 5 - Osiris's Day

Sitre, still shaky from the foreigner's presence, prepared Hatasu for her role in the festival day of Osiris. As she combed her hair, she prepared the child's mind as well…with a another story. "In the beginning of time, Osiris ruled over the fertile Nile Valley. During his reign, grains were abundant and the river rose full. Osiris wished to share these blessings of abundance with the people of surrounding lands. He set off to educate them so they could know about growing grains and honoring the gods. He traveled…not to conquer but to teach. However, Osiris's brother, Set, was jealous. Nut and Geb, their parents, gave Set the barren desert to rule but he resented his brother's rulership of the fertile river valley. While Osiris was away, Set made a plan to take over his lands. As soon as Osiris returned from his journey, Set drew his brother Osiris into a trap and killed him."

"That's when Osiris became god of the dead? Right?" Hatasu knew the story.

"Yes," smiled Sitre. "He now rules over the bas of those who lived a just life. Since that time, those that die are identified with Osiris."

"Like Osiris-Wadjmose!"

"Yes, indeed." She finished the youth-lock and smoothed the few fly-away wisps of red with her hand. "It was his son Horus who returned the land to Maat, winning it back from his uncle Set."

"With the help of his wife, Isis."

"Yes, Isis raised Osiris from the dead and helped Horus

overcome Set."

Hatasu thought about the story of Osiris teaching people of other lands. Her land was, indeed, the center of the universe. Everything was measured by her father's kingdom. It seemed to the princess as though Osiris missed those foreigners in Amurru, however. They could use his teachings on behaving in a civilized manner.

Sitre finished Hatasu's dressing by adorning her with a gold necklace and arm bands, and sent her off to meet the other family members gathering in the gate for the formal procession. Hatasu looked in the direction of the gate but then headed for her father's room instead.

As she approached, she was surprised to hear Amen's voice. "But, Father, Hazor is testing you and Bazor is challenging me. War is the only way to make them respect us again."

Her father's voice answered, "Amen, I'm not going to wage war over this incident. I have other things to think of today. The governors are here from up and down the river. This is the time for them to honor you as my heir and for you to solidify the new loyalties here at home. No more talk of war. The nobleman and governors accepted Wadjmose and now they must make the transition to accept you. It is more important today you focus on the sons of our governors than that son of our subjugated prince."

Hatasu felt nervous about Amen wanting war so she entered the room gingerly, peeking around the corner before she entered. She saw her father standing there very regally, white kilt against bronzed skin, carefully made up with eye-protecting kohl, his gold collar and armbands gleaming. Amenmose stood in front of him.

His youth-lock was long ago cut and his head now freshly shaved. He wore the kilt of a soldier and the neck-collar and arm-bands of the Hawk-in-the-Nest. Hatasu thought he looked handsome and regal. The Pharaoh's manservant stood to the side, waiting to complete his preparations for the day.

"Good morning, Father. Good morning, Amen."

The Pharaoh looked in her direction. Amen grunted acknowledgement, then acted as though she wasn't there. In the few minutes of silence, the servant moved to secure the ritual false beard on the Pharaoh's chin with a sturdy linen string which he tied behind his Pharaoh's head.

Once it was in place, Thutmose turned to his son again, "Amen, your training as Pharaoh must also include an understanding of the deeper meanings of the insignia of royalty. War is only one of the functions of the Pharaoh. This beard, for instance. Do you know why each Pharaoh wears it?"

Amen realized he was being tested. "Because the gods have beards," he said with confident finality.

"Not all gods, Amen, just the gods who bridge the gap between the Great Above and the Great Below. Like Shu, of the creation story…he is the air that comes between earth and heaven, Nut and Geb. He has a beard. Osiris is the god of the dead, whose grain-gift gives us life. Thus, he connects death and life, so he wears a beard. Divine pharaohs wear the beard because they connect the people with the gods."

Amen nodded, apparently resigned. Hatasu found what her father said interesting. Pharaoh Thutmose scrutinized his appearance in the obsidian mirror held by Amen. He nodded approval. The rest of the accoutrements of kingship waited on the nearby stand: The crook, flail, menat beads and, in the place of honor, the Double Crown.

Thutmose motioned to Amenmose. "Son, each of these accruements represents an important aspect of rulership that is not about war. First, the crook."

Hatasu watched as Amen's eyes glazed over but he reached for the striped rod with the curved top and he held it a bit more casually than his father's customary reverential treatment.

Thutmose said, "The Pharaoh carries the crook of the shepherd because our people are herders of animals…and, like the shepherd, the Pharaoh is their leader and protector. You must rule wisely and well. When there is war, it must be for the good of the Pharaoh's flock."

Amen handed it to his father and bit his lip.

Her father moved on. "Now the flail."

Amen took the rod with three beaded extensions on it.

His father explained, "The flail separates the grain from the shaft, for ours are an agricultural people…and it is a symbol of the Pharaoh as judge, identifying the truth from falsehood. As Pharaoh, you must assure the land of justice and seek out the truth."

Amen handed the flail to his father, silently nodding and shifting from leg to leg.

"And the menat beads." The menat, with its many strings of faience beads strung together with the gold counterpoise at the end, sat alone on that stand. His father said, "And the menat beads

96

represent the attraction of Hathor, goddess of love. That means as Pharaoh, you have the magnetism that draws people to you. The use of war and fear is the opposite of magnetism."

Amen's jaw was strongly set and his eyebrows slightly furloughed but he nodded at his father. He shifted to the other foot. The Double Crown was all that was left on the stand.

Hatasu watched as Amen took each part in his hands and placed it on his father's head - first the white, and then, the red crown. His father watched him closely as he handled these sacred objects. Amen's eyes darted to his father's knowing how closely he was watching him now.

"This is the ultimate insignia of kingship," Thutmose said, as his son and heir settled the white, high cone-shaped crowns securely on his head. "The symbol of Upper Khemet, the river valley." Amen placed the second crown with the red head piece that surrounded the white one in the back and had a bee antennae piece that extended in the front. "The symbol of Lower Khemet, the river delta." Thutmose declared with the dignified tone of a formal announcement, "The duty of the Divine Pharaoh is to unite the Two Lands, Upper and Lower: The Great Above and the Great Below. The purpose of war is to protect that union. Frivolous wars weaken, as the many warring groups in the Levant kept that land in chaos until we established our suzerainship over them."

Amen emitted a barely audible sign. He looked toward the door, ready to leave. The Pharaoh's Osiris regalia was complete now.

Hatasu looked at her father with awe. He glowed with an otherworldly light and she thought he was the most handsome man ever to have lived. She tried to imagine her brother, Amen, in that same regalia. It was easier to imagine him in the blue war crown. She felt anxious at the idea of Amen trying to step into her father's role.

It was then her mother appeared in the doorway. She looked beautiful in the crown of the goddess Isis. It was worn over her elaborate wig and was a headpiece that contained the image of a throne. This symbol of the goddess indicated that Isis was the seat of power for her husband, Osiris, for her son, Horus, and for the Pharaoh himself.

Her father smiled his greeting as Ahmose approached. He said, "Greetings, beautiful mother of our people."

She responded, "Good morning, Osiris to our people."

Moving toward the door, Thutmose extended his hand to her and said, "Our governors await us. The presentations from the nomes' governors promise to be pleasing to me. The gods have blessed me with prosperous harvests, in spite of the khamsin."

Ahmose stepped into place by his side and said, "I have received messages from the wives of governors, too. Kharit from the northern town of Zawty sent word she is not able to come. I will miss seeing her. I enjoy her company."

"Yes, I received a message from Kharit's husband, Governor Djehapy. There is something irregular going on in that region. After the festival I will send Ineni down river to see first hand. Ah…" He paused, turning now to look at his heir. "Amen, it would be good for you to go with Ineni on such a trip."

Amen, who had been paying close attention to this part of the conversation, nodded. "I would indeed like to accompany Ineni…perhaps even go on to Itjtawy? …Hmmmm…Perhaps as we could take the army north to the land of the Amurru!"

"Amen! I am *not* going to war!" Her brother raised his eyebrows, cocked his head, and grinned at his father. Amen was the only one who got away with making a point by joking with the great Pharaoh.

Thutmose scolded slightly by shaking his head as he walked out the door with the Queen. The family arrived at the palace gate ready to take their place in the procession. Her father directed his attention toward Amen, ignoring his persistence about war, and continued instructing him as they waited.

"Now, Son, today, you will stand at my side as I give audience to the visiting governors. Several of them have sent their grown sons, like Governor Puya of the Abedju town sent Ti."

"Ah good. Ti is a pleasant fellow," said Amen.

As her father mounted his carrying chair, he motioned to Amen and Hatasu. "The two of you ride together. Amenmose, the people must see your reign will be legitimized by the Princess Hatasu as your consort. She will wear the throne-crown of Isis for you as Ahmose does for me."

Amen looked at Hatasu and made an exaggerated bow. Hatasu suspected he considered it an annoyance she was involved in this 'Pharaoh-business' at all. Wadj was so different. Last year, when Hatasu had ridden next to him, he'd told her funny stories about the different nomes and made her feel like an essential part of this 'Pharaoh business'.

Hatasu stepped into the carrying chair next to Amenmose as her father requested. He nudged her with his elbow, "Red-haired." It was a verbal jab. He knew how she hated to be reminded of her mark of difference.

She scowled and glared at him. "Watch it or I'll put a curse on you." She didn't have any idea how to do such a thing but she was desperate to get him to not tease her and make her mad in front of all the governors.

"Okay, okay…Sekhmet Warrior! …Is that better?"

"Okay, but don't be mean again."

"I promise…for today."

She tried to punch him in the arm with her small fist but he dodged with the teasing edge still in his laugh.

Hatasu calmed herself by focusing on the first part of the procession as she waited. This opening ceremonial pageant was a great contrast to the mournful walk with Wadjmose's khat. Not only was the royal family in formal dress but the music was cheerful and invigorating. The standard bearers passed and then the temple musicians with sistrums, tambourines, and hand clappers came next. The Pharaoh's family took its place next, riding in the litters high over the heads of the crowd, both seeing and being seen.

The people of the town and fields who lined the processional way were in sharp contrast to the formality of the royalty. These farmers, fishermen, townsfolk and palace servants responded to the sounds, smells and sights. As the Pharaoh passed, they bowed low. From her place on the litter next to Amenmose, she could look out on this crowd of faces, bowing and waving to her.

At the temple, they could see the area arranged with a collection of stalls, each shaded with differing bright-colored cloths serving as sun protection for the agricultural products within. There were beautiful finely woven baskets full of fresh, sweet smelling grains on one side, and carefully constructed pens containing bulls on the opposite side—*not* so sweet smelling. The governors stood by their farms' products, ready to be offered by their Pharaoh to Osiris. As Thutmose rode passed them on his litter, each one bowed low. Hatasu spotted her favorite governor, Itruri, of the southern town of El Kab, there with his wife and their daughter, Asat.

As the Pharaoh and Queen's chairs were arranged as thrones on a dais in front of the temple, all of the governors and their attendants bowed again in honor and praise. Ineni, the Vizier, and Huy, the royal scribe, stood by the Pharaoh's throne to note and record the presentation of the individual nomes. Itruri was the first to approach and present the results of his nome's harvest. He bowed his head low and gave the customary greeting and praise. "All praise to you mighty Pharaoh, the Good God Osiris, Protected by the Goddesses, King of Upper Khemet and King of Lower Khemet, Son of Ra, Ruler of all the Sun Encircles. May you live forever." With each customary greeting, Itruri bowed again and again. Thutmose nodded and smiled at his favorite governor.

Itruri's chest expanded with pride as he reported to his Pharaoh. He was Paheri's father and the son of one of Thutmose military generals. He had a look of determination about him…his eyes small and bright, his jaw firm. His ears were smaller than this son, Paheri's, but he also had none of the muscular strength. With Itruri was his youngest daughter, Asat. She had turned into a beauty. At fourteen, her body showed the gentle curves of her budding womanhood and her eyes were soft, brown, and deep. Those eyes were immediately drawn to the young and handsome prince. Last year, she would have offered him only the friendly 'hi' of a playmate. This year, she lowered her head slightly and looked at him through her long lashes…a shy, self-conscious smile on her face. Amenmose was instantly mesmerized. He didn't seem to be able to take his eyes off of her. He smiled back at her…a smile both eager and shy; a characteristic Hatasu didn't think she'd ever seen in him before. She noted that he actually leaned in her direction, like trying to get closer to the sun's warmth.

Itruri presented to his Pharaoh tall baskets containing his finest grains. Thutmose noted the large basket of barley. These small bead-like grains, plump and full, had a most pleasing texture. Inspecting them, Thutmose reached his hand deep into the barley and let it slide through his open fingers.

Hatasu seeing her father do this, wished to do it also. He smiled and said to her in a gentle aside, "These are precious gems, the great gift of Osiris, and our daily bread." As he nodded, Hatasu put her hand deep into midst of the grains, so she, too, could feel its weight and smooth texture. The barley dust rose pale, scenting the air.

Motioning Amen to come closer, their father continued talking to both of them. "Osiris taught the people the art of agriculture. The granaries in each nome hold our wealth. They give stability and security to the people of the Nile in good times and bad. This is the key to our way of life given to us by the gods."

He looked directly at Amenmose and he said, "A future Pharaoh must know how to inspect the grains in front of the people."

Though Amenmose moved to stand physically next to his father, his eyes were more on Asat than on the grains. His hand barely skimmed over the loose barley kernels. Thutmose's expression indicated he recognized Amen's attention to this daughter of the governor. He'd told him to pay attention to the grain.

When the next basket was presented, Hatasu said to him, "This is the beer grain, emmer wheat. Right, Father?"

"Amen, is she right?"

He startled to attention. "Uhhh… yes?" He pulled his eyes away from the young beauty and looked at his father and then for the first time, at the grain.

Thutmose's look scolded his son before he turned to Hatasu. "Yes, this is also the gift of Osiris." She automatically reached into the basket to touch this grain, too.

"The grains of the el Kab nome are of a truly fine quality this year," Thutmose said, smiling at Itruri.

The governors came forward one by one. Each bowed deeply to Thutmose and greeted their Pharaoh with suitable praise and affection. Thutmose in turn acknowledged each of them by name, and for the most part, he expressed aloof affection in return. Only with the Itjtawy governor did he scowl as he asked about some particularity in that town. Each governor also turned to Amenmose and honored him as the Hawk-in-the-Nest. Some were very formal, almost as thought they were uncertain. Others smiled acceptance.

Thutmose turned his full attention to the presentation of the bull. He must choose the one to be sacrificed to Osiris and served at the evening's feast. Each nome's governor's steward paraded their best bull in front of the Pharaoh and Queen. They inspected each of these cattle of their royal estates. Thutmose motioned Amen closer. "Which one would you pick…and why?"

Amen looked at each closely. Itruri's bull stood tall: Large in the chest, with red and brown spots on its white body and great horns that spread out from his head. When this bull had been tethered to a stake and enclosed in a pen, it had snorted loudly and pawed the ground. "I'd choose Itruri's bull," Amen said with finality. "He has a fire in his eyes that I think Osiris would appreciate. Oh! And he also has well developed chest musculature and good formation in his rump."

Thutmose was looking closely at all the bulls and did not notice when Hatasu leaned over to her brother and teasingly said, "You just like the wreath of flowers Asat wove."

"Shhh!" he pushed at her with his shoulder and frowned at her.

Ahhh! She'd found something to irritate him now, too.

Thutmose's attention came back to Itruri's bull and he said, "So, Amenmose, you would choose this one? Yes, indeed this is the best of the heard. This is the one to be sacrificed to Osiris."

Itruri's pride was obvious. Amenmose then looked to Asat and said shyly, "The wreath of lotus blossom is also particularly nice." Hatasu noted how she blushed, for they all knew it was she who had woven it.

Once the bull had been inspected and chosen, the group again formed a procession and returned to the palace. As they made their way back, Hatasu overheard her parents' conversation. "My, how families do grow up! Asat is no longer a child."

The Pharaoh nodded, turning back to look at Asat who was watching Amen leave. Thutmose said to his son, "Amenmose, Asat is a lovely flower but it is your sister here who will carry on our family's destiny for the Two Lands. She is the throne of Isis for you. You are her consort. That relationship must come first. And, it is the sons of the governors with whom you must establish loyalty."

Amenmose looked as his eight-year-old sister with her straight child's body and childish ways. His eyes wandered back to where Asat stood, still watching him leave. His smile deepened as he saw her gentle curves and swells. He turned away and sat a little taller, perhaps assuming a manner fitting the future Pharaoh, perhaps bracing himself for this life of duty.

Hatasu spent what was left of the afternoon with Thethi, Hapuseneb and a few of the children of the nomes. They were pleasant enough playmates, perhaps just trying a bit too hard to please and endear themselves to the royals.

That evening, the many-pillared throne room was arranged with low tables and sitting cushions for the royal family and all the visiting nobility from up and down the Nile. On the walls was painted a larger than life procession of gods and goddesses. The point toward which all the deities moved was the raised dais at the far end of the hall, where the two gold, ornate thrones stood waiting for the royal couple. On the backs of each throne was the image of the papyrus and lotus woven together, the symbols of the united

Upper and Lower Khemet. To the right of the Pharaoh sat Hatasu and Amenmose, side by side.

All the foods from the offering to Osiris had been turned into the sensual aromas of the dining hall. The highlight of the feast was the beef, roasted and spiced to perfection. There were also barley breads and cakes filled with honey, figs and dates and steaming platters of beets, artichokes and beans…all served with garlic, cumin, and thyme. The finest beer made of emmer wheat was offered by serving girls. The ka of the food had been offered to Osiris at the temple and now the blessed food was set out for the guests and governors.

Hatasu sat in her designated place next to Amenmose. As her brother first sat down, he looked at her with a mischievous twinkle in his eye. "Hey, Red Ha…Sekhmet Warrior!"

She was ready to bristle but relaxed as he corrected himself. She made an attempt to be friendly with him by asking, "How was the bull sacrifice?" She remembered Wadj didn't like that part of Osiris day.

"It was pretty interesting," he replied. "It was certainly more interesting than the lesson about the Pharaoh's regalia this morning, or the grains being 'gems' this afternoon."

She looked at him surprised…irritated even…at his dismissal of the things her father saw as important. Wadj would not have complained of father's teachings.

He caught her look and continued, "Okay, so I know I need to pay attention to those things but I remember a time when Father was the warrior Pharaoh…more interested in respect gained in battle than in clothes and symbols." He narrowed his eyes and looked at her directly. "I hope the Amurru make Father angry enough to go to war. Then I would be commander-in-chief of the army of the Two Lands. That would show everyone what a mighty Pharaoh I would make."

Hatasu thought, *'So that's why he's so anxious for war.'*

Amen was drinking more than the usual amount of the beer. He went on, "Back before you were born, Father was a great warrior. When he was co-regent with Amenhotep, and when he was first Pharaoh, he was more interested in battle strategies than in the crook and the flail. I remember when he was such a mighty warrior he had the fear and respect of all. Back then, no one would have come into the palace harbor uninvited!"

As Hatasu enjoyed the flavors of the roasted meat and the sweet breads, she still listened.

"Tomorrow is the day I will shine, riding my chariot at the head of the army in the parade. The blue war helmet will sit more comfortably on my head than the tall Double Crown." He glanced at her briefly, almost shyly, as he said, "The men in the army love me, you know. With the governors and their son's, it feels strange without Wadj, but in the army…they know I'm a warrior, brave and strong. They know the enemy will respect me as they respected Father once…like when he returned from his Nubian Campaign with the King of Kush hanging upside down from the prow of his ship. No, you wouldn't know that. You didn't know father before he was Pharaoh but Wadj and I did. It was before you were born." Amen's beer cup was refreshed again by a serving girl and he sat, silently staring into it for several minutes.

Hatasu said nothing. She had indeed heard about that Nubian war but she knew her father talked more about his building projects now, than his enemies. He said the building that honored the gods were his true legacy.

Amen spoke again, "You don't understand but Wadj understood." There was another long silence. "I do this for Wadj," he added.

His face changed expression and the skin around his eyes reddened. The eyeballs glistened in the lamplight. He blinked hard. A tear drop splashed on his untouched food. He looked up quickly with his jaw suddenly set. Seeing that she saw the tear, he quickly turned away from her and toward Thethi, seated on his other side.

"Did you know, little brother, that father was once a mighty warrior…hanging the King of vile Kush from his boat, getting everyone's respect, even those within our own land that thought they should be Pharaoh instead of him?"

Hatasu could see Thethi's eyes grow larger in alarm at Amen's words. Thethi asked, "What do you mean, someone else thinks they should be Pharaoh instead of Father?"

"Little brother, why do you think old Amenhotep made father a co-regent? He was afraid those arrogant northern Amenenhats would try to usurp the throne again, like they did with our ancestor, Montuhotep IV. But father and Amenhotep were too smart for them." He let out a long sigh and continued, "That's why I must take the Double Crown, even though it is not what I want. I'm doing this for father…No…Really it's for Wadj." His voice got softer. "I do it for Wadj." Then, in an almost inaudible whisper, he added, "And for mother."

Many people had finished their meal and the young folks were gathering in the garden. Amen caught sight of his friends Hetep and Asat moving in the direction of the garden and looking back toward him as though with the hope he would join them.

"Hetep understands. He was there with Wadj and me," Amen said louder. Amen stood up and faced the direction of the garden.

He was about to walk away but stopped and turned to Hatasu. "You know, Pharaoh Amenenhat…There is one thing he said that was true. Being a Pharaoh is lonely and it demands personal sacrifice." He left Hatasu and Thethi still sitting at the table.

Thethi looked at her. "Who is Amenenhat?"

"I guess he's a Pharaoh from the past. I don't know what he was talking about or what it has to do with Father. I just think he wants to go to war to prove he is some big hero."

Hatasu and Thethi also went to the garden to mingle with the governor's children closer to their age. Hatasu kept looking over toward Amen. She saw her brother and Asat walk off together toward a part of the garden sheltered by sycamore leaves.

Chapter 6 - Horus Day

On this, the Horus Day, her father wore the blue helmet of Army Commander-in-Chief. He arrived at the parade grounds driving his war chariot himself. Ahmose, Great Wife, stood straight and alert-eyed by his side; the stomach bump under her linen sheath gave a reassuring hint of her pregnancy. They arrived together for all of the army to see. He was Horus, their divine leader; she was Isis, their goddess mother protector.

Hatasu was relinquished of official 'consort' duty this day, as it was Amen's time to shine in his own right. This was a relief. It was much easier for Hatasu to like this brother from afar. She and Thethi went the short distance to the parade grounds on the Eastern desert outside of Waset with Paheri in his chariot. From her place in the cab with Paheri, she looked out over the desert plain filled with neat rows of men, shields and lance in hand.

In front of each square of men was a row of twenty-five charioteers, their horses brushed and chariots polished. This field was covered with many such squares of soldier-units, spread as far as the eye could see, ready to move in great marching formations, parading in front of their Pharaoh.

Hatasu stared at the incredible mass of men. Around her was a buzz of excitement. A great crowd had come out to view this display of the Pharaoh's military might. Some of the fellahin, or peasants, walked but most of the viewers were nobleman or governors who drove their chariots and watched the parade from the neat arrangement of their vehicles, forming a viewer's section.

Her eyes scanned the crowd looking for the Amurru foreigners. They were there…stony-faced, squint-eyed, and talking intently among themselves as they seemed to be appraising the number of men in his army.

The parade of men began to move forward. Heading it up were the standard bearers, holding high the flag of the falcon-headed god, Horus. Then came the drummers, their instruments suspended from the player's neck by a cord with the two skin-covered ends available to each hand. There were also long-stemmed brass horns, whose musicians blew at regular intervals. They had a character that seemed to call the heart to pride and courage. She could feel both the drum's heartbeat and the beckoning call of the horns. Together, they filled the air with urgent excitement.

Then came Amenmose. He moved forward in his polished chariot, drawn by two fine, brown, prancing horses. Hatasu thought he looked very grand indeed in his role as Commander of the Royal Army! Standing next to him in his chariot was Hetep, his driver. This was the same friend who had been with Wadj when he'd died. Amen stood straight, his gold collar reflecting the sun's light and his kohl-lined eyes scanning the crowds of people…the blue war helmet a bright beacon of his authority.

The town's people who gathered to watch this parade were ready to embrace him as their crowned prince, for they cheered and waved colored scarves. Amenmose, standing tall with his chest expanded, grinned back, taking on an air of masterly authority.

Thethi was excited. "See Amenmose as the commander? He looks so grand!"

Hatasu nodded. He did indeed look very grand!

Paheri said, "Yes, the role of the crowned prince suits him better than he realizes."

After Amenmose came the chariots of Paheri's grandfather, the great General Ibana, and his comrade at arms, General Pennekheb. The two chariots rode side by side.

Again, Thethi excitedly nudged his sister and grinned at his tutor, saying, "There are the two chief deputies, Pennekheb of the Northern Corps and Ibana of the Southern Corps."

Paheri smiled at Thethi's exuberance and enthusiasm. His grandfather, General Ibana, was indeed a celebrity in the army. He'd fought under three Pharaohs and won distinction, wealth and position for himself and opportunity for his offspring. The rest of Paheri's family was at this event also. The chariot of his father and mother were given places of honor near the Pharaoh and Queen. Asat was standing with her parents, her eyes shining bright and fixed on Amenmose.

After these illustrious commanders came the elite charioteers of the Company of Amun. They preceded twenty-five abreast, spreading out across the plain, their well-brushed horses gleaming in the sun and their chariots painted bright colors. In each chariot the warrior held his shield in one hand and his large composite bow in the other, while the chariot driver used both hands to skillfully manage the reins.

Thethi, leaning forward, said, "They are so marvelous! Someday, I will go to war in just such a chariot."

Hatasu nodded, thinking to herself that she, too, might like to be a soldier. They looked so grand; she wanted to be part of it all. She was beginning to really like the idea of being a Sekhmet warrior...a warrior Queen!

There followed a grand procession of men. Each man carried a shield almost as big as himself. Each shield, rounded on the top, was covered with spotted cow skins. Each soldier also carried a long, narrow battle-axe. Throughout the morning, there was one company after another, each named after a god...except for the Sekhmet Unit, named after a goddess. What was at first exciting, gradually became tedious and very boring.

There were *so* many units, one seemed indistinguishable from another. Looking back toward the viewers around the royalty, Hatasu was as interested in the noblewomen who'd come to see the handsome soldiers. They were dressed in their best wigs, jewelry and linen sheaths. There in the midst of them was Asat, her face blushed and glowing as her eyes tracked Amen's movements.

Paheri's brother, who'd been viewing the parade next to his parents and sister, came over to where Paheri and the children were. This brother motioned with his head in the direction of their youngest sibling, Asat. "Looks like we have a romance blooming."

Hatasu's ears perked up but she kept her eyes focused on the soldiers pretending to only be thinking of the parade.

Paheri looked from Asat to Amenmose and then back to his brother. "Perhaps."

"If our sister were to be chosen as a royal favorite, I'll bet I could be assured of an honorable position at the palace and even a well appointed tomb."

"Indeed," came Paheri's quick reply, "a concubine, or second wife, is not a bad postion. You remember, of course, for Amenmose to be Pharaoh, Hatasu must be his Queen and first wife."

"Yes, I suppose it would be complicated."

Hatasu turned from viewing the parade and said, "Yes, if only Wadj was still here, a match between Prince Amenmose and Asat would be a good thing for them and for your family. I wish it were different, too."

Paheri and his brother looked at the princess, thinking for the first time about what this must be like for her.

Hatasu looked back at the field where Amen was positioned at the head of the troops. He intermittently looked back to make sure Asat was still watching him. The princess again felt the longing in her heart for her missing brother, Wadj. It looked like she would be Queen to a Pharaoh who everyone knew loved someone else. The military parade continued. It was more pleasant to direct her thoughts to one day being a soldier herself. Sekhmet Warrior, that's what Amen called her. She would learn to be a warrior like her father, maybe even hang a subjugated chieftain upside down on the prow of *her* ship. Well, probably not. That must have been smelly.

Paheri, wanting to break the tension in the air, offered, "Would you like to hear a story?"

"Yes, yes!" they both said at once.

Thethi added, "Tell us about Horus in battle."

"So it shall be," replied Paheri, smiling. The rhythm of the marching feet, the squeak of the chariot leathers, and the conversations of the viewers fell into the background as Paheri began. Hataus' mind was fully refocused. "When time was still young, Horus set to claim the kingdom that was rightfully his. After Set killed Horus's father, Osiris, Set ruled the kingdom as though it were a desert. And so it would still be, if Horus hadn't fought for it.

First, Horus went to the tribunal of the gods to complain of his uncle's offense and to get justice through law. He presented his case for righteous kingship. The tribunal listened, but Set's case rested on the idea, 'Might makes right!', and he held his rulership by the force of his physical strength.

Since physical strength was his best asset, Set offered to settle the quarrel by challenging Horus to a battle of might. He proposed they turn themselves into hippopotamuses and fight it out in the Nile. Horus agreed. There, in the water, as two mighty river horses, they clashed with each other. There was thrashing and foaming in the Nile as the two huge animals struggled for supremacy.

Set had the physical strength to overpower young Horus and he almost did…but Isis came to his aid. Taking strategic aim at her brother Set, she threw her spear. It pierced, wounded and caught Set. When Set realized he was overcome, he begged her, as her brother, to release him rather than kill him. Taking pity on her brother, she released him to negotiate with her son. Set, master of trickery and deceit, used Isis's mercy to escape.

The war was far from over. Horus challenged Set to fight again, this time in the desert. Set accepted. Out in the desert, Set and Horus again did battle, fierce and awful…but this was Set's territory and using this to his advantage, he plucked out Horus's right eye. Set left him in the desert to die and returned to the tribunal, claiming victory.

This would have been the end of the story but Hathor, goddess of love, went to find Horus. She healed his eye with gazelle milk and Horus returned again to fight Set. The contest drew on for many years. There were many battles, neither one winning, nor the other. The tribunal finally turned to Osiris, now god of the underworld. Osiris insisted his son Horus was the rightful Pharaoh and if his rightful son wasn't acknowledged as the righteous Pharaoh, all who passed before his court of the afterlife would feel his wrath. The tribunal declared Horus as victorious. Thus, Horus avenged his father, reestablished justice and returned Maat to the Two Lands." Paheri paused, looking at the children. "And do you know what happened to Set?"

"Horus killed him!" said Thethi.

"What do you think, Hatasu?" asked the teacher.

"Well, if he'd been killed, he wouldn't still be one of our gods."

"Not necessarily. Osiris was killed and he has great power."

"Well, what happened to him, then?" asked Thethi impatiently.

"Set was given another job. His strength and power is still necessary for our land, only now it is used on the nightly journey to *protect* Ra. He stands at the head of the barque of Ra and fights his great enemy Apophis."

"You mean like the Apophis, the leader of the Hyksos?"

"Right! Set's strength defends Ra from Apophis and the Pharaoh from his enemies. Set and Horus are both needed by our Pharaoh. Horus provides the wisdom of sight and forethought but Set provides the physical strength. Tomorrow we celebrate Set's

Epagomenal Day."

Thethi said, "One day, I, too, will be a warrior like Horus, Set and my father."

Hatasu said, "I will also be a warrior…like Isis when she strikes Set as a hippopotamus…only I won't let him go."

Paheri and Thethi each looked at her, surprised.

Once back in the town of Waset, they joined the gathering at the formal hall set up to receive the foreign tribute. The Pharaoh and Queen sat ceremoniously on their thrones on the dais. Amen sat next to the Pharaoh. The army Generals, Ibana and Pennekheb, sat in places of honor. Hatasu was free of official obligations but, intrigued by the array of foreigners, she was glad the seats for her, Thethi and Paheri were close to the presentation processional.

None of the other delegates were disturbing like the Amurru. The foreign powers, each wearing distinctively different dress, gathered with their retinue and their items for tribute. Hatasu was wide-eyed to see so many different kinds of people in one place. Each group was clustered together in the audience. Huy, the royal scribe, announced each group as it approached the throne.

The first to be called was the vassal from Nubia. The foremost of the Nubians was a tall man. This chief of his people wore an animal skin kilt and lion skin over his shoulders. His hair was short, black and tightly matted close to his head. His face was clean shaven. He came forward and bowed low before the Pharaoh, the Queen and the Prince. The royalty nodded back. The Nubian then motioned to those with him to come forward. Men wearing only short animal skin loincloths carried forward baskets. When Hatasu saw inside the baskets, she realized they carried the precious metal gold. The Pharaoh smiled. Next came men carrying elephant tusks of ivory. Again, the Pharaoh smiled. Another came forward with a number of large bows. The Pharaoh smiled and nodded. Then, Hatasu's eyes almost popped out of her head. Three men carried monkeys on their shoulders as gifts for the Pharaoh.

Thutmose simply nodded, but Hatasu smiled broadly and in her excitement she nudged Thethi with her elbow. "Now, one of *those* would make a great pet!"

Thethi agreed but he was staring at the bows of these archer warriors. Each of these tributes was accepted by servants and marked by scribes.

Next came the representative of Libya. These people of the western desert were light skinned and taller than the Nubians. They wore their hair in a long curl down one side of the fac and feathers extended from their hair on the other side. The men of this land were herders. They bowed low and brought before the royalty a very fine-looking cow, a sturdy donkey and a goat with large heavy udders. Hatasu understood from his broken Egyptian that these animals belonged to a herd waiting outside. The Pharaoh nodded and Huy signaled to a servant and scribe to check and record this tribute.

The trader from the city of Byblos in the land of Syria in the Levant was the next to be called forward with his servants and his tribute. He was a short and rather rotund man. He had black curly hair reaching down to his shoulders and a black, pointed beard. He was dressed in a narrow, richly embroidered, purple robe. This robe was opened in the front to reveal a skirt arranged in layers, alternating with red and blue fabrics. Though his clothes were different than the people of her land, his smile was open and she could tell her father was kindly disposed to him. She heard the Syrian boast to her father this year he brought some particularly fine vintage wines. Thutmose's smile broadened. His servants brought up cedar wood, purple dyes and jugs of wine. As he walked by her to exit, she caught a whiff of cedarwood scent…very pleasing.

Finally, Bazor was called. Like the delegate from Byblos, his hair and beard were dark and curly but his was unwashed. He wore a very tall, cone-shaped hat or crown on his head. Seeing him up close, Hatasu saw his features as coarse; his nose was fleshy and hook shaped. He wore a blue galabeah to his knees and over that a robe that went to the ground and opened in the front, showing his strange shoes. These were metal with pointed toes that curled back toward him. His expression was guarded. He bowed once stiffly before the Pharaoh and ignored both the Queen and Prince. "I bring you these fine horses and chariots as tribute gifts."

Amen sat up taller as though attempting to draw attention and therefore the acknowledgement received from the other delegates. His eyes moved to his father as though expecting he'd insist Bazor honor his son, too. The Pharaoh did not look at Amen but stayed focused on this subjugated prince.

"Now, bring your tribute forward." Bazor motioned to his servants, and several fine prancing horses and two polished chariots were brought before the Pharaoh.

Quickly, Vizier Ineni and General Ibana leaned toward the Pharaoh and whispered in his ear. The Pharaoh nodded. He asked Bazor, "Where is the rest of the agreed upon tribute? According to the treaty between your father, King Hazor and Pharaoh Ahmose, this is not sufficient."

Thutmose's words were slow and deliberate. Hatasu knew this to mean he was angry. Amen knew this, too. He sat back in his seat, his eyes small slits as he looked with distrust at Bazor.

Hatasu, watching this, thought to herself, '*This is what Amen wants, for Father to be angry. Is this enough of an offence for Father to go to war over?*'

The Amurru answered, "It has been a difficult year for us. There are powerful lords to our north also requiring tribute. We bring you fine horses."

These might have sounded like words of explanation, however they were said with a tone of defiance that seemed to say, 'What are you going to do about it?'

"My envoys tell me the weather was good and your herds have multiplied." The Pharaoh's face darkened with anger and his voice started getting louder. A slight smile formed on Amen's lips.

"Your envoys speak only half-truth, Sir. Much of what we have must go to the fierce warrior people to the north, the Mitanni. We still give you these strong horses to show our respect."

The Pharaoh's frown deepened. Amen's eyes were bright with attention to this development. Hatasu's dislike of the foreigners was growing. She didn't trust them.

The Pharaoh maintained his stony anger. "What is this? You let others take the tribute owed to the Two Lands? You have more fear of them, than of Khemet? Must this Pharaoh come in person to your land to collect the tribute?"

Amen crossed his arms in front of him and Hatasu saw a slight nod and smile. Events were unfolding exactly as he'd hoped.

Bazor lowered his head and said clearly, "No Sir, that is not necessary."

Had this really gone farther than Bazor had anticipated? Was he just biding his time? The great Pharaoh then dismissed Bazor from his presence with a flip of his hand and an order to move on and have his tribute registered by the scribes.

As Bazor turned to leave, there was a moment his eyes locked with Amen's. As Hatasu watched, a fist of anxiety tightened around her stomach. It was like the flash of battle-axes. Bazor moved on. She thought to herself, *'That was a threat! How dare he!'* Even more than scared, she felt angry.

As soon as the Amurru delegation left the hall, General Ibana and Vizier Ineni moved closer to the Pharaoh to confer with him. Hatasu saw Amen looking to the Pharaoh hopefully and her father avoiding his gaze as he listened to his seasoned advisors.

Feeling very uneasy about this development, she decided to go outside to see if she could find the Nubians with the monkeys. To her disappointment, the monkeys had been already brought to the menagerie for royal pets. However, she saw the Amurru arguing with the Medjays and the scribes about their tribute.

That night, it was customary for the foreign diplomats to be invited to the feast. Hatasu was able to sit with Thethi; Amenmose had an honorable, and very visible, seat next to the Pharaoh again. She could see Amen leaning toward the Pharaoh and speaking to him with a sense of urgency. She was sure he was still making his arguments for war with the Amurru. She was even hoping now he would succeed.

Her father was stony-faced and formal, giving away none of his thoughts but not silencing Amen either. Hatasu looked away from her family and out toward the banquet room. The hall was very colorful with the faces and clothing of the people from the different lands.

Bazor and his delegation were at the table next to Hatasu and Thethi's. She noted how the foreigner and Amen exchanged glares. She stared, surprised that Bazor had the nerve to show his face after the scanty tribute at the presentation.

Hatasu remembered what Ineni's said at the harbor-lake. *'Was he spying?' 'Was he testing?' 'Was he challenging?'*, she wondered.

Hatasu observed Bazor. Even more than how strange the Amurru looked, it was how he smelled. It was the strong, sweaty smell of an unwashed body and the musty sick-sweet smell of uncleaned horse stalls. Baths and purifications were very important to the people of the Two Lands. Fragrances were valued, allowing one's breath to open to the beauty of the goddesses. Food was also fastidiously attended to. It was meant, as Hatasu had been reminded many times before, to support the continued life of the khet as vehicle of the akh. Eating too much or too quickly was not good for the well-being of either. Evidently, Bazor didn't know or didn't care about these things that were common custom in the Two Lands. He not only smelled in a way that turned the stomach, but he also pushed food in his mouth with his fingers so rapidly, some smeared around his mouth.

At one point, as Hatasu stared at him in disbelief, he opened his mouth wide, strained his stomach and pushed out his chest, letting out a loud belch. An incredibly foul odor escaped of which Hatasu, at the next table over, got an unpleasant whiff. For a least a full minute, everyone stopped eating in shocked silence. Bazor continued on as though the silence was an acknowledgement for a feat well done.

This seemed to be just plain ignorance and bad manners. It was not about spying or even challenging. It was disrespectful but contrary to the incident at the harbor-lake and the defiance at the tribute processional,rudeness here didn't even seem to be his intent. It was more his ignorance.

Bazor looked at her brother and the alabaster lamps reflected a light in his eye like the tip of a spear aimed at Amen's soul. His face seemed dark and hollow; a soulless mass, cruel and threatening. The audacity of this challenge frightened her but also made her angry. This barbarian was so disrespectful to her father, threatening to her brother and insulting to the customs of her land. She could feel the Sekhmet warrior rising in her along with her anger.

As she looked at Amen, however, he was not noticing Bazor. She saw his conversation with the Pharaoh had stopped and his eyes had move in the direction of Asat who'd just entered the hall.

The fine thin linen flowed around her body in response to the rhythm of her gait, giving away as much mystery as it revealed. The coral faience necklace accentuated both the blush of her cheeks and the bloom of her young breasts. She was being seated with her family at a nearby table. Hatasu thought to herself, she wished she had Asat's black shiny hair instead of her red mane. Amen smiled at Asat but a movement from the Amurru table drew Hatasu's attention back there.

Her stomach turned into a knot of dread when she saw Bazor note Amen's attentions to Asat. A menacing smile spread over the foreigner's face; a look that rather said he'd found what he was looking for. Holding a goose bone, its crisp-roasted but greasy skin hanging off, he pointed it at Asat.

Her eyes were dark and shining with the excitement of the evening and the admiration of the young prince. Her budding body was well oiled, graceful and energetic as she smiled back at Amenmose. The evening promised to be a glowing one for her.

Bazor waved his food in her direction. He said to his comrades, "Hmmm, now there's a filly worth a trade." Bazor turned to the Pharaoh and in a voice loud enough to be heard throughout the hall, said, "What would you trade for *her*?"

The Pharaoh's body stiffened. "What was that you said? Surely I misunderstood." His eyes were narrowed in displeasure as he peered at this offensive son of his subjugated prince.

Amen's face was red with fury and outrage. Hatasu wondered again, was this ignorance or a deliberate provocation.

Looking at Amen from the corner of his eye, Bazor continued,

"What would you trade for that filly? The one there with the strange flower on her head and the full set of udders?"

The Pharaoh straightened himself a little and raised his voice. "We do not trade women."

Amen's knuckles were white from his grip on the arms of his throne. He leaned forward as though ready to leap at Bazor. Hatasu thought Amen might attack Bazor right there and then…not even wait for a war.

"I will give you my own horses for her," said Bazor, his muscles bulging as he faced Amen, ready for a fight, that battle-axe gleam in his eye again.

Asat's mother, realizing the volitile nature of this exchange, rose from the table and protectively guided her daughter out of the hall.

The Pharaoh raised his voice now and with a sharper tone said to Bazor, "You are dismissed from my festival hall." He gave a curt and angry nod toward Nakht, the head of the Medjay guards, who immediately moved to escort the troublemaker from the room. He put a restraining hand on Amen's arm.

Bazor's smile was a smirk. He sighed loudly, and before he left, he turned to his countrymen at his table, "By Baal, god of thunder, if I were prince of this land, I'd know real men rule over their women…like a bull over his cows…and trade them if he pleases."

There was a shiver that seemed to pass through the whole room. He attempted to shake off the Medjay who accompanied his exit. He acted as though he was leaving of his own accord but it appeared to Hatasu he was leaving because he'd accomplished his purpose. He'd provoked the Pharaoh and the prince. He walked with a grandiose swagger which was even more enraging to her than his smirk and his rudeness.

'How dare he!', she thought. Then the image of Isis protecting Horus flashed in her mind. It only took a split second. She put her small bare foot out in front of Bazor as he walked by.

The hard muscle of his leg hurt slightly but it was so worth it as he stumbled, looking clumsy and drunk. He caught himself and his hand went automatically to the knife in his belt. There was a gasp from the gathering. The Medjays quickly disarmed him and led him out of the room.

Hatasu had succeeded in her aim…to expose him and make him look like a clumsy fool who trips drunkenly, rather than a warrior of the Levant.

Thethi turned to her and said, "What did you do that for? He could have knifed you!"

"Isis wouldn't have sat by and done nothing if Set was threatening Horus!"

He stared at her, a look in his eye as though she had some kind of frightening magic he didn't quite comprehend.

Amenmose turned back to his father. Though she couldn't hear, she was certain the land was closer to going to war. There was almost a visible sigh of relief from everyone in the hall when the Amurru left but a cloud of apprehension still hung in the air. The men and women of the noble families that had gathered, all seemed to set their faces in an indomitable expression. The older servants, with eyes lowered, scurried about as if they wished to finish their tasks and to get as far away as possible from this monster, Bazor.

"So like the Hyksos!"

Hatasu turned to Paheri and asked, "Why did he say, 'men rule over woman'?"

"The people of the Levant have ways different than ours. When the Hyksos ruled the Two Lands, they forbid the worship of the goddesses and treated women even worse than they treated men."

She pondered these things and spent the night dreaming of monster eyes and flashing battle-axes.

Chapter 7 ~ Set's Day

"By Set, what is Bazor doing in this hunt!" Paheri held his hand on his forehead to shade his eyes, trying to see what he didn't want to believe. Hatasu and Thethi copied him, staring through the desert dust as the Amurru foreigner raced his chariot toward the hunt field.

Everyone else was already engaged in the sport, thus lessening that chance anyone would stop him. He was a dark figure, clad strange in a brown shirt and kilt; a sharp contrast to the local hunters in white linen kilts with bronzed skin on their exposed chest and arms. Bazor's horses, driven hard to catch up with the others were foaming at the mouth, nostrils extended. The chariot was larger and heavier than the ones Hatasu was used to seeing. In spite of its clumsy look, Bazor and his driver handled it with skill and agility.

The Pharaoh gave Hatasu and Thethi permission to view the hunt at close range out in the Eastern desert. They both held tight to the rail of Paheri's chariot as he drove out of the town, past the army barracks and into the barren desert expanse, almost to the shadow of the Eastern Mountains. He stopped a short distance from the area of the actual chase defined by ditch and net. This was the day of the ritual hunt in honor of the god of the wild desert lands. Two herds of animals had been driven to this plain between Waset and the Eastern Mountains. The noblemen, governors and their sons savored this hunt as a demonstration of their prowess and skill in overcoming the chaotic forces of wild nature, as well as exhibiting the positive strength that Set also represented.

Occasionally, the Pharaoh honored a foreign diplomat or prince with an invitation to join them. Hatasu was certain Bazor had not been so honored. That morning, Bazor had been nowhere to be seen.

The prominent men of the Two Lands gathered outside of the city. Their horses were groomed and decorated, their brightly colored chariots shining. Composite bows hung over each hunter's shoulder and the case for the arrows, each with identifying marks, fastened securely to the chariot rail. In each chariot a driver steered, while the nobleman hunter stood ready to aim the bow and shoot the arrows.

The horse and chariot were recent innovations. Before the Hyksos, people hunted on foot and with simpler bows with neither the strength nor range of this composite bow. These new weapons of the hunt also required new strategies in the ritual games. While it had long been the custom for the animals to be herded to this location, in olden times a pre-dug ditch and rope nets confined the animals to a limited space for this ritual day. Now, the enlarged area significantly enhanced the sport of the chase.

The steward of the hunt arranged for the two herds, oryx and gazelle, to be at this location, convenient for the ritual. The scimitar-horned oryx, the larger of the two herds, was about the size of a goat with long, pointed horns reaching back half their length. They ranged from a white or buff color to a red-brown with distinctive markings around their eyes. The dorcas gazelles were about the same size and had long ears, brown bodies with white undersides, and they moved with bounding leaps.

The Pharaoh gave Hatasu and Thethi permission to go with Paheri on the condition they stay back from the hunt—out of danger from the arrows, wild animals and the ever-present sand. So there the children were, holding tight to the chariot rails, their knees bent to absorb the shocks and jolts, moving along the uneven desert.

When the hunt began, Thutmose led the way toward the herd of Oryx. His chariot gleamed in the sun and his horses moved with elegant grace. Most of the noblemen and governors followed him. A second group, led by Amenmose, headed toward the more southern herd of gazelles. From her vantage point, Hatasu could see her brother, bow poised with arrow ready, eager for this display of his prowess in front of the sons of the nobles and governors.

It was then, when both groups were intent upon their prey, focused on their own hunt…Bazor entered the desert. He came, not from the town where he'd be noticed, but from a spot to the south, nearest Amen's hunt. His lone chariot moved out toward the hunt, his driver pushing his horses hard to join the prince's group. These horses were the best of the fine-boned equines he brought as tribute. They pulled this heavier chariot with apparent ease. Undeterred by the leather clothing unsuitable for the desert heat, he rushed forward, leaving behind a thick cloud of dark dust.

At the same time, the Pharaoh's group came close to the oryx. The sudden, startled stampede of these animals across the plain, pulled Hatasu's attention in that direction. As the chariots of Thutmose's followers spread out to make a large crescent behind the animals, the many leaping, charging beasts kicked sand into the air everywhere. She could barely see through the veils of dust as the drivers positioned themselves alongside the beasts of their choice and urged their horses on faster and faster. She watched with excitement as the hunter in each chariot drew his arrow from his chariot case, placed it in his bow, aimed at the animal he chose and let it fly.

Hatasu saw one after another oryx land, more dust erupting in the air. They saw their father go after the head of the herd, a great buck oryx. Because Thutmose was out in front, he could still be seen clearly. The others were becoming more masked by the dust. The children could see the Pharaoh going at great speed as he closed the distance between himself and his prey. Then, running his chariot alongside the beast, they saw him draw back his bow. The arrow flew, landing right in the animal's heart. The oryx seemed to trip on its front feet and fell to the ground with a thud they could feel and a new spray of desert dust.

Hatasu and Thethi cheered from their desert vantage point on Paheri's chariot. Cheers were heard all the way from the town. Paheri explained the oryx, the quintessential desert animal, represented Set. For the Pharaoh to bring him down, indicated his overcoming Set's chaos and claiming Set's strength for all the people. It was a good omen. The Pharaoh's shooting of the buck of the herd was the high point of the hunt.

Paheri and the children turned their attention to the second part of the hunt, Amenmose's group hunting the gazelles. Hetep, his chariot-driver, ran the horses hard but this gazelle buck was fast, moving forward in great erratic leaps. There was more sandy dust on the plain now, due not only to the animals and chariots, but also the northerly breeze directing the oryx dust to the more southerly gazelle hunt.

The details were uncertain, lost in the dust, but…yes…Bazor cut through the group of young hunters, his larger chariot and dark clothing distinguishing him even in the sand cloud. As the children watched, he steered his chariot toward Amenmose.

Paheri had pulled them back a distance. Amen, recognizable by his royal blue war helmet, closed in on the largest, dominant buck of the gazelles. Hetep, his driver, cut the horses into the mists of the stampeding herd, coming up alongside this noble prey. It was just then, that Hatasu again noticed the dark figure of the foreigner. She could see in the shadows, through the dust, the silhouette of Bazor with his bow and arrow poised to shoot.

Hatasu's eyes strained and her heart caught in her throat. Paheri, seeing it at the same time, was utterly silent…bringing his own horse to a stand still. Thethi's throat burst through his attempt to suppress a spasm of coughing. She saw Amen draw his great bow, arrow in place, and aim it at the heart of the beast. She was certain he was oblivious to the danger approaching him.

Bazor's chariot came alongside it and raced past him. Hatasu could see his bow, also ready to let loose its arrow. The dust got thicker and she strained to see. Then…there was a hesitancy…a slowing in the momentum of Amen's chariot. No longer keeping apace with the stampede; gazelle does leaped by their chariot in erratic confusion.

Hatasu heard a holler sounding like pain, and then a scream, as though it were Sekhmet herself roaring. The field erupted into a mass of shadow forms, clouds of dust, and animals stomping. Then, a figure in a chariot formed in the cloud coming toward them…but it was a chariot with just one person.

As it cleared the dust, she saw it was indeed her brother's dusty golden chariot…*but why just one person…the person who was driving it! Where was Amen?* The chariot emerged from the dust and she made out the blue war crown of the prince. She took a breath and let it go in relief…*but then…where was Hetep?*

Now, from the wall of sand in the air, more and more of the hunters emerged, the young men of the Two Lands. Each had two persons in their chariots. The gazelles continued to bound in every direction, keeping the dust stirred up but Hatasu saw another dark chariot drive…not toward them and the town but away, toward the north. She turned back as Amen's chariot was driving past them. There was something huddled on the floor of the chariot cab. *It must be Hetep, but was he dead or alive?*

Shaken by the incident, Paheri turned their chariot back toward the town. Thethi's cough intensified. Hatasu looked down at her brother holding tight to the chariot railing. As they arrived back at the town, they saw the hunters heading for the stables; caked with sand and sweat and their chariots unrecognizable from the gleaming gold and bright paints this morning.

Paheri drove past the wagons poised and ready to go out and pick up the fallen gazelles and oryx that palace cooks would prepare for tonight's feast. The wall of sand was settling, and the remains of the hunt could be seen, spread in random mounds upon the ground. A group of scribes accompanied the wagons, their job to note which nobleman's arrows were found in which beast.

As the children came into the palace courtyard, there were servants scurrying everywhere. Amen's chariot was there, horses still attached and unattended. There was a room in the palace used when someone was sick, an infirmary. Hatasu headed in that direction.

Thethi went with Paheri for some medicine for his cough. She arrived at the sick-room to find Hetep laid out on the bed, bright red blood covering the whole area of his shoulder and chest. His face was pale and his eyes were closed. Queen Ahmose was directing servants to bring water and herbs. A servant was washing the wound in his shoulder and any pressure brought a wince from Hetep he immediately tried to hide.

With relief, Hatasu saw her brother. He was pacing back and forth, up and down the room, casting anxious looks back at Hetep. "Will this be enough for Father? That vile Amurru! I should ride out and challenge him myself...right now!"

"It is better you stay here," said his stepmother, gently but firmly.

"I must go and discuss this with Father." With the momentum already built in his pacing, he catapulted out the door just as Satamun arrived.

Satamun, the Queen's sister, was the High Priestess, God's Wife of Amun, and as a healing priestess of Isis, she specialized in such wounds. Her plain looks and her toothy smile were forgotten as she seemed be bring hope and healing into the room as she entered. She carried a basket, its contents covered with white linen. Her mother greeted her sister warmly. Satamun returned a hurried embrace, scanned the room with her eyes, smiled at Hatasu and then at Hetep. "What happened?"

Ahmose nodded with her head in the direction of a broken arrow lying on the nearby table, "He was shot in the back of the shoulder by the Amurru foreigner."

The priestess looked at her sister with shocked recognition of the implications of this incident. "Hetep is Amen's driver. Was that arrow meant for the prince?"

Ahmose met her eyes, raised her eyebrows and ever so slightly shrugged her shoulders. Satamun raised her hand to her mouth as though to stifle a cry of alarm. "Amen is alright, isn't he? He left here with sufficient energy to say he was not physically hurt."

"Yes, he is unhurt."

"Well, it is Set's day. Some confusion and disorder might be expected…but not this!" The priestess refocused on the young man she'd come to help. Her eyes softened. It was Hetep who now had all of her attention. She watched him closely for several minutes.

It looked to Hatasu that the priestess was matching her own breathing to that of Hetep's. Then, without saying anything further, she closed her eyes and became very still. Hatasu kept watching. She noticed lights around Satamun's head and body. The lights grew brighter and spread out as though they would fill the whole room. She realized if she squinted her eyes, she could make out figures made of light. She thought the figures took the shapes of Isis, Sekhmet and Thoth. Hatasu watched, amazed. The priestess put her hands about six inches over the area of the wound and her

135

hands grew brighter.

Hetep's face softened and seemed to relax. He opened his eyes, then rested deeper into his bed. Only after this change in the lights, did Satamun look around for the bowl of clear water to cleanse the wound again. As she did this, she chanted a prayer to the Great Goddess for her aid. These sounds were low and slow. She took from her basket a small bundle wrapped in clean, white cloth. As she unwrapped it, Hatasu could see an obsidian knife. Handling it carefully, Satamun made an incision in Hetep's shoulder, then with tweezers, she probed until she got a grip on the arrowhead and put traction on it until she freed it from his shoulder. He winced and braced himself against the pain.

The priestess cleaned the wound with water and put herbs and ointment on it. As she bound the wound with fresh linen bandages, she put a red amulet in between the layers of bandage linen. She sang loudly enough for Hatasu to make out her words. *"Isis heal Hetep…As you healed your son Horus…Great Enchantress, heal Hetep,…Save him from all evil things of darkness…As you saved your son Horus."*

After the chant, there were several moments of silence as Satamun sat still. She unfolded another object from her basket. From the fine white linen emerged an ankh made of shining gold. She held it by the loop and pointed the extended end directly at Hetep's wound. Hatasu saw Hetep's colors get stronger. After a short time, Satamun spoke to him in a matter-of-fact way, instructing him on how to ask Isis to enter his dreams in order to heal this wound. Hetep nodded.

Ahmose accompanied Satamun as she left the room. Hatasu followed her mother and her aunt. "It is a very serious wound and he has lost a lot of blood. It will take another day to know if he will recover or if it will fester."

Ahmose nodded.

Then, looking to Hatasu, Satamun said, "So, my little red-haired, Taosid princess, would you like to help Hetep?"

Hatasu thought Satamun had read her mind. "Yes," came her quick reply.

"In the morning, I will return to see Hetep when Ra is still climbing in the morning sky. Meet me here." Satamun turned and walked off in the direction of the temple.

Hatasu and her mother walked to the ceremonial palace where her father was meeting with his ministers. Amen was still pacing the floor. Thutmose stood up and took his Queen's hand as she sat next to him. "Is Hetep going to be alright?"

"Satamun said we will not know until tomorrow," said the Queen. "It was definitely Bazor's arrow that hit him."

"Bazor ran off...escaped. His ships disembarked before we got back from the hunt. Nakht and the Medjays are pursuing him. That arrow was meant for Amen. This forces my hand."

"Then we will take the army. We will subjugate these vile Asiatics once again!" There was a fierceness in Amen's voice.

"Yes, Amen, I must go to the land of the Amurru and subdue that rebellious suzerain."

Hatasu's heart swelled with the rush of purpose she felt in making these barbarian peoples respect her beloved father. For a second Amen's eyes met hers and they each saw in the other the same fire of indignation and purpose they shared.

Chapter 8 - Isis's Day

"What was Satamun doing yesterday, when she pointed the ankh at Hetep's wound?" Hatasu questioned as she walked with her mother toward Hetep's sick room early the next day.

"She was strengthening his sekhem, his own vital energy, so it could heal his khet (body). Though it is necessary to help the khet by cleaning the wound and putting herbal ointment on it, it is the sekhem that must do the real healing. Isis is the goddess who brings healing magic and renewal to his spirit and body. This afternoon, you will join in Isis's ritual dance of the renewal of Osiris. In the sickroom she renews the person; in the temple-dance she renews the community."

"What was the amulet Satamun put in the bandages?"

"That was the 'Knot of Isis'." Hatasu's mother reached into the basket she carried with her and took from its linen wrappings a red carnelian amulet, carved in the shape of the knot. She handed it to Hatasu and said, "It is the blessing of the goddess."

Hatasu fingered its cool redness.

"It symbolized the bond of opposites, between the khet and the ka, the body and the soul. The sekhem binds them together."

Hatasu had worried about Hetep the whole evening before and she was so glad Amen was unhurt. Life seemed precarious, indeed, as she considered she could have lost another brother. Hetep, the son of the mayor of the West Bank, was a gentle young man she thought of mostly as her brothers', Amen and Wadj, devoted friend. As Hatasu and her mother entered Hetep's sickroom, they saw he was awake.

Amenmose was already there, still pacing and saying loudly, "I don't know what it is going to take to get him to declare war!" Then, looking down on Hetep in his sick bed, he said, "How dare Bazor aim at me and almost kill you!"

Ahmose ignored Amen's rantings and sat by Hetep's bed. "How does your wound feel today?"

"It's sore." More of the color had come into his cheeks.

Satamun entered the room with her sistrum and incense. She greeted her sister and niece and came over to inspect Hetep's shoulder. Amen hovered over her looking at what she was about to do. She stopped and turned to the prince. "Amen, it would be better if you found something else to do now and come back to visit Hetep when we have finished."

Amen scowled but looked to Hetep and said, "I'll be back later." His friend nodded weakly.

Once he was gone, Satamun removed the bandages, washed the area and reapplied an ointment from her bag. Then she called Hatasu over. The wound was red and swollen but free of puss. Her aunt asked her to put her hands slightly above Hetep's shoulder and asked, "What do you feel there?"

"It's warm. My hands are hot. They tingle." Hatasu was surprised at how clearly she could feel these things without even touching his skin.

"Good," was Satamun's reply. "It is as I thought. Your sekhem is naturally powerful. When you have the intention to heal, and direct that intention through your hands to the area in need of healing, you sekhem strengthens *his* sekhem. This helps Hetep's khet finish this healing." Turning to the Queen, Satamun said, "I tell you, Ahmose, she has the natural talent to be a priestess." Hatasu was very pleased by this praise.

Her mother, however, said stiffly, "Yes, yes, but her role is still to be Queen."

Satamun returned to Hetep and asked him to tell her his dream of last night. More color was returning to his face as it had the night before when Satamun had done the same thing with her hands.

He told the dream like this, "In the dream, I was carrying a basket of oven fuel. The fuel was on fire but the basket wasn't. This very hot basket sat on my left shoulder, the one that was shot. My sister came to me and said, 'Put that burning basket down'. But I said, 'No, I must carry it'. Then, Amenmose said to me, 'Put that basket down'. But I said, 'No, I can't put it down'. Next, Wadjmose came to me and said, 'Put that basket down'. I said, 'No, no, Wadj, I want to carry this for you'. Then, Wadj became the burning substance in the basket. It got very, very heavy. I wanted to keep carrying it but I couldn't. Then Isis appeared. She didn't say anything. She just touched the basket and it became light and cool. It stayed on my shoulder but now it was easy to carry. She put a staff in my hand and the staff turned to a papyrus stem. And with that, the dream ended."

"You were blessed by a powerful dream!" said Satamun. "Your sadness about Wadjmose's death will no longer be such a burden that it could interfere with you healing. It seems the goddess has plans for you to be a leader."

Hetep's eyes teared-up at the mention of Wadj. "At least this time, a prince didn't die."

Satamun smiled at him. "No, loyal friend. Amen didn't die and neither will you. It will take a period of rest, but you will recover."

"So there will be no need to go to war?"

"I do not speak of war, only of healing."

Hatasu was relieved about Hetep and exhilarated by her experience of her own healing sekhem. She and her mother left together. Her mother said smiling, "Now we are ready for the Isis dance."

Hatasu did a few dance steps on the spot. Her mother smiled and said, "You go along with Sitre and I will see you there."

Holding Sitre's hand, Hatasu skipped into the temple square where they merged with the many women who had come to celebrate the goddess Isis. The mud-brick square in front of the temple was buzzing with women of all ages and sizes. They each wore a simple white sheath that fell from just below their breasts down to their calves. Most women wore their hair long with some hair in front of each shoulder and the rest flowing down their backs. On the ankles and wrists of those who could afford them were bands of faience beads making ever so slight a rattling sound as they moved. Rich and poor, young and old, greeted each other. Sitre held Hatasu's hand a little tighter than usual. She stopped and shared news with her friends.

"So, I heard that the Amurru shot the prince! Is he going to be alright?" a middle aged woman said.

"No, no…the prince is alright. It was Hetep, his chariot driver, who was hurt," returned Sitre.

"The same Hetep that was with Wadj…?"

"Yes, the same. He got a pretty bad shoulder wound. I hear he'll be alright."

"Thank the goddess," several said in unison.

Shaking her head, Sitre said, "Those Asiatics are always trouble."

"I hope it is over with his leaving," said an elderly woman.

"I hear the Pharaoh is very angry…angry enough to go to war."

Another woman who'd joined them said, "Oh, I hope not. My son is in the army. He is a good lad and he is all I have since his father died."

Sitre was silent for a long moment, then looked at the woman with worry in her eyes. "Yes, my dear young husband died in the Nubian war when Thutmose brought our troops south to subdue the king of Kush."

Young Asat had joined the group and she added, "War brings sorrow but it also brings riches. My grandfather has great wealth from his many campaigns in the Levant. He tells stories of the wondrous deeds of war."

A matronly woman agreed with her, "The spoils of war enrich our household and our temple. Wondrous things come home from a war."

Sitre returned, "Wondrous things…if there is a victory."

Everyone looked at her, shocked. "How could you doubt our Divine Pharaoh would not be victorious over these godless barbarians?"

Sitre shook her head and wrung her hands. "Well, at least the Amurru are gone now."

Hatasu was forming her own opinion about her father going to war but she listened to these women.

By now there were many faces in the square, the women in the center and a many-layered circle of men on the outside. Just as the women had gathered to see the men hunt, so now the men formed an audience as the women danced. Asat, practicing her dance, drew Amen's notice. His attention urged her on to even more flowing undulations. His smile when their eyes met, lit up his whole face. Hatasu had never seen her brother glow like this. He and Asat seemed aware only of each other, the crowd of people melted away.

Hatasu continued to look around. Then, she saw the smiling face of her grandmother. Breaking lose from Sitre's hand, she ran to her grandmother, giving her a hug around her waist.

"So, my sweet princess, you are here to dance with the goddess?" asked Senisenb.

Almost before she could answer, her cousins, Meryt with her little sister Isis, ran up to their grandmother, too. Senisenb's arms seemed big enough to encircle all her granddaughters.

"Oh, Grandma, tell us the Isis story before the dance begins," pleaded little Isis.

"But you will see the story in dance."

"Please, tell us in words, anyway," said Meryt.

Hatasu, Isis and Meryt sat on the ground looking up at Senisenb. She began, "In the long ago time, when gods and goddesses still walked the earth, Isis was married to her brother Osiris. They ruled the land well but their brother Set was jealous and killed Osiris by trapping him in a box and sending it afloat down the Nile. News of this was brought to Isis and her grief was terrible. She searched for the body of her husband and traveled everywhere. Finally, her search brought her to the land of Byblos where she found it. Isis brought the box with Osiris's body in it back to the Two Lands.

There, in the Nile delta marsh where she had the powers of the great enchantress, she did her magic. She gathered her herbs, her chants and her magic. She grew from her arms wings…great bird wings." Senisenb spread out her arms along side her like she, herself, had wings. "…and she stood over the body of Osiris chanting the song of renewed life and hope. She gently swayed the wings to the rhythm of breath." Their grandmother moved her arms as though they were wings, up and down they fanned the air. "The breath of the air moved into Osiris's lungs." Her voice held a sense of awe. "The chant moved into his ears and from far away in the land of the dead, Osiris heard the voice of Isis."

Senisenb let her arms rest at her sides and lowered her voice to almost a whisper. She leaned toward the children. "Hearing the call of his beloved, he moved through the doorway between the worlds of the living and the dead. Through Isis's chants and magic, through her love for him, and through his love for her…life returned to his body. The life that returned to Osiris was given back again to Isis and she became pregnant. This was their son, Horus.

But Set unexpectedly came upon his brother, Osiris…restored to life." Her voice became dark with foreboding. "Enraged, he killed him again but this time he cut the body up into pieces. To inhibit

Isis's magic, he scattered the pieces into all the different parts of Khemet, up and down the Nile. Grieved all over again, Isis called upon the help of her sister, Nephthys, and together they searched throughout their land. One by one, they found the pieces of Osiris and in each spot they found a piece, they had a temple built.

They found all of the pieces…except the phallus. It had been eaten by a Oxyrhynchus-fish. This kept her from being able to bring him back from the dead a second time but instead Isis used her magic to fashion for him a phallus of gold, so once she had all the pieces, she could reunite them and bind them together as the first mummy, making him the First of the Westerners and ruler of the Afterlife. Isis then waited for the birth of the son of Osiris, the Great Horus."

The three girls clapped their hands in appreciation. "How did Isis do that magic of awakening Osiris?" Hatasu wanted to know.

"How did she turn into a bird?" Meryt wanted to know.

"How wonderful she had the baby Horus!" said Isis.

"You young ladies have many questions. These are things for you to ponder in your hearts and to study when you are old enough to go to the House of Life. But for now…do you have your dancing shoes on?" she asked.

All three girls looked down at their bare feet, then back up to their grandmother with quizzical looks in their eyes. "Who could dance in shoes? They would surely get in ones way!"

Senisenb smiled playfully. "Well then, you will dance in your dusty feet."

The three girls giggled and Hatasu's cousins pulled her by her arm to get her to practice a dance with them. Senisenb waved them off. Hatasu started to dance as she'd been taught. She expected praise and admiration from her cousin but Meryt wasn't paying any attention. Meryt was doing something completely different. She had recently learned a dance in which she bent herself far over backward until her hands touched the ground again. Hatasu stopped what she was doing to watch her. She tried to imitate Meryt. She fell.

Little Isis laughed and did her version of the backbend, which was to bend foreward. Hatasu frowned at Isis and turned to watch Meryt again. She was jealous her friend could do this move and she couldn't and she was angry Isis thought her failure was funny. She tried again, but fell again, this time skinning her elbow. She wanted to cry because it hurt but she bit back the tears and tried again.

Isis looked sympathetic and tried to offer her an easier way. That made Hatasu all the more determined. Meryt suggested she practice it by first lying on the ground and lifting herself with her arms. The princess felt increasing irritability toward her friend. She spit out impatient words but tried the suggestion, anyhow. It worked! She raised her body up backward as she rested on her hands and feet. Still she was dissatisfied. She wanted to bend backward the way Meryt did. This time, Meryt helped Hatasu by holding her waist so she could bend backward until her hands touched ground. With this help Hatasu did not fall. She'd done it!

Just then, a hush fell over the women. The girls looked up. There at the pylon gate stood her mother, the Great Wife, her sistrum in hand. Today, she was the 'Lady of the Dance'. It was the Queen's role to lead the dance-magic for her people. A queenly smile spread over her face. She called out to her people, "Today, we honor Isis by dancing her story!"

Now, Satamun came out of the temple and stood beside the Queen, her hands held high for clapping. The women knew what to do. They formed a circle and unobtrusively, the young ones were guided into place while the old ones were given places of honor. Hatsu's irritability melted as her body moved with the rhythm. The women around her, just moments ago talking anxiously about the possibility of war, stilled their voices at the sound of the sistrum. The dance began. The women's feet started to move and the faience beads around their ankles rattled. Satamun began to sing the role of Nephthys. *"Hail Isis, Glorious Goddess,…Up my hands raise, and hold…To the sharp angle of invocation."*

Each sister raised her arms, bent at the elbow into the sign of the ka. They moved to the beat made by the clapping of hands and the shaking of the sistrum. Once all the women were moving in harmony with this rhythm, the Queen came down from her pedestal and danced among them. She moved to her right, everyone following. Proceeding slowly, each footstep pronounced, they created their own type of sistrum beat as the ankle beads rattled and their feet made drum sounds on the mud bricks.

Hatasu followed easily. The dance continued from the invocation to the lamentation. *"Oh Osiris, great bull of heaven,…Killed by his brother Set,…Cut into 14 pieces…Osiris is dead…Osiris, Return!"*

The footsteps grew ponderous and heavy as the circle dance

continued. Hatasu felt in this movement the mourning of the great goddess. The steps slapped on the ground heavily. Moving in their rhythmic path, the women bent down in mourning, then raised again in invocation. This lamentation, song and dance, reminded Hatasu of how much she missed Wadjmose. As she looked around, she saw tears in the eyes and on the cheeks of others. The sadness in the people and the music reached a crescendo.

The music shifted again. The tempo picked up. Ahmose chanted to Satamun, *"Says Isis to Nephthys, ...Sister! This is our brother ... Come let us reassemble his limbs ... Osiris, live!"*

The beat and tempo of the hand-clapping and sistrum-shaking intensified. Playing the roles of Isis and Nephthys, the Queen and priestess held hands and led the dance together. Sitre took Hatasu's hand on one side and Meryt took the other. The dance now moved in a sideways step. After making a few fumbling attempts and almost tripping, Hatasu's feet figured out how these steps went.

Next, Satamun sang out, *"Hail Isis, the Great Awakener, ...Who awakened Osiris ... Who carried within the womb ... Horus, the son of Osiris."*

Now came the addition of a hop in the feet and a smile on the faces of all the dancers. Hatasu's youthful energy spilled over into these steps as she grinned up at Sitre and over at Meryt. She saw her grandmother at a little distance, smiling back at her, and her mother was ahead of everyone, leading this gay gathering. *"How beautiful is your face, Great Awakener of Osiris ... We praise thee, Great Awakener of the mighty river ... We sing to thee, Great Awakener of the dance ... We adore thee, Isis, Glorious Goddess."*

Here the Queen led the dancers into a serpentine chain that folded, labyrinth-like, this way and that. Hatasu's feet scurried along as she tried to keep up. Everyone giggled. The women continued to sing the chant even though they were breathless from the laughter. As the dance-serpent wove in and around itself, undulating back and forth, each smiling, laughing face, one after another, passed in and out of Hatasu's vision. Hatasu recognized women by their scents: Jasmine, lotus, patchouli, myrrh, cinnamon, sandalwood, and even an occasional scent of garlic on someone who was ailing. The child thought she must have seen and smelled every woman in the whole town of Waset.

The feelings of sadness and grief gave way to the awakening of Osiris and the river. Comfort and exhilaration spread and was shared by the community of dancers, each experiencing the presence of the Great Goddess in her own way. She even shared a smile with Asat as she moved by, recognizing her sweet smell of musk. Gradually, the dance slowed down. The chorus continued the praises of Isis but now at a softer, slower pace. The Queen led the dancers back into a circle and each person standing in place responded to the rhythm with her feet only. Then, with one loud shake of the sistrum and simultaneous clap of the priestess' hands, everyone stopped.

Chapter 9 - Nephthys's Epagomenal Day

Sitre complained of nightmares the whole time the Amurru was in Waset. Hatasu overheard her telling her mother of dreams of her aunt being chased by an Amurru-Hyksos man intent on raping her. She did indeed look tired and haggard. The dance renewed her spirit but Ahmose, sensitive to her struggle, encouraged her to catch up on her missed rest and to sleep late the next morning.

The Queen herself braided Hatasu's hair and put kohl on her eyes. Hatasu asked her mother, "Today is Nephthys day, right?"

"Right. The doorway between the worlds opens a bit wider today. Nephthys is the goddess who represents what is still unmanifest in Nun. The events of today are about listening to her messages from the Great Beyond."

"I know about that. I want to know what will happen about Bazor and the Amurru. Will Father go to war with them?"

"Perhaps." Ahmose smiled at Hatasu's political concern. "This is the day the Pharaoh consults the oracle and the Amurru question is what he most wants to know."

"Why doesn't he just *know* whether or not to go to war?"

"Well, my dear, the decision to go to war is a complex one. Such a decision could be a destiny or a downfall."

Ahmose finished with her hair. "There are several ways to listen to the goddess Nephthys as the oracle. The astrologer priest listens by noting the movement of the stars. They tells us ways to keep the land in harmony with the Great Above. Priestesses, myself included, look into the scrying mirror, staring until earthly eyes lose focus on this world and begin to see images that are not reflections but visions. These tell us ways to keep the land in harmony with the Great Below. Today everyone participates by whirling the oracle dance in the temple square. Each person has access to the wisdom of the goddess for themselves. Those that want more information then they get themselves will go to the wise women oracles."

"Will there be a prophecy for me? Can I see beyond the doorway to know my destiny?"

"There is already a great prophesy for you given by the priestesses at my purification after your birth. They said you 'shall rule in peace'. But today the prophecy we seek is: What is necessary for the good of the land this year?"

"Can you tell me if I will have to marry Amenmose…for the good of the land?"

"Tradition is that the daughter of the royal line determines the next Pharaoh by her consent to marry him. So, no, you don't *have* to marry him but…you have a duty to choose a consort who will rule. Your father has begun training Amenmose. He wishes for you to be happy with this choice."

Hatasu sighed, "So, yes, I do have to marry him for the land and for Father."

"There is no one else suited to rule."

The child sat in resigned silence while her mother finished kohling her eyes. Ahmose gave her daughter a kiss on the top of her head and said, "I must go to the temple. You go find the musicians and dancers. See what prophecy the dance brings you today. Maybe the goddess will give you another solution."

Hatasu kissed her mother on the cheek and ran off toward the temple square. She found Meryt and little Isis waiting for her. Sitre, looking more rested and refreshed, offered help with the Nephthys Day dance. "This is the day to twirl," she told the three of them.

Hatasu, Meryt and Isis started making circles, going round and round until they were dizzy and giggling. They flopped themselves down on the ground.

"There are some secrets about whirling that can help your dance," Sitre told them. They looked at her expectantly. "The first is, you keep one foot in place and move around it with the other foot." She demonstrated.

The three girls caught on quickly. They spun around the one foot as the nearby tambourines beat a rhythm. But before long the girls sprawled on the ground again, the sky spinning above them.

Sitre called the girls back to her and whispered in the tone of a conspirator, "There is another secret about twirling!" They leaned toward her with wide-eyed nods. "Twirling in one direction feels different from twirling in another. It feels lighter when you turn to the left."

The girls tried it both directions and were amazed how much lighter they felt going to the left.

Sitre motioned them close again. "That works because the left turn comes from the heart and lifts a person from earthly entrapment. That helps you listen to Nephthys."

They all whirled to the left again and it was much longer this time before one after another fell to the ground.

Sitre smiled and said, "Are you ready for the next secret?"

They nodded, giggling at their dizziness.

"If you want to be able to whirl longer without getting so dizzy, you must spin around your center." They waited for her to go on. "Your center is your ab (heart), around which you pivot…your center around which you whirl." Sitre tapped the center of her chest. "Do you think you can remember it all; one foot as pivot, turn to the left, keep your heart your center?"

The three of them tried it again. Sitre watched them, applauding each girl's attempts and successes.

This dance of Nephthys started with the beat of the tambourines slowly, but gradually, speeding up. People gathered in the square and whirled to the music. There were smiling faces, swirling hair and the sound of the feet on the mud-brick court.

Hatasu danced in the midst of it all. She felt exhilarated by the gaiety of the music. Then she felt increasingly dizzy in spite of Sitre's secrets. Still, she danced on. The dizziness changed into a sensation of floating as though she had indeed loosened her bonds to the earth. The floating sensation turned into a feeling of numbness. The dance went on and on. Thanks to Sitre's secret she kept going. When she was finally exhausted Hatasu sat down on the ground but the world continued to spin. This world revolved around her and she felt the stillness of the center…*her* center, her ab.

One by one, others sat down, too, each in silence. Everyone was contained within herself or himself, quiet and listening. Hatasu felt a great peace and comfort all around her. As the sensations of whirling slowed down, she wished for a prophecy, so she listened to the silence within herself. All she heard was the words 'wait, be patient'. This was not the message she wanted.

Just then, the chant began low and sweet. It was the voice of Satamun, the God's Wife of Amun. *"Hail, Nephthys! The Moon and the Sun are One...Lady of the bright crescent and the dark circle,...Mistress of the Night, concealed by the Light,...Multiply my eyes that I may see you in all your forms."*

After the dance and song an old and blind oracle priestess came forward to answer questions from the people who gathered. Her hair was un-wigged. Her natural white tresses hung down around her shoulders. She was very thin and her linen dress hung loosely on her frame.

Hatasu listened as one woman came forward and asked, "Please, will I conceive a child this year?"

The oracle priestess was still for a moment, then answered slowly, "You will conceive a child this year but not bring it to birth. In the fullness of time, however, you will bring a child into your family and she shall be a joy to those about her."

The woman thanked her and walked away with a sad but peaceful expression.

A man came up and asked, "My brother has made a business trip and his return is long overdue. Is he to return safely?"

"Your brother has deceived you. He has taken the profits and spent them in Byblos."

This man's eyes grew wide with surprise, then he tilted his head in puzzlement. Finally, his eyebrows moved together on his forehead and a look of anger moved across his face as he walked away heavily.

Long into the afternoon, the priestess answered the questions of the people.

That evening, Hatasu sought out her mother and found her with her father in the rooftop pavilion. Ahmose was sitting so the fading western sun reflected off the mirror she held in her hand. She was looking into it with a quiet intensity. The Pharaoh sat at an angle from her, his whole body leaning toward her. They didn't notice Hatasu as she approached. She sat herself cross-legged by a potted palm tree, sensing not to disturb them, yet wanting to hear what they were saying.

She recognized the Hathor mirror was a special one; the reflecting surface was silver rather than obsidian. The upper part of the handle was shaped in the form of the goddess' head, the lovely cow eyes and extending bovine ears associated with Hathor, goddess of dance. The surface of the mirror was an egg-shaped ovoid, like the sun as it sits low on the horizon. She watched as her mother gazed into it as though straining to see. Hatasu recognized she was scrying. She listened to the oracle she pronounced from its images.

"It's coming through, darkly," Ahmose said to her husband as she stared at the mirror.

"Can you make anything out?"

"I can make out the god of war, Montu…Yes, he is holding up the banner of victory…but wait…there is something else."

He leaned closer…waiting.

"There is a dark hole in the middle of the mirror's image." She shook her head, not understanding.

Thutmose's body strained to know, his eyes intent on his wife's face. She put the mirror on her lap and looked at him. "I see you will go to war, you will have victory and you will return…but…there is something else…an emptiness. I don't know what the dark hole is in the image."

He leaned back and let out a long sigh. "Well it doesn't say not to go! According to the astrologers, the star omens are in place for a successful campaign."

"Yes, you said Hapu and the astrologer priests confirmed the rightness of the timing."

"He said the planet of the ram (Mars) is moving through sign of Osiris (Orion). As you know, this means war is inevitable. The ram's planet meets up with the large planet (Jupiter), a certain indication of victory. Did I tell you he said with Sirius rising, we have the blessing of the goddess?"

With clear but doleful eyes, Ahmose said, "Yes, you told me. I am sad that you will go away to make this war, Thutmose. Be careful, my beloved, the mirror says to go but there is something hidden. There is something about the dark image in my mirror makes me think of…of Sekenenre (SEC-en-en-ray)."

The Pharaoh put his fingers gently over her lips. "Do not speak of that. That can not happen again. The stars show Amun will lead me and protect me. Banish all other thoughts that bring bad magic." His voice was soft and he looked at her tenderly, "The scrying mirror said I shall return to you safely."

"Yes, it does say that."

Starting to move toward the stairs, he said, "I must call a council of my advisors and meet with them tonight. Tomorrow, I will poise the question to the oracle of Amun in the processional. If it is as I expect, I will announce the war to the people from the Temple of the Ancestor, Montuhotep, tomorrow."

Hatasu realized her father was indeed going to go to war, and she wanted with all her heart to go with him, to fight those vile Amurru right along side her father. She also knew she was female and young but she blurted out from her hiding place as he started to leave, "Could I go with you, even as your sandal barer? Please let me go, too!"

"No, no, sweet daughter." He smiled as he saw her there by the palm. "This war is not for you, but I shall come home with wonderful gifts for you."

Ahmose came toward her and putting her arm around her daughter's shoulder said, "We shall do our part of the battle by bringing offerings to Amun for his victory and we will ask Isis for dreams of his progress."

Hatasu let out a sigh of resignation. "Amen gets to go though, right?"

"Yes, it will train him for his role as Pharaoh." Her mother added to her, "Your training as Queen is different than Amen's."

Hatasu felt frustration rise up in her solar plexus as a burning sensation. He got to go to war with their father. She got left behind. She didn't like it one bit! She scowled. Her father either didn't see or choose to ignore her unhappiness about this. He reached out, patted her red head, turned and left for his council meeting. Hatasu slumped in her chair like a wilted flower. She wished there was a way to get her father to let her go with him.

She looked over at her mother who was again looking closely into her mirror. She thought about that dark spot and lessened her own disappointments to wonder about it. "Who is Sekenenre and why shouldn't we talk about him?" she asked.

After a pause, she looked up and said, "Sekenenre, my grandfather, your great-grandfather, was the great Pharaoh who first stood up to the Hyksos. That is what is important for you to know. The Hyksos are an abomination of the gods. We wish to erase their footsteps and to do that, we do not empower the story with our words."

Hatasu turned all these events over and over in her ab.

Chapter 10 - The Oracle of Amun

Ahmose woke Hatasu before dawn. "I have something very special to show you."

Thethi heard her whispers and begged to come along. The Great Wife nodded and urged the two of them to follow her up the stairway to the roof of the palace.

"Does this have to do with Father and Sekenenre?" Hatasu asked.

"No, my dear," Her mother looked back at her. "We aren't going to talk of that."

She led them on and just before they opened the door to the roof she said, "What I am about to show you is the reassurance of the regularity of the cosmic cycles. Even when there are changes, like war, still the drama of the gods in the sky comfort us with their predictable regularity."

Hatasu relaxed.

As they got to the roof, the sky was dark. The new moon and the dark land allowed the stars to have all the glory. Across the sky spread the Milky Way, the Nile River of the heavens mirroring the great river of the Two Lands. Ahmose directed the children to the eastern side of the roof. There, with her arm around Hatasu and Thethi standing nearby, they looked to the eastern horizon. "Today we are looking for the return of the star, Sothis, Isis's star. This is the morning it rises with the sun after its long journey of seventy days in the underworld."

"Do you see the stars of Osiris's belt?" Ahmose pointed to the three stars in a vertical row, "There they are; see the two bright stars of his shoulders, and those other two stars of his hips." They shone to the left of the vertical stars. "Do you see how he lies on his side?"

Hatasu could, indeed, imagine the figure of a man.

Ahmose went on, "In the sky, Osiris is dead and lies low and still like our river. In the months to come, Sothis will rise a little higher in the sky each night. As she rises, she will push Osiris upright until he stands straight up overhead. The star Sothis pushes Osiris up in the sky, just as Isis raised him up from the dead. At the same time, Isis causes the waters of the Nile to rise with her tears of grief. Thus, we are all renewed."

Just then, through the morning glow over the eastern mountains, they saw a bright star distinct within the dawn sky. "I think I see Sothis!" said Thethi in an excited voice.

"Yes, there she is," said Hatasu pointing low on the horizon.

"This is the herald of the rising Nile!" Ahmose said.

The glow on the horizon grew brighter. Rosy waves spread up and across the hot eastern desert and the sky again gave birth to the day. Ra's light illuminated the land and sky. One cycle of the year ended and a new one started. It was a solemn moment. This day celebrated the renewal of the sun, the renewal of the river, the renewal of the ancestors, renewal of the Pharaoh—and through all these, the renewal of the people. This was the day of the procession of the barque of the god Amun across the river to the Temples of the Ancestors.

Ahmose continued to instruct them, "Sothis is Isis as the Great

Awakener, for it is she who renews the dead. As Isis awakened
Osiris by the power of her love and elevated him to life with the
Imperishable Stars…see those stars to the north that never set and
never fade?" She pointed to their left where the northern stars
glowed their constant light. She continued, "So does she elevate our
ancestors. This year, Wadjmose is among them."

They were all silent as though looking for Wadj in the sky.
Ahmose continued, "Isis's tears for Osiris fill up our river and bring
us the inundation."

Thethi slanted his head to the side quizzically. "But Paheri said
it was Khnum that let out the waters of the Nile for the inundation."

"The Khnum that makes the ka on the potter's wheel?" asked
Hatasu.

Ahmose smiled and went on, "There are many different stories
told to explain each aspect of the world. The story that Isis's tears
bring us the inundation reminds us the tears of grief promise the
renewal of life. Likewise, the story of Khnum reminds us of the
importance of honoring the gods. These stories go together to give
us understanding and balance."

Hatasu and Thethi argued about which story they liked best as
they noisily bounded down the stairs and into the breakfast room.
Thutmose and Amenmose, just returned from the New Year's
ceremonial offering to Sothis at the roof of the temple, sat in their
own animated conversation.

Amen could hardly sit still, he was so excited. "Now that we *are*
going to war, those vile men of the Levant will pay for their
arrogant threats against the Two Lands."

Her father, too, spoke with fervor, "Yes. I, the son of the god Amun, will protect the people of the Nile from the threat of them returning like the Hyksos."

Hatasu knew the oracle had inflamed, rather than soothed, his anger at the foreigners.

Ahmose interrupted, "Until the oracle of Amun confirms this action…"

"Yes, yes…the priests at the temple have been informed an oracle is called for. I will not announce the war to my people until I can tell them I am commissioned by my father Amun."

"The threatening reports from the Levant alarm the council members. The oracle from the stars and the scrying glass assured them," Amen nodded as he reported this. "They see the wisdom of this action."

Hatasu realized Amen had been included in the council meeting. *Another thing he was getting to do,* she thought jealously.

Thethi, just now realizing war was very likely, begged his father, "Let me go with you! I'm good with the throw-stick. I'll kill those wicked Asiatics."

"No, no, my dear son," he said with a smile. "You and your sister will stay home this war but you will come to the Festival of the Ancestors." The Pharaoh gathered himself to his full height and looked down on his two young children. "You two have stayed with your nurse-tutors in the past for this festival as is fitting for young children. This year, you join us for the West Bank festival."

Hatasu thought, '*It was not as good as going to war but it was good*'.

Their father went on, "You shall come to the Temple of Amun with the Queen, Prince Amen and I, and shall witness the Oracle of Amun. You will accompany the processional to the West Bank of the Ancestors. I want my family beside me as I announce this great action."

Hatasu, thinking of her mother's warnings, asked, "Father, what if the Oracle of Amun doesn't say to fight?"

Thutmose frowned and with a dismissive motion of his hand he said, "I am the Son of Amun and I know he wills me to bring him this victory."

Hatasu looked to her mother. Ahmose's face hid any emotion but Hatasu thought her shoulders slumped ever so slightly.

It was a rare occasion when the younger children were allowed to enter the sacred precinct of the Temple of Amun, even though it was next to the palace. As they neared the massive mud-brick wall surrounding the outer perimeter of the temple, the Pharaoh, in an expansive mood, introduced them to its important features, "Look at this wall and tell me what you see."

"The workmen must have been very tired because the wall is sloppy. Look how it waves up and down as it goes along," said Thethi.

Amenmose smiled a knowing smile and nudged his little brother mockingly. He anticipated his father's explanation.

"It is good you noticed, my son, but it takes much work to make sure it waves in that manner. The waves are like the primeval waters of creation. It is made of mud, for it is the blend of earth and river water that is the first stage of creation. The wall's job is to separate the temple from its surroundings and to identify it as sacred space. What is outside the wall is subject to the forces of chaos, inside, the cosmic order of the gods is honored and maintained."

Amenmose gave Thethi a 'poor little brother' grin. Thethi just pushed him, scowled and said under his breath, "Know it all!"

Their father said, "Now you must leave the chaos of your teasing behind as we enter the grand gates."

Both boys…the tall warrior one and the small frail one…turned their attention to what their father had to say about the, as yet un-built, gateway for this entrance. "The pylon walls I will build here will be as the mountain peaks flanking the eastern horizon from which the sun rises. The sun governs the cosmos, giving order and dispelling disorder as it goes. The Creator has instituted kingship likewise to govern on earth, giving order and dispelling disorder. Thus, I must dispel the disorder caused by the Amurru. I must use the courvee tax for the army." (A labor tax required during the period of the inundation when the fields were unable to be worked because they were flooded.)

In a dismissive aside he added, "I'd planned to use the manpower from the tax to build the temple gate this year." With renewed resolve he added, "But when the Amurru are defeated, I will finish this gate and the Temple to Amun will be the grandest temple in all of Khemet!"

The two younger children nodded wide-eyed at their father's grand plans, trying to ignore Amenmose's knowing grin.

Ahmose added softly, "Hatasu, the sanctuary of this temple was built by your uncle, the great Pharaoh Amenhotep."

"Is Amenhotep my uncle, too?" Thethi wanted to know.

"No, he was Hatasu's uncle, because Amenhotep was Queen Ahmose's brother," his father answered. "Mutnofret, your mother, was not related to that Pharaoh. However, you still have a noble lineage. You are related to the Intefs."

"Well, aren't the Intefs my ancestors, too?" Hatasu wanted to know.

"Yes, of course."

"How can she have both Amenhotep and the Intefs? She gets to have too many families!" complained Thethi.

"That's just the way it is," the Pharaoh replied in a tone that discouraged any further questions. Hatasu wondered about it herself.

The royal family now entered the open space of temple within the white walls Thutmose had built the year before. "Amun's name means 'unmanifest'," Thutmose explained. "He represents the hidden force underlying creation. Though he cannot be seen himself, he is the reason all else can be seen. His animal is the ram, for Amun rules the age when the sun raises in the sign of the ram on the spring equinox."

A great many people were moving about within this courtyard preparing for the big event. There was a bit more of a buzz than the usual dignified procession preparation. They knew the Pharaoh was to have an Oracle from Amun. The question hung in the air, *"Would the Amurru attack? Would they try to take over like the Hyksos? What would the oracle say?"* The white-robed priests and priestesses were arranging paraphernalia to accompany the sacred Barque of Amun.

The Pharaoh turned to his oldest living son and with a smile, he said, "Now, Amenmose, Commander-in-Chief of the army and Hawk-in-the-Nest, you made offering to Sothis with me this morning and know the importance of this Temple of Amun for the Pharaoh and for the people. Explain this to Thethi and Hatasu."

Amen had been walking tall, a spring of excitement and anticipation in his step. This was a test by his father. The confidence of his grin faded, for the temple was not his strong suit. "All right," he said, his eyes moving nervously around the enclosure. He began, "This is the first court. Those who've attended the House of Life gather here at festivals. In the center is the Holy of Holies…the dwelling place of the god Amun. Only the Pharaoh and the High Priest go behind those doors and attend to the needs of the god. Today, New Years Day, the god Amun is carried out among the people to bring order and blessing to the land. He is still hidden from common sight within his veiled barque. Today's processional takes him across the river to Temple of the Ancestor, Pharaoh Montuhotep." He looked to his father.

The Pharaoh raised his eyebrows, expecting to hear more. Amen obliged. "Today's New Year's processional is particularly special because while the processional is still in the Temple courtyard, it will pause to act as oracle for the Pharaoh. It is then that our father will ask the Oracle for Amun's commission to go to the Levant to make a great victory in the name of Amun."

Thutmose smiled and nodded. As he was speaking, the children saw priestesses with their sistrums, led by Satamun, and priests with their incense burners, led by Hapu, gathering on each side of the temple doors. Then, amidst sacred songs, six strong-armed, bareheaded wab priests emerged ceremoniously with the poles that support the barque resting on their shoulders.

It was a long, lean boat of shining gold. Ram's heads figures dominated the fore and aft with their short-haired faces and long fur that flowed from behind their ears down their necks. They each had, not one set of horns, but two. One set twisted in a spiral and spread horizontally in a direction perpendicular to the head. The other set framed the head on both sides, pointing backward, then falling in great sweeping curves until the tops pointed forward. Balanced between the ram's perpendicular horns was the round sun with the royal Wadjet cobra coming forth from the forehead. On the deck of the barque between these two grand ram's heads was a four-sided structure containing, veiled within it, the statue of the unseen god.

Each person took his place in the processional as it was carried from its inner sanctuary into the temple courtyard. Music and incense filled the air. The Pharaoh and Queen stood in the processional's way as the barque approached. The Barque of Amun stopped in front of Thutmose.

The Pharaoh nodded his head in honor of the Great God. In a voice loud enough for all priests, priestesses, scribes, noblemen and women in the temple yard to hear, he asked, "Great God Amun, I come to you as your beloved son. I stand here for your holy oracle concerning your favor in overcoming the wretched Amurru threatening your holy land."

Everything was still. Everyone waited. Everyone watched…eyes glued to the Barque of Amun. Hatasu knew this was the way to get the greatest wisdom. This was the Oracle of Amun. The god would give his answer, then they would know. There was still the chance he would say 'no'.

Whatever it was…that dark hole in Ahmose's scrying mirror…that unknown danger reminding her of Sekenenre…would it keep her father from going to war?

The bearers of the Barque looked strained and the platform holding the god Amun started to move is if independent of the will of the pole bearers.

Chapter 11 - The New Year's Day Announcement

Hatasu watched the ornate ceremonial boat containing the god Amun. It moved slowly. The wab priests who carried the front poles, strained visibly under the weight. She could see their arms shake with exertion and the sweat beading on their brows. Clearly the god exerted his will through the priests.

The platform on which the Barque of Amun rested lowered in the front, while the priest in the rear stood steady. The first priest seemed to regain strength and the Barque righted itself. All eyes watched intently. It lowered again…just in the front…and rose again. The signal was clear. It was a nod. The god replied in the affirmative.

A murmur rippled through the courtyard. Scribes stared open-mouthed and then turned to their scrolls, making note of Amun's approval. Priest and priestesses nodded to each other with wise eyes. Students murmured under their breath, nervous excitement in their whispers.

Hatasu smiled. Amun spoke to her father as a god to his beloved son. Eyes turned from the Barque of Amun to the Pharaoh. Solemn faced, Thutmose raised his arms high in the air. "Amun has spoken! I will make war on the Amurru!"

What an exciting moment! The dark shadow in the scrying mirror was forgotten. Hatasu watched as the priests and priestesses moved forward again with the Barque. They loaded it on the river boat that would bring it to the Valley of the Ancestors. This was Hatasu's first New Year's boat processional across the narrow Nile.

She was delighted to be in the midst of this processional, rather than watching it from the palace roof-top.

Boats with banners and musical priestesses led the way, followed by the royal family, and then the boat carrying the Barque of Amun. Hatasu's family traveled in their royal boat; brightly painted and decorated with flags and flowers. Amenmose and Hatasu sat on small thrones in front of and lower than the Pharaoh and Queen. Again Amenmose's new roles as both Hawk-in-the-Nest and Commander-in-Chief needed to be viewed by all and it was legitimized by Hatasu, the sole daughter of the Queen's line. Thethi's seats were in front of and below them.

Amenmose's pleasure in the Oracle shone in the broad grin he gave Hatasu as she assumed the seat next to him. He sat tall in his chair next to her, his eyes shining with anticipation of leading troops into the great victorious war his father was about to announce to the people.

Though Hatasu hoped the Amenmose smile at her meant his friendliness to her would be more than just public show, he immediately turned to a conversation with their father and ignored her. Hatasu's thoughts lingered more on the oracle then on the message. She was astonished. The Oracle was so...large. The previous types of oracles, the twirling dance and the scrying mirror, were small and private in comparison. There was room to doubt in those personal experiences` but the Oracle of Amun...the large Barque, the clear movement of the nod and the witness of so many people...well, there was no doubt. What a wondrous thing!

The royal boat was rowed across the slow moving river amongst boats of every size and description. Everyone, noblemen and farmers, joined in this great New Year's Day pilgrimage to visit and renew the ancestors. In the brightly decorated boats around them, Hatasu could see her friends and cousins. They called back and forth across the water, waving hands, flags and flowers. Hatasu waved back to Meryt and Isis. Hapuseneb whistled from the other side and she called back to him. Grandmother Seniseneb waved from her elegantly decorated boat. Hatasu looked up and down the slender stretch of water, crowded with the many boats.

Voices and tambourines filled the air with familiar melodies specific to this festival. The people of Waset were there for the festival but also to gain the blessing available from proximity to the Barque of their god Amun. The princess was excited to be in the midst of this gay cacophony of sights and sounds. She wondered, though, how many of the people attending this festival guessed that the Pharaoh would announce the plans for war.

Sitre, more excited about the festival than the war, leaned toward Hatasu and pointed to the sand colored mountains in the distance. "Look there, the sacred mountain, el-Qurna. It is the pyramid-shaped peak that shelters and smiles down on the Valley of the Ancestors."

Hatasu's eyes followed where Sitre's finger pointed. The sun-golden triangular peak dominated the western horizon. Between the river and the mountains stretched the valley. First, there were the fertile farm squares of dry cracked earth but then, further back from the river bank, was the rocky desert of the Valley of the Ancestors.

"We begin the New Year with visits to the tombs of our

ancestors, letting them know we have not forgotten them. We share a family meal, telling their stories and inviting dream communication with them. Everyone meets at the ancient Temple of Montuhotep, the ancestor of us all. There, the Barque of Amun spends the night in the inner sanctuary of that temple to commune with the ka of our great ancestor, Montuhotep."

Paheri leaned forward and added, "…where the Pharaoh greets the people and makes announcements for the coming year. That's where he will announce the war in Levant!" Paheri sounded excited.

Sitre continued, "After, is the gathering at individual family tombs. Gifts, food, songs, stories and dances are offered to the kas of the departed and stories are told of their great deeds. We will stay at the Temple of Pharaoh Ahmose, the Queen's father."

"We will sleep in a temple?" Hatasu asked. The temples on the east bank were the ones she was hardly allowed to enter. Now, in one she was to stay the night!

"Yes, indeed." Sitre went on, "This desert land is sacred to the goddess Hathor and the doorway between the worlds of the living and the dead is still partly opened as on Nephthys Day. It is still an easy time, as well as an easy place, to share messages. We sleep in the temples to ease the pathway for our beloved departed to enter our dreams."

Hatasu remembered her nurse-tutor had her own loved one on the other side of that doorway. She seemed eager for the evening's communications.

Thethi spoke with a slight pout. "What about me? If that's

Queen Ahmose's family, it's not mine. Do I sleep in the Intef
family tomb?"

"No, no, dear Thethi," put in Paheri. We will all stay with our
Pharaoh, Thutmose, who chooses to honor his Queen and her
father, the line through which the Double Crown now sits on his
head."

"Won't I even get to see the Intef tombs of *my* ancestors?"

"Before the official meal and story, Thutmose will bring offering
to the tomb-temples of his father Intef VIII and the other Intef
ancestors and I'm sure you can go along."

Thethi settled into his seat with a look of relief on his face.

The river journey was short because the river was low and
narrow and the canal was directly across from the Waset temple
harbor. Their boat entered the canal that led deep into the valley
toward the temple under the mountains. Hatasu's attention was
drawn to the patchwork of crusty brown and cracked land on either
side of the canal. She knew that now, in the drought, the earth was
as dead as their ancestors but she also knew it would spring to life
again with the waters of the inundation.

The servants poled along this ancient water path to their
destination of the harbor lake at the very edge of the sandy desert.
The point at which the fertile fields ended and the desert began was
so defined; it was as though the divine ancestors had themselves
drawn the line. Their living descendants could claim the fields but
the sacred desert plain was forever their own.

Between the grand temple complex of Montuhotep and the el-
Qurna peak, Hatasu could see the towering, buff-colored cliffs

illuminated by the morning sun. The natural landscape gave off a glow. Low on the desert floor, the temple town blushed in the distance. Both dwarfed and protected by the landscape, the temple itself could be seen as a great glory. A causeway stretched from the valley temple, through the gateway of the enclosure wall, and right on through into the sacred precinct of the temple itself.

Over that wall could be seen a glimpse of green trees; a miraculous garden island in the midst of the desert. The temple's terrace rose above the treetops and dazzled with the many colors of relief paintings. The structure was crowned with a pyramid-shaped-structure, a miniature of the great peak of el-Qurna, which rose above it.

They disembarked at the harbor lake and the valley temple where the priestesses of Hathor eagerly waited to greet the royals. These priestesses led the procession from there, dancing and singing along the way; followed by the Pharaoh, Queen, and Prince Amenmose, then the Barque of Amun-Ra, the priests, and nobles, and finally the young royal children, their cousins, aunts, and nurse-tutors and the rest of the towns folk who were not already at the temple.

This last part of the procession was free flowing and Hatasu was allowed to travel with the relatives and children who shifted and regrouped in an easy, casual way. Hatasu took Sitre's hand and asked, "Is the Temple of Montuhotep like the Temple of Amun?"

"Oh, no, my dear, this is a mortuary Temple. It is the sacred burial place that honors a great Pharaoh, Montuhotep, who reigned five hundred years ago. He reunited Upper and Lower Khemet when it was divided by chaos. He reinstalled the wisdom of the ancients."

Thethi wanted to know, "Whose ancestor is Montuhotep? Hatasu's or mine?"

"Both! All of us are descended from Montuhotep. Most of the royalty and nobility of this fourth nome of Waset claim their descent from him, both physically and spiritually."

Just then, Meryt and little Isis skipped up, offering Hatasu their hands to skip along with them. The boys were a short distance ahead practicing marching strides as Thethi told Hapuseneb excitedly about the oracle. Soon they were at the gate of the high, uneven enclosure wall. The procession moved inside and Hatasu got a full view of the building. She thought this was the most impressive temple she could imagine.

As the group moved into the expansive courtyard, she could see past the many people to the two rows of huge statues of Osiris-Montuhotep facing each other on both sides of the central pathway. In front of them was the ascending ramp to the temple proper. In front of the temple, on both sides of the ramp, were the wonderful greens and grays of the grove of trees.

Sitre stepped up, and with a hand on her shoulder, said, "See the giant statues of Montuhotep as Osiris. They are called Osirisids. See how he wears the Double Crown, beard and ankhs, like Osiris?"

Hatasu nodded.

The royal family followed by the Barque of Amun, processed through the courtyard to the temple itself. People danced and made music all along the processional way. The formal part of the procession moved deeper into the courtyard. A broad, high ramp stretched skyward, making the building look, from a distance, like it was reaching to the heavens. As they approached closer it filled their eyes with its monumental beauty.

Just before the ramp began to raise the procession above the earthly level of existence, there were rows and rows of magnificent trees. There were many rows of tamarisk trees; their old, thick, and ambling trunks spread feathery foliage like sheltering arms. Such trees were rare in the desert landscape and Hatasu imagined the fun she could have playing among them with her brother and cousins.

The Barque of Amun and the Pharaoh proceeded up the temple ramp to the second level where there was a columned preamble around the square building. In front of each of the columns there stood another statue of Montuhotep as Osiris. A dark hole of an entranceway was in the center, leading to the inner sanctum and the tomb of the Great Pharaoh of the past, cut deep into the mountain wall. The priest and nobles, along with the royal family, waited on formal seats in front of these columns while the Pharaoh accompanied the Barque of Amun into the inner recesses of the temple.

Hatasu took her place next to Amen again. She'd given up on expecting him to be nice to her, so she just looked out over the crowd in the courtyard. It was hot in the glaring midday sun but she looked down into the cool greenness of the trees, wishing she could be there instead.

Amen did indeed ignore Hatasu and looked instead toward

Vizier Ineni. "How soon do you think the men and supplies can be ready to leave for the Levant?"

"There is much to do, Amenmose. I think it will take at least a month. The men of the adjunct forces, those of the work-tax, need time to travel to Waset. It is customary to give the regular forces a few days with their families before they leave for foreign territories. Supplies must be prepared for transport and arrangements must be made for a supply line into the foreign land. We will feed our troops off the conquered land as much as possible but there must be other arrangement as back up. Weapons must be distributed and accounted for."

"That's much too long." Amen interrupted.

Ineni's eyebrow rose.

"Surely we will leave within the fortnight!" Amen pressed.

High Priest Hapu sat on the other side of Ineni. "I know the war must be fought now but I am worried there are serious problems in the northern city of Itjtawy. We should be wary of the Amenenhet family in that nome. It will take time to set up a plan and make arrangements to assure the wellbeing of the land while you and the Pharaoh are gone."

Amen looked annoyed. "There can't be anything in this land that is as dangerous as the Amurru."

Hapu responded quickly, "The Amurru are dangerous, Amen, but there are other matters to be taken into consideration as well." He turned toward Vizier Ineni. "I'm also worried about Queen Ahmose. She is very close to delivering her child. She looks pale since the Amurru have been here." He turned back to Amen and added, "Your father may wait to disembark for the Levant until after this child is born."

The prince scowled.

Hatasu quickly looked over toward her mother. She did indeed look paler and the stomach bump of her pregnancy looked more pronounced. She wondered about the people from the north who Hapu referred to. This war business was complicated. She wondered, then, what the people in the courtyard might think of this war when her father announced it. She turned her attention and looked out at the crowd of town folk.

There were so many people there to celebrate their ancestors and to hear what their beloved Pharaoh would say to them. There were merchants and sailors, fishermen and farmers, scribes and artists. Many of them were in clusters; like the soldiers gathered in the middle of the courtyard or the noble men and their families closest to the temple to hear the Pharaoh. There was a group of women back by the gateway beating on their frame drums and swaying to the music. They all awaited Thutmose's speech.

At that moment, the Pharaoh re-emerged from the dark inner columns of the temple having left behind, at the sanctuary, the statue of Amun to visit with Montuhotep. Thutmose stepped forward and stood in full view, out of the shadows of the columns. A hush fell over the crowd as they turned to listen to their much-loved leader. He stood tall, the striped nemes headdress coving his head, the image of the royal serpent extending over his forehead. The jewels in his collar sparkled, reflecting the midday sunlight and the white of his linen kilt shone in contrast to brown of his skin.

"I must talk to you, my people, about the greatness of Amun and the many blessings he has given us." He looked down at all the upturned faces. "I must talk to you about the blessings of Hapi, the river god, and this year's promise of a great inundation with the fertile fields and abundant food it will supply. We had great success in last year's harvest and the mighty sandstone wall is completed around the Temple of Amun in Waset."

Hatasu watched the people crowd as close as they could to catch his every word. The people farther back leaned toward the temple, straining their ears to hear what they could.

Thutmose went on, "Our land has come a long way in the fifty-five years since the Hyksos were driven back to Sharuhem. Those Hyksos peoples who live without Ra must never again be allowed to enter the Two Lands to threaten our way of life. For this purpose, the Great Liberator, Pharaoh Ahmose, led the troops of Khemet to the Levant to protect our people and to be assured the descendants of the Hyksos never return."

There were nods of agreement, and murmurs spread through the crowd. "The Hyksos must never return." More people joined in. This agreement got louder and became a chant. "The Hyksos must never return!"

"However," Thutmose's voice resumed. He paused for the chanting to stop before he went on. "Our ministers and diplomats in the cities of the Levant let me know there is new danger." He paused and let the impact of this settle in. "An enemy is rising in power. These people of the Levant are losing their fear and respect for us. During his tribute visit, their ambassador nearly killed the royal Prince Amenmose." He nodded over toward Amen.

The agitation in the crowd almost sounded like a growl.

Thutmose went on, "As your Pharaoh, I must go and bring the armies of the Two Lands to that land in order to subdue these people. Like the great Horus, I must protect the Two Lands and keep it from falling again into chaos. Those of the Levant must never again believe they can find any weakness which would allow them to enter the Two Lands again."

Hatasu could see the heads in the audience nod. Many people, particularly the young men in the courtyard, slapped each other on the back and raised their fists in the air to show their defiance of the enemy.

Thutmose waited for their attention again before he made his final statement. "I have consulted with the Great Oracle of Amun and he has commissioned me to go. As his faithful son, I must fight as the sun god Ra, my father. Like Ra in his night journey through the underworld of the Duat, I, too, must overcome this vile serpent, the Amurru-Apophis. As Horus, I know that Amun would grant me another great victory, as great as the one he granted me in Kush."

A great cheer arose. Women waved colored scarves and danced gaily to their drum music. Hatasu caught sight of young men off to the side engaged in soldierly displays and mock combat. She heard pieces of songs about how the Pharaoh and the soldiers would bring home bounty, enriching them and their land. *Yes!* Hatasu could see that the people knew the wisdom of her father.

Their excitement at the news of war made her all the more eager about the great glory of war, herself. She thought again of how she wished she could go! She could see herself as the fiery Sekhmet battling the ones that rebelled against Maat. But she couldn't do that yet, and the idea of her beloved father being away brought a twinge of distress in her stomach. At the same time, her heart swelled with pride for him. She knew he would do what was necessary to take care of her and the people entrusted to him by the gods.

Once the announcement was made, the official duties were over. Amenmose was quickly surrounded by his older friends and in an excited conversation, imagined their roles in the war.

The younger children were allowed to descend the ramp and were free to play with their cousins. Without so much as a look back at Amen, Hatasu led her cousins toward the grove of tamarisk trees. "Wouldn't it be lovely to make a game inside the grove of trees? We could pretend that we are brave soldiers in the strange land of the Amurrus."

Meryt was reluctant. "Oh Hatasu, I don't know. I think we should play our game someplace else. These are sacred trees."

"Yes, yes, it is forbidden but it would be such a lovely place to ambush an enemy." She was moving in that direction, keenly eyeing the cool shade with its nook and crannies.

Hapuseneb followed close behind Hatasu. "The trees could be like forts, the branches high towers." He looked around to see that no adults were watching before he ducked into the first layer of foliage.

Meryt lagged behind. "What if we get caught?"

"You don't have to come if you don't want to," said Hapuseneb, looking out from the leafy shadows.

Hatasu took her by the hand and pulled her in, saying, "It will be all right."

Thethi took Isis's hand and again checking that no adults were watching, led her into the lovely maze of branches and joined up with the others. Once inside the grove, Hatasu knew it was everything she hoped it would be: Dark and cool, with the scent of tamarisk all around. The feathery leaves tickled as the children ducked past them. The foliage created a roof and the reaching, twisting, low branches of these trees intertwined to create a truly magical space to explore.

Hatasu said, "Now…we are soldiers in the Levant and we're looking for the enemy."

Thethi and Hapuseneb were delighted with the idea. They ran ahead and hid behind the large trunk of one of the trees. When the other three walked by, they jumped out and frightened them. Soon, the children were laughing and chasing each other over, around and through the branches. The manner in which the branches of the trees extended out horizontally made them easy to climb onto and walk along. The boys became more and more daring, egging each other on. Hapuseneb chose a tree and challenged the others to climb higher.

Thethi had stayed in the lower limbs; he was smaller and frailer than his friend. This did not keep him from trying, however. He climbed upward on his chosen tree. Thethi braced against his fear and pushed himself higher up the tree. The branch he was on was narrower and weaker than the others. He climbed still higher, ignoring his increasing fright.

Hatasu felt no caution, just ambition to climb highest. She quickly found a tree equivalent to Hapuseneb's and scampered up its branches until she was at the top.

She called to him, "Thethi! Stop! Be careful!" But no!

Thethi set his jaw and kept climbing. He would be just as strong and brave as his companions, especially his sister. Suddenly…a crackling sound…then a crash…then a howl of pain.

Chapter 12 - The Valley of the Ancestors

Hatasu and Hapuseneb scampered down their trees even faster than they'd climbed them. Little Isis got to him first. Hatasu was close at her heels. Thethi was crying loudly and holding his arm close to his body. The children had barely made their circle around Thethi and ascertained he had not hurt himself too seriously, when adult feet and voices could be heard. They knew they were in deep trouble.

The branches parted and into their leafy world rushed the adults. Three priestesses of the temple surrounded the small group of children and looked down at them on the ground. "What has happened here?" asked the first one.

"Why, it's the Pharaoh's children!" said the second one.

The third one spoke directly to the children, "This is the sacred grove. No one but the priestesses who care for these trees are allowed in here."

The second priestess looked closely at Thethi's arm. "Can you move it?" She gently tested its mobility at the elbow and Thethi's crying increased. "Can you move your fingers?" He could. "Well, it's not broken but it is badly bruised. You are lucky your accident was not more serious. We must find your nurse and have this treated."

"Oh, please, don't tell my father," pleaded Thethi.

"Do you think your father will not notice that your arm is hurt and the tree is broken?" the priestess said as she stood up and brushed the tamarisk needles off her white shift.

Thethi's face showed his misery. The look of fright had lessened on the other children's faces but they knew they, too, would have to answer to their parents and to the Pharaoh.

The head priestess said sternly, "These ancient trees stand for the primeval papyrus swamp of creation. They have stood here with this temple for so long they are old and fragile. A branch like that," indicating the one on the ground near Thethi, "is irreplaceable". She looked back at each of the five children. "Out into the courtyard with all of you and don't come back in here."

The three priestesses escorted the shame-faced children out from the shady grove and into the glaring sunlight. It felt like all eyes were on them. Thethi's cries had softened but he still held his arm protectively to his side.

Meryt whispered to the others, "I told you we shouldn't have gone in there."

Each of the children's tutors seemed to appear from out of nowhere. Sitre's eyebrows came together in a scowl. Her mole was bright red. "What were you thinking?" she demanded, hand on her hips.

"Oh, dear Sitre, it was so lovely and cool in there. We didn't mean to do any harm. Those trees called out to us to play with them. Please don't be cross and *please* don't tell Father."

Sitre's fondness for Hatasu shone through her anger, like sun through a sandstorm. The child knew the ways to warm her heart when she was cross. "I know I can't go to the war with my father in strange lands but at least I can play that I can."

Sitre shook her head but the redness in her mole lessened and she said, "So you were pretending you were soldiers in the Levant?"

Hatasu suspected she was still exasperated.

Her voice was softer though as she said, "Hatasu, this is a place of reverence, not a place of play…especially not a game of foreign war. And besides, you are his older sister. You must watch out for Thethi. He is younger and frailer than you."

"I tried to warn him. Really, I did. You know how he gets. He wouldn't listen. The more you tell him 'don't', the more determined he is to do it."

Sitre let out a resigned sigh and shook her head again. She knew this was true about Thethi.

"Sitre, please say you won't tell father."

"He will know without being told."

The rest of the afternoon was overshadowed by the apprehension of a reprimand from the Pharaoh. Thutmose did, indeed, call his two youngest children to him when he'd finished giving audience to the nomarchs, governors and noblemen with questions about his announcement of war. The children approached him reluctantly as he sat in the royal pavilion waiting for Ineni to complete the final preparations for the procession out of the temple.

Hatasu and Thethi stood before him, looking into his stern, dark eyes. Shaking his head slowly he called Thethi first, and with his penetrating glance he said, "I understand you hurt yourself while you were playing in the sacred grove, Thethi."

Hatasu saw him hug his hurt arm close to himself and blink back the tears forming in his eyes. He blurted out, "Yes,

Father…but…everybody else…"

"You are a prince, Thethi. Remember that! 'Everybody else' is not an adequate reason for doing something. Be mindful of your safety and stay out of sacred places!" He turned away from Thethi and toward Hatasu. In a firm voice, but softer than the one used for Thethi, he said, "You are the older sister. You must look out for your brother and set a good example."

She feared her father knew the 'everyone else' Thethi was following was most likely her. "But…" She started to tell him it was a game of fighting the war with him.

"No buts…no questions…no excuses!" His words were not harsh, yet she, too, fought back tears. To draw her father's criticism was an anathema to her. He dismissed the children by just turning away and redirecting his attention to the processional.

The two children were left looking at each other, both chastened and relieved it was over. Hatasu turned to Thethi. "That could have been worse."

"It would have been better if I'd climbed another tree!"

"True!" She smiled at him. "How's your arm?"

"It will be alright." He stiffened as though bracing against his hurt. Hatasu knew he was mad at himself for having fallen.

The Great Sun God, Ra began his journey downward, slipping behind el-Qurna's peak, cloaking the temple in shadow. People began leaving the courtyard of Montuhotep and moving toward their own smaller family tombs that dotted the desert valley and foothills of the mountains. The courtyards of the ancestors lit up one by one as the head of each family ignited their New Year's fire and each ka priest prepared the offering meal of bread and beer for all to share with their loved ones who'd gone to the stars before them.

The Pharaoh's family was no exception. Thutmose led his family's processional as it went from royal tomb to royal tomb with their offerings of fruit and flowers, bread and beer. They moved to the hillside north. Here was the tomb of Thethi and Amen's mother, Mutnofret. As the offerings were left before his mother's ka door, Thethi held his arm noticeably tighter, his breath whizzed slightly and he let out a few small coughs. Next to Mutnofret's was the empty tomb where Wadj would be buried when his mummification was finished. This tomb was small and simple, showing signs of recent work…for no one expected Wadj would need it so soon.

Hatasu watched Amen withdraw into himself again, showing the kind of grief she had seen during the days right after Wadj's death. Hatasu thought to herself how this visit was supposed to be a comfort but she, too, just felt lonelier for Wadj and wished longingly that he was there with them, alive and well.

She welcomed the distraction of moving on, to the pyramid topped tombs of her mother's royal ancestors. These were each square buildings with garden courtyards. Queen Ahmose left bread and beer offerings at the tomb identified as that of Sekenenre. Hatasu stared at it closely, looking for clues about the 'bad magic'…the thing about which her mother would not speak. There was a picture of a warrior Pharaoh on the outer wall but nothing warning of danger. As marvelous as the war seemed there was still that dark shadow…something to do with the ancestor-pharaoh lying in this tomb.

Sitre noticed Hatasu's thoughtful isolation. "Why are you so quiet, Little Princess?" If there wasn't a clue on the tomb, maybe Sitre, who was so willing to teach her about so many things, would tell her about the mystery concerning this ancestor.

"What is it about Sekenenre that would make Mother anxious about the war?"

Sitre stared at her blankly for a moment, then a sudden light of recognition came into her eyes and she grew pale. "There are things it is bad magic to talk about, Hatasu. They are 'unspeakable'."

"Why, Sitre? Why is it 'unspeakable'?" This confirmed there was something too awful to talk about.

"It just is." Sitre's mole was bright red.

Hatasu knew she would get no further so she approached it differently. Letting out a long sigh the child said, "Sitre, I miss Wadjmose so. His death makes me so sad, though it is not so bad we cannot talk about it. I know something bad happened to Sekenenre and it scares me something bad will happen to my father when he goes to war."

Sitre's face softened. She put her arm around Hatasu with understanding and gave her a hug. "No, my dear, your father will come back with great honor, making our land safer for all of us."

"How do you know that?"

"He is the divine son of Amun-Ra! And he is a mighty Pharaoh with a great army. That's how I know!"

That reassurance gave Hatasu the comfort she needed at that moment. She looked to her father who, strong and handsome, stood by Amen and Ineni. She watched as he threw his head back laughing loudly at some joke. That laughter was music to her ears. *How she would miss it while he was away at war.*

Next, her father led the group to his family tombs, the Intefs. They descended the pathways back to the valley floor and headed into the wadi where his father, Intef VIII's, tomb was cut into the rock wall. It was small and ordinary compared to her mother's family tombs.

Hatasu watched the smile on her grandmother Seniseneb's face as she left the bread and beer offering for her late husband. It seemed a genuine comfort to her. The entire group headed back to the family's main temple-tomb. Hatasu and her family made a lantern-lighted stream of people as they approached the mortuary temple of the ancestor, Pharaoh Ahmose, the Liberator, the Queen's father. This is where they would feast, listen to stories, spend the night and hope for dreams.

Like at Montuhotep's temple, large Osiris statues lined the causeway-approach. They loomed like friendly giants, shadows that guarded and led the family to the temple. Hatasu peered through the gateway to the warm glow of the brazier fires in the courtyard. Lanterns held high, illuminated the pictures on the walls of the Pylon Gate framing the doorway.

There, in bright colors, were larger-than-life depictions of Pharaoh Ahmose smiting the enemies of the Two Lands. On the north side, he strode forward holding a bearded man in Hyksos dress by the hair. Pharaoh Ahmose extended his right arm above his head holding a war club, poised to smite his northern enemy. On the south side he held a black-skinned Kushite by his hair…again, a mighty blow ensuing from the club in his right hand. Hatasu paused, staring at these images.

A voice came up behind her. "That is your grandfather, Pharaoh Ahmose, the Liberator. These outer protective gates show how he protected Khemet and overcame her enemies, north and south." The young princess turned to look into the face of Satamun. Her aunt smiled her toothy grin. "Come, I think you will like the inside even better."

Hatasu followed Satamun through the giant pylons. The princess stopped just inside. The graceful courtyard was a striking contrast to the outside. It was much smaller than the one at Montuhotep's Temple but it had adequate room for the royal family and their serving people.

The child's eyes scanned this temple court. The colors and images here were softer than the warlike pictures on the outside. A rectangular pool of water was in the center of the yard with a sycamore and an acacia tree on each side. The green freshness of these trees relieved any sense of the desert harshness and torches lit the entire area adding to the warm glow. She looked to the left enclosure wall and saw the picture of a woman being blessed by the goddess Hathor, in the form of a cow coming out of the mountain.

Satamun watched the interest showing on her niece's face and said, "That is your great-grandmother, Queen Ahhotep."

Hatasu looked closely. She wore a grand tripartite wig, two parts coming down on each of her shoulders ending in a graceful curl and the third part she knew went down her back. Around her neck, she wore both a traditional collar of carnelian and a pendent with a gold object hanging from it. Her hand extended toward the beautiful Hathor-cow who licked it with affection.

Satamun smiled. "Hathor, the goddess of this valley, honors her as a great queen."

Hatasu looked up at her aunt and smiled, appreciative of her information. She turned to the pictures on the wall on the other side of the courtyard. There she saw a pharaoh in a Double Crown, behind him a queen in the bird headdress of the goddess Mut, and in front of them stood the god Amun with his double plumbed headdress. She stared at the faces of the Pharaoh and Queen in wonder.

Satamun said, pointing, "That is your grandfather, Pharaoh Ahmose, the Liberator, and your grandmother, Nefertari." Reverence deepened her voice. "Amun-Ra, with his tall double plumes, is blessing them."

"That's your mother and father, right?"

"Yes indeed, my child, mine and your mother's."

Hatasu continued to stand by the wall and look into the faces of her ancestors even as Satamun was called away. The child walked up close and squinted at the picture of the woman who was her mother's mother. She looked for features in her face that would say she, Hatasu, belonged. The round face, the dark eyes, the hint of the protruding teeth…these things did indeed look like her mother and her aunt…and, yes…like her. She stared at Nefertari's black hair. There was no trace of red there, though, or in the hair of any of these ancestors. She looked back around the courtyard.

The Pharaoh called everyone's attention to the center of the courtyard as he was about to light the New Year's fire. He stood there, still in his formal attire, but his face more relaxed. As he lit the fire, he recited the prayers. "Blessed Ancestors, Ahmoses-Taos and Thutmoses-Intefs, we invite you to our dinner tonight to share our bounty, and we ask your help and blessing on the war we are about to embark upon." His voice rang out toward the family gathered. "Today is the day we honor our ancestors!"

He looked around at the empty places at the table…each meant for a different loved one who had gone to the stars. "Wadjmose, Mutnofret, Pharaoh Ahmose, Nefertari and Intef VIII, we bring you offerings of food and invite you to visit our dreams." He looked back toward the living. "This is the time we keep them alive in our hearts by speaking their names and telling their stories."

The Pharaoh sat back as the servants heaped the tables high with bread and cold platters of duck meat, figs and dates, onions and radishes. The steward brought the beer around and everyone drank freely. When they'd finished the feast, they all sat in a circle around the fire in the brazier, ready for the telling of the tales of heroic feats.

Chapter 13 - The Tales of the Heroes

"It is time for the telling of the epic story of the heroes of the land," announced Thutmose. He then deferred to the storyteller, directing attention to him.

"These stories are as important as the stories told in the temple during the Epagomenal Days about the gods and goddesses of the East Bank: Osiris, Horus, Set, Isis, and Nephthys. Tonight's stories about Pharaoh Sekenenre, Queen Ahhotep, Pharaoh Kamose, and Pharaoh Ahmose, are about the deified ancestors on the West Bank."

Everyone found seats around the brazier. The flames of the wall-torches added to the flickering shadows that made the pictures of the ancestors dance around them. The darkening forms of the limestone cliffs reached high to the west and north and the bright orange of the moon rose over the eastern mountains, starting its climb up into the night sky.

The Pharaoh and Queen sat side by side in the place of honor, while the other adults sat around in small groups…mostly women with women and men with men. Hatasu sat cross-legged on the ground between her friends Hapuseneb and Meryt. Thethi and Isis were nearby. She'd chosen seats as close as she could to the bard and each of the children leaned forward to catch every word. Hatasu hoped she would find clues to the 'unspeakable' in the story of Sekenenre.

Hatasu's eyes focused on the storyteller. He was a tall man who held himself still taller by his sense of pride in the story he was about to tell. Beneath his black wig there was the evidence of white hair and the wrinkled lines of age mapped his face. One could still clearly distinguish the round face and toothy smile of the Taos; for he was, indeed, the grandson of these heroes and a nephew of Queen Ahmose, making him an older cousin to Hatasu.

He settled himself on a low stool by the fire and its light cast shadows across his face. With a deliberate movement, he reached over the fire and threw myrrh on the brazier flames as an offering. The drift of its smoke encircled each listener, presenting an olfactory gateway to the sacred time and place of the story. That was the signal for everyone to be still.

The storyteller took a sip of his beer and began… "In the dawn of history, Osiris and Isis brought the gifts of culture to the people of the Nile and they instituted sacred kingship. The One Crown of Two Lands united the White Crown of Upper River Valley and the Red Crown of Lower Delta. The divine Pharaoh ruled the land with the wisdom of Lady Maat and thus he freed the people from the fear of chaos. The Pharaohs of old built great temples to keep open communication between these gods above and the people below, thus filling the land with harmony. The House of Life brought the revered teachings to each next generation and as long as a pharaoh wore the One Double Crown and followed the teachings, peace and prosperity flowed through the land, just like our Great River.

"Twice in the history of the Two Lands, however, the pharaohs lost sight of their great mission and they did not practice these teachings. Both times, chaos engulfed the Two Lands. These blind-sighted pharaohs lost the crown; once to regional nomarchs and once to foreign kings. Both of these times, it was the families of Waset who rose up and took on the great mission given them by Horus to reunite the land…to rule again with the enlightenment of Ra and to lead the people back to the wisdom of the ancients.

"First, it was the Intef family and Montuhotep who regained the scattered crowns, protecting the people from the disruption of local quarrels. The second time, it was the Taos family who recaptured the crowns stolen by the Hyksos in the north and the Kushites in the south. Tonight, I honor our Tao ancestors, the Three Warrior Pharaohs: Sekenenre, Kamose, and Ahmose, who won back the Double Crown, and the King's Mother, Ahhotep, who reunited the people in the wisdom of Maat.

"But first, you must hear of the tragedy that befell the land of the Nile. There was a time when the Pharaohs of the Two Lands became lax in their duties to the Lord Ra of heaven. They were forgetful, as if they were sleeping and they were no longer vigilant to protect the sacred regalia of their ancestors. The foreign Hyksos kings entered the land from the northeast and these ignorant men took over the cities of the Pharaoh in the north and dismantled the sacred laws created by the gods and upheld by the ancestors.

"Coming from the Levant, they spread through the land as roving hoards. They destroyed our temples, trampled our crops, killed our villagers and stole the Red Crown of the Delta. The Hyksos' chaos made way for Kush, our enemy to the south, to steal the White Crown of the river valley. And thus, foreigners gained possession of the Two Crowns but they did not know how to use their magic.

"The Two Lands lost the protection of the goddesses of the crowns…Wadjet, the cobra, and Nekhbet, the vulture. Thus, undefended, the Two Lands fell into the hand of Isfet, the goddess of chaos. Everywhere there was misery and despair. Great suffering pressed down on the people in the north, for the Hyksos ruled the delta with tyranny. Great fear swallowed the people in the south as the wretched bowmen of Kush overran the land at the cataracts.

"Before the Hyksos, our wars were limited to cattle raids with the Libyans or punitive strikes on the Kushites. We were a farm people more accustomed to festivals of gods with dancing and music, than to fighting. Our soldiers were the farmers, who provided military service as their work tax during the flood when no grains grew.

"The people of these Foreign Kings however, were a warrior people. They arrived with fierce horses pulling wheeled chariots and they moved swiftly to annihilate anyone or anything in their way. They carried weapons we had never seen the likes of before: bows that shot their arrows twice as far as ours and swords of metal stronger and sharper than our best. They struck terror in the hearts of the strong.

"We had no weapons with which to fight back. Our soldiers had no training to deal with such an enemy and we had no Pharaoh blessed by the gods and strong enough to lead a resistance. The Hyksos set themselves up as rulers over us. Avaris, the delta city close to their homeland of the Levant, was their capital. These nomads, who knew only the construction of tents, took over the Great House of the Pharaoh and robbed the wealth of the land.

"They taxed without repairing the irrigation canals and left unattended the Temple of Ra and the House of Life School. They demanded tribute but restricted ancient worship. This tyranny extended from the delta all the way up the Nile, past Waset. They fostered only worship of their own god, the cruel and angry Ba'al. They had no use for the goddess Hathor and her gentle blessings. They were ignorant of the order of Ra. Instead, these men…the abomination of the gods…honored only Set and the raw power of brute strength. Their footprints trampled every corner of our land. And so it was, for many years."

Here, the storyteller paused. He looked closely at the upturned faces in his young audience. Hatasu's eyes watched his face as the firelight made his features take on the hard, cruel characteristics of the people he told about. Meryt scooted over closer to her, took her hand and squeezed it. She squeezed Meryt's hand back and felt comforted by this contact. Hapuseneb was leaning forward with a fierce look on his face as he pushed the sand on the ground in front of him around with his finger.

The storyteller's voice was a bit louder and prouder as he sat back and resumed the tale. "And then from the nome of Waset, there came a great family." His furrowed brow smoothed out into a smile as he continued. "It started with the Southern Prince, Sekenenre Tao, and his Great Wife, Ahhotep." He paused, letting the names sink into his listeners' minds.

As soon as she heard the name Sekenenre, Hatasu's ears burned with the desire to hear more and her heart beat faster in anticipation. She leaned closer to the storyteller.

He went on, "Sekenenre heard the call of Horus to reunite the Two Crowns. Ahhotep heard the call of Maat to return justice to the people. Together, Sekenenre and Ahhotep did two very important things."

Hatasu listened closely.

"First," the bard went on, "Sekenenre built an army to fight the Hyksos. He called together men from Waset and from neighboring towns. He set up a camp to train them on the west bank of the river behind the papyrus marshes, hidden from the sight of the Hyksos warlords who came to collect tribute-tax. Sekenenre gathered an arsenal of weapons and made bows of composite wood and battle-axes of bronze. Lacking the good boat wood from Byblos, he used the plentiful river reeds and made as many boats as he could. His plan was to fight the Hyksos on the river, where soldiers of the Two Lands were comfortable in light agile boats. They still had no defense against the lethal horse and chariot the Hyksos used on the shore.

"Sekenenre set up a system of spies and messengers to inform him of the enemy's strongholds along the river. The people became hopeful again and men came from many nomes to fight for the Crown in Sekenenre's fledgling army.

"The second important thing done was Ahhotep renewed the spirits of the people by reclaiming the festivals of old. The Hyksos policed their edict of 'no worship of the gods and goddesses' and severely punished the celebration of any of the old festivals. With Ahhotep's plan, the priests brought out the statue of Amun, which had been sequestered away in his inner precinct for many years.

They carried it out into the streets for all the people to be inspired and renewed by its presence. The people celebrated with loud songs and ecstatic dances. They proceeded from Amun's Temple in the northern part of Waset to his Temple in the southern precinct, the sanctuary of the pregnant hippopotamus goddess, Taueret."

The storyteller's voice tensed. "Apophis, the Hyksos king, was a man of great arrogance, ignorance and cruelty. Shortly after the procession to the temple of the hippopotamus goddess, he dispatched a message to Waset. It came as an order. 'Drain the Hippopotamus Marsh! The noise is keeping me awake day and night!'" The bard paused to let the absurdity of Apophis' demand sink in.

Hatasu wondered what Sekenenre would do.

The story resumed. "Sekenenre called together a large council of princes, nomarchs, priests and warriors. Queen Ahhotep sat on the council as did Sekenenre's sons; Kamose, their youngest son, Ahmose and their daughter Nefertari. Sekenenre spoke, 'Apophis tells us to drain the hippopotamus marsh. You would think we had created a man-made marsh just to breed hippopotamuses and annoy Apophis'."

Around the storyteller's circle there were snickers of laughter and shaking of heads from the adults that knew the story. The children sat wide-eyed, listening for what would happen next.

The storyteller continued. "Everyone around Sekenenre laughed at how preposterous that sounded…but it was a nervous laughter because they feared Apophis. Even this far south of Avaris, men and women had felt the cruelty of his retribution and many a family still grieved for a member who had tried to defy him. Sekenenre faced his family and posed the serious question. 'How shall we respond to this demand?'

"Prince Kamose spoke. 'Our festival procession to the home of Taueret, our hippopotamus goddess, has caught his attention. His spies must, indeed, watch us and inform him of whether or not we comply with his edicts.

"Queen Ahhotep added, 'Our spies tell us of the sad state of the Hyksos women who are silenced and enslaved. Could it be they complain after hearing the stories of *our* goddess, and that's what effects Apophis's sleep so many miles from here?'

"The princess Nefertari nodded. 'Our festival of Taueret goes against Apophis's attempt to silence not just the hippopotamuses, but women, as well. He believes all women and their goddess should be silenced. This message makes it clear; He has decided to stretch his long, cruel arm down the Nile once again, to try to clutch us in his grasp.'

"Prince Kamose spoke up again. 'Perhaps the hippopotamus marsh is a coded reference to the army training fields on the West Bank. The river marshes hide our reed boats like hippopotamuses. Also, Set, Lord of the desert and of chaos, takes the form of the hippopotamus. Perhaps Apophis has a spy who has informed him of our plans for resistance and this is his way to warn us to stop the 'noise of our military build-up.'

"This council group grew silent and thoughtful. Princess Nefertari spoke again. 'What if Apophis has not spies but magic that lets him see what we are doing from far away? What if he is *that* powerful?'

"The silence deepened and those around Sekenenre felt fear envelop them. Ahhotep spoke again, breaking the fear in the room. 'Or what if he simply is so old that he is hearing hippopotamuses that aren't there? Perhaps, the demons in his head have finally turned on him?'

"Sekenenre's youngest son, Prince Ahmose, caught the twinkle in his mother's eye and said, 'Mother, are you saying you think he is crazy?' Others smiled at the thought and the spell cast by fear was broken.

"Sekenenre jumped to his feet and said, 'Whichever it is, we must not delay any longer. Perhaps Apophis is referring to the festival, but if he *is* referring to the training camp, we cannot wait for him to crush our rightful actions. We must strike first and use the element of surprise as a weapon. We have an army of three thousand men each equipped with a weapon, trained and ready to fight these northern demons. Now is the time to attack, regain the crown and set our land back on the path of its ancient heritage!'

"Standing nobly at the head of his fleet of small reed boats, Sekenenre and his army sailed north, and Apophis witnessed the greatness of Khemet. But Sekenenre's reed navy was no match for the Hyksos boats made of the cedar wood of Byblos. The leader and his people were forced to fight on land against the horse and chariot. Many of the soldiers deserted the army in terror and despair.

"But Sekenenre passed on to his oldest son, Kamose, his ceremonial battle-axe as well as his fierce determination to regain

203

the Double Crown and the Horus Throne."

Hatasu had listened hard. *What happened to Sekenenre? The tale moved on to Kamose without saying! He must have died, but how? Was that the secret?*

Sitre and the Queen each watched Hatasu from the sides of the courtyard.

Hatasu squirmed in her seat. She was so disappointed. What happened to Sekenenre was 'unspeakable', even for the storyteller.

The story went on. "When Kamose came to the throne as the Southern Prince, almost no army was left. Many had died and many more had run away. They deserted the army, swearing never again to leave their beloved farms and families.

"When Kamose might have given up in despair, his mother, Ahhotep, came forward with a plan. She traveled from village to village, speaking to the families and reminding them of the glories of the Two Lands of old. She urged them to stand up for their gods and their Pharaoh. She called out to the men who had run away frightened from the battlefield and inspired them with her words and her love of the Two Lands. She instilled in them new courage and hope, and the belief they could overcome the chaos of Apophis.

"It was the Great Wife Ahhotep who collected together these deserters and brought them back to her son, Kamose, and to the training fields of the army. Kamose, the Brave, took his place as Prince of Waset and oversaw the renewed training of the troops. He and his mother, Queen Ahhotep, sat in council and planned how to continue the struggle for the Two Crowns.

"They determined that they must acquire better equipment and more soldiers. In order to build wooden boats, she ordered the land's limited number of acacia trees to be cut. Kamose hunted antelope for their horns, built stronger composite bows and trained his archers to be impeccable in their aim and courageous in their assault.

"However, there still was the problem of too few men, no horses and no chariots. They were also in need of metal…tin, which forged with copper, would make their daggers and spearheads as strong as their enemy's. Kamose attempted to send out mining parties to get tin but the Hyksos blocked the river to the north and the Kushites blocked the river to the south. Kamose was unable to get to the tin mines.

"Kamose was determined to capture both crowns, so he set a plan. First, he led his small army south to do battle with the bowmen of the Kush. Driving the Kushites back up river, he reclaimed the Upper River and with it he recaptured the White Crown. With pride he placed the White Crown on his head and declared himself the rightful Pharaoh of the South.

"He took captive many Kushite bowmen and marched them back to his training camp, where he forced them to serve in his army. Now, doubling the size of his military, he had enough men to attack Apophis's forces and now they had access to the mines via the wadi roads from the river. Kamose wanted only to smite the vile Asiatics. Ahhotep wished also to inspire the soldiers to stay the course of battle. She suggested they have a reward to go to soldiers of great valor.

"Kamose designed golden medals of honor, made in the images

of the Nile flies. These winged creatures stuck tenaciously to their targets, just as Kamose wished the soldiers to do with the enemy in battle. All soldiers who did not desert were eligible to win a Fly of Gold. Kamose, the Brave led his renewed army as they sailed downriver in acacia boats.

"At the first outpost of Apophis's in Middle Khemet, the two armies met. Kamose descended upon his enemy. He was fierce, like a breath of fire, and his soldiers were like lions attacking their prey. They won a great victory there. This battle renewed his soldiers' confidence and their commitment to the Double Crown was strengthened.

"Queen Ahhotep accompanied Kamose when he proceeded with his army to the stronghold of the enemy capital, Avaris. The Queen's presence and Kamose's bravery inspired the men to feats most worthy of the Golden Flies of Honor. When they arrived at Avaris, their fleet surrounded the waterways of the fortress and his bowmen patrolled the banks of the river but Apophis stayed within the walls of his fortress and would not fight. The palace women peered from the citadel like young lizards from within their holes.

"Kamose tried to get into the fortress but his soldiers could not breech the thick, high walls. They used a battering ram in an attempt to break down the heavy doors but the doors did not budge. His men built ladders with wheels and rolled them up to the wall to enter the fort over the top but many men died from Hyksos arrows while they climbed. The army plundered the land around the fortress and tried to provoke the enemy into battle but the Hyksos would not come out and fight.

"Kamose tried to starve those who stayed in the fortress by not allowing any supplies to reach them but his own supplies ran low and his men longed to go home to their families for their planting season. Kamose and Ahhotep returned to Waset without having taken Avaris and without the Red Crown of the North but they did have a very great prize. They had taken as plunder the mighty horse and chariot of their Hyksos enemy.

"The people, of the lands Kamose won back, celebrated with a grand festival. The land between the cataracts to the south and the delta in the north was reclaimed from the foreign enemy. He had won back half the kingdom and had gained possession of the White Crown of the Upper River Land, but the Two Lands were still divided, and Chaos still reigned over Maat.

"The deeds of Kamose, the Brave, were great but it was left to Ahmose, the Liberator, to overcome the Hyksos fortress in Avaris, to reclaim the Red Crown and to drive the enemy out of the Two Lands forever." The storyteller paused and called for another cup of beer.

Hatasu noted again, the story had passed from Kamose to Ahmose without saying what happened in between. The storyteller stood and stretched as did the groups of adults sitting in small clusters. The light of the haloed moon floated dreamily across the indigo sky and hung directly overhead. The stars…the souls of the ancestors…dotted the heavens. Over the wall of this temple, one could see the glow of other tomb fires and hear the hum of other families' stories.

The children grew weary, in spite of the excitement of the story.

207

They sought out more comfortable places to recline. Meryt went and lay on her mother's lap. Hatasu snuggled up next to her grandmother, who, smiling, put her arm around her beloved grandchild. Hatasu was tired enough to resign herself to the idea that the way stories were told leaves out how a person died.

The other adults, acting as though there was nothing odd in this, reclined comfortably on mats with the fire between them and the storyteller. The young men of soldiering age jostled with each other, bragging of their intended prowess in battle. The torchlight glowed from the temple walls giving the shadows of the soldiers' wrestling figures giant proportions.

The servants were kept busy refilling cups of beer. The storyteller raised his cup to his lips and drank a big draft of his brew. He put it down with deliberateness and cleared his throat to let the audience know he was ready to resume. "When the ceremonial axe was passed on to Prince Ahmose he was still a young boy; too young to lead the troops of Upper Khemet and too young to drive the Hyksos from their fortress in the delta.

"When he first sat on the throne at Waset he had only one of the Double Crowns. While the tall white headdress was on his young head, it was his mother, Ahhotep, who guided the land as his regent until he outgrew the side lock of youth. It was she who oversaw the administration of the land, working diligently alongside him as she had done with his brother, Kamose, and his father, Sekenenre.

"Instead of rushing back into the battle as Kamose had, Ahmose and Ahhotep took the time to prepare completely before resuming the fight. For ten full years, they planned and prepared and schemed for the dream of regaining the Red Crown and reuniting the Two Lands. They took all the lessons they learned on warfare and prepared an army with an organization that would support the journey to the delta, the battle itself and the food needed by the troops for a long siege of the fortress.

"Thanks to the previous plunder of Avaris, they now had horses and chariots but it would take time to breed these horses into a herd and to train an elite company of soldiers to handle the animals and the chariots. They needed to build a fleet of chariots for themselves. At the same time, they planted a new forest of acacia trees to have a supply of wood with which to renew the navy.

"When the time came, Pharaoh Ahmose and Ahhotep sailed their war ships north, carrying many horses and chariots. The troops adored their Pharaoh, for he was a courageous fighting man as well as a brilliant strategist. Even without the Red Crown, they saw him as their divine Pharaoh.

"Ahhotep again inspired the army with her presence. She fought at their sides and nursed the wounded. The soldiers and their families loved her, for they knew that she herself wept bitter tears when she…like so many mothers of the land…had buried her son, as she had her husband, with a warrior's funeral."

Hatasu heard that Sekenenre was buried in a 'warrior's funeral'. *Another clue?*

"This ancestor, Pharaoh Ahmose, the Liberator, grew to be as clever as Thoth. He sailed past the Hyksos's military outpost at the city of Ankh Tawy and went straight to the ancestral city of the Sun Temple of Ra, Iunu. The people of Iunu met him with jubilation.

They hailed him as a liberator and accompanied him to the temple of Lord Ra, neglected into a sad shadow of its former glory.

"The oracle of Iunu told him that when he won the war, he must bring rich tribute to Ra in the form of Amun of Waset. As long as his family honored Amun-Ra with offerings of war-booty, victory would always be theirs. With the blessing of Ra, Pharaoh Ahmose proceeded with his campaign.

"As he boarded his ship, he was as Ra in his bark, sailing through the hours of night to do mighty battle with the serpent Apophis of the underworld. And like Ra in his nightly journey, Ahmose, too, was victorious. He took his troops past the Hyksos stronghold of Avaris with its thick-walled fortress.

"He was wise, for to win the city, he needed to cut off their supplies from the Levant. For three months the army camped east of Avaris, but when the flood receded and the men in chariots could again move freely on the hard, dry earth in the valley, he attacked a near-by city and overcame it by surprise and by force. By doing so, thus cutting off Avaris from getting supplies from the Levant through that city. He prayed this would shorten the siege and the war.

"The assault on Avaris followed. Ahmose's forces surrounded the city. Again, the Hyksos refused to come out and fight. Once again, brave soldiers of Khemet used the battering ram and the ladder. Once again, they were unable to enter the fortress to claim victory. Once again, they were forced to lay siege. This time, they had the horse and chariot and Apophis had reason to fear them. They surrounded the fortress-town and did not allow anyone to get food or water. They did not let anyone out with a message or call for help.

"Apophis had stored up much grain and water to outlast Ahmose and the army of Khemet. The siege took five years as the Hyksos inside the town tried to outwait Pharaoh Ahmose. Finally, they realized they would die of starvation if they did not get food. They agreed to a treaty in which they would leave the Two Lands, bringing with them only what they could carry…leaving the rest as booty for the soldiers.

"They left Avaris going east into the Levant, to the city of Sharuhem. Ahmose and his army followed them to be assured they did not turn back. Ahmose, the Liberator, accomplished the great victory he had dreamed of. The Hyksos were defeated and he was in possession of the Red Crown as well as the White one. The Two Lands were again united under one divine Pharaoh.

"When the Hyksos reached Sharuhem, Pharaoh Ahmose thought he could return to Waset in peace and place his offerings on the altar of Amun. But once the Hyksos arrived at the city of their brothers, they again gathered weapons and prepared to re-enter Khemet. Ahmose recognized Khemet was not safe until the city of Sharuhem was subdued and defeated, too. He realized Khemet needed a buffer zone between it and these foreign kings.

"For three more years, he led the army in the Levant, again laying siege to that city with battering rams, wheeled ladders and blockades until they, too, were defeated. Apophis signed an agreement never again to enter the Two Lands. It was then that Pharaoh Ahmose instituted the land in the Levant as a suzerain of the Two Lands; a conquered territory that must pay yearly tribute as a sign of respect for the Pharaoh.

"Ahmose returned home, hailed as 'The Liberator'! The victories in the Levant and in Kush reunited the Two Lands and the Great Liberator, Ahmose, wore the Double Crown with the blessing of Amun-Ra.

"However, while Pharaoh Ahmose and the Queen Mother Ahhotep were defending the Two Lands in the Levant, there were malcontents in the midst of the land. There was a prince of the city of Itjtawy, Teti-an, who was a distant descendent of Pharaoh Amenenhat. He had worn the Double Crown before the Hyksos and Kushites stole it. He gathered around him other malcontents and schemed to overthrow Pharaoh Ahmose. He claimed the hard-won crown for himself, saying now the foreigners were gone, the royal line should continue as before…with himself as Pharaoh.

"Ahmose, however, was favored by Amun-Ra and he destroyed that army of treasonous rebels and righteously executed the would-be usurper, Teti-an. Ahhotep oversaw the expulsion of the family of Teti-an from the land, forever.

"Once there was peace, Ahhotep again sent out a call to the fugitives who had left Egypt in fear under the foreigners. She traveled to Canaan, Byblos and Keftiu to tell them they were welcomed home again. They came from all directions, relieved that their home was safe once more and grateful to her for forgiving them their flight.

"Pharaoh Ahmose reigned from then on in peace. He offered great riches to Amun-Ra and restored his temple. Amun smiled on him and on his descendants. Ahmose built great monuments to turn the hearts of the people again toward Lady Maat and the gods of the Two Lands. He left his son, Amenhotep, the Horus Throne and a land protected on its north and south borders by the goddesses of the crown. The ancient wisdom of Maat would again be honored.

"Ahmose had been like Ra, overcoming the vile serpent Apophis in the underworld. As Ra brings light to the land in the dawn of the day, so Ahmose brought light to the hearts of the people of Khemet as he caused the reunification of the Two Lands into one land again."

The storyteller ended with the chant, *"The ancestors are remembered, and the ancestors are great."*

Everyone's voice joined in, *"The ancestors are remembered, and the ancestors are great."*

Hatasu looked at the brazier with sleepy eyes and saw in the flames images of herself as a fiery Sekhmet warrior, worthy of such noble ancestors. High above her the moon started its descent behind the western cliffs of Qurna and the night breezes whispered ancestral messages over the temple walls.

In the light of the embers glow, Hatasu saw where Thethi slept by Paheri, and Meryt and Hapuseneb each sat with their families. She snuggled close into the soft comfort of her grandmother's arms. It felt as though the ancestors were indeed there with them, each with a characteristic energy by which he or she was identified.

Hatasu liked hearing about Ahhotep, who helped the soldiers and who was a warrior herself. But the men…they were the ones who had great victories! Kamose won back Upper Egypt. Ahmose won back Lower Egypt and captured parts of the Levant making it into a suzerain. Hatasu felt such pride that she belonged to these people. This was her family.

Clearly, the Hyksos of the Levant were the vile enemy, just as Apophis was the vile enemy of Ra. *Oh…to do such battle for love of your god, for love of your land!* How she wished it were possible for her go to war with her father. She wished she could do great deeds like her ancestors.

Her mind went back to the Sekenenre part of the story. She could vividly picture the part where he was outraged that Apophis sent his crazy message to silence the hippopotamuses. She could imagine his bravery as he mobilized the soldiers and built a fleet of boats out of river reeds. She could visualize him at the head of his reed fleet sailing north into Hyksos territory.

It started to get fuzzy then. Apophis forced him to leave the river to battle and fight on land. The storyteller didn't say anything more about Sekenenre but moved the story to his son, Kamose. *What happened to Sekenenre? If he died honorably as a warrior, why didn't the bard say that? What could be so terrible, it couldn't be spoken of?*

She thought of the night her mother looked into her scrying mirror, the dark shadow there, her strange reference to Sekenenre and her warning that to speak of it gave power to some bad magic. Frustrated, she looked up at her grandmother. Maybe she would tell her more. "Grandma, what happened to Sekenenre?"

Chapter 14 - Preparations for War

"My dear, you just heard his story. What more do you want to know?"

"What is it about Sekenenre that makes Mother anxious about Father going to war?"

Seniseneb was quiet so long, Hatasu thought perhaps she just wasn't going to answer. Finally, Seniseneb's eyebrows came together and she stroked her upper lip, a gesture she often did when considering something. Finally, she spoke. "War has two faces, Hatasu. One is the excitement of victory and the glory of rich loot. The other face is the anxiety of the women who await the soldier's return. Your father going away to this war really doesn't have anything to do with Sekenenre."

Hatasu did not consider this a real answer. "But, Grandmother…"

With a voice both cheery and determined, Seniseneb interrupted her. "Do you know why the ancestors are buried here on the West Bank?" There was no space for Hatasu's questions as her grandmother continued, "This is the sacred place of the goddess Hathor, the cow goddess with the beautiful face. You can see her on the wall of this temple…there, with Ahhotep." She pointed. "We honor her with music and dance. She is also the goddess who welcomes the dead here in the Western Mountains. I'll bet you can feel her presence." She squeezed her granddaughter closer to her side again.

Hatasu suppressed her annoyance at this evasion. She allowed herself to be distracted because the idea of feeling the presence of the goddess intrigued her. She closed her eyes, the better to sense the unseen. Yes, by focusing on it, she did indeed sense a presence of the goddess, as loving and warm as her grandmother herself. It came from the mountains, not from the courtyard around them as the ancestors' energies did. She felt loved, cared for and nurtured. The energies wrapped around her like a warm cloak on a chilly night. She allowed her anxieties about Sekenenre to be comforted by Hathor.

Everyone now found their places to sleep. This was the time each wished for a dream of an ancestor, a gift to bring back to waking consciousness…a message, a warning, a meaning. Hatasu looked up at the myriad of stars in the heavens. She drifted off quickly, still feeling the warmth of Hathor and imagining Wadjmose felt that warmth, too.

In the morning, Ra rose renewed in the eastern sky, shining rosy light onto the towering mountains high behind them. The royal steward ceremoniously put out the torch fires; dousing them in the traditional way, in the milk of a cow.

The family took their morning bread and beer as they told of their dream experiences of the ancestors. Amenmose had a dream of Wadjmose, in which he felt truly comforted. The Pharaoh reported a dream of Ahmose, the Liberator, with a message of the urgency to bring troops to the Levant and the promising glory. Queen Ahmose dreamed her mother, Nefertari, would protect and guide her spirit at the upcoming birth of her next child. Seniseneb dreamed of her husband, Intef, and felt it would not be too long now, before she would join him in the stars.

Unlike the others, Hatasu didn't dream of anyone in her family.
During her sleep it was Hathor who came to her. As a rosy cow, she
emerged from the mountainside, licked her hand affectionately, and
told the child she wanted her to build a temple to her. She said, 'I,
goddess of love and beauty, will relieve the angers and hurts of the
past'.

Hatasu was the only one who had not been visited by a relative.
She wondered if none of her ancestors saw her as important enough
to visit. She was particularly disappointed she had not had a dream
of Wadj. Surely, such a dream of the goddess couldn't be real. And
if it was, in saying she'd relieve the angers and hurts of the past,
Hathor was saying to stop worrying about Sekenenre…just like her
mother, Sitre and Seniseneb had each said in their own ways.

She prepared to return to her home with the others. An official
procession returned to Montuhotep's temple to escort Amun back to
his East Bank Temple. The royal entourage traveled down the
canal, out to the river and returned to the temple harbor.

Hatasu could see the palace and temple as they moved toward
her home side of the river. Amun's temple was much smaller than
Montuhotep's grand treed building and simpler than the complex
maze of family tombs. She deliberately turned backward again and
watched as the land of the ancestral tombs became more distant.
The festival days were over and life moved forward with the
recurring cycles of the stars and river.

The star goddess, Sothis, had promised renewal to the parched
land…and the river god, Hapi, delivered. The annual swelling of

the Nile's banks began. What had been the narrow stagnant ribbon of water, began to move…then rush…and finally, turn into a strong forceful current. This first stage of the flood, called the Green Nile, carried all kinds of debris: Leaves, twigs, decaying matter from the mountainous headland of the river. It lasted for a day and its putrid smell spread from the riverbank into the land. People pulled their reed boats up onto the disappearing shore and they kept their children away from the rising banks.

It was at this time the Pharaoh announced, "It is time for Wadjmose to go to his house of eternity. The seventy days have passed for his body to become a sah…a mummy. The Anubis priests delayed the funeral because no boats dare to cross while there was so much debris in the water."

Hatasu bit her lip and Thethi hugged his sore arm. There was still this ritual farewell to their brother. She feared it would be painful for her and Thethi. She also knew she would always have a place to visit him on the Feast of the Ancestors and perhaps another year he *would* come to her in a dream.

When the Nile was no longer green and the funeral barge could safely cross the river, they brought Wadj's sah to his house of eternity. Unlike the processional immediately after his death, this one was private. The Pharaoh did not wish to draw the attention of any would-be tomb robbers to its location. Their destination was the small unmarked tomb the children had seen on the hillside during the Festival of the Ancestors.

Hatasu watched silently as the wooden sarcophagus with her brother's sah was brought from the boat up the hillside on an ox driven sled. She stood to the side with Thethi as servants carried the grave goods to be placed in the chambers for him to have for eternity. She noted his favorite chariot, his fine composite bow and the reed flute he loved to play. The coffin was then placed in the same dark chamber.

Amen stood alone a distance from the group, his hands clasped behind his back and his head hanging down. Thethi fidgeted, occasionally breaking the solemn mood with a dry cough. She tried to listen as the lecture priest said his ritual words and she watched as the Pharaoh moved forward with the iron adze to perform the 'opening of the mouth' ceremony. Her father had told her that this act would empower her brother to breathe, eat and speak in the afterlife. Thutmose then formally summoned Wadjmose's ka to come and partake of the food offerings brought for him.

Finally, there was only one thing left to do…the 'bringing of the foot'. The ka priest dragged a broom-like brush across the tomb floor, erasing the last living footprint. The heavy stone door was closed with dreadful finality.

Hatasu and Thethi both startled at the jarring thud sound it made. Thethi leaned his weight against his sister and she hugged him. Ahmose, Amen and Thethi wept but her father stood still and silent.

Hatasu's heart ached. Her eyes burned with tears but she wished to emulate her father's calm. To hold back her tears, she stared down at the pale rocks at her feet.

Then, as clear as the desert wind, she heard Wadj's voice. "I wish for you to be comforted."

It was at that moment she noticed, at her feet, a stone with a star deeply embossed in its surface. Its five points resembled a person; a head, two arms and two legs. It was a star of heaven contained in a stone of earth. Wadj had reached across the doorway of death and communicated with her; not in a dream state but when she was fully awake. She bent and picked it up. This star-stone, just the right size to hold in her hand, was surely a gift from him. Warmth flowed from it and she felt a sense of peace spread through her body.

That night, dinner was quiet, everyone lost in his or her own thoughts. Just before the servant started to clear the dishes, Thutmose cleared his throat. "This was a sad day, for I put my son, Wadjmose, in his house of eternity."

As Hatasu looked up from her plate, she saw the whites of his eyes reddened but no tear watered his cheeks. He went on, "I wish I could go off in my chariot, into the Eastern Mountains, and indulge myself in sadness, but…"

Amen squirmed, for that was indeed what he'd done that afternoon.

Ahmose reached over and put her hand tenderly over her husband's. He continued, "No, my duty takes precedence over my personal grief." He was silent for long enough that Hatasu thought he was finished but he went on. "Our regular visits during the Festival of the Ancestors is my comfort and the divine assurance of my son's eternal life."

Thethi sniffled.

Then, her father lifted his head higher and his eyes recovered their clarity. The difference that came over him was like walking from the inside of Wadj's tomb out into the glaring light of the

Eastern desert. The Pharaoh nodded and his voice took on the cadence of the military drum, "Now, I must turn my attention to preparations for war."

Amen, who had been pushing his roast pigeon around on his plate, leaned over the table toward his father. "Then, we shall leave soon?" he asked.

Thutmose answered, "The military and travel arrangements must be made. Boats, chariots, and weapons need to be checked, counted and assigned. There will be meetings to arrange for food supplies and transportation during the campaign. It is my goal to leave in a month."

"But Father, surely, we want to strike quickly!"

"You heard the story of Kamose. An unprepared army is an army without a victory."

"But that will give the Amurru time to prepare for our coming."

"They were prepared before they ever sent Bazor here to challenge us. To win a victory, the planning is as important as the fighting. These are things for you to learn."

"Then, what can we do to plan quickly?"

Hatasu saw her father's eyebrows come together in annoyance.

"Amen, one month is when we will leave." Thutmose stood up as though preparing to leave the table, his final word said. He stopped, sighed and looked at Amen. "War is more than shooting arrows, driving chariots and comradeship with other soldiers. Large numbers of men must be gotten long distances safely and in condition to fight. There are ten thousand men who need food and water for six months in a strange land. Soldiers without adequate food to eat and drink, do not fight well."

Putting both fists on the table, he leaned closer to Amen. Keeping his voice even he said, "I wish for you to meet with the seasoned Generals, Pennekheb of the North Corp and Ibana of the South Corp, and hear from them how it was done in Pharaoh Ahmose's and Pharaoh Amenhotep's campaigns in the Levant and my campaign in Nubia. There is much for you to learn from them. *Then,* see if you can figure a shorter way."

Amen's face blushed at the Pharaoh's reprimand. Pushing himself from the table he said, "Okay then, I'll look for them immediately." He left the room with brisk steps.

Hatasu wondered how Amen would manage this assignment. This expectation of planning was so different than his natural bent toward direct action.

The next several weeks as the Nile waters rose and spilled over their banks into the cracked earth of the empty fields, the Pharaoh was busy preparing the army for war. Hatasu still wanted desperately to go to war with her father. At first, she schemed about ways to convince him to take her but his 'no' was very final and she vented her frustration in imaginary play with the children of the royal household. She organized games in which she was Queen Ahhotep, leading the armies of Upper Egypt into war against the Hyksos…driving a chariot and killing the enemy with her throw-stick.

She saw very little of her father in those weeks of preparation. He left early in the morning and headed to the army barracks on the Eastern Desert, sometimes not coming home until late and sometimes staying the night out there with his soldiers. She missed him. It made her think of what it would be like when he was gone to war for moons. She felt lonely just thinking about the palace without him.

She went to her mother. "It's not fair men and boys get to go to war, while women and girls must stay home and just *wait* for them."

Ahmose smiled at her and said, "You're right! We can't go to this war but we don't have to stay home and *just wait*, either."

Hatasu's face lit up with a bright smile. "So we can go to the Levant?"

"No, my dear," she said with a laugh. "That's not what I meant. We can travel within our own Two Lands. Your father has asked that we travel with him as far as the northern capital of Ankh-Tawy and await his return there. It would cut weeks of our waiting."

The idea pleased her. But the next week her mother was taken with a spell of weakness and swelling. The healing priestess said her busyness risked the pregnancy. She recommended the queen not travel until after the baby was born.

Hatasu worried about her mother but also feared they'd forego the trip altogether and she'd be stuck with the waiting role again. But the third week, her mother's swelling went down and she was feeling stronger again. She announced that if they weren't traveling with the Pharaoh, she'd still go but would make it a diplomatic trip, stopping at each of the nomes to visit the governors.

On the fourth week the plans changed still again. Chief Priest Hapu upon hearing of the plan he travel with Ahmose, suggested they arrange their trip to coincide with the Spring Planting Festival at the ancient sacred center of Abedju. He thought it would be auspicious for the Queen to officiate at that ceremony.

The army's scheduled departure drew closer. Hatasu was very anxious about her father's leaving. She had a dream of Sekenenre and she began to worry more about her father's safety while he was gone. There was more and more urgency in her play. Instead of Ahhotep, she started playing that she was Isis…battling, protecting and keeping those around her safe. It was as though she was single-handedly warding off the chaos of Apophis.

The more scared she felt, the bossier she became with her playmates and the more she practiced with the throw-stick. Her sympathetic nurse guessed at what was bothering her and talked to the Queen, suggesting Hatasu might cope better with her father's leaving if she had some time with him before he left.

The Pharaoh was in the final countdown for the army's departure and couldn't possibly spare time away but he agreed for her to spend a day with him out at the soldier's barracks. She was very excited about this…until the Queen told her it was Amen who would bring her to the barracks. She knew there was a secondary 'diplomatic' motive in this arrangement. Her mother hoped for a bond to connect between the would-be Pharaoh and Queen.

Amenmose drove his shiny golden chariot into the palace courtyard the next morning. Hatasu was waiting by the lotus pool. She had to admit he was dazzlingly handsome; well-muscled from his bow practice. He had a new manly confidence about him.

"Hey there, Sekhmet Warrior! Are you ready for a ride with the best charioteer in all of the Two Lands?" He smelled of horses and desert air.

She looked at the shiny black horses as they pawed the ground and snorted, making the chariot jump ahead in little spurts. Wadj had died because of an out of control chariot. It gave her pause for a minute but she wanted Amen to see that she was a fearless warrior. She stepped into the cab of the chariot next to her brother and took hold of the handle bar.

She barely had her footing when he shook the reins hard and yelled out to the horses. They jumped ahead with a start. Hatasu bent her knees and held onto the bar tightly. They trotted out of the palace yard through the town streets and out onto the desert road. Her heart beat fast and her stomach tightened but she was determined Amen would not see her fear.

Over the noise of the horses' hooves clattering on the stone road she heard him say, "Now you shall see *my* world, the world of the soldier." He did indeed think his soldier-life was superior to her palace life.

As they moved along the road to the barracks, Hatasu looked up at Amen. He was grinning broadly, the wind blowing the hair back from his bronze face. He looked down at her and nodded. "Fun isn't it!"

There was indeed an exhilaration and excitement in the wind and speed and even in the danger. She pushed her face forward to feel the wind and felt the movement of the chariot floor. Amen continued at a faster pace than Paheri or her father would ever have gone with her. She found herself delighted with her brother's bold chariot driving.

As they approached the camp, they saw the training fields on both sides of the road. Soldiers waved and called out to Amen. He waved back calling out to each soldier by name. Hundreds of soldiers shot arrows at targets and hundred's more practiced throwing spears. There were still more soldiers in a throw-stick practice area.

As they came closer to the camp itself, Hatasu noticed the barrier around the site; first, a shallow pit and then a high mound of dirt. On top of the mound were shields, all painted different colors, individually marked for each soldier. Amen spoke over the din of the chariot wheels, "The camp here is set up just as it will be when we are in enemy territory. The ditch, the mound and the shields make a traveling fort. Isn't that clever?"

Her brother slowed the horses as they neared the main gate. She could see two soldiers standing stiff and tall by the entrance. They formally saluted the Prince and Princess as he trotted the horses through the gate. He saluted the soldiers back. Inside, Hatasu saw the neat rows of tents. There was an avenue that took them straight to the middle of the enclosure.

There, in the center of camp…as in the center of a village…stood the shrine to Amun; a tent decorated in brightly colored pictures and gold hieroglyphs. Next to the home of the god Amun was the large and colorful tent of the Pharaoh.

Amen brought the horses to a halt, threw the reins to a waiting groom, and jumped from the cab. Hatasu, too, jumped the distance to the ground, challenged by Amen's example. She followed Amen into the Pharaoh's tent. Her father was in a conversation with Huy, his scribe. As she and Amen entered the tent, he turned from Huy and smiled a greeting to them.

"Welcome, Daughter!" he said in a robust voice. "Your mother says you wish to see a military city in action before we disembark for the Levant."

She was so glad to see him; her feet did a little dance as she skipped towards him. His face looked as handsome as ever, dark eyes smiling at her. He moved with grace and power, the blue war crown fitting naturally on his head. He smelled of the tent cloth and desert sweat.

Once she was at his side, his attention was drawn to another matter and she had a chance to let her eyes scan the tent room. This was the royal residence from which Thutmose would run his campaign. She felt comfort being able to picture where he would be while he was away. Though it was a tent, it was the most spacious tent she'd ever seen…and the most elegant. The door flaps were pulled back wide and the blessing of Ra filled the first of the three rooms with light. This entrance room was now filled with soldiers, scribes and servants, waiting to do his bidding.

Thutmose's personal scribe, Huy, lifted the tent flap into the next room and she followed her father through the door. Her eyes adjusted to the lantern lights and she looked around to see thick woven mats, painted papyrus wall hangings of Horus and Amun smiting the enemy, a folding-chair throne and a long table.

Her father said matter-of-factly, "This is where I'll meet with my deputies and generals to plan our victories for Amun. This morning there is a meeting of my advisors on the final details to be settled before we leave."

Hatasu felt the excitement in her stomach to be part of this. Just then, the outer tent flap opened. Ibana, the Deputy of the Southern Corps, strolled in with dignified aplomb. Hatasu last saw him at the Epagomenal Days.

He was the grandfather of Paheri. He was a tall man with broad shoulders and a bearing that seemed both humble and proud at the same time. His face wore the wrinkles of many years of smiling back at Ra. A single long scar on his left cheek accentuated these bronze creases. He moved forward with a slight limp. The old wound in his hip, covered by his kilt, was revealed in his walk. He held his chest high…for upon it for all to see was a necklace strung with seven gold ornaments in the shapes of flies.

Hatasu knew these to be the military honors called the Flies of Gold. Each fly, about the size of a ripe fig, had two flat wings looping downwards, a raised body and large, bulging eyes. After the second it took Ibana to recover from his initial surprise at seeing Hatasu there, he winked at her, then offered his Pharaoh the low bow fitting the living god Horus.

Pennekheb, the deputy of the Northern Corps, also seen last at the Epagomenal Days, entered with long, striding steps. He was shorter than his southern counterpart and more powerfully built, reminding Hatasu of a wild bull. His neck was thick and it, too, was decorated with a string of golden flies. His left shoulder was marked with a whitened welt of scar tissue and he wore a dark leather patch over his left eye. The right eye bulged slightly as though to compensate for the loss of the left. He walked with heavy deliberateness as he moved through the doorway. He did not seem at all surprised to see her there in his Pharaoh's tent and the fierceness of his features softened when he smiled in her direction after his formal bow to his beloved king.

Amenmose, who had been in the outer room conferring with some comrade, entered next. His buoyant stride carried him quickly to the center of the room. He bowed before his father. His smooth face and unconstrained step contrasted with the older, seasoned and scarred deputies. He took his place at the council table.

The magician priest, Usermontu, followed Amenmose. His step was soft, light and deliberate. He wore the leopard-skin cloak of the priest and he would accompany the army into battle. He was tall with broad shoulders, looking as much a fighting man as any of the soldiers but his eyes were keen, black, deep set and intelligent. He looked sharply at Hatasu and then did homage to his leader. She did not know this man but found out later he was from the temple of the el Kab nome.

The men stood around the table and waited until their Pharaoh's nod told them to sit. He motioned to Huy to bring a chair for Hatasu and she sat at his left side. Amen was on his right. She was thrilled at this honor her father gave her. When all was settled, Thutmose looked around the room and made eye contact with each of the officers gathered. Each nodded to him, indicating their readiness to give reports.

Amenmose went first. His voice was slightly too loud, betraying some anxiety in his new role. "The provision arrangements were completed yesterday." He looked over toward his father who nodded at him.

Hatasu remembered Amen had thought they should have been able to be ready to go to war in two weeks. It had taken over a month.

Amen continued, "There are ten thousand soldiers traveling to the Levant. Each is allotted a ration of three pounds of grain a day. That makes it necessary to have thirty thousand pounds…fifteen tons…of grain available a day. General Ibana estimated it will take thirty days to get the army to the fertile valleys of the Levant where we will be able to feed the soldiers from the harvests of our enemy's land.

Of the four hundred and fifty tons needed for the month of travel, half of it has been pre-shipped to the frontier fort at Sharuhem ahead of us and the other half we are transporting with us. Arrangements have been made to transport another five hundred tons of emmer wheat by sea to our ally city of Byblos one month from now, for supplies we will need for back up while in enemy territory."

Hatasu's mind lost focus with all these numbers. She looked at Amen's face. He was very focused on the importance of these details. He seemed transformed…not the boy he was at the family meal when, unaware of any of this, he thought the army should leave immediately. She was impressed with his organization and command of his facts.

He went on. "We will be marching through Lower Retennu, the southern part of the Levant, during their harvest season and will be able to avail ourselves of their crops." Amen looked to his father and smiled as he said, "This is a good time to be leaving and not earlier. Our own river is broad and deep without the rushing waters of the flood time, and General Pennekheb tells me the water in enemy territory is most available a month from now, when we will be arriving, providing water for our men and animals."

Thutmose settled himself in his armchair and looked at his son with pleasure. "You have done a fine job on the collection and organization of these supplies. Good Work."

This was a rare compliment. Amen beamed at his father. The generals then gave report on the readiness of their men; Ibana on the Southern Corps, Pennekheb on the Northern Corps. All was in readiness. Thutmose looked to Usermontu. "Have all the appropriate offerings to Amun been made?"

Usermontu answered, "Yes, all is in readiness."

"Have the magical figures been prepared?"

The priest looked toward Hatasu then back at his Pharaoh as though in doubt about speaking of such things in front of her. Seeing no indication that he should not speak, he motioned to his servant who brought forth a basket and opened it. Inside were many small figurines made out of what looked like, to Hatasu, wax. "Yes, Lord, these are prepared and spells have already been cast."

Hatasu wondered about these wax figures but kept her silence.

Amenmose gave the final report, summarizing all that had been reported to him. "All the companies are accounted for and ready to leave. The transport ships have all arrived in Waset Harbor. The last two that needed repairs are now in good condition and the report has come in that the other fleet of boats is in readiness in Ankh-Tawy."

Thutmose asked his scribe, Huy, to bring out the map scroll then motioned to his officers, Ibana, Pennekheb, Usermontu and Amenmose, to gather closer around him at his table. Hatasu stood next to her father. Leaning over the table, he unrolled the scroll. With his large hands, he smoothed out its edges until it lay flat on the surface and he stared at the images thoughtfully for a moment.

Then, turning in the daughter's direction he said, "Here, Hatasu, I want you to see this image of the Two Lands."

She stared at odd images on the papyrus.

"You see here," he said, pointing to a line that moved upward on the page and flared out into the shape of a lotus. "This is the Nile River. It leads to the sea called the Great Green." He moved his finger along the line, past the lotus shape and rested it in what he was calling the Great Green.

The idea of the mighty Nile River being a painted line on a piece of papyrus was amazing to Hatasu.

Thutmose went on. "The Nile is the first path we will travel. We will ride the Great Nile beyond the city of Ankh-Tawy." Then, pointing to a dot just before the line branched out into the flower, he moved his finger along the right edge of the lotus adding, "After that, we will proceed down this eastern branch of the river into the delta."

He stopped and looked at Hatasu to see if she was following him. She nodded, so he continued. Amenmose, Ibana, Pennekheb and Usermontu also nodded as they looked on, as well.

"We will then take the boat out through the delta branch called the Wadi Tumilat and into the green Goshen Valley." His finger moved across the page to the right. "Here, there are old frontier fortresses known as the 'The Wall of the Ruler'. These fortresses stand at the edge of the Sinai Desert, along the ancient travel route between Khemet and the Levant. Military units are stationed there now, policing this land-bridge so as to keep enemies from entering our land."

He continued, "Here we will disembark." He tapped his finger several times to emphasize this point. "We will leave behind our ships to travel by foot and chariot the rest of the way."

He was thoughtful for a moment as though coming to an important transition in his campaign. His finger then moved up the map as he continued, "We will follow this road known as 'The Ways of Horus'. It passes through the barren desert northeast of the delta. We will camp at this outpost," he tapped lightly, "at the conquered Hyksos city of Sharuhem and confer with the commander in charge of the border patrol there."

He rubbed his finger back and forth on a brown-colored area to the right of the Great Green. "From there, we will move into the nearest part of the Levant…the hills and the high plateau called Upper Retennu, or the Land of Canaan. Hopefully, we will not encounter resistance there, for the rulers have sworn loyalty to us. Our real object here is the flat valley of Lower Retennu, called Syria." He pointed now to the brown patch, a bit higher on the scroll. "This is the land of the Amurru who have challenged us and from whom we must demand respect in order to protect our land."

Thutmose paused and turned to his Southern Deputy. "Ibana, you have traveled to the city of Sharuhem and know this terrain. You will advise me about this part of our journey."

Ibana bowed low and said, "It is my honor to serve my beloved Pharaoh."

Then, he turned to Pennekheb and said, "And you served as a royal messenger in the campaign of Pharaoh Amenhotep and have familiarity with the northern states, so you will advise me on matters of terrain and customs in the distant land of the Amurru."

Pennekheb's thick form bowed likewise and he said, "Beloved Pharaoh of the Two Lands, my wish is to be at your service."

Thutmose nodded acknowledgement and proceeded to address his military advisors as a whole. "Maybe our mission will be accomplished in Hazor but maybe, if as Bazor says, there is an expanding, warring people north of them, we may need to continue into the territory of the Mitanni, called Naharin. We will gather information about that land and its people as we travel. Amenmose, as Commander-in-Chief, I put you in charge of the scouts that will go ahead of us to spy out what we will need to know to overcome them."

The Pharaoh now looked up from the map and addressed everyone gathered in his tent. "My suzerains must again see my military might and I will reestablish my position in the area of the Amurru, who dare attempt to challenge my control. I will lay siege to any city that resists, I will engage the forces of the Amurru and, if necessary, the Mitanni. Once this is accomplished and I have ensured the safety of Khemet, I will bring my army home, traveling back the same route."

He looked into the face of each top advisor. He said with triumphant finality, "I will be ready to leave the day after tomorrow."

Each of the men nodded, they were ready to follow whatever orders he gave. The group of men felt the excitement but for Hatasu it was mixed with her melancholy over her father leaving. Thutmose dismissed his men.

He was alone with Hatasu and he was again her father. He spoke in a warm, calm voice, "You are the daughter of Thutmose and you, too, have duties to this land. While I am gone you are to travel with your mother and make strong friendships with the governor's children, for they shall be the backbone of your reign when you are Queen."

She felt a warm glow that he would talk to her like he just had to his generals.

"Now, it is time I returned you to the palace."

She was very pleased she would ride with her father and not Amen again. As they headed toward home in the chariot Hatasu stood tall and balanced. As they were about half-way along the desert road, her father slowed the chariot. "Come, Hatasu, stand up here with me and hold the reins," he said abruptly.

By Sekhmet, he's letting me drive the chariot! Hatasu thought. She felt the thick leather reins in her hands with her father's large, warm hands covering and guiding hers. She leaned up against the front bar of the chariot and looked between the two grand brown horses with their tails flying in the air. Her father guided her hands with a flick of the wrist to communicate to the horses to speed up…and they did. Dust flew out behind them, and Hatasu's knees bent to help her body absorb the bumps of the rough road. She felt safe with her father's body behind her as the hot, desert wind blew in her face. This was a moment she would hold in her memory as a treasure…always.

When they finally stopped at the palace, Hatasu turned to her father and asked if Paheri could teach her how to drive a chariot. Her father thought a few moments then said, "No." After a pause, he continued, "I will teach you myself, when I return."

Chapter 15 - Gold of Honor

The next night there was a banquet for the high ranking generals and their families. When the meal was finished, the young officers gathered around the table of Ibana, the Southern Deputy. Paheri, his grandson, urged him to tell the stories of the wars in which he had served. Thethi's tutor knew his grandfather's stories well and all Ibana needed was to be asked.

Hatasu looked at Ibana and thought to herself how stiff he looked here at the palace, compared to the day before in war tent. She saw a fire begin to glow in his eyes as he began to conjure up the stories of his own youth. He fingered his string of golden Flies of Honor and the gleam of the lamplight reflected of the shining metal.

She turned from Ibana to the young men encircling the table. They were the lucky ones, she thought. They were going to leave, travel to distant land, and fight heroic battles. She knew them as the sons of royalty, the youths of the royal school, and the offspring of governors. These young men would get to be the charioteers, the elite troops, and the platoon leaders that would fight with her father. These were the leaders of the next generation...her generation. There was the sparkle of dreamed-of-glory in their eyes.

Amenmose, too, gravitated to Ibana's family table...not so much for the stories, but because he caught sight of Asat, Ibana's granddaughter. She smiled at him through long eyelashes. With one eye on Asat, Amen leaned toward the old man, and said, "Tell us of your Golden Flies of Honor, Uncle. Inspire us with tales of your bravery."

He turned and winked at Asat. "Yes, I was very brave," Ibana started, with a warrior's modesty. "I fought well and came home with honors from my Pharaohs." Looking around beyond Amen and Asat to the many young faces of charioteers and warriors congregating about his table he said, "All of you, too, must be fearless fighters for your Pharaoh, so that you, too, come home with honors. And if you are very good, you may also win Flies of Gold." He held two of the glowing ornaments on his necklace up so that they caught the lamplight.

More young soldiers gathered around Ibana. "What was it like in the Levant?" a governor's son called out.

"Well, it is a strange place…far different from our land." He shook his head slightly, a faraway look in his eyes. "It is a place that is dry but not a desert. Its water comes from the sky, instead of a river. It is these rains that water their grains, but in a fickle way…more unpredictable than our Nile.

There are periods when the rain clouds in the sky are so heavy, the view of the stars…and sometimes even the great Ra…are hidden from sight. At those times, all things look dark and gray. Sometimes, rainwater comes in terrible storms and fire flashes in the sky. The sky-fire they call 'lightening' is the mark of their god, Ba'al. He is as frightening as his storms. They say the lightning storm means Ba'al is angry.

The kings of the Levant lead their people the same way Ba'al rules their gods. Their kings act with anger and the people obey with fear. For these people, the lightening is more real than the sun and they behave as though they do not know Ra." He stared at the wood of the table as though on it he could see the faraway place.

He went on, while shaking his head, "At other times in that land there is no rain at all and their crops wither in the fields. Their people go hungry and they fight each other for food. It is no wonder they covet our land and harvests." Ibana looked around the table. He enjoyed telling his stories to the young soldiers.

"Their warriors aim to be as fierce as Ba'al," he continued. "They are as strong and brave as any soldiers I have ever fought but what makes them different is that they are full of trickery. They do not know the honor of truth or straightforward combat. They are a very difficult enemy." Then, Ibana said with intensity, "But we are stronger. We are clever without resorting to deceit. Our young men are brave and our equipment is the best. Amun loves us and will give us another great victory."

The folks listening to Ibana, nodded. "Amun will give us a great victory!"

One of the young men asked Ibana to tell how he got all his Flies of Honor. Paheri urged him on, "Tell them, Grandfather."

The old man looked down on his chest and picked up the central ornament…the one that fell in the middle, right over his heart. He held this central one up toward his young friend. He flashed a smile toward his grandson, Paheri. "This was my first Fly of Honor. I did this for my Pharaoh, Ahmose, the living Horus. I did not come by it easily." Ibana shook his head, remembering. "No…it took training, and nerve, and time. One must be brave and stick to the enemy, just like a pesky fly: Stay on him in the face of all fear. Oh, you young soldiers, do not be disappointed if your first encounter with the enemy does not bring you such a reward. Keep fighting and stay true to your Pharaoh and you, too, may win this honor."

Ibana continued, "I see in your bright faces, the mirrored of my own youthful expectations. It takes me back many years, to the time before I'd won my first Fly of Honor."

"How *did* you get your first Fly of Honor?" repeated another young nobleman of Waset pointing at the central pendant.

The old warrior held it in his hand and looked at it closely then raised his eyes to those around him. "I was a young boy when the vile Hyksos ruled the north of the Two Lands and the Nubians ruled the south. My father was a soldier under Sekenenre, who was murdered by the Hyksos."

Hatasu started. There he was again. *Was this a clue to the 'unspeakable'? The Hyksos had murdered Sekenenre! How could that be? He was Pharaoh and god. He could not be murdered. Pharaohs died in time, but not murdered, powerless at the hand of another!*

Ibana went on. "I saw the vileness of the Hyksos with my own eyes. My father taught me it was noble to fight such an enemy. So when I became 16 years old and the Hyksos were still in the delta city of Avaris, I was eager to join the troops of my Pharaoh and offer my youthful might to his aid. At first I worked hard in lowly positions. I was assigned a place in a crowded ship and endured the hardships of the foot soldier. I traveled with the Pharaoh Ahmose's army all the way north, past Ankh-Tawy, the old capital of the Two Lands, even past Avaris, the stronghold of the Hyksos.

On the road I fought off an enemy soldier that ambushed our troop and because of my bravery, the Pharaoh assigned me to a larger ship. But my bravery did not earn me a Fly of Honor…yet. Lots of real flies but no honor," he said, laughing at his own joke.

The boys gathered around him laughed, too.

"Finally, we had a real battle. We attacked the fortress of the Hyksos's sister-city Tjaru. We set up ladders and I scaled their walls. The enemy tried to push down our ladders but I was quick and strong, and I entered their fort from over their walls just as my fellow soldiers succeeded in knocking down the palace gate with the battering ram. My Pharaoh saw me fight hard and well, doing hand to hand combat with the Hyksos soldiers, never shirking from the fight. I sustained a stab wound in my stomach in that battle but I kept on fighting." Ibana pointed to the old scar across the left side of his abdomen. "We had a great victory there. Our soldiers occupied the city of Tjaru and made sure that none of the Hyksos's allies in the Levant could break though our defense and send troops or food to relieve the siege Pharaoh Ahmose was planning to do at Avaris.

"I was given praise but no golden Fly of Honor. But when I recovered from my wound, my Pharaoh promoted me to a better ship carrying his elite troops. There, I had better rations but still no Fly of Honor. I was beginning to think I would never be able to do what was necessary to please my Pharaoh enough for this prize." Ibana again held up his most treasured metal on his string of honors.

"At Avaris it was not as I expected. Our ladders were not high enough for their walls and our battering rams were not strong enough for their doors. Pharaoh Ahmose had us set up our camp at the gates and guard it so no one could enter or leave. Ahmose knew those inside would eventually run out of food and water. He made sure they could see that we helped ourselves to the fruits of their fields and had plenty to eat.

"With no supplies and no way to get a message out for help, they were stranded. We laid siege in this way for many moons. We waited outside the walls and they waited inside the walls."

Just then, Ibana's old comrade walked behind him. Pennekheb's one un-patched eye shone with his own memories of these stories. He slapped Ibana hard on the back and said, "You old buzzard are you stirring up these polliwogs? Are you telling them the first Fly of Honor story? Have you told them yet about Pjedky?"

"No, you old crow!" said Ibana. "I must have been waiting for you to come by, for how could I tell that story without you? Yes, it was at Pjedky that I earned my first fly and it was all because of this ugly, one-eyed scoundrel." He flashed Pennekheb a grin as he continued. "A battalion of Levantines from the Hyksos's fortress of Sharuhem in Upper Retennu eventually made it through our lines at Tjaru and tried to approach the fortress city with reinforcements.

"It was our job to keep them from getting to Avaris and to head them off at Pjedky, a canal to the east of the fortress city. The enemy had many men but we outnumbered them. Hand to hand with battle-axes we struggled, the men of the Two Lands, against the men of the Levant."

Pennekheb looked around at the eager, young faces and added

242

his version of what happened. "The fighting was intense," he said. "They came at us with their battle maces flying." He waved his hand in a circle over his head as though he was waving a real battle-axe. "It was my first hand-to-hand battle. Two men came at me. I knocked one of them out with my first blow," bringing his imaginary battle mace down behind Ibana, as though he'd just killed that enemy of old. "But the second caught me right in the face with his mace." He pointed to the patch over his eye. "I was stunned and in the moment it took me to react he hit me again on the head."

Ibana rejoined the telling. "I came upon this scene, watching this Levantine savagely beating my comrade." He stood up and gave Pennekheb a sound slap on the back. The northern deputy regarded him with soldierly affection. Ibana went on, "Something came over me. I ran forward in defense of my friend. I had no thought for myself but jumped on this enemy from behind and hung on as he flailed about trying to dislodge me. He swung around until he shook me off and I landed on the ground.

"To my dismay, I realized I had lost my battle-axe in the process. I had but a few seconds before this giant man with a hairy face and bulging eyes was upon me again. I had just those few seconds to draw my khopesh. This sickle-shaped knife of mine served me well." He patted the knife tucked into his belt.

"Yes, surely it did," joined in Pennekheb, "for you saved my life that day. If you had not come to my aid I surely would have perished by the mace of that foreigner."

Ibana said, laughing, "And so you lived to plague me with your interruptions of my story." He gave Pennekheb another hardy slap on the back. "As I was saying, I drew my khopesh and thrust it into the enemy's belly. He let out a howl that was lost in the shouts and yells of the battle all around us. When he collapsed to the ground, he was dead. My friend here," Ibana said, nodding his head towards Pennekheb, "was lying as if he, too, was dead…but I saw he was still breathing."

"This old baboon then carried me through the battle back to the medicine tent." Pennekheb draped his arm around Ibana's shoulder, shaking his head.

"But not until I cut off the hand of the ugly Hyksos, so I had proof of my bravery for my Pharaoh." He finished with a tone of triumph. "*That* was when the Great Ahmose finally rewarded me with my first gold Fly of Honor."

The young men around Ibana were all abuzz. Their spirits were high already, but now doubly inspired by this story of bravery they jostled and wrestled each other, joking about how they would do great deeds to win the Fly of Honor for themselves.

Hatasu had shared their enthusiasm right up until this point in the story. At the description of the severed hand for the Pharaoh, she felt a wave of shock come over her and heard herself say, "You cut off a dead man's hand?" She thought maybe she'd heard it wrong.

Amen looked at her strangely with eyes that said he thought she wasn't brave enough to be a warrior. She hurriedly covered up her feeling.

Ibana, however, just nodded and said, "Yes, Hatasu, we bring hands for the commander to count, so he can know how many of the enemies we killed. That kind of bravery pleases the Pharaoh and leads to the reward of gold."

She nodded with a weak smile.

Ibana turned back to the receptive faces of the young soldiers and he held up the Fly of Honor to the right of the center one. "Soon after, I killed another enemy and was rewarded with this second fly. I now thought it would be a worthy challenge to take a live enemy. That capture took place in the farm field to the south of Avaris when Apophis, the Hyksos king, tried to send out a scouting party to bring back food. My Pharaoh sent me as head of a small band of archers to stop them.

Capturing an enemy was harder than killing him. I had to chase him into crocodile-infested waters and carry him back to our camp. That, too, won me this gold of honor," he said holding up the next fly on the string, "as well as the man I captured.

"Eventually, the Hyksos troops surrendered to our Pharaoh. I was rewarded with booty. His Majesty also gave me those I'd captured, as slaves."

Pennekheb looked from the faces of the young men to the face of his old friend and said, "It took us five seasons of the inundation to accomplish the expulsion of the Hyksos. At our final victory, we rejoiced to be home again with our families whom we had made safe by our brave fight."

Ibana said, "But…there are more Flies on my necklace and more battles to tell of. Apophis had established a base in the Levantine city of Sharuhem from which he tried to reinvade the Two Lands.

The Great Liberator led us to Sharuhem and it was my first time out of this land of the gods and onto foreign soil. It took three years for us to take the city of Sharuhem in order to assure the Hyksos would not reenter our land. This battle had been hard for me because I was very homesick for my land on the Nile.

"Again, I fought bravely and carried away booty and captives. I was given another Fly of Gold for my valor. I am proud I could endure these hardships for my Pharaoh." He held up the fourth fly on the string around his neck.

Hatasu smiled and said mostly to herself, "Someday I, too, will win a Fly of Honor!"

Amenmose looked at her quizzically and spoke with a laugh, "Hatasu, women don't fight in wars!"

The chariot ride the day before not withstanding, she really disliked this brother.

Ibana corrected him. "But Amenmose, the great Queen Ahhotep proudly wore three Flies of Honor for her bravery and leadership during the wars of both of her sons, Kamose and Ahmose. I saw her in action more than once and knew she deserved those Flies of Honor. I saw her lead a platoon of bowmen to ambush a Hyksos scouting party. I was there when she led a chariot charge that opened the corridor allowing Kamose to escape capture. And she lent us all courage as she fought side by side with us against the malcontents of Teti-An."

Amenmose tried to save face, saying, "But those were desperate times."

Ibana's eyes misted over in fondness for his heroic queen. He said, remembering those days, "That is true."

Ibana turned back to the group, "In some ways the next battle, the one with Teti-An, was the hardest…for no one wanted to kill our own countrymen. That ungrateful malcontent used the time Pharaoh Ahmose was away at Sharuhem to cause revolt. He actually thought *he* should be Pharaoh. Ahmose overcame his renegade band and executed him."

The old deputy went on about his last three Flies earned in battles with Pharaoh Amenhotep and Thutmose in Nubia. He ended his story with the promise of even greater gains in this coming war. Then, turning toward the other women who had gathered at the outskirts of the group, he said, "We shall tell you great tales when we return. Tales of how we marched into the land of the Amurru making them respect us and know that ours is the land loved by the gods. Amun will give us a great victory and we will bring home to his temple great booty of gold to honor him. And…there is room on my chain for at least one more fly for valor."

The festivities went on long into the night. The young men talked in small groups and slapped each other on the back and called each other obscene names, all in a comradely way. As the evening wore on, many of them gravitated to young women and seemed to engage in intense conversations in corners and in the garden.

Before Hatasu and Thethi finally went off to bed they noticed Amen, hand in hand with Asat, heading towards the garden.

Hatasu's head was full of the glories of war. As she drifted off to sleep her thoughts about war became vivid fantasies in which she could see herself being as great a warrior as her great-grandmother Ahhotep. She couldn't go on this campaign but there would be others.

In the morning, at their last meal together, Thutmose looked to his two youngest children. "Hatasu and Thethi, you know there are gifts at the end of wars but I have gifts for the two of you now, as well."

He motioned Kaf, his servant, who left and re-entered the room carrying in a squirming little puppy. "This, Thethi, is for you," his father said with a smile. "His name is Behka, after a famous hunting dog of one of our Intef ancestors." The boy giggled with delight as the dog licked his face. Within a moment, they were leaping and playing together.

While Thutmose was still smiling at his son's pleasure, Hatasu asked, "Are the enemy's hands really part of the after-war gifts?"

He looked surprised. "No," he said. "The hands are just for counting." Then laughing, he said, "You heard of this in Ibana's story last night. Right?" He pulled her to him affectionately. "Let me tell you about the reason I collect hands." In a tone he'd use to explain something to Vizier Ineni, he said, "Soldiers' uneasiness in killing has been a problem as far back as Pharaoh Sekenenre.

"In our forefathers' days battles were fought to prove strength, not to kill. But the Hyksos fought to kill. Our people needed to match their style of warfare if they were to overcome them. It was Pharaoh Ahmose who found the two ways we use to teach our soldiers to do what is necessary to overcome the vile Asiatics. The pile of hands let them see their success in battle and golden Flies of

Honor motivate them to strive for it. It was the Hyksos who taught us to count our victory in hands."

Her revulsion was calmed, but not eliminated, by his explanation.

Thutmose turned away from this discussion and caught Kaf's eye at the door. He nodded to him. In seconds, Kaf reappeared at the door with her father's gift for her. Her eyes and mouth opened wide as she saw what was in his arms; one of the monkeys she had admired from the Nubian tribute. This monkey chattered excitedly, trying to climb out of the servant's grasp.

When presented to Hatasu, the monkey climbed on her shoulder as if he belonged there and chattered loudly, scolding the servant. She looked up to see her father's warm smile. She felt understood, for he must have known she would need something to help her fill the emptiness of missing him. She threw her arms around his neck in a hug and breathed in the divine scent of myrrh still clinging to him from his morning offering to Amun.

"Now I have instructions for both of you," he said, gathering Hatasu and Thethi within the shelter of his two arms. "While I am gone, you must grow wise and strong in the ways of the gods and goddesses. It is time for both you to learn the holy letters of Thoth. There are great teachers at the House of Life at the towns of Abedju and Ankh Tawy. Sitre will oversee your studies during your travel between temples."

Hatasu showed her pleasure and excitement with a wide grin.

To Hatasu he said, "Honor Sitre's teaching in music and dance, too." To Thethi he said, "Honor Paheri's teachings in discipline and sports." To both of them he added, "Above all, honor the Queen for she has much wisdom to impart to you. If you still wish to learn soldiering and charioteering when I return, there will be time enough to study those things."

Hatasu began to cry. Her father moved his hand comfortingly, stroking the back of her head. "Hatasu, you are a strong dreamer. Look for dreams of me. This will ease your sadness and make your dreaming wiser. Let there be no more tears."

She nodded, forcing her tears to stop.

It was time now to say goodbye to Amenmose. He and Thethi slapped each other on the back and did a couple of wrestling moves that ended in an embrace. Then he looked to his sister and said in an awkward way, "Goodbye, little Sekhmet."

For a moment, she forgot her difficulties with him. He was, after all, her brother. She remembered the warmth she felt toward him the day she rode in his chariot out to the barracks. Amenmose hugged her as though he meant it.

The family accompanied the Pharaoh and Prince to the warship, 'The Falcon', waiting at the harbor-lake. Thutmose looked very grand as the sunlight shone on his blue war helmet and crisp military kilt. Queen Ahmose publicly placed a gold amulet of protection around the Pharaoh's neck. Hatasu noticed Amenmose scanning the crowd of faces until he saw the tearful waving of Asat. Regally, the great warrior Pharaoh stepped aboard his ship. Amenmose boarded with him. Thutmose then gave the official command to cast off.

Hatasu watched the ship slowly float away from the quay. It

glided out into the river and the other warships fell in line behind it until the entire river was filled with wooden ships with oars moving in time to the sailor's chants. Both shores were lined with people waving colored scarves, playing musical instruments and singing of victory to come.

Part 2

Chapter 16 - Neferubity's Birth

The palace felt empty without her father. Even Chi-chi, her new pet monkey, felt like a poor replacement. He climbed around her chattering in an annoying way as she sat by the river looking out in the direction the ships had gone.

"Can I really visit Father in my dreams?" Hatasu asked her mother as she readied for bed.

"Yes, when you are asleep you can spread your ba wings and fly."

"But how can I visit him?"

"I'll tell you." Her mother sat down on the bed and motioned for Hatasu to sit beside her. "Can you feel your ab…right in the middle of your chest?"

Hatasu nodded.

"Now, feel your love for your father there?"

"I can feel that," said Hatasu.

"Can you see his face, in your mind's eye?"

"Yes," she said, hanging her head and shaking it. "But it just makes me sadder because he isn't *here*."

Ahmose put her arm around her and pressed her close. "Hmmm…You need to open the door beyond that sad state of 'missing him' so your ba can fly free again and travel to your father in your dreams."

Hatasu snuggled between her bedsheets feeling the love in her ab and seeing his face in her mind's eye. Her mother tucked the linens tight around her and Hatasu drifted off into a hopeful sleep.

In the morning, Ra was high in the sky when her mother found her still in her bed. "Oh my, Sleepy Head. Well? What do you remember from your dreams last night?"

"I'm still waiting for my dream," Hatasu replied. "Did you dream of him?"

"Yes, and we both came to visit you," Ahmose said. "It seems your sadness still veils your dream memory."

Tears pooled in her eyes but she didn't let them spill onto her cheeks. "How do I get rid of this sadness of missing him?"

"Well, my dear," Ahmose began, "When you feel something strongly, the feelings sets up an abode in your body unless you let it sing to you. You must hear its sound…not words, but *sounds*. You must find where in your body the sadness is living and let it speak for itself."

The feeling around Hatasu's heart was a moan, soft and low. She made the sound, and her mother nodded. The sound got louder and higher pitched. It became like a cry but without tears. Her mother joined in and together they sounded their sadness. Gradually, the sounds began to change. It started to sound like a croon and then finally a melodious chant.

"See?" said her mother, smiling. "The goddess has received your sadness and turned it into a song."

Satisfied, Hatasu skipped off to play with her monkey and her friends. She had a happy expectation that, come night, she would see her father in her dreams. She was surprised when that night she dreamed of her monkey with her father's head. Then, her dream-image of her father changed completely into himself. He seemed to be saying something but she couldn't make out what it was. In the morning, she jumped out of bed and ran to her mother's room. "I did it! I did it!"

"What do you remember?" Ahmose asked.

"He looked like Chi-chi at first. He said something but I didn't understand."

"You are further on your way to being a wise dreamer. Soon, you will remember what your ba hears as well as what it sees."

"What does he tell you in your dreams, Mother?"

Her mother smiled. "We talk about the same kinds of things we would talk about if he were here."

"So, do you know where he and the army are now?"

"They are staying at the Zawty nome tonight. That is half of their Nile journey. Going is slow with so large a number of men and animals to move."

Hatasu's days brightened considerably. Each night, she got better and better at remembering her ba's visits with her father. In the morning, she and her mother talked about anything she missed in her dreams. For the next quarter of the moon, these dreams were the most exciting thing in her life. She went to bed early, got up late and during the day she planned what she'd ask her father in that night's dream.

In the meantime, the gods were doing their work in the land all around. The flood was full and Hatasu started to pay more attention again to waking reality. She watched from the rooftop as the dark water flowed over its banks, swelling each canal, forming fingers, rushing toward the sandy desert edge. Eventually, even the canals could no longer prevent the water's escape and the flood ran lovingly over the fields and farms. It left less and less of the parched brown earth visible above the water, until the town seemed to float, an island in the midst of a wide sea. The waters became a vast expanse spreading from the desert mountains, that gave birth to Ra in the morning, to the desert mountains that swallowed him up at night.

In spite of her father's absence, palace life continued. Queen Ahmose assumed the duties necessary for ruling and both Hapu and Ineni were devoted and loyal to her, responding as respectfully to her as they would to the Pharaoh himself. They reported to the Queen daily about the flooding, the canals and the distribution of last year's grain harvest. Ahmose gave audience to the noblemen from the nomes and attended to the needs of the temple.

She was busy but Hatasu knew that in the late afternoon her mother always took a rest time on the rooftop garden. That part of the day was a lovely island in the Queen's busy schedule. She and her women, Hatasu, and the friends and servants she favored, enjoyed this time as a relaxing interlude.

While Hatasu had been exploring with her dream-ba, Thethi had been bedridden with his cough. This afternoon, however, he was on the rooftop with them. He was well enough for quiet play with Behka, his dog. Hatasu busied herself trying to teach her monkey to bring her a fig without him taking a bite of it first. Hatasu's laughter rewarded the monkey's antics…the women laughed, too. Before long, however, the figs Chi-chi ate filled him up and the little monkey curled up inside an empty pottery jug and fell asleep.

Queen Ahmose sat…almond-eyed, pregnant-bellied, and royal…watching the children play. Her stately tasks were done for the day and she sat enjoying the gentle afternoon breezes. Sitting on a stool to her right was Satamun, her priestess sister; straight and thin, with some gray hair visible under her shoulder-length black wig. Her beautiful, long-fingered hands rested in her lap among the folds of the bleached white linen of her dress. Standing behind the two women was Nefermut, the Queen's personal servant, who had been with her since her infancy.

Now, Nefermut was old and bent, her gray-white hair was without a wig, and her fingers were bumpy and stiff from years of service. Ahmose loved this older woman and included her in this woman's circle as a friend, no longer asking her for service. Off to the side stood Muthotep. She was a younger woman with wide dark eyes, framed with thick black lashes. She had the large breasts of a nursing mother; for indeed, she was to be the nurse for Neferubrity, the princess soon to be born. And of course, Sitre was there, having her own respected place in this palace circle.

Hatasu knew all these women as 'other mothers'. Nefermut soothed skinned knees with ointments, Satamun told her stories about her ancestors, Muthotep saved her choice sweets from the household stores, and Sitre…well, she did everything else. The women talked and laughed softly as they wove lotus blossoms into garlands for the statue of the goddess Taueret, protector of birthing mothers.

Hatasu skipped around their circle. She plopped herself down, cross-legged, on the woven mat at her mother's feet.

The women talked about the height of the inundation this year. It didn't seem as high as last year and it would be important to replenish the grains used for the war. Ahmose listened to their worries as her fingers gently wove the flower stems together. "The milometer reading is well within range of an adequate harvest." She seemed un-rattled by their concerns.

Indeed, as the river swelled with its water, so also Ahmose's body swelled and rounded with her pregnancy. Ahmose carried her pregnancy with grace and beauty. Her regal air disguised any anxiety she might feel. Nefermut, in spite of her age and release from servitude, fussed over Ahmose a great deal; offering her sweet morsels, directing others to brew her special teas, and overseeing the making of special oils that carried reputations for easing the stretch of the skin on the belly.

Satamun put aside her duties as priestess and Great God's Wife, so she could be with her younger sister at this important time. She commissioned a prayer stele to be made, asking the goddess for a safe delivery. Sitre sang her soul-soothing songs. The women were so attentive because they knew of Ahmose's difficulty with past miscarriages and the deep sadness the Queen had felt at each loss. The female friends were also aware that their Queen, though bravely silent, felt the ache of her husband's absence at this time.

Hatasu noted everyone's increased concern. She knew of women who did not survive the birth of their children.

As the afternoon shadows lengthened, Satamun reached for one of the hand drums from a basket and began a gentle, pleasing rhythm. She held the instrument at shoulder height. Moving to the beat, she allowed the rhythm to spread from the drum, to her hands, down her arms and to her shoulders, hips, and feet. Queen Ahmose seemed to catch the music in her hands and clapped out the same song her sister played. Rising to her feet, she began to dance, swaying around the rooftop.

Nefermut added words…a little ditty with a rhyme…and they all joined in. Sitre, too, moved her hips and feet easily as her long fingers urged her drum to bring forth its song. Hatasu naturally imitated their swaying hips. Her mother smiled and motioned for her to dance with them.

Sitre reached out to Hatasu with both her hands. Taking the girl's hands in her own, she drew her into their circle of movement, explaining, "No belly is too large or too small for Hathor's dance of pregnancy."

Satamun looked backward over her undulating shoulders and said to her niece, "The movements of dance open the doorway through which your unborn sister will enter our world and the songs call her to join us."

Nefermut, too, was swaying. Her feet seemed to lighten as soon as the music started. Her steps were slower and smaller than those of the younger women but her smile of pleasure was just as broad. "You will like this dance," she whispered to the princess.

Muthotep's hips swung back and forth. Light on her feet, she'd twirl around in one direction and then the other. Sitre's smiling eyes encouraged Hatasu in her own swaying and twirling movements. In no time at all, the women were moving around the roof to the beating and chanting. Queen Ahmose, her belly heavy and round, moved with a fluid, sensuous rhythm. All the women smiled broadly as they swayed their bellies.

Dance graced each part of palace life. The pregnancy dance honored Hathor, the great goddess of womanly beauty, for whom offerings of dance were more pleasing than any incense or table heaped with food. So, throughout the Queen's pregnancy, this belly-swaying dance had been part of the palace afternoon rest time. It honored the goddess and drew her protection for a safe and healthy delivery.

Each afternoon after that day, when the cooling afternoon breezes began to move the still air, Hatasu heard the call of the women's drums and she moved to join the dancers on the roof. Hatasu understood the dance was a prayer to protect her mother at what could be a dangerous time.

It was as though her mother was two different people that season. She was the very strong, alert ruler of the land, the Queen who discussed important matters and gave rulings to viziers, stewards and priests but she was also the mother expecting her second child, doing the purifications of dance and preening which were enjoyed by expectant mothers throughout the land.

She was still Hatasu's mother, too, and she came each night to sing to her and to tuck her into bed. Hatasu's questions shifted from dreams of her father to questions about the birth of her sister. In particular, she wanted to know more about the comings and goings of spirits through the doorway of death and birth.

One night, her mother smiled and said to her, "Come, we will let the stars answer your questions. We will let them show you where the akh-spirit of your sister, Neferubrity, comes from."

She and her mother walked out amidst the lotus-scented night garden and looked up at the sky. Ahmose pointed straight up into the sparkling night to the stretch of luminescent mist within the deep, warm blackness in the western sky. "It is the Great Mother Nut. Can you see her there, as the milky glow that spreads across the sky from east to west? It is there in the west, where Wadjmose's akh went when he passed through the portal of death. It is as though Nut takes him into her starry self at the evening of his life."

Turning to the eastern sky she continued, "And that is where she births the new day and the new soul at the dawning of its life. Neferubrity's akh comes from Nut, who flows like the Nile River across the heavenly land. There is something else I want you to see." She looked high overhead to the north and pointed out a set of stars. "There, among the 'imperishable ones', we will see the group of stars that picture the goddess of birth, Taueret." She pointed to an irregular line of seven stars in the northern part of the sky. "Those are the seven stars of her back and tail. Do you see it there, just a little this side of Mother Nut?" she said, motioning with her right hand.

"There, Mother Taueret, who we picture as a pregnant hippopotamus, eternally smiles down on mothers and children with guidance and protection."

Hatasu wondered at how the goddesses and gods lived in the sky for everyone here on earth to see. And there…among them all…bulging toward its fullest brightness…was the moon. This was the light of Thoth, marker of time and wisdom. Turning back to look more closely toward Nut, Hatasu said, "How can my sister be in your stomach and with the stars in the sky at the same time? And when will she come through the doorway so she can play with me?"

"Well, it is her akh-spirit that is in the sky-home with Nut. Her khet-body and her ab-heart come through my body and that is what you feel move as you put your hand on my stomach. It is Khnum who makes her ka on his potter's wheel. The doorway is the moment of birth when these parts come together, when we can hold Neferubrity in our arms, and look in her eyes. The ba moves in slowly, coming and going like dreams."

Hatasu mulled this around for a while. "When will she be here?"

Putting her hands on her stomach, she smiled and said, "Oh, about the time the moon is full."

"Do you dream of her?"

"Yes."

"Why hasn't she come to see *me* in a dream?"

"Why don't you invite her into your dreams, Hatasu?" Ahmose smiled.

"Did you dream of me when I was still in heavenly Nut?"

"Yes, indeed I did! I dreamed that Amun, himself, came to me before you were born as sometimes happens when a person is special to the gods."

That night, Hatasu dreamed of a little bird with long, glowing feathers. In the dream it landed on her shoulder then flew away. Hatasu was certain it was her sister's ba-bird and she was delighted.

Hatasu also watched the moon swell into fullness in the night sky. Ahmose's belly continued to swell like the moon.

One day, Hatasu arrived at the roof room to find Nefermut and Muthotep preparing the birth bower. This was a shelter set up on the roof of the palace, so the birthing mother could catch each breeze and the child could have an unobstructed passage from the stars. The shelter kept the sun off those inside and each of the four papyrus-shaped pillars on each side was wrapped with a vine of deep green, heart-shaped leaves with small clusters of yellow-green flowers, called birthwort.

That evening, Ahmose called around her the chosen attendants: Satamun, Nefermut, Sitre and Muthotep. They arrived with their musical instruments: Sistrum, tambourine and nay. Hatasu and Sitre joined the circle with their frame drums. Ahmose was smiling broadly as she walked around, rubbing her stomach or her back, pausing now and then to take a deep breath.

Satamun began a soft tapping on the hand drum. Ahmose's walking and stretching began to take on a rhythm with the drum. Her hips stretched and swayed from side to side with the music and the other women followed her movements in support and sympathy. Hatasu moved her small hips as she saw the other women doing. She understood this was the beginning of the birth and the afternoon passed with a rhythm of dancing and resting, then dancing again.

During one of the rest periods, Satamun motioned for Hatasu to come sit by her side. She asked, "Would you like to hear a story of a very important birth that was attended by goddesses?"

Hatasu settled herself cross-legged and looked at Satamun expectantly. "There was once a great lady, Ruddedet, wife of the high priest of Ra, Rawoser. She carried within her womb three sons, each the child of the Great God Ra. When it came her time to deliver these children through the doorway of birth, she found it difficult and painful.

"Ra called together the deities of birth: Isis, Nephthys, Heket and Khnum. He said to them, 'Go...deliver Ruddedet of the three children who are in her womb. They are my divine sons and they will each one day be Pharaohs in the land of Khemet!'

"Isis, Nephthys and Heket disguised themselves as dancing girls with Khnum, the god who forms the baby's ka on his potter's wheel, as their porter. They went to the house of Rawoser and Ruddedet. When they arrived at the house Rawoser's distress was obvious because even his clothes were on inside out."

Hatasu and Satamun laughed together at the thought. Then, she went on, "The goddesses did a beautiful dance for him, their sistrums shaking and their menat beads rattling."

"Like we do here, right?"

"Right, Hatasu, but in the story, before they finished their first dance, Rawoser stopped them and said, 'My Ladies, your dance can bring me no comfort for my wife is in the pains of childbirth. Her labor is very difficult and I fear for her'.

"Having waited for just this invitation Isis said, "Let us see her. We understand childbirth." Relieved that they claimed they could help, Rawoser invited them into Ruddedet's room. Once inside, they secured the area with locks and with magic to keep the secret of their mission from Ra hidden."

Hatasu's eyes were wide as she listened. She wondered if her mother's birth would get painful.

Satamun went on, "The goddesses could indeed see that Ruddedet was tired from her labor so they began their work quickly. Isis took her place before the laboring mother, Nephthys stood behind her, while Heket's job was to hasten the birth with her magic herbs. Isis spoke to the first of the three infants in the womb saying, 'Be born, Userkaf, Son of Ra'. As she said that, the child slid into her arms. He had a golden complexion and hair as blue-black as lapis lazuli. The goddesses cut his navel cord, washed him and laid him next to his mother. With the ankh of life, Khnum then gave the blessing of health to his body.

"Again, Isis took her place before the mother who was still laboring. Nephthys again stood behind her and Heket again hastened the birth with her magic herbs. Isis spoke to the second of the three infants in the womb saying, 'Be born, Sahure, Son of Ra'. As she spoke, this child, too, slid into her arms. He had a complexion of gold and hair as blue-black as lapis lazuli. The goddesses cut his navel cord, washed him and laid him next to his mother. And with the ankh, Khnum gave health to his body.

"For a third time, Isis took her place before the mother who was still laboring. Nephthys again stood behind her and Heket again did her job with magic herbs. Isis spoke to the third of the three infants saying, 'Be born, Neferirkare, Son of Ra'. This child, too, had…"

And here Satamun paused, so Hatasu could join her in saying, "complexion of gold and hair as blue-black as lapis lazuli. The goddesses cut his navel cord, washed him and laid him next to his mother." Satamun laughed with Hatasu who had indeed remembered all the words.

Smiling she went on, "And with the ankh, Khnum gave health to his body."

"Having delivered Ruddedet of the three children, the goddesses came out of the birthing chamber and said to Rawoser, 'Rejoice! Three sons are born to you! All of them shall be great Pharaohs'.

"The priest of Ra answered, 'My Ladies, what can I do to show you my gratitude? Please allow me to give you this sack of barley for the making of excellent beer'.

"Then Khnum, acting as their porter, loaded himself with the sack of barley and they all proceeded toward the place they had come from. They had not gotten far when Isis said to her companions, 'What have we come for, if not to report back to Ra the wonders we have done for his three children? Let's make three royal crowns and return them to the home of Rawoser hidden in the sack of barley'.

"They magically called up a rainstorm as their excuse to return to the house and asked Rawoser to hold the sack of barley until they returned to his palace. The master placed the sack in a sealed room. At the end of Ruddedet's fourteen days of purification after the birth of her children, she prepared for the feast that traditionally followed the blessing at the temple but the only barley for beer available was that of the wandering musicians.

"Ruddedet decided they would use that barley and replace it before the midwives returned. She was astounded when she heard the sounds of singing, dancing and shouting…the celebration sounds that are performed for a king…when she neared the bags of barley. She and Rawoser opened the sacks together. There they found the three crowns and they knew great magic had been done for them. They knew this was a clear oracle of the future kingship of all three of their sons.

"And, Hatasu, the goddesses were right; for all the brothers became great Pharaohs, truly the divine sons of Ra."

"So, those Pharaohs were sons of Ra, like my father is a son of Amun?" asked Hatasu.

"Indeed," agreed her aunt, smiling knowingly.

Just then, the music of another frame drum announced the arrival of the royal midwives. These healing priestesses were called the 'Sau'. There were two of them; one was older and the other was middle-aged. The first one had very large and intense eyes that seemed to take in everything in the room. The second one had large ears that extended from her shaved head. They each greeted the Queen and her womenfolk and then went about their tasks.

The one with the large ears asked the Queen to sit for a moment while she put her ear to her stomach. Everyone was still as she listened intently. Smiling, she stood up saying everything sounded as expected. The one with the intense eyes went to the ornate box at the side of the room. She opened it and took out three objects wrapped protectively in fine white linen. This dark-eyed Sau picked up the smallest object, unwrapped it carefully and placed on the table.

Hatasu went closer to get a better look. The midwife noticed her interest. She smiled at the princess but her eyes stayed intense. "This is the wand of power," she said.

Hatasu looked at the curved white object with pictures of deities on it.

Satamun was standing by and added, "This ancient wand has been used at birthing in our family from before time. It was used when you were born, when your mother was born and when I was born. It is used to draw a circle on the floor around the mother. This creates a sacred space, a doorway through which the akh of the child can pass safely. Transitions from one side of the portal to the other can have dangers. The Sau priestess," she said, nodding toward the midwife who was continuing to unpack the birth box, "knows how to invoke the deities on both sides to help and protect the mother and the child. This wand helps her to do that."

Hatasu looked at the wand closely. She recognized some of the figures on its surface. "I see Taueret, and I see Bes!"

"Yes, they are protectors of this doorway, just as Anubis is the protector of the doorway at death," the Sau explained, as she unwrapped the next object.

Hatasu looked at each figure, thoughtfully. The Sau unwrapped the second of the larger, longish objects that were fairly heavy to move. As she removed the linen, the princess could see they were common Nile mud bricks—only these were smoothly finished with worn places in the center…about the size of a foot. At one end of each of the bricks was the sculptured head of a goddess. This large-eyed Sau continued her explanation, "This is the goddess, Meskhenet. These sacred bricks support the mother's feet as she gives birth and Meskhenet is the goddess that protects mother and child."

The woman with the dark eyes then took the wand and Hatasu watched as she addressed the deities depicted on the wand. Holding the wand in the middle, the Sau used the pointed end to draw a circle on the floor around the laboring Queen and the birthing bricks.

Satamun leaned over and whispered to Hatasu, "This is the ritual of locking the chamber doors, like in the story of Ruddedet".

Hatasu nodded.

The midwives began to chant. *"This is the doorway...We call to you, oh spirit of Neferubrity...We call to you with the beauty of music and song...Come through this doorway and live among us...We have come to give you our welcome,...Our protection and our love."*

They led the Queen toward the bricks and she put a foot on each of them. Ropes hung from the bower and extended down so Ahmose could hold on to them for balance. The large-eared midwife stood behind her, supporting her and chanting in the name of Nephthys. The large-eyed sau positioned herself in front of Ahmose, in the name of Isis.

The chanting got soft and quiet, and Ahmose began to push and strain. Her face was flushed and she made low grunting noises, reminding Hatasu of when she watched Miu give birth to her kittens. Both of the midwives moved in close around Ahmose and Hatasu could see her mother pushing and concentrating. The attending women spoke soft, encouraging words.

Hatasu was anxious about her mother. She was also eager to see her sister. Satamun and Nefermut supported Ahmose as she lay back on the soft pillows of the lion-headed bed the midwives prepared for her. Then, through the doorway of her mother's body, her sister began to appear. First, Hatasu saw the dark circle of baby hair, then the entire head protruded, facing backward. Slowly, it turned and faced sideways, and then the shoulders slid out and the baby was facing up. The midwife with the large eyes caught the rest of the small body and eased her into the world. And then came the sound…Neferubrity's announcement of her arrival…a soft but clear cry.

Everyone exhaled a quiet sigh of relief, for this was music to their ears. The midwives cut the naval cord, washed the baby and placed her in her mother's arms, just like in the story. Ahmose held the baby close to her heart and the women around continued their soft, gentle chant in between their smiling 'oohs' and 'ahs'.

Satamun motioned to Hatasu to come closer and with her arm around her niece, they looked together into the tiny face of the newest member of their family. Hatasu looked at Neferubrity. She did not look like the babies in the story. Her skin was not gold, her hair was not lapis blue. No, this baby's skin was rosy pink and her hair was like a wet, black cap on her head and two disproportionately large, dark eyes looked back at them. Hatasu reached out and touched Neferubrity's tiny hand and the fingers curled around her own. Hatasu's heart filled with awe and tender love for this new sister.

In that first night's dreams, Hatasu knew her father was aware of Neferubrity's birth before any messenger could have arrived. In that dream, she could 'feel' how her father longed to be there with his family. In the morning, she noted to her mother that now her ba could see her father, hear what he said and even feel what he felt.

"Yes, he knew you would be a wise dreamer," Ahmose smiled.

The first fourteen days after a birth, had been honored as days of purification for a mother since before the time of Ruddedet. Ahmose did not need to do anything but be with her baby and rest. The baby's ka and ba were to come together in its khet in a peaceful, natural way. Satamun came each morning, right after her duties at the ritual offerings to Amun, to do the honorary brushing of the new mother's hair. If the need were to arise, Satamun, as Great God's Wife, was to act as intermediary between the Queen and the royal advisors.

Except in the case of dire emergency, no men were to come to the birth bower until after the fourteen days of purification. Once a mother presented her child to the seven Hathors at the mammisi of the mother goddess Mut, life returned to normal. Ahmose and her sister enjoyed this time. Left behind were their adult concerns and childhood jealousies. They talked of the beauty of the baby and the promise of the continuation of the line of their father and mother, Pharaoh Ahmose and Queen Nefertari. They didn't talk about the disappointment that this was not a boy-child that could blend the bloodlines of the two powerful families.

Satamun didn't mention her son, Taos, or how he would be better than Amenmose as husband to Hatasu and ruler of the land. Ahmose didn't mention Tao's sullen nature that she saw as making him unsuitable as husband to her daughter and heir to the throne. No, those things weren't mentioned. The women just talked of pleasant things…who the baby looked like, the best foods for enhancing breast milk and what ointments were best for the baby's tender skin.

All the while, Satamun brushed her younger sister's hair while Ahmose sat nursing Neferubrity. And they sang together. There were little ditties from games in their childhood, lullabies Nefertiry sang to each of them as children. These were sacred days of purification, when Ahmose was Isis nursing Horus, attended by her sister Nephthys.

Hatasu delighted in listening to her mother and aunt talk of what it was like to be daughters to the great Nefertari. They laughed, saying that neither one of them felt they were ever able to get out from under her glorious shadow.

"It will be different for Hatasu and Neferubrity," Ahmose said. "It is clear from my dreams, and from her birth oracle that she will rule as a mighty Queen…and her sister, here, will be the Great God's Wife like you, Satamun."

"No, no, Dear Sister, surely you remember the prophetic dream I had. I am certain Hatasu will be my heir as a Great God's Wife and high Priestess." Their eyes met in a challenging way.

Nefermut spoke up, "The truth of these two different oracles doesn't need to be known, right now. This is the purification period, a time of peace."

Both the Queen and the high priestess let the matter drop but it made Hatasu stop and think. Hatasu thought to herself, *'No one seemed truly to know what my role is to be…Queen to Amenmose?…Great God's Wife of Amun?'*

In the peace and quiet of the next afternoon, she was alone with just Ahmose and old Nefermut. Hatasu asked her mother, "Tell me the story of *my* birth."

Ahmose had been waiting for this. "Oh, you did not come into this world as quietly as your sister. No, your lungs were strong and you announced yourself with great vigor. You opened your dark eyes wide and looked all around, curious from the beginning. So, you were yourself from the start. When I first saw your red hair, I just knew."

Hatasu giggled, delighting in this story about herself.

Ahmose continued, "The priestesses of Hathor, at my purification, said you would 'reign in peace'. All of this pleased your father and me but I was not surprised. I'd had a dream before you were born in which Amun told me you are his daughter and your name should be Khnemet Amun Hatshepsut…'The one who is joined with Amun, the foremost of noble ladies'."

Old Nefermut had been in a corner of the room, quietly weaving flower garlands. Now, she came forward and spoke in a soft but insistent voice to Ahmose. "Perhaps, this is a good time to tell her the meaning of your dream."

Ahmose said nothing. She had long ago decided *not* to tell her daughter that part because it was so against the usual way of things. Its implications would bring much hardship. Perhaps, if she didn't tell her, things would follow a more normal path.

Hatasu looked back and forth between them, curiously.

Nefermut waited.

Ahmose took a breath.

Nefermut continued gently, "Tell her about your dream of Amun being her father and how that is similar to the dream of other Pharaoh's mothers."

Ahmose gave out a deep sigh this time, giving her old friend a look that showed her distress at having been pushed into this. "Well yes, that dream of Amun's presence was a highlight of my life. And Seniseneb had such a dream before your father was born." She looked gently at Hatasu. "But Mutnofret also had such a dream before Thethi was born. We know it doesn't always mean that child will become Pharaoh." Turning to Nefermut, "I think you give it too much weight. I believe my dream is for Hatasu to be Queen."

"Did you have such a dream of Nefertubrity?" Hatasu asked.

"Well, no. I've had plenty of dreams of her but none that she is a daughter of Amun."

Nefermut, smiled, shrugged her shoulders and turning a knowing look toward Hatasu, shuffled back to the corner with her flowers. Hatasu stared at Nefermut, then turned to her mother. "So…I might become *Pharaoh*…like father?! What did my oracle say?"

"At my purification, one of the priestess interpreted the signs to mean you would 'reign in peace' as a *Pharaoh*." There were several moments of silence. Ahmose frowned slightly as she looked at her daughter's open quizzical face.

Hataus asked quietly, "But, who would I marry if I were Pharaoh?"

Ahmose's, shoulders seemed to drop in resignation as she said, "That is certainly part of the problem. Just as there needs to be a below to reflect the above, a woman and man need their compliment in each other. The way of Maat is the balance of two opposites. The people need to see that balance in their Pharaoh and Queen. To rule wisely, the Queen must unite the above and below in the spiritual realm as the Pharaoh must unite them in the outer world. It is theoretically possible for one person to balance these two opposites within herself but it is a very hard and lonely job. No one would choose to carry the burden of rulership alone. I do not wish this for you. I wish to protect you from the strain of such a hard life."

Hatasu listened, her eyes wide. There was comfort in a world that was fixed and certain as when she was to be the Queen to Wadj. Even being Queen to Amen was preferable to this confusion. *Pharaoh? Queen? God's Wife?* Hatasu folded her arms in front of her and with a stamp of her small bare foot, she said, "I don't care about that oracle priestess or what the dream says. I want to be a Queen like you and have a Pharaoh husband like father!"

Chapter 17 - Journey to the Place of Truth

Fourteen days after the birth, it was time for Ahmose to receive the purification and for Neferubrity to receive her blessing at the Temple of the mother goddess, Mut. There was a small procession to the temple where the seven Hathor priestesses were consulted about the baby's fate. Ahmose brought her offerings in thanksgiving for her healthy child. The priestesses met the royal entourage at the pylon gate to the temple complex. Each had the red ribbon of Hathor around her head and each held a sistrum in one hand and the menat beads in the other. Each was an oracle who had trained her inner sight. One by one the priestesses put down their musical instruments and held this child saying their words of prophesy over her.

"The goddess tells me this child shall bring brightness and happiness to her family."

"By the grace of Mother Mut, this little one shall love all sorts of music and song for that will feed her ba-soul."

"This is a child who will love small animals and bright colored plants."

When it came to the last priestess, she looked deeply into the baby's eyes, then scanned the area around her body. With a compassionate smile at the Queen she said, "This child has a strong connection with the goddesses Isis and Nephthys and she shall bring you, her mother, closer to understanding the world of the gods." Then she handed her daughter back to the Queen.

Ahmose stayed, as though waiting to hear something more but

the priestesses turned and walked back into the temple. As the royal entourage turned and departed, Satamun leaned toward Ahmose as though she were offering her words of reassurance. Hatasu knew something was wrong but she didn't know what. She pulled on Sitre's hand as they all walked back to the palace. "What happened?"

Sitre kept walking and said, almost in a whisper, "The priestesses left out anything about a long life or any of the deeds of adulthood. This may mean that Neferubrity may not stay with us for long."

Hatasu was shocked. Maybe her mother's lack of an Amun dream for her sister meant she was less likely to be Pharaoh or Queen but surely she'd live to grow up! Feeling herself as a protective big sister, she burst out, "Well, we must make this a place where she wants to stay!" She did not want to lose another sibling! The rest of the way home, Hatasu thought about what could make Neferubrity want to stay. When they arrived at the palace, Hatasu caught up with her mother and said, "Neferubrity hasn't met the river yet. I think she would like the water."

Ahmose stared at her baby. Without taking her eyes off her, she answered simply, "Yes," and they took the path down to the steps of the royal bathing area.

Feeling very much the big sister, walking next to her mother who carried the baby, Hatasu chattered on and on telling the little one about everything along the way. "This is the papyrus, its stem and its tufts. Neferubrity, can you hear the kites sing as they sweep through the sky?"

The flood was high so it didn't take very long to be at the water. Ahmose unwrapped the baby's cloth and held her ever so gently so just her toes could feel the water. Hatasu watched the baby's eyes open wider as though surprised at the sensation. She kicked her legs and feet and was again surprised when they splashed. Hatasu laughed and splashed a bit in front of her. The baby smiled and kicked her feet in the water some more. Everyone joined in the laughter as Hatasu put more water on her feet. Then, Ahmose lowered Neferubrity into the blessing Nile.

Hatasu, loving the water, waded in, knelt before her sister and dunked herself in, disappearing. She then popped up, laughing. This startled Neferubrity and she started crying. Hatasu was quick to comfort her with soothing, reassuring words as she had seen her mother and the nurse do. Her baby sister smiled again.

That night, at a feast in honor of the royal birth, the barley beer flowed plentifully and the halls rang with the music and dancing of the local nobility who had gathered to celebrate the new princess.

Once the fourteen-day purification was over and the ritual blessing of the baby at the temple, Ahmose returned to her duties at the ceremonial palace. Neferubrity began to suffer from stomachaches and frequent fits of crying. Each time Muthotep nursed her she would pull her tiny legs up tight to her belly and bellow out her discomfort in a voice much larger than her tiny self. Her nurse was often unable to comfort her. She kept her dry and fed, and spent hours rocking her in her cradle or pacing with her up and down the nursery floor, jouncing her gently up and down as she sang every lullaby she knew.

The Queen, too, did everything she could think of to comfort her child. Satamun was called and her advice for herbal teas, amulets and soothing songs was followed. Nefermut brewed a peppermint drink and the palace artisan made an amulet of Bes. Ahmose made incense offerings to Isis and Taueret. Still, Neferubrity cried.

On one of Satamun's visit, Hatasu asked, "Why does she keep crying?"

"Oh Niece, it is hard for Neferubrity's ba, so used to living unencumbered in its home in Nut. It must get used to the heavy garment of her khet. She must learn about being nurtured by woman's milk rather than the milk of Nut, herself. No milk is as sweet or as easy to swallow as the goddess's. That is why she cries. Singing and music is food for her ka. The harmony in a song takes her to the place where Maat dwells. The magic sounds, words or music bring health and ease pain."

It was true. The only thing that seemed to help at all was music. The lullabies soothed Neferubrity. Ahmose and Mutnofret sang until their voices were hoarse. Hatasu helped, too. She would often sit with her baby sister and sing her the lullaby her mother sang to her:

"May the Wings of Isis enfold you. Safe may they always hold you." She would sing on, ending with the hopeful line, *"Now, sleep gently within her wings."* Hatasu's lullabies helped. As a big sister, she was delighted to discover she had some ability to partake of the soothing magic. At special moments, Neferubrity quieted her cries, un-squinted her eyes and looked up at her sister. Sometimes, if Hatasu made an unusual sound or a funny face, the little one would

produce a smile or even a soft cooing sound. These were precious moments and rather than turn away in frustration at the baby's frequent crying or questionable fate, Hatasu's affection for the little one grew.

Ahmose talked things over with Satamun and Hatasu knew her mother's mind turned, as any mother's of Khemet would, to sympathetic powers in the other world. It was to her own mother that her ab-heart reached out. The great Nefertari was known to be 'powerful of magic' and her magic was strongest across the river at the village that she had founded for the royal artisans. The worried mother had a stela made of stone which contained offering prayers to Nefertari for good magic that would give health to her child.

There was still a priestess-chantress in the village trained by Queen Nefertari, herself. That was the magic Ahmose wanted for her child. Once the stela was completed, she planned to bring Neferubrity to this village for Nefertari's healing.

Ahmose, remembering her own happy childhood trips with her mother to visit the artisans of the town, decided to bring Hatasu as her mother had brought her. When she told her daughter of the pilgrimage to the West Bank Temple, she was surprised when Hatasu asked if Thethi could come, too. Ahmose paused. Hatasu pressed her mother. "Mama, he's been left out of the activities and rituals for Neferubrity. I know he feels bad about it."

"Not this trip, Hatasu. Our group must be small and inconspicuous."

"Oh, Mother, I feel sorry that he has missed so much."

Remembering the time her mother brought her and her sister to this village at the same time, brought a smile to her face. She said, "All right, call your brother and I will tell you both about the trip."

She gathered the two children in front of her and with a twinkle in her eye she said, "Do you know what a secret is?"

"Something that others don't know," Hatasu offered, her ears opened wide with expectation.

"Something you don't talk about," Thethi added, truly pleased he was included.

With the word 'secret', the Queen had the children's full attention. "Yes," she said, "some things are kept secret because they need to be protected. You must honor those secrets with your silence. It is because I believe you understand this that I have decided to take you on this trip." The two small faces with wide eyes nodded their consent. "The place we are going to is one such secret. You haven't been there before because it is a hidden town. My mother, Queen Nefertari, founded this town especially for artists. Your father, the Pharaoh, deems it wise to keep it hidden. Ineni and Satamun know of it and will accompany us tomorrow. The purpose of our making the journey is to seek healing for Neferubrity. I am bringing a stela as an offering to my mother, Queen Nefertari, the deified."

"Can we bring an offering, too?" Hatasu asked.

"Perhaps you'd like to bring a flower from the palace garden?" Ahmose liked the idea. Both children were quickly out the door, talking excitedly about the next day's adventure and about what kind of flower they would each offer. Ahmose called them back and silently put her finger to her lips. They resumed their quest for an offering, this time in silence.

The garden was just below Ahmose's window and inadvertently they heard her conferring with Ineni and Satamun about the trip. The Queen addressed her brother-in-law and sister. "I am very worried about Neferubrity and I have arranged a trip to the Place of Truth to make offerings to Queen Nefertari. I have commissioned a stela and sent a message to Merit, the chantress of the temple there. I pray that my mother will grace her granddaughter with comfort and health. I plan to take the reed boat because it will be least conspicuous. The children will accompany me."

There was a pause and then some alarm in Ineni's voice. "Beloved Queen, perhaps it is best to just bring the infant? Is it wise to bring the others?"

"I have decided to bring Hatasu and Thethi as my mother brought me and Satamun as children."

"I bow to your wisdom, Mother of the Two Lands but I wonder of the Pharaoh's wish that The Place of Truth remain a secret, with 'No one seeing. No one hearing'."

The children grew still, straining to hear every word.

"Oh, Ineni, surely you do not think he meant to keep it a secret from his children," she replied.

"Surely not, Wife of my Brother, but perhaps he would like to take them there himself."

"Ineni, I know the secret nature of this place is crucial to his plan but I do not believe the secrets will be endangered by the children's offerings for their sister's health or by them encountering the artisans." She added, "And it will give me comfort to take my children to the temple of my mother before our long sojourn in the north."

Ineni's voice warmed. "I know Neferubrity worries you and the strain of the Pharaoh's being at war bears heavily on your shoulders. However, I share his concern that any who know of the town will eventually find the tomb."

After a measured silence, Satamun's voice was heard. Her tone was cautious, "Ahmose, my dear sister, I understand your wish to bring our mother's granddaughters, both of them, but I wonder why you would choose to bring Mutnofret's son."

The children looked at each other. Thethi shifted uneasily.

"Satamun," Ahmose said in a firm voice, "he is also the Pharaoh's son! It is good for his training as possible future vizier to include reverence for our mother, the great Queen Nefertari."

"Reverence for our mother, yes. Exposure to the secrets, no!" Satamun's voice was just as adamant.

"My Sister, I am not talking of exposing either of them to anything more than the location. There is little danger in Thethi having this information. Queen Nefertari supported the Pharaoh's ascension to the throne. I believe she would welcome this son of his and not begrudge him the knowledge of her temple. I wish that he be included in this ritual blessing of his Neferubrity."

Satamun's voice answered, "Things are not quite the same as when our mother brought us to the village. She was dedicated to renewing the lost arts and training those suitable to promulgate them. She wished us to know of these things."

Ineni joined in, "Now, the Pharaoh wished these arts to serve eternity without the disturbance of the profane or the vulgarity of the thieves that can plague royalty. This plan requires more secrecy than Queen Nefertari's vision."

The Queen nodded thoughtfully. "I thank you both for your council of concern. Queen Nefertari built a town to enhance the learning of the sacred arts and Pharaoh Thutmose built a wall to protect these sacred secrets from dishonor. I shall bring the offspring of Queen Nefertari and the offspring of Thutmose and teach them both the importance of the magic arts…and of discretion."

The God's Wife added softly and the children strained to hear, "I'm sure the Pharaoh's son, young as he is, is capable of being discrete. It will also serve as a test of his worthiness."

The Queen seemed to ignore this last comment but Hatasu felt her own discomfort, which only increased her protectiveness for her younger brother. For Thethi, the comment stimulated his customary response of determination to prove himself.

The next day, a boat was packed with offerings for the temple and gifts for the villagers. The children carried their own offerings. The six of them boarded an inconspicuous reed boat and headed across the broad expanse of river. The oarsmen rowed for a long time, as the river was just beginning to shrink from its full width. Ahmose, held Neferubrity. Satamun and Ineni sat quietly in the shade of the boat pavilion. As they started off, the children gathered around Ahmose as Hatasu showed her brother how to play with Neferubrity. He was more easily discouraged than she by the baby's fussiness. Wrapped in a sling around her mother, the little one eventually fell asleep to the rocking motion of the boat.

Ahmose continued her preparation of the children once they were underway. "You know how Queen Nefertari guided the land when Pharaoh Ahmose was away at war…much as I do now, and you know it was she who kept it stable as a djed column, raising it up and offering the people her help and leadership. You know that when Ahmose, the Liberator, died, she ruled the country as regent for her son, Amenhotep, and when this son was Pharaoh, Queen Nefertari was always at his side, strong and wise."

They nodded and she continued, "There is more for you to know about her. She was not only Queen but also God's Wife of Amun, the role that Satamun now carries. Pharaoh Ahmose recognized Queen Nefertari's great gift of wisdom for her people and created that position for her. She was thus High Priestess and he was High Priest. She was Queen as he was Pharaoh. She used her power to bring the ancient magic of music and art back to life as he used his power to bring stability and Maat to the land and people."

Satamun added, "If the secrets of these arts fall into the wrong hands, as they did with the Hyksos, they could be lost or destroyed. Therefore, those who study these magical arts must do so in protected privacy."

Ineni interjected, "'No one seeing! No one hearing!' These are your father's words. He foresees the need to keep the magic of the arts not only from foreigners but also from malcontents within Khemet. It is from the threat of thieves that he wishes to protect the village. Your father's plan is truly ingenious, for robbers won't steal something if they don't know it exists. The success of his plan depends upon the loyalty and discretion of those of us who are entrusted with the knowledge."

The two children observed the intensity of Ineni's eyes as he spoke to them. They each squirmed a little.

Ahmose directed her next words toward Hatasu. "Your grandmother was very proud of this village of artisans. She named it 'The Place of Truth' after the divine patron of all artisans and craftsperson, Ptah. He is known as Lord of Truth because he is the creator god that crafted the world with the sound of his heart. The people…the artisans and their families that live there…also carry a great love for your grandmother. Out of that love, they have built a temple that honors her and Pharaoh Amenhotep as deified ancestors."

The two children nodded understanding. They promised again to keep the secret and went off to lie on their stomachs at the prow of the boat, watching it plow the water, as the rower inched them closer to the western mountains.

If the children talked softly, the adults couldn't hear them at the prow. Thethi broke the stillness with a whisper, "Protecting secrets from Hyksos and thieves is pretty exciting. I've never had a 'secret' before."

Hatasu was silent. She stared toward the shore. Finally she said, "I have a sort of secret. Well, I don't think it is quite the same thing as this secret but I'm not supposed to talk about it."

Thethi stared at her, his eyes wide.

"Do you remember in the story of the ancestors, the Pharaoh named Sekenenre?"

"I remember."

"Well, I think something happened to him that is not in the story and when I ask about him everyone tells me it is 'unspeakable'."

"Wow. Do you think, just like Ineni didn't want us to know about this secret village, there is another secret they don't want us to know?"

"I think it is different, Thethi. There is something of the 'unspeakable' thing that feels scary. This 'secret' feels exciting."

Thethi went on, "Sekenenre was a soldier. Perhaps the scariness of the 'unspeakable' is a call for the courage of a soldier, a call to be brave. 'The warrior goes after the enemy, even the enemy of ignorance'. Paheri says that to me all the time."

Hatasu thought of Amenmose calling her a Sekhmet warrior. She didn't decide to leave the 'unspeakable' alone because it was scary but because those she loved had asked her to.

Her brother would not let the subject go. "Maybe there is something at this secret place that will tell us something about the 'unspeakable'. How did you find out about it in the first place?"

"When father first talked of the war, Mother said, 'Remember Sekenenre' and he told her, 'That can't happen again. We won't talk of it'. No one will tell me what it is about. Everyone I've asked has said it is 'bad magic' and forget it."

Thethi said, "I wonder why."

"Maybe it is enough that we are being allowed in on this secret, now."

"But it seemed like the 'unspeakable' is a soldier-secret. I remember Senisenb saying that there are two faces of war. One face is glory and the other isn't. Do you remember?"

"I remember but I don't know anything more. I think something bad must have happened to Sekenenre. He was murdered or something. All I could really tell from the tale on the night of the ancestors was that he gathered an arsenal of weapons and led the local princes in a reed navy to fight the Hyksos. And then, his son, Kamose followed after him."

"What bad could happen to a Pharaoh? He is the divine Horus!"

The boat entered the canal path and it followed the path right up close to the edge of the desert where Mentuhotep's temple could be seen in the distance under the huge rock cliffs. This canal path then turned to the south and traveled along, close to the line that marked the tillable land and the desert.

The small troop disembarked from the boat and began their trek toward what looked like nothing more than a hill of sand. Ineni, the two women, the two children and the baby proceeded up the hill along the path. Hatasu and Thethi playfully pretended to be doing a military march with an occasional interruption for a mock battle. This left them behind the adults and they had to run to catch up.

As they neared the adults, Hatasu exclaimed, "I don't see a town here! Where are we going?"

Ineni responded, "This town is hidden from common eyes, remember? It is a secret because it contains a treasure."

Thethi kept silent as they walked on. They were following a path that clearly had been trodden by many feet before them. "This path must go someplace!" he said.

Hatasu was unable to contain her curiosity about this new bit of information. "Treasure? What's the treasure?"

"Well," her mother said, "you know that music and art are magic and they hold power. That power is meant to help us. Those who make pictures and songs must go through much training to learn how to make such magic. This magic is very powerful. It is not meant for those of ignorance or unbridled passions. That's why it is secret."

"Secret from Hyksos and thieves, right?" asked Thethi.

"Yes." Ineni nodded.

"The ability to create such beauty is a gift from the gods and goddesses," Satamun said. "Both the gift to create beauty and the beautiful things created are treasures that bless our land. These artisans have special jobs. They enable the royal family to survive into eternity by preserving their images in pictures and statues. Because of this, the artisans are honored and protected by the Pharaoh. Their art is a treasure for all of us."

They rounded the hill and a short distance away, they could see a white wall, like that which hid East bank temples from common eyes. "Is that a temple wall?" Hatasu wanted to know.

Ineni answered, "No, this is the wall your father is having built for the town itself, not for the temple. The wall keeps it hidden. I will be inspecting this wall to see how the work is going."

As they approached the entrance, a tall, straight-standing woman came out to meet them. Black hair fell over her shoulders and dark eyes shone from a mature face. She bowed first to the Queen, then to the vizier, and finally, with added warmth in her smile, to the Great God's Wife. Each of the visiting group nodded back, acknowledging the greeting and homage. "The servant of the Beautiful Place of Truth welcomes you, Queen Ahmose, Vizier Ineni, Great God's Wife Satamun and Royal Children. How good to see your shining faces. The workmen gangs are away working on the Pharaoh's Temple of a Million Years (mortuary temple). They will be very sad to learn they were not present for your visit."

Ahmose and Satamun also wore big smiles. With formality, the Queen spoke for the group. "Yes, Sahte, we also regret not seeing them. You look well. How is your family?"

"They are well, Your Highness. You look beautiful, like your mother. It is a great joy that both the daughters of the divine Queen Nefertari visit us together…just like when you came as children with your mother." She also greeted Ineni, with more formality, but still with warmth and respect. She seemed to be saving up her greeting for Hatasu. Now, with her full attention on the princess, she bowed very low. "You must be the red-haired child the oracle said would 'rule in peace'."

Hatasu was shocked by this reference to the oracle her mother told her about and she found it strange to receive such a low bow.

This woman of the Place of Truth turned next to Thethi and with a slight bow she said, "I am honored, son of my Pharaoh."

Neferubrity was crying again. In spite of Ahmose's soft cooing sounds, she couldn't be comforted. Sahte put her hand on the head of the crying infant and said, "May the great Queen Nefertari bring you comfort and healing." The baby quieted.

Now inside the gate, the women and children of the village came out to greet them, carrying their sistrums and tambourines, chanting a welcome. Hatasu looked around. The houses made quite a pretty picture. They were made of white-washed mud bricks, each with a bright red door. Across from the houses was an open space where roamed a couple of cows, several sheep, and many ducks and geese.

Ineni excused himself to inspect the wall and Sahte led the rest of them through the streets to where a second gate opened at the other side of the village. As they walked, the village people followed them. Ahmose smiled warmly and with her free hand she reached out to them. She laid a hand on one woman's shoulder and touched a child on the head. Some of the folks she called by name. Satamun, too, was greeted with warm familiarity and she responded in a generous, regal manner.

Hatasu watched her mother and her aunt and she noticed how these village folks beamed as they walked among them. It was as though they were Isis and Nephthys, the divine sisters, who had themselves come to visit them. As they passed through the second gate, Hatasu could see that around the hill to her right was a temple.

Her mother called to each of the children and drew them close to her. "This is the village temple to Queen Nefertari. The main temple has three rooms. One is for Amun, one is for Hathor and one is for Ptah. Next to it is a side chapel dedicated to Queen Nefertari and Amenhotep. That is where we are going."

An old woman stood by the temple. Ahmose exclaimed with pleasure, "Oh, Merit, how good to see you again!"

Merit did indeed look old and frail. Her frame was bent and her muscles were sagging. She wore a simple sheath in the manner of a priestess and a red ribbon of Hathor encircled her shaven head.

Deep wrinkles spread from her smiling eyes. She walked with a cane, though it was unclear if the object was for support or authority. Three mature women stood around her and were very solicitous to her. Merit was clearly the respected elder. "Welcome!" Merit said. "The chantresses of the Place of Truth welcome you."

There was a quality in Merit's voice when she spoke that dazzled Hatasu and made her want to be near this woman even though she had never met her before. The Queen introduced her children. The woman looked at Hatasu closely, her black eyes piercing through her as she took in every inch of the child, stopping at her red youth-lock. Then she bowed low, as Sahte did. She righted herself. As intense as her eyes were, they betrayed a loving warmth and endless interest. She addressed Hatasu in a matter-of-fact tone, "I knew your grandmother well. She was my teacher. As I am always honored by visits from her daughters…," She nodded her head toward Ahmose and Satamun, "so I am honored to meet her granddaughter. I see much of Queen Nefertari in you."

Hatasu felt slightly uncomfortable as though the old woman was seeing something the child didn't. Thethi and Neferubrity were then introduced. Merit spoke to the Queen about the healing ritual for her child, then urged the small group into the temple of Queen Nefertari.

Hatasu and Thethi were anxious to see what was inside. In the niche of the holy of holies were the two statues, just as her mother said. They sat in stone, side by side. Her grandmother wore the great Nekhbet crown. There, over her forehead, were both the vulture head of Upper Egypt and the cobra head of Lower Egypt.

Amenhotep wore the Double Crown of the Pharaoh, white for Upper Egypt and red for Lower. Her right arm was protectively around him, showing her hand on his shoulder. The ankh was in her left hand. He carried the crook and flail of kingship in his right hand and another ankh in his left.

With Ahmose's permission, Merit took Neferubrity in her arms and began to sing to her. This song had a very different quality from the chanting of the girls. Merit's voice was mature and lovely with a deep ka-stirring quality to it. Her voice was soft as she directed it to the infant with sustained notes that gently wrapped the baby in a blanket of celestial vibrations. The room seemed to fill with the music and the walls themselves enhanced and amplified the sound sensations.

Hatasu saw lights around Merit, the way she had seen them around Satamun when she'd done the healing on Kamose. Neferubrity began to smile. When Merit stopped singing, the room seemed to go on humming a while longer. When it stopped, everyone was smiling. The Queen and the children then proceeded with the offerings they had brought. Ahmose laid her gifts of the flower garland on the offering table, Hatasu placed the lotus she brought from the palace pool and Thethi placed the stick soldier he'd brought. A strong young boy from this village, who had been sent back to the boat to get the stela Ahmose had commissioned, brought it forward to be placed in the chapel. This piece of stone art was inscribed with her prayer to her mother for protection of her youngest daughter.

Satamun and Sahte directed the children back toward the village, leaving their mother to her private conversation with her mother in the temple. As they walked back, Sahte explain to the children, "Under the Hyksos, most of the temples of the land had decayed. Not only the buildings themselves but also the traditions and the learning were endangered. What had once been a mighty river of beauty at the time of Mentuhotep became but a small and hidden stream. There were a few great kas that held the traditions and passed them on in secret for the hundred and fifty years of foreign rule. Once the foreigners were expelled, your grandmother fed this small stream with the waters of her vision and her patronage. To renew these gifts of ancient art and beauty, she and your uncle created this place where the magic is safe from any forces that would cause distress to the sacred traditions that are carried on here. Our people make the stone come alive with the beauty that perpetuates the ba of the people and of the Pharaoh. Gradually, more people are being trained in the almost forgotten arts of magic."

Sahte went on, "Queen Nefertari and Pharaoh Amenhotep were generous to us and gave us all we need to live happily as we do this work. It is because of this generosity and foresight that the workers here honor their spirits and made statues of them so they may live forever. Now, Queen Ahmose and Pharaoh Thutmose support and protect us. We are happy people and we praise the goddess."

Ahmose rejoined them and she promised future gifts of rare fresh fruits, extra grains, the finest materials for brushes, paints and chisels. Sahte presented her with a small, but beautifully sculptured, image of the goddess Mersegert; deity of nursing mothers and of the harvest…a favorite goddess of this village.

The small troop departed the village and progressed toward their boat, tired but warmed by the connection with the ancestors, the healing music and the adulation of the people. Neferubrity, oddly enough, was awake and smiling. She was very alert and responsive to Hatasu's chatter and attempts to entertain her.

Thethi began to catch on. He learned how to make 'baby talk' to get her to coo back at him. The baby even offered him one of her rare smiles which went a long way toward warming him to her.

Ahmose smiled her most relaxed smile in weeks. It was a contented group that returned from the secret town. As they neared the palace harbor, Ahmose reminded the children, "Remember, this is secret. Not a word must be breathed of the place or the people we visited today."

The children nodded.

Then, Hatasu asked her mother a question, "Does this mean that the Place of Truth is 'unspeakable', like Sekenenre?"

"Sekenenre is not secret. We speak of him in the Tales of the Ancestors." Her words were sharp, possibly even impatient, that the subject came up again. "He is your great-grandfather and a very important ancestor to remember but there are some things that happened to him that are not spoken of because words bring images to the heart that create disturbance. Be content with that, so you are not disturbed!"

Hatasu again resolved to let thoughts of the 'unspeakable' go. Her mind was filled with the beauty of the art and music from the secret village.

But Thethi did not wish to let the 'unspeakable' go. The secrets of the Place of Truth interested him less than the still-forbidden information about the warrior's story.

As they came down the hill toward the canal where their boat was tied up, they heard some voices to their left. Ahmose's face lit up. "Oh, the gang of workmen is at Thutmose's mortuary Temple. We shall say hello to them and the children can see the artist's magic and what it does of their own family."

After a short walk, they came to a temple with its pylon gate and a limestone wall around it. Hatasu felt the soft north breeze blow warmly against her face as her vision filled with the partially decorated pylon gates. There was the grid of many small squares onto which was being drawn a scene of her father's defeat of the Nubian forces in his war there. A group of artists were standing on a scaffold working on the images.

The small group entered the temple. As they went through the gate, they could see the changes in the pictures there. The structure of this mortuary temple was like that of Ahmose's but the pictures were all of Hatasu's father and the members of her own family. Hatasu and Thethi loved the one of the whole family hunting birds in the papyrus swamp. It was almost completed, just awaiting the addition of this newest offspring. The pictures seemed so real, Hatasu felt she could almost step right into the swamp. There on the boat in the swamp were representations of each person in the family. Their father's large form dominated the scene. He held the throw-stick high over his head with one hand and the other hand grasped the feet of a duck, its wings still flapping. Standing behind him were his wives: First Ahmose and then a smaller figure of Mutnofret. Thutmose's feet were spread in a wide stance. Between these figures was Hatasu, easily identified by her red hair. Wadjmose, Amenmose and Thethi were behind him.

Hatasu felt the sadness of missing Wadj as she looked at his picture. It looked just like him and she wanted to walk into the picture and be with him. The two children stood staring at the picture.

Ahmose came up behind them and put a hand on each one's shoulder. "You see the magic here. Wadj and Mutnofret live forever because of the artist in the Place of Truth."

Chapter 18 - Beginning of the Nile Journey

Neferubrity's relief and calm continued. She became more and more alert and active. Everyone in the palace breathed a sigh of relief and the members of the royal household turned their attention to preparations for the journey to Ankh-Tawy.

It was almost as big a production for the Queen to leave as it had been for the Pharaoh to head off to war with his whole army…at least it seemed that way to Hatasu. There appeared to be an army of servants and they filled many boats. There were not only the usual personal servants for the Queen and the children but also the Queen's favorite kitchen servants, fragrance makers and weavers. Both children wanted to bring their animals, so an animal keeper was needed.

In the two moon-cycles since the Pharaoh and his army left Waset, several messages had arrived from the Pharaoh. Ahmose, though she trusted her scribe, Yuf, made a point of reading these letters herself. Ahmose allowed Hatasu and Thethi to be present and they heard the political as well as personal passages. In his first message, the Pharaoh expressed delight at the birth of his daughter, concern about her health problems and relief at the Queen's smooth delivery. His next messages he acknowledged the improvement in Neferubrity's health but then focused on political matters in Waset. He recommended a formal reminder of the transfer of authority to Satamun, Great God's Wife of Amun, while the Queen was away. He included the personal information that her son, Tao, had petitioned to join the army and Thutmose made him an officer with royal rank.

Hatasu sat at her mother's feet, straining to hear every word. This letter went on, "Be sure to plan adequate time at Abedju, oh Gracious Queen. There is a promising young initiate there and I wish you to see if his talents are as exceptional as reported. Governor Puya of that nome is steadfast in his loyalty and deserves the distinction of fine gifts."

Ahmose smiled and nodded as she read this. "Be alert in the town of Zawty," she continued reading his words. "There are questionable circumstances in need of attention. I assured Governor Djehapy you would give his concerns a fair hearing. The needs of the army kept me from attending to the matter as I would have liked. There are also rumors about irregularities in Itjtawy. I could not tell if there was any substance to these reports. Ineni, Hapu and Nakht will be of good assistance to you in these matters."

Hatasu wondered if she should be worried about things in Zawty and Itjtawy but her father sounded so matter-of-fact and her mother showed no alarm, so the princess assumed there was no real danger for them on their journey.

She delighted in the next part of the letter that told of her father's travels. He apprised the Queen of the position of his army, along with its progress toward Retennu. He informed her they had arrived in good order in the city of Sharuhem. This Asian city, now a frontier out-post of Khemet, had a regular army unit in residence. He sent newsy information about his plan to allow the soldiers to rest there several days as he sent scouts north to determine the disposition of his suzerains. He wrote of his confidence in the

Queen's ability to secure the allegiance of the governors at home for they were as important as the maintenance of respect abroad.

He ended with, "Oh Queen, Mother Goddess, Mut to our people, I wish I were by your side and these were times of peace but things being as they are, I entrust the Two Lands to your protection and your wisdom. The image of your loving eyes gives me confidence that the Two Lands are well cared for in my absence. I send my love to Hatasu, Thethi and little Neferubrity. Amenmose sends his regards."

Amenmose's regards seemed an afterthought. He was probably so busy having fun soldiering that he didn't give the women-folk at home another thought. Hatasu kept this to herself, while she and Thethi went off and practiced with their throw-sticks, both wishing they were as lucky as their brother, far off in Sharuhem with their father.

The preparation for the Queen's journey continued and the cousins huddled together in excitement as they watched dark-skinned, white-kilted workmen fitting the boats to leave. The harbor was a busy place with people scurrying to and from, packing the boats with personal items as well as things needed for the trip.

Hapuseneb pulled Hatasu by the hand, pointing out the wonders being loaded on the boats as gifts for the heads of the nomes they would visit. "Look at that statue of Osiris! I wonder which nome will get that."

"I'll bet it goes to Abedju!" exclaimed Thethi. "But look at the basket of turquoise stones!"

Muscles rippled across the servant's backs as they placed the heavy baskets on the boat deck, arranging them securely and making room for more items. Next came a line of men carrying amphora angled on their right shoulders. Hatasu saw them first. "Look there. I'll bet that's the special wine brought from the Oasis."

"It's a lucky nomarch that gets favored with that as a gift," said Hapuseneb.

"I'll bet those wicker chests have fine linen in them and that would be my favorite gift," said Meryt.

The children skipped along the quay, darting between the workers and the boats that would bear them north. A banquet was held the evening before they departed. The morning they were to leave, Hatasu, Thethi, Hapuseneb, Isis and Meryt were all in high spirits. They gathered at the quay to board their respective ships. Seniseneb and Satamun were at the quay to see them off.

It was hard for Hatasu to leave her grandmother and aunt behind. When Seniseneb embraced Thethi and Hatasu in turn, she pressed them close and clung to each a little longer than expected. Facing the two youngsters again, the children's paternal grandmother mother took off the upper arm bracelets from each of her arms. Bending each bracelet a bit smaller, she gave one to each of her grandchildren. The wonderful design of the Eye of Horus looked back at each of them. "May Horus look over you and protect each of you, my children." Tears were welling up in the old woman's eyes. Hatasu hugged her grandmother closely.

The Queen's public good-bye to Satamun was a public presentation of a staff; the sign of authority, entrusted to her royal sister, the God's Wife of Amun, while the queen was away from Waset. The private farewell between her mother and aunt, that Hatasu witnessed the night before, was much more reflective of the closeness they'd shared over Neferubrity's birth.

When Satamun said farewell to Hatasu, she squatted low to her level; a very unusual thing for her to do. Then to her surprise, her aunt pressed into her hand a small roll of papyrus. She said warmly as a personal confidence, "You will see your cousin, Tao, before I do, for he will return with the army via Ankh-Tawy. Will you bring this to him for me? I know the two of you will like each other." Hatasu felt honored by this task and gave Satamun a warm hug before she walked onto the ship, leaving a smiling Great God's Wife.

Satamun offered a slight formal bow to Thethi. It was a public gesture of farewell. Thethi had come to expect nothing more.

Hatasu turned now toward the Queen Ahmose's ship, 'Hathor Rising'. It was made of fine cedar wood and it had a deckhouse in the middle decorated on either side with twelve thin columns crowned with lotus blossoms. The stern, also shaped like a lotus blossom, rose high in the air and bent forward. Under this was the place for the sailor who steered the ship with a large, long oar used as a rudder.

The prow of the ship came to a long blunt end, upon which was a sheltered seat for the captain. He sat with a long pole in his hand and a keen eye pealed for signs of sand bars, shallows or hidden islands. Both the prow and the stern rose in a way that the captain and the steering crew could communicate with each other. The captain would call directions back to his crew, who would skillfully negotiate the channels.

Five sets of rowers manned the oars on port and starboard. The canvas sails were tied to the boom because they would be of no use until the journey home. The wind always blew from the north, so to travel north, one relied on currents and oars.

It the center part of this ornate and beautiful floating vessel was the throne-chair of the queen. Ahmose stepped on board and took her royal seat under the canopy held up by the brightly colored, lotus topped columns. Hatasu and Thethi followed her on board. They stood on deck waving to those on shore, blowing kisses, calling good-bye. Hatasu had Chi-chi on a leash and the monkey chattered loudly in the direction of shore. The rowers skillfully moved the boat forward and she could feel the water under them as the boat slipped through the canal that connected the palace-lake with the river.

Once on the river, the breeze blew against her face as the current carried them forward with increasing speed. Two herald-boats, be-flowered and emitting the sounds of frame drums and nays, led the way. The Queen's boat followed and then the boats of the noble families like Ineni and Hapu. Trailing behind were the many smaller boats of servants, supplies and gifts.

In the early morning light, Hatasu watched as the river moved them in the direction of the rising sun. She looked back again and could still see the proud figure of her aunt and the more bent figure of her grandmother standing at the shore growing smaller and smaller. Finally, even the tall temple flags of the Temple of Amun faded into the distance. In the far distance, she could make out the farmers' mud-brick homes at the edge of the flood land, back where the waters met the desert and mountains.

The flow of the water could be felt beneath the creaking wood of the boat. The current was still strong from the inundation and it carried them toward the north at a cheerful pace. It was the middle of the month of Koiak and the river was returning to its banks. All that could be seen was the expanse of brown earthy mud stretching over the emerging fields on either side of the river. The outline of the fields and the pattern of the canals were re-emerging. Creation was again coming forth from undifferentiated Nun.

Hatasu found this journey oh-so exciting. She had been on papyrus skiffs for family picnics in the marshes and on ceremonial boats to cross to the tombs on the West Bank but she had never been on a traveling boat, at least, not that she could remember.

Wadjmose and Amenmose each had told her stories of the northern lands. They spoke of the remains of great temple cities to the west of their palace at Ankh-Tawy. They described gigantic pyramids; buildings whose points reached like a stairway to the heavens. They also told her of the great stone statue of the Sphinx, with the body of a lion and the head of a Pharaoh. Paheri told both children of Abedju and how fortunate they were to be visiting that sacred place of pilgrimage.

While she loved the promise of adventure, mostly she longed to relieve the constant ache of missing her father. It felt like she was going to meet him and that thought made her heart beat faster in anticipation. Her mother warned her it would be a long trip. There were many nomes that must be visited along the way, many nome governors whose allegiance must be attended to. Hatasu comforted herself with her regular nighttime dreams of her father and her daytime activities were calculated to make him proud of her.

By midday, the river bent again and they sailed into the afternoon sun, past the town of Naqada where lining the banks of the river, groups of people waived brightly colored cloths and called out praises to the Queen and Pharaoh. The Queen and children waved back. Hatasu amused herself with her monkey and Thethi curled up and took a nap with his puppy. Hatasu settled into a long day on the boat.

In the afternoon, the river turned north again toward the breeze and soon it was crowded with boats. They were approaching the sacred nome of Abedju. There the children could see in the distance the large bustling temple town. The main town of the large ancient center spread across the western bank in front of the mountains and stretched beyond the cultivated land. The land had emerged around it; rich, dark black, waiting now for Ra to liberate it from the moisture that delayed the plowing and planting. The network of canals and irrigation ditches were in plain sight.

Hatasu and Thethi were sitting eagerly at the prow of the boat and the Queen joined them as the boat sailed past a large pyramid, a brightly colored temple and a cluster of low brick structures. Standing on deck with a hand on each of the children's shoulders, the Queen explained to them about what they were viewing. "Abedju," she said removing her arm from Thethi's shoulder and extending it to indicate the entire area of this west bank, "is the sacred city where Pharaohs have built their temples and tombs since long ago, before the Two Lands were united. We will stay at the royal mooring palace here at Abedju, a comfortable residence, for the duration of the planting festival."

Both children looked to the busy harbor and town before them. Flags were waving and the wind carried the faint sound of music as though the festival had already begun. Chi-chi, high on the mast, chattered away and Behka lay peacefully at Thethi's feet.

Puya, the Governor of Abedju, and his family were at the harbor lake to greet and welcome the royal family when the Queen's boats pulled up. Puya was a large man by comparison to others in the Two Lands. He was tall with expansive shoulders and a slightly bulging abdomen that hung over his kilt. He seemed to move with the same ponderous slowness as the sacred animal of Osiris, the bull. His face was thoughtful and his bovine-like eyes were peaceful and intelligent. He was not only the governor of this nome but also the high priest of Osiris so his head was shaved and the great leopard-skin robe of official occasions draped over his huge shoulders.

His wife, Neferiah, stood next to him. She was as tiny as he was large. She was almost two heads shorter than her husband and so lithe and thin she appeared to be a child, belying the importance of her role as mistress of her house. With bright, alert eyes, energy radiated from her body and her face shone with friendly anticipation at entertaining the royal family. Her dress was of finest linen and her necklace of gold.

Puya and Neferiah had two sons. The oldest, Ti, commanded a

unit in the Pharaoh's army but the younger son, Puyemre, stood next to his parents. Evidence of his youth-lock remained in the cut of his hair. He wore the kilt of the young adult but looked as though he would be more comfortable in the unencumbered freedom of his unclad years. He looked twelve or thirteen years old. His height was between that of his father and mother. He had the large, deep eyes of his father and the agile body of his mother. Under his arm was tucked the nay, a reed instrument.

His eyes followed Hatasu with intense focus, a look of surprised recognition. Most people lowered their eyes when introduced to royalty. Puyemre didn't but Hatasu wasn't offended. She liked that he looked at her and smiled.

The governor's family had their large black dog with them. He was on a leash held by Puyemre. He sat beside his waiting masters with canine beauty and alert and calm dignity. Perhaps the dog felt his young master's shock at seeing the red-haired princess. Perhaps he spotted the royal pets, Chi-chi or Behka. Whatever it was, he let out a series of sudden, unexpected barks.

Before Puyemre could quiet him, Behka responded with high-pitched puppy barks. Chi-chi became excited by the noise and frantically climbed down from her perch on the mast and onto Hatasu's shoulder. Thethi and Paheri's attention turned to calming Behka while Hatasu and Sitre tried to sooth Chi-chi. Chattering in a scolding manner, the small monkey clung all the more tenaciously to her mistress's head. Sitre tried to help Hatasu disengage the creature but Chi-chi clung on resolutely. Hatasu's red hair had been neatly tamed into its braid but the monkey's shenanigans completely disarranged it. Strands of fiery red burst forth all over her head. The two of them were a tangled mess.

Rather than being upset, Hatasu found her pet's behavior amusing and she laughed as she tried to disentangle him. It wasn't until Paheri came to their assistance that Hatasu was freed, the monkey was calmed and the royal group returned to some semblance of order. As they disembarked, Paheri had Chi-chi, Sitre had Behka and the Queen had the hands of Hatasu and Thethi.

Hatasu, with a halo of flaming hair, managed to walk ashore with playful dignity. Hatasu was vaguely aware that she looked like quite a spectacle for she could see the young Puyemre looked at her with a bit of shock and a lot of awe. With a smile still on the face of the prince of Abedju, he stepped forward to greet the royal family with grand bouquets of flowers. Never taking his eyes off Hatasu's amazing hair, Puyemre took his nay and played a lovely tune in honor or their arrival. It was then that Hatasu first noticed the ring he wore on his left hand. It was a turquoise colored image of a scarab beetle set in gold. As she watched his fingers move to produce the notes on his instrument, Hatasu wondered why he wore such a ring.

Once official introductions had been arranged, the governor's family accompanied the royal guests to the Abedju palace built by Pharaoh Thutmose. Puyemre seemed both eager and shy at meeting Hatasu. He hung back, reticent, as his parents exchanged formalities with the Queen.

Hatasu looked about as she entered. The palace was fairly large and quite comfortable. It had a lovely garden with lotus pools, sycamore trees and apartments for dignitaries visiting the town for the sacred festival. Hapu and Ineni's family had already arrived and the cousins were pleased to be reunited. This added to the feeling of comfort.

Puyemre and his family left the newcomers to allow them to settle in and freshen up for the banquet that evening in their honor. The banquet included finely-cooked, roasted and stuffed pigeon, delicious bread and vegetables preserved from last year's harvest. Dignitaries from Abedju and neighboring towns were crowded into Puya's dining hall and spread out into the garden.

The Queen stood and spoke graciously to the gathering, praising the upcoming festival of Osiris and extolling the greatness of Pharaoh Thutmose. She promised he would return from this war with safety, glory and riches for the people of Abedju as well as for the Two Lands. The Queen commended this nome for its support of the Pharaoh's military mission, acknowledging their soldier-sons who were fighting with the Pharaoh in the Levant to overcome the vile serpent Apophis, now in the form of the Amurru.

She presented Governor Puya and this nome with the fine diorite statue of Osiris the children had guessed was for here. There were many bows to the queen in gratitude for such a gift. Ahmose went on to say she was also glad to report the military expedition was going smoothly. The army had left Sharuhem and come to the walled city of Jericho where they were met with the respect due from their suzerain.

Throughout the banquet, Hatasu noticed that Puyemre was staring at her...or more precisely, at her hair. Now, she knew all too well that her hair was an oddity but she didn't like anyone to draw attention to it. Whatever the reason for his staring, she wanted it to stop. After the meal, she stood up and walked over to him. As she approached, she could tell he was flustered and his face grew red.

Before she could blurt out her complaint, he took a step toward her and said softly and clearly, "My deepest apologies to you, Princess. I did not mean to be rude to you by staring at your hair. I hope you will not find it impertinent if I tell you the true reason for my offensive eyes." He paused as she cocked her head, curious about his meaning. He took this silence as an indication to continue. "I have had several dreams in which a red-haired person led me on a path to a place I wished to go. I have never before seen anyone with red hair. It was like you stepped right out of my dream and into my life and that shocked me. Please forgive me, Princess and I will confine my willful eyes."

A smile formed on her face. At least he was not acting like her brother Amenmose. She would not argue with dreams. She decided to use his contriteness to satisfy another of her own curiosities. She responded, "I'll forgive you but in exchange, you must tell me about your ring."

He stepped back a bit and involuntarily touched the glazed steatite scarab on his finger. A momentary panic came into his eyes as though she asked him something he was forbidden to disclose. "This was given to me by my father when I entered the House of Life as a neophyte. It reminds me to make choices that benefit the building of the temple of my akh rather than my worldly or selfish gains." He paused, looking worried. With hesitation, he said, "I fear that even speaking of such a secret thing might be contrary to my progress."

Impressed but unsatisfied, Hatasu ignored his concern and asked, "What do you mean, 'building the temple of your akh'?"

"It is through learning the Greater Mysteries that we develop and unite the ba, the ka and the akh; building and perfecting the spiritual temple of our bodies through living worthy lives. The rituals and festivals, the Lesser Mysteries, are for everyone. The Greater Mysteries are only for those who are willing to tread a more difficult path in order to journey from the darkness of ignorance to the light of wisdom." Then he looked very flustered and said quickly as he nearly ran from her, "I've said too much. Please don't tell anyone I've told you this."

Chapter 19 - Abedju

The next morning, Hatasu planned to ask her mother about Greater and Lesser Mysteries, bodies as temples and scarab rings. She figured she just wouldn't let her mother know where she got the ideas but her mother left no time for questions. She was intent on giving out specific instructions for Hatasu and Thethi for their stay at Abedju. "There are private rituals here that will take all my attention. I will be involved with this day and night for the month we are here."

Hatasu and Thethi looked at her with some alarm in their faces. She smiled reassuringly. "You will enjoy the public festivals. There are two of them; the enactment of Osiris' story and the First Planting Festival. Sitre and Paheri will look after your needs in the mooring palace, the young nobleman, Puyemre, will show you around this nome and help you at the time of the public festivals." She paused then and looked excited about the next news. "And…you will each start your classes in the Abedju House of Life. I have arranged for the master teacher, Rekh, to begin teaching you hieroglyphics, 'The God's Words'."

Hatasu's eyes lit up. "I will finally learn the magic on the walls of the temples?"

"Yes, My Dear, you will be taking the first steps in that direction."

Thethi complained, "You mean I'll have to sit still at the temple all day."

Ahmose raised her eyebrows and tilted her head toward him.

"Yes, it is an honor to study in this House of Life."

Thethi grumbled and kicked the dirt at his feet.

While Hatasu was happy about the House of Life, she was still concerned at what her mother said about being unavailable to them in this strange city. Sitre, Paheri and Puyemre were only some comfort. "But Mother, what is so important at the temple? In Waset you go to the temple but we still see you every day."

"This time of the year, Abedju is the place of one of the most sacred rituals of initiation. It is very strenuous for those that have earned the privilege to participate. Those that successfully emerge from this ordeal are empowered with the skills that connect our Two Lands to the Great Above. These people are very important for the wellbeing of the kingdom. It takes a full moon to accomplish it and your father and I agree that no effort be spared to assure the success of the young men and women with kas gifted in the learning of the sacred sciences.

During the years of Hyksos rule, these rituals could only be conducted with great risk of discovery and death, and so the training in the ancient wisdom almost died out. When Ahmose, the Liberator, took the Double Crown there were few people who knew the wisdom taught by the ancients. The greatness of your father's reign, and of Amenmose reign, is dependent on the cultivation of this knowledge, so my participation is very important. Between Sitre, Paheri, Puyemre and Rekh, you will be in good hands. After the final ritual, we will continue on our way toward Ankh-Tawy together."

Thethi, still pouting about the temple school, now looked around the strange palace. With the Queen's talk of leaving them, an alarmed look spread across his face and he started to cough.

"Come now, Thethi, it will be okay." Ahmose tried to cajole him into this plan but no relief lightened his face. Ahmose sighed, "If you really feel you are not ready for the House of Life then it is not right for you to go. You can consider it again when we get to Ankh-Tawy."

Thethi's face lightened. "Can I practice the throw-stick with Paheri?"

"Yes," she said. "Go ahead and find Paheri and let him know the change of plans."

Once he'd left, the Queen turned to Hatasu. Smiling, she said, "The House of Life is a privilege for those who want it."

"I do want it, Mother."

"Well then, tomorrow is an important day for you. I will go with you as you start your new life as a student."

Hatasu was pleased. She would miss seeing her mother, of course, but the idea of finally attending the House of Life and learning like her older cousins Meryt and Hapuseneb was exciting to her. She was also pleased that Puyemre would show them around. She rather liked this older boy with the scarab ring and his secret information. Maybe he would even tell her more about the Mysteries. "What is the enactment you said would happen?"

"This festival for Osiris is celebrated by the entire town, acting out the events of his story over five days."

"Will you be there?"

"Yes, but even then I will be there in my ritual role. I will be back to being your mother once both the festivals is over."

That evening she wondered about what her mother was going to be doing and she also wondered about Thethi not wanting to start school. He'd been her companion in most things, so it would be strange to do this without him but certainly his reluctance didn't hold her back.

The next morning, her mother greeted her with, "Are *you* ready for this new life as a student?"

"Oh yes, I am ready!" Hatasu replied quickly.

"You, too, can wait until Ankh-Tawy if you wish."

"No, no, I want to go to the House of Life."

Accompanied by Ahmose, Hatasu walked the short distance to the main temple of Osiris. As she came up to it, the princess saw it had the same structure as other temples. They approached the mud-brick walls and walked through the towering pylon gates with colored flags flapping in the north breeze. At the far end of the courtyard, she could see two statues of the god Osiris flanking the entrance to the inner temple. Each stood tall, like the Osirian statues at the temples of Mentuhotep, with the Double Crown of kingship reaching toward the sky. The mummified body stood, his arms holding the crook and flail folded across his chest. The long, curved beard of a god extended from his chin and his face was the color green of new vegetation.

The entrance pathway divided the courtyard in two, a round pool on each side. The tent-covered pavilions of the House of Life classes lined the side walls of this courtyard. Rekh, the teacher-priest, read a script written on a whitewashed board in front of the would-be scribes. The young students sat poised to copy the script onto the ostrakas (shards of broken pottery for writing) on their laps.

The teacher read aloud, using a rod to circle each word's representations as he read, "'Great are the advantages reserved for the scribe, the ones who tread the path of the gods. They will spend all their lives in joy, richer than their peers'.'" The teacher stepped back from the board and addressed the pupils, "These are the words of a text of ancient wisdom. Learn each word's meaning as well as its letters." He then left his students sitting cross-legged in the shade of the tent and walked toward the Queen with a smile of greeting on his face.

He was dressed humbly with the shaved head and simple white kilt of a priest. His mouth was thin as if he had no lips. His eyes held Hatasu spellbound. They were gray with dark specks. The intense focus of his eyes set him apart from more common men. Then she noticed his hand and the ring he wore. It was like Puyemre's, only larger.

As Rekh approached, he bowed low before the Queen, saying, "I am honored to teach the daughter of the royal family in our House of Life. I understood the young prince would join us as well."

"The princess is you sole student. The prince is not ready for the House of Life, yet."

Rekh nodded acknowledgement then he turned to Hatasu whose eyes and ears were wide with wonder and excitement. "Seba Hatasu," he asked, "are you prepared to embark on this journey?"

She answered simply, "Yes, Honored Teacher."

He repeated, "Are you willing to embark on this path of learning that will require you to turn from idle pleasures to disciplined study?"

This requirement sounded more difficult. Her mind darted to Thethi's freedom, playing with the throw-stick, but it was only a momentary doubt. She was truly anxious to begin her learning. "Yes, I am willing," she replied.

He asked her again, this time his tone serious enough to give her another pause. "Are you ready to die to your childhood ways of ignorance, to be born again to the ways of the wisdom of Thoth?"

Hatasu looked to her mother who did not seem alarmed by this strange question and gave her daughter no other indication of how to answer. Hatasu faced the teacher and replied, "I am ready to do what I must to grow in wisdom and understanding."

The adults smiled and nodded. Her new teacher said, "You will call me Sebai (teacher). You have just passed the first test."

She looked to her mother, who was smiling at her. "You have made a good start. I must go now. Learn well from Rekh." She hugged her mother tightly, knowing she wouldn't see her for a full moon's length of time.

The teacher formally bowed to the Queen as she left the temple courtyard. Sebai turned to Hatasu. "The next step is to purify yourself in the temple pool." Rekh proceeded to one of the temple pools. "Each time one enters the temple, one must purify oneself here."

Accustomed to bathing in the garden pool at the palace, Hatasu stepped into the water unencumbered by any linen dress and she easily submerged her naked body into the purifying pool. She stepped out onto the dry mud-brick of the courtyard, the drops of water beading on her brown skin. She looked to Sebai Rekh.

"Next, you will learn to use your instruments of writing and set up your place to study."

She looked toward the other students who were under two separate tents. For the first time, she became aware that they all had been watching her. Puyemre was among a group. She knew they'd be looking at her hair and she felt a slight dread of dealing with their questions or teasing.

It became clear, however, Sebai Rekh did not allow for such foolishness. He simply announced that she was a new student, her name was Hatasu. She nodded and smiled at the other students. Her new Sebai took Hatasu to a side area in the canopied enclosure and there she saw a reed mat on the floor with a set of a scribe's equipment laid neatly in a corner of it. There in the center was a scribe's palette…for her! It was a narrow, rectangular piece of wood with a central longitudinal slot in which reed pens were kept. Two round depressions were at one end holding blocks of black and red ink. Several medium-sized reeds were resting on the mat near the box along with a small bowl, a flint blade, a piece of sandstone and a small bag with a drawstring.

Noticing the light dancing in Hatasu's eyes, Rekh interjected, "I see you are excited and eager to use the palette but discipline is a very important part of your learning. You must be patient. First, you will learn the proper way to sit for your studies."

Definitely not feeling patient, Hatasu quickly folded her legs into the position in which she had seen scribes sitting all of her life.

Rekh smiled, and said, "All right, the next step is to understand that writing is about words and language, the gift of Thoth, the god of wisdom. Words and sounds have power. By writing these sounds, we capture the power. It is important to honor them and learn with precision."

Anxiously eyeing the palette, Hatasu swiftly answered, "Yes."

"Okay then," Rekh said, "these are to be your tools for writing. You see the reed? That is your pen." He took the flint knife, cut the end evenly, and put it to his mouth to chew it into a brush end. "This is how you make a simple river reed into an instrument of writing." He took a second reed and handed it to Hatasu to chew.

Following her teacher's example, she soon had her first instrument for writing.

Rekh went on, "This bowl is for the water you need to wet the paints so they come alive."

She dipped the brush she had made into the water and then rubbed it on the block of black paint in the palette case. Hatasu watched with growing impatience as Rekh then drew a dot on an ostraka. Her tutor then nodded for her to do it. Hatasu drew a great fat swirling line. She looked back at her teacher, very pleased with herself, but Rekh was frowning and shaking his head.

"We start with a dot," he said. "The dot is the center, the beginning, the creator. You must not run ahead of yourself. Now, here, take this piece of sandstone. It will erase your mistakes. This is an important part of your equipment, for learning entails many mistakes."

Hatasu frowned. Her excitement about using the reed overcame her reticence with this new teacher. "I like my swirl," she said. "It was fun to draw. I don't think it is a mistake."

"Then we will stop our lesson for today, until you are willing to abide by the discipline of your studies." Sebai collected the materials and stood up to leave.

Shocked and horrified at such a prospect, Hatasu said quickly, "No, no, Sebai! I'll erase it and do the dot." Hatasu took the sandstone and quickly rubbed it against the beautiful swirling line until it was just a shadow.

Sebai Rekh put the materials back down on the mat and said, "Okay then, draw the dot and concentrate all your energy into that one spot, for it is the beginning and the end...the navel of the world."

Hatasu looked at her teacher carefully. The navel of the world sounded a whole lot more worthwhile than just a dot. She made her first dot. She was instructed to work on these 'navels', which she did...fat ones, tiny ones, ones with lots of paint and ones with very watery paint.

Next, Sebai instructed her to draw on lines...again, all kinds of lines. Finally, he said to draw circles.

As she was working, Hatasu saw Puyemre doing his writing. She also saw other students staring and pointing at her hair. She pretended not to notice but Puyemre stepped up and told them to stop. They laughed at him but he didn't back down. Hatasu smiled at him across the distance of the courtyard and he smiled back.

When it was time to stop, Sebai Rekh said to Hatasu, "You have begun your journey in the House of Life. You are now a 'seba', meaning, 'student'. I will show you the temple hieroglyphs for 'seba' but then you must learn the practical writing before you begin learning this sacred language."

Taking the stylus and an ostraka, he drew first a roll of papyrus, then above it a five-armed star and finally a loaf of bread. "This is a scroll that you will learn to read. This is a loaf of bread, for knowledge will feed your spirit. This is a star, the light within you that learning enables you to shine forth. Lack of knowledge is ignorance and that is darkness. Knowledge illuminates and brings us to the truth of Maat. Today, you began your journey."

With that, Hatasu put the stylus in the palette and she placed the stone, flint and bowl into the drawstring bag. Student and teacher rolled up their mats and put them on shelves against the wall, ready to be reclaimed for the next day's work. She returned to the mooring palace with Sitre, bubbling over with all the newness of the school. She really missed her mother. She was the one she most wanted to tell about it.

Thethi was not interested and wanted to tell her about his adventures with the throw-stick. It was Hapuseneb and Meryt, who'd started at the House of Life in Waset, who most understood. Puyemre also listened to her excitement. He came in the late afternoon and guided the royal cousins around the Abedju nome.

She fell into the schedule like the other students who started their days with purification, chants and dance exercises. Hatasu gradually learned the combination of sounds and tones that made up the songs to the gods chanted each morning. Her body became accustomed to the movements and positions of the gods and goddesses shown on the temple walls. She would then settle herself on her mat to complete her assignment.

The next day, Sebai Rekh explained, "The writing you must learn first is a short-hand version of the temple writing. It is used in everyday documents like letters, inventories and contracts. It takes up less space and is quicker to write. You must know this type of writing before you go on to learn the sacred language of the temples."

"You mean I am going to have to learn how to write short-hand first and then learn how to write all over again? As a princess, can't I learn to read and write the sacred words first?"

Rekh's frown deepened in disapproval. "No," he said, "you must be patient like everyone else and learn in stages." In a crisp, firm voice, he continued, "Knowing the script writing is important for a Queen. A wise Queen, like your mother, reads reports for herself and does not rely solely on servants and scribes who can misinform either by ignorance or intention."

Hatasu thought about her mother's wisdom and the letters from her father that Ahmose read, herself. She started learning and practicing the strange squiggle Sebai identified with sounds. She practiced the letters and sounds Seba taught but she was often distracted by what the older students were doing.

Puyemre was in the group of more advanced students. Each morning, Rekh stood at the white board with writing on it for the older students to copy. It looked like a lot of scraggly lines to Hatasu; not at all like the sacred writing on the walls of the temples.

She focused her attention back on her lessons for she longed to be able to read and write the way Puyemre and the older students could.

This first part of the time in Abedju passed pleasantly, even though Hatasu's mother was unavailable. Each day had an established rhythm. Mornings were spent at the temple with Rekh and afternoons with Thethi and Neferubrity. Neferubrity was smiling often now and making cooing sounds. Hatasu sang her songs and brought her pretty and bright things to hold in her little hand, and chew on.

Hatasu, Thethi and the cousins continued playing warrior games and practicing with throw-sticks. At night, the princess dreamed of her father. Puyemre occasionally joined the troupe of royal cousins and entertained them with anything from rides on his father's donkey, to fishing trips in his boat, to tours of the ancient cenotaphs of long-ago Pharaohs. He and Hapuseneb became particularly good friends. Together they built, from reeds and string, traps for small animals and cages to keep them in. Puyemre measured things very carefully and Hapuseneb seemed to be the only one of his friends to have the patience and perseverance to join him in this task.

There came a day that stood out in Hatasu's mind. Rekh read what he'd written on the board for the older students to copy before they began their assignment as he always did. She listened with her usual curiosity. "Do not become arrogant because of your knowledge and do not think you know everything," he said. "Take advice from the ignorant as well as from the wise, for you can never know all there is to know." Rekh emphasized the placement of each of the letters then left the novices to their task.

Hatasu returned her own attention to her letter practice. When the morning's lesson was over, Rekh took his red paint and made corrections to both her letters and his older students' writing. This one particular day, Puyemre had many red marks. Sebai Rekh finished correcting the governor's son's writing and said, "This is too many mistakes for you, Puyemre. I am wondering if you are a boy with ears on your back, hearing only when you are beaten." He took the rod with which he had been pointing to the letters as he'd read them and raised it as though to hit Puyemre across the back. The governor's son stiffened his body. Rekh lowered the stick without hitting him, and said to him simply, "Pay better attention tomorrow."

Hatasu knew this must have been very embarrassing for her friend but she didn't want to embarrass him further by saying anything. That afternoon, she meandered in the direction of the governor's palace. A broad path went from the palace down to the Nile. Reaching out into the river were quays where many boats were tied. Hatasu could see a lone figure sitting on the bank staring out at the river. She ventured down the path that traveled through some papyrus thickets. Sounds of birds and frogs surrounded her and grew louder as she moved toward the river.

There, looking thoughtfully across the moving water, was Puyemre. She squatted beside him. "Wow! What noisy frogs you have here at Abedju! My brother, Wadjmose, taught me to hunt and catch frogs. He said the best time to catch them was when the Nile first starts to rise, but it sounds like you have plenty of frogs as the river returns to its banks, also."

"Yes, certainly frogs are something we always have an abundance of," he said absentmindedly.

"Do you know how to hunt them?" she persisted.

"Certainly."

"Well, would you help me? I'd like to be able to draw animals and I should like to see a real frog to draw it tomorrow."

For the first time, Puyemre cracked a smile and showed some enthusiasm. "I could do that. We could use my reed boat. It is right here. I could take you into the papyrus thicket. You shall see all the frogs you wish."

The boat was made of reeds tied together with a flat place large enough for her to sit and him to stand as he poled the boat along the shallow marsh. The flat reed surface was drawn up at each end, prow and stern. She sat back on her knees as Puyemre poled the skiff forward into a pathway through the papyrus growth that was freshly recovered from the floodwaters. This was just how Wadjmose had taken her frog hunting in Waset. It made her feel both excited and sad. "You will see many frogs but I know a place where a grand old bullfrog lives. We'll be able to find him by his song."

As they moved through the water path next to the long thin stems of papyrus, ducks could be heard, then seen, as the children's presence disturbed the birds into flight. The great, throaty call of the bullfrog grew nearer and nearer as they moved through the water. They came to a muddy sandbar. As they approached, the "ke...rer" sound of the Nile frog was a commanding presence.

Puyemre motioned to her to be still as they glided around an island of mud. There, they saw many frogs stationed on the shady bank. In the center of them all was a large, fat frog with a deep, throaty croak. As his song rang out, she could see his throat extend and flatten. Suddenly, to her surprise, he opened his mouth, extended a long, curled tongue, captured a dragonfly with it, and drew the tongue and bug into his mouth. Startled by this sudden action, Hatasu jumped. Her movement startled the frog that, just as suddenly, jumped into the water and disappeared beneath the surface into the underwater stalks of papyrus.

Puyemre laughed. "You've never seen a frog catch his dinner before?"

She laughed, too. Splash…splash…plunk…plunk! One frog after another escaped into the cool Nile mud. As they headed back to the quay, Puyemre caught a large frog and handed it to her. She held it carefully in two hands, feeling its slippery body pulse in time with its tiny heartbeat. She studied the frog, noting the shape of its head, the curve of its hind legs, the proportions of its body, and the shades of color in its skin. She was preparing to draw a perfect frog the next day with her stylus and ostraka. She insisted upon catching another one by herself and in doing so almost fell into the muddy water. Their laughter mingled with the sounds of the frogs, the ducks and the wind through the thickets.

She wanted to take the frogs home but Puyemre discouraged her, saying they were happier by the river where they had water, mud and bugs. "Unless you have a way to give them these things, it is more respectful to Heket, the frog goddess, to leave them here."

Hatasu remembered when Wadjmose used to tell her the same thing. On the ride home, each of them seemed lost in thought. Hatasu's quiet was related to her nostalgic feelings of missing her brother.

Puyemre abruptly broke the silence, "I usually do my studies very carefully!" He shook his head. "During today's lesson, I did not do well because I was very busy in an argument with myself. I did not like what we were told to write. I *do* want to know *everything!* The wise teacher Ptahhotep says that is arrogance. The opposite of arrogance is humility and it was an embarrassing lesson to learn today."

"I thought Rekh was mean to you."

"Not really, Hatasu. It is as important to learn virtue as it is to learn script. Without virtue, I would not be ready for the next initiation. My father says the discipline of virtue is essential for the building of the temple of the akh."

The next day, Hatasu was enthusiastic about drawing her frog and showed Sebai. He looked at her illustration with close attention then said, "You have observed the Nile frog well. Would you like to see the way a frog is drawn in hieroglyphs?"

"Yes, indeed!"

He made several red marks over her black lines. She had to admit the frog looked more realistic with his changes. He just smiled at her and moved on to start the day at the board, writing out the lesson for the older students. He had Puyemre read it aloud. "Consider how badly things fare for those with the careers of farmers, soldiers, bakers and gardeners. But not so with the scribe who directs the work of all these people. For him, there are no taxes, because he pays his tribute in writing. Take heed of this! Learning to be a scribe is worth all the hard work."

Hatasu noted, also, that Puyemre went right to work, although not before he shot her a sideways smile. She went back to copying her letters and Rekh again came around to see her work and again he used his red ink to correct the hieratic letters she made. Puyemre's copying met with Rekh's approval that day.

Each day after school now, Hatasu spent time with Puyemre and Hapuseneb; sometimes drawing, sometimes making boxes or make-believe villages out of small stones. On one of these days, Puyemre called their attention to how the fields gradually were emerging from the flood. They were still oozy wet with black mud and it would be a while before they were ready for planting. "Soon, it will be time for the Passion Play of Osiris. It's really the best part of the year," he told Hatasu. "This is five days that everyone takes part in. I think you will really like it."

The day before the festival enactment was to begin, Sebai Rekh stood at the head of the small group so as to instruct his seba (students) on their role in the enactment. "Tonight the moon is dark. It seems to die," he started. "This new moon of the planting month is the time to commemorate the death of Osiris and the planting of the seed." Rekh turned to the children from Waset. "Do you know the story of Osiris?"

Hatasu answered, "Yes, of course. He was the great ruler and leader of the people. We celebrate him on the first Epagomenal Days."

"Yes, indeed, he was our greatest ruler but in these five days we remember that he was killed by his brother Set and his son Horus fought with both his wits and this arms to win the land of his father back from his uncle." Rekh went on. "In this festival of Osiris, he dies like the seeds we plant in the earth each spring; the tribunal of the gods pass judgment on his killer and Horus does battle with Set to establish his rulership and re-establish Maat. The community acts out Osiris's story as a sacred play in the temple square and on the streets. You will play your parts, right along with everyone else." He looked at the upturned faces of the children. "You will each have a guide to help you."

What fun to be part of this! Hatasu and Thethi had Puyemre to help them which pleased Hatasu even more. The next morning, Hatasu and Thethi met Puyemre at the temple and he led them toward the village where the townsfolk were already at a peak of excitement in the courtyard. Market stalls offered sweets and delicacies to eat. The adults were dressed in their finest clothes and perfumed oils. Puyemre pointed out to the children that these people were already playing their roles, participating in the banquet Set gave for his brother when he planned to trap him in the jeweled chest.

Next, the crowd of people parted to make way as temple priests carried an ornate wooden chest in the direction of the river. Hatasu was pushed and jostled along by the agitated crowd moving toward the Nile.

Pulling on Puyemre's arm, Hatasu managed to ask, "Is that Osiris?"

Puyemre answered with a simple, "Yes," as he, himself, was getting caught up in the passion all around him. "Come," he cried, "we must keep them from dumping the chest with Osiris in the river! His brother Set has tricked him and locked him in that box."

At that moment, it was real to Hatasu that Osiris was caught in the chest and she *must* keep the chest from being dumped in the river. Two groups formed, one representing the forces of Light and Horus, Osiris' son, and the other the forces of Darkness and Set, the slayer of the god. If the conspirators reached the river Osiris would be carried away to his death, yet again. Hatasu and Thethi stayed close to Puyemre and the three of them were swept toward the river with the crowd. She joined with a group of men who struggled with the priest-actors, trying to deter them from the death of their god. She pulled on the conspirators, trying to free the chest from their grasp. In spite of the opposition, Set's men reached the river and with a great flourish of strength, they threw the chest into the water.

Helpless, Hatasu watched it be carried away by the river current. She felt a terrible void in her body. The whole crowd became silence. The chest floated down the river. Then…everyone shifted from their roles in the struggle for Osiris into their roles as mourners for their god-king. Women let out loud, sad cries. They tore at their hair and covered themselves with dirt. Men, women and children displayed the wild abandon of grief. The sound of the drums and the sistrums were slow and mournful as the people dragged themselves from the river and back to the village.

That night, Hatasu cried herself to sleep. She cried for the death of Osiris, she cried for the death of Wadjmose and she cried for her absent father. She even cried a little for missing Seniseneb and Satamun, who were still back in Waset. She wished her mother was there to comfort her but it was Sitre who held her and stroked her red hair until she fell asleep.,

The next day was designated a day of mourning for Osiris. The courtyard was filled with people singing out sorrowful chants and expressing all their unspent grief of the past year. Hatasu's mother, the Queen, and Puyemre's mother, the governor's wife, played the roles of Isis and Nephthys, leading the people in their mourning. She was glad to see her mother but there was no opportunity to be near or talk to her. She looked instead for an opportunity to ask Puyemre more about the Greater Mysteries and the Lesser Mysteries. He seemed to be deliberately avoiding the topic.

The third day of this festival was the enactment of the tribunal of Set before the gods, charging him with the killing of his brother Osiris. The crowd gathered this time in the first courtyard of the temple. The Queen, Puya, Hapu and other officials sat on the dais as members of the tribunal.

One wore the headdress of the Set-animal. He presented his case. "I am the rightful ruler." Set stood unbowed before the tribunal. "The kingdom is rightfully mine as the son of Nut and Geb, (sky and earth). It was unjust that they gave the leadership to Osiris in the first place." Set went on, "The land should be mine, because I am the strongest and 'might makes right'."

The tribunal argued, "No, no, you are unfit to rule because you plotted and killed your brother, Osiris."

Everyone on the tribunal agreed but Set responded, "There must

be a battle to determine the winner. The strongest shall be ruler!"
The tribunal agreed to this.

The crowd called out, arguing against Set and championing their
beloved Osiris. Hatasu heard Puyemre call out a heated rebuttal,
"Down with Set. Horus is the true ruler of our hearts."

Puya, leading the forces of Horus, called out, "We will battle
with all our strength to overcome Set and establish Horus. It is in
that way, we return Osiris to his rightful place as ruler of the
underworld."

The whole town was ready for the battle the next day. That night
in the palace, Thethi, Meryt, Hapuseneb and Isis each spoke with
vehemence and personal indignation. They agreed that they would
do battle for Osiris. Each was in fighting mode, well prepared from
warrior games. Hatasu reclaimed her identity as a Sekhmet warrior,
and remembered Isis's heroic defense of Horus against the
hippopotamus. On this fourth day, they were ready!

When Puyemre came to the palace to get them, he was visibly
taken aback when he saw Hatasu's uncharacteristically tough
demeanor…even though he, himself, was in battle mode. Once at
the temple courtyard, the priest and older students were put in
strategic places to choreograph the battle. Wrestling was allowed
but no blows. Puyemre showed Hatasu and Thethi how to pretend
fight.

The priestesses played music to set and temper the mood. Drums
kept the feeling high, though the flute softened the intensity. Hatasu
was matched with girls about her size. She'd never wrestled before
but she caught on quickly to the holds and bested one opponent

after another.

As lots were drawn to play Set, so also lots were drawn to play Horus. The main battle scene, taking place in the square in front of the temple, was the ritual encounter between Horus and Set. By overcoming the strength and trickery of his Uncle Set, Horus took his rightful place, and thus re-empowered Osiris.

Hatasu was certain her father would be proud of how well she fought with Horus for Osiris that day. All of her heart and determination was in it. The tired children returned to the palace to the comfort of a good meal and to their tutor-nurses. They each compared notes of their own heroics.

The fifth day was the grand processional. The statue of Osiris was paraded through town on his barque. He was reborn, crowned with the crown of Maat and returned to his rightful place in his temple. The crowd cheered loudly. The great god had returned from the dead! The forces that obstructed him had been overcome. Each person in the town, including the children, knew that he or she had helped make it happen.

Osiris was restored! The crops would be plentiful! Their festival was a success. Hatasu felt elated.

Walking together back to the palace that last day of the Osiris Enactment, Hatasu dared to ask Puyemre, "Can you now tell me about the Lesser Mysteries?"

He paused for a minute, considering what he could say. Then he looked at her and said, "Sebai Rekh already told you. Osiris is the seed we plant in the ground. When we bury the seed, it dies. We do not see it anymore. But all the while, the seed is trying to come forth. The soil, like Set, opposes it. The seed must battle with the forces of resistance as the tribunial resists Osiris. In the final battle, the seed bursts through the crust of the earth and is triumphant in coming forth and growing to give us new food. It rises tall and renewed like the Djed pillar. The renewal of Osiris and the emergence of the seedling give us bodily and spiritual food for the next year."

"So that is the Lesser Mysteries! That is what everyone is reminded of in this festival." Hatasu paused, then resumed, "But Puyemre, what then are the Greater Mysteries?"

Puyemre was quiet.

Hatasu said softly, almost in a conspirator's whisper, "When Rekh talked to me on the first day of school, he asked me if I was ready to die to my childhood ways of ignorance, to be born again to the ways of the wisdom of Thoth. Does that have anything to do with the Greater Mysteries?"

Puyemre flashed Hatasu a huge smile of surprised pleasure. "I haven't told you a thing, right?"

Chapter 20 - Between Abedju and Zawty

After the Festival Re-enactment of Osiris, Hatasu's mother vanished again. There was another half-moon before the Festival of Planting and Hatasu reassured herself by remembering that her mother said she would be with her again once they left Abedju. But now…she missed her. *Where could her mother and the secret rituals be?* She could see there were a number of small funeral temples in the vicinity of the Osiris Temple but the only sign of activity was the comings and goings of the occasional ka priest. She knew whatever her mother was doing, it was large and important. *Where was she?*

After the enactment, the children returned to their school schedules. Once she put her mind to it, Hatasu learned how to write quickly. Sebai Rekh taught her the basic letters of the hieratic print and the sounds that went with them…well, the consonant sounds, anyway. The vowels, a, e, i, o, and u, were not expressed in letters.

"These vowel sounds are like the wind," he explained to her. "The consonant sounds are like the doorway. It is the energy of the wind that gives the structure of the doorway, life."

This is the way she learned to read and write. There is the khet (body) you can see and the ka (spirit) you know but don't see. As she put the sounds together into words, she had to recognize them and know the 'wind by its doorway'. She caught on quickly and was soon reading the proverbs and sayings Rekh posted for the older children.

Ever impatient, Hatasu tried to understand the temple 'words of the gods' on her own, even before Sebai Rekh was willing to teach her. She examined the pictures on the temple walls around her. One day she snuck her scribe's tools out of the classroom, and tried to reproduce the picture language on her ostraka.

Puyemre saw her leave with her stylus. He followed her to the outside wall of the main courtyard. "Looks like you are impatient to learn the temple writing!" He smiled down at her. "Perhaps I can help you read and draw some of these symbols."

She noticed the many pictures of their friend, the frog. Puyemre told her the reason the frog was on the walls, as well as in the water, was because the frog was sacred to Heket, a goddess of childbirth, and associated with magic and the process of spiritual rebirth. "Look," he said pointing to a frog picture. "This picture shows the frog and writes the name in hieroglyphic letters. This triangle mark stands for the 'k' sound."

Hatasu nodded.

"Now, these two signs that look like mouths, stand for the sound of 'r'. The 'e' sound is the wind that gives the word life. All together it spells out 'kerer', the word for frog and the sound it makes. The *word-names* sound like the actual *thing*."

"You mean like 'miu' is the name of my pet, and it is the sound she makes when she calls her kittens?"

"Yes, exactly." Still staring at a row of frog pictures, he continued. "See, as a hieroglyph each frog is drawn from the same angle and they look exactly alike. You could draw them in different ways, just as you can look at them from different angles, but the hieroglyph is always the same way."

336

Hatasu sat down cross legged with her ostraka and stylus and worked to reproduce the exact curve of the frog's back and the exact proportions of her front and hind legs, the positioning of her eyes and mouth. When she finished…after several erasures…she looked up at Puyemre and said, "Let's go around to the other side of the temple and see if there are frogs there." Before he could respond, she'd collected her things and moved toward the back of the temple.

He followed, protesting. She focused her attention on the temple walls looking for kerer (frog) pictures as Puyemre called to her more insistently to come back. She turned away from the temple and noticed the pathway that went from a small door in the wall. It seemed to end abruptly, than vanish between a cleft in a rocky wall and the bent and broken branches of a shrub tree. Puyemre, with some urgency in his voice, called her to see hieroglyphics around other corner of the temple.

Hatasu ignored him, and said, "Puyemre, this path goes into that stone. Is there something there?"

Alarm filled his voice now. "No, no, Hatasu. Come see this hieroglyph of Heket."

"But," she neared the cleft and started to slip her small body between the rocks. The sound of chanting filled her ears.

Puyemre grabbed her wrist. "No, Hatasu!"

She looked back at him with surprise. She tried to jerk her wrist from his grip. He whispered urgently, "Please come away from that path. If my father finds out I was here with you, he will banish me from the Mystery School. He would say I am unworthy because I can not keep its secret."

She saw great pain in her friend's face at the very thought of
this. She allowed him to pull her to a far side of the larger temple.
The two of them sat with their backs against the sun warmed stones
of the temple. Hatasu watched him closely, tears welling up in his
eyes as his rapid breathing returned to normal. "What was that,
Puyemre?" she finally asked. "Is that the Temple of the Mysteries?"

His body slumped into the hieroglyphic pictures behind him. He
spoke now with resignation, "It is where the rituals of the Initiation
of Osiris take place. It is underground…like the seed." He looked
over at this red haired princess whose passionate interest in sacred
mysteries repeatedly disarmed his spiritual will and again drew
from him sacred secrets.

She leaned toward him eagerly. "Have you been inside?"

"No, Hatasu, not yet…and I probably won't be able to, now."

Her heart went out to her friend at the thought he could be
deprived of his heart's desire, for she too felt that same desire to
learn in her own heart. "I can keep a secret, Puyemre. Some day I
want to go through the rituals of the Great Mysteries, too, and I can
start keeping its secrets now."

Relief and gratitude flooded his face for a second but tensed
again, for she'd not finished with her questions. "What do you
know about the initiation this year? Mother says there are people
whose skills are important for the future of all the land."

His eyes glanced off. "Hatasu, my father…well, there is one he
spoke of. Something about his training is unusual because he is a
commoner. I think I remember a priest saying he has shown special

talent during his training...almost like the famous architect, Imhotep."

This made her thoughtful and full of wonder about this man. *Would he succeed in his initiation as her mother hoped?*

She kept her word. She did not sneak back to the hidden temple. Puyemre began to trust her more. He taught her to make little Hekets out of the drying Nile mud. Sometimes Hapuseneb joined them in their play. He was interested in making things out of the mud, as well. He had learned much in making the reed structures earlier in their visit. Puyemre and Hapuseneb started making model temples out of the moldable mud. Often, there by the receding river, the three friends spent their afternoon; the two younger ones, unclothed with their youth-locks still in place, the older boy, head shaved and dressed in the kilt of a young man.

Hatasu was fascinated by their discussions of temples and how they were built. Puyemre taught them to take the mud and, like Khnum, mold it; not into human bodies as such but into temples. He rolled the moist clay in his hands to make columns and flattened the mud to make pylon gates and built it up to make walls. They made the clay into temples of many different shapes and sizes. Puyemre explained, no matter what the shape of the temple, always the sanctuary in the middle was the heart, just as the heart of a man is his center.

The waters of the inundation receded and the mud gradually dried. Hatasu noted how the fields changed while they had been there in Abedju. When they first arrived, it was a black watery soup they'd waded in. About the time of the Osiris Re-enactment, it was a thick paste that oozed between their toes. Now, finally, it was firm enough to mold and soon it would be hard enough to walk upon. That was when it would be ready for the plow and the promise of seeds.

When the day of the Planting Festival arrived, Hatasu, along with the other students of the temple school, met at the site of the Festival Field. Sebai Rekh gathered them together and said, "Last night the moon was round and full. Today is the plowing and sowing ceremony. The planting of the seed means its death. We celebrate this because it is necessary for its new life as a food grain. Osiris, god of the underworld, presides over the First Planting."

As Hatasu watched, Governor Puya, dressed as the High Priest, came from his residence to the ceremonial plot of land to be plowed. She saw her mother take her place as royal witness. Hatasu felt the pull on her heart. How she wanted to run to her! But she knew better. She'd have to wait. She let her attention be drawn to the animal-handler who led two grand bulls from their stable. Their black backs, all washed and brushed, shone in the light of Ra. Next, a servant carried the polished, tamarisk yoke out into the field next to the bulls. Finally, a temple priest appeared with the sacred black-copper plow, used only in this ritual.

Amid much censing and singing, the sacred bulls, the sacred yoke and the sacred plow were harnessed together. Hatasu watched as Puya directed the plow through the field and the lector priest chanted the ritual prayer. *In the Duat, where the sun goes down under the horizon, that is the place of transformation and rebirth. Similarly, under this ground, the seed is buried so life will return.*

Then, her dear friend, Puyemre, came forward. He stood tall by his father and looked proud, for he had the honor of carrying three bags of seeds: Barley, flax, and smelt. Hatasu noticed the way he held himself with dignity. Governor Puya began his task of plowing the first of three fields. He walked forward, one hand on the handle of the plow and one hand holding the flail to urge the bulls along. The dirt welded to the fertilizing plow and Puya recited the holy prayers of hope for an abundant harvest.

Puyemre walked behind him with the bag of barley seeds, scattering them into the furrow of the upturned earth. He let his eyes steal a glance over toward Hatasu. She flashed him a big smile and he smiled back as he scattered the flax in this next furrow row. His father plowed the third row. Puyemre scattered the third seed bag…the smelt.

With the first rows planted and blessed, the small group proceeded back to the stable. There the bulls were ritually honored, cleaned and put back in their stable to rest. This was the official beginning of Proyet, the sowing season. The agricultural year had begun.

Now all the farmers of the land were poised to plow their own fields, which were officially blessed by Osiris, in this ritual of the First Planting. The same crowd that mourned and fought at the sacred drama at the opening of the festival, now rejoiced and celebrated the great triumph of their god and the promise of an abundant harvest. There was feasting and dancing in the town but the festivities ended at sundown for each farmer would be up early the next day, plowing their fields.

During her visit to Abedju, the moon god, Ah, had shrunk from full glow into a dark shadow in the sky and then grew luminous again, round and full. Hatasu felt something changed within her this month, just as the moon changed. She'd given up some of her will to Sebai Rekh's teachings but like the moon she was refilled, for she was now a junior scribe. And this moon introduced her to Puyemre, one who turned out to be such a dear companion in her adventures.

She was sad it was over now and she must leave Abedju and Puyemre. Her mind turned toward her mother. How she longed to be with her again and see the smile in her almond eyes and hear her sing the 'Wings of Isis Lullaby'. The next morning when Hatasu did indeed have her mother back, she followed her around not letting her out of sight. Ahmose busily oversaw the servants who were packing up their things for the continued journey. She stopped frequently and gave her daughter a hug and Hatasu knew her mother missed her, too.

That morning, two messengers arrived almost simultaneously. One of them bore the seal of the Pharaoh. Ahmose had a servant send word to Ineni and Hapu. The two came immediately. Nakht was already there. Ahmose sat in her ornate chair, positioning herself to read the missives. Hatasu and Thethi gathered around her. Each was anxious for word of the Pharaoh's safety and success. The Queen broke the seal and read it aloud. "'Greetings, my beloved Queen. I am grateful to Isis and Horus to hear of the improved health of Neferubrity. I long to see her and hold her in my arms. I am content to hear of Hatasu's entrance into the temple at

Abedju and her progress there'."

She beamed from ear to ear at her father's mention of her.

"'It is good that Thethi's breathing problems have not been depriving him of strength to train his dog with Paheri. I send my greetings to all the good people in the eighth nome and warm greetings to Puya, Neferiah and their son, Puyemre. Their son, Ti, sends his greetings, and I can commend them that he has in all ways conducted himself in a manner to make them proud.

"The army is faring well though the men are homesick already. We arrived at Megiddo yesterday and found things in good order. There is, however, much talk of trouble to the north. Considerable forces gather here but they are friendly and have done nothing to provoke a disciplinary action. The ruler has agreed to send one of his companies along with us as it benefits him, too, to be rid of the threat from the north. The leader of these northern peoples, the Mitanni, is Barranta. He is reported to be ruthless and power-hungry. Our soldiers are tired of marching and ready for a battle. We head for Hazor tomorrow.

"Stay vigilant on your travels north down our great river and keep me advised concerning the plans we discussed. Bring my greetings to each governor and to the people of each city. I thought of you at the planting festival. The people here have a festival but it does not have the heart and soul of Abedju. Your Pharaoh, Thutmose'."

The Queen looked up from the papyrus and with a light sigh, she smiled at her advisers. "Things are going as planned. We can announce to the people of Abedju that Thutmose continues to have a successful campaign."

She turned, then, to the second scroll. A messenger from Zawty carried this scroll. Upon it was the seal of Governor Djehapy of that city. Expecting only the usual preparation for their arrival, she opened the scroll and read while the children were still in her presence. "'Lady of Two Lands, Goddess Mut to her people, Great Queen of the Two Lands, I, Djehapy, governor of Zawty, greet you with deepest respect. We happily anticipate your visit and joyful preparations are being made for your arrival.

"However, it is advisable for you to know that there is disquiet in our city. The caravan traders have brought messages of dissent from one whose family was exiled to the el Kharga Oasis. Your presence would turn the ears of my people away from the troublemakers and toward the royal blessings of the Pharaoh. Your devoted servant, Djehapy, governor of Zawty'."

Ahmose looked surprised as she turned to her vizier. "Ineni, what can you tell me of this difficulty in Zawty?"

"I know nothing of this 'dissent' from the oasis but Zawty's position as the destination of the Darb el Arba'in Caravan trail would make them the first to know if there were signs of trouble. The town, itself, has had recent difficulties with grain storage, due both to the devastation from the recent khamsin and to rodent infestation. Our Pharaoh has sent aid to the nome for both. At that time, Djehapy expressed concern that the grain shortage would have an effect on trade, which is of great worry for his townsfolk," Ineni reported.

The Queen nodded slowly and said, "I remember Djehapy from

his visits at the day of the tax, Osiris's Day. Thutmose talks of him as an excellent administrator. His consistent displays of loyalty moved my husband to gift him with golden armbands."

Ineni tilted his head toward Nakht and said, "Perhaps you have more information about the situation at the oasis?"

Ahmose turned to her military adviser. "Your Majesty," Nakht began, "the exile of the rebellious family of Teti-an effectively silenced any dissenters since Pharaoh Ahmose sent them to that remote place. Pharaoh was merciful to have refrained from executing the children of that family as he did the traitor, Teti-an, himself. There have been isolated reports of minor trouble in the last year or so. A grandson of Teti-an, who is coming into his manhood, is known for his angry arrogance." As Nakht spoke, his black face was open, and his eyebrows slightly shifted down in an expression of thoughtful concern.

The Queen nodded as she listened to Nakht. She said, "It was the apprehension about such situations that moved the Pharaoh to wish us to take this trip. Thutmose feared there might be some trouble but we had not expected it from the oasis." The Queen's dark, round eyes looked from man to man then rested back on her vizier. "We must find out for ourselves the seriousness of the situation and then decide a course of action. If there is threat that goes as far as treason, I am prepared to act to protect the Pharaoh and the people."

"Ahmose," Ineni spoke after a thoughtful silence. "I am concerned about Djehapy's words: 'Disquiet', 'dissent' and 'discontent'. We don't know if this is an early sign of possible trouble or if there is already danger there. We do not want to walk into danger unprotected. Perhaps having more personal guards would be advisable for you at this time."

Nakht nodded and said, "That can quickly be arranged."

She shook her head and said, "No, fear is for those who are outside of Maat. I do not want armed forces following me around. I do not want to give the people of the Middle of the Two Lands to get the impression that I seek protection from them. If Djehapy perceived I was in immediate danger, he would have indicated it. These are my people. We want the loyalty of our people. I go to the people of my land with the protection of the two goddesses, Nekhbet and Buto, upon my brow. To the people, in the Pharaoh's absence, I am both Hathor and Horus."

Hatasu noted the strength in her mother's unwavering tone. She turned to her scribe, Yuf, who was sitting cross-legged, his papyrus on his lap and his stylus in his hand. "Send a message to Djehapy," she told him. "Inform him of our imminent arrival." She paused a minute and then added, "Yuf, take another letter to Satamun inquiring about the wellbeing of Waset. We have not had any word from her."

He bowed his head in agreement. "Yes, Your Majesty, Mother Mut to your people. Both messages will be dispatched shortly."

Rising from her chair and proceeding toward the door, the Queen turned and said, "I thank each of you for your council. I wish to continue on our journey as quickly as possible. We shall leave very early in the morning. Please prepare your families to leave before the rising of Ra. Inform the captains of my plan."

The children had inadvertently been privy to a session of the

Queen's council. The dangers discussed both raised Hatasu's anxiety level and her determination to be as brave as she saw her mother being. Once Ineni, Hapu and Nakht bowed out of the room, Hatasu approached her mother cautiously. The queen started walking in the direction of the banquet hall and motioned to her daughter to walk alongside of her. Thethi trailed along, too. "Why would this person from the oasis cause trouble?" Hatasu asked, trying to grasp the situation.

Thethi quickly jumped into a swordsmen stance with an imaginary knife in his hands. "I'm ready to fight them!" he said.

Ahmose chuckled at Thethi and said, "I don't think that will be necessary, Son." Putting an arm around each of the children, she drew them near. "It is sad that there are those in our land who are rebellious. The Pharaoh is the son of the god and through him the blessings of the gods flow to all the people. Only ignorance and passion could mislead men to rebel against him. Perhaps there are such men in el Kharga Oasis but we do not know that, yet. A wise ruler takes the time to gather the facts. He neither acts prematurely nor is paralyzed when action is necessary."

She went on…talking more to Hatasu for Thethi was busy in a make-believe battle with imagery rebels. "There is some concern," she said, "which is why your father wanted us to make this trip while he is gone. Renewing our contacts with both the governors and the people of the nomes reinforces their loyalties and strengthens the unity of the Two Lands. There are other safeguards set up, too. Pharaoh Ahmose saw to it, after the rebellion of the nomarchs with Teti-an, that the power in the land must reside in the pharaoh.

"There are now governors in the nomes rather than princes or nomarchs. They are chosen by the Pharaoh and answer to him. The position of governor is not passed down from father to son. In the past, nomarchs became like little pharaohs of their nomes. This kept the Two Lands divided and caused a weakness that allowed the Hyksos to take over. Now, the governors must swear loyalty to the Pharaoh and bring him yearly reports of their nomes. They must travel to Waset, so they are reminded that Waset is the one and only capital city.

"We, the Pharaoh and I, also visit each nome to renew the loyalty of the nobles and to be assured of their continued loyalty and the accuracy of their reports. We want to rule our people in peace, neither allowing corruption nor using unnecessary force."

After the gathering, Ahmose returned to her room early to be rested for their start in the morning. Hatasu begged to stay in the Queen's room that night. She still felt a bit scared about the possible difficulty of rebellion. Her mother agreed and her bed was made up in her mother's suite. Hatasu relaxed as she lay in her bed watching Nefermut brush out her mother's hair. Hatasu spoke her questions from her cot. "How can you tell if people are planning deceit against father or the land?"

"You are referring to the message from Djehapy?"

"Yes, how will you know if he is really loyal? Do you have to wonder about everyone, even Puya and Puyemre?" Hatasu asked.

"Think with your heart, dear. What does your heart tell you about your friend here in Abedju?"

"When I think of Puyemre and hold him in my heart, I feel him as a loving and loyal friend."

"This is wise, Hatasu. Listen to your heart."

Nefermut continued to brush the Queen's thick black hair. Even with her stiff fingers, she still knew just how this nightly ritual soothed and relaxed her. She sang gently, softly as she brushed. After a few moments Nefermut, not servant but trusted friend, said to her, "You will know just what to do if you encounter difficulties. I know you will. You are more like your mother than you give yourself credit. Just as the great Queen Nefertari knew how to make wise decisions, so will you."

Ahmose smiled and looked up at the old woman. "How is it you always read my mind? You always know what I need to hear."

Hatasu realized her mother was not always as confident as she looked. Once Ahmose was in her bed, Nefermut blew out the lantern and retired to her own chamber. Hatasu lay down between the cool sheets and stared at the ceiling of the darkened room feeling very small and alone again. She looked over toward her mother's bed and in a little girl voice said, "Omm (Mommy) could I sleep with you?"

She could see the smile and nod, even through the shadows. Ahmose lifted her sheet and made room for her. Hatasu bounded into her mother's bed. Her mother smiled and snuggled her close. The child breathed in deeply the lotus scent of her oils and felt the ache of the month without her melt away.

The next morning, the boats of the Queen and the councilmen were waiting at the harbor-lake ready to set out again. The boats were boarded and ready to be headed down river before the rest of the town was even awake. The Queen wished to leave quickly to avoid any delay caused by the congestion of boats. In a short time, everyone would be up and there would be a bustle of activity as the pilgrims began their journey home from Abedju.

For the entire moon of this festival, the town of Abedju had bulged with activity and people. Now, it would shrink back to its customary size and focus its attention on the spring planting and the customary care of this year's crops. The river would be a mass of boats; large and small, some traveling upriver toward Waset and some traveling downriver, just like the royal entourage.

Ineni, Hapu, Nakht and their families were continuing with them all the way to Ankh-Tawy. The Pharaoh had planned their continued council to the Queen before his departure. It was also planned that Ineni would oversee an architectural project in the north and check on the promising young initiates and architects in the temple city of Khemenu. The Queen determined the children and their tutors would travel together in Ineni's boat and the vizier and her other councilors would confer on her boat.

Hatasu was pleased to be traveling with her favorite cousins. Meryt, Isis and Hapuseneb were all together with her again. In the back of Hatasu's mind, however, was an unsettled feeling. *Was there real danger in the northern city? What would her mother do about it with the Pharaoh away?* Her mother and father, when they were together, always had answers. *Could her mother, alone, face the challenges?*

In her thoughtfulness, she had fallen behind those who had

already boarded Ineni's boat. As she walked with Sitre to the gangplank, the dawn fog was melting and the vision of the sacred city slipped through the lacy veil of morning.

It was just then the figure of a young man came walking through the haze. Hatasu paused, looked closely and to her surprise…it was Puyemre! Dear Puyemre had a farewell gift in his hand. She waited as he drew near. He stood tall over her as he shyly handed her the small gift he had worked on well into the night. It was a small mud temple. Inside was a perfectly modeled sculpture of Heket, the frog goddess of magic and rebirth. Scratched on the bottom was the word 'Heket', written in both hieratic and hieroglyphic.

Hatasu wished she had something for him in return. She looked at him 'with her heart', as her mother said and she saw him as one whose loyalty and love she could trust. Her response came from her heart and she threw her arms around his neck. She gave him a quick hug, then ran up the gangplank onto the boat. Once upon the deck, she turned to look back and saw the surprised, somewhat embarrassed smile on her friend's face. He turned and vanished back into the morning fog.

On board, the captain directed the bustle of activity, inherent in making final preparations to cast off. The crew scurried about, freeing the vessel from its mooring. The sound of shouted orders and creaking oars claimed her attention as the boat moved away from the Abedju quay and into the river's current. Once underway, she looked at her surroundings. Ineni's boat was similar to her mother's, only smaller. The cabin in the center was not as prettily nor elaborately painted. There was still a captain at the bow, a steersman at the stern and rowers on each side.

The five children, Aunt Nefermose, Aunt Ahhotep and their tutors, all stood on the deck watching as the holy city of Abedju faded into the distance. The early hours on the river passed quietly. Whatever the concerns were with the distant governors, they faded from thought as the boat floated along. At the moment, the river and the land were at peace with each other and the gentle scenes of villages passed in front of their eyes. Farmers on both sides of the river plowed their fields with their long-horned oxen. Groups of women, who brought their linen and their children to the river to wash, waved and sang songs of praise as the royal boats passed. Any threat of conflict seemed far away.

Sitre sat with Hatasu who was at her writing lessons. Hatasu looked up periodically to scan the river for her mother's boat or to observe the occasional hippopotamus with her young calf beside her in the marshes or to listen to the 'peer-wit' call of the lapwings that flocked over the sprouting grasslands. When noontime finally came, all of the children were freed from their lessons and encouraged to enjoy the entertainment planned for them.

It was then, Hatasu first noticed the young man sitting in the bow of the boat. He sat in the position of a scribe as he was working on some papyrus. He also seemed to notice her…and not just because of her hair. Aunt Nefermose called the children together and led them toward this young man and introduced him as a storyteller. The five children eagerly gathered around this man, who was perhaps twenty years old. Hatasu saw him as a rather short and plump person with a large and protruding nose that was even more angular than the Thutmose nose. His eyes were bright and keen. A kind of glow was around him. He, like Puyemre and Rekh, wore a scarab ring. She wondered if he were the special initiate her mother and Puyemre spoke of.

He looked up at them from the papyrus he was apparently studying and they watched as a mischievous smile crept over his face. "Let me see. What would be a worthy story for royal children? Hmmm… Well, we are all sailors today, right? How about I tell you the story of a sailor? Maybe a story about a sailor who found…*the land of the gods*?"

Hatasu was immediately entranced. Her large, black eyes opened wider. She watched this storyteller carefully. There was something familiar about him, though she knew there was no way she could have met him before. All of the children took their places around him, sitting cross-legged and looking with open faces to hear his story.

He began, "I shall tell it to you as though I were the sailor:
'I once sailed into the Great Green Sea.
Our ship was large. and magnificent to see.
We traveled to the royal mine,
With the finest crew that we could find.
Seasoned sailors who could read the sea,
They were wise in whatever weather may be.
Their hearts were as brave, as lions are free.'
A sudden storm came upon us. Sharp winds and hungry waves devoured our ship and swallowed the men…all but me. The swelling waves of the great, angry sea carried me alone to an island.

Its sandy beaches led to an inland of beauty and plenty. All manner of foods were growing, ready to eat. Just as I gave offerings to the gods in thanks for my safety, a great rumbling came from the land. I feared I would perish. Out of the sea rose a giant serpent with golden scales and lapis eyebrows and the long beard of a god. It reared up and I thought again I would die, this time of fright of this thing.

It spoke to me in a woman's voice. 'What brings you, brings you, Little Man? What brings you to this Isle? Speak quickly, before I burn you, Little Man…burn you as one who has never been!'

I mumbled, as best I could, through my panic. In my fright, I hardly knew myself. She took me safely in her mouth and brought me to her house.

She asked again, 'What brings you, brings you, Little Man? What brings you to this island in the Great Green Sea?'

This time I told her, *'I once sailed into the Great Green Sea.*
Our ship was large, and magnificent to see.
We traveled to the royal mines,
With the finest crew that we could find.
Seasoned sailors who could read the sea,
They were wise to whatever weather may be.
Their hearts were as brave as lions are free'.

The golden serpent said to me, 'Fear not! Fear not, Little Man! You are safe with me in this place of magic. This is the isle of all fine and lovely things, Little Man. You will be blessed with four months here. Then your sea comrades from Khemet will bring you home, Little Man, and you will tell of the joy of your suffering, overcome'.

'I have such a story of my own,' she went on. 'Once, on this isle, I lived with a large and wonderful family. I particularly loved my small daughter, who was brought to me by prayer. But a falling star destroyed them all while I was away. When I found their tangled corpses, I wanted to be dead, too. I tell you this to encourage you to savor your family and friends when you return to them'.

As I heard her story, my compassion for her grew. I wanted to tell her all the wonderful things I knew. 'When I return,' I told her, 'I will tell my story to all. I will sing the praise of your beneficent powers. I will tell the Pharaoh and council and they will bring fleets of the fabled wealth of the Two Lands to this goddess, so loved by men who live in a far and dimly known land'.

This golden serpent laughed. 'Little Man, Little Man, This is Punt I rule! This is the land of myrrh, incense and sacred oils. This wealth makes the fabled Two Lands look poor in comparison. No, it is not for you, Little Man, to return with gifts but I shall give gifts to you. I have a request for you, though. Tell this story, Little Man. Tell this story in your city. Let my name be known to your people, Little Man. Let your people know the gifts of Punt. You have found favor, Little Man, in this land of the gods. So you will carry home with you not just this story but the fabled wealth of Punt'.

When the ship from the Two Lands arrived, just as she said, the golden serpent with the lapis blue eyebrows had it loaded with many good things of Punt. There was myrrh, oil, perfume and spices, giraffe tails and elephant tusks, hunting hounds and long-tailed monkeys. There were also great lumps of incense. I offered thanks beside the sea for the Lady of the Isle and those on board did likewise.

When I returned to my Pharaoh with the gifts of the Goddess of Punt, he made me a Royal Follower with servants and fame and I continue to tell my story just as she asked.

" 'I traveled into the Great Green Sea.

Our ship was large and magnificent to see.

We traveled to the royal mines,

With the finest crew that we could find.

Seasoned sailors, who could read the sea,

They were wise in whatever the weather would be.

Their hearts were as brave, as lions are free.

A storm blew us port and lee.

Punt was the isle that rescued me.

Busied with a meal to hunt,

I met a goddess on the Isle of Punt.

Her eyebrows were lapis lazuli,

And she had golden serpent scales of all to see.

The land had the wealth of the incense tree,

Which the goddess sent back home with me'."

Hatasu had been absolutely transported. The images formed brilliant pictures in her mind. For the hour of the telling of the story, this land of Punt was more real to her than the boat she rode on.

Thethi's question broke into her trance, "Do storms at sea really make such trouble?"

"I hear it is indeed true," said the storyteller.

"Then, it does take very brave men to sail such ships," said Thethi.

Meryt commented, "Oh, that poor serpent who lost her whole family!"

Isis added, "Oh, that was such a lucky man! He returned with such wealth and found favor with the Pharaoh!"

The images still singing in her head, Hatasu watched the storyteller's face as the other children asked their questions. When she finally spoke, there was intensity in her young voice, "I want to know more about Punt. I want to visit this land and meet the god, myself." Her statement came out almost as commandingly as if it were a Pharaonic decree.

Not being quite sure how to respond to this young princess, the storyteller said, "No one has been there for many generations. This story is from the reign of Montuhotep, from a time when the Two Lands were united and our wise Pharaoh had both peace and wealth for trade. Since the Hyksos have not cared about the land of the gods, they neglected the trade routes to Punt and perhaps those routes are now lost." The young man squirmed a bit, feeling uneasy from the child's questions.

Hatasu went on, "Storyteller, what is your name? Where do you come from?"

Visibly taken aback, he answered, "I am Senenmut of Armant. As a student of the temple, I am traveling to study architecture at the temple of Thoth in Khemenu."

Nefermose, wife of architect Ineni, smiled at the children's pleasure in the story and said to Senenmut warmly, "May you be as good at designing temples as you are at telling stories!"

By now, Ra had begun to sink in the western sky. The children's attention was diverted as the tutors and mothers gathered at the port side of the boat, pointing toward the cluster of buildings and the harbor of many ships. Aunt Nefermose said with anticipation, "There is the city of Zawty!"

Hatasu turned. The western mountains all along their trip had made a high, buff-colored backdrop. They now dissolved downward to a sandy corridor fanning out from the town to a lower western horizon. This opened the view from the river to a glimpse of the desert beyond. Other cities they passed had great mountain walls that kept the Set-ruled red lands of the desert at bay and there were only the deep crevices of the wadis that allowed commerce with the caravans of desert traders. Here, the desert seemed to part the mountains and come right down to touch the fields, then to reach out to the river itself through its uneven slopes. In the center of this corridor was a roadway, distinguishable by its lighter color and broad, snake-like pattern, winding down the slope and through the fields, right into the bustling town.

The town of Zawty was on a mound, a spreading hillock, with broad flood plain of irrigated fields on both sides and a booming riverfront filled with boats, people and brightly colored market stalls. Whitewashed mud-brick houses clustered along the streets. As their boats drew closer, Hatasu could see the estate of the governor and what must be their own mooring palace set off high on the mound, just a little below the fluttering flags of the temple.

The captain's voice called out to the men at the steering oars and they headed the boat toward the docks. The children could see the quays and the gathering of the people of Zawty. They sang and waved colored scarves, celebrating their arrival. Hatasu's stomach fluttered. *What would they find in this town? A loyal governor or a dangerous malcontent?*

Chapter 21 - Trouble from the Oasis

The Queen's royal barque leading the flotilla of boats was first to pull into a quay. The children's boat took the next spot and then came the smaller boats that carried the servants, belongings and supplies. The new arrivals filled the city's already bursting harbor. The shoreline and marketplace were crowded with people. Some had come to see the Queen and some to trade with the recently arrived caravan.

Hatasu scanned the gathered crowd looking for signs of trouble. Colored scarves brightened the air and the frame drum beat out catchy rhythms. People offered the usual welcome chants of praise, "Welcome, Queen! Welcome Goddess Mut to her people." But something was, indeed, different here. People looked thinner and sadder. There was a slight edge in the voices of the chanters and a slower pace in the steps of the dancers but there was no clear sense of imminent danger.

Hatasu's attention was drawn to the governor's family, positioned to greet the royalty. The governor held himself erect and tall, his black wig framed his aging face and kohl framed his tired eyes. He wore a collar of gold and faience, suitable for his high station, and a pair of gold armbands, the Pharaoh's gift for loyal service. He held his staff of office tight in his hand. His kilt was bleached and starched to perfection, the sandals on his feet were made from new reeds.

His wife stood beside him and was his equal in height, though she was considerably younger than he. Her eyelids were painted a fine blue above the deep kohl, her wig was pleated in fashionable layers and she wore a thin, glittering chain of gold around her neck. The linen of her tunic was very fine, indeed. The craftsmanship of the weave and the delicateness of the thread were obvious from the grace with which it fell about her body. Just below her breasts was a band of brilliant purple, deep and alluring.

The daughter was as tall as her parents. She was about thirteen years old, painted, pleated and robed as elegantly as her mother. She was thin, almost stick-like and seemed poised precariously between being a child and an adult…the body of a child, dressed as an adult.

Thinking of her father's directive to befriend provincial families, Hatasu hoped for a friendship; if not as satisfying as that with Puyemre, at least a pleasant connection. She wondered what this governor's daughter might know or think about the trouble coming from the oasis.

Hatasu was glad Chi-chi and Behka were sequestered away with their animal handlers. She had a chance of disembarking with dignity…well, at least her hair was still neatly pleated. That, however, did not protect her from her hair still drawing stares. She and her brother came forward for their introductions to the governor and his family. The two adults smiled formally but the daughter's eyes widened and for an awkward second, stared at the red hair. She caught herself almost immediately and lowered her head into a formal bow. This, the princess was informed, was Tutkharit, the daughter of Governor Djehapy and his wife, Kharit. Hatasu hoped her hair would not deter a friendship.

Djehapy greeted each person in the royal entourage with respectful familiarity, which he had gained from his visits to Waset at tax time. He bowed deeply, reverencing the Queen. He had a broad, welcoming smile, and his eyes extended their eagerness to please and honor her. Kharit managed to convey a sense of warm personal regard to not just the Queen but to each of the family members. She was especially warm in greeting Ahhotep, Hapu's wife, for their families were friends.

The visitors formed into the procession and moved toward the Zawty mooring palace. Thethi and Hatasu walked with their tutors behind the Queen. Muthotep carried Neferubrity, who fussed, and the other families followed. Ahmose set a leisurely pace, as she chose to walk rather than ride in a litter. She smiled and waved to people as she went, reaching out to touch those who extended their hands to her.

Hatasu noticed a unique thing about this town, was its number of cats. They were everywhere; sitting perched on doorsteps, chasing fat, furry mice and squabbling with other cats. She also noticed for all the people who came forward to reach out to her mother, there were just as many who hung back…watching…silently…their cold eyes following their progress to the mooring palace. *Was this a sign of danger?* She looked to her mother. Queen Ahmose waved warmly to the smiling, expectant faces. Several times she stopped and called a greeting to someone hanging back in the distance. Each time, it had the effect of softening the look in their eyes…and sometimes even eliciting a smile, a wave, or even some movement forward toward the welcoming crowd. Wanting to be a queen as gracious and effective as her own mother, Hatasu waved and smiled…and noted they waved back to her, too.

Once inside the mooring palace, Hatasu could see it was less ornate than the one at Abedju and the garden was smaller but the rooftop offered a lovely view and a refreshing breeze. Unlike the ritual center of Abedju that drew like-minded people, Zawty was a prominent trading center. It buzzed with the excitement of the unfamiliar and the unknown, not all of which was dangerous. She again took her cues from her mother, who appeared not only comfortable, but pleased with the exotic elements around them.

This mooring palace distinguished itself with lovely and unfamiliar objects the children had never seen before; like the wall mats whose designs were more reminiscent of desert sand patterns than of river flowers. Hatasu asked Sitre about the things she saw.

"This is a trade city," her tutor said, as she unpacked things for the night's comfort. "You remember the story of the sailor who brought wonderful things from Punt via the sea? Well, here, things come from the desert; some of them wonderful, some of them dangerous."

"Do you think anyone will cause trouble while we're here, Sitre?"

"No, my dear, your mother is wise enough to keep things in hand. And besides," she said with a twinkle in her eyes, "there are way too many cats here for anyone to cause trouble." Sitre laughed and Hatasu felt annoyed. Her nurse was not taking her seriously. She'd have to wait and see what she could determine on her own.

That evening started out in a relaxed way with the greeting

banquet. Governor Djehapy had the fatted calf ritually slaughtered and roasted in the custom of honoring beloved royal guests. Kharit, the governor's wife, ordered the table filled with the usual array of foods: Breads and beer, roast pigeon and goose, onions and radishes. Delighted, Hatasu and Thethi spotted the abundance of plump, delicious dates.

The dinner conversation started out with the typical polite exchange of pleasantries. Everyone was so calm and polite, she thought maybe there really was no danger. Letting herself relax a bit, she gave way to her hunger, and reached for one of the dates dipped in honey and presented on an unusual platter.

Queen Ahmose smiled at her hostess and said, "Kharit, this dish is very beautiful. What unusual pottery! I believe I've seen similar in the Lower of the Two Lands. It is from Keftiu (Crete), is it not?"

Hatasu took a look at the serving plate. It had wonderful swirl designs in white over black with delicate red-drop shapes strategically placed to accent the white curves. This plate offered an obvious contrast to the familiar, yet plain, Nile mud pottery amphorae for wine, which was standing against the wall with the decoration of white lotus flowers.

Hatasu was licking the honey from her fingers as Kharit smiled in reply, "Yes, My Queen. It is a trade item from the artisans of the Keftiu."

Ahmose nodded as she bit into one of the fresh dates from the platter. "The dish is as lovely as the dates are delicious. It is remarkable to combine dates from the desert oasis and pottery from the sea islands. This truly is a wonder of trade and a blessing of the gods."

Djehapy said, "Yes, our position allows us to benefit from trade with many places: The Oasis, the Delta and even foreign places like Keftiu and Byblos."

Turning to Kharit, the Queen said, "I noticed that your trading has brought you the noble purple dye of Byblos. It is very lovely on your sheath."

The governor's wife smiled, softening her features. "Yes, on rare occasions, some of this dyed cloth is available at a high price. I was blessed by Hathor to come upon an opportunity to trade for a piece. It is so hard to attain."

"And the fine weave of your shift. Do you weave it here or trade for it?"

"This is my own humble work," she said, with obvious pride.

As Hatasu listened, her mother skillfully turned the conversation to the matter of her concern…the threat from the oasis. "I received the message that there may be trouble, as well as benefits from being a crossroads of trade."

"Yes, indeed, we are troubled," Djehapy replied. "This is not the usual trouble of raids on the caravans. It is much worse." His brow furloughed and he shook his head as he talked. "The traders from the Oasis have brought a plague of sedition and calls for nothing less than the fire of Sekhmet." The governor's words were pressured and he spat out the syllables. "It is the soul-illness of treason." He then turned to the queen, and reining in his anger, he addressed Ahmose with a bow of reverence. "Your presence is the great remedy, Lady Mother. Even as the people accompanied you to the mooring palace, I saw their faces begin to relinquish their angst. But that wretched treasonous criminal and his band of outlaws..."

The Queen leaned toward him. "So, what *is* this dissent from the Oasis that disturbs my beloved people of Zawty?"

Djehapy seemed to sink into himself and his face darkened. "The traders bring poisonous messages from one who has been exiled, one who now seeks to return to the Nile Valley. I fear he plans to lay claim to power he says is his. His messengers incite the people with discontent and he plants thoughts of rebellion. I have warned those people who listen to him that they are asking for the angry fire of Sekhmet and the swift justice of Maat." Djehapy spoke with renewed vehemence.

"Who is this?" Ahmose asked.

"They say his name is Setmose, born of Set, the god of the red lands of the desert. How appropriate," Djehapy said bitterly.

Kharit's voice came from deep in her throat, as she added, "It is of great concern that the people are listening to these rebels but they are listening because of the hard conditions they have endured recently. You know from my husband's reports to the Pharaoh. We have suffered a shortage of grain since the khamsin destroyed this year's crop. The open gateway in the western mountains, which positions us so well for trade with the desert, also makes us vulnerable to the ravages of the desert storms that again have destroyed our grains. This problem of insufficient grain makes the people's bellies hungry and leaves them nothing with which to trade."

Ineni responded, "Yes, the struggles and hardships of the people in your nome are known to the Pharaoh. He sent grain and aid to help your people and relieve their burden." That one eyebrow was raised but his tone was not inquisitive.

The governor answered, "Yes, our Great God Horus, Pharaoh Thutmose, sent aid. We received grains from his own stores. He sent men to help dig out our irrigation canals in time for the inundation and he arranged for cats to be sent to subdue the infestation of mice." Bowing at the waist, he added, "We are eternally grateful to our Pharaoh, Thutmose."

Hatasu's eyes brightened. *'Ah'*, she thought to herself, *'that's why there are so many cats in town!'*

Kharit's bow of gratitude was less deep and she spoke up again, "However, before the Pharaoh's aid arrived, the spoiled grain supplies caused disease and the rodents had already spread a fever among our people. Many families were grieved by loses of loved ones. I know these people. They would not listen to the rebels if it weren't for their hardships. Likewise, their discontent would dwindle and disappear if the troublemakers didn't feed off it."

Kharit smiled, bowing her head again, and said softly, "We rejoice at your arrival. Your presence alone is like the menit beads of Hathor. Our townsfolk look to you for help and protection."

The Queen nodded, and then turned to Djehapy, ignoring the reference to the delayed response to the earlier khamsin problem. "What else do you know of this Setmose?" she asked.

Hatasu was listening hard.

"He is the grandson of the malcontent, Teti-an of Itjtawy.

Though Pharaoh Ahmose executed Teti-an for treason, he exiled his sons, rather than executing them also. This man's grandson has become the arrogant and angry young man who sends messages through the trading caravans traveling from el Kharga Oasis to Zawty. The gossip is this: Setmose dreams of a return to his ancestral home in Itjtawy. He has gained sympathizers here. He finds company in the troubled souls of the women in the marketplace." Djehapy looked at the Queen sideways, as though fearing to even say the next piece of information. "He tells them that Thutmose is not the legitimate Pharaoh. He is not of the line of Tao *nor* the Amenhat family before the Hyksos occupation."

There was silence at the table for a full minute. The intensity of Ineni's reaction was like an explosion that made Hatasu jump in her seat. "That is ridiculous!" There was a fire in his eyes and they seemed to glow dangerously. "It is Amun, himself, who chose Thutmose in the oracle, and Amenhotep made him his co-regent." With effort, Ineni calmed himself, but he pushed away from the banquet table and began pacing; hands grasped behind his back, feet stamping against the mud brick floor. His face solidified in a deep frown. Hatasu had never seen her uncle so angry.

In contrast, the tone of Ahmose's voice was calm but hers words were spoken with cold precision. "This treason is as awful as Set, himself. The people must, of course, be protected from it."

Vizier Ineni stopped his pacing and looked up, the anger was still dark flames in his eyes. "Has the distress of your people blinded them both to the truth of Maat and to what Pharaoh Thutmose has done for them?"

Kharit responded slowly, carefully…trying to allay the royal righteous anger and illicit royal support for their plight. "There is no excuse for listening to treason but I fear that in the people's grief and pain, they entertain their own dreams that a past time was better for them. The years of the Hyksos rule increased trade with the Levant and gave them a taste for what is available through foreign ports. The current disruption in trade feeds their discontent. I pray you recognize the difference between Setmose and the people of Zawty and protect my people rather than include them in your righteous wrath." Her shoulders rose and tightened as she spoke, her eyes moving from the Queen to Ineni, and back again.

The Queen responded, "I see this difference but wonder if there are ring-leaders within the town."

"I know of none. Just a murmer of discontent born of their grief and worry."

Nakht, who had been attending silently up to this point, put both of his large black hands squarely on the tab as he drew himself forward to speak. His deep, full voice gathered all eyes to him. He was the guard, commissioned with protecting the Queen's safety, as well as that of the land. His focus was clearly on the troublemaker from the Oasis. "Do you know what Setmose plans to do? How large is his band of outlaw-followers? Have there been any attacks? Any armed battles?"

Djehapy shook his head and gave this report, "No attacks. We caught some raiders last week…the ones that are the usual menace to caravans. One of these raiders told border police that a man at el Kharga, Setmose, is gathering men, mostly desert raiders, nomads, outlaws and other such disenfranchised persons."

Nakht nodded. "Those types of fighters are easy to draw but they have more capacity for disruption than loyalty to any leader."

The Queen said, "But Djehapy, here at Zawty, you have the largest police force, aside from the cataracts going to Kush and the Horus Road that protects us from the Levant. Is that force not enough to manage raiders and traders that cause such a threat?"

Djehapy replied, "The police force helps with the swords of raiders but not with the words of traders. While Setmose is free to dream of sedition, we are not safe…and neither are the Pharaoh and his family. Men of soldiering age have all gone with the Pharaoh, so there is no one here for Setmose to recruit. On the other hand, there are few men available to defend the city if attacked. Our police force protects us from raiders. They are not trained nor prepared to meet a band of rebels."

"Do you think," asked Queen Ahmose, "that getting rid of Setmose would be enough to take care of the problem here?"

"Indeed, it would," Djehapy's voice came quick and strong. "Without his instigation, the matter here would die a natural death."

But Kharit added her perspective, "I believe removing Setmose would eliminate the outside threat but there is still the trouble for the people of the nome." She reached out and placed her hand over her husband's. "Which makes them vulnerable to rebellious thoughts, in the first place. The governor and I want our people to look toward Waset with loyalty." Djehapy smiled at her and nodded.

Queen Ahmose responded, "What would they need to do that?"

Almost relieved, Kharit leaned forward gracefully in her chair. "Their appetite is wetted for the novelty and wealth of things from the Levant. They are traders. Even our farmers are traders. The grandfathers tell tales of the wealth of the barbarians…of horses, timber and purple dye. Our people believe that trade is what makes them rich and what makes their temple rich."

The Queen nodded pensively, drumming her fingers on the cleared table, looking back and forth between governor and wife. "Djehapy, you fear the threat of outsiders' ideas and attacks. Kharit, you fear the vulnerability due to the people's want and suffering, here in the city. Do the two of you disagree about what is needed?"

The husband and wife looked at each other and smiled. Djehapy spoke, "No. Really, we both agree that both issues are important. There are two problems, here. One problem is what is brought from the outside, the ideas of sedition and the other is the problem within the town itself, the vulnerability of people who open their ears when they should be shut." Kharit smiled and nodded in agreement.

The Queen moved a delicate index finger back and forth over her lower lip in a thoughtful manner. "I would like to see your town and consider all possible options."

Djehapy said, "Tomorrow we had hoped that you would do just that…and allow the people to see you and be reassured by your presence and support."

The Queen answered, "Yes, Ineni and I will see your records. I know that Hapu also wishes to visit your temple and speak to the priest there. Nakht would like to meet with your desert police guards to gather information about Setmose. Yuf will, of course, make notes."

Djehapy bowed his head, and said, "All has been arranged. We thought, also, that the children would enjoy visiting the marketplace with our daughter, Tutkharit."

Hatasu's eyes lit up. She looked over at Tutkharit, who smiled back at her. Thethi broke into her thoughts by jabbing her with his elbow. "I'll fight off those troublemakers. If we see them at the market place, I'll take care of them…you'll see. How could they question my father's legitimacy?" Paheri bent over and whispered something in Thethi's ear. The boy made a face and slumped back in his chair.

The plans decided, the conversation shifted to the report of the Pharaoh at war in the Levant. Queen Ahmose told of Pharaoh Thutmose's progress through Sharuhem, Jericho and Megiddo not meeting with any resistance. She anticipated that by this time, he must be at the city of Hazor, where he expected more trouble. She also spoke frankly that her husband's aim in the war was to eventually secure and increase trade. This would, indeed, aid the Zawty community.

"Not if we have no grain to trade," persisted Kharit.

Ahmose turned to her, and said, "You think you need another trade item besides grain to help the situation?"

Kharit responded, "Yes, that might help, but what? Cattle? Vegetables? It needs to be something that stores better than grain and doesn't attract mice."

Hatasu noted her mother's thoughtful attention as Kharit made her points. The next morning, Hatasu awoke to the smell of desert sand and caravan donkeys. The loud *he-haw*-ing of these animals filled the air as they were driven to the river to drink. This sound mixed in with the *baa*-ing of goats and the shouted orders of the children who tended them.

The sky was a particularly clear color of blue as Hatasu stood on the roof of the mooring palace gazing in the direction of desert. The sun rising on the other side of the river, shone with particular glory on the mountains and the wadi (canyon valley). This was the pathway by which the desert blew into the Zawty's main street. She stared hard at the mountain opening, thinking its road led to a dangerous place where a bad man was trying to defy Maat and her father. She could see the well-beaten road that came out of that wilderness and reached all the way through town, coming to a halt at the river. The trader's donkeys were now traveling along it for their morning watering.

Turning away from the caravan route, Hatasu noted the square fields formed by the irrigation ditches and canals made a patchwork of different shades of tan and brown. About a quarter of the fields had been plowed and planted. Farmers were out moving along the furrows with their ox and plows and seed bags.

At the junction of where the sand-road came into town and the dirt-road led to the river, she could make out a cluster of tents. At the western perimeter of this tent-city was the corral for the donkeys and goats. This temporary village outside the royal city was alive with activity of people going here and there. A steady stream of people carried bundles to the market area. She could also see the town and its complex system of broad and narrow streets, seeming to converge at the river quays. There was much activity as people loaded and unloaded boats. The market stalls were being set up and stocked for the day. Scribes and administrators were registering every significant activity and transaction. The sounds of the morning bustle filled the air and mixed with the chanting that came from the temple. These seemed like the activities of a normal day, free of all threat.

Tutkharit arrived right after breakfast to take the royal children on the town tour. At thirteen-years-old, she moved with womanly grace and carried in her hand several small bags tied at the top. The small troop of children walked along the wide, central street that connected the desert trail through the town to the market place and harbor. Tutkharit walked several paces ahead, followed by Thethi, Meryt and Isis. Hatasu kept her pace quickened so as to keep up with Tutkharit. Hapuseneb trailed along behind.

As the young guide walked briskly, she talked just as rapidly, telling tales of her city's tale of woe. There was a proud sense of authority in her manner, just as there was with her mother.

"There are the storehouses for the grain we trade *with*. There should be wheat and barley there but the mice ate what the sand didn't destroy." Tutkharit pointed to the buildings on their left. "It is necessary for us to eat the grain the Pharaoh sent us, and therefore, we have little or nothing to trade with." Then, still walking quickly, she turned toward another row of mud-brick, round-topped buildings. "There are the buildings that store the items traded for; dates, wine and alum. They are stored here for the tax for the Pharaoh." In an aside, she whispered a confidence, "The desert is dry and boring but the things that come out of it are remarkable, particularly the date and wines."

Turning back and pointing to the broad ribbon of heavily packed sand that wound down from the desert plateau to the marketplace, Tutkharit said, "The desert road that brings these things to us is the Darb el Arba'in. Along it travels the desert traders who go back and forth from the el Kharga Oasis, carrying the dates, wine and alum from the people who dwell in Oasis villages. Most of the traders are nomad people. They are not like us. They are dirty and do not know the customs of the people of the Nile. They cover themselves with cloth. Father says it's to protect them from the desert sun but I say to conceals their dirt and their crimes." She said these things matter-of-factly to the group. "The people whose goods they carry, the Oasis dwellers, are much like our own Nile farmers. Some of them occasionally travel here with the caravan on business or family visits. I will introduce you to one such person at the market when we get there.

"There is a third group of people we hear about, but seldom see. They are the desert raiders who attack the caravans and steal their goods. They are terrible people, not only dirty but vicious and clever. We only see them when our police capture the culprits and bring them to town for execution."

"What about the malcontent, Setmose?" Hatasu wondered how Tutkharit saw the situation.

"He is like the desert raiders." Her eyes flitted around to see who might be listening. "Only he's scarier. Some people are afraid he will attack our village. But my father says the Pharaoh and the

Queen would never let that happen. Now that I have met the Queen, I think he is right, and she will protect us from the danger of Setmose."

Hatasu nodded, liking this young woman, with her hope and confidence in her mother, the Queen. They arrived at the place where the main street came to the marketplace and the docks. The conversation stopped as Tutkharit turned, guiding the group into the corridor between the markets stalls and the boats quays. The traders' stalls formed one row; the boats moored in the harbor formed the other. They faced each other with a wide area between for travelers and traders. The royal boats were brightly colored in contrast to the simpler boats of fishermen and merchants. There was even one large, wooden vessel made for traveling long distances…possibly even from the Levant. There were also small reed boats, like that in which she had ridden with Puyemre. These little boats, carrying fish or passengers, scooted in and out, dodging the larger boats.

The market on the other side was a row of stalls, each with a canopy; some brightly colored, some faded and dusty. They were mostly of thick linen and all were held up by poles to give shade to the traders, the men and women who sat behind the wares they displayed on blankets or baskets. This row had empty stalls, like teeth missing in a smiling mouth.

Tutkharit said, "The caravan arrived yesterday. They heard of the Queen's arrival. People come to trade with each other, even when Zawty has not grain to trade itself. The empty stalls you see in the market row are usually occupied by Zawty merchants. The nomad traders, who recently arrived, set up their tent city on the desert side of town. They take up many of the market stalls for a week or so, trade their wares and are off again to the Oasis, or even further. They will be back here again in a moon or so."

Hatasu turned to the market, noting its activity and the thin and sad people that were buying and selling. This market was indeed different from the one at home in Waset. There was also a strange disorder to it. The nomad traders' children ran around behind the stalls. They were smeared with dirt, their hair knotted and they were hitting and throwing things at each other. Their donkeys were now herded a short distance from the market stalls and they were tended by the children. The smell of these straggly animals affected the entire atmosphere of the market. In a corner of their pen was a heap of the large, dusty, woven baskets used to transport items on the donkeys.

Tutkharit led them into the market corridor. The vendors called out greetings and invitations to passers-by to buy their wares. Most of these traders were women, some were old men. Many greeted Tutkharit by name and she explained that these were townsfolks with whom she and her mother trade regularly. Some called out to the royal children as well, particularly Hatasu and Thethi.

They passed stall after stall of people selling different qualities of linen, dyes and bleaches. Tutkharit kept walking and told them that one of her mother's distant cousins was a trader from the Oasis and they would stop and buy some dates from her. Hatasu noticed the people that looked like they were not the tent-wearing nomads but townspeople. She saw a woman and child each with ash and dirt on their heads and she knew they were mourning a loved one. She saw an old man with a hollowed face and protruding ribcage and she knew he'd suffered hunger and illness.

They finally came to the stall of a gray-haired, older woman, dressed in a coarsely woven brown sheath with a faience amulet of Bas on a cord around her neck. She sat upon a many-colored blanket on which there were also many baskets of dates. When the old woman saw the group approaching, she called out to Tutkharit. The wide smile of greeting multiplied the weathered lines on her face and exposed the toothless interior of her mouth. "Cousin Tutkharit, so glad to see you today! So, these are your royal visitors?" Her voice was raspy but pleasant. She bowed low before the children, which called attention to them from passersby and vendors.

"Yes, yes, Tchet, these are our royal visitors." Turning to her guests, she said, "This is Tchet. She is our favorite trading cousin and she comes here just to bring us wonderful dates from the Oasis." She said this with a teasing grin and then continued with emphasis, "For very high prices!"

"You know I am always fair! I ask only fair trade of grain."

"Yes, yes. Today, I wish for some dates for my guests." Tutkharit placed one of her tied packages on the ground in front of her.

Tchet picked it up and felt the heft of it. Then, she opened the tie at the top and looked inside, feeling and examining the quality of the grain. She nodded seriously then looked up at Tutkharit and smiled. "This will buy you half a basket of dates."

"Now, Tchet, you said you were fair. This much grain should afford us at least one whole basket of dates. They are very small baskets."

"Oh, Tutkharit, these are very hard times. You will make me and my family very poor. We would all starve if we gave away our dates for so little."

Their young guide looked at the old woman, shaking her head and smiling. "Well, we certainly wouldn't want your family to starve! Will a little grain from this other bag be enough for a whole basket?"

The five cousins watched in awed silence. They'd seen people at the marketplace before but their own needs were provided for. This was the first time they actually witnessed the act of bartering.

Tchet took the other bag, felt its heft and emptied half of it into the larger container of grain at her side. She nodded and smiled at her young relative.

Shaking her head but allowing a smile to open her face, Tutkharit said, "Old woman, you are a hard trader." This was said as though being 'a hard trader' was both a virtue and a term of endearment.

Smiling, Tutkharit took the baskets of dates and offered them to the children. The woven basket was heaped high with the oasis fruit at the exact peak of ripeness and flavor. Thethi loved dates. They were his favorite food. He reached out and took three in one hand. He put the first one in his mouth then the others. His eyes closed and he moved his head slowly from one side to the other as he savored the sweet, ripe taste. "Mmmm! These are good!" He moved his mouth around so he could liberate the sugary flesh and spit out the pit.

Isis followed Thethi's lead, put a date in her mouth, and joined in his exclamation of delight. Tutkharit urged the others to try some, too. Hatasu and Meryt grinned at each other then looked at the dates in the basket. Each girl chose a fine-looking sample and allowed it to melt in her mouth as she savored the perfect flavor and meaty sweetness. Hapuseneb took his turn and before long the two boys were shooting the pits out of their mouths, using each other as targets, laughing as they did.

Smiling at them, Tchet said, "I have gifts for my new royal friends." She took from behind her a basket of small stones. These were interesting stones from the desert with designs of swirls and circles like imprints of strange, shelled creatures. "Do you like?"

The girls each picked one and turned it over to inspect it closely. "Thank you so much, Tchet."

Tchet then turned to Tutkharit. "How are your wedding preparations coming?"

"Oh, very well. Mother and I have finished most of the linens and the furniture father had commissioned is begun." She turned to her young guest and added, "I am to be married to Qenu, the son of the governor of the Beni Hassan nome, when he returns from the war in the Levant." Hatasu and Meryt both looked at her with renewed respect. She would soon be the mistress of her own household.

Tchet continued, "You tell your mother I have kept aside for her the very best of the alum for the linen-dying you are planning to do.

I also was able to trade for some natron from a boatman from el Kab. I knew you'd need that for the linen bleaching. I had to trade quite a quantity of dates for it but I knew the natron was the very best and it is just what you would want."

Tutkharit smiled a 'thank you' at Tchet. Her youthful, well-oiled skin was a sharp a contrast to the old woman's leather-like wrinkles. It was like looking from a desert to a river. "My preparations are close to finished, and soon my beloved Qenu and I will be making offerings to Hathor for children. How is your family? I hope all are well since your last trip here."

Tchet shook her head. "What worries me most is my grandson. He is a reckless youth and he has been listening to that trouble maker, Setmose. Our family threatened to disown him but still he persists in his madness. He even tried to use our family trade connections to get Setmose some khopesh swords. He was such a fine young man before he listened to that criminal!"

"Oh, dear, Tchet, I'm so sorry to hear that. When the Queen gets rid of Setmose, I'm sure your grandson will return to his better self."

"Maybe, if he is not punished right along with him. My grandson also spoke of Setmose's connections in the north. I think there is more to this issue than eliminating Setmose."

Thethi had been listening even though it seemed he was busy shooting date pits at Isis. He looked at the old woman and blurted out, "I'd show that Setmose. He can't threaten my father." Taking a defiant stance, arms crossed over his chest, with a deep frown on his face, the boy looked more like his father than Hatasu had ever seen. His strong words were new to her. His brashness alarmed her.

Hatasu pulled him away from the stall, remembering how her father told her to look out for this troublesome brother. "Thethi, it is a dangerous thing to challenge this criminal!"

"He must stop telling lies about Father!"

At that moment, Hatasu saw a nomad watching them from the shade of a tree. The eastern sun caught the glint of his eyes from inside his hooded robe. He pulled the hood forward, further hiding his face as he moved toward the group of children.

Chapter 22 ~ Setmose

Tutkharit saw the hooded nomad, too. "We must return to the house," she said with urgency in her voice. Tchet left her stall and placed herself between the children and the stranger as she helped Tutkharit usher them in the direction of Djehapy's walled manor.

Thethi was still standing boldly, his arms crossed in front of him. He didn't notice the hooded stranger. The other children quickly followed Tutkharit. Hatasu took Thethi's hand and pulled him along. As they retraced their steps back through the market place, more nomads gathered, seemingly coming from nowhere. Each focused on the children, moving closer, surrounding them, their faces hidden in hoods. The road to the house stretched into the distance in front of them. Cold fingers gripped Hatasu's intestines as the group of children started to race-walk toward safety.

One of the hooded figures pushed forward blocking Hatasu and Thethi's path. Hatasu darted forward and escaped his grasp. Thethi, who now understood, hesitated as though he wanted to turn and fight this man. The stranger was so close, she could smell the donkey dung on his clothes and see the scar over his left eye.

Suddenly, Hatasu heard Nakht call out, "Halt!" in a tone that said alarm. She and the other children broke into a run, heading toward the shelter of Tutkharit's house. Behind them they could hear shouts and scuffling.

At the door, Hatasu turned back and saw the unit of their own black Medjay guards, armed with batons and staffs, locked in battle with about ten hooded, robed figures. As soon as all of the children were in the garden, Sitre slammed the door shut and bolted it. Sitre and her aunts hugged each child tight and checked them all over to make sure each one was okay.

"Where is Mother?" Hatasu asked Sitre. Thinking if she and Thethi had been in jeopardy, so, too, was their mother.

"She is there, on the roof." Sitre pointed above them to the roof room. Hatasu could see her standing tall, flanked by Djehapy, Ineni and Hapu. The Queen's hand shaded her eyes as she focused on the fighting in the street below.

Leaving Thethi in the safety of the garden with Paheri, Hatasu ran to the stairway, bounding up the steps to the roof and her mother. As she looked out over the scene, police batons and battle staffs were a blur going every which way. Whack and thud sounds were loud, as wood made forceful contact with muscle and bone. She saw Nakht's wood stick strike hard against the side of the leader's head and he fell to the ground. Nakht and his band of Medjays, along with Djehapy's desert police, surrounded the robed nomads group.

Nakht pulled back the hoods and exposed the men's faces. The man who threatened her looked up to where she and her mother stood on the roof top. There was the most awful gleam in his eyes. A chill went though her body. Nakht and his men put wooden handcuffs on each of the men, connecting all of them with a sturdy rope. A group of townspeople gathered now, talking and pointing. Nakht looked up to the Queen and saluted her. She acknowledged him with a nod of her head. Nakht led them off in the direction of the desert, each forced to walk bent forward by their shackles.

"Where is he taking them?" Hatasu asked.

"There is a thick walled building that will be well guarded until we bring these treasonous criminals before a tribunal. I believe we have captured the troublemakers," Djehapy answered.

Hatasu breathed out a sigh of relief.

Ineni's eyebrows were drawn together as he spoke next, "A tribunal must be gathered quickly. These men must be interrogated. It is important to have swift justice, leaving no doubt in the minds of the townspeople of the strength of the Thutmose family and the blessing of Maat. No threat to the royal children is tolerated."

Djehapy nodded vigorously. "Yes, yes! These men are not from our town. I believe it is Setmose from the Oasis. Their ominous behavior toward the royal children…that was terrible."

"They fought as men who have practiced using weapons. These were certainly not simple trading or herding nomads come here to exchange goods," Hapu said.

It was then that Nakht burst onto the roof room. "We have Setmose in custody. The trader, Tchet, identified the leader as this grandson of Teti-an."

"Then, he *is* the treasonous one!" Queen Ahmose spoke clearly.

"Thank the gods he is caught! My people need no longer fear him or be bothered by his sedition," said Djehapy. "Execution is the prescribed punishment for treason but it is still necessary to follow legal procedures."

The Queen reached over and placed her hand on his arm. "I must rely on you to form a tribunal as quickly as possible. Hapu and you shall be on it. I will be the judge in the place of the Pharaoh. Vizier

Ineni," she turned to her brother-in-law, "shall examine the criminal before the tribunal and pronounce a verdict, making sure that Maat is served."

"When would you like to have the trial, Your Majesty?" Djehapy asked. "It could be ready this afternoon."

"Ineni, does that give you enough time?"

"If we had the tribunal tomorrow afternoon, we would have time to find out if he acts alone or has more gang members in the desert."

"Nakht, take a troupe out into the desert with a gang of the police and see if there are any others that might try to stage an attack or a rescue. Tomorrow will be time enough to act swiftly."

Smiling warmly at her royal guard, the Queen said, "Nakht, thank you for your quick and effective action in protecting the children." He bowed low before the Queen, pleased at her acknowledgement.

Hatasu walked to her mother and put her arms around her skirt. The realization that real danger, even death, could have come to her dear mother, left her feeling wobbly inside. Her mother's hand trembled slightly as she rested it on her daughter's shoulder. Hatasu became aware that for all the firm decisiveness, her mother, too, was shaken by the incident.

Hapu stood on the other side of Ahmose and the three of them looked out over the town square that still held a gathering of people, mostly women, old men and young children. There was a buzz of anxiety and excitement. Hatasu remembered the adult men were away at war with her father. They did, indeed, need royal protection at this time. As their men were away fighting for their Pharaoh, it was only right that the Queen and royal family protect them from *this* trouble.

Kharit walked up behind them. "I am so sorry to have had the royal family endangered in my nome but it is *not* my people that would harm you. You see them there in the street, alarmed at their exposure to such a criminal as Setmose. They will be relieved when this matter is put to rest."

They walked toward the stairs, descending to the garden. Lady Kharit looked to the Queen and said, "It would be better if you and the children did not venture into the town again, until it is certain that all of the rebels have been rounded up. However, we could visit the weaving shed within our manor. I would be so pleased for you to see our fine operation and it would distract you and the children from the danger."

Ahmose agreed and as they walked through the garden, the girl cousins ran up and were invited to join them. As the women walked along, Hatasu asked her mother, "Why does this Setmose cause such trouble?"

"Well, Setmose and those who follow him are men without Ra. It is up to the Pharaoh and now to us, to protect Maat for the people."

"Yes, but what did he want with Thethi and me?"

"We will find out more tomorrow at the tribunal but if Setmose wanted to overthrow the Thutmoses as the ruling family, he must have seen you as the easiest target. But, you are safe now."

As the small group walked to the shed, Hatasu noticed the wall surrounding the manor house, offering them safety. It was whitewashed and its protective thickness was disguised by the bright garden flower design painted on it, a mature reflections of the flowers sprouting in the pond and flower beds. She took comfort that it kept any lingering danger at bay.

The small group proceeded to the working area in the rear of the manor house. There, amidst the household grain storage, grinding stones and bread-making ovens stood a white-washed mud-brick building marked with a larger-than-life striding image of the goddess Neith...red crown on her head and weaver's shuttle in her hand.

Tutkharit met them just outside the door. The Queen smiled toward the young woman and made polite conversation, "I hear from your parents that you are to start your own household soon? What are your plans?"

She blushed slightly then proceeded to speak, "Yes, I will be starting my own household with Qenu, the son of the governor of the Oryx nome. As soon as he returns with the army, I will join him. Then family and friends will accompany us on the bridal procession, carrying things by flotilla to my new home down river. My mother is finishing the beautiful linens she is preparing for me and I am waiting for the furniture my father has commissioned."

"I wish you much happiness in your new life, Tutkharit."

Standing outside the weaving shed, Hatasu could hear chanting. It was a mesmerizing, repetitive sound. As they opened the door, Hatasu could make out the words, "*Oh Neith, Great One of Sais, Your glory unfurled, Spinner of destinies, Weaver of worlds.*"

The Queen, her daughter and her nieces were ushered into a large room of people who were busily at work. As they entered, the workers stopped chanting as they all stood up and bowed low before their Queen. Kharit spoke to the overseer and introduced her to the Queen as Bekat. Ahmose smiled warmly and then nodded to the other women, encouraging them to continue.

The chant began again as their nimble fingers did the tasks assigned to them. There were five women in all, each attending to her responsibility at differing stages of making a piece of linen cloth. First, Hatasu noticed the rover; a young girl only slightly older than herself, who loosely twisted the fine, young flax fibers together, rolled the tentative string carefully into a ball and placed it in a spinning bowl in front of her. Next, there was an older girl who was a spinner. She stood to the side of the rover and spun the contents of the bowls into a thin, sturdy thread with her spindle. Hatasu recognized the loom that stretched long on the floor, threads carefully wound at both ends of its wood frame. Two mature women sat facing each other over the growing piece of linen, each handling a shuttle and skillfully managing the delicate threads woven into the warp. The fifth woman was Bekat, the overseer; an older woman with drooping breasts and a wrinkled face. She directed each phase of the work.

Tutkharit squatted to the floor beside the loom and moved the gauze-thin material between her thumb and first two fingers. In an enthusiastic tone, she announced, "This fabric on the loom now is for a fine banquet dress. Isn't it exquisite? I shall be a fine lady when I am mistress of my household with Qenu."

"Yes, indeed. It is beautiful," said the Queen.

Tutkharit went on, "There are other thicker and heavier pieces that have been finished and are in the boxes in the storehouse waiting to be transported."

"Won't you miss living with your mother and father?" Meryt wanted to know.

"We will visit often, as our families do now."

Isis piped up, "I am never going to leave my mother and father's house. My husband will have to come and live with me there."

Everyone chuckled and no one bothered to correct her naïve notion. Setting up a new separate household was simply what marriage was...except for the royal family, who married siblings to protect the blood line. Hatasu's mind went to her own situation. She was one of the few who would actually have Isis's wish. Though Hatasu's marriage meant she would be in her parent's household, she felt none of her new friend's excitement at marrying Amenmose. She wondered if Amenmose knew Tutkharit's Qenu; if they were friends, like Tutkharit and her.

The sounds of weaving and chanting, brought her back to the present. Hatasu looked around her and noticed the high windows and thick, whitewashed walls that protected these women from the heat of the sun. The women worked on, the rhythm of their chant matching the rhythm of their shuttle. "*Spinner of our destinies, Weaver of worlds.*"

Hatasu thought to herself how she and Tutkharit had such different destinies; one marrying her love but living away from her family...the other having the comfort of home but with a brother-husband who didn't even like her. *What worlds would the goddess Neith weave for the two of them out of the threads of these destinies? And how might those destinies be different if Nakht hadn't acted so quickly?*

As the shuttles moved back and forth weaving the cloth, the chants wove a melodic soul-cocoon that contrasted a wedding-linen–preparing-world inside with the Setmose-threatening-one on the outside. Over the sounds of the shuttles and the chants, Hatasu heard Ahmose ask Kharit questions about how they achieved the fineness of thread and the evenness of weave. Kharit explained how she chooses the young, tender shoot for such fine weave and older, tougher plants for coarser fabric. Hatasu heard her mother say, "Since it is the very young sprouts of the flax plant that make the threads of your linen so fine, then it need never go to seed except to replant."

"Yes," the governor's wife answered.

The Queen nodded thoughtfully and asked, "Do you think linen would be a possible trade item for Zawty?"

Kharit raised her eyebrows. "Well, it would store well and not attract mice. A weaving industry in the Oryx nome down river is successful but they produce thicker, sturdier, less delicate cloth."

Ahmose went on, "You could trade it to acquire the grains you need. Would you be interested in setting up more weaving sheds and producing more of this fine fabric as a trade item? When our Pharaoh has made the trade routes to the Levant safe again, it will be a valuable commodity for the women and families of Zawty. This would be a way to help your people be free from the threat of storm?"

"I think it would work," said a thoughtful Kharit.

Hatasu smiled, watching her mother tighten the bonds of the friendship between the two families.

It was arranged that the next day the chosen tribunal would meet in front of the temple. The Queen felt there was still an element of danger, so she ordered that the children not be allowed outside the governor's walled manor. She did not, however, say they couldn't watch the proceedings from the roof.

Hatasu, Thethi, Hapuseneb and Meryt sat cross-legged on the roof facing into the temple square. Paheri sat with them. Little Isis opted to stay with her mother and Sitre made it known she was content to let Paheri be with the children because she 'never wanted to see those ugly faces again'.

The four friends looked down to the tribunal; nine upright men and women of the town sat in chairs in front of the temple, talking among themselves. Townspeople gathered around. Hatasu could see in the distance, from the direction of the desert pathway, Setmose and the nine other men being brought in, handcuffed and tied.

They were escorted by a company of Medjays with Nakht at the lead. The prisoners were made to stand in front of the tribunal. Relieved of the hooded robes that comprised their nomad disguises, they stood with shaved heads in dirty white loincloths. Most of them were young men about Amenmose's age. Setmose was the oldest, probably in his thirties. Some had scars on their body and all looked disheveled.

Hatasu could see Ineni standing before the man thought to be

Setmose. Ineni looked very angry and poked the man repeatedly in his chest. The man struggled with his restraints and yelled at Ineni and then at the Queen. Hatasu was very tense, fearing for her mother, but she stood tall. Hatasu heard the words clearly shouted by the rebel, "Your family usurped the crown from the Amenhat in Itjtawy."

Hatasu looked to see how the townspeople reacted to this. They booed Setmose. The tribunal discussed the case. Ineni stopped questioning the prisoners and joined them. It took only a few minutes before the Queen stepped forward with the announcement of the verdict. "Setmose is found guilty of treason and is sentenced to death."

The prisoners were led away. Not toward the desert from which they came but down to the river. Each of the prisoners struggled against their bonds and against the Medjay who escorted them. The townspeople dispersed.

The children could hear the screaming and hollering as the men were dragged toward the river. "What's happening now?" Hatasu asked Paheri.

"They are going to be executed. The sentence for treason is death."

"But where are they going? How will they be executed?"

"Well, since they are going to the river, it is most likely the Queen decided the manner of execution to be by crocodile."

"They will throw all of them to the crocodiles?"

"Yes, the crocodile does not leave any part to be mummified and therefore the criminals will not have a body to gain entrance into the Field of Reeds. It is the worse possible punishment."

The screams were full of intense terror. They grew fainter with distance. Then, there was silence. Shortly after, the townspeople began filtering out of their houses and moved toward the temple. Women carried frame drums and colored scarves singing the praises of their Queen. As she made her way back to the governor's house, she reached out to the hands extended to her and accepted the well wishes of the people along the way.

As Ahmose reached the doorway, Hatasu ran along with the other children to greet her mother with questions, "Why was he after us?"

Her mother said, "Setmose won't bother you, any more. He would have held you hostage to get to me. His plan was to disarm the Thutmose family and set himself up as the ruler. If he had done away with Ineni and I, it would have been easy for his band of renegades to take over this town of women and expand from there."

Djehapy, Nakht, Hapu and Ineni walked through the gate. Nakht said, "It is a good thing for us those nomads are so notoriously unreliable. They, of course, just disappeared into the sands and abandoned him."

Ineni said, "The other men said he promised to pay them with swords and gold. Where do you think he planned to get these items to pay them with?"

Djehapy said, "I do not know for sure, but there is rumor some people in Itjtawy are sympathetic to Setmose."

"Or who may use him as a pawn for their own ends," added Hapu.

"We deal officially only with Amenhat, your governor at Itjtawy," Djehapy continued, "I really don't think he is involved with rebels. Our temple priest sometimes deals with a priest named Usersobek. I have heard whispers this high official of the Itjtawy temple complains, like Setmose, that the Pharaoh should come from that old, royal city."

The Queen joined them and said, "Now is the time to be grateful to Amun for his…and Nakht's…protection against Setmose."

They entered the building. Hatasu was distressed at the possibility of a new threat and decided to find Thethi and Hapuseneb. She had a strong desire to practice with her throw-stick. At that night's banquet, relief flooded the room. No one spoke again of Setmose. There was a great expression of warmth shown toward the royal family. Many of their most prized trade items were presented to the Queen by various local merchants, all dressed in their finest garments and jewelry. Even Tchet had exchanged her sturdy linen sheath for one with a fine, bleached weave and presented Ahmose with an exquisite piece of purple cloth.

Hatasu and Meryt sat with Tutkharit and laughed over silly jokes and made up stories to tell each other of their possible futures.

At the end of the meal, Queen Ahmose spoke to the people gathered. There was absolute stillness as every ear listened. "My beloved children of Zawty, you have been very gracious to me and I thank you for your gifts. I also have a gift for you. I know you have suffered much from the wind and the rats. They have deprived you of your health, your food and your trade items. Therefore my gift to you is a new crop to free you from this suffering. It has been arranged, you will have a new item to trade that will not be so dependent on such forces of nature.

"You shall grow flax and harvest it while it is young; too young to interest the rodents, and long before the winds are bothersome. You will weave this flax into bolts of clothe that will bring a fine trade, both along the Nile and beyond it. You shall gain renown as the weaver of the finest linen in the land. I shall build ten new weaving sheds and ten new looms. You shall receive grains from the Pharaoh's own stores until your trade has grown sufficiently to trade for your own. Messengers were sent to all the nomes to bring you all their flax seeds to be planted this season to begin your change; no longer growing wheat but rather trading your fine linen for what you need."

The women looked from one to the other. A murmur spread through out the gathering. Then, a great cheer went up. The people danced and chanted her praise, "*Great goddess Mut, mother to her people.*"

After dinner, the royal family returned to the mooring palace where her mother called her advisors together to discuss the events of the day.

Ineni scowled as he said, "It was a good day's work to have executed Setmose. There is no doubt about his guilt. But I'm not sure the weaving shed plan is going to address the real problems here in Zawty, itself. I know Djehapy and Kharit are loyal to Thutmose but they govern a very difficult nome. There have been too many times that Zawty has been the vanguard of trouble with the north."

Hapu added, "The network of trade places Zawty in a strategic position between exiled rebels of the Oasis and ambitious priests of Itjtawy. It is a place for opportunity as well as trouble for the Thutmose family."

Ahmose said calmly, "At this present time, I see the legitimate hardship of the people. The signs of hunger and illness can be seen on their faces. I believe the making of a marketable linen is a good solution to their problems."

Hapu spoke to Ineni, "I think it will bind these people to us in loyalty and cause them to turn away from past alliances with Itjtawy."

"Perhaps you are right. Time will tell," Ineni said.

Hatasu asked, "Mother, why is there such tension between Zawty and Itjtawy?"

"Well, my dear, this is the land of a five-hundred year-old feud. It is by no accident that we call our country 'The Two Lands'. It is very important to keep the two parts united. Long before your forefather Montuhotep, our beloved land was ruled from the northern city of Itjtawy but there was confusion in the Two Lands about who should be the rightful Pharaoh. The people of Zawty favored the rulers from Itjtawy, against Montuhotep, who was the successful reunitor of the Two Lands. These tensions continued between Waset and Zawty under the yoke of the Hyksos and they resisted the unification offered by the armies of Kamose. Our job now is to bring peace and prosperity to all of the land. We must not let the history of our conflicts blind us to present opportunities for unity."

Chapter 23 - River Dangers

The next day, Hatasu noted that Sitre deviated from the usual morning tasks of bathing and braiding. Once the traditional princess pampering was complete, her nurse reached into her own traveling basket and took out a necklace with a stone pendent. She placed this new amulet around the Hatasu's neck, companion to the turquoise pendant of Bes.

She looked down at the new pendant. It was a wonderful blue with lively specks of gold glittering on its surface, almost as though it was solidified river water reflecting the golden sun. It was in the shape of a fish. "What is this?" she asked.

Sitre had already started the incantation. *"Protect this wearer from any danger of drowning. Make her safe on the river."* Once she finished, she offered a satisfied smile to her royal charge and explained, "It's a magical catfish. Now, I don't have to worry."

Hatasu looked at it carefully and said, "It's the fish that swims upside down, isn't it?"

"Yes," Sitra replied, "it is the fish that has the power to protect those on the river."

After breakfast, they preceded as a royal group back to their boats, the other children also wearing new fish amulets. Sitre tried to hurry Hatasu along, distracting her from further thought about why, at this point in the journey, she gave her this magic. It was easy to be distracted as Governor Djehapy and his family escorted them to the quay. Townsfolk again lined the street, this time whole heartedly waving and singing the praises of the Queen and Pharaoh.

She smiled as she went, honoring many individuals with an extended touch of her hand, a wave or a nod. Behind her walked Hatasu, alongside Sitre, Thethi and Paheri and Muthotep carrying Neferubrity. Hatasu recognized many faces in the crowds. There were merchants they had seen at the market, priests and administrators she saw at the tribunal and landed squires from the banquets. Hatasu waved and smiled, following her mother's example.

The crowd no longer held back as they had when the royal group had first arrived. Now they leaned toward her, waving with both hands. Her mother had truly re-won their hearts. At the quay, there was a formal goodbye to Djehapy, Kharitand Tutkharit. The governor's family reverenced the Queen, expressing deep gratitude for her help in restoring order and giving hope for new prosperity. There were messages and gifts to be carried to Khnumhotep and Qenu's family at Beni Hassan. At last, a warm farewell to all.

The children were to travel in the boats with their parents on this leg of the journey, so Hatasu boarded the bright-colored vessel of the Queen. The animals, Chi-chi and Behka, who had remained safe onboard the ships during this short visit, were ecstatic at the sight of their masters. Chi-chi squealed and chattered as she ran to and fro on the deck. She climbed up Hatasu, eluded her grasp to jump down, then climbed up the mast. The princess giggled as her monkey repeated the whole performance again. Behka, on the other hand, barked loudly at the sight of Thethi and jumped up to lick his face. Thethi knelt down and petted his dog's head and rubbed his ears while the huge, rough tongue kissed his face. Neferubrity, too, reacted. She clung tight to Muthotep but stretched out her chubby baby hand toward, first the monkey, then the dog, making her own squealing sounds.

It wasn't until they pulled out into the river and were out of sight of the waving, singing and dancing townsfolk of Zawty, that the animals and children calmed down sufficiently for Hatasu to notice some things were different. Her attention was drawn to the sailors checking and tightening the ropes that secured anything that could move on deck. "Why are you doing that?" she asked one of the sailors.

"Well…" He stopped and looked at her. "The river will be a little rough today."

"What does that mean?"

This sailor, like each of the sailors, had dark hair cut close to his scalp, weather-bronzed skin and muscles bulging under the surface of his arms and legs. He wore the short linen kilt of the sailor of the royal ship. His kohled eyes squinted, protecting him from the reflection of the sun on the water. In a gruff voice he told her, "The spirits of this part of the river are restless. Winds blow down from the eastern mountains with the fury of marauding desert raiders and sandbars lurk under the water like crocodiles waiting to ambush."

Hatasu's hand went to the amulet of the fish at her throat.

Another of the sailors working with him, spoke up, "Now don't you be scaring the little princess!" This sailor had a mole beside his nose but the same short black hair and tied kilt. He turned to Hatasu and said, "Don't you worry, Royal Miss, we have been past these parts many times. This is a good crew, seasoned in the ways of the river."

Hatasu caught the similarity to the words of the sailor in the Punt story. She braced herself with inward courage.

"Yes," said the first man, "We have methods to elude the winds and dodge the sandbars." Shaking his head, he continued, "No wind raiders or crocodiles will get us."

A third sailor, taller than the others, piped up wanting to be helpful. "This will be as easy as swallowing honey cake. Nothing like the difficulties of the cataracts at Swenet on the way to Kush. Now *that* is a dangerous river. It has hidden rocks like teeth that chew a boat up and swallow it in its great swirling mouth. No, this stretch of waterway is like the river god playing with us, saying 'Let me push you here. Let me trip you there'. We know his game and how to play it. We will be fine."

The second sailor, seeing the princess' eyes grow wider and her hand clench around the lapis pendant, knew his friend was creating fears rather than allaying them. He tried again in his own way, "Our beloved river god, Hapi, just gets a little rambunctious between Zawty and Kusai. We haven't lost anyone overboard in…oh…two years or so."

Hatasu's eyes widened still further. At this point, the captain came out of the cabin doing his own check of things on the deck and taking in the sailor's conversation with the princess, he said in an authoritarian manner, "The river god protects those with the blessing of the fish." He nodded at her magic necklace. "And the sailors made their offerings to Hapi, before we left port. Our ropes are strong, objects tied down. When we get to the rough places, you children will be safe inside the cabin."

Hatasu stood a little taller. "Oh, no, please, can I stay on deck and see how the river plays? I can be as brave as the sailors. I want to learn the ways of the river." Her imagination was triggered by the description of the shipwreck sailor in the story. "I want to see the clever ways you tame the wind and dodge the sandbars."

Thethi had overheard them as he was standing next to his sister and took hold of her hand. He said defiantly, "Me, too," with only a bit of doubt in his voice.

The captain and the sailors stared at the children with puzzled looks. They had expected the children to need comfort, not to challenge such things. "Well you must speak to the Queen but I am sure she will be most concerned with your safety."

In contrast to the sailors' warning, the river they were traveling on was calm and quiet. The sailors all took their places at the oars, five on each side of the boat. They used the strength in their bulging arms to move the boat along with the flow of the current. There was only the usual wake of the traveling boats, the creaking sound of the oars and the sound of small flocks of birds splashing and chirping.

Her mother was busy so Hatasu settled down with Sitre to practice the lessons from Sebai Rekh. This dear nurse-tutor knew what would inspire her to study her scribal arts and she gave *The Story of the Shipwrecked Sailor* to copy. Sitre assured her there would be time to get some lessons done before the river turned temperamental. Hatasu fell into the delight in learning the first symbols for: '*I once sailed into the Great Green Sea. Our ship was large and magnificent to see. Seasoned sailors who could read the sea, Wise in whatever weather may be. Their hearts were as brave as lions are free'*. She made lots of mistakes but Sitre patiently guided her through the words with her red pen, until she felt very proud of herself and was certain her father would be proud of her, too. As the morning wore on, however, she was more and more vigilant to the slightest sound or movement that might indicate the river was changing.

Copying the lines about the storm that blew upon the sailor in the story kept her even more on edge. Anxiously, she waited for the river's mood to shift. She jumped as a flock of ibis took flight, flapping their wings for take off from a marshy cove. She relaxed again as their flapping turned into an airborne glide. She went back to her ostraca and reed pen. Again, she startled as a large fish jumped out of the water and landed back with a loud splash. She relaxed as the water surface returned to the disruption caused only by the wake of the nearby boats. She returned to her writing. She startled a third time when Behka barked at Chi-chi, who was teasing him. This time, she looked around.

Over at Ineni's boat, Merit and Isis waved to her, but she could see their boxes were tied down, too. On Hapu's boat, she could see Hapuseneb and his parents sitting among their boxes. Her cousins were studying papyrus with their tutors, too. Still, she could feel only the usual north breeze as they passed the peaceful, broad fields of green on both sides of the water. The young sprouts showed their tender heads and gave a light green blur of color to the fields. As during the journey from Abedju, she was aware of the farmers moving in their neat rows with their plow animals, tending the soil and weeding the plants.

Then, in that moment of peace, the captain came out from the cabin. With a certain flourish, he took his place on the deck in the prow of the boat. The rows of sailor on each side of the boat sat taller and ten pair of eyes turned to watch him as they kept the rhythm of their strokes. The captain's clear, musical voice called to the steering man at the stern.

Hatasu became fully alert. She put down her stylus and ostraca. Her eyes followed the captain's eyes as he looked over the rowers to make sure each was in his place and alert. Each sailor met his eyes, indicating readiness. Then, he looked down the river. Hatasu turned her head to see, too.

The green, east bank vanished. In its place were giant, sand-colored cliffs looming close to the river's edge. The water's surface stirred into waves and what had been the calm, steady current carrying them along, began to swirl and twist serpent-like around unseen forms under the surface. As they moved toward this turbulent water, they felt the wind blowing against them. It blew down from the cliffs, stirring up the waters and pushing against anything in its way. The strong current continued to carry them as the wind tried to push them to the west bank. The rowers responded with strong strokes.

The captain spotted the first sandbar and called back to the steering man. He moved the great rudder oar to one side, the boat navigated to the other side. As Hatasu looked over the side of the boat, she could see the sandbar they missed just under the surface. Sitre tried to usher Hatasu to the cabin. Hatasu and Thethi both begged to be allowed to sit just outside the door so they could continue to see this exciting passage.

The Queen emerged from the cabin and stood tall in the doorway, the wind blowing the hair back from her face. Looking down at the children, she said, "You can sit by the doorway, if you promise to go in if I tell you."

The two of them nestled into their seats next to each other, grinning. The river continued to carry them swiftly, even splashing its waters onto the deck. The rowers added their power to the turns; left side rowing hard to turn right, right side rowing to turn left. They also had to row against the wind so it didn't push them to the west bank. They dodged one sandbar after another throughout the long afternoon. Some swirling waves splashed high enough onto the deck to wet their faces. There was the creaking sound of the oars, the clear note of the captain's orders for turns, the wind roaring in their ears and the water, splashing and swirling as it rushed past them and sometimes on them.

Hatasu felt a clear excitement. All of her senses were alive. Thethi assumed his great 'brave soldier' attitude. He whispered to his sister, in a conspiratory way, "Maybe we will be shipwrecked? Maybe the goddess of Punt will find us?"

The brother and sister looked at each other and recited together, "'*A storm blew us port and lee, Punt was the isle that rescued me. Busied with a meal to hunt, I met a goddess on the Isle of Punt.*'" They laughed together and the afternoon passed with the captains skillfully guiding the royal boats safely through the obstacle course.

Before the afternoon ended, the river and the winds finally

slowed down. The waters flowed more smoothly as the limestone cliffs receded, leaving more room again on the floodplain. The children claimed they were actually disappointed there had been no shipwreck.

Sitre interrupted their fantasy, by saying, "I think you are wishing to see the goddess. Well, you know there are easier ways to do that, than with the unpleasantness of a shipwreck. I'm just glad to finally be at Kasai. This boat-dance with the river is too hazardous for my taste."

The governor of this capital of the fourteenth nome greeted them. The mooring palace they proceeded to was small and simple but the banquet put on by the governor was aimed to honor and please. The Queen again waved to and smiled upon the people, re-winning hearts wherever she turned.

The day on the rough water left Hatasu feeling she was in a tired haze, unable to focus on these, yet another set of new surroundings. Ahmose drew the children to her, once they were settled in that night's lodging. The wind, jostling and excitement of the boat had exhausted them.

Their mother sang them the lullaby, "*May the wings of Isis enfold you, Safe may they always hold you, May your dreams be of wondrous things, Now sleep gently within her wings.*"

As her mother tucked the linen sheets cozily around her, Hatasu asked, "Can we go to Punt? Can we plan a trip, instead of waiting to be shipwrecked?"

Ahmose smiled as her daughter asked, "Is it possible to visit Punt the way we travel to the nomes?"

"So you would like to see the goddess of the marvelous land of Punt? No one has been there for many generations. The sea routes have been lost since the Hyksos who never cared for the land of the gods or the sacred incense it offers. But, I may have a surprise for you. Do you know who that is, that Queen Goddess of Punt?"

"How can she be a goddess if it is a serpent with a beard?"

"Hatasu, think. You, who have learned this story so well…think of what is on your father's crown? Who is that looking out over his forehead?"

"Why, that's Wadjet, the royal cobra goddess of Lower Egypt." Her eyes got bright and wide in recognition. "She's the protectress of the Pharaoh, the uraeus on his crown. But, why the beard if it is the goddess? The serpent goddess on Father's crown doesn't have a beard."

"You're right. The serpent goddess of Punt is different from Wadjet. As a matter of fact, it is the goddess Hathor. But, why do you think Hathor would have a beard as the Goddess of Punt? What other god is known for his beard?"

"Amun and Ptah."

"Yes, they are each creator gods, who bring heaven to earth. There are two others and one of these is the key."

She thought back to the creation story. "Well there is Osiris, who separates the living from the dead, and Shu, the god of air, who separates heaven from earth."

"There…now you've got the idea! Shu has the long beard like the ruler of Punt and that's what the beard on this goddess means. At Punt, it is her role to be the mediator between heaven and

407

earth…the above and the below…like Shu. Now, would you like to see a temple to this Lady of Punt?"

She sat upright in her bed. "Can we? Really, Mother, can we? Oh! Could our cousins come with us?"

"Well, Hatasu, I must tell you this is not like other temples you have seen. Temples must be kept up and repaired and worshipped in. The Hyksos didn't keep up this temple any more than they kept the secrets of the trade route to Punt. The priestesses here were run off and the treasures looted. The Hyksos allowed our priests to keep up some of the temples to our male gods, which were located closer to their capital city, but our goddesses' suffered neglect. This temple is now an ancient ruin, a neglected memory of a past glory. Would you still like to see it?"

Hatasu was certain she would. Thethi, Hapuseneb and Isis were playing that they were sailors with 'hearts braver than a lion's' and they were not interested in going, but Meryt was as excited as Hatasu to see the ancient ruins. The Queen indicated she wished this pilgrimage with her daughter to be a private affair.

The governor's daughter, Senbi, was to be the only one to accompany them as guide. She was shy and quiet by nature, so she kept to herself how puzzling it was that anyone, let alone the Queen, would want to see such a run-down mess. Senbi was a little older than Hatasu, yet still free to go unclad. Her skin was browned by the sun, not yet paled to yellow by the expectation she be indoors doing house chores. Her features were similar to most young people of Khemet, distinguished only by the smallness of her mouth. It seemed only a slit; her lips thin and even her smile seemed to be in miniature.

The small group set off for the temple. Senbi led the way, carrying a basket of dates and bread for a picnic lunch. They followed an overgrown pathway that many centuries before had been a major thoroughfare. It led them out of town to the north, tracing the slight eastward curve of the river. They had not followed Senbi long, before they got their first view of what had once been the temple gardens.

Now, tall weeds blew in the northern wind. Beyond the straggly green scrub appeared the ragged outline of broken walls and toppled pillars. Sand blew around the remains of the building, as though the earth was trying to swallow it up. There was one section where the roof was still in place. The wind whistled and howled as the small group moved closer; they thought they heard human voices.

"Perhaps, there are still some old priestesses caring for some part of this holy memory," Ahmose said, half to her self.

Senbi's small mouth spoke softly, "I don't think so, or my father would know of it."

As they got closer, they distinctly heard children's voices muffled in the wind.

"What is that moving on the ancient roof?" the Queen asked aloud. "Could it be an animal? Oh no…it's children *playing*!" Her voice grew in alarm and distress, "How could this be…a holy spot left to the games of children?"

Hatasu thought her mother quivered as though she was going to cry. They quickened their steps, moving past the crumbling gateway, into the chaotic remains of temple garden. Hatasu looked up into the face of her mother. Tears filled her eyes as she looked at what used to be a magnificent tribute to the great goddess of all women. They kept walking and entered what was left of the pillared hall. There, the columns, with the once brightly colored smiles of the goddess of beauty, were fallen facedown in the dirt. Ahmose kept walking, looking at the open roof that exposed the paintings and carvings to the harsh elements. The offering table in front of the sanctuary was empty of flowers and the holy of holies was unprotected. The sacred statue had been looted.

Half a dozen children, along with their sheep and goat, had been engaged in a lively game of hide and seek. They had stopped their scurrying around and peered cautiously around pillars and down from the remains of the roof. Ahmose and the royal children were an unexpected intrusion upon their playscape and it was clear to Hatasu, from their comfort, how many years they'd played here. Hatasu looked up into the un-kohled black eyes of a young girl peering down from a hole in the roof. She quickly vanished back over the edge. The princess turned to see two tall boys staring at them from behind a ragged-edged wall by a fallen column. They did not vanish but kept staring.

The Queen raised her hand to her mouth, her eyes reddened with unshed tears. Hatasu supposed this was heartache for the destruction of this once beautiful old temple. All was still; the children were silenced. There was only the lonely sound of the north wind making a mournful echo through the empty halls.

Standing a bit taller, the Queen looked around at the young

shepherds. The scraggly nomad children viewed her with alarm in their eyes. Several of them ran off. She called them back and in a kind and queenly voice, she asked, "Come back. Do you know what place this is in which you play?"

One of the oldest children stood by a damaged doorway. Another two peeked from around piles of fallen stone. The little girl from the roof had come around and was standing, holding the hand of a girl who was a taller version of herself. With gentle, encouraging tones, Ahmose coaxed them out of hiding and as the royal children watched, five scraggly children stepped shyly forward…each looking a bit like the goats they tended with tangled, matted hair and bodies spotted with dirt.

Two had the darker skin of the Nubian Medjay. All of them were painfully thin with the extended bellies of hunger. Their eyes showed fear of this strange woman. In their ordinary life, they would never expect to encounter the Queen of the land. They feared the lord of the estate would be angry and punish them severely. They stood still as though numb with shock.

Sensing this was the case, Ahmose continued to speak to them softly, "Don't be afraid. There are no punishments from me, just teachings for you about this place. Come, we will share our bread with you."

The children's bodies relaxed. None of them moved to bow, unlike the official reverence shown to the royals when they visited villages. Hatasu watched her mother for clues on how to behave toward these odd-looking children. Ahmose motioned them to come closer. "Come, have some bread." The governor's wife had packed them a more than abundant lunch. "As you eat, I will tell you of the glorious history of this ground you play on."

The children eyed her suspiciously as they snatched the bread from her hand, pushing it into their mouths. After a couple of bites, the littlest of the children said, "Would you like some of the milk of our goats to drink with the bread?"

The pail for collecting and drinking the milk was dirtier than Hatasu could imagine drinking anything from. She was relieved when her mother said, "Thank you, we have water with us."

The little girl busied herself again in eating her piece of bread. When the children's eating slowed down and the bread was all devoured, the Queen talked to them again. "This used to be a grand temple to the great goddess, Hathor. It is she who brings us love and beauty. She is a mother to us all, offering her protection and the joyful things of life."

The tallest boy spoke up for the first time, "What do we know of the joyful things of life? Our work is hard and if a jackal should lessen the number of our flock, we are not only poorer, but our backs feel the pain of the stick as well."

"Yes, I see your life is hard, but Hathor softens even such hard lives as yours with the gentle touch of a mother's hand or the beauty of the paintings on these walls. There was a time when only princesses and priestesses could see these pictures. Now you, too, can bathe in their beauty. It takes special eyes to see such things. Do you have such eyes?"

The smallest girl piped up, "I think the pictures are pretty. Sometimes when we come here, I put a flower in front of that picture of the beautiful lady. The others laugh at me, but I do it, anyway."

A second boy said, "If this…'goddess'…is so important, how did she let her temple get so destroyed?"

"Goddesses and gods bless us when we give honor to them. It is in paying tribute to Hathor that she blesses your life with love and joy. It is *humans* who have forgotten this and have allowed this temple to fall to ruin…not the *goddess*."

The tallest girl had something to say next, "This goddess is nothing but a cow…a pretty cow but just a cow. See her cow ears?"

"Yes, here she is pictured as a cow. What living thing is kinder in giving her children milk for them to grow strong? What creature is more motherly, than the soft-eyed cow? But, she is pictured in other ways, too. Come look at these pictures on *this* wall." Moving across the cracked alabaster floor, she pointed to the opposite wall. "See…here she is a beautiful woman with a crown of cow horns, with the sun, itself, sitting between them." Pointing to an adjacent wall she added, "See her sign here? It is the falcon god Horus inside a square house. It is she who healed Horus of the eye wound he received by Set. It is she who is the consort of great Horus, the warrior." Beyond the broken door jam, her eye caught the flash of still bright turquoise. She continued teaching, "And here she is goddess of the beautiful stone, turquoise."

All of the children followed her from wall to wall as she explained, "Here she is goddess of wine and inebriation, and here we see her with the head of the cow and the body of a woman nursing her son, Ihy." Turning to Hatasu and Meryt, she pointed to yet another picture, barely visible, the paint worn by blowing sands. "And *here* is Hathor…as Queen of Punt!"

Hatasu stared. There, indeed, was a beard of lapis lazuli.

Ahmose turned back to the shepherd children. "This is not a place for play. This is holy and sacred ground. I commission you to honor and protect these ancient ruins of the goddess. Someday, a Pharaoh will rebuild this blessed spot but until then, I ask *you* to safeguard it against further damage. Bring flowers to the place in front of Hathor's pictures if you like, but do not play in the holy places nor on the fragile roof. Can you carry out this wish?"

The tallest boy stepped forward, his chest held high. "Yes," he said, looking around at the others, his dark eyes meeting each of theirs. "Yes, we can do that." There was a pride in his voice of having been given an adult's job.

The others nodded their heads, murmuring, "Yes", too.

This oldest boy, then asked, "Who shall we say has given us this commission?"

"Queen Ahmose, the Mother Goddess Mut to the people of the Two Lands."

Their mouths fell open and they all looked very confused. The tall girl, still holding the little girl-child's hand, gathered herself first, and bowed deep and low before the Queen.

Ahmose smiled and said, "Rise, go now, tend your flock of animals, and remember what you learned about this place."

Meryt and Hatasu held hands as they walked back to the town with Ahmose. Hatasu asked, "Senbi, who are those children?"

"Those are the 'animal people' from the desert," she said. "They are not from the Two Lands but they come here from the east. They live in the red land of Set, raising herds of sheep and goats and living like animals in tents, moving from place to place. My father says they are the Hyksos who never went home where they belong. He doesn't like them but in the dry season, he lets them bring their animals to the river for water. Mother says they will never go back to the Levant as long as Father makes it so comfortable for them. He responds that they have been living this way for so many generations, it would be a great deal of trouble to teach them another way. He doesn't like them and he doesn't like their ways but he says they do not cause trouble, either…as long as they get the water they need."

That night, Hatasu dreamed of Hathor, with her crown of cow horns, taking her to Punt…only it wasn't an island. Instead, it appeared in her dream as the garden of a beautiful temple filled with many delicious fruit trees, brightly colored flowers and blue-water pools alive with white lotuses, tilapia fish, and great, green, croaking bull frogs. It seemed so real, she could smell the sweet incense of the trees and hear the north wind rattle the leaves like the seeds of a sistrum. The feeling of having actually been in Punt was so strong, it stayed with her though the next day and could be easily recalled for the rest of her life.

They left early the next morning, as the boat crew had another day of hard rowing. All six children went on the Queen's boat this day and were content to make up their own stories and play games of senet. Hatasu and Meryt played with Neferubrity but largely, the boat was quiet.

Hatasu began to think of the people she missed: Her father, her grandmother, her brother. *How much longer would it be before she would see her father?* She went to her mother with her questions. Ahmose told her it would be a while before they reached Ankh-Tawy. There they would wait for word from the Pharaoh about his success and news of when he would journey home.

Hatasu sat in a lonely mope for the rest of the afternoon. Even the captain's warning calls for sandbars had lost their excitement…since she knew if they were shipwrecked, they wouldn't be going to Punt.

Her mother came, sat beside her and put her arm around her. "Our land is large and river trips are long but you are learning about our land as we go. Your father is proud of you. He realizes how much you've learned about each place we've visited."

This brought a smile back to her face. "What is he proud of?"

"Well, you notice how each town has a different character and you've met the important people at these places. You befriended quiet Senbi at Kusai, the young Mistress Tutkharit at Zawty and the easy-going Puyemre at Abedju. The next towns also hold things your father wants you to know."

"What other things do we see before we reach Ankh-Tawy?"

"Our next stop will be at Khemenu, the city of his patron god, Thoth."

Chapter 24 - Khemenu, City of Thoth

Khemenu (KEM-en-nu) was but a two-hour boat ride from Kusai. Queen Ahmose sat under the sun protection of the canopy, side shades pulled up so she could see the fertile lands float past. Hatasu sat next to her. "Our next visit is to Khemenu, the center of magic."

"Even more than Waset?"

"Even more than Waset. It is the place of the Sacred Mound of Creation and of the Temple of Thoth, God of Wisdom and Magic."

Hatasu sat on the edge of her seat, straining to get her first view of the 'town of magic'. As it came into view, she could see the white-washed houses glistened in the sun and eventually the brightly colored pylon gate of the temple with its high flags fluttering in the northern breeze. When they pulled into this quay, it was something else that caught her attention…large monkey-like creatures, some of them on leashes and others roaming the streets. Her first reaction was to thank the goddess Chi-chi was safe with her animal handler, for she would have made a ruckus for sure at the sight of such animals.

One of the people in the greeting party, even had such a creature on a leash. It had intelligent eyes, a gray face with a long dog-like snout and a silver, shaggy mane that covered its head, upper back and chest. He sat at attention. Hatasu thought she saw it bow to the royal family, just like his masters did. She pulled on Sitre's arm. "What is that animal? It looks like a big, fat version of Chi-chi."

Sitre laughed softly, as she bent to whisper in her ear. "It is a baboon, the holy animal of the god of wisdom, Thoth."

Hatasu was staring at the baboons so intently that at first she didn't even see the royal governor or the high priest and his family. The Governor, Tjay, stood alone...no wife or child. He was thin and wizened looking. His long white governor's kilt accentuated his stick-like appearance. In marked contrast, Maatmose, the high priest, stood with his priestess-wife and their dozen or so children. This whole family looked round, almost fat...certainly not magical. The smooth contours of Maatmose's shaved head reflected the sun's light and his leopard-skin robe flared to contain his rotund body. His wife, Zita, was the sister of Tjay. She was a stout version of the governor and their children ranged from a babe in arms, all the way up to a grown daughter with her own baby. There were a couple of gaps in the sizes...likely for the sons away at war with Thutmose's army.

All three adults, Tjay, Maatmose and Zita, held the tall wooden staffs that proclaimed their position of authority. This she could see, was where the magic was. These staffs were not ordinary staffs but instead resembled living snakes. Staffs were usually chosen for their straightness but each of these staffs bent into serpentine waves; undulating up from their tail on the ground to a head that veered off to an angle above the owner's hand. Each hand that held the serpent staff also wore a scarab ring, not unlike Puyemre's.

Hatasu stared. *What were the staffs made of; wood or an actual snake? Was it the light on shiny material or were they moving?*

Ahmose greeted the governor and high priest and priestess warmly and proceeded as though the staffs were normal. Her mother then extended her arm out to her and pulling her close said, "I want you to meet Djehuti."

The young man came from behind the governor's family and bowed low to the Queen and princess. This was the first time Hatasu laid eyes on this cousin. He was the son of the Pharaoh's sister, who had long since gone to the stars. The Queen inquired about his health and his studies at the House of Life, as Hatasu took in his unique appearance. He was about the age of Wadjmose and wore the simple, bleached linen kilt of a student…no staff, no ring. Hatasu noted his familiar Thutmosid nose as well as his hunched shoulders and the limp with which he stepped forward when the Queen spoke to him.

The Queen moved on with her greetings and Djehuti took his place among the other students of the House of Life. She winked at him and he smiled back at her. The processional finally moved forward along the broad paved avenue that led from the quay directly to the grand pylons of the Temple of Thoth. Hatasu noted the happy and healthy looking people who waved as they passed. The houses they went by were neatly built, orderly and freshly white-washed and painted.

Just beyond the temple, she got a glimpse of the shining waters of the inland lake but the road veered off to the right and they headed for the mooring palace. As they walked along, the street swelled with enthusiastic well wishers, many of whom also had pet baboons with them. These creatures traveled on all fours, tails high in the air. The people eagerly jostled each other to get closer to the royal procession, chanting, *"Hail to the Queen, Mother to her people.*"

Following her mother's lead, Hatasu smiled and waved. The frame drums beat, the sistrums sounded and even the baboons danced.

This mooring palace was a bit larger than others. Thutmose had recently built a new addition for his visits to honor his patron god. In the garden, two statues of baboons faced east and west, while two ibises looked to the north and south. The pool in the center gave off the heavenly scent of the lotus and date and palm trees offered islands of shade. Under one of these trees, Hatasu spotted a whole family of baboons; a long silver mane marked the male and the babies on the laps of the two smaller brown ones indicated they were females.

"Those are your father's baboons," Sitre told her.

"Oh what fun!"

"We'll see how much fun you think they are tomorrow morning!"

"Why?"

"You wait and see," was all Sitre would say.

At the greeting banquet, Hatasu continued to look for the magic her mother said this town was known for. She was not disappointed.

After the meal, the governor announced the entertainment…a magician. "Good evening, Royal Highness and other distinguished guests," began the middle aged man with gray lining his black hair and a twinkle in his eyes. "Tonight you are going to be entertained…by your meal." He waited and the townsfolks, familiar with his trick, smiled knowingly. He directed his comments past them and toward the table of royal children. Little Isis's eyes were so large, they filled her whole face. Hapuseneb sat back with his arms folded across his chest, a 'show me' look on his face. Thethi leaned forward and squinted, all the better to see, and Meryt attended to the magician as though he was the usual entertaining harpist.

Hatasu, having checked her companion's reactions, turned back to the magician. She, herself, was curious about the whole scene where magic, so much a part of their everyday lives, was to be used to entertain. This was a rarity.

On cue, the serving person arrived with a tray of after dinner treats…sweetbread in the shape of people. As she walked by him, he said, "I'll take two of those, please." He picked one that was clearly meant to be a boy and the other a girl. He held them up for all to see. "Now," he said, as he leaned them against a plate so they seemed to be standing up. He took his wand, a wavy stick…a smaller version of the governor's staff…and he waved it around the two figures. He said some indistinguishable sounds and then the words, "By Thoth, come alive."

Hatasu gasped as she saw the bread figures begin to move on their own. At first, their movements were jerky and slow but gradually they loosened up. She applauded in delight.

The magician continued, "And now, Mister and Misses Bread, I'd like the fine people here to see you dance." He directed his wand toward a flute lying idle against the wall, and with a snap of his wrist and a point of the wand, he said, "Play"!

And it did! A lively dance tune came out of the flute and it moved about as though someone was holding it but Hatasu could see no one.

He turned back to the bread people. He snapped his wrist and made another strange utterance, then waited…Sure enough, the bread people moved to the rhythm of the flute. They moved their little arms and legs, picking up their feet, touching hands and whirling each other around. "Very fine!" the magician exclaimed. "Now, bow to your audience?" And that is just what they did.

Hatasu and her cousins all clapped in great appreciation. Obviously pleased with the audience's reaction, the magician turned back to the sweets. "Mr. and Mrs. Bread, it is time for you to say good night and return to your old selves." He moved the wand over them again, making more strange sounds and then saying, "It is done." And they again lay still and expressionless. They were again 'just' after-dinner sweets. The magician picked up the boy and bit off his hand. Chewing it, he said, "Hmmm."

Hatasu turned to Sitre. "How did he do that?"

Her nurse smiled and shrugged her shoulders. "Clearly by magic."

The governor stood up as the magician bowed and left the room. "Honored guests, I also have a story for you about magic. It is cautionary tale of a very foolish prince and a lesson about the wisdom of using magic only for its true and beneficent purpose." He motioned now to a young man who stepped forward. He looked just like a younger version of the high priest, Maatmose. His dark hair was neatly arranged and his eyes shone with the love of the story. All the children's eyes moved to their young host.

He began, "There was once a prince who loved knowledge more than wisdom. His name was Neferkaptah (nef-er-KA-pa-ta). He was a powerful magician but he was always looking for more powerful spells. One day, he overheard an old priest talking about a hidden location of magic spells written by Thoth, himself.

'What is this? You know the whereabouts of the lost book of Thoth? The Emerald Tablets?'

'You must not ask about this magic,' the old priest warned him. 'It will bring you trouble'.

'I must know!' returned the prince. 'What is in this Book of Magic?'

'There are only two spells in it,' this old priest said. 'If you read the first spell aloud, you will enchant the Great Above, the Great Below, and the Earth in between. You will be able to understand every beast and bird and to summon the fishes of the deep, just like a god. If you read the second spell, even if you are in the Land of the Dead, you will take your own form again and see the sunshine, the moonrise, and the gods themselves'. But then, the old priest added, 'What I say is true but a wise man would also heed the warning of the gods. Such knowledge comes at its rightful time when the person proves himself worthy. Those who go looking outside of the due course of study, ask for trouble!'

The foolish prince could not listen to the old priest's warning. He could only hear of the magic and power of the ancient book. He promised the old priest anything he wanted to hear in order to get the information of its where-abouts.

The old man said, 'The Book of Thoth is hidden in an iron box at the bottom of the river. Inside the iron box is a box of bronze and inside the box of bronze is a box of sycamore. Inside the sycamore box is a box of ebony and inside that, a box of ivory. In the ivory box is a box of silver and in the silver box, a box of gold, and in that box, the Book of Thoth. And there are snakes and scorpions guarding all the boxes'.

Neferkaptah determined he would go to the place the old priest spoke of and claim this magic for himself. He and his beloved wife sailed on to the city of which the old priest spoke. The people of the city met them and a wise old woman came forward and said, 'This book has been buried here a long time. It was buried for a reason. It is not wise to bring it to the light of day'.

Still, Neferkaptah insisted he must have this knowledge. He was already a great magician, and he knew what to do. He molded a boat of pure bee's wax and breathed life into its crew. He loaded the vessel with sand and launched it towards the middle of the river. When the boat stopped of its own accord, the prince knew they had reached the right spot. He threw over the sand so the water was divided and there was a strip of dry land in the middle of the river. He went down into the riverbank reciting spells, for he could see the snakes and scorpions all around the iron box.

His spells worked on all creatures, except for one huge serpent that had wrapped itself around the iron box. This snake would surely not deter this magician prince. He cut it in half with his bronze axe…but the two halves joined up again and the serpent turned on him and tried to crush him. Neferkaptah clenched his sharp knife and cut him in half again but this time, he threw sand between the halves so they could not rejoin.

He was at last free to open the boxes; first the iron box and then the bronze, next the sycamore, the ebony, ivory and silver…until he came at last to a slender golden box. He carefully opened this box and there, inside, was the Book of Thoth: The tablet of emerald green stone covered with ancient hieroglyphics of the two spells the old priest had promised.

Right then and there, he recited the first spell and felt the magic power course through his body. And yes, he was able to enchant the Above and the Below. And yes, he was able to understand the speech of animals and fishes. But this was not enough for him. No, he went on to read the second spell. By its terrible power, he saw the sun, moon and stars in their true form and the glory of the gods, themselves. His face shone with the pride and joy of his new knowledge.

He made a copy of the words of the spell and dissolved the papyrus and drank it down so to make it his own. He was pleased with his success. But the god Thoth was not pleased! Thoth went to Ra, the god of gods, and told him there must be justice. Thoth said, 'This arrogant prince has received knowledge, in an unlawful way. He has killed the seven guardians and he has broken into the seven boxes. He has stolen the spells for himself and he does not know how to use them for the betterment of mankind but uses it only for his own power. This can not be allowed'.

Ra knew what Thoth said was true. It could not be allowed, even of a prince. It was not long, before the prince and his wife were sailing home. It was then, that their trouble started. They had not gone far when his beloved wife fell into the river and drowned. In great grief, he tried to use his new magic to revive her. He succeeded in bringing her back from the dead, just long enough for her to tell him of the displeasure of Thoth for gaining the spells illegitimately. She died in his arms. In great grief, he traveled on but before too long, he, too, fell into the waters and died.

The crew returned home to the prince's father, the Pharaoh, with the terrible story of the secrets of the Book of Thoth. The Pharaoh was a man wiser than his son. With respect for Thoth, he buried the book deep within the temple of learning with a warning that no one was to gain the knowledge of these spells without the blessing of Thoth and respect for the power they wield.

And so it is today; the study of magic spells in the Khemenu House of Life is coupled with training on the right use of magic."

Hatasu spoke up right away, "How does one get the blessing of Thoth to learn the right use of magic?"

The governor stood up again. "I'm so glad you asked."

He was smiling and turned to a group of youngsters just rid of their youth-locks and wearing student-kilts. He nodded toward them and they said together, "In the Khemenu House of Life!"

Hatasu's heart set its course by these words. Back at the mooring palace that evening, Ahmose came to tuck her daughter into bed. Hatasu asked eagerly, "How did the magician do that tonight? And the staffs…are they really snakes? And when can I enter the House of Life in Khemenu?"

"One question at time! About the House of Life…you must be a bit older and a bit more learned in your letters…but soon. About our entertainer tonight, he used his words, his wand and his will to animate the bread, much like Neferkaptah did in the story to animate the boat and sailor he made of bee's wax. Only our magician tonight used it to honor his Queen, not for his separate personal power."

"Is that like the wax figures Father had in his war tent before he left for the Levant?"

"Yes, indeed. Wax soldiers are a magical aid to battle."

Hatasu lay back on the bed and thought about this. "And the staffs are wands, too?" she asked from the bed.

"Indeed, but they are only magic in the hands of trained magicians. For anyone else they are just staffs." Ahmose went on, "There is more for you to learn, and as the story says, you must learn it at the right time. You are already on your way to knowing the magic of dreams and as you know from the dance we did to calm the khamsin in Waset, the magic of weather is one of my gifts. Your father has the magic that makes the people love and follow him, and governor Tjay has the magic of running his nome in harmony, justice and loyalty to the Double Crown."

"You mean everyone has a different kind of magic?"

"Well, sort of. Everyone has the potential to learn and apply the natural laws that produce magical results but it's more natural for some people than others…kind of like the artists. Everyone can draw a line or a circle but the artists that fill the temple walls with pictures of gods have a natural ability. But they are also trained to use that ability."

Hatasu nodded. She had a lot to think about. The next morning came abruptly. There was great commotion in the garden. Hatasu and Thethi jumped from their beds and rushed out to the garden to see the baboons on the easternmost section, facing the spot on the horizon from which the sun would soon emerge. All three of the adult animals were jumping up and down, emitting shrieks and howls.

Throughout the city, echoes of the same performance could be heard from household to household. Amused by these antics, Hatasu and Thethi jumped up and down imitating the baboons and laughing. Gradually more and more light could be seen, until the sky turned to a rosy glow. The baboon shrieks reached a crescendo as the gold of the glowing sun showed itself over the Eastern mountains. Hatasu and Thethi laughed out loud at their own frenzied attempts to keep up with the animal's enthusiastic display. The animal's dancing increased in intensity, until the beams of light lit their faces and reflected off the silver of the male's manes. Once the sun god Ra was secure in its place in the sky, the baboons quieted down, wandering off to shady places and attended to their grooming.

The children continued to do their imitation of baboon howls and they danced their way to breakfast with the Queen. "Why do the baboons make all that noise?" Hatasu asked.

"They give honor and praise to the great god Ra as he rises each morning. It is because of this wise action that they are Thoth's animal."

"Oh. We gave praise to Ra right along with them this morning.

Does that make us wise enough to be magicians?" Ahmose smiled at her daughter's mischief.

Djehuti came to collect the children for their day's outing. Hatasu was enthusiastic about seeing more of this city of magic. As they walked, his pronounced limp and hunched over shape became even more obvious. Thethi asked, "What happened to your leg?"

"When I was a child, I developed a very high fever. The doctor and my mother didn't think I would live. My father made many offerings to the god Thoth, that he would use his magic to spare my life. The medicine and spells worked and I recovered from the fever but I was unable to walk. My parents sought still more magic and they brought me on a pilgrimage to this temple. The waters, the incantations of priests and priestesses, and the blessed, healing dreams that happened in this holy place, restored my ability to walk. That is why I study medical magic here…to become a priest of Thoth, to help others who suffer as I did."

Hatasu's heart warmed to him, both because of his hardship and his courage. Thethi shieded away from him, as though Djehuti's physical deformities reminded him of his own vulnerabilities.

"Which would you like to see first, the Sacred Lake with the Mound of Creation or the Temple of Thoth?"

After a short discussion, the children agreed to the Sacred Lake first. Djehuti led them along a broad, white limestone pathway to a large round body of water with an island in the middle. They walked under palm trees, surrounded by the cackling sound of many geese nesting and eating all around them. There were groups of people walking around the lake whose sparkling waters reflected the morning light. Djehuti let them know the other individuals were pilgrims, honoring the sacred mound of creation and seeking the source of magic. Their young guide announced, "This is the spot that empowers Khemenu and makes it the best place to learn and practice the magic arts. The geese represent the Great Cackler from whose egg all life came." Djehuti then asked, "Are you ready to see the Temple of Thoth?"

"I am ready," Hatasu said with a good-natured stamp of her foot.

Djehuti smiled at her and said, "Then let's go. This building, itself, is so magnificent." He picked up his pace, and clearly, his limp was no hindrance to his enthusiasm. Djehuti explained as they went, "This part of the pathway is lined with Persea trees, the Tree of Life. Seshat, Thoth's consort, writes the name of the Pharaoh on the leaves of this sacred tree so that he will live a long life."

Flocks of the long-beaked ibis birds whitened the ground as they moved about pecking with their curved beaks. "The ibis is as much the sacred animal of Thoth as the baboons. They hunt and peck for food as Thoth does for wisdom." They approached the temple and Djehuti and the children stood beneath the massive pylon gate looking up at the brightly colored pictures of Thoth; the broad shoulders of a man and the head of an ibis. He held in his hands the stylus and papyrus of the divine scribe. The magic of hieroglyphic writings filled the rest of the walls. Over the doorway, beneath the picture of the winged solar disk, were large deep hieroglyphs.

Hatasu recognized the symbols and feeling so proud she could read them now, recited aloud, "*As above, so below.*" Hatasu turned to Djehuti. "Why does it say that there?"

"That is a famous teaching of Thoth. The Above and Below are actually one and the same…two parts of the whole…like the Two Lands, Upper and Lower Egypt, are two parts of the same country. That is the basic principal behind all magic."

Hatasu thought of the times her parents used that proverb. Hatasu and Hapuseneb walked at Djehuti's pace and plied him with questions about the magic he learned in the House of Life. "In this House of Life, one learns about the intricacies of writing and reading for Thoth is the god of scribes. You learn about herbs and medicine because Thoth is the god of healing. You learn about the stars because Thoth is the god of time. You study numbers, geometry and the proportions of things because Thoth is the god of wisdom. Each of these is a part of Thoth's magic teachings."

"Tell us more about the secrets," Hatasu begged.

"Oh, no, dear cousin. The *secrets* are things I can *not* talk about. I can tell you the subjects that honor Thoth but the details…no. Remember the story of Neferkaptah." Seeing the look of longing on Hatasu's face, he continued, "If you are found worthy to study in this temple, you will earn the right to unlock the secrets of 'The Emerald Tablets'. Then you would know the language of heaven and earth-the Above and Below."

Hatasu set her jaw. She must find a way to be worthy to learn these secrets, soon. They returned the mooring palace, where Hatasu thanked Djehuti, and went into the garden looking for her mother. She was sitting in the garden with a scroll resting in her lap. "Is it a letter from Papa?" Both children bounded towards her.

"Yes, this is, indeed, from your father." A smile brightened her face as the two children crossed the room to her side, eager for their father's words. She said, "Your father's message is from Hazor, the city of the Amurru, which Bazor comes from." She paused, looking back at the scroll.

"Well, has he done mighty battle with him?" Thethi asked as he assumed his warrior stance, imaginary bow and arrow in his hand.

Hatasu, also excited, responded to Thethi's clue and poised in her 'Isis against Set' position, imaginary spear held high.

"Yes…yes, he writes the army of the Pharaoh attacked the area around Hazor by a razzias, a quick surprise attack. There was a clash with the Amurru warriors and he struck fear into their hearts. There is no doubt, they will respect him with tribute, now. He writes that they captured many hands and his soldiers suffered only slight wounds. He says Hazor, Bazor's father and ruler of the city, again swears loyalty to Khemet."

"Then, Father will be coming home!" Hatasu exclaimed in glee.

"No, my dear, his work is not finished." She put the scroll on her lap and her hands rested on it. "At Hazor, he learned more about the enemy to the north. These Mitanni, of which Bazor spoke, are a fierce warrior people, who are trying to expand southward into Hazor's territory. The Pharaoh must take his army farther north to settle matters with them, directly. He ordered more supplies sent by ship to the port of Byblos. It will be a while yet, before he will be coming home." Ahmose looked sad and tired.

"Oh," said Hatasu, crestfallen.

"Well, what else does he say?" asked Thethi. "What battle will he fight next?"

Her brother's enthusiasm for their father's further victories, revived Hatasu. "That is all he said in his letter," the Queen said. "It takes time for his message to get to us so it is likely he is at Byblos now. The Two Land's relationship with that trading city of the cedar woods has always been friendly. It is a safe place to store food for the troops. There is a chance that there was fighting on the way to that city, however."

She wished she could be there, fighting alongside her father, like Amenmose. "Does he say anything about our brother?" Hatasu asked her mother.

"He says he fought bravely in the raids and took his first hand."

Hatasu had not had any dreams of Amenmose, at all. She suddenly wondered what it was like for him at war. That night, after the banquet, lying in her bed, Hatasu thought about the letter from her father. She closed her eyes and tried to imagine what it was like for her father in the far-off land. She wished very hard to have a dream visit with her father where he was. She imagined herself with a soldier's spear; her father standing beside her, commending her for her great bravery. She drifted off to sleep and found herself standing in her father's war tent.

He was seated in his traveling throne and smiling at her. "You wished to visit me here, you who are so naturally strong in dream magic?" There was the usual fatherly smile on his face. "What would you like to see?"

"I wish I could be a warrior now, and fight with you."

Moving as though he were floating rather than walking, he motioned to her to leave his tent and vanished through the walls.

She followed him out and found herself on a hillside looking down on the army campsite. It spread a long distance on a flat plain. She could see the outline made by the shields, the rows and rows of tents, and the area fenced off for horses and chariots. Beyond this, she could see the buildings of a fine city. Her father extended his arm, motioning for her to look at the sea beyond the buildings. Then, he turned her back around facing the land. He pointed to the hillside, crowded with tall evergreen trees. "These are the great cedar trees, fine wood that make strong ships and beautiful doorways to temples. They smell of inspiring incense."

The next thing she knew, she was herself, standing among the trees, rather than looking at them from a distance. She felt she could almost reach out and feel their flat evergreen needles. A piece of bark had fallen from a tree and her father pointed out its red color. He encouraged her to smell the scent all around them. The trees were tall, reaching up to the starlit sky. She could see the moon, full above them. Just as quickly as she arrived among the trees, she now found herself and her father at a boatyard. Many docks with numerous large ships lined the shore.

Beyond that was an expanse of water like Hatasu had never seen. Even at the height of the inundation, one could see land on the other side. Here, the water stretched on and on forever, marked only by the reflection of the moon that made a broad, bright pathway into the water's unknown vastness. She looked back up into her father's face and asked, "Where is the fighting?"

"Not here. We had a battle in Hazor and another on the road here. Armed men came from behind shrubs and ambushed us. We overcame them easily but one of our men was killed and a couple were wounded. We are in Byblos now. These people are friendly traders who like our grain and linen too much to fight us."

She remembered that her mother thought he was in that city. Hatasu looked back at the city. A temple stood out. "What is that?"

"That is the temple to Baal and the building next to it is the temple of Ishtar. I do not want you to enter this city. There are spirits there that are foreign to us. We use magic to protect us but the people here built their magic on their fear. From that, they have created thought forms of demons. They empowered the demons by worship and fear. It is only when you attend the House of Life that you will learn to protect yourself from these things. Now, give me your word that you will not try to come back here on your own. Do you agree?"

"Yes, Father, if you wish."

"Now, your ba must return to Khemet. Continue with your studies and give your mother a kiss on the cheek for me."

Before she even answered, he vanished. She opened her eyes to find herself in her bed in the mooring palace in Khemenu, the same full moon shining through her high window. Her father had heard and answered her wish.

The next morning, she rushed into her mother's room to tell her about the dream. She planted the kiss on her mother's cheek and bounced off to start her day. There was a sparkle of pride in Ahmose's eyes, as she thought of her daughter's special magic.

The royal children were scheduled to spend this day at the home of the high priest and his many children. Their home was a short distance from the temple on a shady street. The mistress of the house, Zita, welcomed them graciously and five of his children who were closest to the ages of the visitors joined with them in the lovely garden. They family had a couple of young and very playful baboons. The children were immediately engrossed in play with them. Their nurse-tutors brought them a large and delicious lunch, and afterward, they all sat in the shade of Persea trees.

Hatasu asked her questions, "Have you studied it in the Khemenu House of Life? Can you do magic, like make sweet cakes dance?"

Seshat, the daughter of Maatmose, laughed. "No, that Si, the magician at the banquet, loves to do that trick. My teacher keeps telling me to be patient and not 'open the box' before it's time."

"No, It's pretty unwise not to honor Thoth and learn magic without his approval."

"Well, I suppose it's good no one can use the magic illegitimately again," Hatasu said.

There was a strange silence. Then, Pi, the second youngest son of the priest, spoke. "I wish that was so."

"What do you mean?"

"Well…there is a rumor. I hope it is not true but there is talk of a priest in Itjtawy. A servant told me he has dreams of this magician haunting his sleep with images of demons and fearful threats if he does not do his will."

The older son, Mrib, laughed out loud. "You believe that servant? He is just scaring you."

Hatasu looked over at Hapuseneb. He looked back at her with

alarm.

Mrib saw the look. "Our father and our uncle Tjay are both 'great of magic'. Besides governing well and honoring Maat, they keep our nome safe by magic protection."

"What do you mean?" This was very interesting to Hatasu.

"Magical figures protect our nome. Even if there were someone who would use evil magic…even retched magic like the Hyksos did…they couldn't get past the magical guardians."

"How do you know?" asked Hapuseneb.

Mrib continued, "I was out training my chariot horses along the northern boundary of our nome and my horse tripped on a strange clay figurine. I stopped and looked at it closely. It was a magical image of Sekhmet. It raised my curiosity so I rode the whole length of that boundary line and I found many of them, all facing out; protecting us from anything harmful outside our nome."

The second son, Pi, said, "That servant had the dream when he went north to visit his cousin. He said many people in the nomes north of us are troubled by bad dreams, illnesses and fears due to the evil priest in Itjtawy. He said that priest uses magic, not of our Two Lands but of the peoples from the Levant; magic that builds fear and harms rather than protects. You don't have to believe me, but…"

Hatasu thought of what her father said in her dream about the magic of thought forms, built of demons and empowering them with fear. *What would this mean as they traveled further north?*

Chapter 25 - Usersobek

Leaving the high priest's house, Hatasu said good-bye to the children of the family. Now, with threatening magic right here in their own land, Hatasu was anxious to see her mother. But when she returned to the palace, there was a crowd waiting to see the Queen…tall ones and short ones, old ones and young ones. Each looked distressed; lines of worry on their faces and dark sleepless circles under their eyes. She heard whispers that sounded like snakes hissing, "Usssss er sssssso bek".

They were talking about Usersobek. *What could have happened? Was there an ominous change in the situation?*

She realized she wasn't going to get to see her mother, so disappointed, she went to her room. There, she found Sitre packing up her things. "Are we leaving so soon, Sitre?"

"Your mother has decided to depart first thing in the morning, again. It seems she's in a hurry to get to Itjtawy."

"Why are there so many people to see her? Is something wrong?"

"Whatever gave you the idea something was wrong, my child? People always want to see the Queen, and she just wants to get to Itjtawy, and then on to Ankh-Tawy." This made sense but Sitre's worried hands wrung round each other. The mole on her chin darkened. "Come now," Sitre said to her, "your mother is busy, so I'll sing you your lullaby tonight." As she sang, the music seemed to sooth them both.

The next morning, soon after the sun rose, Hatasu boarded the boat with her cousins. She noticed that the high priest, Maatmose, boarded her mother's boat and this surprised her. Soon, he, magic staff in hand, huddled in council with her High Priest, Hapu. Sitre told her they'd be stopping at Beni Hassan. "Khnumhotep, the governor there, is one of the Pharaoh's favorites. I believe the plan is to stay there only a short time."

Recognizing Beni Hassan as the home of Qenu, Tutkharit's fiancé, Hatasu wondered, "Is there protective magic in Beni Hassan like there is Khemenu?"

"Every place in Khemet has magic but Khemenu's magic is unique." She smiled reassuringly.

Hatasu turned and watched the river. The rowers of the Queen's flotilla moved them along rapidly, enhancing the current's speed. It wasn't very far before Hatasu noticed an abrupt change in the landscape. There was a clear line where the grains were noticeably shorter than the grain fields close to Khemenu. Up until this point, the fields of grain lining the river banks stretching sun-ward, gave a feeling of luxuriant emerald wellbeing. She thought she saw a clay statue of Sekhmet protruding from the stalks of grain. The wheat on the Khemenu side was emerald green and tall. The grain north of it was shorter and grayer-green in color.

Hapuseneb, sitting next to her, leaned toward her and said, "That must be the boundary between Khemenu and Beni Hassan, and that must be the Sekhmet statue Pi talked of. The protective magic ends here."

A chill went down her spine. Ahhotep and Nefermose, her two aunts, whispered their concerns to each other. The air felt different, thicker and heavier. Hatasu decided to distract herself from worry by attending to her baby sister. Neferubrity was cranky. She was almost six moons old and was sitting up, trying to crawl, and wanting to put everything in her mouth. Hatasu sat and played with her. She had a wooden paddle doll with shaggy yarn hair and a painted face. As big sister, Hatasu made up a song to entertain Neferubrity and acted it out with the doll. When the baby went down for her nap, Hatasu's worry returned.

She sat out on the boat deck, thinking about what her father said in her dream about the harmful magic in he Levant. She thought, too, about the rumors in Zawty about the rebellious priest. They arrived at Beni Hassan mid-morning. Governor Khnumhotep met them with singers and dancers, and the usual bowing and reverencing but the air was thick with clouds of incense and tired looking people wore multiple amulets around their necks.

Khnumhotep and his wife Kia were advanced in years, with stooped bodies and white hairs showing beneath their formal black wigs. The governor's staff was serpent like but all the rest were straight. With them were the wives of three of their grown sons away at war and an assortment of children. Qenu, Tutkharit's beloved, of course, was also in the Levant with the Pharaoh.

Hatasu looked around, for unlike in Khemenu, no one here seemed strong enough to keep the danger at bay. The old Beni Hassan governor was anxious to hear news of the Pharaoh, the war and his sons. A messenger had arrived for the Queen from Lower Retennu in the Levant that morning. They immediately headed for the palace.

During the procession through the town, the people prayed loudly; songs of praise, spiced with chanted spells for protection. When they arrived at their lodging, Hatasu saw it was an old nomarch's palace, refurbished. The rooms were large and grand designs decorated the painted columns. Finely woven mats covered the floors and brightly colored figures covered the mud-brick walls.

Ahmose received the messenger from Retennu. The governor sat nearby as she read it. "Warm greeting to My Beloved Queen Ahmose and to my loyal governor, Khumhotep. Ahmose and Ineni, the grains arrived safely at the Byblos port in good condition. It is good for you to know I have engaged the enemy in the first battle. We fought on the road outside of Hazor. My brave soldiers killed many of the enemy and we declared it a victory."

Hatasu recognized the things he told her in her dream but in the dream, he had spoken of the death of a soldier and the wounds of others, which were not mentioned, now.

"Though my heart longs to be able to bring my soldiers home to Khemet, circumstances here demand that I stay. It is necessary to fight a new offensive with an enemy in the north. There is no protection for the people of Khemet without overcoming these northern peoples. My time here is difficult, for part of this battle is with the fearful state of the people of the Levant. They live in ignorance and do not know Ra or Maat. Their magic was full of demons and evil forces. It would be difficult enough if it was just the soldiers I must overcome but I must also deal with the mashmashu, their wizards of evil magic. I, Pharaoh Thutmose, assure you of the greatness of my army and the greatness of

Amun's love for me."

Ahmose did not hide the worry on her face. The children were ushered out of the room and into the garden. Hatasu followed Sitre to the lotus pool. She worried about these mashmashu, the wizards of evil magic in the Levant. She had questions she wanted to ask Sitre. She started to formulate her worry into a question but as she opened her mouth to ask, her nurse pounced on her verbally, "Not now! Just go to your room and take a nap. If you cannot sleep, at least rest."

These questions of magic seem to make Sitre tense and nervous, too. Maybe there would be another time to ask.

At the banquet that night, the royal children were seated separate from the other children and adults. This was different but in some ways it was more relaxing. Hatasu didn't mind…until Hapuseneb leaned over and said to her, "I think something is happening here they don't want us to know about."

Only then, did she notice that there were local servants posted all around the children's table. Across the room, she saw her mother. Armed guards stood behind her. The governor, Maatmose, Ineni, Hapu and Nakht seemed to be sitting close to her, talking with a certain sense of urgency. Yuf stood nearby, as though he expected she might need his services. Hatasu opened her ears to the other conversations around her. She heard the words 'Itjtawy' and 'Usersobek' again.

Hapuseneb picked up on the whispers, as well. He leaned toward her again and said, "My father spoke to me once about a kind of magic that can cause harm. He called it the 'Left Handed Path'. He said it was brought here by the Hyksos. I'll bet that is what Maatmose's son, Pi, was talking about and I'll bet that's what the Pharaoh was talking about with the mashmashu magic of the Levant. I'll even bet that's what this priest in Itjtawy is using."

"But a temple priest *has* the knowledge of Amun-Ra. I don't understand what could make the priest in our land turn to the left-hand path," said the princess.

"Didn't Djehapy say something about Usersobek questioning Thutmose's right to be Pharaoh, and his wanting Itjtawy to be the capital again…instead of Waset?"

Hatasu shook her head. "How can he think such things?" Fear flashed through her body and tightened the knot in her stomach. *If someone used magic to get their own way and to hurt the people rather than help them, what would that mean? Could he steal the Double Crown from her father and move the capital from Waset to Itjtawy? Well, if the 'left-handed magic' could keep the wheat from growing tall and green, and could frighten people until they looked like they were sick, maybe it could steal the Crown.* The next thought was even worse than the last. *But to take the crown, the evil magician would have to do away with her father and mother!* She let out a sigh of relief. *They are god and goddess. Even magic couldn't kill them before their time,* she thought. *What would her mother do to protect herself and the people here and what would her father do to overcome the mashmashu in the Levant and protect himself and his army?*

Later that night, when Ahmose came to sing Hatasu a lullaby and tuck her into bed for the night, she had in her hand a white wand like what was used at Neferubrity's birth. "Mother, what are you doing with the wand?"

Ahmose looked at her daughter with tender protectiveness. "Well, my dear, there is some trouble brewing in the north, in Itjtawy, but like the trouble at the Oasis, we are taking care of it. Now, I'm going to draw you a magic circle and this will protect you while you sleep. You must stay in your bed tonight and not leave until Ra rises in the East. Do not try to visit your father in your dreams until I tell you it is safe again."

Hatasu felt fear and her small body began to shake under her linen covers. Seeing this, her mother said softly, "You must call upon your courage."

She told her mother of what her father told her in the dream of the fear and magic in the Levant. "Is that magic and the priest in Itjtawy the same?"

Ahmose didn't answer. Instead she walked to one of the traveling boxes and recovered one of her own amulets, the one of Sekhmet. She returned to Hatasu's bedside and slipped the cord around her neck, patting the image of the goddess on her chest. "It is time for you to be a Sekhmet warrior again and overcome your fear. This amulet, plus the magic circle, will keep you safe. It is important that you muster your courage. Not all battles are fought on the battlefield. Many are fought inside oneself, to overcome fear that can rob one of strength and wisdom. What your father was referring to is fear, the first weapon of an evil magician. If he can generate fear, he can use it to spin his enchantments and bind his victims in the web of his will."

With an act of will, she looked into her mother's eyes. They took a deep breath together. As Hatasu let out the breath, she felt her body relax and her fear lessen. "How will this amulet, this circle and this courage protect us tonight?"

"In our House of Life, this magic is used to engage the forces in the Duat to help and protect the ones still living here. The people of Retennu use magic and fear as a weapon. Fear robs you of the defenses of the goddess and leaves you vulnerable to attack. That is why you must use the magic of Sekhmet and the circle to ward off fear and give you courage."

"Will you and Father be okay, too?"

"Yes, we both are skilled in the power of magic that protects. Now, I will sing you your lullaby. You must sleep." Ahmose's sweet voice sang the words, "*May the wings of Isis enfold you, Safe may she always hold you...*," and Hatasu snuggled into her bed.

Her mother then took the ivory stick and dragged the end gently on the floor around her bed, chanting strange words Hatasu couldn't make out. As she finished, Hatasu asked, "Did you do this for Thethi and Neferubrity?"

"Yes, now go to sleep. I'll see you in the morning."

Hatasu watched the shadows on the walls and listened to the night sounds until she fell asleep. Her dreams were strange and muddled. Shadows darted back and forth around the edges of the circle. She thought she remembered the howl of large cat.

In the morning, there was a commotion when she and Sitre arrived in the garden for breakfast. A guard was giving orders. Nakht was standing cross-armed and spread-legged behind the

Queen and Hapu and Maatmose were standing next to her, forehead furrowed. Hapuseneb was already there with his father.

Hatasu went up to him. "What happened?"

"My father had a dream last night, warning that the Queen must get to Itjtawy immediately."

All six children tried to get their tutors to answer questions about the danger and its meaning.

"There is a magic threat coming from Itjtawy," said Sitre. "Our Queen is great of magic, herself. It is a time when we must all be careful and brave." Her arm encircled her princess, protectively.

During the morning, the children huddled together comparing notes on their experience the night before. Each of them had similar nightmares of threatening shadows. Shortly after noon, it was announced the boats were ready to be boarded. The children were to stay together and travel on Ineni's boat, the Queen on another, conferring with her advisors. Old Khnumhotep joined the Queen's council.

Hatasu's hand clenched the Sekhmet amulet in one hand as they boarded the boat. Thethi reached for her hand, and she held it tight, listening to see if his breathing changed. Everyone seemed alarmed. The fear of one person seemed to spread easily to another. As soon as she could, Hatasu gravitated toward Hapuseneb. He understood more of what was happening, and that brought her comfort.

Over the next several days, they boarded the boat early in the morning and traveled long hours. There were three towns they stayed at between Beni Hassan and Itjtawy. As they traveled north, the growth in the fields became more and more stunted, the color faded and the fear in the people became more and more palpable. The number of amulets that hung from their necks weighed down both children and adults. The people looked haggard and tired. As they got closer to Itjtawy, some even looked pale and sick, some had bandages or open sores. They all looked to the Queen with frightened pleading eyes.

The Queen's entourage stayed in each town only long enough to sleep. There was no time to see their temples or to get to know the families of the governors. The children were kept together, even sleeping in the same room at night. Sitre, as priestess, was in charge of all the children and it was she who drew the magic circle at night. The priestess in her came to the fore; she knew the rituals and chants of protection and gave voice to them with authority.

And so the three days passed with thinking of magic, talking with Hapuseneb and watching the stunted fields go by on the western banks. The nights were filled with threats and fear. Sitre would tuck Hatasu into each new, unfamiliar bed and cast a circle around her with a chant of protections. She would then proceed to repeat this with each of the cousins. She would end the ritual by drawing the white bone wand around the whole group of children.

For those three nights, in Hatasu's dreams, chaos and fear threatened to penetrate those circles. By the third day, she had a hard time trying to keep her mind from the threat of danger creeping in. She distracted herself again with comforting Neferubrity. When she was able to entice the baby to coo and giggle, it calmed her a bit. Thethi's breathing began to get raspy and she knew he was scared. When he wanted her to play soldier with him, her heart wasn't in it, but she did because she hoped it would help him feel better. She missed her mother and wondered what was happening on the other boat.

Sitre was comforting and went easy on her lessons and told reassuring stories of hope and courage but Hatasu's greatest comfort was Hapuseneb. He alone seemed to be able to understand and willing to talk about what was happening. He, too, remembered the feeling of chaos in his dreams. "I think it is what the original chaos of Nun must be like," he confided in her. Hatasu thought about the confused images in her own dreams. "I believe there is a mighty battle of magic going on and our bas feel it even inside the protective circles," Hapuseneb went on.

She looked over at Thethi, apparently unaware of the tensions as he picked fleas off his dog. "Do you think the other's feel it that way, too?" she asked.

"Most people are not as naturally sensitive to such things. It spares them this distress."

Tensions seemed to grow each day. The air got thicker, the crops were sparser in the fields and everyone was exhausted from lack of sleep.

On the third day, just as they neared the port for Itjtawy, a loud roar issued from the river bank. Startled, Hatasu jumped. Everyone on the boats looked to the source of the bellow on the shore. A hippopotamus cow stood facing the river, its huge mouth opened to its full extent. She let out another thunderous sound as she started moving toward them. Hatasu could see a whole section of the grain fields had been destroyed…eaten or trampled. A herd of hippopotamuses stopped their eating and looked toward the sound. Leaning on the boat rail, Paheri shook his head and grumbled, "It's bad enough the grain's growth is stunted…but these hippopotamuses are wrecking havoc with the whole field!"

The rowers and the current kept them moving them down river. Hatasu strained to see what was happening as they moved by. She heard Sitre complain in agreement with Paheri, "Those animals run rampant and destroy so much, the villagers will hardly have anything to eat."

Hapuseneb leaned toward Hatasu and whispered, "It's Usersobek's 'left-hand magic'. I just know it."

"How could he affect the animals as well as the grains?"

"Well, you see how sick and sad the people look in the last towns." Then he stopped. In that moment, they both saw why the hippopotamus ran toward the river. A large crocodile slid down the bank and into the water. Hatasu saw a young hippopotamus struggling to escape the crocodile's mouth.

The rowers saw it too and picked up their pace. A powerful croc tail could overturn a boat and endanger them all. The crocodile made a loud splash as his tail navigated him into the deeper waters. The mother hippopotamus gained momentum as she ran. Even the river seemed to shake at her thunderous charge into the water. She headed straight for the crocodile. The huge water-horse followed the croc into deeper water. This caused a large wave that rocked the boat.

Hatasu held tight to the railing. The boat crew acted quickly to move away from the angry animals. The crocodile dove under the water with the baby hippo still in his mouth. The mother hippo was close after them; their battle fought under the water. All Hatasu could see of them was the churning of the water, then a spot of red appeared on the surface. The color spread and the agitation continued. The rowers strained at the oars and put all their bodies into getting the boats away from there.

Hatasu stood at the stern peering into the growing distance between the boat and the animals, straining to see the outcome of the battle. For the sailors, it didn't matter who won. Either animal, if wounded, could destroy them.

Paheri was watching closely, too. Once they had enough distance for safety, he said, "What an odd thing. I've never seen a hippo attack a crocodile, even to protect her young. This is a strange omen."

"It is indeed," Sitre's voice quivered as she spoke.

It was not lost on Hatasu that the name Usersobek means 'powerful is Sobek, the crocodile god'. Nor did it elude her that the hippopotamus was the representation of the goddess, Taueret. *Was this really an omen, a predictor of her mother's encounter with the evil priest?*

The children were still shaken from the churning waters and animal chase when their boat pulled into its mooring in el-Saff on the east side of the river. The boats of the Queen and her advisors docked on the west bank across from the town. With no fanfare or delay, the Queen disembarked and proceeded along the road that went to Itjtawy.

Sitre told Hatasu they were to stay on the boat until the Queen returned. If she was not back before nightfall, they were to spend the night at the home of the headman of that village. Hatasu and Hapuseneb stood side by side on the deck of their boat as the royal procession started off.

The Queen was dressed in her most formal and regal attire, sitting high on her litter over the heads of the four guards who carried her. She carried in her hand one of the snake-like staffs. They proceeded along the roadway to the city of Itjtawy and the resident temple of Usersobek. The procession was long, as a large group of priests and royal magicians were like an army themselves, led by Queen Ahmose.

Hatasu watched until every one had grown small and lost from sight in the distance. Then, the children waited. Hatasu held tight to her Sekhmet amulet and remembered her mother's words about fear making one more vulnerable. Everyone seemed stiff and quiet.

The Queen had not been gone long, when the sky began to take on a very odd, gray cloudiness. It was a storm sky but not the cloudless yellow sky of a khamsin. Clouds, seldom seen in this land, gathered thick and billowy, darkening the sky. Then to the utter amazement of all, the clouds dumped their watery contents. Hatasu had never seen rain before. The drops of water were large, heavy and cold. When they pelted upon the skin, it hurt at least as much as the sandstorm winds.

Sitre and Paheri hurriedly ushered the children into the shelter on the boat and pulled down the side awnings. The sky seemed to crackle. Light flashed across the darkened heavens and a sound greater than a thousand drums shook the very earth and turned the river water to churning. The rain made a peculiar sound as it pelted the canvas roof and it wasn't long before the rain started dripping down from the ceiling.

Paheri went to make the necessary arrangement with the headman to bring the children to his house. Servants arrived at the boat holding thick linen over their heads to protect the children. Once safe in the building, the children huddled in a corner, the youngest ones giving into their fear. The headman and his wife were, themselves, very frightened and spoke of the terror of demons that Usersobek had instilled in their hearts. Neferubrity cried loudly. Isis whimpered and clung to Meryt, who distracted her with clapping and rhythm games. Thethi's breathing had gotten labored and he looked around with large, frightened eyes. The headman and his wife had no herbs or oils available, so Paheri gently sang to him.

One of the servants stood in a corner looking down at the floor, mumbling chants of protection. Hatasu noticed Hapuseneb standing by the door and joined him. Together they looked directly out toward the thunder and lightening that seemed to come from the direction of Itjtawy. Great streaks of light flashed across the western sky and another flash from farther west seemed to answer it. They came one after the other and the roaring noise of the thunder shook the ground...louder than the hippopotamus's roar.

Hatasu felt the spray of the rain, cold and wet against her face and body, as it splashed on the ground and building. She took deep breaths, as her mother had taught her, to calm her fear. "What do you think is happening?" she asked Hapuseneb.

"I think it is weather-magic. The battle is being fought with lightening. The Queen is known for her ability to control the elemental forces of weather. This is a good sign."

She looked again in the direction of Itjtawy where the sky was lit up at random intervals. It frightened her but she looked anyways. The irregular line of light, set off a momentary glow and she thought she could see the buildings of the town that must be Itjtawy. Then, complete darkness again.

In the next streak of light, she thought she saw a figure. It was dark, like a new moon, but she could make out its outline. High in the sky, many times larger than any human person, she saw an image of a man in a priest's leopard skin cloak. He was clean shaven but his eyes were blacker than the inside of a crocodile's mouth. He held in his hand a serpent staff and he directed it into the sky.

It was then, as lightening flashed from the end of his staff, that she saw the other figure…again, gigantic in the sky. This figure she recognized, instantly. It was as light as the moon when it was full, and she saw mother's winged crown and the flow of her linen shift. Ahmose's eyes looked like they were burning white embers and she directed her staff back at the priest figure. Lightening again lit the sky and the male figure seemed to sizzle with the light. She saw his mouth open, just as the thunder shook the walls and the foundation beneath her.

She looked over at Hapuseneb. He was staring in the same spot. "What's that?"

Her voice was a frightened whisper, "I think the Queen is

fighting Usersobek as her akh." She kept staring at him, as though it didn't register.

"You know," he turned and looked at her, "their shining spirit bodies, Hatasu. The magic battle takes place with their spirit. It is the strength of the akh that will determine the winner."

She turned back and forced herself to see what was going on in the lightening-filled sky. She saw the dark figure, again. This time, the image of the crocodile god, Sobek, stood behind him. Hatasu remembered the time her aunt Satamun healed Hetep and she could see Isis, Sekhmet and Thoth behind her. Now, she looked over at the figure of her mother, etched in light in the sky.

At first, she could see nothing but blackness behind her but then, faintly, she saw the glowing image of Sekhmet, her lion fierceness lending all her force and strength to the Queen. Just then, the dark figure pointed his staff directly at the Queen…and when the next lightening flared, it seemed to go right through her. Hatasu saw her mother's light body shrink in size and seem to fall back where the bolt of light hit her.

The child hid her eyes with her hands. She couldn't bare to look. Hapuseneb, touched her arm gently and said, "She's alright. Look, my father and the other magicians are with her."

Hatasu dared to peek through her fingers. There were, indeed, more light edged figures in the sky. She recognized Hapuseneb's father, Hapu, Maatmose and Khnumhotep. Lightening flashed, one after another in quick succession. The thunder was deafening. Hapuseneb put his hand on her shoulder and began to sing, at first softly, then gradually louder. It wasn't really a song, just the names of the deities sang over and over again; "Isis, Sekhmet, Thoth." His voice became more and more clear and confident. She joined in and found it easy to follow him.

The threat of impinging fear lessened noticeably as they sang. It even seemed as though it could somehow help her mother in the battle. Sitre, Paheri and Muthotep readily added their voices. Soon, Meryt joined in. Thethi and Isis both seemed calmed by the way the singing changed the atmosphere in the room. Thethi found it difficult to breathe well enough to sing and Isis's little voice was rather lost in the sound of other voices, the rain on the roof, and the thunder in the distance.

"Isis, Sekhmet, Thoth, Horus, Ra."

The headman's wife complained, "Why do you sing at a time like this? We are doomed! Usersobek will swallow us all."

Hatasu realized that they could not see the akhs battling in the sky like she and Hapuseneb could. However, when they lessened the singing, the fear seemed to be waiting right at the doorstep, ready for its chance to re-enter. The group started up again. This time, the headman's wife joined in and sang, as well. They sang on and on. Gradually, the lightening flashes grew farther apart. The thunder seemed farther away.

Hatasu looked back toward the Itjtawy sky but now it was just black. The lightening stopped and there was no light to see. Silence seemed to settle on the land. The only sound was the water dripping from the roof of the house. Hatasu looked over at Hapuseneb who now was sitting, holding tight to his knees. He looked back at her. "Is it over?" she asked.

"I don't know."

"Who won?"

"I don't know."

For the rest of the night, Hatasu sat there at the doorway, staring at the road to Itjtawy, straining to see her mother return. There was nothing but stillness. Her small body shook in the chill and damp of the night. Hapuseneb sat next to her, looking for his father's return, too. He put his arm around her and his warmth stilled her tremors.

When the sun came up in the morning, the sky was absolutely clear and blue again. She saw water still dripping from plants and puddles dotted the roadway back to the river quay. All surfaces glistened in their wetness. "What does it mean that Mother is not back yet?" she begged Sitre, as her nurse paced back and forth across the small room.

"It takes time to travel back to the river," she answered weakly.

Villagers and servants milled about the waterfront, gathering in small clusters. They talked in excited, nervous tones; of the storm, their fear of Usersobek, and their hope that it was the Queen who was victorious. In early afternoon, steam rose from the land as the sun's heat drank up the puddles.

Hatasu sat staring at the road that vanished in the direction of Itjtawy. At first, it was hard to distinguish if she saw people or mist in that distance. She strained to make it out. The forms slowly got closer and clearer.

Hapuseneb called out, "Someone is coming!"

Villagers lined the bank, craning their necks to see. They voiced their trepidation, aloud. Were these Usersobek's henchmen come to punish them for harboring the Queen's children or were they messengers of the Queen, coming to tell them of their freedom from the wicked high priest's tyranny? Finally, they could see the outline of the litter, but still…was it Usersobek's?

Hatasu was the first to make them out clearly. The sun reflected off the gold of the Ahmose's winged crown, and she knew. The Queen was indeed victorious!

Hapuseneb kept staring. His mother, Ahhotep, walked closer…staring. Nefermose was by her side, with Meryt and Isis.

Hatasu looked again. There was no sign of Hapu or Ineni.

Part 3

Chapter 26 - Ankh-Tawy, The White-Walled City

The Queen's sailors rowed her to the east bank. The village, headman to humble peasant, cheered and danced as her ship approached the quay. Hatasu was aware of how Hapuseneb and Meryt kept looking for their fathers, who weren't with the returning group. She thought her mother looked older but her manner and movements were, if anything, more regal and commanding than ever.

Queen Ahmose stood on the ship's deck and spoke to the crowd, "With the power of Amun, I have overcome Usersobek. The evil magician of Itjtawy's rule of fear is over. His spell is broken. Chaos is defeated, and Maat is restored."

The people cheered. The release of the tensions was visible…for all but Hapu and Ineni's families.

The Queen went on, "Usersobek, overcome by his own demons, threw himself into the river and drowned. He was thus duly self-executed for his treason against the gods and the Pharaoh. Usersobek's assistants have been removed from their positions and stripped of their power and their property. These men will do you no more harm."

A great cheer sounded. Ahmose then turned and looked directly at the strained faces of Ahhotep and Nefermose. She smiled warmly at them and said, "My loyal councilors are safe. Hapu will stay in Itjtawy to administer the holy places until priests who are loyal to Maat take their positions in the city and temple." Ahhotep and Hapuseneb exhaled their breath in relief. Ahmose then looked to

Nefermose, Meryt and little Isis as she said, "Ineni will supervise the redistribution of the lands confiscated from the evil priest." The deep furlough left Nefermose's brow, and Meryt and Isis smiled.

Hand drum sounds and dancing feet filled the dockside. The townsfolk made way for the Queen. She gathered her children around her and announced, "Tomorrow, we will sail toward the City of the White Walls. There, we await the return of Pharaoh Thutmose and the army of the Two Lands."

That night, in the humble dwelling of the headman of el-Saff and his wife, Ahmose tucked Hatasu into bed with a lullaby. It was the first time in the many days of growing tensions that her mother put her to bed and without the need of the magic protection. Hatasu longed to know about the battle. She had never seen her mother prepare in any way. She seized this opportunity and asked, "Omm, what happened last night? How was the magic battle fought? I've never seen you throw a spear or drive a chariot."

The Queen looked down, thoughtful. "All you need to know is that the physical plane is not always the field of battle. When you go to the House of Life, you will learn more of the magic of the akh and how it is used for good and for evil. The exercises of a spiritual warrior are discipline of the will and the heart, rather than the skill at arms and horsemanship. Last night, skill in magic was what was required for victory. Usersobek's plan to overthrow the Pharaoh is foiled."

Tucking the sheets tight around Hatasu, Ahmose said, "Tomorrow, we sail into Ankh-Tawy, the great city of the north. We must be ready to set sail at first light so we can see the city in all her glory."

Lying back on her bed, Hatasu was half resigned to the limited knowledge of magic battles and shifted her attention to anticipation of the next day's adventures. She let her mother's kiss and song usher her into a world of dreams…in which her mother was the mighty Isis, yielding a lightening bolt spear into a Set-crocodile with a shaved human head of a high priest and the coarser, harsher features of the men of the Levant.

The next day, the air still had the smell of humidity as it was saturated with evaporating rainwater. The ubiquitous desert sand, bound now with moisture, was temporarily confined to the earthy ground. Everywhere the eye rested, sparkled bright with color, for everything had been washed of its ever-present dust in the rain's cleansing powers.

The emotional atmosphere was cleansed, too, as though the ka of each person was freed from a heavy garment of fear. The night's rest was deep and rejuvenating as it was no longer troubled by Usersobek's attacks on the sleeping spirits of the royal family. Scowl lines vanished from the foreheads of the adults. The sober tones and cautious restrictions on the children's activities, disappeared. The celebration banquet that evening was alive with dancing, singing and praising the victory of the Queen and High Priest, Hapu and Vizier Ineni, who freed the land of Usersobek's evil influence.

The next morning, as Ra began to glow on the eastern horizon, Hatasu stood on deck close to her mother. Ahmose's arm reached around Hatasu's shoulder, drawing her close to her. They stood together looking out over the river that was just beginning to reflect the rosy colors of dawn. Then she gave her daughter a squeeze and said, "I remember well, the first time I saw Ankh-Tawy's shining white walls. My mother, also, arranged for us to arrive with the dawn so I would see it in all its glory. She said to me, 'Ankh-Tawy is the Queen of cities. See how she dresses in finest white, pleated linen'." Ahmose smiled to herself at the thought of the irrepressible Nefertari.

Looking down at her daughter, she continued, "I have loved it ever since but you will find different kinds of wonders here, than in Waset. Look there, to the west." She leaned forward and pointed in the direction of the west bank. The bright rays of the sun's shining fingers were just beginning to light the golden tips of the pyramids beyond the fertile stretch of green. "There are the temples of those who ruled our land in the long ago, when Ankh-Tawy was the capital and the single greatest city in the land, before Waset was the seat of the Pharaoh and before Itjtawy was the place of rulers, before the Hyksos."

Hatasu, still sleepy from the early hour, strained to see clearly. The current moved them along swiftly, for the river was full from the added water of the rainstorm. From a distance, she saw the shiny white structure of the wall. Getting closer, it loomed large, stretching the distance along the riverbank. This wall was unlike other walls. It was neither smooth, nor covered with brightly painted pictures. No, this grand expanse of gleaming white was arranged with a repeating pattern of indentations that made an incredibly beautiful pattern of gleaming light and deep shadow.

Hatasu's eyes were wide with wonder now, and she thought of her grandmother calling it a 'Queen of a city', and this wall being her fine, pleated-linen dress.

"Ankh-Tawy is also called 'Hikuptah'," said Ahmose. "It means 'Temple of the Ka of Ptah'. Ptah is the creator god, sacred to crafts persons and this is where the Nile Valley meets the Delta, the junction of the two lands, Upper Egypt and Lower Egypt."

As they floated by the wall, the play of light and shadow danced across its face, enlivening it by the moving reflection of water and waves. Beyond the wall was the bustling harbor. A long line of quays reached out like fingers into the river. There was no sheltered palace-harbor like at Waset and Abedju, no protective space the ships could pull into. These piers extended right out into the river.

Music floated toward them from the city side of the river. Several rows of white-robed priests and priestesses were neatly assembled on the shore by the royal quay. With sistrums, frame drums and clapping hands, they joyfully chanted a welcome. In the center of all the priests and priestesses was a tall and portly man. He wore the leopard skin of a priest over the long skirt of a governor. The staff of authority stood upright in his hand.

The royal boat was ushered into its docking space as men wearing loincloths scurried around with strong, thick ropes, securing the boat to the wharf. Behind the mayor and the temple personnel, the people of the city anxiously awaited their opportunity to get a glimpse of this Queen who saved them from the oppressive influence of the evil priest. The electric storm lighting the night sky had been their announcement of the battle and proclamation of her victory. Those educated in magic understood its meaning; the common folks felt only the palpable difference in the physical and emotional atmosphere.

The Queen disembarked, looking royal, indeed. She stepped from the boat and offered her official smile to the greeting party. The mayor, Rahotep, bowed low before the Queen. He added an exaggerated flourish with his hand. He waited deep in the bow with an overstated humility, ignoring her quiet hand motion to rise.

Hatasu watched this pompous display with a suspect eye. The same men who had tied up the boat were now unloading it in an orderly and efficient manner under the direction of a matronly-looking woman. The princess looked at the woman closely, wondering if she was the steward of their house here in Ankh-Tawy. She was in late middle-age, with a strained but smiling face. Her skin was lighter than Hatasu was used to seeing to the south in Waset but she had the same straight, black wig that came down to her arms.

Rahotep gave a speech that professed his great loyalty to the Pharaoh. In the middle of his exaltation of his accomplishments, there came the sound of footsteps running hard down the central street. The crowd buzzed as a messenger made his way through, finally appearing in front of the mayor and Queen. He was a servant with a loincloth and shaved head. He was breathing so hard, it was difficult for him to get his words out. His brown skin glistened with the exertion of getting there. His face was pale and strained. The crowd hushed. What message could be so urgent as to interrupt this ceremony?

"There is a messenger," he panted, struggling to get his breath.
Hatasu saw her mother stiffen.

"Out with it, boy." Rahotep seemed annoyed that the messenger
arrived during his speech.

"A messenger…from…the Pharaoh!" He was still breathing
very heavily. The people of the crowd strained to hear what else the
messenger had to say.

The Queen motioned to the matronly woman to bring some
water for this runner. She handed him a ladle of liquid. He drank
eagerly, then said, "He comes from the war; he is wounded." He
stopped again to catch his breath.

Ahmose's face strained. "Is his news good or bad?"

"He did not say."

Rahotep, now direct and without flourish, asked, "Well, what *did*
he say?"

Turning to the mayor, the servant bowed his head and answered,
"He arrived on a Levantine trade boat docked at the north quay.
When I told him you were at the main harbor to greet the royal
party, he said he would wait and give his message directly to his
Queen."

During this exchange, Hatasu felt reassured by the composure on
her mother's face. Her own dreams around Itjtawy had been
troubled but there had been none of her father in half a moon. She
did not believe anything awful could happen to him without her
knowing about it first in her night travels. Still, doubts crept in. *Was
something wrong? Why did the servant look so pale?*

The mayor said, condescendingly to the Queen, "I advise we

continue our formal greeting. If we conclude in haste, we might alarm the citizens of our great city."

The Queen spoke as though she had not heard his tone, "We will proceed to the palace now. Any further ceremony may be performed at this evening's banquet. We will move the procession forward with directness but not with haste." She smiled at him benignly, nodding her head once. He followed after her.

Ahmose and the children were carried by litter through the broad, central street of this grandest of cities at the crux of the Two Lands. The step of the litter bearers was lively but the paved way to their destination at the palace seemed endless. Every fiber and nerve of Hatasu's body longed for the news of her father and…she hoped …reassurance of his safety.

Hatasu moved her eyes from the destination to the crowds who lined both sides of the street. Many sang out greetings, "Hail, Oh Queen, who saved us from Usersobek!" But there were also many faces that looked strange and unfamiliar to her. They had lighter skin and sharper Levantine features. Finally, the palace gates rose before her and they arrived at their destination. The design on the gate walls was like that at Waset but there were areas not yet painted and even parts of the wall still under construction. The gateway was wide and contained a large window opening in the area above it, which faced the northern gate of the city. The procession moved through this gateway. The palace was different from the homey, sprawling, flat building of Waset, just as the exposed, long, finger-like quays of Ankh-Tawy river harbor were different from the still waters of the protected harbor lakes of the southern capital.

This palace had rows of windows that stretched skyward, up three floors. Like the wall, the white-washed mud-brick exterior of the palace was brightly painted in some places and still unfinished in others. Inside the walls, the garden opened before them with the comfortingly familiar sight of a lotus pool surrounded by ornamental trees and plants. The greenery had the statue of small recently planted shrubs.

It was there by the pool, she first caught sight of the messenger. He was a young man in a warrior's loincloth with the sandals of a soldier. His large, brown eyes looked wild. What might have been a handsome face was disfigured with the red welt of a scar close under his left eye. It took Hatasu a moment to realize there was something else in this scene that alarmed her. The man's right arm was missing just below the elbow. The red end of the stump hung half-way down his side. He held a scroll in his left hand. Hatasu looked back to his face and only then recognized that his rounded head, almond-shaped eyes and slightly protruding upper teeth were similar to those found in the Ahmose family. Yes, surely, this was the son her Aunt Satamun was so anxious for her to meet. Even more alarmed, she thought, 'What must the news be that a royal prince carries it instead of a servant messenger and a wounded one at that?'

Queen Ahmose was unable to stifle the gasp that escaped from her mouth when she first saw him. "Tao!" she exclaimed, as she stepped forward to embrace her nephew. He stiffened and bowed formally, blocking the family embrace. She motioned for him to rise and said with due ceremony toward the returning war hero, "Greetings to you, Captain Tao, son of my sister, the Great God's Wife." She averted her gaze from the stump. "What news do you bring from your Pharaoh at the war front?"

He bowed again. He seemed to be making an extreme effort to keep emotions under control. "Yes, Your Majesty," he said, his tone formal, further distress revealed in the terse pronunciation of words. "The Pharaoh is safe and well but the battle with the Mitanni was terrible. Not all our soldiers fared as well as I did." His voice had a stoic steadiness, even if his eyes glistened with unshed tears.

Hatasu heard the words that her father was safe but she knew something was still terribly wrong, or Tao, a prince, would not be standing before them like this. The Queen's body braced, as her eyes, too, filled with tears. "I see the war has been hard on you..." she said gently. "You have offered much for your homeland."

Tao interrupted her, "I am not here to speak of my hardship but to bring you the message from the Pharaoh." He pulled his body up straighter and taller. "It was against my wishes that I return before the rest of the army. It was only at my Pharaoh's command that I returned to deliver this message to you in person." He handed her the papyrus scroll with his right hand.

Hatasu felt an aching terror in her heart, as her eyes were fixated on where Tao's lower arm and hand used to be. He kept his eyes lowered to the ground and his body erect in a way that suggested his sense of dignity, in spite of his pain.

Ahmose looked at the Thutmose's seal on the scroll, then looked back to Tao. "Tell me the news. I'd rather hear it, than read it," her voice quivered.

"As you wish." Tao bowed his head. "The Prince, Amenmose has been slain in battle." With this information spoken out loud, he made a choking sound and was unable to go on.

Hatasu stared at him. Her breathing stopped and the world around her took on an eerie light. Time slowed down. *Had she heard that right? Amenmose is dead!?! A second brother dead?*

The Queen stared as though the information had not registered. "Your Pharaoh, Tao…you said he was alright?" her voice was a strained whisper.

"Yes." He raised his head and looked at her. "Amenmose's death was not in vain. The Pharaoh won the war with the dreadful Mitanni. He will be bringing the army home, as soon as a treaty is signed with the Mitanni leader."

Hatasu felt relief at this reassurance of her father's wellbeing. She realized *that* was the worse of her fears. Then her mind returned to Amenmose and tears welled up. She tried to be a brave daughter to her father but she blinked hard and several tears escaped and plunked onto her cheeks. It had not occurred to her that Amen could die. She had only thought of him as getting accolades from the Pharaoh and experiencing the glory of being at war with their father.

Tao's words broke through her thoughts, "I offer you my condolences, Queen Ahmose." He looked like it was difficult for him to stand on his own, now. A servant moved toward him to support him. He shook off the help and said to Ahmose, "I beg your leave, Queen Ahmose. I am weary from travel and wish to retire.

The news I bring grieves me deeply for Amenmose was my friend and comrade, as well as my prince. I wish to rest alone."

The Queen nodded. "Go, Tao, and rest well. We will share more news when you feel stronger."

Hatasu watched as he moved, a lone figure with a limp, toward the doorway into the palace. A servant trailed along behind him.

The Queen nodded to the servant, "See to it that my nephew has every comfort and he has the best of doctors."

Once Tao disappeared indoors, Ahmose looked at the scroll resting on her lap. She broke open the seal and in silence looked down on Thutmose's words. The group of nobles that accompanied the procession, began to murmur. Queen Ahmose stood up from her chair, scroll still in hand and spoke, "Please go home now. We will speak more of these things at the banquet this evening, after the royal family has rested."

Ahmose silently turned and made her way to the door of the palace. Sitre and Paheri guided the children after her. They could see the women of the household tearing their clothes and throwing dirt on their hair. Even after they entered the palace, they could hear them wailing out their grief.

Hatasu held onto Sitre's hand as they entered. What would have, under different circumstances, been viewed as a magnificent entrance hall of this Ankh-Tawy palace, Hatasu hardly noticed. The world had taken on a feeling of unreality like she was watching everything from outside herself. This was a strange and alarming sensation. She blindly followed Sitre up one flight of stairs and then another. She was in a daze, unable to make her thoughts congeal.

When they came to the private apartment for the royal family, Thethi's breathing had gotten raspy, so he and Paheri were shown to their rooms first. Hetka, the matronly woman from the quay, led Hatasu and Sitre to the princess's new room. It was arranged similarly to her room in Waset, with a niche set up with a bed. There were plain, undecorated walls and a window not quite as high as in the low, sprawling building she called home in the south. Hatasu sat on the bed and tried to get her bearings with this strange 'unreal' feeling.

Hetka started helping Sitre unpack her things, putting them neatly in ornate wooden boxes against the bare walls. The two women worked efficiently together. "Great joy and great sadness seem to go hand in hand for this Pharaoh's family," said Hetka as Sitre took the oils out of the traveling box and placed them in an orderly fashion in the box.

They were talking as though Hatasu wasn't even there. It felt fitting, as she was experiencing herself as nothing more than a ghost or a shadow. Thoughts of Amenmose's death…and images of Tao's arm…swam in her head.

"One knows there must be a price for victory, but…" Sitre sounded distracted by her own emotions. "Oh! Amenmose!" she said. "That is too high a price…to lose the second son." Then, looking toward Hatasu, "…and a second brother, so soon after Wadjmose. It is a great weight the Pharaoh must bear for his people and their safety."

This last statement stirred Hatasu from her fog. Unshed tears burned her eyes but she thought of her father's lack of tears at

Wadj's death. She wanted to be like him and not like the women who wailed in the streets. She lowered herself to the floor and sat cross-legged in front of her traveling box. She started to rummage through it and picked up her yarn-haired paddle doll. She tried to look at it but she couldn't see through her watery eyes.

She turned to Sitre. "Amenmose's ka will be with Wadjmose in the stars of Nut, right? That's what my father would say." Looking up, she saw Sitre nod an affirmative answer. After another moment, she asked, "How will they prepare his body for the great transformation if he is so far away?"

Sitre put down the folded linen sheets she was unpacking. She squatted to Hatasu's level and enfolded her arms around her. "Dear heart, Amenmose will indeed receive all the necessary rituals for his journey to Nut," her nurse spoke through her own tears.

Hatasu buried her face in Sitre's shoulder and surrendered to the sobs that shook her body. Gradually the tears subsided and she sat back. "So he will be among the imperishable stars with Wadjmose?"

Sitre nodded.

"He would like that."

"Yes, he will be brought home purified and ready to be laid in his house of eternity on the West Bank of Waset, so we can make offerings to his ka on the festival of the ancestors."

Hatasu wiped her eyes and blew her nose in the linen Sitre offered her. "Satamun told me that as I grew, I would get used to people going through the doorway of life to live among the stars. She has people she loves on both sides of that veil, you know."

Sitre looked at her with sad eyes.

The child continued, "I am glad for her that Tao returned from the war."

Sitre and Hetka exchanged troubled looks. After a pause, Sitre said, "It will be a hard life for him, much different from what his mother had planned for her only surviving son." Her long, thin fingers rested passively, brown against the folded white linen.

Hetka nodded, her black, shoulder-length wig swaying with her head. "There is a sting to having had a dream dangled in front of you and then having it cut short…" Her words trailed off, as the image of the shortened arm dangling at the side of the proud son of the Great God's Wife came to their minds. "I'm sorry," she said, putting her hand over her mouth as though to force back the words.

Sitre shook her head back and forth. "Hetka, it is true. Everyone knew Satamun wanted Hatasu to marry Tao rather than her brother because that would keep the Double Crown in the lines of Taosid. It was Seniseneb who urged that Hatasu marry her brother to shift the line to the Thutmosids. Now, both dreams are dashed."

She waited a minute, then continued, "Well, not completely dashed. There is still Thethi. But his health is so poor and…" Her words trailed off again.

Slumped over her small body, the princess said softly, "My consorts keep dying. Who will survive to be Pharaoh? It would be okay with me for it to be Thethi. I just don't want Thethi to die, too." Hatasu's thoughts shifted back and forth between her possible consorts. "Wadjmose and Amenmose have gone to the stars and they can't rule from there. Thethi is sick a lot and often scared, not good for a ruler. Perhaps Tao could still rule. He has royal blood, he's a war hero and he's still alive." She sat straighter, out of her slump and looked to Sitre and Hetka.

"No, he couldn't," said Sitre, shaking her head slowly. "Dear one, the Pharaoh must be physically perfect to represent the god Amun among us. He would be unable to hold the crook and flail with only one arm. Tao knows he's been robbed of any chance to dream that dream again," Sitre's dark eyes seemed to deepen as she spoke. She turned back to the traveling box, now empty. She closed it and turned to Hetka. "The servant can take these boxes to storage. Hopefully, it won't be long before we need them to return to Waset." The two women left the room to find the appropriate servant.

Hatasu was left with her sad and confusing thoughts. There was even more compassion for her cousin as she realized what all this meant for him. She continued to rummage through her box again and pulled out a neatly rolled and tied papyrus scroll. She held it up and exclaimed to herself, "This is the message Satamun gave me to give to Tao when I saw him! Maybe if I bring it to him, it will cheer him up."

During the banquet that evening, Ahmose announced to the nobility of Ankh-Tawy that the Pharaoh had a great victory…that he had been triumphant in the Levant. A great cheer filled the hall. When the room was quiet again, she continued with the news of the demise of Amenmose, the heir to the throne, the Hawk-in-the-Nest.

A hush fell, as the seriousness of this news settled heavy in the hearts of all. The battle had been won to keep them safe from the outside but what would become of them without a clearly identified heir to the throne? Few of the landed lords there knew Amenmose but they all knew what he represented for their future. Thethi's name was brought up as the next probable heir, and Hatasu's, again, as his Great Royal Wife. One of the priests brought up the prophecy of Hatasu's rule and the lack of any such prophecy for Thethi. It was known that this matter would not be settled until Thutmose announced his decision when he returned.

As soon as Hatasu could leave this domain of strangers, she did so. Talk of prophesy of her ruling made her uncomfortable. Thethi followed her out to the lotus pool in the garden. The familiar plants, even in an unfamiliar setting, still gave her comfort. Her brother's breath had been wheezy since the afternoon. She waited for him to catch up with her.

His jaw was set and his eyes were frightened. He picked up a stone in the pathway and threw it hard against the garden wall. "What do you think father will do?" he asked through his wheezing. "You are a Taosid and that is important. You have always been his favorite. I think he will choose you."

"Thethi, I don't want to be Pharaoh. I'd rather be Queen, like mother. I guess I'd rather be Queen to you, than to Amenmose."

Thethi took a stance like he'd seen his father take, feet spread wide, fists on his hips. "If I were Pharaoh, I would be a mighty warrior and kill all those people of the Levant who killed my brother and took Tao's arm." He stamped his foot on the crushed-stone pathway for emphasis.

Hatasu said, "We would build great temples and make the

people strong at home."

The wheeze lessened as he directed his fear into anger. He picked up pebbles in the walkway and used the wall as the target, aiming each stone as though it were a spear shot at the heart of the enemy. Then, he turned on her and showed his doubt, saying, "But there is no prophecy about me as there is about you."

"There may still be one. Who knows?"

"Well, when I'm Pharaoh and you are Queen…" His voice trailed off, as his imagination failed to complete the picture.

"We could work together, as mother and father do," Hatasu said, completing the sentence. She thought that it always seemed to be her job to take care of her younger brother. *If he couldn't take care of himself, how could he take care of the Two Lands?*

"The doctors say when I'm an adult, the breathing sickness is likely to go away. Then, I will show everyone that I can do great things."

His sister encouraged him, "We can do great things together." Some of the feeling of numbed fog that she'd been walking around in since the announcement of Amen's death, seemed to lift a bit as she tried to consol Thethi. Feeling a bit more like herself, Hatasu sat down by the lily pool and after a short silence, said, "I didn't always like Amenmose, but I loved him as my brother. I didn't want to be his Queen, but I didn't want him to die. And poor Tao, poor Satamun. What will happen to him?" She took one of the stones and tossed it slowly, sadly, into the pond. Its circular ripples spread outward but were interrupted as they met floating lotus pads.

Hatasu wished her father was here now, to squat down next to her and put his arm around her. He would remind her how Amenmose's ba had journeyed to the starry arms of the goddess, Nut, and how everything would be all right. She wished Seniseneb was there, so she could cuddle up next to her soft body and feel comforted. But, it was just she and Thethi in the garden. They sat close together and took what comfort they could from each other's presence.

Her mind trailed off to the disturbing image of her cousin Tao, with his dangling half arm and the horrible look on his face. She leaned over the now-still water and thought to pick a perfect lotus, sending its fragrance into the evening air. She could bring it to Tao, she thought, remembering the papyrus note still in her room. Back in Waset, the flower had cheered up Hetep when he was hurt. Consoling Thethi helped her feel better, maybe something nice for Tao would help, too.

Unfamiliar with this new palace, she went to Hetka to get directions as to where Tao might be. The house matron shook her head slowly and said, "It may not be a good idea to see him, now."

The determined child thought for a moment and said, "Well tomorrow, where would I find him, then?"

"His room is in the family guest quarters on the far end of the third floor, where your room is, also."

That was all she needed. Carrying the papyrus scroll and the single sweet smelling blossom, she walked to Tao's room and knocked softly at the door. There was no answer. She knocked a little harder. Still no answer. She began to think he must be asleep and she didn't want to disturb him, but she tried one last time.

"Go away! Just leave me alone! I don't want anything to eat. I don't want any of the healer's teas and I don't want anyone's sympathy or pity. Now, just go away!"

Hatasu stood frozen. No one had ever talked to her like that, before. Well, maybe the note from his mother would cheer him up. She slipped the papyrus under the door, then laid the lotus blossom on the floor. She turned to walk away and the door opened. Tao was holding the papyrus in his single hand. His face was blotchy. The carnelian-colored scar contrasted sharply with the paleness of the rest of his face. His eyebrows were low and bushy over his reddened eyes. His hair was mussed and in disarray.

In a small voice, she said, "I didn't mean to disturb you. Satamun wished me to give the message to you and I thought it would cheer you. Please don't be mad at me."

"Hatshepsut, I didn't expect you," he said.

Hatasu was surprised. No one ever called her by her formal name. She scarcely knew he was referring to her. He went on, "I am not good company, right now. I'm sure I know what my mother says in her note. It was meant for different circumstances. Please go…be with your family and do not waste your thoughts on me."

She bent to pick up the flower on the floor. Extending her hand, she offered it to him. He'd already turned and was closing the door. He was gone. The lotus was still in her hand. The feeling of fog returned. That night, she slept in her new bedroom with its undecorated walls. Falling asleep was easy…the first time. But in the middle of the night, out of the stillness of the sleeping household, came a piercing scream. She sat bolt upright. There were scurrying sounds in the hallways and Sitre came to her side to assure her that everything was okay.

Hatasu was all the more puzzled, for clearly, everything was not okay. She thought first of Thethi and worried that he might have had a breathing attack brought on with the news of his brother's death, but the scream had come from the other side of the palace. Thethi's room was not far from hers, and the more she listened, she picked up the familiar sounds of his troubled breathing and his nurse-tutor's soothing chants that usually accompanied the herbal tea. On the other side of her room, she heard Neferubrity. Her crying sounded the same as it did this afternoon when she had an earache.

Hatasu heard Muthotep walking back and forth with the baby, singing lullabies. Sitre smiled weakly. It was obvious there was more than one person in the household who was distressed. "It's been a long and difficult day for everyone. Now just try to go back to sleep," she said.

Hatasu tried but her own anxious thoughts disturbed her. Thoughts of both Amenmose and Tao hung heavy in her heart. She knew the scream was from Tao. He had sounded so frightened. She didn't know if she felt sorry for him or if she was afraid of him. This was a different kind of fear than the fear in Itjtawy. There, someone was actively trying to hurt them. This was different. She was afraid to see the stump on his arm, afraid to see the distress in his eyes as he averted them when someone spoke to him, afraid of why he would scream out in the middle of the night, as though some evil mashmashu were chasing him in his night travel.

Her eyes popped wide open at that thought. She looked around her room and was unsettled by the absence of the protective image of Bes, who watched over her in Waset. She lay there wishing for a dream visit from her father when the scream came again, more muffled, as though coming through many doors. There were thrashing sounds. This time, she didn't wait for Sitre to come and comfort her. She got up and padded along the corridors to Tao's room.

She moved quickly and silently, close to the wall, hoping no one would notice and question where she was going. She pushed open the doors that separated the royal apartments from the guest rooms. Continuing down the second corridor, she arrived at the room she had visited earlier in the evening. She peered around the open door jam. Torches filled the room with artificial brightness. The table by the bed was knocked over. The bed linens were tangled in disarray.

Tao, himself, paced frantically back and forth within the small space, pulling at his hair with his one remaining hand and making jerky movements with the stub that was left him, responding as though it had forgotten that half of it was no longer there. His eyes looked wild, defiant, frightful. A priestess was in a corner of the room, preparing a medicinal tea while she chanted softly. A man paced along with him, talking to him in a reassuring voice.

She could hear him saying, "You are no longer in Retennu! You are home in Ankh-Tawy. The battle was won. There was nothing you could have done to save Amenmose." The third time this was repeated, Tao's eyes focused on the man next to him. His frantic movements slowed and he took a tentative look around him as though noticing his surroundings for the first time.

In looking around, he saw Hatasu. He turned on her, fiercely. "What are you doing here? Don't you *ever* tell my mother of this," he demanded. "She must not know the truth about her only surviving son. Not only can I not succeed as a solider but I can't control my dreams as a priest." His eyes took on a glaring, ferocious light that penetrated her to the core.

The priestess in the corner came forward and handed the priest the tea she'd been preparing. She moved quickly to Hatasu. Putting her hands on her shoulders, she turned her around and ushered her out the door. It was just as well she had no time to respond, for Hatasu had no idea what to say to her distraught cousin. She looked back toward his room, from which she now heard sobbing. The woman ushered her to the other side of the first door which separated the guest apartments from the royal rooms. This priestess squatted down so that she was level to the princess and looked her squarely in the eye. "Tao must not be disturbed, anymore. You must stay in the royal apartments."

Hatasu looked into the face of this very beautiful woman. Her eyes were the shape of an almond and they were black like a starry night. She had a small nose and a delicate mouth. Her teeth were straight with no sign of the upper protrusion of the Tao family. This beauty contrasted with the firm harshness of her voice.

Hatasu felt embarrassed that she had inadvertently done something wrong, and in her own distraught state, her eyes welled up with tears again. She blinked the tears back and blurted out, "What's wrong? Why is his ka so ill? Does Usersobek still have power to hurt dreams? Do the mashmashu chase him in his sleep? What makes his dreams frightening?" She stamped her small foot on the painted mud-brick floor to overcome her inclination to cry.

The young woman's black hair hung over her slight, white shoulders. The red ribbon of the temple was tied around the forehead. She let her hands slide down Hatasu's arms and she took both her hands in her own. "Indeed, war battles can wound the ka as well as the khet, Hatshepsut."

The child was taken aback again at being addressed by that strange, formal name. The priestess continued, "It is as though Set binds him to the moment in time that he wishes he could change. His dreams keep returning him to the battles in Retennu, in the Levant."

"Can't you draw the magic circle around him before he goes to slee, to keep out hurtful spirits?"

"We have tried but he carries these memories within him. The bone wand did not work. It is not the Usersobek dreams. I have worked with many of those. The mashmashu magic may be part of it but most of the trouble seems to be coming from inside Tao, not outside."

"What can you do? What will help him?"

"I am Sihathor, priestess of Sekhmet. I make him brews. I recite the old chants. I call upon the ferocious goddess of war and healing, to do battle with these memories that wound his ka. Hopefully, Sekhmet will favor us with healing."

The child nodded, satisfied. "Please tell him I will keep his secret. I will honor his request."

Sihathor smiled and still holding the small hands, stood to her full height. "Go now to your own sleep. May your dreams be of healing." She released her hands and urged her in the direction of her own room.

Hatasu returned to her bed and lay awake thinking. When sleep finally came, it was filled with images of Tao and his ka struggling with each other; a sort of wrestling match that neither could win.

The next morning started slowly, as no one had slept well. The new halls echoed in the stillness. Ra had risen across the river. Hatasu did not wish to stay in bed for more disturbing dreams. She thought she'd explore this new place. Thethi would have been her preferred companion but she knew he would be exhausted from last night's illness, the worst he had experienced since Wadjmose's death. He would be in no shape to practice either his swordsmanship or throw-sticks. She was somewhat relieved, for soldiering didn't seem quite the same since she had seen what it had done to Tao.

Though the weight of sadness slowed her movements, she did not wish to stay in her undecorated, unprotected room. Careful to stay away from Tao's side of the house, she wandered down the stairs and started to explore this new palace.

It wasn't long before she heard Sitre call her. "There you are, my dear!" she said when she found her. "Your mother wishes you to have breakfast with her this morning. Come, I don't think you have seen the roof garden, yet. You will like it. That is where your mother waits for you."

Hatasu followed Sitre to the roof of the palace where there was another garden with a lovely canopied shelter and potted trees arranged for shade. Ahmose sat under the canopy, a table piled with sweet breads and bright fruits in front of her. Thethi sat to her side, looking tired and haggard with dark circles under his eyes. She ran to her mother and gave her a kiss on the cheek.

"Do you like this new palace?" her mother asked, as she pointed to the place set for her at the table.

"Well, I like everything except my bedroom." She sat where her mother indicated.

Tilting her head to one side in surprised curiosity, her mother asked, "Why?"

"The walls are plain. There is no protective goddess, no stories, to brighten them."

"We are in the city of Ptah, god of craftspeople. I will have someone from the temple paint you a picture of Bes, like the one in Waset. You can then think of your room as your temple, with Bes honoring its walls!"

Hatasu thought for a minute while she chewed her morning bread. "I would rather have a picture of the serpent goddess, Queen of Punt, for she is in the Land of the Gods, far away from the Levantines."

"When Hereptah, the master craftsman, comes to discuss the decoration of the family's gathering room, I will talk with him about decorating your room, too."

Hatasu smiled, more with relief than anything else. Just then, Muthotep arrived with Neferubrity, who was rubbing her sleepy eyes. Her earache from last night had been relieved by Muthotep's healing magic. When the baby saw her mother, she held out her chubby arms and Ahmose rose from her seat to take her. She planted deep kisses into each of her baby's soft cheeks and bouncing her up and down, she sang her a little ditty. The baby pulled at her mother's nose and tried to poke her eyes. Ahmose gently shook her face free of the little finger and blew kisses into her neck. Neferubrity giggled, then snuggled her head into her mother's shoulder. The mother smiled as she swayed back and forth, her loving arms holding the little one close, one hand gently cradling the baby's head of dark, straight hair.

Hatasu left her morning bread half eaten and went to her mother's side. She reached up to take her baby sister's hand and called, "Ubriti! Ubriti!" which had become her nickname.

The little one lifted her head from her mother's chest and pointed to her big sister. "Ha!" she called out.

"Ha-ta-su," the big sister said slowly, trying to teach her to say her name.

"It seems as though 'Ha' is her own special name for you. It will change, soon enough," Ahmose said, as she took the baby to her seat.

Neferubrity squirmed and her mother lowered her to the floor. Ubriti scurried off on hands and knees with a protective Hatasu close behind. She found a leaf from a potted palm tree and started to put it in her mouth. Hatasu took it away gently and said, "Wait a minute, Ubriti. I'll get you a piece of bread." She scooped her up and brought her back to the table to join the others. As the baby gummed the crust of bread against the incoming teeth, Hatasu asked her mother, "Is Tao coming to breakfast with us?"

"No, my dear, he is preparing to travel today. He plans to return upriver to Khemenu, where he had been studying before he went to the Levant. There is a famous dream healer there and it is hopeful she can help him with his nightmares."

Hatasu nodded, saying nothing about the previous night and turning her attention back to her baby sister on her lap.

Chapter 27 - City of Craftspeople

Hatsu stood on the rooftop of the Ankh-Tawy palace the morning after the celebration banquet announcing the Pharaoh's military victory. As she looked out over the palace grounds and beyond the garden wall to the greater city, the snatches of conversation overheard the night before kept running through her head. Her mother's official announcement had only informed the guests of the Pharaoh's triumph. Nothing was said 'officially' about Amenmose's death.

Hatsu understood it was better not to alarm people…or to leave room for unhealthy speculation about the next Hawk-in-the-Nest. When the Pharaoh returned home it would be time enough, for he would then be able to quell speculations with the announcement of his own choice of the next heir to the Double Crown. The lack of an official announcement did *not* mean people didn't know.

Everywhere she turned, reports of the death of Amenmose rippled through conversations. This morning, the overheard words haunted her mind. "Who will the Pharaoh choose this time?"

She had heard a local nobleman say, "It is no secret that Thutmose's one remaining son is in such poor health. He won't be able to withstand the rigors of rulership…if he survived to adulthood."

A woman standing next to him had responded, "His first daughter, Hatshepsut, is very promising. There is a prophecy about her, you know."

Hatsu had startled at hearing these words from a stranger.

"Yes," that person had continued, "but it is a prophecy that she will be a Queen."

Hatasu had relaxed a bit, again.

A much older man wearing a necklace of golden flies made another remembered comment, "It is possible the Pharaoh could name a successor from his army, in the manner that Amenhotep named him."

Hatasu had assumed he was a trainer at the Ankh-Tawy army barracks. Hatasu mulled all these words over in her mind as she looked out over the awakening city of Ankh-Tawy. She wished her father was already home. The squawking of a small gaggle of geese, herded by a boy hardly older than herself, drew her attention to the yard below her. Indeed, the entire palace community was waking up and beginning its usual activities as though the world hadn't been turned upside down. The bakery, the weavers, the animal herders and the gardeners came out to begin their service to the palace. It was very similar to the activities in the Waset palace yard and at each other mooring palace she visited.

She felt some relief that her rooftop perch was high enough, she did not hear the continuing gossip…about last night's banquet…about Amenmose's death…about the speculation of who would be next in line for the Double Crown. She looked beyond these servant's activities to the spreading boulevards of the city beyond the mud brick enclosure of the palace walls. She could see two large temples, much larger than the one in Waset. People came and went through their pylon gates. The smell of incense and the sound of chanting escaped over the walls.

From the direction of the riverbank, she heard the merchant's calls to sell their wares and the creak of the ship's riggings. To the north, she could see the tips of giant pyramids and in-between was the city with so many people, all concerned about the royal choice. She made out the large mansions of the wealthy, the smaller homes of the craftspeople and the tiny hovels of the workmen. The mud huts of the farmers were clustered in the areas close to the fields. From where she was, it looked like everything went on as normal…even with Amenmose's death…even with the Pharaoh's victory.

The foggy feelings of un-realness, enveloped her again. She decided to look for her mother. Coming down the stairs into the family's apartment from the roof, it took a few minutes for her eyes to adjust to the dimmer light of the room. Her mother was there, in conversation with an old priest. Gradually, she could see clear enough to take in his appearance. He was dressed formally, in a long, linen skirt and a close-fitting cap. She noted that he wore a gold armband…a gift showing the Pharaoh's favor…and an ornate faience neck collar. His skin was light but his features were soft and familiar, like those of the people of Waset. He had considerable rolls of skin around his waist and his face was full, almost round.

Ahmose noticed her daughter and turned away from the priest and said, "Ah Hatasu, I want you to meet Hereptah (he-re-pa-ta). This is the painter who will bring the blessings of the Ptah, the god of craftsman, to this northern palace. We want this new palace to be ready and pleasing when your father returns. Hereptah is the head of the group of artists who will bring comfort and beauty to our family chamber, here."

Hatasu said a polite hello to Hereptah, who bowed to her formally. She then looked around and realized the as-yet-unpainted-walls were covered with a grid of small squares, gray on the white-washed surface. Her interest and curiosity brought her out of her emotional fog. "Oh, can Hereptah paint pictures in my room, too?" She looked up into her mother's face, eagerly. "I need a protective image to look over me at night."

"Of course, my dear, what image would you like?"

Without a moments thought, she said, "I'd like a picture of the serpent Queen of Punt. I want her to be the protective deity in my sleeping room."

"The serpent goddess of royalty?" Hereptah's eyes opened wide and his breath gasped a bit.

Hatasu went on, in singled minded excitement, missing the painter's surprise, "Yes, she would need to be covered with golden scales with lapis eyebrows and a long, royal beard." As she spoke, she moved her hands in the outline of her body to indicate the 'golden scales' and ran her fingers over her eyebrows while talking of the lapis. She cupped her hand over her chin, pulling down on it to show the placement of the beard.

The priest bowed his old, capped head respectfully and said, "The serpent is a powerful protector of royalty but I would have thought it was premature…I mean, I would have thought that the young princess would have chosen the more common princess protectors, Bes or Isis."

Hatasu looked at him, blankly. She had no idea what might be 'premature' about it.

The Queen, however, understood the priest's meaning. "It is not the serpent goddess, Wadjet, protector of the Divine Pharaoh that she is asking for, Hereptah. It is Hathor, the goddess of Punt."

Hatasu caught the emphasis, this time.

The priest stammered a bit, "Yes…yes…of course." He bowed once to her mother and then once to her.

'*Strange!*' Hatasu thought, '*Why is he bowing to me?*'

Her mother turned back to Hereptah and continued with her instructions, "These rooms must be ready when the Pharaoh returns. I must find things that will cheer him in his sorrow." She turned her attention to study the bright colored pictures on the papyrus Hereptah held. Hereptah's voice was smooth and melodic as his finger identified objects on the scroll.

"As Your Majesty requested, the repeating papyrus pattern will be along the north wall and it will contain pictures of the royal family: The Pharaoh, the Queen…" He paused awkwardly. These were the places originally filled with the images of Amenmose and Wadjmose. He looked sideways at the Queen. Hatasu's own eyes watered as she saw her mother brush a tear from her eye. The Queen motioned for the artist-priest to go on. He did so, softly. "Hatshepsut, the Divine Daughter," he nodded in her direction, "Thutmose II, the son by Mutnofret and little Neferubrity."

Hatasu was surprised to hear the formal names referring to her brother and herself. She tried not to think about the empty spaces meant for her two older siblings. Their home was in the stars now, not in this family room.

The priest paused a moment, then turned around to the south wall, sweeping his hand along the bottom section. "Alternating buds and blossoms of the lotus will be here on the south side and above it will be a table of food: Bread, grapes, dates and a goose." This was sufficient distraction to recover the moment.

Ahmose ran her thumb and finger thoughtfully on each side of her chin. "And the pattern of plants should be alternated with the ankh for life. I believe the Pharaoh would find that comforting."

"Yes, Your Highness, as you wish," said Hereptah. "We will start tomorrow morning."

"Good," said the Queen, smiling. "I expect the Pharaoh will be home before the moon turns full again. There is much to do before then." The sound of Neferubrity's crying could be heard in a distant room. Ahmose moved toward the door leading to her chamber. She nodded toward the house matron. "Hetka will show you out."

Hatasu stepped forward. "When will Hereptah do my room?" she blurted out. "I want my room to please my father, too."

Hereptah smiled, amused at the princess's enthusiasm. "I shall bring sketches for the princess' approval when I come tomorrow. That is, if this is pleasing to Your Majesty." He bowed low.

Hatasu looked to her mother, eyebrows high in expectant questioning. Ahmose nodded her consent. "As long as the Pharaoh's rooms get finished, first." She continued with quick steps in the direction of her crying child.

The next day, after her lesson-time with Sitre on the roof, Hatasu hurried to the family room where the Queen and Hereptah were watching as the gang of artists drew on the walls, filling in the grid of squares with the pictures of the people and plants discussed the day before.

"Ah, Hatasu, come see the pictures," her mother said, looking up at the sound of her footsteps. Ahmose extended her arm to welcome her.

Hereptah produced the papyrus scroll he carried under his arm. "I've made two sketches for you to choose from," he said, as he unrolled the scroll before her. The first picture was of the golden-scaled, long-bearded, lapis eye-browed serpent Queen of the land of the gods. The other one was the gentle-eyed Hathor, depicted with a very beautiful human-like cow's face with the same gold and blue coloring of the serpent.

Hatasu looked closely at each picture. "Ooh!' she said, leaning toward the cow-faced Hathor. "I like the Queen of Punt as the beautiful cow-woman, like the ruined temple at Kasai but I also want her to look like in the story where she is the serpent. I want both pictures on my wall."

"So, you would like both pictures?" asked the priest.

"Yes, the serpent Queen of Punt on one side and the Hathor cow on the other."

Hereptah looked to Ahmose, who nodded. Hetka entered the room to announce that Ramose, the mayor, and the Ankh-Tawy council were waiting in the throne room for their meeting with the Queen. Ahmose said to Hatasu, "Run along now and let the artists do their work undisturbed."

"Oh, Omm (mother), please may I stay and watch? I'll sit very still."

Moving quickly in the direction of her meeting, Ahmose said over her shoulder, "As long as you don't slow down the workers with your questions."

Hatasu sat herself in a corner and watched the artist draw out the pictures within the grid of lines. Before very long, Thethi wandered into the room, too, and squatted by her. "What are they doing?" he asked.

She had not seen much of him the last several days because his breathing problems had occupied most of his time since the news of his brother's death. He was either dealing with the demands of the illness or acting so irritable about it, that she didn't want to be around him. "Shhh! Omm said not to disturb them because the room must be painted by the time Father returns."

In a softer whisper, he tried again, "They're drawing pictures of your family inside the squares, right?"

"Right."

He was silent for a few more minutes. Then, he said, "We could do our own drawing."

"Oh, no," she looked directly at him, shock in her eyes. "We can't draw on their pictures."

"No, no, I mean we could get ostraka and draw our pictures on them."

In no time, the two children had ostraka and stylus. Hatasu made an awkward attempt to draw a grid like the one on the wall. Thethi copied hers. The afternoon passed quickly. Hatasu filled her grid in with her version of the Queen of Punt, while Thethi drew figure of soldiers fighting in the Levant.

The fading light signaled the end of their work for the day, so Hereptah directed his gang of workers to pack away their materials. Hatasu ventured to ask him, "Why do you make the grid?"

Hereptah seemed glad to answer her question. "The grid helps us reproduce the picture exactly. You see, it is easier to copy the curve of a line within a small square than it is to reproduce a whole figure of a man or woman. The paintings are magic. *'As above, so below'*. Everything in our paintings direct us in alignment with the above and thus aid in the preservation of the order of the cosmos."

She nodded and looked intently from the artist to the emerging line drawings on the wall. The following day, with a fresh pile of ostrakas, she approached her drawings with a new intent of trying to copy the artist's work. Thethi drew, too, but he would start coughing and need to leave with Paheri for medicine.

At the end of that day, Hereptah came by and commented on her drawings. She again used the opportunity to asked him, "How come, in your pictures, people look the same, but different?"

"You mean, why the eye looks like you are staring straight at the figure but the nose looks like you are viewing the figure from the side?"

"Yes, that's what I mean. Also, the shoulders face us but the feet go sideways, like the nose. Why is it like that?"

The master craftsman smiled at her and said, "Yes, in drawing people…particularly sacred people…our usual ways of seeing, are not enough. We want to make sure we see the most important things."

She thought for a minute and asked, "You mean the ba, the ka and the akh?"

"Well, those are the most important parts but what I mean are the important parts you can see with your earthly eyes."

She looked blank for a minute. The artist continued, "I mean, first, the eye, which takes in the light of Ra and leads us to understanding. Then, there is the nose, which takes in life and breath. And then the heart, whose home is in the chest and by which we know the truth. The feet are important because they indicate will and movement."

He looked at Hatasu to see if she understood. Hatasu was listening attentively. "The paintings are magic, Your Majesty," the artist went on. "We want the eye to be whole so we draw it that way. We want the nose free to breathe life so we draw it full. And we want the chest to have full space for the heart, the place of knowing. Feet must move us forward. Everything must follow formulas that direct us in alignment with the above and thus aid in the preservation of the order of the cosmos."

He directed his attention back at her drawing ostrakas, and taking his red pen, he made some simple corrections that improved her drawings. "You have a very good eye for drawing, Princess." She felt very pleased.

"How about me?" asked Thethi.

Hereptah looked over at his stick-like figures within a wobbly-lined grid and said, "Perhaps some day…with training…yours will be as good as your sisters."

He scowled and then gave Hatasu a glaring look. Hereptah had barely turned his back to leave, when Thethi bent over to Hatasu's ostraka…and with his stylus, drew a thick black line through the middle of it. Very hurt, but mostly shocked, Hatasu stared at him for a minute. Then she grabbed his ostraka out of his hands and deliberately dropped it on the floor, seeing it shatter into pieces. She stomped out of the room as he let out a loud howl of complaint.

That evening, there were reprimands and apologies. By the next day, Hatasu and Thethi were cohorts again. They entered the artist's workspace to find the gang that did the line drawings had left and a gang of painters had taken their place. The picture came alive with the colors of blues and reds and greens they mixed right there in their small jars.

The figure of their father, the Pharaoh, was painted in with the deep red-brown. The painters had gone to lunch and Hatasu and Thethi were able to walk right up to the picture and look into the painted face of their father. It rather took her breath away. This picture of him made her longing for him all the more intense.

She was curious about this new paint and reached out a tentative hand to see if it were still wet. Another part of her, however, felt as though the magic was so real, she might actually touch her father through the picture...as though touching her father here, could help her know what is real and move her out of the fog that still came and went in her mind. She reached her hand out and at that moment, reversing their usual roles, Thethi exclaimed, "Oh, no! Don't touch it! You'll get in trouble."

There was something about that moment and his telling her what to do… She meant to pull her hand back but instead it made contact with the red-brown wall. As she touched it, she realized that the picture was, indeed, fresh and sticky with wet paint. She pulled her hand away quickly, but the smudged evidence of her behavior remained behind to incriminate her.

Her mother had said not to distract the artist or slow down their work! She tried to cover up the smudge by rubbing it but it just made it larger. She looked at her hand. The sticky brown proof of her guilt stared back at her. Her heart beat fast as she thought, fearfully, of the displeasure this would cause.

Thethi savored the reversal of their roles. "Now you've done it. Boy, are you going to get into trouble, this time."

She looked straight at her brother and wanted to smear the still wet paint on his face. But she didn't. There was a linen cloth folded on the floor. She took it and tried to wipe her finger clean. This faded the color but didn't get rid of it. She ran to her room where the morning wash-water was still on its table but that didn't help, either. Her scrubbing only drew Sitre's attention.

Hatasu tried to hide her hands behind her back but her nurse asked to see her hands. The princess didn't want dear Sitre to know of her misdeed. She stood there silently and hung her head, keeping her hands where they were. Sitre came forward and gently took the child's hands, bringing them out in front where they could be seen. The evidence was clear.

Hatasu blurted out her excuse, "I didn't mean to mess the sacred picture! It just looked so much like Father. I wanted to see whether it was wet or not."

Thethi was looking around the doorway, hiding his snickering behind his hand. Sitre sent Thethi off to Paheri, then turned to

Hatasu. In a calm voice, she said, "Oil will clean this up." She went to the basket in which were stored the fragrant unguents. She applied a little oil to Hatasu's hand and with minimal rubbing, the dye came off onto the linen cloth.

Just then, angry voices came from the family chamber. Returning from lunch, the artist must have just spotted the hand print smudge in their work. Hatasu's stomach felt queasy and she so wanted to run and hide. Sitre looked at her squarely, and said, "You are a princess. You must honor Maat by telling the truth. As the daughter of the Pharaoh, you must face up to what you have done."

Hatasu gathered herself up to her full height and holding onto Sitre's words…'she was the daughter of the Pharaoh, she must honor Maat'…she walked toward the family chamber and the angry artists. She stepped in the room and they fell silent. She spoke in a clear voice, louder than she intended, "It was I who smudged the painting. I am sorry."

Hereptah asked, "Why, Princess? Why would you disturb our magic?"

A horrible thought entered her mind. She had disturbed the magic alignment with the above. She swallowed hard, then said, "I did not mean to disturb your magic, it just looked so much like my father. I am willing to do whatever I must do in order to make this right by Maat."

Faces relaxed, drained of their intensity. A sympathetic smile moved across Hereptah's face. He nodded. "We will go to the Queen. She will know the wisdom of Maat."

Sitre, Hereptah and Hatasu went to Ahmose. Hereptah explained the problem. Ahmose was not nearly as angry as Hatasu had feared she would be. "Hatasu," the Queen said leaning casually on the left arm of her chair and looking pensively at her daughter, "it seems you are in need of some useful direction for you curiosities. I believe you are ready to re-enter the House of Life." Ahmose turned to Yuf and said, "Please bring a message to Ptahhotep that Princess Hatshepsut will begin her studies at the House of Life at the Temple of Ptah tomorrow morning. I, myself, will bring her to meet her new sebai."

Yuf, who was clearly fond of Hatasu, smiled and bowed his way out of the room. Hereptah also nodded his satisfaction with that judgment. Ahmose dismissed the others but required her daughter to stay.

Hatasu was greatly relieved. She had wanted to return to her studies anyway, so this was hardly a punishment. She had just one fear left. "Mother," she asked, "Father doesn't need to know about this, does he?"

"Hatasu, we are all becoming like Keperi, the beetle. What is important is making wrongs right. Maat and justice help us to regain balance when we lose it. Even the Pharaoh's daughter is not immune to the need for this. As a matter of fact, the welfare of the Two Lands is dependent on the balance and truth in the royal family. Owning up to something is an important lesson."

Resigned, the young culprit nodded. Ahmose reached over and drew her daughter close in for a hug, saying, "There are better ways to satisfy your questioning at the House of Life."

The next morning, Hatasu and her mother went to the Temple of

Ptah. Hatasu carried her writing palette over her shoulder and with a bounce to her stride and a smile on her face, she was ready for her first day at the House of Life in Ankh-Tawy. Her heart swelled as the eastern sun shone full on the brightly colored pictures of Ptah on the pylon gates. They moved beneath the flags fluttering high above and the gateway opened up into a huge courtyard. The princess felt the excitement of entering the bustling craft center of the realm.

In the center of the courtyard was a statue of Ptah. Hatasu recognized the unique representation of this god. It was a man standing erect, wrapped entirely in mummy linens, except for his head and hands. Over these wrappings and covering on his shoulders was large collar like Hatasu had seen her father wear. The close-fitting cap of a craftsperson covered his head and he had a wedge-shaped beard. His hands held a waas scepter, a djed column and an ankh.

All around him was a vast community of busy temple workers plying their crafts. Along the north wall were mud-brick apartments with canvas tent tops to shade the craftspeople. Along the south wall was an elaborate animal pen.

A tall, elegant-looking priest came toward them with extended strides. He moved across the courtyard quickly on long legs. His face was thin, his eyes were deep and black and his mouth was small and soft. He, too, wore a long skirt and a tight fitting cap. He met the small entourage. "Greetings, my Queen. I am Siptah (si–pa-TA), and I am here to welcome Hatshepsut…" He bowed to her, "our young princess, into the House of Life. It is my honored duty to greet you and bring you to Ptahhotep, the High Priest of Ptah, and the director of the House of Life. He will determine your next step on the path of knowledge."

The Queen accepted his bow and allowed Siptah to lead them into the temple courtyard. He stopped in front of the large statue of Ptah in the center of the square. Turning to Hatasu he said, "Your studies here begin and end with Ptah. He is a creator god." Siptah continued, "Every creature came into being through that which the Heart of Ptah thought and the Tongue of Ptah commanded. Therefore, every kind of work and every kind of handicraft is part of the creation of Ptah."

This was different from the creation story she saw during the Epagomenal festival, but she accepted it because her mother taught her there were many different stories about the same thing, allowing different aspects of a truth to come to light. Siptah then walked her in front of the statue and stood a little distance from it. "Noticed what Ptah stands on?"

Hatasu looked at the unusual pedestal under the statue. It had a slant on the front side. "When you study hieroglyphs," Siptah went on, "you will know this plinth-shaped pedestal Ptah is standing on is also the hieroglyph for Maat, as Truth and Justice."

Hatasu's ears seemed to open a little wider to hear reference to her recent increased concern for Maat's truth. Siptah continued, "It also represents the measuring rod used by craftsmen. It says Ptah is the measure of our worth and the source of ethical and moral order in the world. He is called the Lord of Truth. Here, in the House of Ptah, you will study the language of the gods and the crafts of drawing and painting."

Her excitement showed on her face. Siptah turned then and walked toward the canvas-covered stalls that were the workshops of the craftspeople. He said as he walked, "Our courtyard is the workplace of the artisans who honor Ptah by their craft."

Approaching the first work area, he said, "This is the place of the wood crafters, who make furniture, boxes and other useful objects." There was the sound of sawing as men bent over pieces of wood. He kept on walking and said, "And here are the artists who work in gold and make objects of beauty for the Pharaoh and the temple." There was the sound of hammering on soft metal as men worked on small, gleaming pieces of jewelry. "Here is the pottery shop."

Hatasu saw women working on small bowls in front of a kiln. They walked by more stalls. There were those making faience, those sculpting alabaster vases and those working with bronze to make weapons. In each of the stalls, there were several workers. One appeared to be a master craftsman, wearing the tight-fitting skullcap, and the others were younger workers studying under the master's guidance.

Hatasu thought about the secret village of the artisans that decorated the tombs in Waset. This art was so out in the open, no secret here. She knew she couldn't ask Siptah about the difference between the two groups of artisans because that, itself, would betray the 'secret village'.

They came to the end of the stalls of the craftspeople and Siptah took the group to a room in the north temple wall. They entered a doorway into the north wall and found themselves in a dark and cool chamber, out of the glaring heat of the sun. Bent over a table with an open papyrus scroll in front of him, and many rolls of papyrus in neat compartments in the wall behind him, was an old man with the skullcap of a craftsman and the leopard-skin robe of a priest.

As he looked up, Hatasu could see that his eyes were the color of the day-sky. She then noticed his hands; the fingers were lumpy and gnarled. They moved slowly and carefully across the papyrus in front of him. She could see the beautiful pictures, in contrast to the deformed hands. He put his pen down carefully and rose slowly and stiffly to greet the Queen and princess. As he stood, he was bent at the waist into a perpetual bow. He placed his staff in front of him and leaned on it heavily as he started to shuffle his feet forward, one and then the other. "Greetings, Queen Ahmose, mother of our people," his voice quivered with age.

Hatasu could see why this High Priest didn't come, himself, to greet them. He moved his body slowly in Hatasu's direction. He said, "Greetings, Hatshepsut. You have come to begin your study in the House of Life of the Temple of Ptah."

Hatasu bowed respectfully and nodded. "Yes, Sebai, I wish to know the language of the gods and to study the mysteries."

"Then, you shall begin right away! I understand you have already been through the preliminaries at the Temple of Abedju. Today, you must write something for me so that I might know where to place you in this school." Ptahhotep returned to his chair and sat, bent over. Siptah came forward with an ostraka and Hatasu sat in a scribe's position on the floor. With her pallet arranged before her, she wrote out the first lines of the 'Story of the Shipwrecked Sailor'.

When finished, she brought the ostraka to Ptahhotep and he looked at it closely for several minutes. "You have learned the elementals of script writing….Yes, yes…you are ready to start the study of the hieroglyphs." His light blue eyes looking directly into her eyes. He said, "It is time for you to purify yourself in the temple pool. Then, Siptah will bring you to your class with Sihathor."

Siptah did as Ptahhotep instructed. Leaving the darkness of the High Priest's study, they walked under the bright blue canopies… first to the temple pool for the purification and then to what would be her classrooms in the House of Life. They approached a small gathering of youths, boys and girls and a woman teacher.

As they got closer, Hatasu realized the teacher was the same person she met the night she visited Tao's room. Indeed, it was the same almond eyed woman with the beautiful features. As the royal group approached, she bowed deeply. "Greetings, beloved Queen, esteemed teacher, and royal Princess."

Siptah nodded to her and turned to Hatasu. "This is Sihathor, the sebai of the language of the gods."

Smiling at Hatasu, she said, "We have met. I am looking forward to teaching you. Now, come and meet the other students."

Hatasu was delighted, for she already liked this priestess. She looked around at the others. Each had on their lap an ostraka on which they were writing. There was a board with a phrase written out for the students to copy, like she had seen at the Abedju temple school. She took in the group of boys and was surprised to see her friends and cousins, Hapuseneb and Meryt! Sihathor introduced her to the others.

Ahmose left her daughter, saying, "You now start your studies, here. Learn well. Sitre will meet you at the end of the day and walk you back to the palace."

Hatasu smiled goodbye and settled down on a mat with her pallet and an ostraka. She felt a sense of satisfaction for she was now a student who could attend on her own, without her nursemaid. The afternoon passed quickly. When the class time was over, the children were told to put away what they were working on and to tidy up. Hatasu followed the instruction and then walked with the others toward the gateway to go home.

Sitre was waiting for her as promised and Hatasu started giving her nurse an enlivened description of her class, when Sihathor approached them. The priestess asked, "Did Siptah show you the Ka of Ptah?"

"I saw the statue of Ptah."

Sihathor and Sitre exchanged a knowing look. Smiling, the priestess said, "Your introduction to the Temple is not complete without seeing the Ka of Ptah. Come, I will show you."

The three of them walked to the south wall of the temple. There, they came upon an ornately decorated animal pen with a large, black bull inside. The pen was immaculately clean and adorned in a most pleasing design of repeating images of a glorious bull.

"Why is this bull in so elegant a pen?" asked Hatasu.

"Ah, this is the Ka of Ptah," replied Sihathor. "He is the sacred bull who contains the ka, the great fertilizing ardor, of Ptah, the creator."

Hatasu's brow furrowed in question and her eyes squinted as though to see clearer. "So, the god Ptah has a ka as people do, only his ka is an animal, a bull?"

"Yes," Sihathor said, smiling at her. "A person's ka accompanies that person in life. It is the ardor or yearning for its highest spiritual self, its akh. In the animal kingdom, it is the bull that is most known for its ardent fertilizing powers. It is this force of passion…the ardent desire…that create and makes things happen. That is why the Ka of Ptah is incarnated in a bull. We honor this bull as we honor Ptah."

"What makes this bull so special?"

"Ptah lets us know his chosen calf by certain signs and markings. First of all, a celestial ray must conceive him, either a moonbeam or a clap of thunder. He must be black with a double pyramid…a white diamond…on his forehead. Upon his back, must ride the markings of the great vulture goddess, Nekhbet. Under his tongue must be a node in the shape of a scarab; Keperi is our symbol of becoming or self-creation. Also, there must be two tufts on the bull's tail, one white and one black. None but this one sacred calf will do and sometimes it takes months to find him."

"It is amazing that they *ever* find such a calf!"

"It is truly the work of the great Ptah."

Hatasu watched as the bull ambled around his pen with an occasional snorting sound from his nose and an intermittent pawing motion on the ground with his hoof. She could see the spread wings of the great vulture goddess extending down each of his sides, the body white across the bull's back. He pranced and kicked up his heels. The group of watchers were amused by his antics and made comments on his good health and vitality. After a while, he slowed down.

A hush fell on the crowd. Sihathor explained, in whispered tones, "The priests interpreted his behavior as an oracle prediction. The oracle priests were awaiting omens."

The Ka of Ptah sauntered around the outer fence, tossing his large head from one side to the other, snorting restlessly. As he rapidly approached where Hatasu was standing, his size and briskly aggressive movement alarmed her. She backed away from the wall as he approached. The bull stopped. He turned out toward where she stood. He kicked up his hind hooves, snorting. Then, he lowered his huge head and rubbed it against his right forepaw. It looked incredibly similar to a formal bow.

The attending priests, gasped. They all turned toward the red-headed princess. No one looked more surprised and startled than Hatasu, herself. This Ka of Ptah seemed to hold himself suspended indefinitely, staring into Hatasu's eyes. She stared transfixed back at him. Finally, she bowed her head to him, as though acknowledging a foreign dignitary. As soon as she did that, he raised himself from his position, pranced almost daintily along the wall, and preceded back into his honorary enclosure.

The scribes wrote rapidly on their papyrus scrolls. The rest of the people, one by one and in small groups, bowed to the red-haired princess. She didn't know what to say or do. So, like she did with the bull, she simply bowed back. This seemed to create even more of a stir.

Sihathor seemed pleased, but Sitre put a protective arm around the princess and led her quickly away from the crowd. Things were a bit of a blur on the hurried walk back to the palace. Sitre took long strides ahead of Hatasu, holding her hand tightly, pulling her along.

The nurse was too intent and preoccupied to turn around as Hatasu questioned, "What just happened? Why are we in such a rush?"

Sitre answered as she continued full-speed ahead, "Your mother must know, right away. The priest will be sure to waste no time to tell her and I want to tell her first."

Hatasu thought the news must be very bad. She must have done something really awful, this time.

Chapter 28 ~ The Oracle

Sitre led Hatasu directly to Ahmose in the throne room. She rushed in unannounced, interrupting a meeting the Queen was having with the Ministers of Agriculture and Ineni, who had recently returned from Itjtawy. The Queen looked up from the scrolls laid out before her.

"I apologize for the interruption, Your Majesty," said Sitre, bowing to Ahmose as she rushed past Hetka. "I think you'll want to know this, right away." Then, without even waiting for the ministers to be dismissed, she blurted out, "The Ka of Ptah has recognized Hatshepsut!"

This was unusual behavior for Sitre and it was hard for Hatasu to tell if her nurse was excited or upset. Hatasu decided, based on the color of the mole on her face, she must be very angry and she braced herself for big trouble. She was also cringing at the use of her official name and wondered why Sitre would all of a sudden refer to her in this overly formal way. Sitre had said the bull 'recognized' her. *What did he recognize? That she had entered the House of Life? That she had disrespected and smudged the picture? Oh…what must she do for Maat to be restored, this time?*

The Queen looked from Sitre to Hatasu. She sat bolt upright, her eyes widening and her attention immediately focused on her daughter and her nurse. The ministers, too, opened their eyes wider as they stared at the child. Each of the men gathered up their scrolls and backed out of the room without waiting for a formal dismissal. They exited, bowing to the Queen and, to Hatasu's amazement, her, as well. All except Ineni…his one eyebrow lifted high on his forehead; he maintained his position standing behind the Queen.

"Thank you, Sitre," Ahmose said, once the ministers were gone. "Tell me what happened."

Sitre was still a bit breathless from the rapid walk. "Sihathor suggested Hatasu would like to see the Ka of Ptah. The bull was lively, prancing along the outer wall. When he came to where Hatasu stood, he not only stopped, but he formally bowed to her, foreleg forward and head down. He didn't arise from this bow but held it. Then…" She shook her head and her eyes grew wider. "Hatasu bowed back!"

That must be what it is, Hatasu thought. It was bold and out of place for me to have bowed to this sacred bull.

"She bowed back?!" repeated the Queen. She looked to her daughter, and, for the first time, saw the anxiety on her face.

Hatasu blurted out, "I didn't mean to be disrespectful! I thought the bull was playing with me and I was just playing back. I'll be more respectful, next time."

Her mother's mouth turned up into a broad smile. "Daughter, you are not in trouble for this. Whatever the details of the interpretation, the Ka of Ptah has certainly given you an honor. The priests of the temple will help us understand the meaning of this omen but it is assuredly not a problem of disrespect."

She had no sooner said that, then there was a commotion in the entrance hall. Hetka came to the door and bowed. "A delegation of priests from the Temple of Ptah is asking for an audience with Your Majesty." Ahmose nodded to Hetka who ushered them in.

The first was Ptahhotep, with his sky-blue eyes and gnarled fingers. He disembarked from his ornate carrying chair and walked into the room bent over his walking stick. The next was Siptah, striding in on his long legs, elegant in his movements. He positioned himself to the right of the High Priest. The third was Sihathor, the lovely, smiling priestess-sebai who had led Hatasu to the bull's pen. She seemed to float effortlessly to her place to the left of Ptahhotep. In unison, they bowed before the Queen and then Hatasu.

As High Priest of the temple, Ptahhotep began. Leaning heavily on his stick, he raised his head and shoulders to look directly at the Queen. "Your Majesty, the Ka of Ptah has honored the princess with an oracle."

"Her tutor, Sitre, has just informed me."

With obvious effort, he used the stick to push himself up still taller and said, "The bull bowed to her in front of a small gathering. This is a very confusing oracle, due to the present circumstances." After a short pause to catch his rasping breath, Ptahhotep continued, "Siptah," he nodded in the direction of the tall priest, "a priest trained in the interpretation of oracles, informs me that he believes the Ka of Ptah's honor to Hatshepsut was recognition of her being a powerful future queen."

Graceful Siptah actually looked awkward. He shifted self-consciously from one foot to the other and said, "This oracle happened in front of a small gathering of temple staff. The oracle of the future Pharaoh is expected to take place in the Temple of Amun in Waset, in front of large gatherings and during a festival. I believe this can not be an official oracle to designate a Pharaoh. It must be a confirmation of what we all expect. Hatshepsut will be a great Queen."

Ptahhotep then turned and nodded to his left. "Sihathor, our junior priestess, also trained in interpretation of the oracles, reads this oracle sign differently."

Sihathor stepped forward and faced the Queen. "With all due respect to our head of the House of Life and distinguished High Priest, I was the only one of the three of us present at the time of the incident. I saw the bull's behavior. I read this oracle as a confirmation that Hatshepsut is to be the Pharaoh, the successor to Thutmose." Sihathor looked back at the other two priests, firm in her position, yet respectful of them.

Ptahhotep shook his old head in jerking movements. "The Ka of Ptah has given us an oracle but one that is very confusing to interpret. Though I respect what Sihathor says, I do not believe this oracle was clear enough to break with precedence and support a female as Pharaoh. I, as High Priest of Ptah, believe this oracle recognized Hatshepsut as a future Queen."

Ineni spoke up from his position behind the Queen. "But why else would the oracle recognize Hatshepsut now, if it weren't as Pharaoh? It is not the Queenship we are concerned with. It is the line of Pharaoh. Nine moons ago, we thought the Double Crown was secure with three possible royal heirs. Now, two of the Pharaoh's sons have passed to the ancestors, while the nephew is maimed. It leaves us Thutmose II and his survival into adulthood is uncertain. Why didn't the oracle choose him or at least someone suitable for Hatshepsut to marry?"

Ptahhotep's head bobbed, whether in anxiety or agreement, was unclear. "Perhaps another form of divination to clarify the situation would be helpful, then?"

The Queen looked at the three oracles and after a thoughtful moment of silence, she replied, "Pharaoh Thutmose will be home soon. We will await his judgment. He will make his announcement about his intended successor and thus end the controversy."

Ptahhotep nodded, apparently satisfied and said, "You are wise, my Queen. It is good to make no public announcement of this oracle. Our Pharaoh will return soon and he will make the final announcement of the oracle and determine if it is to be interpreted as Hatshepsut is to be Queen or Pharaoh. I fear confusion over these interpretations will increase the uncertainty in the people and encourage, rather that diminish, speculation."

The Queen nodded agreement and exchanged formal bows with the priests. Ptahhotep remounted his carrying-chair and the two lesser priests followed his exit. The Queen turned her attention to her daughter.

Hatasu's head swam with the conflicting interpretations. The old questions arose again, against her will. *Would these excited people make her be Pharaoh?* She thought about the dream of Amun and the prophecy of ruling in peace. *She'd stand firm. She would be Queen like her mother. What did she know of being a Pharaoh!*

She was used to the idea that she would be Queen to a male Pharaoh, ruling at his side. She had understood her marriage was very important for the wellbeing of the Two Lands, whether the marriage was to Wadjmose, Amenmose, Thethi or perhaps even Tao.

Ahmose called, "Come here, daughter." Hatasu stood before her mother, who reached out and placed her hands on each of the princess's shoulders. She seemed more resigned than the last time this subject came up.

The princess looked into her mother's eyes and said, "Sihathor thinks the oracle-bull is saying that I am to be *Pharaoh*, not *Queen* to a Pharaoh?"

"Yes, that is so."

"You think I am to be Queen?"

"Yes, that is so, too."

"I remember Satamun saying she thinks I am to be the next Great God's Wife."

"Yes, she believes that to be so."

"Does it matter at all what I want?"

Ahmose heaved a deep sigh. "You are of the royal family." Her voice was gentle, "We each must respond to the will of the gods in order to keep the world in balance, whether it happens that you become Great God's Wife, Queen or Pharaoh. It is the responsibility of our royal blood to follow the path that is given to us. If we don't, the world will return to chaos."

Hatasu crossed her arms and protruded her lower lip. She said firmly, "I want to be Queen! Thethi can be Pharaoh. Pharaohs are men. I bowed because I was playing with the bull, not because I want to be Pharaoh! I want to be Queen, like you."

Ahmose smiled at this last comment but she went on with more warmth in her voice, "Oh, dear one, either way you are called to a great task for your people. I agree, to be Pharaoh would be a hard road for a woman."

Hatasu stomped her foot and burst out, "I don't want to be Pharaoh! Stupid old bull!" She crossed her arms tightly in front of her and pulled both her eyebrows down toward the bridge of her nose.

Ahmose sat back on her throne-chair, moving her head back and forth slightly. Worry lines appeared on her brow. "If this is your destiny, child, it will unfold in a way that you can't refuse it." Ahmose paused and let out another sigh, then said a bit more briskly, dismissing the subject, "Time will tell the will of the gods. In the meantime, life goes on and you still must study each day at the House of Life and apply yourself to your lessons."

Hatasu stomped out of the throne room. She plopped herself on the floor on the other side of the door. Sitting still, she listened, unobserved, to the conversation between her mother and uncle in the next room. She could hear her mother nervously pacing up and down the room saying, "I am painfully aware of the void left by Amenmose's death and the precarious and uncertain situation of Thethi's continued ill health. I know this can lead to the dangers of speculation." Hatasu heard her talk in a rapid, pressured way.

When she slowed down, Ineni's voice went on, "I think you are wise to postpone any announcement until the Pharaoh's return. While I was in Itjtawy, I did hear people speak of their concern about the transmission of office. There are those in that city who would not readily acknowledge a female as Pharaoh."

The Queen responded, "Yes, Ineni, I would much rather Hatasu be Queen. My true reason for wanting to postpone an announcement is the hope it isn't true, for her sake." She paused, then went on. "However, Ptahhotep's wish to postpone it makes me wonder. Is there someone else the Ptah priests have in mind to be the next Pharaoh? While it is true an announcement of the oracle's indefinite interpretation could open more speculation about the next Hawk-in-the-Nest, the Oracle's nod to Hatasu would also undermine any other candidate for consideration."

"If that is so, Ahmose, I do not know about it."

After the oracle, things changed for Hatasu, particularly with Sitre and Thethi. Her nurse seemed to think that it was her personal responsibility to assure appropriate training in dignified behavior, for she was convinced that Hatasu would indeed be the next Pharaoh. Thethi, on the other hand, withdrew from her. He made teasing comments like, "You, the Pharaoh …*huh*! You're a girl. You'd look pretty funny with the beard of the gods as the Pharaoh."

She tried several times to say she didn't want to be Pharaoh but Thethi just turned his small back and walked away. Hatasu felt alone and miserable. This distance from Thethi was another loss. As her mother had instructed, she continued going daily to the House of Life and she concentrated on practicing her writing with the other students. It seemed Ptahhotep had been successful in keeping the oracle quiet among the students, for to Hatasu's great relief, no one said anything to her about it.

At home, the painting in the family room was finally completed and Hereptah and his group of painters started on her room. At the end of each day, Hatasu stayed far away from the bull's pen at the temple and instead hurried home with Sitre to see what had been done in her room. There, she was very careful to not touch anything on the walls. At last, there came the night she slept in her newly painted room.

When her mother came to her room to sing to her, they admired the painting together. "Yes, you will be well protected here, now," Ahmose smiled.

She would indeed sleep better under the smiling lapis eyes of the Goddess. Snuggling into her cot, Hatasu looked up at her mother and said, "I had a dream visit with Father last night and he said he was on his way home. Do you know when he will be here and can see the beautiful pictures in my new room?"

The Queen looked off in the distance. "I had hoped the Pharaoh would be home for the first harvest festival, the celebration of the first fruit of the goddess, but he sends me word he has been delayed in Lower Retennu." Looking at Hatasu again, she said, "But he promised he'd be here for the last festival, the one dedicated to the god, Min. By the time the moon is full in Payne, the Pharaoh and the army will be safely back in our own Two Lands. By then, the crops will have been gathered, measured and recorded. The Pharaoh will be here to receive the reports and to bless the final harvest…and of course, to see your new room," Ahmose smiled.

Looking at her mother sleepily, Hatasu said, "It seems he has been gone forever."

"Yes, but it won't be so long, now. Time will pass quickly as we have much to keep us busy, before he gets here. First, we must officiate at the opening of the harvest season. I think you will like watching the activities of the peasant-fellahin. After the harvest festivities in their own nomes, the nobles and their families will be arriving from up and down the Nile to be here in Ankh-Tawy for the Pharaoh's return with their sons in the army."

"When is the harvest festival?"

"When the moon is dark, showing her face only as shadow, that is when the first of the grains will be ripe and ready. That day, peasants make it a celebration as they cut the first crops from the fields and thresh them, loosening the grain from the shaft. Then they do the winnowing, separating out the grain heads to be stored for food, all with a spirit of fun and with lots of music. When the moon is full again, there will be the final harvesting festival, this time more formally to the god, Min. By then we know the full extent of this year's crop. They'll be all measured and recorded for taxation and the storage."

On the day of the first harvest, Hatasu rode in the litter with her mother. Usually, Thethi would have been with them and Hatasu was alarmed at his absence. "Is Thethi all right?" she asked.

"He had another attack last night. Sihathor says he is not well enough to be out of bed today." Worry lines creased her brow and were mirrored in her daughter's. This meant his illness was getting worse, rather than better.

They rode through the main avenue of Ankh-Tawy and out toward the farming town to the west. This festival took place not in the mighty temple of the god like in Waset, but out in the fields themselves, like the planting festival at Abedju. Sitre, with her watchful eye, walked alongside the litter. Hatasu smiled and waved to the city people as her mother had instructed her to do. She watched her mother carefully and behaved as *queenly* as she could.

As the processional left the city, her attention turned to the squares of fields within the irrigation ditches. In spite of the evil magic retarding the grain's growth along the Nile, this region's harvest recovered in time for it to look abundant. Most of the square fields were still the malachite green of ripening grains, but there were also the sections of golden stalks ready for the harvester's scythe. Hatasu noted the particular smell of the field barley. She enjoyed the sound the kernels made as they swayed in the gentle breeze, noting the difference between the song of the still-green grains and the dryer rattle of the ripe, gold ones.

As the litter neared the farming village, the dwellings appeared dusty brown against the desert sands. A growing numbers of peasants crowded along the road, looking for a glimpse of the Queen.

"There is the red-haired princess!" she heard. Some women threw blue cornflowers to honor her. "Look! It is the princess the oracle has predicted will be heir to Thutmose!"

Hatasu was shocked that these people knew about the oracle. Young boys ran alongside the litter, waving and singing, "Hail to Queen Ahmose and Princess Hatshepsut."

Surprised again, she continued to smile and waved. She had promised her mother she would. Sitre seemed to beam with pride in her certain belief that 'her' Hatasu would one day be the grand Pharaoh.

The faces were different from those of the city folks. There were many children, playing running games, all brown-skinned from the sun and free of clothes. Several young women were round-bellied with pregnancy but there were few young men…only those who had been too young to join the army at the time it left for Retennu. Those still on the farm were bronzed and muscular from their work in the fields. There were also the old, bent and infirmed. Some had extended stomachs; some walked with the help of a crutch or cane; some had toothless smiles or reddened eyes. All wore coarse, homespun linen and simple amulets as necklaces.

All those who were able, danced and sang. These people laughed and drank their beer. Music, dance and incense permeated the air. The royal procession came through the fields of grain where the actual activity of the harvest was taking place. Hatasu could see the people harvesting the emmer wheat. The work song rose in the air. She watched the men as they moved along rows of the grain, rhythmically taking a bunch of grain heads in one hand and with the sickle in the other, they cut the stalks below the heads. They then placed the heads in baskets to be carried to the threshing floor.

A young woman ran alongside the litter and offered Hatasu a grain-weavings with which to make music like the dancing children all around her were using. Stalks of grain were woven into patterns and used like rattles; shaken, they elicited the same sound as the wind through the fields. These same rattles were later hung on their walls as blessings of abundance and fertility. Hatasu shook the one offered her and made smiling eye contact with the young peasant woman who gave it to her.

They came at last to the cluster of the simple, mud-brick, one-room houses of the fellahin-peasants arranged around a large public square. In the middle was a sheltered stone stela. This was the local shrine of the goddess of the harvest. In front of it was a stone table for her offerings. The villagers and farmers, men, women and children were in a festive mood, buzzing like a hive of happy bees. They made way, bowing as the Queen's litter moved to her place of honor in the center of the harvest activities.

Hatasu, in the litter next to her mother, could make out several different centers of activity. Here she saw the threshing floor and winnowing areas and the storage silos. The headman of the fellahin town and his wife ceremoniously presented the stalks of emmer wheat, first to the Queen for her nod of approval, and then they placed them on the offering table. They did the same with stalks of barley. All the people sang the praises of the goddess of the harvest.

Hatasu imagined herself as an adult doing the same queenly tasks. From there, the Queen smiled her blessings on the village's offerings to the goddess. This was a much more raucous festival than official royal ceremonies Hatasu had seen before. The dances and songs were much influenced by the goddess's gift of beer. The best of the local brew was brought out and it was apparent that many of the celebrators were feeling its effect.

Hatasu, loving so to dance, started to get down from the litter to join them but Sitre's hand reached across the seat and took hold of her arm. "No," she said softly. "The princess only watches this festival."

Confused, Hatasu looked to her mother but she was busy talking with the village headman. She sat back down with a scowl and a pout, frustrated with the limitations placed on her freedom due to her recent 'recognition'. It seemed this oracle brought restrictions as well as confusion. Looking around her, Hatasu stood again and wanted so to get out of the litter and walk among the people. "Come, Sitre, let's go dance with them! Pleasssse?"

"Oh, no; only the peasants dance at this festival. You must maintain your dignity before your future subjects."

Hatasu's heart sank. She looked at Sitre with disbelief. She'd hoped that she would be free to have some fun; she did not want to end up stiff, with a painted on smile and an arm sore from waving. Sitre took hold of her hand as though she could read her mind and knew what she longed to do. They walked together through the crowds. There were young girls passing out honey-sweetened breads made from the newly-threshed grains and others were distributing beer.

Hatasu reached for the small cake-breads that were sticky with honey. She had a sip of the beer and then noticed that Sitre was honoring the goddess with her own cup of brew. That and the bread, now occupied both her hands.

Just about then, a woman, newly arrived from Waset for the celebration, approached Sitre and expressed great delight in seeing her. Hatasu saw her opportunity. She looked to the royal litter and saw her mother in conversation with a magistrate. She looked about the crowd and each palace attendant was engaged, except for Yuf. Her mother's scribe was watching her. She paused. Then he winked and smiled at her. It was as though he knew how she longed to mingle with the others. She trusted he would not tell on her. She looked back up at Sitre who was still in lively conversation with her friend. This was her chance. She moved quickly away from her tutor-guard, and without a backward glance at Yuf, she slipped through the crowd of people, their bodies creating a veil that hid her from her caretaker's sight.

Chapter 29 - Mutsi and Ferit

Hatasu found herself in an adjacent square. She looked around to assure herself there were no spying eyes to report her to Sitre. Slinking along, she tried to look as inconspicuous as she could. She turned her attention to the sun-browned field, workers carrying baskets of the newly harvested barley on their shoulders. They dumped their contents onto a threshing floor, a circular enclosure of beaten earth.

A bright-eyed boy, wielding a two-thonged whip, walked behind a team of oxen, driving them over the barley, their hooves crushing and separating the grain from the stalk. Other workers forked more barley under the oxen's feet, while still others gathered up the crushed grain and shoveled them into piles for the winnowers. They sang a lively song and each person did their tasks for the threshing with an energetic step.

"*Thresh for yourselves, oxen, chaff for you to eat, barley for your masters to eat. Don't let your hearts grow weary.*"

The rather raucous vitality of the activity excited Hatasu. There was nothing in palace life with quite the raw physical energy of this fellahin-peasant harvest celebration. She wanted to be part of it…to be like them…singing…working.

"*Thresh for yourself, oxen,*" she joined in with a full voice.

Almost immediately, a young man next to her turned and stared. "Look," he cried out, "it is the red-haired princess! Look, she sings with us!"

To her great alarm, everyone in her vicinity turned and looked at her. "Oh, no, please, shhh," she said, looking around the square to make sure no palace people saw her. She moved away quickly, ducking back into the crowd. If such a commotion drew Sitre's attention, her freedom would be over. She found herself in an area just south of the threshing floor. There were only the local farmers, mostly women. She knew she must disguise her red hair.

This was the winnowing area, where the baskets of oxen-crushed grain were brought. People, mostly young girls her age with large scoops in each hand, tossed the grain in the air and allowed the north breeze to carry away the chaff, re-catching the barley heads.

Hatasu noticed they all wore headscarves to protect their hair from the falling chaff. *That was what she needed...a scarf!* Looking around, she spied a discarded head-covering lying on the ground at the edge of the winnowing area. Hatasu picked it up, shook it off, and put it on her head, careful to cover both the redness of her hair and the youth-lock of royalty. Feeling a bit safer in her disguise, she looked more closely at people around her.

Here, there was such a variety of people. In Waset, there were either brown-skinned people or the very black people of Nubia. But here, there were many different shades of skin, textures of hair and shapes of eyes. Everyone around her joined in the harvest celebration, tossing the grains in the air, watching the chaff blow off in the wind, and singing the traditional winnowing songs.

Now, with the scarf of a winnower on her head, she picked up two scoops and stepped into the midst of the activity with the others. She tossed the grain in the air. Some of the kernels of grain landed back in her scoop; more landed on the ground around her.

She watched others to see how they did it, then she tried again, catching more this time and emptying what she caught into a large container.

She attempted to sing again, her voice more tentative this time. *"This barley will make our beer, the wind will free it from the chaff."* No one seemed to notice her as different from anyone else this time. So there, amidst the haze of floating grain chaff and the laughing work songs of the women and girls, Hatasu was able to join in the festivities. She began to relax and allowed herself to become more daring at the task. She threw the grain a bit higher and realized she had to compensate for the breeze by backing up a few steps to catch it again in her scoop.

Bam! Hatasu collided with not one but two young winnowers, girls about her age. Each turned in surprise, grain scoops still in hand. All three broke into giggles. Hatasu quickly sized up each of them. One wore a plain, unbleached, homespun scarf over short-cropped hair. Around her neck was a cord with a small linen bag, dirty with wear, on her browned skin. The other child wore a bleached linen scarf over a black wig and a necklace of cowry shells. Her skin was a lighter, more yellow shade. Hatasu recognized the first girl as a sun-colored peasant child while the other was a more house-bound child of some noble people of the city.

She was nervous again that they would recognize her. Was her red braid sufficiently hidden? She remembered her turquoise amulet of Bes and wondered if it would give her away or protect her. Neither girl reacted as if there was any thing out of the ordinary.

They each went back to gaily throwing the grain in the air. Hatasu threw up another scoopful of grain, and measuring the height a bit better this time, caught it in her scoop. She followed the farmer-girl as she ran to empty the scoops into the grain basket for the silo.

A few more tosses and the girl with the homespun scarf pointed to a jug of water cooling in the shade of a solitary sycamore tree. The others followed her lead. There, still laughing from their exertion, they dropped to the ground and exchanged names.

"My name is Mutsi," said the girl with the shell necklace. Her voice was soft and clear. "What are your names?"

"I'm Ferit," the peasant girl said, with a throaty voice.

Hatasu felt two sets of eyes on her. *Should she tell them her real name? There were others with the nickname of Hatasu.* She decided to risk it. "I'm Hatasu," she said, hoping the common people all thought of the princess by her formal name, Hatshepsut.

Mutsi and Ferit each just nodded…no other reaction. Hatasu let out an unperceivable sigh of relief. Ferit took a drink from the jug and passed it to Hatasu. All three chuckled as the water escaped the corners of her mouth as she laughed. Serit drank next. They rested with their backs against the tree trunk and looked out on the others winnowing, and beyond them to another group of youngsters in the barley field nearest them.

This group, moving among the stubble of the recently harvested stalks of grain, caught their attention. Those children jumped around, laughing and squealing as though something delighted them. "What are they doing?" Hatasu asked.

Ferit, living the life of a fellah in these fields, knew exactly what they were doing. "They're catching snakes," she said.

The three girls got up and walked closer to the fields. Hatasu could see a girl holding a small, green snake with a golden-yellow belly and a necklace below its head in the same bright color. "I caught a sedbu!" a peasant girl was saying. Hatasu watched as she held a snake in her hand and it wrapped its thin body around her arm. She raised her hand up over her head and she danced in a circle, singing, "See the lovely child of the harvest goddess."

The other children clustered around her, and when she brought her hand down, others wanted to pet it. "*Thank you, little sedbu, Thank you for helping our fields, thank you for eating bugs, thank you for protecting our harvest,*" she sang to the little snake and the other children joined in.

Hatasu thought of how in Zawty, cats protected the harvest from rodents, while here, the snakes protected it from bugs.

A short distance away, another child found another field snake and did the same as the first child. The two girls who found the snakes called to each other across the short distance. "Let's bring them to the goddess!" They began dancing toward the shrine of the harvest goddess, Renenutet, continuing their song. Other children searched among the newly-cut barley to find their own snakes to offer the goddess.

By the offering table, in front of the shrine, was a basket ready for these snakes. The adults watched and smiled as the girls danced in the square with the creatures. The songs expanded, from songs of simple thanksgiving, to praise for the snake's ability to shed its skin and bring forth new life, dying like the seed put in the earth, to emerge again in its plant form.

Ferit parted the grain stalks. She was so familiar with these fields and their creatures that she found and caught one for herself quickly. Hatasu wanted to find her own. She looked down the rows of cut grain. Ferit offered to help her and said, "Look around clusters of stalks."

A young girl nearby, added her advice, "Catch only the green ones with the gold necklace. Others have a bite that can kill."

Hatasu pulled back and stared at her. A taller girl laughed, "Don't worry. The dangerous snakes are in the desert and mountains. These fields are full of these little friends of the goddess."

Ferit took Hatasu's arm and pointed toward a cluster of barley stumps. "Look, there's one now."

Hatasu scrambled after it as it wound its body through the stubby stalks. Kneeling on all fours, she was able to catch it. It was a small one. Ferit laughed and called out, "It's a baby! You caught a beautiful little sedbu." Hatasu felt unsure holding it. It squirmed in her hand in a most unusual way.

Mutsi ooh-ed and ahh-ed at Hatasu's courage but couldn't quite bring herself to go after one. Ferit caught a snake for Mutsi, then showed both her new friends how to hold the creatures properly. "Here," she explained, "take its body in your hand like this and let it wrap itself around your arm. It won't hurt you. It will only bite you if you squeeze it and even then there is no pain or poison in it. Hold it gently, like that, and see how it responds and dances with you."

Hatasu treated her snake very tenderly as she held it up just like the others were doing, singing the praises of the goddess's little friend. Mutsi was obviously less comfortable but the dance, itself, was enthralling, and before long all three children joined in with their dance-snakes. Ferit demonstrated, holding the snake high. The other two girls, tentatively at first, began to try it. Hatasu loved it. For her, the snake was just another animal friend, like her cat and her monkey.

They danced with the others toward the stela of Renenutet, stepping around in circles, moving their arms in slow undulations in imitation of the snakes themselves. When they arrived at the Renenutet stela, they gently put their snakes in the basket at the foot of the offering table. Hatasu stood before the offering table and looked up at the stone stela with the carving of Renenutet, the goddess of the harvest and the abundance of the fields. Renenutet sat upon her throne, with the body of a woman and the head of a cobra. Around her flared throat, one could see the traditional three-part hairstyle of the goddess, and upon her head was the two-feathered crown of divinity. Sitting on her lap, nursing from her breast, was the god of the grain, Neper.

The girls went back to the shade of the sycamore. Ferit fingered the amulet bag at her throat as she looked out on the children who continued to dance with the snakes. She commented, "My great-grandmother says we are very lucky to be able to have this festival. She says when Apophis, the Hyksos, ruled this land, he wouldn't allow it."

"My great-grandmother tells stories, too," said Mutsi. "She says

Apophis brought chaos and suffering like the Apophis serpent, the enemy of Ra. The people of the Levant have only one goddess, you know; her name was Anat. She liked blood sacrifice. Can you imagine that? My grandmother says Apophis didn't allow our festival to Renenutet or the worship of any of our goddess, even Taueret."

Hatasu remembered the ancestor's story about Apophis sending the ridiculous messages to shut up the hippopotamus that were 'keeping him awake'. "I have heard stories, too," she said. "What stories does your family tell about when the Hyksos were here?"

Mutsi said, "My family is grateful that we can gather to honor the goddess, too. My grandmother tells stories of when she was a child and she saw Sekenenre murdered. She was a young woman when Ahmose, the Liberator, drove the Hyksos out."

Hatasu's eyes grew wider. She heard Mutsi say clearly that Sekenenre was murdered. *Certainly this wasn't true. A Pharaoh can't be murdered!* She leaned forward as her new friend talked.

Ferit said, "My great-grandmother won't tell us about the Hyksos years. Those stories give her nightmares. But, every festival she tells us how lucky we are."

"What else did your grandmother tell you about Sekenenre?" Hatasu asked Mutsi, trying to hide the urgency in her voice.

"She doesn't like to talk about Sekenenre, either. She just says he did great things. She talks more about Ahmose and our liberation," said Mutsi. "My father told me she saw some terrible things when the Hyksos ruled. She still has nightmares and sometimes she talks to herself. People say she is touched." Mutsi pointed to her head and made a face. "My mother says that's what happens when a person lives through terrible things. Grandma prefers to tell us stories about when her grandparents managed the herds of the Pharaoh, before the Hyksos came. Now, she reminds us to be thankful that our beloved Pharaoh Thutmose protects us from the possibility of the Hyksos ever coming back. I am proud that my brother and my uncle are among the soldiers who fight for our Pharaoh and our land."

"I, too, have an uncle who was called to leave our field of barley to fight in the far, strange land to keep us safe," said Ferit.

Hatasu's heart ached at hearing these stories of people suffering. *That poor woman!* She wondered if her nightmares were like Tao's. *What could she do to make things better?* Ferit's next question was directed at her, distracting her from such feelings. "What stories does *your* family tell?"

"Oh, they tell of Pharaoh Ahmose but also of Nefertari and how Queen Ahhotep helped the Two Lands. I have heard the stories from Waset."

"That is where your family is from?" said gentle Mutsi.

Hatasu nodded.

"Is that amulet around your neck special to Waset?" she asked.

She caught her breath a bit as she reached down and touched the small turquoise pendant of the protective god, Bes. She hoped this didn't give her away but she answered, "It is Bes, protector of children."

"You must be from a noble family to have a stone amulet."

"Sort of," Hatasu answered, smiling inwardly at her secret.

Then, directing attention away from herself, she asked Ferit, "What is that you have around your neck?"

"It is an amulet bag. My grandmother paid a magician much linen for me to have this."

"What's in the bag?"

"It is a fang of a cobra, a tooth of a crocodile and a papyrus with a very powerful spell written on it. It will keep me safe from all samana demons, she says. Samana demons bring harm to people who aren't careful. My father died of a snake's bite because he wouldn't wear the amulet my grandmother gave him. I don't want to die like my mother and father did."

"What happened to your mother?"

"She died in the time of plague, last year."

"Who takes care of you?"

"My grandmother and grandfather. But I must work hard to help them. My grandmother is weak and tired much of the time because she has the blood-in-urine disease. It is I who must grind the grain and make the bread. It is hard but I have cousins and aunts who help." She said this in a resigned voice and Hatasu wondered at how her own life would be different without her mother and father…even if they weren't Pharaoh and Queen. Ferit went on, admitting her further plight with acceptance, as though it were a common occurrence. "Grandmother gets weaker and grandfather fears she will soon go to the ancestors."

Mutsi joined in, "I have a cousin with that blood-in-urine disease. The doctor was called and made him a tea to drink. His urine is clean again, now. Would that help your grandmother?"

"The doctor has come many times. Many times she has drunk the tea. It gets better for a while but then it returns. Her urine gets red and she gets bloated, full of water, and very tired."

Mutsi continued, "My father is a timber merchant who trades with Byblos. There, they say samana demons cause illness. They have mashmashu-magicians who overcome the evil magic but my mother says the magic of the Levant is dangerous." Turning toward Ferit, she asked, "Do you think your grandmother is sick because of the evil magic from the Levant?"

Ferit's eyes grew large and frightened. Her voice got small, almost a whisper, "I have an aunt who believes my grandmother's sickness is because of their evil magic, but my grandmother is as afraid of the mashmashu healers as she is of the samana demons."

Mutsi stood a little taller and spoke up, "My mother says we have all the magic we need, right here. Our priests know how to fight the foreign magic."

Hatasu thought of Thethi. "I have a brother that is sick with a breathing illness. I've seen the priestess of Isis use their chants and herbs of the Two Lands and he's gotten better. They don't talk of foreign demons or gods."

"Maybe there aren't as many samana demons in the south. I hope they don't bother your brother while you are here in the north," Ferit said.

Hatasu felt the knot form in her stomach. Thethi had been sick and irritable since they'd arrived in Ankh-Tawy. The thought of her youngest brother being made ill by foreign demons terrified her, even if she didn't believe they were the real problem for Thethi.

She didn't want either friend to see how scared she was, so she turned toward Mutsi, nodding toward her necklace of cowry. She asked, "Are those your protection?"

"Yes, these shells are symbols of the goddess and they bring her blessings and protection."

Hatasu wanted to know if they kept her safer from illness and foreign magic. But just as she was about to ask, there was a sudden commotion on the other side of the square. She turned to see where the sound was coming from…and there she stood. A red-faced Sitre loomed larger than life. Her mole was scarlet and her formal black wig was askew. She easily would have frightened anyone who knew her less well. Sitre pointed toward the group of girls. A small group of palace staff clustered behind her. She shouted loudly, "There she is! Bless the goddess, she is safe."

Everyone in the square stopped what they were doing and stared in the direction Sitre pointed. People backed up to open a broad corridor between the angry nurse and the embarrassed princess. Hatasu turned to her new friends. Their faces had each blanched white with alarm. She thought to herself that Sitre was scary enough looking for her new friends to think perhaps she was the personification of just the kind of demon they had talked of. "It's okay," Hatasu said with a sheepish smile. "It's my nurse."

Sitre started to close the space between them, so Hatasu got up and walked to meet her, sparing her friends the fright. Sitre was scowling, and the bright red mole contrasted against her pale face. When they met in the middle of the corridor of people, Sitre squatted low and she hugged her tight for several minutes. People recognized it as an understandable scene of a mother re-finding a lost child and they returned to their business and celebrating. "Hatshepsut, how could you have done this?"

Hatasu heard the tension and pressure in her voice. "Oh Sitre, I'm sorry I upset you. I had such a wonderful time. I caught a sedbu for the goddess and…"

Sitre pulled back and looked at the child. "You played with wild snakes!! You are the Hawk-in-the-Nest, now," she interrupted, speaking softly but with a sudden firmness in her voice. "You must be mindful of your safety and behave with dignity." Her immense relief now gave way to disapproval. She reached over and removed the scarf. "What is this rag over your beautiful hair?"

They were still in full view of her new friends and Hatasu heard the girls behind her gasp as her red youth-lock was exposed. Sitre seemed not to notice them as she brushed the remaining chaff from the princess's shoulders. Her nurse's face regained its composure slowly and gradually her mole gave up some of its redness. Hatasu felt her own face redden with the awkwardness of being 'found out'.

Sitre stood up and gradually returned to her usual self. She said, "It is time for the processional back to the palace." Taking Hatasu's hand firmly in her own, she proceeded to the royal litter. But Hatasu, with a mischievous smile, turned and sent a secret wave to Mutsi and Ferit. They each were still wearing an expression of shock.

As she climbed into the riding chair next to her mother, Yuf caught her eye and gave her a conspirator's wink. Once she was again within the confines of the palace, Sitre set about scolding Hatasu for her impropriety of mixing with the fellahin and merchants, now that she was the most probable Hawk-in-the-Nest. This was another annoyance about the whole oracle business. She heard Sitre's words like they were the buzzing of flies in her ears.

As soon as she could get away, she went to Thethi's room. Even though she knew it wasn't so, she wanted to assure herself that he was *not* a victim of the foreign magic. She also figured he was the only person she could talk with about Sekenenre. She tiptoed into his room and found him still in bed. He opened his eyes and looked at her. Encouraged, she said, "I found out more about the Sekenenre puzzle!" She hoped the news about Sekenenre would rekindle their old camaraderie, and of itself, make him feel better. A slight glimmer of his old interest rose in his eyes. Encouraged, she continued. "I talked to someone who knows of Sekenenre."

He tilted his head, squinted his eyes and looked at her. It was the first time in a long while that he let his eyes meet hers. "What did you find out?" he asked.

Hatasu was heartened to hear a little of the old Thethi in his voice. "I met the daughter of a merchant whose grandmother told her Sekenenre was *murdered*."

His face brightened with surprise for a second then he squinted his eyes even more suspiciously this time. "Why would you, the Hawk-in-the-Nest, want to share anything with me now?"

"Oh, stop it, Thethi!" she exploded suddenly in frustration. "Stop blaming me for the oracle!"

"I can hardly get out of bed," he said, "let along share an

adventure." She saw how pale he looked in his bed, his chest pulled in all hollow-like from his troubled breathing. He went on in a small voice, "The oracle seems to be true. I couldn't be Pharaoh, like this." He tried to sit up as he said this to her but immediately his breathing became labored again. Discouraged, he plopped back down on his little cot. He looked at her with large, red eyes.

She tried to reassure him…and herself. "You'll get better," she said. "You've been sick before and the medicine of the Two Lands always makes you well."

He just closed his eyes. With a worried sigh, she walked out of the room. Trying not to sound discouraged, she said as she left, "Just get better."

She went to see her mother. That was the person who would know the answers to her questions. She couldn't tell her about Sekenenre, but maybe she could ask about sickness and maybe even talk to her about the things her new friends said. Hatasu found her in her room, rocking Neferubrity. Hatasu had tears in her eyes when she entered the room, asking, "Why doesn't Thethi get better?"

Ahmose got up and put the baby into her bed. She motioned Hatasu to follow her out of the room. "Sihathor is our best healing priestess and she is working with herbs and chants," she said, once they were out in the hallway.

"He doesn't play with me anymore. He doesn't even tease me!" she complained.

"He needs time and rest. Recovery takes a while."

After a moment's thought, Hatasu's face brightened. "The stela at Nefertiry's temple made Neferubrity better." After a pause, her shoulders sloped and she remembered, "But Nefertiry's temple is so far away in Waset." Tears formed in her eyes again.

"Well, my dear, there is also a healing temple here in Ankh-Tawy. I have business at the healing Temple of Sekhmet tomorrow and you could come with me and bring a stela for Thethi's recovery."

Hatasu's face lit up. "Could I?"

The Queen's eyebrows rose and she smiled. "Well…you must give me your word that you will stay out of mischief."

"I'll be good…really!" A disturbing thought entered Hatasu's mind. *Would the healing priestess be able to overcome the illness if it was caused by foreign magic?* Her mother was the person to ask about this but she again thought of the risk that she would be upset at her for going off without Sitre at the festival. She decided she must have answers so she'd risk it. "Could the reason Thethi doesn't get better, be because of samana demons?" She watched her mother with apparent casualness, observing her out of the corner of her eye as she fiddled with her fingers.

Her mother's eyes turned toward her quickly. "Where have you gotten this idea?" Her eyebrows came together and her face seemed to darken. Then, nodding her head thoughtfully, she relaxed and added, "Sitre told me you joined the festivities with the common folk this afternoon. Is that what makes you speak of samana demons?"

"I met a peasant girl there. She said her grandmother is sick with the 'blood-in-the-urine' disease. She talked about samana demons from the Levant. Could those demons be keeping Thethi sick, too?"

Ahmose shook her head, frowning. "It will take much to cleanse the land of their ignorance and fearful beliefs of the Hyksos." She sighed loudly. "Thethi's illness is certainly not related to foreign demons."

Hatasu let out a little sigh, this time of relief. The subject was open, so she decided to go on. "What is the 'blood-in-the-urine' disease? Does it come from the foreign demons?"

"No, our people have done battle with that disease here in Khemet as long as the people have had canals."

"Mutsi, a merchant girl I met, talked of mashmashu magicians for the samana magic sickness. Do they help at all?"

"My, you were busy at the festival! You met a peasant girl and a merchant girl and got yourself all kinds of misinformation."

Hatasu watched her mother faintly smile as she shook her head. She seemed more distressed about the misinformation than about Hatasu's impropriety. She waited for Omm to talk again. Her mother explained, "Thethi's breathless disease and the 'blood-in-the-urine' disease have nothing to do with samana magic or the Levant. Their treatment has nothing to do with foreign magicians. It is our priests of Sekhmet, like Sihathor, who have always used their magic to battle these diseases as well as plagues and other sicknesses that disturb our people."

Hatasu was listening closely. "So...is there anything else the Sekhmet priest can do for Thethi and for Ferit's grandmother?"

Her mother was silent a moment before she said, "Bringing the stela to the temple is good Egyptian magic. I believe he will recover this time, as he has other times. As for this peasant's grandmother, the recovery of the peasants is not so certain. When we bring the offering stela to the Temple of Sekhmet tomorrow, you may ask the priest that question yourself."

Hatasu liked the prospect of learning more about what would help her friend's grandmother. "Mother, you're not upset with me for meeting people at the festival, are you?"

"Daughter of the Pharaoh, these are your people, too. It is a good thing you are interested in the farmers and merchants, as well as in the governors and priests you met on our way here. A wise Queen mixes with the people and understands their struggles."

Hatasu's heart rested a little easier. It was early afternoon the next day before the Queen was ready for the trip to the Temple of Sekhmet. Hatasu waited patiently outside the council room door until the ministers of agriculture-harvest and the ministers of canal-works filed out of their meeting. Finally, Ahmose was ready to go to the temple.

Mother and daughter walked hand in hand, accompanied by the servant who carried the stela. Ahmose spoke to her daughter as they went, "I want you to understand that the healing magic of the Two Lands is the very wisest and best in the entire world. Foreign magic lacks the illumination of Ra. The goddess is our best hope of healing illnesses like this. You've seen it work before. Here, you will see the healing power of Sekhmet. She is both our most fierce deity and our most compassionate.

"In Ankh-Tawy, it is she who overcomes enemies of Ra and it is she who brings us back to peace. Just as the Pharaoh does war in a land that threatens our peace with chaos, so the priests of Sekhmet do war on the forces that threaten chaos within a person's body. Sickness means there is a lack of Maat's balance within the khet, the physical body, and Sekhmet returns it to balance.

"What you encountered at the festival was the local people's superstitious beliefs, learned from foreigners, who are ignorant of our wisdom. Our festivals are meant to enlighten people's hearts and open their ka-spirits to health and balance. Even so, some people are still influenced by foreign ideas and fears. The spirit world of the Two Lands has many loving and protective deities that teach as well as heal. They are your best defense against illness."

They passed under the breeze-blown temple flags and just inside the pylon gates was a large statue of Sekhmet. Up until now, all of Hatasu images of Sekhmet were in her mind: The fiery lion, the fierce khamsin winds, the punishing daughter of Ra. Now, she looked at the official image of this goddess in this statue of Sekhmet in all her grandeur. She had the body of a woman, the head of a lion, and she strode forward, her left foot extending like a Horus statue. But, she was very much a goddess. Her hair came down over her shoulders and extended to the gentle swellings of young breasts. A mane framed her lion face and two small ears protruded through it. Extending from the top of her head was the large disc of Ra. In front of it was the raised, hooded cobra of the sun. Her eyes were dark shadows, looking like shiny beads that could actually see, and the whiskers on her face made her mouth seem real. In her left hand she held the wadj scepter in the exact center of her body. Her right arm was extended down her side and in that hand she held an ankh. She was frightening and awesome and beautiful, all at the same time.

Sihathor, her teacher at the Ptah Temple, and another tall plain looking priest walked across the courtyard toward them. They bowed formally as they approached the Queen. Ahmose spoke first, "Greetings, Sihathor."

The priestess offered a formal greeting, "Oh, Great Queen, Mother of Her People, the Temple of Sekhmet is honored by your visit."

With a nod, the Queen then motioned to the servant to come forward with the offering stone. "We have with us the stela to be offered at the sanctuary of Sekhmet for Thutmose II's recovery."

Hatasu watched the stone as the servant carried it. It was flat, with a rounded upper portion and a squared-off lower portion. Under the arc at the top was a carved image of the winged sun disc. Below that, was a picture of the god Horus as a child with a youth-lock on his head and his finger to his mouth. In the lower section of the stone were hieroglyphs requesting health for Thethi.

Sihathor motioned to a shaven-headed wab priest to come and receive this stela. "Great Queen, the place in the sanctuary is prepared for the stela."

Hatasu watched as her mother, Sihathor, and the young priest carrying the stela, walked through the second pylon leading to the sanctuary; the most effective place to leave this stone prayer but forbidden territory for her. The other white kilted priest stayed with her to show her around the temple. As they walked toward the colonnade along the side of this center court, she started asking her questions, "Are you a priest of Sekhmet, too?"

"Yes, I use herbs and surgical instruments, as well as chants and spells."

"Well, besides my brother, I am also worried about a friend whose grandmother has the 'blood-in-urine' disease. She thinks it is from the samara demons. Mother says it is not samara demons and it is Sekhmet who can help with such a sickness. Do you think you can help her?"

He took a minute to reply, "The samara demons feed on the fear they generate, but our goddess, our magic, and our medicines are stronger than their fears." He smiled and continued, "So you'd like to learn about how Sekhmet heals the khet of 'blood -in-urine' disease, and maybe even how she heals the ka of the fear of samana demons?"

Hatasu nodded.

"Well, I shall tell you. The trouble is the canals breed worms, not demons, when they are not kept clean of human waste. If a person drinks or wades in the canal, the worms get into his blood through his skin. These worms devour a person's energy. If the sickness goes untreated, the body swells up…especially the stomach, and eventually the person dies. It is this information of what causes the problem, that protects the people's kas from fear of demons."

"That is the illness my friend said her grandmother has. She said she has drunk healing teas many times and still she is sick. Can Sekhmet help her?"

The priestess went on. "There is a treatment that uses a mixture of wormwood, pond weed and beer. Let us know who she is and we can send a Sekhmet priest to administer the potion and perform the magic chants."

Hatasu was very excited. "Oh could you? She is the grandmother of a girl named Ferit and she lives in the farm village where we had the Festival of Renenutet."

"I will see to it that it is arranged. A priest of this temple will go out to that village. The main thing, however, is the enlightenment of Ra to overcome ignorance. From now on, she must avoid dirty water. This is difficult, because women do their laundry in the canal rather than lugging their soiled clothes to the river. This is the problem. The illness will return if she does not heed this warning to stay out of the canal water."

"But you will teach her and help her, right?"

"We will do our best."

The princess was satisfied.

Chapter 30 – The Pharaoh's Return

Hatasu and the priest walked together toward the columned passageway and the storerooms behind the columns. When they reached the colonnade, Hatasu's eyes slowly adjusted to the dark and her skin felt the relief of the coolness. She looked around. Hanging from the ceiling beams were bunches of dried plants. There were shelves on which were jars, each marked with its own special sign. There were also baskets on tables against the rear wall, all holding different tools for preparing cures. Several priests were preparing treatments. They paused at their tasks, bowed, and continued their work.

Hatasu breathed in, smelling the exotic scents of the dried herbs and concoctions. She wandered in and out of the various rooms, each room having a healing purpose: One for preparing herbs, another for storing surgical knives and equipment, and still another had a library of medical papyrus. In each room, men in white kilts attended to their tasks.

After a while, she heard the Queen's voice echoing through the colonnades as she was talking to Sihathor upon her return from the sanctuary. "I want to make sure you have all you need. The low-river season of illness, the time of the plagues, will be here soon. Do you have a sufficient supply of the sour pomegranate wine that worked so well last year?"

Hatasu walked into the sunlit courtyard toward her mother. Sihathor nodded. "Yes, we have a storehouse with many amphorae of the wine."

"This year, we have the added concern of the soldiers returning with wounds and foreign diseases," the Queen said.

Sihathor agreed. "We may need more linen for bandages but I've made arrangements with the local weavers." She looked down at the scrolls she carried. "Our supply of aloe, capers and thyme are sufficient for inflammations. We have enough poppy plants for the relief of pain. Our moringa oils, honey and beer are abundant for mixing the herbs. The priests have examined and sharpened the surgical equipment. I believe we are ready for both the plague season and the returning soldiers."

The Queen reached out and touched Sihathor on the arm. "Thank you. Hopefully our soldiers will return healthy, but it is better they return wounded, than not at all. May the low-water-plague be light this year."

"By the grace of Sekhmet, I hope you are right," Sihathor responded.

Hatasu had reached her mother's side and Ahmose nodded to her that it was time to leave. As they reached the gate, Sihathor bowed formally to the Queen, reciting her prescribed litany of praise. She also bowed to Hatasu. On the walk home, Hatasu felt a new confidence…for Thethi and for Ferit's grandmother. She asked her mother, "When will Father be home?"

"Soon, My Dear, the army is but a few days march from Ankh-Tawy. It won't be long now."

Hatasu's heart beat faster at the very thought on seeing him again.

Back at the palace, Paheri reported Thethi was sleeping peaceful for the first time in a month; his breath was free of its rasping sound. Indeed, magic and healing of The Two Lands was the most powerful in the world.

During the next three days of waiting, Hatasu's small body tingled with excitement at her father's return. People arrived daily from the nomes and Hatasu was thrilled to see her friends again: Tutkharit from Zawty, Djehuti, and the children of Maatmose from Khemenu. Catching up with these friends lessened her disappointment that Puyemre was not coming, though his parents, Puya and Neferiah, were there to welcome home his brother, Ti. The pervasive air of bustle and the hum of activity, added to her exhilarated state.

Sitre gave her the task of weaving garlands of flowers for the amphora and pillar columns, and to still her non-stop chatter, she taught her a welcome-home song. "*My heart beats in gladness. The sycamores bow to welcome you home. The lapwing-birds let go of their sadness. All sing of your welcome home!*"

"What will it be like?" Hatasu asked. "When father and the army come home? Will it be like it was when they sailed away...? People waving scarves and playing frame drums in an orderly way that really took all day? Or will it be like the Beautiful Festival of the Valley, when the Pharaoh addressed everyone at the Temple of Montuhotep? Or maybe more like the harvest festival here in Ankh-Tawy, where everyone drinks beer, dances and sings?"

"A little bit of all of that." Sitre smiled. "They will be marching, not arriving by boat. It is more of a 'Grand Entrance' than a processional, and it will take all day for all of the military units to get through the north gate of the city. It will be treated as the grandest of festival, with beer, wine and sweet breads passed out to everyone. I'm sure he will give a speech, but when or where I don't know."

"I can't wait to tell him all the things I've learned, and how good I've been."

"That probably won't happen right away, Hatasu. There are many people who will be anxious to see him. He has many official duties to perform when he returns."

"But surely he wants to see me, and Ahmose and Thethi and Neferubrity."

"Surely he does, but he must make sure he gives thanks to the gods and greets the governors of the nomes that have traveled to see him…"

"Too bad for them! I'm his daughter, and I've waited a long time and traveled a long distance to see him, too."

"Indeed, you have." Sitre smiled at her impatience. "I'm just telling you, so you won't be too disappointed if you don't get to see him by yourself until a day or two after he arrives."

"Well, I would be disappointed!" The flower stems she was weaving got tangled up with her finger. She pulled at them and broke the strand.

Just then, old Nefermut came into the room with Muthotep carrying Neferubrity. With excitement in her voice, Nefermut said, "Let me tell you, when Pharaoh Ahmose returned from his campaign in the Levant, he brought all kinds of treasures: Levantine pottery, exotic purple dyes, incredible gemstones and even some of the treasures stolen from our temples."

Young Muthotep bounced a squirmy Neferubrity as she walked. She asked, "Do you think Thutmose will bring things back, too?"

"I'm sure he will have wonderful things."

Muthotep looked at her with wide eyes. "I do remember my mother had a bluestone necklace my father brought back with him from that campaign. She treasured it. He also had two cows and a slave he said was from his brave service to the Pharaoh."

"Yes, indeed, war brings us women rich rewards of waiting for our men's return."

Ahhotep, Hapuseneb's mother, was sitting near them with Neferiah, Puyemre's mother. They also were weaving flowers for the decoration of the banquet hall. Ahhotep spoke up, "The only gifts I want is for my son, Saamun's, safe return home, sound in body and mind. That would be gift enough, for me."

Neferiah responded, "And I also want that for my son, Ti. Though I would love the gifts of colored dye and gemstones for jewelry, they would be as nothing if my son were not safe."

Hatasu put the broken garland on her lap as she looked to the group of women, knowing her brother was *not* coming home safe. It was more pleasant to consider what gifts she might get from this war. "Do you think the Pharaoh will bring gifts to me, too?"

Nefermut, realizing how their wishes would bring to mind Hatasu's loss, hesitated a minute, then said, "Oh, I'm sure he will have something special for you, his little lotus blossom."

"Oh, what do you think he will bring me?"

"I don't know, but I'll bet it will be special."

Thethi and Hapuseneb came through the room carrying their
throw-sticks. Her brother called to her, "Want to come practice
throwing with us? I want father to see how good my aim has
gotten."

Hatasu was so glad to see him up and about. After the stela had
been placed in the temple, his recovery had been rapid. Frustrated
with the blossom weaving, Hatasu turned to Sitre. "Can I?"

"Go ahead but don't let your brother get over tired." Turning to
Thethi, she said, "You will need your energy for viewing the formal
entry into the city and you won't want to miss the award banquet
when your father gives out the Golden Flies of Honor, would you?"

"I'll be fine," he called over his shoulder as the three of them
headed for the practice area. Turning to Hapuseneb, he held the
throw-stick like a dagger and invited him to some swordplay. "At
the banquet we will get to hear of the great battles and the enemies
my father overcame." It seemed to Hatasu that he was back to his
old self, over-compensating and pretending that he'd never been
sick…or that he'd never be sick again.

Hapuseneb said, "I'll bet my brother Saamun has battle stories,
too. Won't he be surprised to see how I've grown and how good
I've gotten at the throw-stick?"

Thethi and Hatasu were silent again, for a minute. Amenmose
would never get to see their changes.

"I'm sorry," Hapuseneb said, realizing the predicament.

Hatasu spoke up first, "That's alright. I'm happy for you to have
Saamun come home, like we are happy our father is coming home."

"Yes," said Thethi. "It just feels strange…no Amenmose."

"I bet I can throw further than either of you!" Hatasu challenged, again moving the talk away from areas of discomfort. She had practiced with the throw-stick in each of the nomes they traveled through but the last weeks had been too busy.

The three of them arrived at the throwing field ready to hone their skill. Thethi's residual weakness limited the distance of his throw, but Hatasu's reach was far and her eye for the target exact. Hapuseneb's skill was somewhere in between.

Later that afternoon, Asat arrived with Itruri and Kam, her father and mother, from Waset. She looked radiantly beautiful with a flush about her skin and a look of expectation in her eyes. It occurred to Hatasu that she didn't know Amenmose was dead. *How sad for her!*

Ineni greeted them and as they spoke, Hatasu saw Asat's face turn ashen white. Her mother put her arm around her in support and comfort. Other visitors from Waset brought news that Senisenb, Hatasu's grandmother, would not be making the trip to Ankh-Tawy but would await her son in Waset. Hatasu would have been sad if she wasn't so surrounded by other new arrivals.

As the time of the Pharaoh's arrival neared, Hatasu also watched her mother do a most interesting balancing act. During the day, she was the ruler and the protector of the people, concerned with her meetings with the Steward of the Harvest and Overseer of the preparation for the celebration of the Pharaoh's return. In the evening, however, she was a woman who wanted to look beautiful for the husband she had missed during his long absence. Hatasu watched Nefermut apply special treatments for her hair and bring out her most precious beauty creams for the Queen's face.

Ahmose looked over her specially woven, fine linen sheaths. "Which one do you think I should wear, Nefermut?"

"The one with the border of gold threads mixed with deep purple, of course."

Hatasu watched Nefermut polish her mother's jewels until her collar, crown and arm bans had a brilliant luster.

The night before the army's grand entrance into Ankh-Tawy, Hatasu climbed to the palace roof and could see the lights of the military camp far off to the north. When Hatasu's mother slipped out the back door of the palace with just Nefermut, Hatasu guessed she was going to see Thutmose before the formal reunion. She called to her mother and begged to be allowed to go, too.

Her mother smiled gently and said, "No, dear, you will have your time with him tomorrow."

"You promise?"

"I promise."

She dreamed of her father all night and the next morning she awoke to the buzz of the palace staff putting last minute touches on their preparations. Nefermut was scurrying about like a Kushite monkey, making sure everything was just right for Ahmose's role in the ceremonies of the day. Her mother did, indeed, look beautiful, and Hatasu thought she looked calmer than she had ever since her father had left.

Muthotep was also scurrying around, getting Neferubrity ready. Sensing all the commotion, the baby was excited but also easily upset. Hatasu knew Sitre would be anxious to get started on her own preparations but she evaded her and went to the nursery. There, she offered to hold Neferubrity as Muthotep completed some tasks. Hatasu bounced her sister up and down and carried her back and forth across the room making soothing sounds, until the baby stopped her fussy crying.

Then, she sat down on a stool with her and said in her most comforting way, "Neferubrity, do you know what is happening today? Your father is coming home and you are going to get to meet him for the first time in this life! You and I are so lucky to have such a grand and wonderful father. He has been away fighting a very important war and now he is home safe. Everybody is so excited. Now, you want to look lovely for him, so you must stop crying so your eyes will not be red and puffy. Try very hard to be good and to cooperate with Muthotep, so Father will be proud of all his children. Okay?"

Neferubrity's eyes, momentarily distracted from crying, watched her sister's face with interest. Suddenly, she reached up and pulled on her sister's red youth-lock. Hatasu made a face of mock displeasure and shook her head, pressing kisses into the baby's cheek as the little one let go of her hair. Neferubrity giggled. Hatasu laughed and gave her sister a big hug. She returned her to Muthotep, who was ready to take the baby back.

Sitre was calling and Hatasu hurried off in that direction. Once Sitre had finished her ministrations, and braided, oiled and bejeweled the princess, Hatasu was off again to see how her brother was doing. Thethi was dressed in his finest collar, and oiled and braided by Paheri. Just a few days before, she had doubted he would be able to join the festivities, at all. In her general excitement…and relief…she threw her arms around him and hugged him. He looked surprised at his sister's demonstration of affection.

When the appointed time came, Ahmose, Hatasu, Thethi and Neferubrity took their positions in the Window of Appearance. This opening was in the bridge between the two great pylons of the palace. From there, the crowd could see the royals clearly as they smiled down on their people and waved to them. From there, also, they could look out over the broad avenue that stretched to the great gate at the north end of town through which the victorious army would pass.

Before them, they could see the streets lined with the many, many people who had come to greet their victorious Pharaoh. It was a great mass of color; people waved colored linen scarves and palm fronds and everyone sang in jubilation. There were clusters of people from many of the nomes along the Nile. Many had their standards raised high over their group so the Pharaoh could easily see who was represented.

From their high vantage point, the royal family could see beyond the people in the street, out to the gate to the north. Hatasu watched the approaching line of chariots and foot soldiers, captured horses and wagons of booty. First to come through the gates were the military musicians. There were two trumpeters, each with two long-stemmed brass horns put to their mouths; out of the cups at the horns' ends, came one single note. The trumpeter blew loud and long to announce the entrance of the Pharaoh. Drummers marched beside them wearing drums that looked like long, narrow jars. Each was attached with straps around the drummer's necks, their hands in position to beat out a rhythmic march.

This music was slightly different from what Hatasu remembered from the music played before they left. It had a slightly exotic quality to it…perhaps something learned from one of the foreign lands they visited. Whether it was the music or just the occasion, Hatasu was wonderfully excited.

With mounting tension, she looked for the first glimpse of her father…but next came the standard bearers. One held aloft the fan shaped as the lotus, the flower of Khemet, with alternating red, yellow and green petals, and with red and white streamers flowing in the breeze. The standard bearer carried a fan shaped as the papyrus of Upper Egypt in similar colors, again with streamers. Then, a third standard followed with the head of the war god Montu, with the solar disc and feathers of Amun.

Finally, there came two perfectly matched black horses with flowing black manes and shining brass harnesses, pulling the chariot of her father, the Pharaoh. The Pharaoh moved through the grand gate of the city. She could hear the sound of horns and the beating of the drums but they sounded far away. Her immediate attention was on the magnificent figure of her father. He was truly the god of his people. Yes, he was the son of the sun, with all his glory.

As he moved through the gates, a wondrous cheer went up from the both sides of the passageway. He proceeded along the avenue at a measured pace. His horses pranced, lifting their hooves high with each step. Thutmose looked around, savoring his triumphant return to his people. He waved his hand and nodded his head to those he recognized along the way. The rhythm of the warrior's drums now mixed with the frame drums and sistrums of the women and priestesses.

Hatasu felt her heart beat in her chest. It swelled with gladness. She caught her breath, experiencing the expanded feeling of great love she had for her father. She had never seen anyone or anything look so grand. She waited as he moved forward to his Queen at the Window of Appearance at the palace. It was like watching the great Horus arrive at the temple of his beloved Hathor. He came along the broad avenue driving his polished…though dented…chariot, and wearing his blue war helmet. He waved gaily to the people as he passed but he was always turned with half his attention toward the palace.

Hatasu bent toward her baby sister and said, "Look there," pointing to their father, still just off in the distance. "There is our father. He is coming to us. See all the people cheering for him? They cheer because he is the very grandest of Pharaohs!"

Neferubrity looked up into the face of her big sister and then followed her arm out to her pointing finger. Hatasu was nodding, "Yes, there he is!" Looking back to the baby, she clapped her hands and Neferubrity did the same. Hatasu looked over at Thethi, her one remaining brother, healthy again, and the two of them shared a broad happy smile.

The generals of the army moved through the gates behind the Pharaoh. Everyone could clearly see Ibana and Pennekheb in their chariots. A sharp pang went though Hatasu's heart. She realized…again…Amenmose was absent. A strange kind of loneliness stabbed low in her chest. She was *so* happy to see her father, happy Thethi was well again, yet so sad that Amenmose was dead…gone to the stars.

She looked closely at what came next. A pair of oxen pulled wagons carrying two sphinxes and a giant statue of the goddess, Hathor. Another great cheer went up when the people saw this. Ahmose leaned over to the children and said, "The Pharaoh recovered these treasures taken by the Hyksos as booty from our temples and palaces. The people recognized them and that's why they cheer."

There were several more wagons with statues and objects with special significance. Next came the standard for the Company of Ptah, the legion local to this area. The first row of elite chariot drivers was followed by the foot soldiers walking with their shields all held uniformly…or almost.

As they got closer, Hatasu could see that many of the soldiers had wounds that made either walking or carrying the shield difficult. The companies that had been neat squares of military precision during the military parade in Waset, now seemed to straggle along like a snake of ants. These men were followed by many soldiers with ropes to which were attached many horses; enough for a large herd and great breeding possibilities for years to come.

The Company of Amun came next, carrying its standard. Next, came foot soldiers herding a large number of cows. Then, there was another company and still more wagons. The procession went on and on.

Hatasu could see off in the distance, beyond the wall, there were many more herds of horses. These were just the best and finest. There were also miles and miles of soldiers in their units, headed with their banners and charioteers and followed by the shield and spear carrying foot soldiers. As the army passed by, the people lining both sides of the road cheered and cried. They passed around the jugs of wine the Queen made available for the festivities. Young girls danced gaily and women looked frantically at the faces of the soldiers, seeking their beloved sons, husbands or brothers.

The scene was a blur of emotions. All the while, the procession moved forward toward the palace. Hatasu could see Asat with her mother and father, Itruri and Kam, standing by the palace gate. Asat, having been told that Amenmose was not returning, looked pale and drawn. Hatasu felt very sad for her. The princess looked back to the processional and watched the survivors come through the street.

The Pharaoh led the processional directly to the palace; he climbed the stairs and greeted the Queen and children with embraces. Hatasu held him tight in her hug, breathed in the scent of his skin, all desert sun and sacred oils, and she remembered a thousand images of him before he left. Then, he looked for the first time on his second daughter and smiling, kissed her on the forehead. The family then stood together in the Window of Appearances waving out over their people.

Hatasu looked up at him adoringly. Thethi, gathering his

strength, stood at his full height. Once reunited with his family, they accompanied him in the procession to the Temple of Sekhmet to bring her an offering in thanksgiving for his victory and then to the Temple of Ptah, to do the same. These first official duties fulfilled, Thutmose need only wait for the rest of his army to pass through the gate.

This was his time for his children as Queen Ahmose promised. It was this day Hatasu held in her heart through all the haze of activity in the days that followed, in which she hardly saw her father. This is what she had wished for.

Neferubrity took a while to warm up to her father for he was a stranger to her, despite Hatasu's best efforts to explain his relationship. But at last, she finally gave him a half-smile and stopped clinging to Muthotep whenever he came near. Thethi, still somewhat pale, was glad to be there and rallied his fading energy. Thutmose expressed his relief that his ill son was showing good signs of recovering but it was Hatasu who most basked in the glow of her father's presence and attention.

When Hatasu told him about all the things she had learned in order to make him proud, he favored her with an open and warm smile. She went on about what she had learned about the language of the gods at the House of Life, how she had trained her monkey, her current excitement about decorating her room with the Story of the Shipwrecked Sailor, and the many friends she had made on her voyage down the Nile.

Thethi squirmed as she went on and on but their father never interrupted or seemed impatient. He listened carefully, as Hatasu sat close by her father's side feeling his warmth. Then, he turned a worried smile toward deep-eyed Thethi, who told his father of his great care of and pleasure in his dog, Behka. Thethi also talked about how far he'd come on his training with the throw-stick, and said he was ready to learn the bow and arrow. Thutmose nodded slowly and thoughtfully.

The Pharaoh motioned to Huy to bring him a basket. This scribe of her father's was more bronzed and muscled than she'd ever seen him before. Inside the basket Huy carried, Hatasu spotted objects wrapped in fine, white cloth. Her eyes sparkled as the Pharaoh spoke, directing his words more to Hatasu than to Thethi, "Would you like to see what I brought back from the Levant," then nodding toward her brother, "for each of you?"

Her eyes were big and her father was thoroughly enjoying her anticipation. "Hatasu, you are now the oldest, so you shall go first." This shocked her. Even with the commotion about the oracle, she had not thought of her position now as the oldest of his children. It was both a proud and lonely feeling. Her eyes followed her father's hands as he took the first object from the basket. He moved very slowly to tease her.

As she took the object in her hands, she could feel its weight. It was not a large package, but her hands gave way a bit as he placed it in her palms. Putting it on her lap, she un-wrapped it quickly. There before her very eyes were the most amazing colors she had ever seen. It was deep blue…like midnight over the palace garden…with specks of gold streaked through it. There were several stones and they seemed to capture the sky itself. They were set within magnificent gold.

Hatasu's mouth fell open. This was a woman's collar, a very regal, adult's collar. She immediately wanted to put it on and he helped her fasten it. She felt it, heavy and cool around her neck. It was big for her she realized, as she raised her hand to feel it. She looked to her father's eyes for approval. She wondered if she looked as grown up as she felt.

Pharaoh Thutmose was smiling and nodding; his pleasure in giving her this item was obvious. "Hatasu, it will not be long before you are a woman. You look beautiful in this now, and your beauty and loveliness will only grow."

She threw her arms around his neck. As she hugged him tight, she felt the metal of his collar clank against hers. Thethi had been squirming, uncomfortable with the way their father was favoring her. His turn finally came. His father turned to Thethi and asked, "You are still as interested in studying the military and war?"

Thethi's eyes brightened as though perhaps his father did understand him. "Yes, I want to be a great military leader, like you."

Thutmose's face rewarded his adulation with a smile. "Then, I think you will like what I brought you!"

His gift, too, was wrapped in cloth. Receiving the veiled but heavy object from his father's hands, he grinned broadly. This object's weight, too, lowered his hands a bit. It was longer than Hatasu's gift and, as Thethi unfolded it, there, gleaming before his eyes, was a thrusting dagger with a gold handle and a ribbed bronze blade. It was a fine weapon; however, Thethi quickly saw that there were no jewels on it as on his sister's collar.

Thethi's father smiled as though he did not notice his son's reticence. Her brother tried hard to hide his disappointment but Hatasu noticed. The Pharaoh said, almost in the tone of a military command, "You, too, are growing rapidly and will soon be ready to study weapons, not wooden daggers but real ones."

His gifts for Ahmose were dazzling and abundant. There was lapis jewelry, magnificent pottery, a bolt of vibrant purple cloth, and best of all, a small statue of Amun that had been stolen from her family during the Hyksos reign. Once the gifts were given, Thutmose told the family that he must go and oversee the arrival of the rest of the soldiers but they would see him again at the banquet that evening.

Hatasu went to the roof top and watched the continuing line of soldiers, but as Ra was sliding down the Western sky, the soldiers who arrived toward the end of the line were the wounded ones: Walking with crutches, bandages and some being carried. She was glad the healing temple was ready for them.

That evening was the celebration dinner; again, her father belonged to the people as their Pharaoh, while she was lost in the sea of other adoring faces turned toward him. The columns of the hall and the amphorae were entwined with lotus and papyrus. The aromas of breads, fruit and roast meat filled the air. The palace swelled with court officials, governors, army officers, important citizens and their families.

Pharaoh Thutmose sat on his throne on the dais in the grand columned hall of his new palace in Ankh-Tawy. Hatasu watched him closely. He looked down over the governors, ministers, nobles, and priests, and their wives. He looked out over the soldiers, generals, deputies, commanders and young heroes. He looked to his Queen, sitting and smiling on the throne next to him. He looked to her, her brother and sister…his only remaining children.

She saw him then turn his attention to the surroundings, perhaps gladdened to be in his homeland again. Moving between the columns and the table of people, the palace staff was serving the excellent wines and beers brought from the Levant. The people settled into their seats and turned their eyes to their Pharaoh on the dais at the head of the room. He was their Pharaoh and god, and he was ready to address himself to the gathered dignitaries.

Hatasu, like everyone else in the room, couldn't take her eyes off him. He stood to speak and an anticipatory hush fell over the room. He smiled beneficently. His voice, full and resonant, filled the hall. The upturned faces and smiling eyes of the people spoke of how each of their hearts was so gloriously open with love of him.

He began, "We have a great victory. I have made the boundaries of Khemet as far as that which the sun encircles. I have made strong, those who were in fear; I repelled the evil from them. I have made Khemet the superior of every land. I am a favorite of Amun, Son of Ra, of his body. I am his beloved Thutmose. I am given life, stability, satisfaction and health, while shining as King upon the Horus-throne of the living. I am the joy of his heart, together with his ka, I am like Ra, forever."

He paused as this glory he spoke of radiated from him. It shone and ennobled each of his subjects in the room, for they partook of his glory. Hatasu wondered when he would say something about Amenmose but he continued along the same lines, "The great god Amun commissioned me to go to the Eastern Lands to bring back that which had been stolen from us, and to secure the tribute and respect of these neighbors so they could no longer threaten us.

"As a good son, I did as the god commanded. I mounted my chariot. I marched the soldiers of the Two Lands. I increased our sphere of influence in the Levant. My army marched into the lands of Canaan, and in fear of our might, the cities of Sharuhem and Jericho paid tribute. I marched into the land of the Amurru. There, the city of Hazor in Galilee resisted me, yet were overcome by my might.

"I continued northward, through the friendly seaport merchant cities of Byblos and Ugarit, whose position of power has kept them more independent of the savage forces of destruction. I marched on, to the banks of the great Euphrates River, to recover the treasures of our temples that had been so vilely taken from us. There, I set a stela so all could see the glory of Amun and the great deeds I do in his name. But it was there, that the terrible forces of the Mitanni came upon us. Their chariots were large and heavy. They wore clothes with metal scales like a serpent. I fought a mighty battle against them near the city of Carchemish and then made a treaty-contract with them. For fear of me, they will honor the Two Land's sphere of influence in Canaan and Amurru and I give to them the territory north of the Orontes River in Naharin."

Thethi nudged his sister with his elbow. His face shone with the excitement of this tale of war.

The Pharaoh went on, "With the recovery of our stolen treasures and the rich tribute of many suzerains, we continued our victorious march home. Our land is once again safe from the chaos of the Levant. Amun blessed us and led us in the battles against a fierce and vile enemy. Like the barque of Ra overcoming the enemy of the serpent Apophis, we are again victorious. I give thanks to the gods Amun, Sekhmet and Ptah for their protection and for the victory they granted us."

The people cheered and waved their colored cloths. There were a few minutes, before the gathering quieted down again.

Thutmose's face showed strong emotion, as though he were trying to bring it under his control before he spoke, "The army of this Pharaoh fought bravely and well. These soldiers are most deserving of the honors they will be given tonight. I first want to honor those who returned to the ancestors while on the battlefields of Naharin, and to Amenmose, their commander-in-chief...and my son". His voice cracked a little but he quickly went on, not leaving space for grief or comments.

Hatasu longed to hear more. She waited.

"And now is time to honor those whose bravery helped win our victories. First, I would like to honor the Great Wife," he said, holding out his hand to Queen Ahmose and raising her to stand beside him. "Her magic protected me in the Two Lands, as Buto and Nekhbet protected me in Canaan and Naharin." The cheers resounded again. The Queen was dear in the hearts of the people. "She has truly followed in the tradition of her ancestors, Ahhotep and Nefertari, for she maintained Maat in the land during my absence.

"And now, I honor my soldiers with the Golden Flies of Honor to wear around their necks. To win this honor, one must be as tenacious as a fly upon the enemies of the Pharaoh. I wish to recognize first, my Chief Deputy of the Northern Corp, Ibana. I, myself, witnessed his bravery. He distinguished himself in Naharin as he has in the past. There, he captured an enemy chariot, its horses and a warrior. This was a great feat, for the warrior he caught gave us much information about the one with whom we were fighting. So, this first of the Flies of Honor goes to Ibana."

The old soldier's face beamed. As the other Golden Flies gleamed from his chest, he rose from his seat, and bowing before his Pharaoh, he gratefully received his honor. The table of his family, with Itruri, Kam, Paheri and all Ibana's grandchildren, cheered loudly. Asat was at the table with her family but her eyes were red and distant.

"Next, I wish to recognize my Deputy of the Southern Corps, Pennekheb. He, too, led the troops well. He captured over 20 hands and brought to me a chariot and a horse of the enemy. I give to him another Golden Fly of Honor." Pennekheb rose and limped forward to receive it.

He turned next toward a young man Hatasu had never seen before. "This Golden Fly," he said, holding it high in the air, "goes to General Nebra. He was great in the leadership and inspiration of the men under his command, and he presented me with the largest number of hands, thus aiding greatly in the destruction of the enemy." The young man who stood up to receive this honor, had strong, handsome features, broad and bronzed shoulders and a charismatic air of confidence.

Hatasu had never seen him before but he looked vaguely familiar. Then, she noticed that the loudest applause was coming from the table of the mayor of Ankh-Tawy. Yes, certainly this man held a resemblance to Rahotep, the grandiose leader of this northern city. As Nebra approached his Pharaoh to receive his honor, Hatasu thought his mouth looked hard and determined; his jaw was set firmly.

After Thutmose placed the honor around his neck and offered him a broad smile of affectionate acknowledgement, Nebra turned first to the Queen, bowing his head in acknowledgement of her and then…his eyes sought out Hatasu's. He bowed his head to her, too. The smile he offered her softened the hardness of his features and made him devastatingly handsome.

Her father was already on to honoring the next hero. He called Saamun, Hapuseneb's brother. Hatasu drew her breath in sharply as she realized he had only half of his left ear but he was grinning widely while Hapu and Ahhotep looked on proudly. He, too, had brought his Pharaoh many hands and had captured a whole suit of metal when he captured a Mitanni soldier, who was now his slave.

Next she recognized Ti, the brother of Puyemre, for he looked like an older version of her friend except for the large red scar on his neck. Puya and Neferiah, applauded loudly. Ti was acknowledged for his great skill and accomplishments in defensive battles, especially when the troops were ambushed on the road in Canaan. He was more modest in his smile and his stance, simply accepting the honor instead of reveling in it like the ones called before him.

Qenu stood tall and dignified, when he was called. He wore the Gold of Honor with a kind of nobility. The Pharaoh honored him for his energy and expertise at siege warfare. Only his brother, Baqt, was there to represent his family. Hatasu felt sad for him about that, but clearly the enthusiasm of Tutkharit and her family made up a bit for the lack of the others. Many soldiers, from their places through out the room, added their cheers. The princess noted how popular Qenu was with his men.

Hetep, friend to both of Hatasu's brothers, got his Gold of Honor. As he walked forward, his company of charioteers and elite archers applauded. The honor and the cheers brought a smile to his face but the slowness of his movements betrayed a deep sadness. Hatasu wondered if he had been with Amenmose when he died, just as he had been with Wadjmose at his death. She could almost feel the sadness dripping from him. The Pharaoh honored him for his great bravery, both in the open battlefield and in his encounter with the Mitanni.

Once the long list of awards was finished, Hatasu and Thethi were free to wander around the banquet hall to hear the stories the soldier heroes were retelling to each other and their families. These tales of war seemed to energize Thethi. Hatasu was particularly interested in Ti's account of how much better everything in the Two Lands is, compared to the Levant.

Ti launched into a story of how Qenu rescued him in the siege of Hazor. Qenu and Tutkharit had joined their party, and Qenu grinned, saying how Ti had saved him during the ambush on the road to Byblos. Saamun was enjoying his younger brother's wide-eyed admiration but Hatasu could see Hapuseneb's face close down as Saamun spoke with admiration of the warrior way of the Mitanni. On the other hand, Thethi's admiration seemed to grow along with his curiosity about these foreign ways.

Nebra joined the group, and made a joke…bragging about how he had saved all of them. Qenu and Ti jousted back at him, reminding him that the Pharaoh, himself, had saved him.

Thethi urged Nebra on. "Oh, tell more about *that!*"

Smiling broadly, Nebra began, "I had killed many of the enemy and the Pharaoh admired my strength and courage. I had recommended a strategy for the battle with the Mitanni. Our Pharaoh liked it and he tried it, but as I was fighting valiantly…at least 20 Mitanni armored soldiers against just me…a whole unit was caught between the River Euphrates and their advancing troops. I was glorious in battle but I was so outnumbered."

He looked over toward Hatasu to see if she was impressed. "Just when I thought a Mitanni soldier was going to run me through with his sword…there was the mighty Pharaoh! In his grand, golden chariot of Amun, he swept through the tangled mess of fighting men and with his mighty bow, he shot an arrow straight into the heart of the enemy, freeing me to kill the other 19 enemy soldiers, myself."

The group around him laughed good-naturedly. "Yes, you and at least sixty others of your troop."

"But of course!" he said, as though that was what he'd meant all along.

Thethi was impressed with his story and that pleased Nebra, but he kept looking at Hatasu. The group moved on to other stories with different soldiers. Nebra moved closer to Hatasu and began to speak, "Beautiful Princess, I have heard great things about you. I am honored that you are present to see me receive this award."

The hard lines around his mouth melted when he said sweet words but they reappeared quickly when he was still. She felt uncomfortable and glanced to the dais where her parents remained seated. Her father was watching this interaction. He neither smiled nor frowned. He just watched.

She sensed Nebra wanted something from her. She didn't like the way it felt to be near him, so she excused herself and looked for an escape from the crowded room. She edged her way toward the garden. She would have preferred if Thethi had come with her but he was enthralled with the stories. He was resisting Paheri's urgings for him to retire and save his strength.

She went out to the garden by herself. The area around the lotus pool was amazingly quiet after the cacophony within the grand hall of the palace. She was relieved to be alone. It took a while for her eyes to adjust to the moonlight. She moved toward the edge of the pool to sit down; she found herself thinking of her grandmother, Seniseneb, back in Waset. *What would she think of all this? She would, as always, be proud of her son, the Pharaoh. What would she say about Nebra, with the handsome face and hard mouth?*

In her mind's ear, she imagined a conversation from home in Waset. *Satamun would say, "He acts as though he were in line to be the next Pharaoh."*

And Seniseneb would reply, curtly, "But he isn't."

Then it dawned on her. Nebra could see her as his ticket to becoming Pharaoh, just like her father, who by winning the favor of Princess Ahmose and being a military hero with Pharaoh Amenhotep, became Pharaoh Thutmose. That must be what Nebra had in mind. She felt very vulnerable, exposed to men's ambitions.

It was just then she noticed she was not alone. An old woman was sitting under one of the trees against the palace wall.

Chapter 31 - Miriam's Story

Hatasu looked closely at the woman in the garden, almost thinking it was her own beloved grandmother, Seniseneb. But no, this woman was older; her hair was whiter, her face more wrinkled and her shoulders more bent forward. She was sitting on a stone bench next to the lotus pool, her face turned up toward the moon. Hatasu noticed how the light and shadow animated her features as it danced through the leaves of the sycamore tree.

There was a girl sitting beside the old woman. She looked more closely and realized it was Mutsi! Hatasu's face lit up as she recognized her friend from the festival. Mutsi smiled shyly. The princess immediately forgot her worried thoughts of Nebra, for she immediately hoped that this was the great-grand mother who told the story about Sekenenre!

Mutsi gently tugged at her great-grandmother's arm and said, "This is the girl I met at the harvest. This is Hatasu."

Hatasu's smile was shy also, wondering what Mutsi thought after seeing Sitre's scene at the festival. Mutsi gave no clue that she realized Hatasu was the daughter of Pharaoh. Hatasu bowed and said, "Greetings, Grandmother."

The old woman pulled herself up to her full, seated stature. Looking toward Hatasu, she replied, "Greetings, young one. So you are the red-haired friend Mutsi told me of from the harvest?"

"Yes, we met at the festival. Why aren't you inside at the banquet?" Hatasu asked.

"Hathor's tree smells so lovely in the moonlight." She tilted her head back and breathed deeply of the fragrance. "The goddess is smiling on the Two Lands, tonight. Pharaoh has come home with a victory and my grandsons returned safely with the army. I am so grateful." Her voice quivered with her advanced age.

"We have much to celebrate but why aren't you listening to your grandsons' stories of the Levant, inside," Hatasu persisted.

"Oh, my old head is already too full of stories. And besides, stories of war bring…memories. Life is good, now." She shook her head slightly.

Was this her opening? She was afraid to ask. She might be told again that this story was 'unspeakable'.

Mutsi came to her rescue. "Grandmother, Hatasu wanted to know the story of Sekenenre."

There was a silence. Hatasu held her breath, wondering if she would really tell it, so she urged her on, "I am a lover of stories. Perhaps you would like to empty your head of a story for us. I would as soon listen to your stories as any of the warriors inside the hall."

The old woman scrutinized her again. "You are a lover of stories? …Hmmm, yes… And you want to know of Sekenenre." She put gnarled fingers over her lips, as though considering the situation. "Not many people want to be reminded of *that* story. Some say it would be better if that story were lost. But I, Miriam, think maybe not; maybe this next generation should know what could happen without a wise Pharaoh. It will help them be grateful for Thutmose and his protection."

Her eyes moved away from Hatasu's, and with darting glances, she looked behind her as though scanning the garden for trouble. She rocked slightly, settling into her seat on the stone bench. "This seems like a safe enough night. I will tell you about Sekenenre."

Hatasu and Mutsi seated themselves cross-legged on the warm stones at Miriam's feet. They each looked up into her moon-shadowed face. Hatasu would finally hear the story of her great grandfather.

"But, I must tell it as my story," Miriam began, "and I must start it before I ever heard of the great Sekenenre. I must start my story when I was a young girl, safe in the bosom of my family."

She brought her hands down to rest peacefully in her lap, leaning toward the upturned faces of the girls. "We lived here in the city of Ankh-Tawy among people of the Two Lands, like ourselves. But Apophis, the Hyksos ruler, took for himself the red crown of Lower Egypt." She spoke this with undisguised scorn in her voice as though *he* could be a Pharaoh to us.

"The year that I was fourteen, I had many suitors who flattered me with poems comparing my loveliness with that of a flower or a gazelle. That 'loveliness' became my curse, for once this Hyksos looked at me, he became intent that he should have me as his own." She drew her eyebrows together and shook her head to emphasize her objection.

Hatasu searched her face for the remnants of this youthful beauty through the wrinkles and sags. She found it in the depths of her dark eyes.

"Now, my family had once been officials to the Pharaoh," she went on. "But then, those foreign kings raided the land. The father of Apophis moved through Ankh-Tawy with soldiers and never-before-seen chariots, and my father's family lost all its lands. My family never betrayed their allegiance to the true Pharaoh. My father told me his family learned to hate these invaders. He knew Maat frowned upon the passion of hatred but how could he not hate those who robbed his people of land and titles, and neglected and defiled their temples? My family saw many of their people suffer at the injustices brought by these strangers. Everywhere, chaos threatened to overwhelm the land because of the foreigners' strange ways. Hate and fear were rampant. Maat, herself, seemed lost to us. The sacred teachings and festivals honoring the goddesses and gods were forbidden. The Hyksos rulers deliberately created fear to force people to bend to their will."

Hatasu listened with a bit of impatience for the part about Sekenenre.

"When Apophis decided he wanted me, he threatened my father and mother. If they did not send me to him, he would increase their taxes to punish them. My mother and father said, 'No, you cannot have our daughter'. But Apophis raised the taxes so high there was no food for my younger brothers and sisters. Finally, my parents were without means to resist him, so Apophis's henchmen carried me away to his palace harem in Avaris. I remember the sounds of my mother's wailing above my own panicked screams."

She stopped and was silent for moments, wringing her hands, twisting them tightly into each other. Hatasu held her breath, forgetting for the moment about Sekenenre. She was shocked at the terror this woman must have felt being pulled away from her mother.

The grandmother began again, "When I arrived, the Hyksos women's quarters were a frightening place for a young girl of the Two Lands, but not as frightening as the palace kitchen where I was sent when Apophis lost interest in me. My family had been educated scribes so my father had taught me to read and write when I was quite young. This gave me an advantage with the kitchen staff and I soon stood out as capable. Standing out was not a good thing in the Hyksos court. Apophis came to me in the kitchen and ordered me to poison the food of an opponent. I tried to refuse but he threatened to kill my family. His political enemies found out about the plan and escaped before they ate the food I had poisoned."

Here she paused for so long, Hatasu thought she had stopped her story before ever getting to the Sekenenre part. But suddenly the old woman started pounding her fisted hand against her knee. "But Apophis killed my father in front of me. He said it was to teach me a lesson for trying to disobey him," her voice spit venom.

Just as suddenly as this statement erupted from her, she crumbled into herself, her head in her hands. Hatasu could hear the ache of her wounded heart in her moans. This behavior frightened Hatasu. She wanted to ease Miriam's pain but didn't know how. Her mind raced. She thought of her fears for her own father's death when he was at war…but he was the Divine Pharaoh. That kind of thing couldn't happen to him.

Mutsi moved to the bench closer to her grandmother offering soothing words. "You do not have to tell us more," her granddaughter said.

Miriam sat silently for a long while, her breathing deepening and slowing. Eventually, she placed her hands deliberately on her lap, leaned toward Mutsi and said, "No, it is better if I tell it." Her voice was firm. "These things must be known. I tell it to you because this land must never let down its watchfulness nor lower its defense against those who, without the wisdom of Ra, do such acts of cruelty."

The old woman wrapped her arms around her frail body and she stared off into the distance for a moment before she began again, "After that, I was unable to do any kind of work because the terrible nightmares kept me awake all night and awful thoughts chased me through the day. Useless to him, he kicked me out of the palace altogether and I wandered the streets begging for food. There was no family, no temple, no gods and no priests to go to for help. No courts for justice."

The princess's heart burned with anger at the meanness of Apophis.

"It was at that low point in my life, that I first heard of Sekenenre." Miriam's voice softened, here. "He was the ray of hope in the darkness all around me. He was the rightful Pharaoh, the son of Ra. He had gathered an army of men to free the people from this foreign impostor. I gathered what rag-tag bits of hope I could and I prayed to the goddess. I huddled with other disenfranchised souls living in the streets of Avaris and listened to the urgings of Maki, a young man who said Sekenenre would arrive and free us."

Hatasu was glad the story had finally gotten to the Sekenenre. This was similar to the story she'd heard at the Festival of the

Ancestors in Waset. But just as she settled in to hear of her great-grandfather, Miriam's voice rose, loud and angry. "What kind of a people does not honor the dead?"

Hatasu startled at the sudden expletive.

"Well, not these barbarians. The Hyksos violated every code of decency."

Hatasu and Mutsi looked at each other, wondering *what* she was talking about.

"Sekenenre did indeed come, just as Ra said he would. He surrounded the city and began the siege. Apophis realized he had underestimated this Southern Prince, so he agreed to settle the conflict by hand-to-hand combat. It was to be a battle between Apophis and Sekenenre, a fight of honor. Sekenenre's army stood a distance behind him and Apophis's army stood to his back. I found a place on a wall, far from the contest, for I was intent to watch."

She breathed out loudly, jerking her head from side to side. "Woe to me, that my eyes ever beheld such a tragedy! Apophis's generals viciously violated the agreement and attacked Sekenenre. They came forward with axes and clubs and spears. Defenseless against such treachery, he lay lifeless in the center of the square for only a second, and as must have been preplanned, Apophis' men captured the body and carried it inside the walled city."

Her head was shaking vehemently now, as if to deny this event actually happened. Her whole body trembled. "Apophis laughed. Yes, he actually laughed!" She started rocking back and forth. "It is that sound that most haunts my dreams." She put her hands over her ears and pulled her head down to her lap. "I think I will never be free of it."

Hatasu sat numbly in the silent moon shadow. She didn't know what to say. *And how was she to understand that Sekenenre had been betrayed and murdered? Why hadn't the god Amun come to the aid of his son, the Pharaoh?*

Miriam regained her composure, while Hatasu was still battling with these ideas. "An attempt was made to rescue his body immediately, but the Hyksos forces had the advantage of surprise. Queen Ahhotep and Prince Kamose petitioned Apophis for the body. He denied them access to it. He placed the decaying khat of the Pharaoh high on the wall, in full view, but out of reach. The Hyksos prevented the mummification of the body in order to torture the entire nation with a 'lesson'. He said, 'Your magic is gone! All magic is now in me…Apophis!'"

Hatasu felt dizzy, as though she were spinning. She reached out and put her hand firmly on the ground, reassuring herself the earth itself was not actually moving. This information…it didn't have anyplace to 'fit' in her mind.

Miriam was still speaking. "I heard of schemes to get the body. For days, no one had any luck. Finally, a group of loyal men residing inside the city succeeded in stealing the corpse and in a daring move they brought it to Kamose, Sekenenre's son. Kamose escaped with it to the south where he could prepare his father for his journey to the stars. Several of the brave men who recovered the khat of Sekenenre weren't able to escape with Kamose. They were caught, killed, and left hanging upside-down at the gate of the city as a warning to the rest of us of what happens to those who aid the southern Pharaoh."

Hatasu was stunned. *So this was the 'unspeakable?'* She felt nausea in her stomach. *How could this be? Apophis was wrong! A Pharaoh is Divine, a son of Ra himself, but how could it be that he did not have enough magical power to protect himself?* The very idea that this could have happened, turned her world upside-down.

No wonder her mother didn't want her to know this story. That night before her father went to war, he had reassured her mother that 'it could never happen again', but the cruel Asiatic foreigner had indeed again overcome the protective magic of both her brother, Amenmose, and her royal cousin, Tao. She looked back at Miriam, who was silent now.

The old woman's eyes were closed, and she seemed drawn into herself. She started shaking her head and whimpering, "No Apophis! "Stop!"

Hatasu stared at her, sorry she'd ever asked her to suffer the telling of these memories.

Mutsi put her hand on her grandmother's arm, and called her name. Miriam pulled away and shouted louder, "No! Apophis, No!"

Mutsi called her name louder. She shook her arm gently, as though waking her from a dream.

Hatasu remembered what she saw happen to Tao. Sihathor told her. 'Set binds the person to the moment he wishes he could change'. Perhaps that is what was happening to Miriam so she said, "Grandmother, the Hyksos are gone. You are here in the Pharaoh's garden. You are safe now."

Miriam stopped murmuring. She opened her eyes and looked

straight at Hatasu. Then, with frightened eyes, she looked around the garden. Gradually her body relaxed and she nodded gently at familiar objects.

Hatasu said, "Rest now. Let the story be."

"This is really the Pharaoh's garden?" Miriam asked.

"Yes, Grandmother, you are really safe here."

"The mashmashu demons of that night still have the power to grab my ba and bring me back to those wretched moments. It is like a nightmare that swallows me up when I am wide awake."

Hatasu reassured her again, "You don't have to tell us any more."

Miriam looked around again, nodding at the sycamore tree and moonlit path. "No, it is better if I tell the rest of the story. I will not let the Hyksos magic win. I will not let them keep me stuck in the horror. I must tell the good ending. I must go on."

The old grandmother pushed her chin up high. "The world plunged into blackness that night with the irreverent death of our holy hope. But gradually, bits of news came of Kamose." Her body relaxed into the stone bench. Her eyes looked directly at the children. She went on. "Valiantly, Kamose continued the fight. News, often no more than rumors, spread through the walled city but they offered hope and promise. We rejoiced when Kamose arrived with a new army but he was driven back and soon after that news arrived that he, too, died.

"Again, great darkness filled the land but messages still came from the Queen Ahhotep. This kept hope alive. In the ten inundations that followed these tragic events, there was misery and drudgery, but we knew there was still a royal family in whom we could hope, and this encouraged a group of us inside the walls of Avaris to plan for the overthrow of these ka-killing foreigners.

"I was part of a spy system that used codes to communicate with messengers of Queen Ahhotep to prepare for the eventual defeat of Apophis. It was like the dry season, when the river is low. The waters of hope were scarce but as long as there was a trickle, we could survive. There were times I don't know how I managed, between the terrors at night, and the memories during the day.

"No doubt, I survived because of the love of Maki, the brave and noble man who became my husband. He worked within the Hyksos city as a spy for Ahhotep, mapping weaknesses in the fortifications, secretly storing up primitive weapons and getting messages to Ahhotep of political weaknesses in the Hyksos king. He gave us his hope, as well as his love, and through those years we had three sons. He held me and reassured me when the demons chased me at night, and he taught me to focus on the future I wanted for my sons, during the day.

"News began to trickle in that Ahhotep's youngest son, Ahmose, had come of age and was preparing an army. Our hopes were renewed. Surely this time, with our help, he would at last be able to overcome these monsters. It was a glorious day when we first spied the army of Ahmose, the Liberator, from the city walls of Avaris."

Miriam's voice had gotten firm and strong again and she sat up straight in the moonlight. "The army of the true Pharaoh encircled the city. He laid siege and it took weeks. Water and food were scarce. We, still bound to the Hyksos, were unable to leave the city so we used every means we could imagine to sabotage our enemy from within. Finally the siege worked, and out of food and water, Apophis tried to escape into the night. He tried to slip away at night, unseen…a coward trying to save himself.

"We let Pharaoh Ahmose know of his plan and the army of the Two Lands chased him all the way to the Asiatic city of Sharuhem and made sure he would never come back. It was Queen Ahhotep who flung open the doors of the cursed city of Avaris, releasing us from our years of confinement in the sorted world of the Asiatic foreigners. We returned to my family's ancestral lands and reclaimed them from Hyksos overlords.

"Pharaoh Ahmose renewed the Temple of Ptah and reopened the Temple of Sekhmet. We were able to send our sons to temple schools and our grandchildren are again able to learn the wisdom of our ancestors. Our rightful Pharaoh and Queen led us into a time of peace, bringing justice back into the land and rebuilding our temples to our goddesses and gods.

"One of my grandsons went to Heliopolis and became a priest of Ra, another became a general in the army, and a third, Mutsi's father, became a merchant."

She tightened her arm around her great-grand daughter. "I am an old woman, now. I've seen 75 inundations and four Pharaohs. Thutmose is a good Pharaoh. He maintains peace at home and protects us from our enemies."

Surely these Hyksos were the abomination of the gods! Hatasu understood anew why her father had to go and fight the foreigners. He would not let them treat the people of the Two Lands like that again. She glowed with love and admiration for Ahhotep. She set the thought in her heart that she, too, would work for her people as her great-grandmother had. Never again, as long as she could prevent it, would such evil overwhelm the people of her land.

Miriam smiled at the two children as she ended this tale. "You must always be grateful that you are able to worship at the temple festivals."

She smiled in the direction of her granddaughter. "I think it is time for me to go home. By this telling, the goddess has freed me from the burden of these memories!"

"I will remember the story and am grateful for what we have now," said Mutsi.

Hatasu bowed as a sign of respect for her and her story. "Thank you for the story, Grandmother." Hatasu watched as Mutsi guided her grandmother's steps toward the palace gate.

She stayed in the garden, with the shadows looking like images of Hyksos with demon faces. She didn't know what she had expected to hear about Sekenenre. *Adventure? Magic? Certainly not a tale that threatened the divinity of the Pharaoh! Why hadn't Sekenenre's magic and his spiritual power been strong enough to save him?*

That night, she awoke with a terrifying nightmare of a hideous demon-man who was chasing her. He dragged behind him a body she knew was Sekenenre. Many people were looking on, crying. They were all bound in loose mummy wrappings; only their faces were showing and they each had the same fright in their eyes Miriam had. She could hear their cries, 'No, Apophis, No'. The

Hyksos-faced demon laughed at them. 'You are all bound to me….bound to the moment you wish you could change….bound to me by your fear and hatred'. His laughter rang out, again.

Hatasu screamed in her sleep. Ahmose came running. Hatasu tried to hide her knowledge of Sekenenre when she told the dream. "It was terrible. A mashmashu demon was chasing me…dragging the body of an ancestor Pharaoh behind him. Many people were crying and they were bound up, wrapped around and around like mummies, with live heads, crying, 'No, Stop, No!'"

Her mother held her close and comforted her. Once she was calm again, she asked, "You heard the story of Sekenenre, didn't you?"

Hatasu looked down at her bedclothes. She was distressed at the displeasure in her mother's voice. "An old woman told me the story. She said telling it reminds us to never let down our watchfulness, nor allow such treachery to come to our land again."

"Your father's army has protected us from the return of such treachery without the need of telling that story. The Wise Ones of Old teach us to not speak of these things because those images of fear and hatred empower those demons, like they just did in your dream," Ahmose told her.

"Mother, I am sorry I didn't follow your instructions. But…but…why didn't Sekenenre have enough magic, as a son of Ra?"

"Sekenenre's magic was good but what we have learned about these northern invaders is we must have greater physical manifestation of power, as well as the spirit manifestation of it.

That's why the Pharaoh's army has the horse and chariot, as well as the magic wax figures. It was, for us, another lesson in the teachings 'As above, so below'."

Hatasu thought about it for a minute, then asked, "Why, then, did Amenmose get killed…like Sekenenre…and why did Tao get maimed? Father told you what happened to Sekenenre couldn't happen again!"

"Death and wounding is part of war on this earth level below. Neither initiation nor enlightenment protects any of us from death. We all must die. It is death by treachery in battle that your father said wouldn't happen again…in this war."

"But what about the poor people like old Miriam who still suffer from those demons of fear and hatred in their lives?"

"It is sad, indeed."

Hatasu looked to her mother and said, "When I am a Queen like you, I want to help people with nightmares, like old Miriam. Is there a way for Miriam to get rid of those awful memories, like the medicine that get rid of parasites that cause the blood-in-the-urine disease?"

Her mother said, "Healing priests have herbs that help, but it is the temples of the gods, and the festivals of the seasons that do the most to keeps people's minds focused on their attunement to the Great Above. That is what most helps a sad and frightened mind to heal."

"Then, that is what father must see to. The ruined temples must be rebuilt and everyone must be able to go to the festivals."

Her mother nodded, as she tucked her into bed again.

As Hatasu fell off to sleep, she knew her world had changed. She had passed out of childhood. The story of Sekenenre showed that divine magic was not enough, as she once thought it was. No one was truly safe. Of itself, it was not sufficient for her survival. She'd have to be cleverer and more skillful in the Above and in the Below. She wondered how she would do it.

Chapter 32 - The Elephant Hunt

In the morning, Hatasu took her throw-stick out to the practice field. She didn't want to think about the events of the night before. Another child might have been frightened by her realizations but she thought of her great-grandmother, Ahhotep. *How did she manage? Did she find ways to align with both the above and below...spiritual and physical...protection?* However she did it, Hatshepsut would find a way to understand Ahhotep's wisdom; she, too, would protect herself and her people.

Her mind moved into greater resolve as she hit her target, again and again. Finally tired and her arm sore, she walked back through the warming morning air to find her father and show him her accomplishment with the weapon. She longed to be comforted by his presence. Hatasu found her father in her mother's room. She stood at the door and watched as he paced back and forth, his hands folded behind his back and his head looking down toward the floor.

"Protecting the land from foreigners is not enough. It is my responsibility to bring Maat to the people," he was saying adamantly.

She stood there, part eaves-dropping, part waiting to be invited in. The Pharaoh went on, "A clear succession must be assured now. Everyone can tell how sick Thethi had been. At the banquet he was so pale and thin."

"Yes, my Dear," said Ahmose, "Thethi's illness has given us great worry."

"My point is...is it wise to name another heir who might die before he reached the throne? There are already rumors that the loss of the two sons I've named heirs is being interpreted as a bad omen."

"There was the oracle. The Ka of Ptah bowed to Hatasu. Some of the priests interpret that as she is favored to be your heir."

"Yes, yes, you spoke of that. I think that could be the solution." He rubbed his chin and looked at her thoughtfully. "She is healthy and strong. She shows promise in magic skill with her dreaming. I see signs of enlightened leadership and interest in the workings of politics. She certainly is dear to my heart."

Ahmose let out a heavy sigh. "I wish you could see another way, Thutmose. Such a role would be hard for any woman. There are those who would oppose her but whatever your decision, Hatasu or Thethi, it will set the quibbling to rest for now."

Thutmose rubbed his chin thoughtfully. "Well…I have another possible idea."

Just then, Ahmose spotted Hatasu. "Ah, my dear, how are you feeling this morning?"

"I've come to find Father to have him come see how good I've gotten at the throw-stick."

"Very fine, daughter, but I will have to see that later. I must go now to a meeting with the mayors and governors about the sedition in Itjtawy. Perhaps this afternoon we could go to the practice field together."

The afternoon passed with Hatasu waiting but her father never came out of the meeting room. Many servants entered and exited carrying papyrus book, messages, food and drink. She figured she'd get to see him at dinner. She knew she would feel better if she were with him.

Dinners before the war were usually just the immediate family: Her mother, father, brothers and herself. Sitre informed her dinner this night would be in the banquet hall. When she got there, she was surprised to see so many guests. There was Ibana and Pennekheb, Ineni and his family, and Hapu and his. She was most surprised to see the mayor, Rahotep, and his son, Nebra. Hatasu took her seat next to Thethi.

The conversation was full of military jokes, comradely laughter and boasting of war exploits. Hatasu watched as her father smiled at Nebra and laughed at his jokes. Even worse, Nebra kept smiling in her direction. Each time she looked away with a scowl, hoping it would discourage him.

Thethi, on the other hand, kept looking over at Nebra and pulled himself up to his full sitting height as he mimicked Nebra's straight warrior posture. Thethi laughed loudly at a joke Nebra made about the lack of formality at meals out on the campaign. Nebra, however, was only coolly polite to him and dodged his questions about soldierly life in the field.

After the meal...and several passes of the wine jug...the conversation turned to stories. "How about that elephant hunt!" Ibana said. He pushed Pennekheb with his elbow. "Not bad for an old soldier, if I do say so my self."

"Not bad at all, Old Friend." Thutmose gave out a hearty laugh.

"That creature sure was quite a giant!" Pennekheb said.

"What's an elephant?" Hatasu asked.

"It is the biggest creature I have *ever* seen!" said Hapuseneb's brother.

"And it gave us the best hunt!" another young general added.

"Certainly did!" said Ibana.

"What happened? How did you come to hunt this elephant?" asked Ahmose.

"Ah…would all of you like to hear the story?"

"Oh, yes!" the women and children of the group replied.

"Well, I shall tell you the story of my elephant hunt." Thutmose sat back on his throne and leaned over on the right arm of his chair.

Hatasu settled herself into a comfortable position for listening to her father's story. She so loved just being in his presence and watching his charismatic interchange with the others.

The Pharaoh began, "An elephant is bigger than any animal we have here in the Two Lands, even bigger than a hippopotamus. It stands almost as tall as a tree, it is all gray, and it has a long nose that goes way out in front of her. Its legs are like tree trunks, ears large and flapping like the sails on a ship and a tiny tail like a rope. Strangest of all, it has giant white horns that grow out of its mouth. These animals live in great herds on the marshy plains in the part of the Levant called Amurru.

"After we did battle with Barratarna, King of the Mitanni in Naharin, and he signed an agreement of respect and peace, he asked me to seal the treaty with a royal elephant hunt. These Mitanni are fierce in war and I had to outdo him in the hunt also, in order to maintain the respect that would keep the peace. We came upon a herd of these creatures at the border of the area of our treaty.

"A hunter must know his animal, its habits, its likes and dislikes, what will lure it and what will enrage it. In our travels, I had watched these herds from afar with fascination but I knew Barratarna knew them much better. One might think that because they are so big, they can't move quickly…or one might think that because the herd is led by an elephant cow that there is no danger…or one might think that because they seem so peaceful when eating in their herds, they can't pose a threat. But, I had seen two elephants fight with their tusks. I knew these beliefs were wrong.

"These brave generals," Thutmose nodded to Ibana and Pennekheb, who nodded back, laughing. "They said to me, 'No, no, this is not a good creature to hunt. It is too dangerous'. But I said, 'Yes, yes, I will hunt this animal and I will kill it in front of the King of the Mitanni'. Indeed I did!" Then, smiling and looking around the table, he added, "And my generals hunted with me." Their voices rose in cheer.

"We went after the biggest elephant, the head of the herd. I mounted my chariot and took my best composite bow and straightest arrows, and I trotted my horses out toward the herd, along with Barratarna and his generals. We all moved forward slowly until we got close to the biggest one. The Mitanni sent a decoy out in front of this apparent leader of the herd; she took the bait and started to run. With that, we raced our chariots alongside each other, until we were beside the huge animal. From that vantage point, Barratarna shot!

"The animal staggered at first, but then turned on the king and started to chase him, almost touching him with his tusks. Three of his generals drove up on the other side of this mountain of an animal and finished him off, pummeling him with arrows until he fell with a tremendous thud."

Hatasu's eyes were wide as she listened.

"I thought I had lost the opportunity to outdo my opponent. But then…out of nowhere…there came charging at incredible speed, the largest animal I had ever seen. She was so large, I thought, truly, she was a goddess herself. Surely, no creature could be that big. When she ran, her huge feet made the earth shake. She let out a bellow that made my ears hurt. As she crossed the field, I saw the passion of rage in her eyes. It was like flames reaching across the distance, attacking me even before her huge body could carry her to my destruction.

"In my heart, I called out to Amun, 'I am your son! I can feel your power! This hunt I do for you. I do it for your honor!' I instructed my chariot driver, Nebra, here, to move my horses forward as though I was going to charge right into the creature; but a few feet in front of her, Nebra veered to the left, giving me full view of the beast's side. I shot her in the neck as we moved past. The plan worked! Nebra was as brave as any soldier I've ever fought with. With nerves of iron, he drove the chariot straight toward the charging elephant and veered at just the right second. The elephant's bulk was too immense for her to be able to make a turn after us, just as I had calculated. She immediately fell from the force of just one of my arrows."

Hatasu's small body was tense with the anticipation, urgency and the danger of the tale. His magic had been enough, that day.

Thutmose then relaxed and smiled as he continued. "Our men ate well of elephant meat that night. Barratarna honored me by cutting the tusks from the elephant he had fallen and ceremoniously presented them to me. He said, 'I, too, should honor a god who could hunt so valiantly and so well'."

The men cheered again and turned to each other re-telling their own part in the great hunt.

"There will never be another hunt like that one!" said Ibana.

"Those are true words, old friend," said the Pharaoh. "But we have different kind of hunts here. It is not necessary to impress enemy warriors. No, on the Nile we hunt to impress the goddess and our womenfolk."

After a few moments pause, Thutmose added, "In two days, I will convene the tribunal that will hear the cases of those accused of treason while I was gone. Before that, I think we should relax with just such a duck hunt with the ladies." There were nods of approval and a buzz of families making plans, for the hunting of these waterfowl was a sport for the whole family.

Thutmose then, taking another drink from his wine goblet, tapped his goblet with his ring until he had everyone's attention again. "I have an announcement to make. I have decided to make a presentation to the young hero, Nebra." Holding his drinking mug high now, he said, "To the brave charioteer, Nebra, I wish to give a fine reed duck-hunting boat with which to join the hunt in the marsh tomorrow."

Hatasu was shocked! She realized that by this gift, he was also letting it be known that he was considering Nebra as his heir to the throne. Thethi choked on his food. Nebra accepted with a huge smile.

With his chest puffed out, understanding the full meaning of this gift, he leaned toward Hatasu. "If it would please Your Majesty, I would be greatly honored if I could have the pleasure of having the lovely Hatshepsut in my humble boat."

Hatasu wanted to scream, "No!" She felt the hairs on her arms stand up at the thought of being on a boat with Nebra. She so wanted to go on the bird hunt…but with her father, not this bragging, grandiose boy-man. She wanted to revert to the temper tantrums she would have used at four-years-old but she tried to be more diplomatic. "I thank you," she said in her most queenly manner, "but I prefer to go on the boat with my parents."

"Nonsense, Hatasu," came her father's booming voice. "You will be perfectly safe with this hero of our land. I wish that you to become better acquainted with Nebra."

Chapter 33 – The Duck Hunt

She was trapped. Yes, this meant without a doubt that her father had set this up and he wanted her to marry Nebra and to make him the next Pharaoh. *But what about Thethi?* She stared at her father with her jaw set but she knew there was nothing more to be said…at the moment.

She excused herself from the table and went directly to the women's quarters so Nebra could not follow her. She plopped herself on a mat at the base of a pillar to consider what to do about her predicament.

Who then should walk in, but her cousin Meryt. "Hatasu," she said, "why are you here all alone when you could be with that dreamy Nebra? Isn't he the handsomest of all the men? You are so lucky that your father likes him…and that he likes you!"

Hatasu looked at her through squinting, suspicious eyes. "Well, I don't feel lucky! I feel like a knucklebone to be moved around the senet board. I do not want to go in Nebra's boat tomorrow!"

"How can you say that? What I wouldn't give to go in his boat, pick lotus blossoms for him and admire his manly beauty."

"Well, I wish you could go for me. I don't like him. Yes, he is handsome, and yes, he is a war hero…but his bragging and all the attention he gives to me are like a fancy kilt with glittery trim just to impress. He wants to be Pharaoh and I'm just his way of getting what he wants."

"Surely not! What a mean thing to say about such a handsome hero. If you don't like Nebra, is there someone else you do like?"

"For me, my choice has always had to be someone who could be a Pharaoh, someone as grand and royal as Ra himself, for he would need to be the Son of Ra, like my father. I would have liked it to have been Wadjmose." She paused, a look of sadness coming over her serious, young face. Then shaking her head, she stood up and headed for her room. She said over her shoulder, "I thought it would be Thethi, not some stranger." She went to her room to consider what she would say to her father in the morning so he would change his mind and let her go in the boat with him.

The next morning, Thethi was not at breakfast. Hatasu sat next to her father. As he was eating his figs and bread, she looked up to him pleadingly, "Please do not make me go in the boat with Nebra."

"Don't talk nonsense. You are soon to be a young woman. It is time for you to enjoy the attentions of a suitable young man in the duck hunt."

"But I don't like him!" She decided not to bring up the matter of Thethi.

"Hatasu, he is a fine soldier, well able to organize and plan successfully. Don't you find him handsome?"

"Yes, but that doesn't mean I like him."

"Perhaps you could learn to like him?"

"Why should I have to?"

He stopped and put his piece of bread back on his plate. "I have my reasons, child. For today, I want you to conduct yourself with royal dignity and seek out his good qualities."

He was neither going to relent on this directive, nor admit his plan of naming Nebra his heir. She frowned and her lower lip protruded out in a pout. *Why couldn't her father tell something wasn't right about Nebra?* Unable to escape her fate in this matter, she determined to do the best she could. To make the trip more tolerable, she decided to take along the throw-stick. It would impress her father that she had learned to throw so well. He would be able to see this, even if she was in Nebra's boat.

The Pharaoh led the royal family to the quay. Hatasu held her mother's hand. The Queen had been oddly quiet about the situation of Hatasu going with Nebra.

The atmosphere was gay as the select group of nobles of Ankh-Tawy gathered at the harbor quay with their reed boats. Besides Nebra and his father, Ineni was there with Nefermose. Hapu and Ahhotep were there. Saamun was there with Asat. Of course, Ibana was there. As head of the royal navy, he was in his glory on the water. Qenu was present with Tutkharit.

As they approached the reed boats, Nebra bowed low before his Pharaoh and Ahmose. He then offered a second bow to Hatasu. She acknowledged it with a nod. After that little bit of encouragement, he offered his hand to help her step into his boat. His hand was moist, cold and clammy. She withdrew her hand as quickly as she could, without offending her father. She looked to her mother in the Pharaoh's boat, so she could copy what she was doing. Hatasu placed herself in the goddess position of kneeling on one knee with the other knee up to steady herself. Her mother smiled and waved to the relatives in the other boats. Hatasu did the same.

The boats were made of the fine, bound reeds. They were

broadest in the middle, giving plenty of room for the women to sit. The bow extended out over the water ahead of them, held together with cords colored lapis, carnelian and turquoise. The stern end extended off the water at an angle, again bound in similar colored cords.

Nakht was present with a small contingent of Medjay, a necessary precaution until the matter of the rebels was decided. Everyone was dressed in the finest clothes. Men wore startlingly white kilts and gleaming neck collars. Women wore their best wigs, linen sheaths and brightly colored neck collars. Duck hunts were neither strenuous not dangerous. This was a family social event.

Hatasu had been on duck hunts in the marshes of the south but never in the Delta marshes. In Waset, the marshes were flatter, more covered with lotus, with only the occasional inlet where papyrus grew tall. Many of those trips had been with Wadj. The marshes in Abedju, which she had explored with Puyemre, were also more like mud flats, as she had been there only shortly after the inundation.

As they headed downriver toward the great reed marshes of the delta, the Pharaoh's boat led the way and Nebra's boat was next. All the men had their throw-sticks tucked into the waists of their kilts as they poled their skiffs downriver. Hatasu looked to her father. She thought to herself, *"Now that is handsome."*

She looked back at Nebra. His muscles rippled under his bronzed skin. He tried to enter into light conversation with her. "Why do you bring a throw-stick, my lovely one? It is not the usual ornament of a lady and I have my own trusty stick, renowned for bringing down marsh birds."

"I did not bring it for you. I brought it for me."

"But surely you do not intend to hunt! This is the sport of men. The princess is more suited for simply enjoying the fruit of the hunt, presented her by her suitor."

She looked at him tensely, saying, "This princess looks to the goddess Isis and to her great-grandmother Ahhotep. Each was skilled at the throw-stick." He was so audacious to refer to himself as 'her man'.

Nebra held his tongue for a minute in shocked silence. Then, he continued, "Those were wild and desperate times, both when Isis fought Set and when Ahhotep fought the Hyksos. Maat rules again, and it is no longer necessary for females to fight."

Hatasu noted that he knew his history, even if he didn't understand her nature. She said, "Well, my father doesn't seem to agree with you, for he has blessed my soldierly training." She noticed a slight shake of his head, as though in disbelief. A mischievous thought jumped into her mind. If he wanted to talk, she'd talk to him. She said, "You are truly a brave man to invite me on your boat, Nebra."

"This is not bravery but pleasure, beautiful Princess. Bravery was for the war in the Levant. Now, I have the delight of the duck-hunt." Talking of his bravery relaxed him a bit. His smile softened the line of his jaw but did little to alter the glint in his eye.

With great, pretended seriousness, she went on, "You mean you are not aware of the danger of courting this princess? Surely, you know of the curse."

He paused a moment, the tension re-gathering in his shoulders. He said stiffly, as though his line was practiced, "I am aware only of your loveliness. Surely, one as blessed by the goddess as you, is joking if you speak of a curse."

"Oh, you don't know." She looked down and shook her head, as though overcome by shyness. "I did not mean to alarm you." She tried to hide from him the twinkle of glee in her eyes.

"No, no, my dear, a soldier as brave in war as I am, is not easily scared. Do tell me."

"It is not complicated," she said in an airy fashion. "It is just that anyone who courts me will be cursed with an early death. Already, this has been true, for you know both of my brothers have died very young." She watched him from the corner of her eye and noticed with satisfaction that he pulled back a bit from her. She went on, "If it seemed to you that I have been avoiding you, it was only to protect you from this terrible fate."

"I have no fear of such things as curses," he said, though without conviction. "I wear the great amulet of Montu." He watched her warily out of the corner of his eye as he continued to pole towards the marsh.

She was grateful that his conversation slowed. Just then, the marsh thickets came into view. With Nebra's chatter slowed by his thoughtful distraction, Hatasu was free to enjoy the delights of nature. The many busy birds filled the marsh with their chirping, quacking, squawking sounds as they went about their business of gathering food. The papyrus thickets spread out over a great distance, stalks tall, swaying above the heads of the men standing on the boats. As their boat approached the thicket, she momentarily forgot her boating companion and looked up at the papyrus umbels swaying in the gentle northern breeze, supported by their slender reed stems.

There was a great teeming commotion of life behind the wall of green growth. They came to an opening in the reed bed. A wide avenue formed, allowing the boats to enter the thicket. Great walls of green rose on both sides of Hatasu's boat, towering over her. The sound of the birds was so loud; she could not hear anything else. The quacking of ducks, the honking of geese and the *poo-poo* call of the Hoopoe bird…all these sounds seemed to swallow her up. She found this exhilarating and exciting.

As more of the skiffs moved into the water avenue, the birds became agitated and grew still louder. After a brief look to the princess to see how she was doing, Nebra put his hand on the throw-stick at his belt, ready for the Pharaoh to start the hunt.

Hatasu watched as her father ceremoniously took his throw-stick from his belt. Masterly, and with the most excellent form, Pharaoh Thutmose took the first aim at one of a number of ducks that exploded into the air when a servant rustled the umbels. Raising his right hand high above his head, he hurled the throw-stick at the duck in the center. It found its mark and hit the duck right on the neck. The stick immediately found its way back to his boat.

The people in the other boats gave out a cheer and each man let fly his own throw-stick. Hatasu took her stick from her decorative belt and, like Nebra and the other men in the nearby boats, she stood poised to throw. A distinct look of distaste came over Nebra's face. Clearly, he expected her to miss but her throw was straight and true. Down came her duck. He mumbled under his breath in tones of disapproval. Nebra's throw-stick hit his target with a great deal of force, actually opening the neck, and causing the bird to bleed. This was *not* considered good form.

The others, Ibana, Ineni, and Hapu, each caught up in their own hunt, registered neither surprise nor irregularity at Hatasu's participation. Hapuseneb was also putting their throw-stick practice to the test, but Merit and Isis, on their parents' boat, kept the demure posture of the traditional female. Only Rahotep seemed to notice Hatasu's behavior. He frowned in the direction of his son. To Hatasu's pleasure, Nebra's tension grew.

There was a growing excitement in the air around them. Hatasu cheered like the other women when the hunters got their prey. Boats moved into the thicket to collect the ducks. As they did so, more birds flew up into the air. It was then, that she saw the hoopoe with its pinkish-brown plumage, black and white wings, and erect crest. It flew into the sky and she witnessed the full drama of the patterning of its feathers.

She looked back. Nebra was more impressed with the bloody duck he had killed. He backed the boat out of the thicket and he held the gory creature high for her to admire. She put on an exaggerated show of admiration, just enough so he knew she was mocking him. The cold light came into his eyes again. They traveled farther into the marsh, waiting for the next opportunity to down a duck.

This was a leisurely time to enjoy nature. Hatasu turned her thoughts to the appreciation of the marsh birds. She exclaimed with delight when she saw the large pied kingfisher hover over the water before diving after a fish dinner, its black and white feathers a blur. It returned to the surface with a fish speared in its long, black beak.

She was even more excited when she saw the small flash of iridescent blue contrasting with the orange belly. She recognized the small kingfisher and called out to Hapuseneb and Meryt in their nearby boats to see it, too. They shared her excitement. But Nebra took aim again, setting his sights on that same small kingfisher. Hatasu saw the throw-stick hit its neck and she let out a shriek of horror as it fell into the marsh. She looked back at Nebra, who was standing in the boat with a self-satisfied look. He had done this deliberately to get back at her.

She angrily said, "Duck hunts are not for killing kingfishers!"

"Oh Princess, I did not mean to offend you! I meant to impress you. It was so much smaller than a duck, so it took more skill." He said this with mock sincerity. The servant brought the bird's limp body back to the boat. He offered it to her. "Because you admired it so, I wished only to offer it to you as a gift."

The appalled look on her face seemed to delight him. "I do not want such a gift," she said, unemotionally pushing it away toward the other ducks. She turned her head away from him, directing her focus toward the marsh wildlife.

It wasn't long before Hatasu spotted an ichneumon, sleek and brown like a cat, climbing a stalk of papyrus and heading for a purple gallinule, a fairly large bird with a stout, bright-red bill and bluish-green plumage. The bird was busy feeding on young papyrus. It was tugging on the well-rooted marsh plants with its strong legs and then stripping off the greenery with its sturdy bill. It was oblivious to the approaching predator.

The princess watched. She reached for her throw-stick and aimed at ichneumon's hind leg. She had not noticed that Nebra had taken aim at a duck at the same time. Nebra threw his stick toward a fat, red-breasted goose, but at that moment Hatasu stood up to throw her stick. Her throw rocked the boat; her weapon found its mark and the marsh predator let out a screech…running off into the thicket and leaving a startled gallinule looking around.

In doing so, she tipped the boat in such a way that Nebra lost his balance, missed his target and tumbled backward. His loud splash drew her astonished attention away from the rapidly escaping ichneumon and the startled gallinule and she exclaimed in surprise when she saw him in the water. Laughter broke out in the other boats.

Nebra stood up in the shallow water, his fine kilt drenched and muddy from the river. His perfumed wig dripped into his eyes. She giggled, because he looked funny all wet and very angry. He got back on the boat and turned all of his attention on getting as many ducks as he could. Nebra said to her coldly, "You missed your mark. The ichneumon got away. If you'd aimed a little higher, you would have gotten his neck and killed him."

She looked at him, surprised. "No," she said. "I meant to hit him on the leg, to scare him away from the gallinule. If I'd meant to hit him in the neck, he would be dead."

He looked at her and shook his head darkly. There was that cold fire in his eyes. She shook her head with a mock sadness. "Perhaps the curse can take more than one form. Perhaps your falling into the water is a warning to you. I do not wish another of Khemet's heroes to die because of me."

Meryt caught up and walked beside her toward the palace. "I doubt your monkey, Chi-chi, could have made such mischief today!" Meryt was smiling, and then she broke into a laugh.

Hatasu paused a minute, and then with relief, laughed with her. "Yes, well, I hope it is enough to make him stop courting me."

Back at the palace, her father didn't speak to her. He went directly to his private quarters. She could hear him pacing back and forth. She comforted herself by going to Thethi's room and amusing him with the story of Nebra's fall into the river. They laughed quietly. It was important certain people didn't know they found humor in Nebra's embarrassment. She didn't tell him about her made-up curse. Even though it was fiction, it frightened her a bit.

Finally, her father called for her. She was ushered into the opulence of his private quarters and she approached her father, who was sitting silently in his large, gold chair. When she got close, he said, "Sit!" indicating the chair next to him.

Hatasu had a sense this was not going to be an ordinary scolding. He began, "Daughter, there are reasons why I asked you to be nice to Nebra today." He paused and Hatasu braced herself for what was to come. "You are a daughter of this Pharaoh. This heritage carries with it heavy responsibilities for the welfare of the people. This care entrusted in royalty by the gods is not always easy. The

Pharaoh and his family are called upon to turn away from their own choices and toward their duty, regardless of their own wishes."

She feared her father was going to see it as her 'duty' to apologize to Nebra. But he went on in an unexpected direction, "It is my sacred duty to maintain Maat for the people of the Two Lands. That includes providing for a successor. I had felt assured that with three sons, I offered the people that security. This is no longer so. Within this year, two of my sons have been taken to the West, and my third son is too frequently ill, which makes him inconsistent in his schooling; and thereby unable to learn the things that are necessary to rule. My hope now falls to you." He paused again and looked at her closely. She squirmed at bit.

"You know of the oracle of the goddess at your purification and your mother informed me of your recognition by the Ka of Ptah. These are irregular prophecies, speaking of an unusual destiny for a woman. Whether you become Queen or Pharaoh, I wished to ease the hardship of this oracle for you by giving you a consort with whom you might rule. It is unlikely that your mother will bear me a boy-child, and with your two oldest brothers passed to the stars, and with Thethi so ill most of the time, I sought out another who might ease your burden of rulership as your mother does for me. The people are anxious to hear of my plans for a successor. The nobles want to be assured of an heir; otherwise, there may be danger of competing candidates and this would be a threat to all my plans."

Her head began to spin as she thought, *'He is going to tell me he still wants me to marry Nebra!'*

But he went on, "Your uncle, Amenhotep, faced such a problem when he had no suitable heir. Amun chose me as his son and your mother loved me. I thought a similar solution might protect you from the solitary burden of protecting the people from the threat of chaos. Nebra would make a good consort. He is from the line of Pharaoh Amenenhat and thus has royal, divine blood."

Hatasu butted in, "There must be some other way! I would much rather have Thethi as my consort!"

The Pharaoh's eyes wandered off into some far distance. He turned now to look at her face, as he said gently, "I know you love the gods and the people of this land and that you want the best for them. Your royal duty and your fate is to protect them from the chaos of the power struggles that will overwhelm the land if there is not a clear succession…which is what will happen if Thethi is named and then passes to the stars. The heir named this time must be stable and certain. Do you understand, Hatshepsut?"

This talk had a very strange effect on Hatasu. It felt like her father, the Good God and Pharaoh, had taken her into his confidence like an adult. She felt warmed by the glow of his talking. This no longer seemed like a scolding. But the thought of being married to Nebra was still too distressing for words. She was also troubled by the implications of his doubt about Thethi's survival.

She would try to make her father understand. "Father, Nebra is not right! When I was in Abedju with Mother and we heard of trouble in the oasis, I got scared and doubted everyone." Her father started to interrupt but he closed his mouth again and listened. "I asked mother about how I felt and she said, 'Think with your heart'.

Then, I knew that Puyemre was a loyal and faithful person and I need not fear concerning him."

Thutmose smiled and nodded approval. She went on, "When I think with my heart about Nebra, I become very afraid. I want very much to do as you say because I love you, but Nebra could be no comfort to me."

A dark storm seemed to come over his face. "You understand that what you ask could mean you could have to rule alone?"

She nodded her young head.

"Go, then. I must think on this some more."

Chapter 34 ~ The Judgement of Maat

The next day was the tribunal. As was his duty, the Pharaoh had to put aside personal concerns and feelings to sit in judgment on the case against Sobekhotep and Amenhat. The charges were the worst in the land…treason.

The plaintiff was the Two Lands…Egypt, itself. Ineni, in his role as Vizier, and therefore as priest of Maat, was to present the evidence before the Pharaoh. Usersobek, being dead…it was the mayor, Amenhat, and priest, Sobekhotep, who would be brought before the tribunal. Ineni would present the case against the two men to the Pharaoh.

In this formal and official role, Thutmose went by his throne name, Okheperkare. It meant 'Powerful is the transforming of Ra'. He would listen to all the advisors on the tribunal and then it would he who would proclaim the judgment and punishment. Thutmose-Okheperkare wished to make an example of this case to all mayors and priests, so he planned to hold the proceeding in the grand hall of the palace.

Hatasu had been somewhat left to her own devices after the catastrophic duck hunt and audience with her father. Her curiosity about the 'magician of Itjtawy' was great and no one told her she couldn't go. The priests of the House of Life were all expected to be at the tribunal; therefore, there was no school. Sitre had relatives, a brother and a cousin, who had been away in the war and she was given time off to reunite with them. Thethi's breathing attack, following his father's choice of Nebra for Hatasu, was severe but not prolonged. Paheri was still watching him closely and they had gone this day to the chariot stables.

Hatasu used this unusual freedom to make a plan with Hapuseneb to sneak into the royal hall where the tribunal was meeting and to hide behind one of the grand pillars. Many nobles and high administrators took their places in the royal hall.

Queen Ahmose entered first, beautiful and dignified in the crown with the golden wings of Mut, emphasizing her role as mother of her people. Hapu arrived in the leopard-skin robe. Ahmose and Hapu were prominent in this judgment, for it was their magic that had subdued and overcome these enemies.

Ineni, as priest of Maat, and the Vizier entered next; the Vizier wore the formal long, white skirt, and carried the tall staff, of authority. Ibana took his place wearing the white, short kilt of a soldier with many gold Flies of Honor glittering from the chain around his neck. Many scribes were in attendance to record the proceedings and Huy and Yuf, the scribes of the Pharaoh and Queen, led them. The tribunal was complete.

Nakht, wearing the simple white kilt of the chief of the Pharaoh's guard, came in leading the two accused men with their hands tied behind their backs. This was the first time Hatasu had seen these criminals. Sobekhotep had a look of defiance about him. He was clean-shaven, and though his robe was wrinkled, it was washed. Mayor Amenhat, on the other hand, was unshaven and his white skirt was soiled and in disarray. He walked with his head down and he looked frightened. The prisoners stood before the seated officials.

Once everyone was in place, a hush of expectation settled over the crowd. Only then, and with great dignity, did Pharaoh Okheperkare enter the Hall of Justice. He strode forward wearing his Double Crown of the North and South of the Two Lands and, holding across his chest, the royal hook and flail.

Regally, he addressed those present, "This tribunal is convened here at the Royal Palace rather than the hall of the Vizier Ineni because of the extremely grievous character of this crime of treason, of which these defendants have been accused. Thus, the petitioners of Upper and Lower Egypt come to receive judgment in the Hall of the Pharaoh, himself. The crime of treason is particularly heinous because it is an affront against the Son of Ra and the goddess Maat. An attack on Maat threatens all people of the Two Lands, for without Maat everyone would be thrown into the darkest chaos of Isfet.

Precisely because of the lawlessness of these acts, it is essential that this court be conducted in the ways specified by the law. It is important everything is done in a precise and lawful manner to let these men plead their innocence. It is also important that the Vizier and court officials bring forth the facts in their evidence against them.

I, as the Son of Ra, shall act according to the rules set forth by the god Thoth and the legal precedents preserved in the 'Record of all Judgment'. I will do what is specified therein. I will not make an improper judgment; biased behavior is abhorrent to the god. I will not dismiss a petitioner before you have heard his words. The court in which you sit contains a hall with a record of all judgments. I will not act as I wish in matters where the law is known. I will act according to the dictates of Maat. Vizier Ineni, bring forth the evidence against Sobekhotep and Amenhat." The Pharaoh took his seat on the grand dais at the head of the hall.

Ineni stood and walked toward his Pharaoh. "Great Pharaoh Okheperkare-Thutmose, there stands before you first, Sobekhotep, lecture priest of the Temple of Itjtawy. It is established that the high priest, Usersobek, was a criminal and acted with treason…to overthrow you by means of magic. He was overcome due to the strength of Great Wife, Ahmose, and High Priest, Hapu." He nodded with reverence in their direction. "Once overcome and stripped of his magic powers, Usersobek drowned himself in the river, which is his right under law.

"Sobekhotep was associated with Usersobek in duties at the temple and at the temple school. There are many here who will testify to his traitorous behavior. He practiced acts of heka-magic against his town, controlling by fear all those around him. He taught this hateful magic and his plans of sedition in the House of Life in Itjtawy. He used his powers to steal cattle from the temple and from the commoners alike. He and Usersobek schemed together to amass wealth from the temple and the people, so as to overthrow Maat and to have another Pharaoh, Usersobek, himself, in place of the Good God, Okheperkare."

Ineni bowed before the Pharaoh when he finished his speech. Sobekhotep stood stone-still, arms tied behind his back, and his blank eye staring into space. No expression. Several people…a high-ranking scribe, a landowner and a priest from the Temple of

Ptah…came forward with evidence for his criminal behavior. Students who had been sent to the Itjtawy House of Life came forward with tales of cohesions and abuse of power.

Okheperkare-Thutmose asked, "If this man was so powerful, where is his power now?"

Hapu had the answer. "His powers were contained within his staff and in his secrecy. The staff has been destroyed by fire and his secrecy has been exposed."

"Is that so?" the Pharaoh asked the man on trial.

Sobekhotep just stared into space. No answer.

The Pharaoh, with all the dignity of his office, addressed those present. "It is necessary for the serving of Maat, that we listen to what Sobekhotep has to say in his defense."

Sobekhotep was pulled forward, hands bound behind him. The guards stationed him in front of the Pharaoh to answer the accusations. Okheperkare spoke directly to him, his own calm face betraying no emotion. "You are entitled to speak now. This is your opportunity, if you have anything to say in your defense."

Sobekhotep turned his head slowly to look defiantly at the Pharaoh. He spit out angry words as though they were daggers to pierce Thutmose. "It is not I who am the traitor to Maat." A silence hushed the Great Hall. The man's audacity was great but the whole hall listened. "It is you, unjustly wearing the Double Crown that is not rightfully yours. Amenhotep should have chosen one of royal, divine blood, not an…Intef."

The Pharaoh's ancestral name was spoken with derision and hatred. There was an angry rumbling among the crowd. Thutmose's supporters were shocked by this assertion. Nakht quickly stepped closer and gave the traitor a blow across the face. He was silent again. The advisors whispered among themselves. An unsettled murmuring spread over the rows of those assembled.

The righteous anger of the Pharaoh's voice rose over the din, "If that is your defense, then it condemns you. We need to hear no more." With a brush of his royal hand, he said, "Take him away."

Nakht dragged him toward the door but the crocodile in Sobekhotep was now aroused and he raged at the Crown as he left. "It is not over, Thutmose Intef. Others are poised to follow in my footsteps to continue this battle!"

"Halt!" commanded the Pharaoh. "Who is it that is poised to follow in your footsteps?"

Sobekhotep sealed his mouth tight with a grin. Just then, Hatasu noticed stealthy movement behind an adjacent pillar. She nudged Hapuseneb. He saw it, too. Ineni stood and asked if anyone here had any knowledge of other plots. "If so," he warned, "step forward now. Anyone found withholding information will be considered a conspirator as well."

There was silence for a long moment. Then Ptahhotep, the old priest from the temple of Ptah spoke up in a shaky voice, "Our mayor, Rahotep, has been very friendly with the priests of Itjtawy. He withdrew his son from the temple school of Ptah and sent him to the temple in Itjtawy to study. He encouraged other parents to do the same." His blue eyes looked around the room for others who knew this was true.

Another person, an administrative scribe in the service of the mayor, spoke up, looking around nervously, "Rahotep has become very wealthy in a very short period of time." He continued with rapid speech, "But his words are always loyal and praising of the Pharaoh so it can't be true that he is involved."

A soldier spoke up and said, "I fought with Nebra. He is loyal to the Pharaoh to a fault. Surely, his family could not be involved in this treason."

"Surely not," said the Pharaoh, clearly distressed at this turn of events. "Where is Rahotep to speak for himself?"

Everyone looked around. He was nowhere. Ineni and Nakht were commissioned to go to his house to summon him. Many people murmured with their own suppositions of what might be going on. The Pharaoh consulted with Hapu and Ahmose, each finding this turn of events quite unexpected. However, in the name of Maat, the possible treason had to be investigated.

Hatasu nudged Hapuseneb and whispered, "Nebra! Those bad feelings I had about him…maybe I had them because he is part of the conspiracy!"

They waited. Finally, Ineni entered the hall first, wearing a most distressed expression and carrying a box in his hands. This was a box easily recognizable by Hatasu because her mother had one like it. Ahmose took it out whenever she needed to do magic. She had also seen one like it in her father's tent before he left for the Levant. It was the box of the magician with the wax figures.

An official and determined-looking Nakht followed, leading Rahotep, hands bound behind his back. Rahotep's head was bowed low. All of his grandiose posturing was gone. He looked frightened.

Ineni approached the Pharaoh, opening the box in front of him to display a set of wax figurines. Ineni explained, "Rahotep was attempting to destroy these as we entered his house."

High Priest Hapu stepped forward to examine them. "Yes, Your Majesty, they are high quality wax figures constructed for harmful magic. And this figure," he said, picking one up and turning it over in his hand to inspect it fully, "is in the likeness of you."

Okheperkare took this figure from Hapu's hands. His face was growing red with anger. His jaw was set forward and muscles protruded and trembled in front of his ears. He looked accusingly at Rahotep. Meanwhile, Nebra, also bound, was being led into the room behind his father.

Hapuseneb pointed and said in a whisper, "Hatasu, you were right!" She sat back, leaning for support on the column.

"Thank the goddess his plan was discovered in time!"

"I didn't like him," Hapuseneb said, "but I didn't think he was part of conspiracy of rebellion!"

Okheperkare stood in front of the tribunal, the imposing figure he was, his feet spread wide and his arms folded across his broad chest. He looked first to Rahotep, then to Nebra. "Each of you has the right to defend yourself and to explain why these magical figures with spells for the destruction of this Pharaoh were in your possession." His deep voice quaked.

Nebra spoke up as he struggled against his bonds, "I knew nothing of this."

His father spoke through his teeth, "Shut up, boy. Say nothing!"

"But I have nothing to say! I don't know what you were doing with these magical figures."

Ineni spoke, "Apparently your father had Usersobek prepare these figures so that once the Pharaoh declared you his heir, he would then cause Okheperkare Thutmose to fall ill by magic means. This figure here is identified as Okheperkare Thutmose and here, is Usersobek's mark."

Nebra looked to his father with shocked disbelief. "You told me to be brave for my Pharaoh and endear myself to him, for I, too, am of the royal blood of the Amenhats."

His father's darkening face silenced Nebra. His words, which attempted to claim his own innocence, had clearly condemned his father. Realizing the immensity of what had just happened, he looked away from his father to his Pharaoh.

With a sad and slow voice, Okheperkare Thutmose declared, "The evidence here is indisputable." Rahotep looked at him with a set jaw. Gone were the grandiose flourishes and pretty words of his false loyalty. The same hard, hateful line of his mouth that Hatasu had seen in Nebra, revealed itself on the father's face. Cold eyes looked at Thutmose. Nakht pulled him from the royal presence.

Nebra was still standing there. He descended to his knees. "Your Majesty, I am innocent of what my father planned. I beg of your mercy."

"Nebra, I am deeply saddened by these events. Precedent governs our tribunal. I follow what is set down as pleasing to Maat. This crime is too heinous to respond to with anything but swiftest justice. Treason toward the son of Ra is the greatest of crimes for it threatens all the land with chaos and great suffering."

A tinge of sadness tempered the anger in his face as he spoke to Nebra. He continued, "Still, you have the right to speak in your defense. Is there anyone you can call to refute these charges against you?"

"I could call the thousand men in the division I led in the land of the Mitanni," Nebra responded. "You, yourself, saw me fight there, and have so recently honored me with this Fly of Honor." He used his chin to nod to the gold pendant still hanging around his neck. "Surely you, yourself, must remember when I fought bravely against the enemies of Your Majesty. I did this with honor and love for you."

"Did your father encourage you to rebel against this Pharaoh?"

"My father encouraged me to endear myself to you, to open the possibility that I, as a descendent of Amenhat, might again serve the Two Lands. Any father would encourage his son to serve his Pharaoh and win his favor. This does not mean I am a traitor."

"It is true," the Pharaoh admitted. "I have witnessed your loyalty and bravery to this Pharaoh in the battlefield. But what of the accusation that you left the House of Life in Ankh-Tawy to study with Usersobek in Itjtawy? If he was teaching treason or the dark use of the magic arts, surely you must have known that!"

"No, no! I was a student there only a short time before I was called to the war in the Levant."

"What, then, can you tell me of what he taught? He said he trained others to follow in his footsteps..."

This was a trap question and Nebra knew it. "You would have to speak to others about that, for I do not know."

The Pharaoh turned his attention away from Nebra, asking other students from Usersobek's school to step forward. Raneb, a student who was attending at the time Nebra was also present, testified that Usersobek and Sobekhotep particularly favored Nebra, and that in the short time he attended, Nebra had received ample instruction from the priests. Nebra shook his head adamantly and struggled against his bonds. He knew this testimony was weighing very strongly against him.

At the Pharaoh's indication, Nakht led him from the room. The Pharaoh looked to the next accused, Amenhat, the mayor of Itjtawy. Ineni, holding firmly to his staff of authority, presented the case against Amenhat. He said that Amenhat, as mayor of the city in which traitors were conspiring, surely must have been aware of and been a participant in the crimes.

Amenhat bowed low before the Pharaoh, begging, "Please, Your Majesty, all health, life and prosperity, I am faithful to you with all my heart, and I have always been. It was the magic of Usersobek and Sobekhotep that blinded me to what they were doing. It was only after Ahmose and Hapu had broken their spell, that I came back to being myself. Please believe that I am innocent of these charges."

"Is there anyone here who will vouch for you?" the Pharaoh asked.

Amenhat looked around in a forlorn manner. Djehapy, the governor of Zawty, stood up and spoke, "Though I am mayor many miles away, I have always known Amenhat to be fair in his dealings and to represent the wishes of the crown in all ways. As the news of

Usersobek's tyranny spread, we simply heard less and less from Amenhat."

Another man spoke up and then another, each in Amenhat's defense.

"I have heard your case," the Pharaoh said. "I will now meet with the tribunal and announce my judgment."

All the prisoners were led out of the hall and those in the Great Hall were dismissed. They were to be called back when the judgment was to be announced. Hatasu and Hapuseneb, hidden behind the pillar, remained unnoticed. Okheperkare sat in the center of his circle of ministers.

Once they were alone, Okheperkare stood up and stormed around the room. His anger was apparent. "Well!" he exclaimed. "Sobekhotep and Rahotep deserve to die as the law requires. They deserve to be impaled. I'd like to kill them with my own hands. How dare they go against this son of god?"

Queen Ahmose stood up and paced beside him. "There are still the laws of the land," she said. "As always, you are Maat and will follow the precedents of the laws given us by Thoth."

Ineni said, "It is essential that justice be swift and effective, for all opposition must be eliminated. These ideas of treason are very dangerous to have growing here in the Delta. I am now worried about all the students who have attended Usersobek's House of Life. The danger to the land may be more widespread than we thought."

Ibana sat fingering his Flies of Honor. He said slowly, "You were mighty and fierce in battle against the Mitanni. These traitors here today are as much your enemies as the Mitanni were."

The Queen spoke up again, "In our land, the Pharaoh must have two faces. The face of Sekhmet is for the enemy outside our land and the face of Hathor is for building love for himself within his own land. The precedence is that the treasonous one must die but the Pharaoh may not want to go to his judgment of Maat with that death on his heart. It is better that the criminal be given the opportunity to do that final deed himself as Usersobek did. Sobekhotep and Rahotep deserve to die but it should be done in the way established by the gods."

Ibana went on, in his slow thoughtful way, "Those in the Levant have laws, too. They are different from ours. Their king kills their subjects for much lesser crimes than these. Our soldiers have seen this. They would understand if you were to decide to kill the traitors yourself. It would show them that your strength here at home matches your strength in the Levant."

Queen Ahmose nodded to Ibana, saying, "But we do not send our soldiers to fight in the Levant because we wish for them to become like the foreigners. For every soldier who is used to killing, there are many more of our citizens wishing only to be protected from the ways of the Levant…protected from their laws, protected from their magic and protected from their diseases. This is all the more reason that your justice must be true." Turning to the Pharaoh, she said, "Thutmose, follow the letter of the prescribed law of this land."

Okheperkare-Thutmose carefully attended to this discussion, calming himself by listening to others debate. He said, "What is most important is maintenance of Maat. That is why I took the army to the Levant. Our structures, our ways and our peoples must be preserved as the gods have given them to us. Because Maat must be preserved, it is my sacred duty to wipe out this wave of treason.

"I feel the personal sting of betrayal by those I thought trustworthy; there is no question about that. The question is, what judgment will most effectively deliver Maat to the people, both now and in the future? Without a doubt, Sobekhotep and Rahotep must die; they may kill themselves or they will be impaled upon a stake to execute them. Neither will be allowed a House of Eternity; they will wander forever homeless in the afterlife.

"Their families shall not benefit from their corruption; therefore, their possessions shall be confiscated and used to compensate those from whom they stole. All reference to the traitors shall be purged from papyrus and tombs. They shall cease to exist."

Everyone in the tribunal nodded in agreement. Okheperkare continued, "I am at peace about these judgments." He paused. "But Nebra…it is he who most disturbs my ka."

High Priest Hapu spoke up for the first time, "I believe he is guilty. I also believe he is dangerous. There were too many opportunities for him to have learned left-handed magic under Usersobek's tutelage. The seeds of ambition planted by his father have grown into a tree. The Setmose trouble in the Oasis is likely to repeat itself here with Nebra if you merely exile him."

"Yes," the Pharaoh said, "but he served well and faithfully in the foreign lands. He became like a son to me when my own son was killed. I placed affection and hope in him. I do not wish to have him killed. I think it would be more just to displace him in the area of Faiyum and to keep a close eye on him there."

Ibana agreed, "I saw him in the Levant as a brave and loyal soldier. He has endeared himself to many. There is a chance he will direct his life into more useful pathways than those of his father and Usersobek."

"I don't like him," said Ineni. "There is something false and strange about him."

Queen Ahmose said, "Well, he could receive a lashing or be sent to a work gang in the mines."

Ibana added, "Or you could have his tongue cut out. I've seen that punishment work to prevent the abuse of words of power in the Levant."

"I think Faiyum is enough punishment for Nebra," Okheperkare said with finality of tone. "Now, Amenhat…his case is different. Hapu, do you think he was under a spell from Usersobek?"

"It is very possible. Usersobek's magic was strong, and in general, he used it to bind people in fear of him. When Ahmose and I entered that area, all the people who weren't directly involved with the temple looked like they were sleep walking."

"Ineni, what was your administrative contact with Amenhat like over the past year?"

"It was very sparse. His reports were concise and to the point, always saying everything was fine. This manner of writing was odd, because he is usually a very sociable person. Our attempts to probe the situation were obstructed until we arrived in Itjtawy ourselves. Then, I found him to be friendly, but he seemed…disoriented. He appeared to be trying to hide his ignorance of the things that had been going on within the last year."

"Queen Ahmose, what do you think?" the Pharaoh asked.

"I agree with what Ineni and Hapu said, but if Usersobek's magic did indeed affect him, I believe he is too weak-minded to hold the position of mayor. We need someone at the head of each nome whom we can trust to be strong enough and loyal enough to ward off such crimes before they grow to such dangerous proportions."

"So, I will replace him as mayor of Itjtawy and he must return any goods appropriated from the temple, the throne or the people. Perhaps his position could be given to Qenu of the Beni Hassan nome."

Ahmose and Ineni nodded together. Ineni said, "I believe that would be a good choice."

Okheperkare nodded and continued, "My final judgments, to be carried out by Ineni and Nakht are as follows: Sobekhotep and Rahotep are to die by their own hand or by impaling. Their estates are to pay back the stolen amounts and they are each to forfeit their tombs." Each person of this tribunal nodded their heads.

"Nebra is to be exiled to Faiyum immediately and to be forbidden to hold any office throughout his life."

Ibana said, "Do you expect him to be a farmer? No office for him? Isn't that a waste of his talents?"

"He can apprentice to a craft…anything but military or priest crafts."

"I still think he is dangerous," said Hapu. "Perhaps the Kharga

Oasis would give him less opportunity to be a future danger."

Ineni shook his head. "Perhaps Elephantine instead? There are less likely to be Amenhat sympathizers there than either Faiyum or Kharga."

"Yes," agreed the Pharaoh. "Elephantine is far enough away from the centers of power and it is still an area loyal to the realm. Perhaps he could be a scribe at the quarry there. It is true about the use of his talents. It is decided: He is to go to Elephantine. Now, bring the men in to hear their sentencing."

The doors of the Great Hall were opened again and the people returned to hear the judgment of their Pharaoh. Nakht returned with the four accused men. They lined up in front of the tribunal. The Pharaoh addressed Sobekhotep and Rahotep first. "Each of you is to die for your treason either by your own hand or, if you fail at that, by being impaled upon the stake."

He looked at them threateningly and continued, "The gods despise such criminals. When each of you stand in the Judgment Hall of Osiris and face the 42 Assessors, and when you are asked for your Declaration of Innocence, your hearts will betray you. When your hearts are weighted against the Feather of Maat, with all its lightness of truth, your hearts will tip the scales, for they are heavy with their misdeeds and their lies. Thoth, the scribe of the gods, will make note of how your hearts betray your crimes against Maat; and Amemait…the monster with a crocodile's mouth, a lion's front quarters and a hippopotamus's behind—the one called the 'Devourer'…will eat your hearts and you will forever be deprived of the joy of the Field of Reeds."

Weeping and moaning were heard from the relatives of the criminals. The rest of the hall was silent, considering the gravity of the Pharaoh's words. After a few moments, Okheperkare turned to the young man who he had hoped would be his daughter's husband. "Nebra, you are to be sent to Elephantine. You may hold neither an administrative, priestly nor military office. You are to depart immediately."

Nebra stared with a look of numb shock. Within a day, he had fallen from the exalted height of his Pharaoh's regard to the despair of exile. Yet, he was also relieved, for he, too, could have been sentenced to death like his father. He let out a barely audible mumble, "It is true. Anyone who courts Hatshepsut is cursed."

The Pharaoh paused only a moment, and turning next to the mayor of Itjtawy, he said, "Amenhat, you are to return all goods that belong to others and you are to be relieved of your office of mayor." He bowed repeatedly, knowing that his Pharaoh was just and merciful. He had been spared being sentenced to death…the fate he most feared. He now had time to make amends and lighten his heart with good deeds so that when he did pass, his heart might not outweigh the Feather of Maat.

Each of the criminals was led from the room to carry out the sentence he had received. Okheperkare then looked to the others gathered, saying, "You are dismissed. Today, you have honored Maat by your presence and your testimony. Remember well the lessons of loyalty."

Okheperkare stayed in place until everyone, including the tribunal, had left. Hatasu and Hapuseneb, not wanting to be detected, feared moving until the Pharaoh was gone. To the young people's great surprise, the Pharaoh stood at the edge of his dais and faced the pillar behind which they were hiding. "Hatasu and Hapuseneb, you can come out now." His voice was calm.

'Oh, no!' Hatasu thought. 'We're caught!'

They peeked around the brightly colored column and saw the stern face of their Pharaoh. "Come along, come up here," he motioned to them.

When they arrived at the foot of his throne and looked up at his noble face, Hatasu was shaken but she stood tall, ready to take whatever consequences there were. She was fortified, however, in her knowledge that the trial had exposed Nebra's falseness, proving that she had been right in her feelings about his character.

"What did you think of the trial?" he asked.

Was this a trick question? Hatasu decided not to hesitate. "It showed I was right about Nebra," she said.

"Yes, indeed you were. You are a better judge of character than I gave you credit for. Hapuseneb, what did you think?"

"The laws of our land are wise and I honor Maat. When I am a man, I would like nothing better than to honor Maat as a judge to protect the land from Isfet."

"Would you? Well, the next time you wish to observe justice, you can ask rather than hide behind a pillar." With a nod of his head, he said, "You can go now."

As they were leaving, the Pharaoh called once more to his daughter, "Hatasu, where did Nebra get the idea that that anyone who courts you is cursed?"

She squirmed. "Well…um…I wanted him to leave me alone…and I figured telling him he would be cursed, would help."

"I thought that might be it," he said, raising his eyebrow and nodding. "All right, you can go now. Find Sitre and see if you can stay out of trouble, for at least a little while."

Chapter 35 – The Pharaoh's Announcement

Hatasu and Thethi noticed nothing alarming about the scene when they approached their father in the garden the next day. There was nothing to give them a clue that this was the point from which both their lives would change forever. Sitre and Paheri had come to get each of them and said simply that their father wanted to see them.

The Pharaoh was sitting under a canopy with the Great Wife and around him were his loyal attendants: Ineni, Hapu, Nakht, Ibana. Wearing his usual nemes headdress and his broad royal collar, their father smiled at his children as they came down the path. There was nothing to warn them of what was on his mind, but they should have known. Once they were under the canopied enclosure, he motioned to them to sit in the two smaller chairs placed on the dais for them.

There was expectancy in the air as the adults all sat quiet, alert. Thutmose began, "I called this meeting because I have come to a decision about the succession to the throne." Ahmose looked down at her hands, while Nakht twisted his ceremonial spear in place and Ibana fingered the Gold of Honor on his chest. Hatasu held her breath.

"It is my decision that…" Everyone leaned a little toward him to hear. "Hatshepsut, my daughter by the Great Wife Ahmose…shall be Pharaoh after me." He extended his arm, motioning for her to walk toward him.

There was silence. Ineni, Nakht and Hapu exchanged glances.

Hatasu felt her heart catch. She was alarmed but not surprised. She looked to the Queen, who smiled pensively and nudged her toward her father. Throughout her childhood, Hatasu had seen herself as Queen, even when the oracle controversy raged, but now, her father decided she would be Pharaoh…and her mother, apparently, accepted it.

She simultaneously felt her body soften in resignation and straighten with the new purpose. She wanted so to live up to her father's expectations.

Thutmose put his arm around her tenderly and said, "Hatshepsut, you are the true Hawk-in-the-Nest. You have the ka of a Pharaoh and always had this quality since you were born when the sun rises…in the sign of the royal lion. It is this royal ka that will enable you to be the intermediary between the gods and the land, the Above and Below. You have within you the ability to lead and care for the people of the Two Lands. As with all Pharaohs before you, you must now go through the preparations at the House of Life. I shall oversee your training in this, myself."

Being the chosen one was frightening but the prospects of both the House of Life and time with her father distracted from her fears.

Ineni cleared his throat, "What are your plans for Thutmose II? I thought you would have chosen this son as you did your other sons of the Intef-Thutmosid line."

"Ineni, the rebel's questioning of the legitimacy of our Thutmosid line makes it a less stabilizing choice than it was with Wadjmose or Amenmose. The Taosid line of Queen Ahmose is accepted as the royal bloodline. Hatshepsut carries that blood."

The Pharaoh turned then to his son, whose face looked to him for the answer to what his role would be. "Thutmose II," his father said, "since you have been born, it has been expected that your position would be as Vizier, like my own brother." He indicated Ineni. "It is my wish that you continue in that plan but I also know how you have dreamed of being the commander-in-chief of the army. Therefore, I have decided that you will stay here in Ankh-Tawy and study military arts. Paheri will stay with you. In periods when your health is strong enough, you will practice soldiering. At others, you will attend the House of Life at the Temple of Ptah and learn the skills of a Vizier. This plan has the added advantage of being near the healing temple of Sekhmet where the stela, offered for your health, has been so successful."

Thethi smiled. This did indeed please him. Because of his bouts with ill health, he had feared he would be denied his dearest dream of a military training.

Hatasu interrupted, "Thethi and I won't be together?" Though there had been conflict between the siblings since the oracle, she did not remember a time he had not been her companion.

"No," her father said, his hands both placed decidedly on the arms of his throne. "Each of you will undergo different training. Thethi here in Ankh-Tawy, you in Waset."

Hatasu looked to her brother and he looked back at her, his eyes showing the fright she felt.

Nakht, the head of internal security, stood to speak his concerns, "Your Majesty, Lord of Two Lands, how can the oracle intend this girl-child to command the respect of the doubters and questioners at home and abroad? There are rebels among us. They could use your appointment of your daughter as an excuse to overthrow your order. Please, Pharaoh, reconsider. Choose your son Thutmose. How can you overlook him for a daughter…even if he is not of Tao blood?"

Hatasu's stomach tightened. *He was right. How could she manage rebels?*

"Nakht," replied the Pharaoh, "she is to be my heir. I will admit it seemed very odd when the first oracle spoke this prophesy of her ruling at her purification ceremony, so I blessed the interpretation that she was to rule as Queen to first my son Wadjmose, and later to my son Amenmose, empowering the Thutmosid line with her Taosid blood. Both those sons have passed to the stars. I believe the gods had always seen the future Pharaohs to continue within the combined Thutmosid-Taosid line; thus, my daughter by the Great Wife is the suitable heir."

The Queen looked down at her hands, rubbing her intertwined fingers together. She looked up and addressed her husband, "I know the prophecy and oracles, well. Still, my Pharaoh, a woman is better suited to be a Queen. Strong women like my mother, Nefertari, and grandmother, Ahhotep, served their land and people well, but no one asked them to sacrifice their female natures. At least you could have Hatshepsut marry Thutmose II and name them as heirs together."

"The oracle didn't say that. It is Hatshepsut, alone, who is the heir. The people need to know, this time their Hawk-in-the-Nest will indeed be able to rise to be their new Horus. Thutmose II is frequently ill and it would be demoralizing for the people to be disappointed by the loss of another planned successor. This time, the announcement of the heir *must* come to fruition. It is Hatshepsut who can provide the people with a stable transfer of power. While the choice of a female is unusual, the threat of another loss of an heir is a greater danger as it potentially opens the door to another conspiracy of treason."

Hatasu bit on her thumb nail. Thutmose sat back on his throne and crossed his arms over his chest. "Once she is named Pharaoh, she can name her consort, as long as he has divine blood; but the people need to know now that it is *she* who will rule and that they have a certain succession to protect them with Maat."

After a respectful pause, old Ibana, the war general, spoke up, "Divine Pharaoh, Lord of the Two Lands, I see your wisdom for the stability for the people within the Two Lands but what about the foreigners? How could this young girl, strong willed as she is," he nodded and smiled at Hatasu, "captain the barque of state against the brutal Mitanni? You, Great Pharaoh, have just returned from the Levant. These are difficult times. We have just fought a difficult war. The Two Lands have enemies to the north in Retennu and to the south in Kush. We need a strong Horus on the throne to hold the Mitanni to their treaty. Those to the north do not regard women as capable. Please reconsider Thutmose II, for even a weak male voice may be heard more strongly than a strong woman's voice."

Hatasu's hands began to shake a little but her father reached over and put his strong fingers over hers and she felt calm again. He said, "Ibana, I have made a good peace in the Levant. What will be needed for the next ruler is diplomacy. Hatshepsut can do that as well as any man. The wars have been fought; now is a time to consolidate our victories. We must use the wealth and manpower from our conquests to rebuild our temples and to renew the ancient wisdom. With this war, I have made the land safe from the outside; now we need to return to the gods of the Pharaohs before us. Hatshepsut will be able to do that but you, my old friend, must also work closely with Thethi to keep the army strong so that no one mistakes diplomacy for weakness."

Ibana's eyes followed the Pharaoh's arguments and he nodded his head slowly, more in resignation than agreement. When her father said she could do these things, Hatasu began to think maybe she could.

Hapu shook his head and looked straight at his Pharaoh. "I honor the oracle's choice and see the strong spirit in Hatshepsut. I pray she is strong enough to withstand the initiations in the House of Life."

"I believe she can." Thutmose looked from person to person. His jaw was set. Thutmose put his hands on the two arms of his chair to propel him into a standing position. With a definitive nod, he said, "It is decided! I shall announce my decision to the mayors, governors and priests at the banquet tomorrow. Hatshepsut is the now the Hawk-in-the-Nest. I will make the official announcement of it to the people at the Festival of Min."

Hatasu felt as though a powerful wind had carried her away and she had no say as to where it would take her; but like the wind of the khamsin a year ago, when she backed into her father at the palace gate, she felt any storm would be alright as long as he was there. His presence and his surety was like a sheltering arm around her. If he said this was how it should be…for the god Amun and for the people of the land…she believed it was true. It wasn't that she didn't still have doubts that she could do all he said, it was just that she believed her father could make all things possible.

While the palace staff prepared for the banquet to make the announcement to the nobles, Pharaoh called Hatasu to him. "I have instructions for you for tonight's banquet." She looked into his face and felt the joy of being the focus of his attention and training. "You are to sit beside me at this banquet as I announce you as the Hawk-in-the-Nest.

"I will teach you your first lesson in how to build loyalty for yourself as future Pharaoh. The important thing for you to know, is that though the Pharaoh must rule with a firm hand; his people will best follow him for love, not for fear. You must seek out noblemen who are loyal to you and build on their loyalty by rewarding it.

"After I announce you as my successor, I will be giving out the spoils of the war to my loyal governors and their families. These gifts, rewards for loyalty, help garner support in each of the nomes so the whole land may be governed in peace and security. Your presence at the banquet will connect you with these gifts in the nobles' minds and their loyalty to you will be fostered through your positive connection with me."

She nodded her head to whatever her father said. She had also seen what happened to those who were not loyal.

Later, the governors, nobles, priests and their families arrived at the palace hall in all their finery. Okheperkare-Thutmose stood,

Hatshepsut by his side, and welcomed them one by one as they entered his hall for the feast. Once they were all gathered, and before the meal was served, he began, "My Majesty wishes to inform you tonight that I have a grand announcement to make."

The hall quieted to listen. They were all waiting for the news of his heir and most understood the meaning of Hatshepsut's presence next to her father. His voice broke through the anticipatory silence, "We again have an official heir to the throne. It is my daughter, Hatshepsut, who is now the Hawk-in-the-Nest."

There was silence, then murmuring. "A girl-child as a Hawk-in-the-Nest is unusual…but at least it is a clear succession," said Djehapy of Zawty.

"The oracles said she is the one to rule us," said the priest, Siptah from the Temple of Ptah.

"So be it!" someone called out. "We shall celebrate our new Hawk-in-the-Nest…Hatshepsut!"

A cheer went up and the people began to sing and dance in her honor. If the oracle and their Good God, Thutmose, said it was so…it was so.

Their Pharaoh called for their attention again. "Now, my dear people, the clear succession is the first thing you have to celebrate. The second thing is…I have something for each of you who have been faithful and loyal while I was away. After our meal, I will distribute among you a share of the booty of war."

The banquet was merry; people were secure again in the knowledge of the succession and happy in the anticipation of what might be their gifts. Once the meal was over, Pharaoh Thutmose began the distribution of booty. Each visiting family received riches for the major temple in their nome, as well as gifts of cattle for their herds, bolts of cloth for the women, fine wine or precious woods for their households and slaves to do their manual labor.

Each person who came to receive the gift from the Pharaoh, bowed once to him and once to Hatshepsut. The celebration went deep into the night and many of the local leaders wore broad smiles. Hatasu could hardly keep her eyes open but her father insisted she be there for each of the gifts dispersed.

From that point on, everyone seemed to be bowing to Hatasu all the time. This became more and more an annoyance to her. The good part was she had more time with her father. He talked to her about what he was doing and why. Everything he said, she listened carefully, adoringly. She felt some confusion and doubt that she would ever be able to learn to do what her father does, but when she was with him, even these doubts melted away.

He also included her in his royal schedule. "I meet with my council in the morning. I want you to sit in on this meeting. You are to be there."

That night, she lay looking up at the ceiling over her bed niche. During Sitre night time bed preparations, she'd been all abuzz, excited that 'her' Hatasu would be Pharaoh. Her mother tucked her into bed, sang her a lullaby and said soothing words but Hatasu saw the sadness and worry in her eyes. It would do no good to talk about it that night. The Pharaoh had spoken.

The next day, Hatasu sat at the place her father assigned her. The usual group of his advisors was assembled: Ahmose, Ineni, Hapu,

Ibana, Nakht and the scribes, Huy and Yuf. Okheperkare-Thutmose started the meeting by instructing Huy and Yuf to bring in the map-scroll of the delta area of the Two Lands and the Levant and to unroll it on the table before them.

He addressed his councilors, "There is more I need to tell you, dear council, of the disposition of our suzerains in the Levant." Leaning over the table, he pointed to the familiar areas on the scroll-map. "These are the familiar suzerains: Sharuhem, Jericho, Galilee and Hazor. And further north are the two great sea trading cities of Byblos and Ugarit." He made circles around these areas. "What I am to tell you next, is what we did not know until we went to the Levant."

Ibana sat back with his arms folded, looking smug in his knowledge of what his Pharaoh was about to say. Ahmose nodded, and Ineni and Hapu looked at each other quizzically.

"North of Ugarit is an area that used to belong to the people of Yankhad but this has changed. A savage people called the Hittites swept through this area with a mighty army and destroyed the people of Yankhad and their two large, prosperous cities, Alalakh and Aleppo. The Hittites attacked them, killed their king, burned their buildings and stole their treasures. Then they moved on to loot and destroy the cities and people to the east, between the Euphrates and Tigris Rivers."

He indicated the V shape of those rivers then continued, shaking his head, "This 'attack and abandon' strategy created a political vacuum, a ripe fig waiting for the king of the Mitanni to pick...which he did.

All this has happened in the fifty years since Pharaoh Ahmose brought the army of the Two Lands into Canaan. These are changes that affect us. Now there are not one, but two war-like peoples far to the north who are building up power. The Hittites destroyed and moved on but the Mitanni rapidly expanded south after the Hittites left. The Mitanni leader, Barratarna, started demanding tribute of our suzerains to their south.

Bazor stopped his tribute to us and started looking south to expand his power. Thus, both our suzerains and our home land were indeed being threatened by these Mitanni. The Hittites and Mitanni are more vicious and chaotic than the Hyksos."

The Queen said, "It's hard to imagine any people worse than the Hyksos."

"It is true, my dear. I saw with my own eyes the ruins of the city of Alalakh. There was nothing left to rebuild. Our concern now, however, is with the Mitanni. They are fierce warriors with fearsome battle equipment. They are organized and have the intention to control and govern for their own profit. It is they, who are moving south into the void left by the Hittites' chaos. It is from them, I have made the Two Lands safe…for a while, anyhow."

Ineni, leaning on his Vizier's staff, sat forward in his seat and said, "What do you mean…'for a while'?"

"Their king made a contract with me. He will keep it. Therefore, it is good as long as he lives. But these are an expanding and warring people. There will come a time when they will want to expand southward, again. We must prepare for that. My treaty with the king will give us maybe thirty years of peace in which to build up our spiritual and military strength. The gods are moving time forward and the future in the Levant is full of turmoil. We must use this time to build protection for Khemet."

Ahmose sat straight and said, "From my journey down the Nile, I can see much to do to strengthen the land and people here at home."

"What are your recommendations?"

"I see three main areas to address. First, there are the buildings, like the Temple of Hathor at Kusai, that need to be restored and worship to the goddess renewed. Second, the trades, like the budding linen industry in Zawty, that need help for the people to establish strong trade partnerships. And third, the spirits of the people, like the folk in Itjtawy, need to be strengthened so a priest like Usersobek cannot deceive them."

"Yes, indeed those are very significant areas for attention," Thutmose said.

Hapu added, "I see a couple of areas, too. I'm concerned about our soldiers who need to be healed of wounds of war by the priest of Sekhmet and Isis, as well as the ka of the soldiers need to be protected from the Levantine superstitions of samara demons and mashmashu magicians. On the other hand, craftspeople and artisans need renewed training to honor and record the transactions between the Pharaoh and the gods."

With a grave face, Thutmose nodded. "Yes, all these things need to be done in this land so we may live firmly in the ways of Maat as taught by the ancient ones. It is important to have suzerain tributes to reinforce our temples and to bring them back to the full power they had before their decline in the Hyksos times. Ongoing tributes give us wealth, without the drain and expense of war."

Ahmose was about to say something more but Ineni's voice pushed into the dialogue, "It is fine and good to honor the gods and to encourage training but the Mitanni could still be a physical threat."

Hatasu listened, anxious about this warring threat in the north. She wondered what her father would say.

"Ineni, dear brother," he said, "yes, they could be a threat in the future. They have numbers and equipment we never could have imagined until we saw it with our own eyes. It was only by the blessing of Amun, our rapid surprise attack, and our clever strategies, that we were able to win the battle this time. It was far better that we withdrew with the treaty we have now, than to put our soldiers of the Two Lands up against their deadly war equipment. It will take us many years of trade and tributes to gather the specialized materials to equip ourselves in order to be a realistic match for them.

"We have returned with samples of their metal clothes that make our arrows bounce off them and fall to the ground. We have returned with enemy chariots that withstand their rough terrains, yet still are agile enough to turn quickly. We learned this lesson from Kamose and Ahmose; we will bide our time and build our skills and equipment. One day, my son, or the son of my daughter, will lead an army back to the Levant with war-clothes of metal scales like serpents and chariots, faster, more rugged, than the Mitanni's."

The Pharaoh turned back to his council, and leaning forward on the table, resting on his knuckles, he addressed his high priest, "Hapu, it is true our soldiers are more vulnerable to superstitions and false beliefs of the Levant, like fears of the demons and the magicians of the foreign lands. There needs to be a time of peace to rebuild spirits…not just the spirits of the initiates but also the wounded and frightened spirits of the farmers, the merchants….and our soldiers.

The gold in the temple gives them a sense of the wealth of their gods and their gods' ability to protect and care for them. That will aid their healing. The grand festival processionals that I have planned will also help."

Hatasu nodded and smiled, thinking of Tao and Miriam and her own anxiousness to help those like them.

Ineni had more to say, "But, my Pharaoh and my brother, what makes you think Barratarna will keep his word to you as you expect? The people of the Levant, with whom we have dealt with in the past, have been notorious for saying one thing and then doing just the opposite. What will keep him from attacking our suzerain or even Khemet, itself?"

"I believe he will keep his word. He swore by his god, Mitra. This is a god who protects oaths and contracts. Barratarna, like all Mitanni I met, fear their gods and particularly honor this one god after whom their people are named."

"The Hyksos may have feared Ba'al but that only meant they were more fearsome, themselves," replied Ineni.

"I have made a good Treaty of Peace, I tell you," said the Pharaoh. "Now, we must plan for the future with peace. It is what I have decided." He paused a minute, then continued, "In the meantime, I have commissioned a general to be in charge of designing metal coats for our soldiers, such as the mariyannu, or Mitanni soldiers wear. Another military person is working on breeding a superior chariot horse and a third is working on building a chariot with better maneuverability."

Before I leave for Waset, however, I will oversee the Harvest Festival of Min; I will use this festival to communicate with my people that Hatshepsut is the Hawk-in-the-Nest."

Ineni nodded. "I am your servant in making all that you have said be so. As for now, everything is ready for you, as Horus, to take on the role of the mighty and fertile Min."

"This is very good timing," said the Pharaoh. "We celebrate the fertility of land, our prosperous victory abroad and the official announcement of my heir."

The Festival of Min began at its cosmically appointed time, the end of the growing season of Pert. The water had receded out of all but the major canals. The water in the river itself flowed only in the deepest channels, leaving exposed islands and sandbars. On the day of this festival, however, the people were turned not to the river but to the river's gifts, the grain-filled silos.

Renenutet's festival celebrated the beginning of the harvest season, while Min's festival celebrated its completion. Now, all the grain had been gathered and stored in silos and grain bids. The harvest was safe from late-season threats like locusts, windstorms or hippopotamus raids. Now was the time the Pharaoh knew the land would sufficiently feed his people.

Pharaoh Thutmose was content, for the reports from Upper and Lower parts of the Two Lands told of adequate store of grain despite the khamsin in the south and despite the magic storms around Itjtawy. The gods were smiling on him and his land. He had victory in the Levant; he silenced the rebels with Maat and he had a Hawk-in-the-Nest. With these things, the people were assured that he had the love of his father, Amun-Ra.

The Festival of Min itself was very official and royal. The people celebrated it on a grand scale and it reminded the people of the dynamic relationship between their Pharaoh and their god, between this world and the spiritual one. The Pharaoh took the role of Min-Horus, the Powerful, and it was through his ability to relate to this god that all the blessings of fertility were to flow to the people in the coming year.

Thutmose called his daughter to him. "Hatshepsut, you will stand next to me at the presentation of the harvest to the god Min. You are simply and profoundly the Hawk-in-the-Nest, not the first born son like Wadjmose and not the commander like Amenmose. You are the one with the ka of a Pharaoh."

Any doubts she had were numbed by his words and his conviction they were true. She stood tall in the aura of his grand personality. What he wanted became what she wanted, too. On the morning of the day before the new moon, Hatasu prepared for the ceremony. Sitre had her youth lock braided and her skin oiled.

Her mother came into her room carrying a small object. She held it up and Hatasu could see a gold chain interspersed with silver cowry shells and turquoise beads. Smiling, the Queen said, "This girdle jewelry was mine as a girl. I think it is the perfect day to give it now to my daughter."

She fastened it around her waist and then took the marvelous blue necklace, which her father had given her when he returned from war. Putting it on Hatasu, she said, "You shall wear this today for the ceremony, for truly you will look royal in it."

Ahmose was wearing her own royal, winged headdress of Mut, her makeup was perfect and her dress was of finest linen. Looking back into Hatasu's box, she brought out the arm-band given to her by Senisenb when they parted in Waset. "This will go nicely."

Sitre beamed with pleasure, seeing her beloved charge looking so grand. Ahmose handed Hatasu her own mirror with the head of Hathor on the handle. As the girl looked in the mirror, she saw her smoothed red youth-lock and her kohl-framed almond-shaped eyes. All these were familiar features, yet she felt so different.

She felt a little outside of herself, watching this day happen. She proceeded to the front hall with her mother and nurse. There, awaiting her, was her father with his tall Double Crown and royal jewelry. She saw his eyes take in her bejeweled appearance. A satisfied smile spread over his noble face. He nodded to Ahmose and they prepared to embark upon the litters that were to carry them to The Temple of Min.

As usual, many people lined the processional way to the temple. The nobles assembled; men were in their black, curled wigs, women in their sweetest-smelling oils and children with their brightest eyes. The peasants lined the processional way wearing their garments of coarse, homespun cloth with amulet bags hanging from their necks and their eyes bright with wonder at the glory of their god-king. Anticipation filled the air. This was their glimpse of 'He who bestows abundance'…their god and Pharaoh.

White-robed, bald-headed priests were carrying the litter for the royalty and the barque for the god Min. The statue of this god appeared with a crown and mummy wrappings of brilliant gold, while his face, upward-reaching arm and extended penis, were bitumen-black. The gold garments represented his radiant abundance and the black-skin was the fertile land. On his head, he wore the gold, fitted cap of the craftsman. Around the cap was a band holding in place two tall plumes reaching skyward and long ribbons that fell to the ground behind him.

Amidst the music, incense and dancing, Okheperkare-Thutmose was an image of grandeur in his Double Crown of red and white. Hatshepsut, who followed with her mother, kept her eyes focused on her glorious father. She could almost see the spirit form of the great goddess Nekhbet, with her protective vulture wings, overshadowing him. In Hatasu's eyes, her father glowed, khet and ka, body and soul. Always handsome but now the personification of Horus and Min, she felt him to be absolutely glorious.

The sensations of the heart-throbbing drums, the musk-scented incense, excited her. Hatasu's young heart swelled in her chest with love for him. She was awed and frightened at the idea that she was to follow in his footsteps. *How could she be this to the people?* She looked around to the faces of the others, in which she saw the same expressions of love for their Pharaoh. They all felt themselves to be his children, thus allowing them to participate in the Pharaoh's sexual fertile connection with Min. *How could she ever live up to this?*

The destination of the processional journey was the grain field of Min's Temple. There, a canopy waited in a central cleared area under which was the staircase throne, a barque station and an offering table. Once all the participants arrived, it was time for the chief act of the ceremony. The priest places the barque, carrying the image of the god Min, on the barque station and the Pharaoh takes his place behind the offering table. The Vizier of the Land presents the Pharaoh with a scroll with the report of this year's harvest and Thutmose presents it on Min's altar.

The Pharaoh was ready to speak to his people. He stood tall and noble before them. "My people," he announced, "we have harvested not only an abundance of grain but also a great victory that will protect our people from the Levant. We give thanks to Min. I have another great announcement for you. The oracle has made clear the choice of my heir." He waited for the crowd to hush with anticipation. "It is my daughter, Hatshepsut, 'foremost among women', and it is she who shall sit next to me as my heir and it is she who is to be the ruler after me. Honor her in all things."

He then extended his hand to Hatshepsut, who was standing a short distance behind him. She stepped forward with her eyes seeing only his glorious figure. She stepped up next to him on the dais and turned. There was a sea of expectant faces turned upward. A cheer rose up from the crowd. They had accepted her because their divine Pharaoh had said so. She heard none of the questions and concerns brought up in the council. She simply saw in the faces around her, a readiness to love her father and to follow wherever he should lead them.

He went on, "The oracle said that Hatshepsut, this daughter, shall rule in peace and that she shall do great things."

A cheer went up among the people who were standing around the center of the festival. Hatasu was only vaguely aware of the murmuring on the outskirts of the crowd. The procession returned to the Temple where Min would be cared for by his priests until the next Harvest Festival.

As that day ended, everyone seemed to be bowing to Hatshepsut, as well as to her father. She watched the Pharaoh and did as he did.

Chapter 36 - The Sphinx

The next day, her father said to Hatasu, "Before I left for the Levant, you said you wanted to learn to drive a chariot. Today, I will teach you!"

Her eyes lit up. This was so much better than sitting through another meeting or procession. She beamed and hugged him.

Smiling at her enthusiasm, he said, "I am driving out into the Western Desert to see the ancient temples and you will come with me. First, we will go to the stables to oversee the harnessing of my horses."

It took three of Hatasu's running steps to keep up with each of her father's long, godly strides. Once at the stable, the Pharaoh told the groom, "Prepare Magnificent and Splendid. Harness them to my sturdiest desert chariot."

Hatasu breathed in the pungent smell of the stable, a mixture of horse and hay, while the groom brought the horses from their paddock. As the chariot was pulled from its housing, Thutmose brought his daughter to stand in front of the pair of waiting stallions. He stroked the heads of first one, and then the other, and offered each a measure of feed from his open hand.

"Look here, Magnificent," he said to the first horse, "your princess has come today to accompany us. And, Splendid," he said, turning to the second horse, "we are going to take the princess on a grand ride. She will learn to drive the chariot today and you must both be on your best behavior for her."

Then Thutmose said to his daughter, "Here, hold out this bit of feed for Magnificent. Hold your hand flat…with the feed in your palm, so he won't confuse your fingers with the food. There…see how he likes it?" The horse lowered his huge head to take the feed from her small palm, and with his soft fat lips, he gathered all of the feed into his mouth. "Now, pet his nose. Feel how soft it is?" She reached up and cautiously patted his upper lip. He let out a soft whinny.

Magnificent was larger than any other animal that Hatasu had befriended. They turned to Splendid and did the same thing. Her father said in his teaching tone, as he stood comfortably leaning on Magnificent's neck, "The people of the land are like these horses. They are a grand and dear people worthy of good leadership, but they can be strong willed, and if left to their own devices they would lead themselves into chaos. They need strong direction. Like the horses, the people must be cared for; fed, organized and directed toward Maat.

The Pharaoh has the duty to be wise toward the people. Sometimes the people, like the horses, will try to pull in different directions. If the driver is not strong in directing them forward, they will be torn apart…or worse still, topple the chariot with the Pharaoh in it. The strong Pharaoh must pull the people together and lead them forward, always in alignment with the Great Above, just as a we lead a team of horses toward the ancient Temples in the desert."

The groom attached the chariot to the steeds and bowed to his Pharaoh when he was finished. Thutmose checked the harnessing himself and then said to his daughter, "Come, mount the chariot. I will drive us out of the city and then you can take the reins."

They headed toward the Western Desert, out of Ankh-Tawy, out past the harvested fields of grain, out past the farmer's village, out along the desert. They rode north toward the temple complex of Harmakhis, the Sphinx. As the Pharaoh drove the team, Hatasu stood beside him; the scenery swiftly moved past them.

When they got to the desert, he pulled the horses to a halt. "Now, *you* drive the horses. Tell them to go ahead." He demonstrated as he spoke, "Flip your wrists, like this." The movement started in his arms, went through his wrists and sent a ripple along the reins. "At the same time, say, 'Go ahead'." The two horses smoothly moved forward together.

Hatasu's hands fairly itched to try it. She reached her hands toward the reins but her father continued, "Now, this is how you tell them to stop." He pulled back on the reins, while saying, "Whoa!" The horses came to a halt.

He stepped aside from his central place against the rail of the chariot. Hatasu stepped forward. He handed her the reins, positioning them in her hands. She moved her wrists and the reins shook slightly. The horses moved forward a couple of steps, shaking their heads a bit.

"Try again, this time a little firmer," her father commanded.

Quite nervous, she flicked her wrists more deliberately, putting her whole arms into it. This time, they lunged forward. Her father put his hands over hers, and talking to the horses, he steadied the reins. They began to step ahead more steadily. Then he let go and she had the reins again by herself. As they moved ahead, she felt the thrill of the movement and her knees, loose beneath her, responded gracefully to the desert bumps. Her father smiled and gave her a brisk, military-like nod of approval as they went forward.

Once they were out in the desert, he said, "Now turn your chariot." He waited a moment to see what she'd do. She remembered what she had seen done in chariots before. She pulled back on the left rein. "That's it…firmly." Then, he said louder, "Don't jerk their heads!"

She let up on the reins again and looked up at him. The horses smoothed out the turn; the chariot moved left and they headed out toward the Western Desert. It was then that she experienced the full visual impact of the ancient sacred site of the pyramids. Still holding tightly to the reins, she caught her breath! She saw the huge structures: The giant Sphinx and a complex of temple buildings high on the Giza Plateau in front of them.

"Ah, yes," said her father, "those are the ancient temples that hold the secrets of the wise ones."

She felt the desert wind against her face as the horses followed the incline of the road leading to the plateau, the better to view the imposing buildings. They moved ever closer and she could better appreciate the largest pyramids and the huge reclining lion with the human head. Her father's voice seemed to share her sense of awe as they drew nearer to the complex.

"Our ancestors built the great pyramids as Temples of Initiation. The Temple Complex in front of it is a grand House of Life…for the most advanced students of the ancient wisdom." As they got closer, Thutmose directed her to drive toward the Sphinx. Once there, he told her to bring the horses to a halt. It took his help to pull the horses to a complete stop.

Hatasu and her father stepped down from the chariot in front of the enormous stone creature. Her father hobbled the horses so he and his daughter could walk around and explore every angle of the man-headed lion. She strained her neck, looking up at the huge head with the face of a man, a nemes headdress and uraeus on his forehead. He stared out in the direction of the river and its long body reclined in feline repose.

The wind on the exposed plain howled and she had to yell for her father to hear her. "Why is this giant Sphinx out here in the desert?"

His deep voice carried better than hers as he said, "He was built many ages ago, when the spring of the year began with the stars of the lion in the eastern sky. Thus, we have the lion-bodied Sphinx on this desert plateau that looked to the lion in the sky. Now the year begins with the stars of the ram in the eastern sky and Amun guides us as a ram-headed god in Waset. As ages pass, the heavenly constellations of stars change. The astrologers call this the 'progression of the equinoxes'." He led the way around the great body without trying to talk again.

In the rear of the Sphinx she could view the pyramids. In the front of it was the square valley temple and beyond that she could see the dry outline of what would be a temple harbor when the inundation returned. She noticed the movement of priests in each of the temples below them but the pyramids were absolutely still.

Her father guided her steps into the enclosure between the giant stone paws of the lion, guardian of the mysteries. These two paws stretched out in front of it with a space between them, offering protection from the desert wind. There was a wonderful feeling of safety and warmth in the sheltering arms of this guardian beast. The walls of the paws were a meter over her father's head and this made it still enough to hear each other talk.

He guided her to the back of the area…against the sphinx and there he sat on the packed sand, and patting the spot next to him, motioned for her to join him. He began to teach again, "This is a crucial time in the life of the Two Lands. By fighting the wars in the Levant and in Nubia, we now have the peace, and the wealth needed to rebuild according to the ancient wisdom. The army is still very important but more for keeping peace than for fighting. However, you can still be a warrior like your great-grandmother, Ahhotep, as you told Paheri. I will teach you to shoot an arrow straight to its mark. From seeing you with the throw-stick, I think it will be easy for you."

He had a mischievous smile and looked at her out of the corner of his eye. She giggled a bit but then she thought of how her way of seeing things had changed over the months her father had been away. They were sitting together within the arms of the sphinx, backs supported by his giant chest containing his ab (heart).

"Father, I've been thinking. Senisenb said there were two faces of war. Now, I understand more of what she meant. When you went to war, I dreamed of the glory; but now, I also see the sadness, with things like Amenmose dying and Tao getting wounded. I know that war can kill even a Pharaoh like Sekenenre. Mother told me there are also spiritual warriors who use discipline of the will and the ab (heart). She said I would learn these things in the House of Life." She looked up at him.

He was staring out toward the horizon, beyond the paws. He spoke with his gaze still focused in the far distance, "War has been a sad necessity in the Two Lands. The oracle says you will 'rule in peace'. The foreign occupation, the wars in the Levant, the influx of strangers in trade and as slaves…these foreign influences distract our people from the wisdom of the ancients. Your mother tells me you have had conversations with local children about samara demons and mashmashu magicians. You can see how ignorance confuses the mind with fear and cruel passions wound the soul with pain. The years of peace are an opportunity to rebuild the temples that were lost to the Hyksos and to heal the hearts of the people. This is a mighty battle and there are many things you will need to know to rule with Maat."

He turned suddenly and looked into her face, "With or without war, the Pharaoh must have the ferociousness of the lion to gain the respect of the foreign rulers." Looking up at the figure looming over them, he continued, "Like Harmakhis…this Sphinx who protects these temples…the Pharaoh must be the lion to protect his people. He must be able to smite those who threaten and to keep the rebellious ones out of the sacred precinct of our land. If the army is strong and powerful, the Pharaoh can have respect without going to battle.

"But within the Two Lands, with our own people, there must be love; both the love of the Pharaoh for his people and the love of the people for their Pharaoh. Remember this wise saying, '*The tongue is the sword arm of the Pharaoh with his people*'. Your best weapon is persuasion. Like Osiris, you must teach. Use your words to dispel the darkness of ignorance. It will be your job as Pharaoh to bring the people home to the wisdom of the ancients. But as you saw with Usersobek, Sobekhotep and Setmose, anyone who threatens that ancient wisdom must be dealt with swiftly to protect the greater whole."

Thutmose stood up and brushed the sand from his kilt. Hatasu followed his example and walked along side him to the opening of the enclosure of paws. Before they exited into the wind again, he said, "To accomplish this goal of bringing the people to the wisdom of the ancients, you must spend many long years in study. You must apply yourself. In the time of the pyramid builders, there were great and wise rulers, learn the old texts written by them. Before the Hyksos, this wisdom was taught from generation to generation. This wisdom was our strength. The foreigners tried to destroy it. The most powerful weapon to overcome the enemy of ignorance is the sword of truth and knowledge. To protect and teach your people, you must educate yourself in the wisdom of the Great Mysteries.

You have done well in the outer court of the House of Life. Now, you will begin the more difficult studies in the inner temple in Waset. There, you will walk through the second pylon gate to the inner sanctuary and prepare for your first initiation into The Lesser Mysteries. In time, you will return here for the initiation into the

Greater Mysteries at this temple, here."

She looked from the Pyramid, back to her father. "What will I study there, that is so different from the hieratic and hieroglyphic writing?"

"Writing is just the first step. What you will learn in the school of mystery is to be born again as a Daughter of Amun Ra. To be a child of the Sun God, you must know and do many difficult things. When you are a Daughter of Amun Ra, you will be able to guide the people of the Two Lands and to be the intermediary between them and the gods. It is the Pharaoh who must be able to connect the Great Above with the Great Below. Only then, can the people live in harmony with all that is. You must know the wisdom of the Followers of Horus, who have gone before you. Do you know the story of the first three sons of Ra…Userkaf, Sahure, and Neferirkare… and how Ra sent Isis to deliver these three sons?"

"Oh, do you mean the story of Ruddedet?"

"Yes, indeed," replied her father and Hatasu basked in his smile of approval. "Our greatest Pharaohs, like those first sons of Ra, taught by putting the wisdom they acquired in the Great Mysteries into the architecture of their temples. As a Pharaoh, you, too, must build a temple that expresses the truth of the Great Above of the Mysteries in the earthly materials of the Great Below. In that expression of truth and wisdom, you will bring blessings and healing to the people. It gives them a way to overcome ignorance and heal passions. In order to accomplish the task of your temple, you will need to learn the terrain of the night sky, the magic of painting the gods, and gather a council of talented and loyal followers to pull it all together and build your vision."

"Father, I don't see how I can do all this. What if I don't succeed?"

"You are the best one to do this. You must do it."

Hatasu was quiet. She looked down at her hands on her lap.

Then Thutmose began walking again toward the horses, saying, "Come, there is something more I would like to show you." He un-hobbled the horses and they remounted the chariot. He drove them up the hill toward the huge pyramids.

The brilliant white limestone was so bright, it hurt her eyes; the brightly painted hieroglyphs on the sides were dazzling. As he drove the chariot between the two largest pyramids, he told her the names of the builders. "This one was built by Khafre and the one over there is by Khufu." He continued to drive around Khafre's pyramid, and as he came out the other side, he pointed toward the third and smaller pyramid. "That one is Menkaure's." He directed the chariot to an area next to Menkaure's causeway which was littered with rubble.

A smaller causeway led to a flat-topped, mastaba tomb. There were the remains of what looked like a town around it. Thutmose again hobbled the horses and he and his daughter walked around the ruins. They approached the gateway of the mastaba and he walked up to the granite that lined the doorway and brushed sand off a carved image. "Come, look here."

Hatasu walked behind him and looked at the figure on the doorframe. She looked, and then she looked again, closer. "How could that be?" she asked. "It is a person with the three-part hairstyle of a woman, yet it has the uraeus and beard of a Pharaoh!"

"Her name here is Khenkawes, meaning 'In Front of the Ancestors'," said her father. "Perhaps you will recognize her as Ruddedet? It says here in hieroglyphs...can you read them?"

She read aloud, "'The King of Upper and Lower Egypt, and Mother of the King of Upper and Lower Egypt'."

Her father continued, "She was the mother of the first three kings to hold the title 'Son of Ra'...Userkaf, Sahure and Neferirkare. I know you think the role of Pharaoh is only for men and that is part of the reason you doubt you can do it and think your younger brother should be Pharaoh. I wanted you to see, this hasn't always been so."

Hatasu stared hard at the image. "Ruddedet was a Pharaoh and a woman?!"

"Yes, this is true. You, too, can be a Daughter of Ra, a woman and a Pharaoh."

Hatasu moved her fingers in the warm loose sands as she stared up into her father's face. Thutmose turned from her and looked up at the sky to see where the sun was and how much time they had to get back to the palace. "Our time is short, and we have a ways to go to get home." They returned to the chariot.

Hatasu again stood behind the horses and held the reigns. Her father stood behind her this time, and with his hands over her hands, urging the horses to trot quickly in a southerly direction.

The End

Bibliography

Assmann, Jan, translated by Andrew Jenkins. *The Mind of Egypt: History and Meaning in the Time of the Pharaohs.* MA: Harvard University Press, 2002

Baines, John and Jaromir Malek. *Atlas of Ancient Egypt.* NY: Facts on File, Inc. 1980

Breasted, James Henry. *Ancient Records of Egypt: The Eighteenth Dynasty – Vol. 2.* Champaign, IL:University of Illinois Press. 2001.

Brier, Bob. *Ancient Egyptian Magic: Spells, Incantations, Potions, Stories, and Rituals.* New Haven: Yale University Press. 1972.

Bunson, Margaret. *The Encyclopedia of Ancient Egypt.* NY: Gramercy Books. 1991

Clark, Rosemant. *The Sacred Tradition in Ancient Egypt.* St. Paul, MN: Llewellyn Publications. 2000.

Cooney, Kara. *The Woman Who Would Be King: Hatshepsut's Rise to Power in Ancient Egypt.* NY: Crown Publishing. 2014.

Ellis, Normandi. Translator. *Awakening Osiris: The Egyptian Book of the Dead.* Grand Rapids, MI: Phanes Press. 1988.

Ellis, Normandi. *Dreams of Isis: A Woman's Spiritual Sojourn.* Wheaton, IL: The Theosophical Publishing House. 1995.

Ellis, Normandi. *Feasts of Light: Celebrations for the Seasons of Life based on Egyptian Goddess Mysteries.* Wheaton, IL: Quest Books. 1999.

Erman, Adolf. Translator H.M. Tirard. *Life in Ancient Egypt.* NY:

Dover Publications. 1971.

Filer, Joyce. *Egyptian Disease*. Austin: University of Texas Press. 1995.

Foster, John. Translator. *The Shipwrecked Sailor: A Tale from Ancient Egypt*. Cairo: The American University in Cairo Press. 1998.

Hall, Rosalind. *Egyptian Textiles*. Aylesbury: Shire Publications. 1986.

Harris, Geraldine. *Gods and Pharaohs from Egyptian Mythology*. NY: Eurobook Limited. 1981.

Healy, Mark. *Armies of the Pharaohs*. Oxford: Osprey Press. 1992.

Houlihan, Patrick. *The Animal World of the Pharaohs*. London: Thames and Hudson Ltd. 1996.

James, T.G. *An Introduction to Ancient Egypt*. Oxford: University Press. 1979.

Lehner, Mark. *The Complete Pyramids: Solving the ancient Mysteries.* London: Thames and Hudson. 1997.

Lichtheim, Miriam. *Ancient Egyptian Literature, Vol. 1*. Berkeley: University of California Press. 1973.

Manniche, Lise. *An Ancient Egyptian Herbal*. Austin, TX: University of Texas Press. 1999.

Naydler, Jeremy. *Temple of the Cosmos: The Ancient Egyptian Experience of the Sacred.* Rochester, VT: Inner Traditions. 1996.

Nunn, John. *Ancient Egyptian Medicine*. London: British Museum Press. 1996.

Pinch, Geraldine. *Magic in Ancient Egypt. Austin.* University of

Texas Press. 1994.

Redford, Donald. *Egypt, Canaan, and Israel in Ancient Times.* Princeton: Princeton University Press. 1992.

Regula, DeTraci. *The Mysteries of Isis: Her Worship and Magick.* St. Paul, MN: Llewellyn Publications. 1995.

Roberts, Alison. *Hathor Rising: The Power of the Goddess in ancient Egypt.* Rochester, VT: Inner Traditions International. 1997.

Roehrig, Catharine, editor. *Hatshepsut: From Queen to Pharaoh.* New Haven: Yale University Press. 2005.

Shaw, Ian, editor. *Egyptian Warfare and Weapons.* Buckinghamshire: Shire Publications. 1991.

Tyldesley, Joyce. *Hatchepsut: The Female Pharaoh.* NY: Viking Press. 1996.

Tyldesley, Joyce. *Judgment of the Pharaoh: Crime and Punishment in Ancient Egypt.* London. Phoenix Paperback. 2000.

Tyldesley, Joyce. *Daughters of Isis: Women of Ancient Egypt.* London: Penguin Books. 1994.

West, John Anthony. *Serpent in the Sky: The High Wisdom of Ancient Egypt.* Wheaton, IL: Quest Books. 1993.

West, John Anthony. *The Traveler's Key to Ancient Egypt.* Wheaton, IL: The Theosophical Publishing House. 1995.

Wilkinson, Richard. *Reading Egyptian Art: A Hieroglyphic Guide to Ancient Egyptian Painting and Sculpture.* London: Thames and Hudson, Ltd. 2000.

Wilkinson, Richard. *Symbol and Magic in Egyptian Art.* London: Thames and Hudson, Ltd. 1994.

Wilson, Hilary. *Understanding Hieroglyphs: a Complete Introductory Guide*. Lincolnwood, IL: Passport Books. 1993.

The Author

Kathy Timpane Medbery lives in Mansfield Center, Connecticut with her husband and cat, Bahari.

www.ingramcontent.com/pod-product-compliance
Lightning Source LLC
Chambersburg PA
CBHW060239030726
47493CB00024B/1350